Schweizer Anglistische Arbeiten
Swiss Studies in English

Begründet von Bernhard Fehr
Herausgegeben von Andreas Fischer (Zürich), Martin Heusser (Zürich),
Daniel Schreier (Zürich)

Band 143

Martin Mühlheim

Fictions of Home

Narratives of Alienation and Belonging, 1850–2000

narr\francke\attempto

Bibliografische Information der Deutschen Nationalbibliothek
Die Deutsche Nationalbibliothek verzeichnet diese Publikation in der Deutschen Nationalbibliografie; detaillierte bibliografische Daten sind im Internet über http://dnb.dnb.de abrufbar.

Einbandgestaltung: Martin Heusser, Zürich
Illustration: © Laura Barrett, London

Die vorliegende Arbeit wurde von der Philosophischen Fakultät der Universität Zürich im Frühjahrssemester 2014 auf Antrag von Prof. Dr. Martin Heusser und Prof. Dr. Fritz Gutbrodt als Dissertation angenommen.

Die Druckvorstufe dieser Publikation wurde vom Schweizerischen Nationalfonds zur Förderung der wissenschaftlichen Forschung unterstützt.

Dischingerweg 5 • D-72070 Tübingen

Internet: www.francke.de
E-Mail: info@francke.de

Satz: pagina GmbH, Tübingen
Printed in Germany

ISSN 0080-7214
ISBN 978-3-7720-8637-3

Table of Contents

"I kept my head down, staring at the gravel lane, as if immersed in a book, a series of beautiful and soothing words spelled out across the roadside to lead me home." Scott Heim, *Mysterious Skin* (276)

Acknowledgments

Writing this book was a lengthy but never very arduous process. The latter is thanks to the many friends and colleagues in the English Department at the University of Zurich who were willing to listen to half-baked ideas, ask the right questions, and, if necessary, to distract me with intelligent or silly conversations – whichever was needed at the time. In particular, I would like to thank those among them who gave me feedback on one or several chapters: Antoinina Bevan Zlatar, Nicole Frey Büchel, Simone Heller-Andrist, Laura Marcus, Diane Piccitto, Rahel Rivera Godoy-Benesch, and Christa Schönfelder. I am especially grateful to Sarah Chevalier and Anja Neukom-Hermann, whose insightful comments on the manuscript helped me to identify and correct some major argumentative flaws. In addition, I am indebted to my supervisors, Martin Heusser and Fritz Gutbrodt, as well as to Pam Morris and Randall Stevenson, for their support, encouragement, and useful suggestions.

Many friends already appear in the previous paragraph. Of the others, I would like to mention Normand Beaudry, Patricia Chronis, Pascal Dubacher, Nicole Eberle, Francesca Falk, Landson Ferrer de Albuquerque, Claudia Holy, Frances Ilmberger, Susan and John Jay, Daniela Landert, Ezequiel 'Pato' Lentz, Veer Nanavatty, Arnaud Praplan, Daniela Schönenberger, Marcel Schwendener, Larssyn Staley, Nicole and Dieter Studer, Daniel Weibel, and Katherine J. Williams. Without them, I would feel less at home in the world.

I agree with the narrator of Salman Rushdie's novel *Midnight's Children*, who suggests that "[m]ost of what matters in our lives takes place in our absence" (14). This book could not have been written without the – direct or indirect – support of unnamed strangers who harvested, sold, or cooked food; cleaned rooms; drove buses, trams, and trains; paid the taxes that financed my research; or worked in mines and factories to produce cell phones, furniture, and other goods I use in my daily life. The boundaries of home are permeable, and far too many of its comforts depend on the exploitation of others. I thank all of you, whoever you are, as well as those who strive for greater equality and justice.

Without the unwavering support and affection of my parents, my brother, and his family I would not be able to feel as passionately about home and belonging as I do. They have made me feel safe, accepted, and loved, and it is thanks to them that I know how much joy home can bring.

Prefatory Note

This study is driven by an explicitly political agenda: to counter right-wing discourses aimed at monopolizing the meaning of belonging. The success over the years of such discourses among the Swiss electorate has seriously complicated my affection for the land I call home, and though I write from a position of safety and privilege, my – far from traumatic – memories of growing up gay in a heteronormative society have left me not entirely unfamiliar with the feeling of being out of place. This inquiry into the concepts of home and belonging is thus to some extent a deeply personal matter. Nevertheless, I will refrain from using the first-person singular in the remainder of this study, opting for the 'inclusive we' instead. This constitutes an attempt on my part to create a sense of communal endeavor. Should anyone find this stylistic choice alienating or awkward, then this may serve as a salutary reminder of how easily gestures of inclusion can turn into strategies of coercion, even if not intended as such. Fair warning, dear reader? Let us go then, you and I.

Introduction – Theories of Home: Alienation and Belonging in Steven Spielberg's *E. T.: The Extra-Terrestrial*

Abandoned by his loved ones and exiled from home, E. T. is arguably the most famous illegalized alien in motion picture history.[1] At the beginning of Steven Spielberg's film, we see E. T. and others of his kind peacefully exploring their terrestrial surroundings – when suddenly a group of humans appears, aiming to capture the foreign 'invaders.' While the other aliens reach the safety of their spaceship, thus managing to elude their human pursuers, E. T. is left behind, stranded on an unfamiliar planet. In panic, E. T. runs off and hides in a field behind a suburban house, where he is later discovered by a ten-year-old boy named Elliott, whose own home was recently disrupted when the boy's father left his mother, Mary, for a younger woman. Initially, E. T. and Elliott are afraid of each other, yet soon fear is replaced by fascination. Elliott smuggles his new-found friend to the safety of his room, where at one point the boy places his hand on a globe that stands on his desk. Looking at the alien, Elliott explains: "Earth. Home."

In describing earth as home, Elliot's point is evidently not that all humans feel perfectly at home in the world; the boy is not referring to profound feelings of belonging, but simply notes that earth is, for better or worse, the planet we humans inhabit, and where we must try to live our lives. And yet, it would be misleading to suggest that Elliott uses the word *home* merely as a spatial marker, for he is in fact interested in learning more about E. T.'s history. More precisely, Elliott tries to explain the meaning of the word *home* because he wants to find out what kind of being E. T. is: where he comes from, and how he got here (Kath Woodward 48). Home, in other words, also raises questions about origins and the journeys we make, and therefore has a temporal as well as a spatial dimension (Agnes Heller 7; Cecile Sandten and Kathy-Ann Tan 3). Moreover, home involves our relations with others: those with whom we share our places of

1 I would like to thank Antoinina Bevan Zlatar and Anja Neukom-Hermann for their comments on the first draft, as well as Sarah Chevalier for her feedback on the final version of this chapter. Some of the arguments presented here are based on my essay "Resisting Governmental Illegalization: Xenophobia and Otherness in Steven Spielberg's *E. T.: The Extra-Terrestrial.*"

shelter; those with whom we feel we belong but from whom we may at present be separated; and those with whom we are forced to struggle and engage because we simply have no other place to go (Jan Willem Duyvendak 120). Finally, even if we limit ourselves to the meaning of home as merely a kind of habitat – the place where we happen to reside – the concept's range remains nothing short of astonishing. Home, as we try to explain it to others, can denote small-scale places of shelter – a house, for instance, or a tent – but also neighborhoods, nations, entire planets: "Earth. Home" (FIGURE 1).[2]

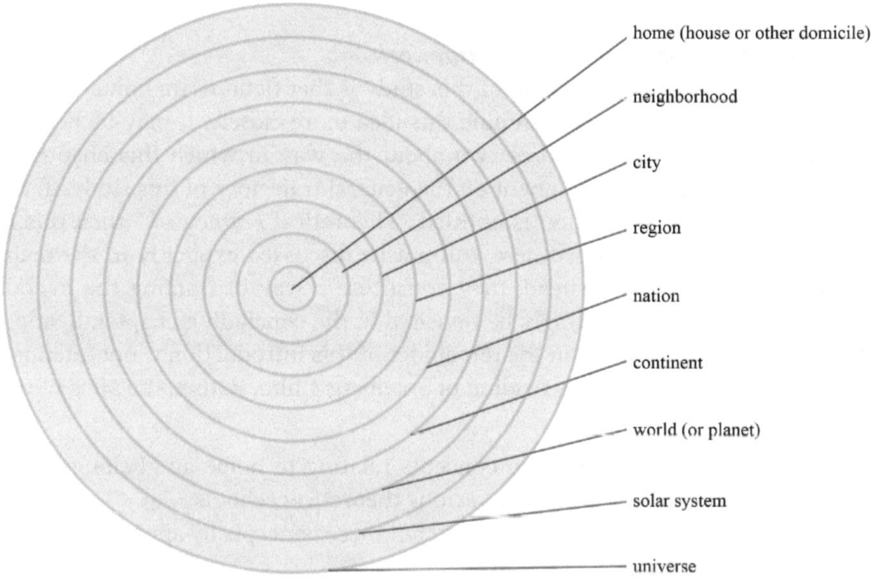

FIGURE 1: The idea of home ranges across various scales (diagram adapted from Fox 19).

This conceptual range is far from a critical disadvantage. Rather, home is a powerful tool for literary and cultural analysis precisely because it is a multi-scalar and open concept that allows us effortlessly to relate our smallest and most intimate concerns to matters of truly global importance. Indeed, it is by focusing on the manifold dimensions of home – as a place of residence or shelter; as a network of given as well as of chosen relationships; as a repository

2 The diagram simplifies matters, of course. For example, it is possible to have more than one home (e.g. the apartment where one lives and the house of one's parents, where one grew up). For some of us, the diagram would thus have to have more than one center.

of both individual and collective ideals (Alyson Blunt and Robyn Dowling 100; Fox 6); as a story of origins, waypoints, and destinations; or as a site of violence and exclusion (Rose Marangoly George 9; Sandten and Tan 8) – that we can develop critical questions, especially in situations where the term's multiple meanings are difficult, or indeed impossible, to reconcile. As a theoretical concept, in short, home allows us to explore a dialectic movement of alienation and belonging that, in turn, is able to generate extraordinary passion, in all the senses of that word: desire and yearning; fervor, agony, and rage; but also feelings very much like love.

Fictions of Home: Theoretical Framework

The core theoretical assumption of this study is that fictions are home-making practices, and we will soon examine this idea more closely. It may be helpful, however, first to say a word or two about the way in which this chapter is structured, as well as to comment on the general trajectory of this study. If, for instance, this first subsection is entitled "Theoretical *Framework*," then this is because the ideas developed here will not be discussed explicitly in the main chapters of this study. Instead, they constitute a way of framing the overall argument, and will accordingly be revisited in the concluding chapter. In addition, the discussion of *E. T.* in the remainder of this introduction is not intended to develop a comprehensive reading of Spielberg's film. Rather, the aims of the discussion are:

(a) to introduce key ideas and concepts relating to home and belonging, as they have been proposed by various theoretical schools;
(b) to exemplify the interpretive power of these concepts by applying them to Spielberg's film;
(c) to indicate, roughly, which of these ideas and concepts are central to which of the six main chapters of this study.

We will also examine briefly the choice of primary texts, as well as some important caveats regarding the scope of the overall argument. The introductory chapter does not, however, summarize the findings of the six main chapters; these will, instead, be presented in the conclusion.

If, in this chapter and the ones that follow, the argument will often have a meandering quality, then this is a matter of conscious choice, for in order to 'get' home – in the sense of understanding it – we must be willing to travel wide and far: to explore its connections to the wider world, as well as its complex internal relations. Home-making thus requires a degree of patience, and the style of the argument is to some extent meant to reflect this fact. At the same time, being patient is not the same as tolerating aimlessness or boredom, so that a plea for the former ought not to be misconstrued as an appeal for the latter.

The key ideas formulated in the remainder of this introductory chapter can be summarized in the form of seven partly overlapping precepts:

1. Even in a secular analysis of home, we must bear in mind the foundational, metaphysical dimension of questions of belonging. This means to consider, among other things, religious beliefs and motifs (such as the idea of a transcendental home) as well as agnostic or atheist accounts of existential angst or trauma (in the sense of a not-being-at-home in the world).
2. References to other texts (especially canonical ones), as well as to established generic traditions, can be understood as home-making practices because they add a dimension of familiarity to an unfamiliar text. However, at the same time, we need to analyze carefully the precise way in which these intertextual references relate (a) to the text in which they occur, and (b) to each other, as this may alert us to important intertextual entanglements, which in fact serve to defamiliarize and critique the tradition.
3. Familiarity, predictability, and a sense of control are essential features of homely homes; they arise, among other things, from habitual practices and ritual actions, and they constitute 'energy-saving devices' that allow humans to focus their limited mental and physical resources on tasks of their choice (rather than having to expend all their energy on the challenges of everyday life). However, too much familiarity can constitute an obstacle to understanding and (self-)knowledge, which is why alienation effects and defamiliarizing practices are necessary tools for critical inquiry (whether deployed in works of art or by critics, scholars, and other analysts).
4. It is by no means a coincidence that the terms *community* and *communication* are so similar to each other, as communication is central to the establishment and maintenance of a sense of home. One factor that facilitates successful communication is a shared cognitive background (established, for instance, through shared experiences), while another crucial factor is the distribution of communicative resources. As this distribution is unequal, some will find it easier than others to establish and maintain a sense of home (e.g. in the case of diasporic communities).
5. Psychoanalysis provides us with powerful concepts for analyzing home – both through Freud's notion of the uncanny and, more generally, through complex techniques of decoding that allow us to unearth the unconscious

forces that shape personal as well as collective identities, and which influence the very form of works of art.

6. Even the supposedly private home is a site that is permeated by relations of power, and we must always take into account the political forces that help to shape the home (as well as the individual and collective identities associated with that home). These forces include:
   (a) the marginalization of others on the basis of race or ethnicity;
   (b) cultural discourses about ideal homes – including the construction of 'normal' as opposed to 'deviant' forms of desire – and how they are diffused through various media, even in the home itself;
   (c) the gendering of domestic space and how it relates to structures of domination (e.g. patriarchy as a social system);
   (d) class relations (e.g. the production of social stratification through economic inequality, and how it appears in, and sustains or undermines, particular types of home).
7. Any critical analysis of home must focus not only on the content or ingredients of home, but also on their formal arrangement. Indeed, the core theoretical assumption of this study is formal in nature: that the concepts of fiction and home are structurally akin to each other because they involve the same form of fictionalizing negotiation between the two realms of the real and the imaginary. One implication of this assumption is that a better understanding of fiction also contributes to our understanding of home and belonging.

Evidently, each of the subsequent chapters constitutes an attempt to follow these precepts, and they may be judged accordingly.

Two caveats, however, are in order. First, the fact that this study covers only texts from between 1850 and 2000 means that all claims and findings must be treated with due caution when applied to earlier periods. Second, the six primary texts discussed in the main chapters do not constitute anything like a representative sample of fictions of home. One simple reason for this is the sheer number of texts that explicitly make home and belonging their theme. A quick search on Amazon.com, for instance, yields 16,944 titles in the category "Literature & Fiction" that feature the word *home* in their titles, and this is of course only the proverbial tip of the iceberg, as the theme of belonging can easily be central to a novel that does not announce this fact in its title.[3] At the same time, the principle of selection for the primary texts used in this study is not entirely random:

3 The search was performed on August 2, 2017.

three of the texts are English (*The Mill on the Floss*, *Mrs. Dalloway*, and *Union Street*), while the other three are American (*Moby-Dick*, *Absalom, Absalom!*, and *The Virgin Suicides*); three of the texts were written by men (Herman Melville, William Faulker, and Jeffrey Eugenides), while the other three were written by women (George Eliot, Virginia Woolf, and Pat Barker); and the texts date, roughly, to the beginning, the middle, and the end of the period covered in this study (i.e. 1851 and 1860; 1925 and 1936; 1982 and 1993). There is thus at least some socio-historical breadth to the corpus, though serious limits remain (e.g. all the English authors are women, whereas all the American authors are men; all six authors are white). At the same time, one aim of the six readings presented in the main chapters is to open up each of the primary texts to a wider range of themes, and thus hopefully to make it easier for readers from various backgrounds to discover, perhaps in unsuspected places, a little piece of that place called home.

The fact that home is such a fundamental and complex concept also means that it would be difficult to provide a comprehensive overview of the previous critical literature on the topic. Fortunately, this is also to some extent unnecessary, as Alison Blunt and Robyn Dowling's study *Home* (2006) constitutes an excellent survey of key concepts and debates (with a particular focus on the fields of geography, sociology, and anthropology, but by no means limited to them). Moreover, it is difficult to think of a more concise definition of home than the one suggested by Blunt and Dowling, who contend that home is "a *spatial imaginary*: a set of intersecting and variable ideas and feelings, which are related to context, and which construct places, extend across spaces and scales, and connect places" (2; original emphasis). Home, for Blunt and Dowling, is thus neither purely imaginary nor entirely reducible to the places and contexts that form the concept's material basis.[4] Crucially, the phrases "variable" and "related to context" in Blunt and Dowling's definition also hint at the temporal dimen-

4 Elisabeth Bronfen uses a slightly different term in the subtitle of her study *Home in Hollywood: The Imaginary Geography of Cinema* (2004), but the terminological reversal – 'imaginary geography' vs. 'spatial imaginary' – arguably signals a difference in emphasis rather than a fundamental disagreement about the components that must enter the equation.

sion of home noted earlier (highlighted as well by Sandten and Tan 3).[5] To render this aspect more explicit, we ought perhaps to amend their formula and say that *home is a spatiotemporal imaginary.*[6]

The dual quality of home as simultaneously extending into the realm of the imaginary and into spatiotemporal reality, in turn, constitutes the main reason why analyzing fiction can contribute to our understanding of the phenomenon of home as such. In *The Fictive and the Imaginary* (1991), Wolfang Iser rejects the conventional binary opposition between fiction and reality, positing instead that we ought to envisage a triadic relationship between the real, the fictive, and the imaginary. According to Iser, a fictional text necessarily incorporates aspects of lived reality, but at the same time it is never reducible to this referential dimension. Instead, the act of fictionalizing also involves components and effects

5 Other texts will be discussed throughout, but it may be useful to provide a list of the most important recent studies available in English here: Gaston Bachelard, *The Poetics of Space* (1958); Witbold Rybczynski, *Home: A Short History of an Idea* (1986); Nancy Armstrong, *Desire and Domestic Fiction: A Political History of the Novel* (1987); Rose Marangoly George, *The Politics of Home: Postcolonial Relocations and Twentieth-Century Fiction* (1996); Raffaella Sarti, *Europe at Home: Family and Material Culture, 1500–1800* (1999); David Morley, *Home Territories: Media, Mobility, and Identity* (2000); Peter Blickle, *Heimat: A Critical Theory of the German Idea of Homeland* (2002); Michael McKeon, *The Secret History of Domesticity: Public, Private, and the Division of Knowledge* (2005); Bill Bryson, *At Home: A Short History of Private Life* (2010); Jan Willem Duyvendak, *The Politics of Home: Belonging and Nostalgia in Western Europe and the United States* (2011); John Hill, *At Home in the World: Sounds and Symmetries of Belonging* (2010); Judith Flanders, *The Making of Home* (2014); Imogen Racz, *Art and the Home: Comfort, Alienation and the Everyday* (2015); Michael Allen Fox, *Home* (2016); Thomas Barrie, *House and Home: Cultural Contexts, Ontological Roles* (2017). In addition, there are many shorter contributions, the most thought-provoking of which include: Doreen Massey, "A Place Called Home?" (1992); Mary Douglas, "The Idea of Home" (1993); Orlando Patterson, "Slavery, Alienation, and the Female Discovery of Personal Freedom" (1993); Agnes Heller, "Where Are We at Home?" (1995); John Durham Peters, "Exile, Nomadism, and Diaspora: The Stakes of Mobility in the Western Canon" (1999); Douglas A. Marshall, "Behavior, Belonging, and Belief: A Theory of Ritual Practice" (2002); Nicholas Howe, Introduction to *Home and Homelessness in the Medieval and Renaissance World* (2004); Marco Antonsich, "Searching for Belonging: An Analytical Framework" (2010); Cecile Sandten and Kathy-Ann Tan, "Home: Concepts, Constructions, Contexts" (2016). See also David A. Ellison, *Home* (2009) and Klaus Stierstorfer, *Constructions of Home* (2010).

6 While it may seem tempting to replace the adjective *spatiotemporal* with the term *chronotope* – which Bakhtin defines as "time space" and which he coined to express "the intrinsic connectedness of temporal and spatial relationships that are artistically expressed in the literature" ("Forms of Time and the Chronotope in the Novel" 84) – I refrain from doing so because the term, in Bakhtin, applies specifically to artistic representation, whereas the definition of home provided here is intended to cover non-fictional uses of the term *home* as well.

that do not form part of the represented reality, and which must therefore stem from some other source. Iser suggests that this other source is the imaginary, and in his view the act of fictionalizing constitutes the creative force that negotiates between the imaginary and the real. More precisely, the act of fictionalizing 'de-realizes' the real by relating it to the imaginary, just as it gathers or 'concretizes' the free-floating impulses of the imaginary into a comprehensible shape or *Gestalt* (*The Fictive and the Imaginary* 1–4).[7] The fictive, in short, is the result of a dialectical confrontation between the real and the imaginary, and as such it is precariously poised between these different realms.

Considering that fiction's precarious negotiation between the two poles of the real and the imaginary also applies to the concept of home, we may now propose that home is itself very similar to fiction: not in the sense of being 'untrue' or simply opposed to the real, but in the sense that any particular idea of home is the result of a fictionalizing act that intermingles the real with the imaginary (and vice versa).[8] Fictions of home are therefore not merely narratives that happen to thematize the dialectic of alienation and belonging; they are also, as fictions, structurally akin to the mental processes that allow for the construction and maintenance of home in the first place. More specifically – as Franco Moretti suggests in *Signs Taken for Wonders* (1983) – fictional texts constitute formal *compromises* between the real and the imaginary, and as such they train us "without our being aware of it for an unending task of mediation and

7 In the German original, the key passage runs: "Das Oppositionsverhältnis von Fiktion und Wirklichkeit würde die Diskussion des Fiktiven im Text um seine entscheidende Dimension verkürzen; denn offensichtlich gibt es im fiktionalen Text sehr viel Realität, die nicht nur eine solche sozialer Wirklichkeit sein muss, sondern ebenso eine der Gefühle und Empfindungen sein kann. Diese gewiss unterschiedlichen Realitäten sind ihrerseits keine Fiktionen, und sie werden auch nicht zu solchen, nur weil sie in die Darstellung fiktionaler Texte eingehen. [...] Bezieht sich also der fiktionale Text auf Wirklichkeit, ohne sich in deren Bezeichnung zu erschöpfen, so ist die Wiederholung ein Akt des Fingierens, durch den Zwecke zum Vorschein kommen, die der wiederholten Wirklichkeit nicht eignen. Ist Fingieren aus der wiederholten Realität nicht ableitbar, dann bringt sich in ihm ein Imaginäres zur Geltung, das mit der im Text wiederkehrenden Realität zusammengeschlossen wird. So gewinnt der Akt des Fingierens seine Eigentümlichkeit dadurch, dass er die Wiederkehr lebensweltlicher Realität im Text bewirkt und gerade in solcher Wiederholung das Imaginäre in eine Gestalt zieht, wodurch sich die wiederkehrende Realität zum Zeichen und das Imaginäre zur Vorstellbarkeit des dadurch Bezeichneten aufheben" (*Das Fiktive und das Imaginäre* 20).

8 Arguing from a Jungian perspective, John Hill makes a rather similar claim about home: "As a symbol it mediates between outer reality and inner truth" (5).

conciliation" (40).[9] Fictions themselves, that is to say, are best understood as symbolical home-making practices, in the broadly Marxist sense that they invent "imaginary or formal 'solutions' to unresolvable social contradictions" (Jameson, *The Political Unconscious* 64).[10] Conversely, if fictions are imaginary attempts to reach formal compromises between real-life contradictions, then this implies that one important task for literary critics is to unearth the problems that fictions attempt to solve (i.e. to 'unpack' the conflicting forces that led to the fictional compromise in the first place).[11]

And yet, even though home is structurally akin to fiction, the concepts differ in two important respects, the first of which has to do with different types of truth claims. The question of truth in fiction is, of course, a thorny issue (e.g. Eagleton, *The Event of Literature* 106–166; Lamarque 220–254), but for our purposes it will suffice to say that fictional texts involve three basic truth claims:

(a) claims about what is true within the fictional world or with regard to the fictional text (i.e. *intra-fictional* truth claims);
(b) claims about the adequate representation of types of real-world phenomena, or kinds of real-world experiences (i.e. *generalizing* truth claims);
(c) claims about the correspondence between, on the one hand, information provided in the fiction, and, on the other, a particular state of things in the real world (i.e. truth claims of *one-to-one correspondence*).

Crucially, these three truth claims differ with regard to the grounds on which they can be contested. In the case of intra-fictional truth claims (e.g. 'In Shake-

9 If Elisabeth Bronfen asserts that "a knowledge of the uncanniness of existence haunts all attempts at devising protective fictions that will allow us to make sense of the contradictions and contingencies of reality," then she is in effect expressing the same idea, albeit in a psychoanalytic rather than a Marxist idiom. After all, the phrase "unending task" in Moretti's formulation signals that he, too, regards the formal compromise effected by any fictional text as inherently precarious and unstable.

10 Perhaps it is this idea of fiction as a home-making practice that Martin Heidegger has in mind when he claims, in "... Poetically Man Dwells ..." (1951), that "poetry first causes dwelling to be dwelling" (213), defining poetry as a way of "measuring" (219): "This is why poetic images are imaginings in a distinctive sense: not mere fancies and illusions but imaginings that are visible inclusions of the alien in the sight of the familiar" (223). The German original runs: "Darum sind die dichterischen Bilder Ein-Bildungen in einem ausgezeichneten Sinne: nicht bloße Phantasien und Illusionen, sondern Ein-Bildungen als erblickbare Einschlüsse des Fremden in den Anblick des Vertrauten" ("... dichterisch wohnet der Mensch ..." 195). Robert Mugerauer succintly sums up Heidegger's view: "The poet attempts to find a true home by wandering out into the foreign" (119).

11 For a brief account of the intellectual lineage that defines fiction as an imaginary solution of real-life contradictions see Haslett (67).

speare's play *Hamlet,* the protragonist marries Ophelia'), the information provided in the fictional text itself forms the only basis on which we may accept or reject such a claim ('No, the text makes it very clear that Hamlet and Ophelia never get married'). In the case of generalizing truth claims, by contrast (e.g. 'Jane Austen is right when she writes: "It is a truth universally acknowledged, that a single man in possession of a good fortune, must be in want of a wife"'; *Pride and Prejudice* 5), we must refer to evidence pertaining to the real world when formulating a counter-argument ('What about men who are attracted to other men?').[12] In the case of fictional truth claims of one-to-one correspondence, finally (e.g. 'In 1991, Zurich was the capital of Switzerland'), readers are free to take note of divergences between the fictional world and real life ('In fact it was Berne'), but as it is essential to the game of fiction that constraints on truth claims of one-to-one correspondence be playfully suspended, such divergences do not constitutes lies, or even inaccuracies. Instead, counterfactuals in fiction prompt a series of interpretive questions: What is the function of these divergences within the fictional text? Do they contribute to or detract from the text's aesthetic and rhetorical effectiveness? And is it morally justifiably to 'play around' with the particular facts in question? Even in the case of fiction, in short, truth claims of one-to-one correspondence remain open to critical debate, but they cannot be challenged directly on the basis of their divergence from fact – and this is what distinguishes the fictional compromise between the real and the imaginary from the structurally analogous compromise of home as a spatiotemporal imaginary. In the case of truth claims about home, constraints on one-to-one correspondence remain in full force, and it is therefore legitimate to challenge any divergences of this kind directly ('No, Dietikon is *not* your home because you have no relation to that place and in fact don't even know where it is').

If these different rules for how to challenge truth claims provide us with one criterion theoretically to distinguish the concept of home from that of fiction, then the second criterion pertains to these concepts' respective degrees of closure. In the case of fiction, the compromise between the real and the imaginary is necessarily expressed in a definite shape (i.e. a finished product, such as a written text or a film). By contrast, home as a spatiotemporal imaginary remains, for the most part, implicit, or is expressed piecemeal, either by individuals or by

12 As Lamarque rightly notes, literary truth "is not always to be found spelt out explicitly in literary works," which means that readers are often "called upon to construct their own generalizations" (236). Accordingly, the opening line of *Pride and Prejudice* is used here as a simplified example, for the sake of the argument. In the context of Jane Austen's novel, it should, of course, not necessarily be taken at face value.

collectives, in evolving communicative situations. Home as a mental structure is thus generally fuzzier, and likely to be less internally consistent, than fiction – which means, conversely, that the pressure to find satisfactory compromises is much higher in the case of fiction, as fiction must give a much more clear-cut form to the compromise between the real and the imaginary than is the case for constructions of home. This, in turn, allows us to speculate that the need for fictions becomes particularly acute precisely in those moments when socio-historical pressures bring to the fore certain contradictions in the (usually implicit) spatiotemporal imaginary of home. Fiction's formal compromise, though perhaps unable truly to resolve such crises, at least serves temporarily to dilute and reduce the contradictory stresses that threaten our sense of home and belonging – which is merely to reiterate, in slightly different form, that fiction itself is a home-making practice.

The Metaphysics of Home: Religion, the Canon, and Existential Trauma

As we have seen, home is a spatiotemporal imaginary, and as such it is concerned with our place in the world, both in the sense of our geographical location and of our position within the larger scheme of things. Accordingly, an inquiry into the nature of belonging may quickly lead us beyond questions of daily existence, toward the realm of metaphysical speculation. More specifically, inquiries into the nature of home are likely to spark questions of a religious nature because religions tend to hold forth the promise of a final, transcendental home. In the Judeo-Christian tradition, for instance, humanity appears as tragically fallen: expulsed from Eden, and exiled in the desert of earthly existence (an idea powerfully expressed, for instance, in John Milton's *Paradise Lost*). As John Durham Peters observes, there is thus at least one similarity between Judeo-Christian and poststructuralist thought, for in both these traditions human identity is seen as inherently incomplete and discontinuous with itself ("Exile, Nomadism, and Diaspora" 22).[13] According to Peters, Christian discourse in particular has come to be suffused with nomadic imagery, with St. Paul's ideas being particularly influential: "The human body for him is a temporary, mobile dwelling in which mortals sojourn on earth" (27–28). In this view, humans are wanderers on the face of the earth, and only in death, when we have finally left our nomadic bodies behind, is it possible for us to recover our transcendental home in God, with whom we will forever rest in peace.

---

13 Note, however, Thomas Barrie's important caveat that "estrangement from the world is found pan-culturally and trans-historically," albeit with different inflections and evaluations (4). For Barrie, one of the functions of architecture may be precisely "to ameliorate humanity's homeless condition" (6).

Steven Spielberg's *E. T.* explicitly draws on this religious narrative of alienation and belonging in order to enhance the significance of little Elliott's quest. As already noted briefly, Elliott's own father is absent from the home; he has left the mother and moved to Mexico with his new partner. Elliott longs for the absent father, and E. T. assumes the role of a Messiah who will guide the boy towards a new sense of belonging. Indeed, as Thomas Sebeok has noted, *E. T.*'s emotional power depends to a large extent on its "subliminal religious infrastructure" (662). Spielberg's film tells the story of an otherworldly being who, we will find, has the power to heal little Elliott's wound when the boy cuts himself on a sawblade; a being who dies, is resurrected, and who, in the final scene, ascends once again to his heavenly home (Alexander 25; Tomasulo 275). The film's religious subtext is also apparent visually, as when E. T.'s glowing heart alludes to the iconographic tradition of the Sacred Heart of Jesus (FIGURE 2).[14] In fact, even the film's advertising campaign has incorporated this religious dimension, with official posters pointing to Michelangelo's depiction of the creation of man in the frescoes of the Sistine Chapel (FIGURE 3). In *E. T.* – as in many texts about home – a protagonist's attempt to find a place in the world thus assumes a profoundly metaphysical dimension, and it is arguably for this very reason that the eponymous heroine of D. H. Lawrence's *Lady Chatterley's Lover* (1928) includes *home* in her list of the "great words" (the others being *love*, *joy*, *happiness*, *mother*, *father*, and *husband*; 62; ch. 6).[15] At the same time, to say that Elliott's quest gains in metaphysical depth, as well as emotional resonance, through the film's use of religious imagery is not to argue that *E. T.* is in fact a religious film; the point is, rather, that intertextual references affect our reactions to the film. More generally, references to religious and other texts that are widely familiar can enhance the spectator's sense of belonging, as they place the individual work of art within a larger system of meaning.

Historically, it was the literary canon – or in Matthew Arnold's famous phrase, "the best that has been said and thought in the world" (*Culture and Anarchy* 5) – that was to provide men and women with a sense of belonging to a higher order that was not, strictly speaking, transcendental, but that at least

14 Another visual reference to the Judeo-Christian tradition comes when the spaceship that takes E. T. back home leaves behind a rainbow – an allusion to the biblical story of the flood, after which God places a rainbow in the clouds as "the sign of the covenant" between him and all living beings (Genesis 9: 8–16).

15 If, in Lawrence's novel, Lady Chatterley also believes that "home," like all the other great words, has somehow been "cancelled for her generation" (62; ch. 6), then this bleak assessment has much to do with the traumatic impact of World War I (Stevenson, *Literature and the Great War* 48) – as well as with the novel's rejection of industrial-capitalist modernity in general.

transcended the spatiotemporal limits of these individuals. Indeed, the term *canon* – which originally referred to the list of biblical books "accepted by the Christian Church as genuine and inspired" (OED) – itself bears witness to the quasi-religious function envisioned by Arnold for the monuments of high culture. In fact, Arnold and other Victorian thinkers (e.g. Thomas Carlyle) had quite explicitly conceived of 'high culture' as a means both to cultivate the soul and to ensure social cohesion in the absence of religious certainties (Philip Davis 133–134; Eagleton, *Literary Theory* 21). Agnes Heller has captured well the utopian hope embodied in this high-cultural home that, ideally, would form the basis for universal belonging:

> This home is not private, everyone can join it, and in this sense, it is also cosmopolitan. The assurance that everyone can join, refers both to the works that this home entails and to the visitors who enter with nostalgia and a quest for meaning. [...] At the outset few works were admitted, now almost everything is. At the beginning there were also few visitors but later their number began to grow. Now, this, originally European [...] home is visited by millions with all possible cultural backgrounds. (9)

FIGURE 2: The iconography of the Sacred Heart of Jesus is reflected in E. T.'s glowing heart. (Screenshot from *E. T.*; © by Amblin/Universal Studios, used by permission)

FIGURE 3: Michelangelo's depiction of the creation is echoed in official ads for *E. T.*

Heller herself notes, however, that the canon, as envisioned by Arnold and others, can only fulfill this function of creating a sense of universal belonging if it remains limited and exclusive; as soon as too many works are included, the canon's ability to serve as a discursive home begins to crack and, ultimately, collapses (10). The Arnoldian ideal of the canon as home is thus in one sense inherently contradictory, for it can only serve as a discursive medium of universal inclusion if it simultaneously remains thoroughly exclusive in terms of the works it incorporates. Many will, in other words, not be directly represented in this assembly of high culture, and will therefore simply have to trust that those who are included will speak on their behalf. The logic of canonization thus resembles closely Victorian arguments for a limited franchise – a parallel that is arguably not accidental.

At any rate, those who happen to be unfamiliar with the canonical texts that, supposedly, form part of "a common cognitive background" (Heller 10) may find that intertextual references can also have a profoundly alienating effect. Comedies, for instance, are a highly allusive type of genre – and therefore they travel rather less well across cultural borders than other types of texts, for as Franco Moretti has observed, "laughter arises out of the unspoken assumptions that are buried very deep in a culture's history: and if these are not *your* assumptions, the automatic component so essential to laughter disappears" ("Planet Hollywood" 99). When exposed to a comedy from a very distant time or place, we may thus not experience the relief of shared laughter, but instead find ourselves puzzled and disoriented. More generally, allusions to unknown texts may confuse rather than reassure, provided the allusion is nevertheless recognized as such. In *E.T.*, for instance, the film's religious infrastructure arguably does not feel particularly alienating for anyone because it remains largely subliminal; it is perfectly possible to watch the film without ever realizing that it draws on biblical imagery, so that even those who are unfamiliar with the story of Jesus are unlikely to feel excluded from the film's intended audience. However, *E.T.* also contains a reference to *Peter Pan* (to which we will return later), and because this reference is more explicit, it is possible that those who have never heard of this text will, at least momentarily, feel alienated by its intertextual inclusion.

Let us briefly recapitulate the relation between religious transcendence and the literary canon as a secular attempt to replace a lost metaphysical home. Victorian intellectuals not only worried about statistics that indicated a sharp decline in religious observance, but also themselves suffered from a sense of metaphysical 'unbelonging' prompted, among other things, by Darwin's theory of evolution; at the same time, they hoped that the secular religion of high culture, as encapsulated in the canon, might serve to alleviate the socially disruptive effects of unbelief or agnosticism (a term that, tellingly, was coined by T.E. Huxley in 1869; see Philip Davis 57). This is not to suggest that there was, at some moment in the nineteenth century (or, indeed, in the century that followed), a total collapse of religious belief amongst each and every segment of the population.[16] Rather, the point is to emphasize that those who have no faith in a transcendental home also lack that sense of metaphysical belonging that religion has, for many, been able to provide. Bereft of a metaphysical home, these unbelievers may therefore seek other, more secular types of spiritual shelter.

Following Georg Lukács, we may describe the condition that results from a loss of faith as "transcendental homelessness" (40–41): a sense that human existence is purely contingent, and that humankind is adrift in a universe that is indifferent to human happiness or suffering. Secular individuals can, in other words, no longer find comfort in the idea that life is securely anchored in transcendental meaning, but instead experience the Heideggerian anxiety of finding themselves thrown into being or *Dasein* (*Being and Time* 131): an existential angst that Heidegger explicitly describes as a sense of "not-being-at-home" (182; see Agnes Heller 4; Mugerauer 43; O'Donoghue 139).[17] Dominick LaCapra has suggested the term structural or existential trauma to express the disturbing nature of this experience, though at the same time LaCapra is careful to distinguish this phenomenon from what he dubs historical trauma, which by contrast "is related to specific events, such as the Shoah or the dropping of the atom bomb on Japanese cities" (*History and Memory after Auschwitz* 47). In the case of *E. T.*, we might therefore say that the film threatens to elide the distinction between the existential threat of transcendental homelessness, and Elliott's more limited, historical trauma of losing the comforting presence of his father. More generally, moreover, we may regard trauma as one of the most dramatic symptoms of not-being-at-home in the world, and the discussion of Herman Melville's

16 Indeed, C. A. Bayly argues that, from a global perspective, the nineteenth century in fact witnessed an expansion of the major world religions (7), and while secularization certainly gained ground in twentieth-century Britain (e.g. Turner 49), religion remains central in many other countries – very much including the United States (which, incidentally, would make it possible to read *E. T.*'s messianic subtext as simply a cynical attempt by Hollywood producers to convert Americans' faith in religion into the more tangible stuff of box-office gold).

17 In the German original, the relevant passages are: (a) "Diesen in seinem Woher und Wohin verhüllten, aber an ihm selbst um so unverhüllter erschlossenen Seinscharakter des Daseins, dieses 'Dass es ist' nennen wir die *Geworfenheit* des Seienden in sein Da, so zwar, dass es als In-der-Welt-sein das Da ist" (*Sein und Zeit* 135); (b) "In der Angst ist einem *'unheimlich'*. Darin kommt zunächst die eigentümliche Unbestimmtheit dessen, wobei sich das Dasein in Angst befindet, zum Ausdruck: das Nichts und Nirgends. Unheimlichkeit meint aber dabei zugleich das Nicht-zuhause-sein" (188).

Moby-Dick in chapter one will revolve precisely around such questions as transcendental homelessness and how it relates to existential and historical forms of trauma.

Growing Up: Redefining the Meaning of Home

Returning to the discussion of Spielberg's *E. T.* and its second important intertext, *Peter Pan*, we must first note that, in J. M. Barrie's story, the process of growing up is conceived as a dialectic of exile and homecoming.[18] Early on in the story, Peter Pan – "the boy who wouldn't grow up," according to the subtitle of the original stage version (179) – leads Wendy and her two little brothers away from the family home, taking them with him to Neverland. There, Wendy and her brothers have all kinds of dangerous adventures, but ultimately they return to the family home where, in time, they grow up and become adults. Years later, when Wendy tells her daughter Jenny about her adventures in Neverland, the girl wonders why Wendy is no longer able to fly, which apparently she had been capable of as a child. Wendy, however, knows exactly why adults, unlike children, remain earthbound: "they are no longer gay and innocent and heartless" (174; ch. 17). And it is true that Peter appears heartless throughout Barrie's story; we learn, for instance, that with regard to heroic deeds, "it was his cleverness that interested him and not the saving of human life" (82; ch. 4). Indeed, as Annie Hiebert Alton rightly notes, Peter's heartlessness is that of a very small child who "seems unaware of the feelings of others" (174n1). Accordingly, as an eternal child Peter is free from the ties that bind one to others, and can simply do whatever he pleases.[19] This freedom, however, comes at the cost of familial belonging, for as we learn at the end of a chapter entitled "The Return Home" – in which Wendy and her brothers are reunited with their parents – Peter "had ecstasies innumerable that other children can never know, but he was looking through the window at the one joy from which he must be for ever barred" (169; ch. 16). In *Peter Pan*, in short, there is an irreconcilable conflict between, on the one hand, freedom from interference with one's desires, and, on the other, the freedom to belong and be part of a family home – with everyone except Peter eventually opting for the latter.[20]

---

18 For a recent, book-length study of Barrie's story (including adaptations and sequels) see Kirsten Stirling, *Peter Pan's Shadows in the Literary Imagination* (2012).

19 See Ann Yeoman, *Now or Neverland* (1998) for an extended Jungian reading of Peter Pan as a *puer aeternus*.

20 This may, of course, be a misleading dichotomy – but the point is that the text establishes it as such.

The idea that as children we enjoy a greater degree of freedom than is the case later in life may, of course, be merely an instance of nostalgic idealization – and nostalgia is in fact a crucial concept in any discussion of home because it can be understood, like trauma, as one particular symptom of alienation and unbelonging. According to Kimberley K. Smith, the term *nostalgia* was coined in 1688 by the physician Johann Hofer, who used it to describe a severe, even potentially fatal illness diagnosed among Swiss mercenaries, and in Hofer's view caused by the mercenaries' physical absence from home (509). In the course of the eighteenth and nineteenth centuries, Smith continues, the concept's meaning broadened and complicated: "Once defined simply as a desire to return home, to a specific *place*, nostalgia was gradually being conceptualized as a longing to return to a former *time* – and usually a time the patient only *imagined* to be better" (512; original emphasis). Smith's main point, however, is that we should not simply dismiss the longing for the past as "mere nostalgia," but instead regard nostalgic desires "as a valuable basis for social critique" (523). While we may all agree that it is impossible to simply return to a past state, nostalgic subjects may nevertheless have perfectly valid reasons for rejecting the current state of affairs. More generally, nostalgia is an expression of individual or collective values and desires that, as such, may very well be legitimate.[21] If Elliott, for instance, longs for the time before his father left the family home, then a certain degree of nostalgic idealization may well be involved, but this does not invalidate the boy's desire to be reunited with a person he loves. At the same time, Roberta Rubenstein suggests that "nostalgia, or homesickness [...] is the existential condition of adulthood" because the process of growing up turns as all into "exiles from childhood" (4–5) – an idea symbolized in *Peter Pan* through adults' exile from Neverland.

At any rate, the implications of growing up as depicted in *Peter Pan* match precisely some key concerns of *E. T.*, as the latter, too, tells the story of a child who must learn to respect the feelings of others as part of the process of coming of age. The importance of a respect for the feelings of others is made clear early on in Spielberg's film when Elliott, after his first brief encounter with E. T., fails to convince his mother (as well as his brother and sister) that he has really stumbled upon something unusual in the field behind the family's suburban home:

21 See Jan Willem Duyvendak: "Nostalgia is not necessarily problematic, so long as we understand that nostalgia says more about contemporary society than it does about the past" (107; see also Kirk 606; Peters, "Exile, Nomadism, and Diaspora" 30).

> MARY
> [M]aybe you just probably imagined that it happened.
> ELLIOTT
> I couldn't have imagined it! […] Dad would believe me.
> MARY
> Maybe you ought to call your father and tell him about it.
> ELLIOTT
> I can't. He's in Mexico with Sally. (Mathison 63)

Elliott's mother is evidently shaken by her son's heartless reference to the father's new lover, and eventually leaves the kitchen in tears. Michael, Elliott's older brother, is furious: "Damn it! Why don't you… grow up? Think of how other people feel for a change!" (Mathison 64). Michael thus explicitly defines Elliott's task as the need to be more empathetic, and it is thus significant that Mary will later read the story of *Peter Pan* not to him, but to his little sister, Gertie, who is still young enough to be "gay and innocent and heartless," whereas Elliott has already left behind the stage of infantile narcissism and begun his journey toward adulthood. Indeed, the film's *mise-en-scène* during the sequence discussed above emphasizes Elliott's transitional state, as Elliott is shown sitting on one side of a rather oddly-shaped, triangular kitchen table, with Gertie placed on her own on another, and both Mary and Michael positioned at the third (Figure 4). Elliott is thus situated symbolically between a very small child and two more adult figures, while at the same time the framing of the shot makes him appear as still closer to his younger sister. The remainder of Spielberg's film then tells the story of how Elliott is saved from the error of his former, childish ways by his encounter with E. T. the Messiah. Accordingly, when at the end of the film E. T. is ready to go back home, it is no longer Elliott, but Gertie who is in need of spiritual guidance from the alien, whose message to her is as simple as it is clear: "Be good" (Mathison 146).

FIGURE 4: Elliott is placed symbolically between a small child and two more adult figures. (Screenshot from *E. T.*; © by Amblin/ Universal Studios, used by permission.)

And yet, above and beyond these rather homely pieties, the film's juxtaposition of *Peter Pan* with elements from the story of Jesus Christ also has some rather more unsettling effects, which becomes apparent if we examine closely the scene in *E. T.* in which the two intertextual references are most explicitly intertwined. The scene in question occurs roughly in the middle of the film and shows Elliott and E. T. hiding in the closet of Gertie's bedroom while Mary is reading to Gertie from *Peter Pan*. The passage Mary reads to Gertie tells the story of how Peter tries to save the fairy Tinker Bell by breaking the frame of the fictional world and appealing to the children in the audience:

> MARY
> "Her voice is so low I can scarcely tell what she is saying. She says, she says she thinks she could get well again if children believed in fairies. Do you believe in fairies? Say quick that you believe!" [...]
> GERTIE
> I do, I do, I do! (Matthison 104; cf. J. M. Barrie 145).

It is precisely during this scene about children's belief in fairies that Elliott, hidden in the closet, cuts himself on a sawblade and starts to bleed, which prompts E. T. to heal the boy's wound with the gentle touch of a finger (Mathison 103–104). This surprising juxtaposition suggests a parallel between, on the one hand, a belief in the healing powers of a Messiah, and, on the other, a belief in fairies – as if the two were one and the same.[22] This, in turn, illustrates the extent to which intertextual play can develop a dynamic of its own, with various

22 For a different (and more detailed) reading of the parallels between *E. T.* and *Peter Pan* see Patricia Read Russel's essay "Parallel Romantic Fantasies."

strands of references becoming entangled and sometimes tied up in complicated knots. Put differently, the interplay between *E. T.*'s combined references to *Peter Pan* and to the story of Jesus Christ shows that the use of canonical intertexts may – intentionally or not – lead to moments of friction that end up defamiliarizing the well-known originals.[23] In this way, literary traditions are opened up to critique – as is the case in George Eliot's *The Mill on the Floss*, which we will examine in chapter two, and which, like *E. T.* and *Peter Pan*, revolves around the problem of growing up, the protagonists' occasionally nostalgic relation to home and belonging, and the critical use and reexamination of established discursive traditions (including genres such as the *Bildungsroman* and tragedy).

The Question of Racism and the Politics of Home

In the case of *E. T.*, we can widen the political scope of intertextual critique if we focus on a third set of references that relates, on the one hand, to other films featuring aliens, and, on the other, to one of the most canonical of English novels: Daniel Defoe's *Robinson Crusoe*. Admittedly, *Robinson Crusoe* is far less prominent a presence in the film than is *Peter Pan* or the story of Jesus. Nevertheless, relating *E. T.* to Defoe's novel helps us capture more precisely some of the film's political import. The most famous section of Defoe's novel tells the story of how Crusoe ends up stranded on an island that he soon regards as his "little kingdom" (109). Accordingly, many critics have insisted that the novel's ideology is deeply colonialist; after all, it depicts a white man appropriating new territory that he subsequently defends against native 'intruders' – with the exception of one, whom he turns into his personal slave, imposing on him a new name, a new language, and a new religion (e.g. Carter and McRae 154–155; Stam 71–74). Given this colonialist ideology, one may begin to wonder for whom, precisely, the canon comprises "the best that has been said and thought in the world" – and critiques of this kind have of course long been central to the larger project of postcolonial studies.[24] In the context of our discussion, however, it is sufficient to note that the story of *Robinson Crusoe* contrasts markedly with Spielberg's

---

23 A more detailed account of the idea that intertextual frames create various kinds of friction can be found in Simone Heller-Andrist's monograph *The Friction of the Frame* (172–244).

24 One classic example of such a critique is Chinua Achebe's attack on Joseph Conrad's *Heart of Darkness*, a text that Achebe regards as profoundly racist because it portrays Africa as "a place where man's vaunted intelligence and refinement are finally mocked by triumphant bestiality" (783). Note that J. Hillis Miller has formulated a nuanced reassessment of Achebe's argument in an essay entitled "Joseph Conrad: Should We Read *Heart of Darkness*?" (*Others* 104–136).

E. T., whose title character, like Crusoe, is stranded alone on alien shores, but who, unlike Crusoe, harbors no aspirations to dominate the natives.

The contrast between *E. T.* and *Robinson Crusoe* is all the more remarkable if we bear in mind that, in the decades following the 1950s, a large number of American films featuring aliens had revolved precisely around the threat of invasion (e.g. Booker, *Alternate Americas* 5). This is not, of course, to claim that there had never before been films in which aliens were portrayed as benevolent creatures. For instance, in *The Day the Earth Stood Still* (1951), the alien Klaatu is on a mission to save rather than destroy the human race by forcing it to abandon its self-destructive ways. Moreover, Spielberg himself had previously scored a huge box-office hit with *Close Encounters of the Third Kind* (1977), which also features benevolent aliens. The point, however, is that, in *E. T.*, the agents of the government behave as if the aliens were aggressors (as many other fictional aliens – including Crusoe – in fact had been). Home is, in short, not a pre-political space, but a conflictual terrain that usually involves the systematic exclusion of those perceived as alien (Rosemary Marangoly George 9).

One way to account for the irrational fear exhibited by the government agents in *E. T.* is to use Stephen D. Arata's diagnosis that imperial centers may at times suffer from an "anxiety of reverse colonization." In a reading of Bram Stoker's *Dracula*, Arata argues that the Transylvanian Count serves as a mirror-image of Western colonizers: an alien from the East who has spent much time and effort to acquire useful knowledge about the Occident, and who plans to use this knowledge "to invade and exploit Britain and her people" (638). According to Arata, Stoker's novel must be read against the backdrop of a *fin-de-siècle* perception of decline of Britain as an imperial power (622). This narrative of imperial decline, in turn, explains a widespread anxiety of reverse colonization, which Arata defines as the impression that "what has been represented as the 'civilized' world is on the point of being colonized by 'primitive' forces" (623). Arata insists, however, that geopolitical fears are only half the story, with metropolitan guilt constituting a second key ingredient:

> In the marauding, invasive Other, British culture sees its own imperial practices mirrored back in monstrous form. […] Reverse colonization narratives thus contain the potential for powerful critiques of imperialist ideologies, even if that potential usually remains unrealized. (623)

In Arata's view, then, anxieties of reverse colonization project the colonizing practices of the metropolis back onto the screen of an alien Other, who may then serve as a fantasied scapegoat figure.

If it is true that Dracula constituted a projection of late Victorian British guilt, then E. T. – that dark-skinned alien who secretly enters a white suburban home – perhaps fulfills a similar scapegoat function for a guilt-ridden United States Empire.[25] William Alexander, for instance, argues that *E. T.* is suffused with markedly racist sentiments. In the film, Alexander contends, E. T. is subliminally associated not only with monkeys (by being shown next to a monkey doll; FIGURE 5), but also with primitivism (he comes from the woods and possesses magic powers) and with the 'non-white' places of the earth (at one point E. T. is shown standing in front of a globe on which the audience can see Asia and Africa; FIGURE 6). For Alexander, the verdict is therefore clear:

> [Spielberg's film] brings the threatening, righteously angry figure – the unemployed black youth, the guerrilla fighter of Central America who has said 'enough' to the centuries of hunger, the starving Latin American child, the napalmed Vietnamese peasant we are trying to forget, the minimum wage worker, the potential disrupter of suburban comfort and economic status – into the suburb. (33)[26]

E. T., the illegalized, dark-skinned alien, violates the boundaries of white suburbia, and the government acts quickly to try and re-establish control over the imperial nation's privileged social space.[27] Moreover, on the larger scale of the national home, the U. S. government's determination to capture any illegal alien also involves an act of force against its own citizens, whose suburban home is invaded in *E. T.* by state officials (FIGURE 7). As the internment of Japanese

25 The fact that the color of E. T.'s skin cannot simply be dismissed as a random and insignificant feature is nicely summarized by Adam Roberts, who observes in his study of science fiction: "Aliens, as popular consciousness knows, are differently coloured: green-skinned, blue-skinned or (more latterly) grey-skinned. Skin colour, in other words, is reflected by SF [i.e. science fiction] as the key vector of difference" (105).

26 Alexander in fact argues that *E. T.* as a whole is a racist fantasy in which the symbolic representative of the oppressed turns out to be reassuringly "good-hearted and harmless," and is ultimately sent "back to where he came from" (33). I have tried to defend Spielberg's film against this particular charge in my essay "Resisting Governmental Illegalization," and would only like to add here that the association of E. T. with Jesus is potentially anti-imperialist in its implications, for as Terry Eagleton notes, Christ was murdered "by the Roman state and its supine colonial lackeys, who took fright at his message of mercy and justice, as well as at his enormous popularity with the poor, and did away with him in a highly volatile political situation. It did not help that a number of his closest friends were probably Zealots or anti-imperialist revolutionaries" (*Trouble with Strangers* 289). However, for a reading that is closer to Alexander's, see Robin Wood (160).

27 The suburban home and lifestyle of Elliott's family in *E. T.* is, of course, inextricably entangled with the history of race relations in the United States. For a more detailed discussion of this problem, see chapter six of the present study.

Americans during World War II (David M. Kennedy 748–760) or more recent US policies in the wake of 9/11 or have shown, when 'homeland security' is supposedly at stake, the oft-proclaimed sanctity of the private home quickly becomes irrelevant for the very powers supposed to protect it.[28] Both these historical examples highlight the crucial analytical importance of relating particular, small-scale homes to their broader social, cultural, and historical contexts – and it is precisely the politics and ethics of homes situated in a metropolitan center that will constitute a key theme in the discussion in chapter three of Virginia Woolf's *Mrs. Dalloway.*

FIGURE 5: E. T. happens to hide right next to a monkey doll. (Screenshot from *E. T.*; © by Amblin/ Universal Studios, used by permission.)

28 Likewise, when placed in the context of South African history, the term 'homeland' is itself decidedly unhomely, as it was used by the Apartheid regime to designate ten preponderantly rural areas assigned as mandatory places of residence to the country's black population (Butler, Rotberg and Adams 1).

FIGURE 6: The globe next to E. T. shows two 'non-white' continents: Africa and Asia. (Screenshot from *E. T.*; © by Amblin/ Universal Studios, used by permission.)

FIGURE 7: Government officials invade the home they are supposed to protect. (Screenshot from *E. T.*; © by Amblin/ Universal Studios, used by permission.)

The Return of the Repressed: History, the Family, and the Freudian Uncanny

While homes in general are shaped by larger power structures, the particular agents of domination often reside in the home itself, with some inhabitants exerting a truly tyrannous control over the minds and bodies of others (Douglas, "The Idea of Home" 277). Children, for instance, are often seen as key inhabitants of truly homely homes, but many parents do not grant them much "agency in the running or representation of these homes" (Blunt and Dowling 115). Such familial domination in fact plays an important part in *E. T.*, for it is because Elliott's mother would surely not allow E. T. to stay that the boy hides him from her. Indeed, given that Elliott at one point literally keeps E. T. in the closet, his fear of parental sanction may productively be read from a queer perspective: the alien, it seems, must not come out. More generally speaking, what counts as a 'proper' or 'homely' home very often depends on individuals' physical and moral conformity to cultural ideals and prejudices, and the supposedly private family home often serves as one key site where these values are passed on to future generations.

To some extent the formative influence of childhood homes explains the widespread assumption that learning more about someone's home tells us something about the kind of person they are. As we have already seen, it is precisely this assumption that motivates Elliott to convey the meaning of "home" to E. T.: the boy wants to find out where the alien comes from in order to understand what kind of being he is. Such a "conflation of home and self" is, as Rosemary Marangoly George points out, a central trope in various disciplines: "literary theory, architecture, sociology, political science, geography, philosophy and psychology" (19). At the same time, Marangoly George highlights the danger inherent in conflating home and self, as those who are homeless, or who happen to live in 'deviant' homes, may easily come to be judged as faulty selves (24). This is all the more so because, as Blunt and Dowling observe, in any given society or culture "a central feature of imaginaries of home is their idealization: certain dwelling structures and social relations are imagined to be 'better'" (100). Historically specific ideals of a 'stable home' help explain, for instance, why 'unsettled' nomads have repeatedly been regarded as a threat to societal order, with the nineteenth century in particular witnessing a worldwide onslaught on nomadic ways of life (Bayly 434; Osterhammel 173).

In addition, the formative influence of childhood homes is one reason why the family is of such crucial importance to the discourse of psychoanalysis. In her study *Figurations of Exile*, Barbara Straumann even suggests that psychoanalysis is "the most paradigmatic critical discourse of twentieth-century culture to address questions of identity and belonging as well as the fundamental dislocation subtending all subjectivity" (13). Freud, for instance, famously used a bourgeois domestic metaphor when he argued that the ego "is not master in his own house" (*Introductory Lectures* 285), and such concepts as the family romance and the Oedipal triangle between mother, father, and child, are of course central to psychoanalytic endeavors. In addition, in later texts – such as *Group Psychology and the Analysis of the Ego* (1921) or *Civilization and Its Dis-*

contents (1930), Freud explicitly addresses the question of belonging to larger social structures.[29]

The most frequently evoked text by Freud on the issue of home is, however, his essay on the uncanny: a type of fear that arises when one is confronted with something that seems other to oneself, but which in fact represents a repressed, unassimilated part of the self. Noting that the German word *unheimlich* ('uncanny') not only contains the word *heimlich* ('secret,' 'hidden,' or 'covert'), but is also related to the homely and familiar (e.g. *das Heim, heimelig*; "The Uncanny" 126–134), Freud argues that the uncanny is best understood as "something that was long familiar to the psyche and was estranged from it only through being repressed" (148).[30] The double or *Doppelgänger* is, for Freud, one particularly frequent motif associated with the uncanny (141), and E. T. in fact functions as the uncanny double for Elliott. As Julia Kristeva notes, initially one's encounter with the double "is a shock" (*Strangers to Ourselves* 188) – and in Spielberg's film, shock is Elliott's first reaction at seeing E. T. when the boy stumbles upon him in the field behind his suburban home.[31] Crucially, E. T.'s reaction mirrors Elliott's precisely, and they flee from each other in panic. In time, however, Elliott overcomes his initial reaction of shock and coaxes E. T. to the safety of his room. There, E. T. soon becomes sleepy, and Elliott, too, drifts off to sleep, as if to emphasize the extent to which they mirror each other. In a later sequence, in the course of which Elliott explains the contents of his room to E. T., the alien tries to eat Elliott's toy car, prompting the boy to exclaim: "Hey, wait a second!

29 Another example for the psychoanalytic concern with home would be the collection of essays by D. W. Winnicott, *Home Is Where We Start From* (1986). Examples from Jungian or analytical psychology would include John Hill's *At Home in the World* (2010) as well as the essays published in *On Home and the Wanderer*, a special issue of *Spring: A Journal of Archetype and Culture* 85 (2011).

30 The German original runs: "[Das] Unheimlich ist wirklich nichts Neues oder Fremdes, sondern etwas dem Seelenleben von alters her Vertrautes, das ihm nur durch den Prozess der Verdrängung entfremdet worden ist" ("Das Unheimliche" 264).

31 Jung's concept of the shadow is in fact very similar to Freud's notion of the double. This becomes apparent, for instance, in Jung's essay "Archetypes of the Collective Unconscious": "[T]he meeting with ourselves belongs to the more unpleasant things that can be avoided so long as we can project everything negative into the environment. But if we are able to see our own shadow and can bear knowing about it, then a small part of the problem has already been solved" (20; § 44). The German original runs: "[D]ie Begegnung mit sich selbst gehört zu den unangenehmeren Dingen, denen man entgeht, solange man alles Negative auf die Umwelt projizieren kann. Ist man imstande, den eigenen Schatten zu sehen und das Wissen um ihn zu ertragen, so ist ein erster kleiner Teil der Aufgabe gelöst" ("Über die Archetypen des kollektiven Unbewussten" 23). For a good summary of Jung's concept of the shadow see Murray Stein, *Jung's Map of the Soul* (105–124).

No! You don't eat 'em. Are you hungry? I'm hungry" (Mathison 69). The emotional parallel between them thus continues, and while Elliott goes to the kitchen to grab some food, E. T. explores the boy's room and finds an umbrella. Suddenly, the umbrella opens and startles, not only E. T., but also Elliott, who is still downstairs in the kitchen. This moment makes it clear to the audience that there is a mysterious telepathic link between the two – and Freud explicitly mentions telepathy as yet another motif typically associated with the uncanny (141).

Given E. T.'s function as Elliott's (initially) uncanny double, there is a good case to be made that the alien in fact represents Elliott's unconscious. Thomas Sebeok, for instance, has pointed out that E. T. and Elliott are not merely friends, but in a profound sense "identical, as the boy's very name, *E*llio*tT*, insinuates" (661). From 'Elliott' to 'E. T.' by means of condensation and displacement: we are faced with two of the crucial mechanisms of the Freudian unconscious.[32] Moreover, in one scene in Spielberg's film E. T. makes a notably appreciative noise when seeing Elliott's mother, Mary, in a tight-fitting Halloween costume, as if Elliott's Oedipal desire for Mary had been displaced onto his alien friend. In fact, a scene was cut from the final version of the film that would have rendered this Oedipal dimension much more explicit, with E. T. going into Mary's room and leaving some candy on her pillow to imply "that E. T. had a crush on Mary" (Mathison 104). One may therefore speculate that the filmmaker's decision to cut the scene constituted an act of censorship in the precise psychoanalytic sense of an attempt to repress inadmissible desires.

Another sequence, at the end of which Elliott kisses a girl in school, not only strengthens the idea that E. T. embodies Elliott's unconscious, but also suggests that even desire itself – that seemingly innermost part of our nature – is in fact shaped at least in part by public forces. In this complex sequence, the film intercuts two different scenes: on the one hand, we see E. T. exploring the family home while everyone is away at school or work, and on the other hand we follow Elliott's adventures in the classroom. Throughout the sequence, the telepathic link between E. T. and Elliott is emphasized, as when E. T. drinks some beer that he discovers in the fridge, which leaves not only him, but also Elliott notably inebriated (with E. T. bumping into the kitchen cabinet, and Elliott winking at a pretty girl and then slowly sliding off his chair, onto the classroom floor). Both the alien and the boy eventually recover their wits, and we see E. T. watching TV while Elliott is now in biology class, where he and his classmates are expected to anesthetize frogs and then to dissect them. Elliott, however, when looking at

32 For a brief summary of these mechanisms see Freud, *The Joke and Its Relation to the Unconscious* (20–21).

the helpless, lonely frog on his desk, is suddenly reminded of E.T.; muttering "Save him" to himself, the boy first frees his own frog and then proceeds to liberate the others (Mathison 88) – which, unsurprisingly, leads to chaos in the classroom. The film now cuts back to E.T. watching TV, and we find him watching a "soppy love scene" from the movie *The Quiet Man* (Mathison 90). E.T. watches engrossed as the male protagonist grabs the arm of his female counterpart, pulling her close in a dramatic sweep and kissing her as passionately as only movie heroes can. Next, we return to the classroom, where Elliott will soon re-enact this heterosexual fantasy scenario with the pretty girl he had winked at earlier on. The scene thus bears out Slavoj Žižek's claim that cinema "doesn't give you *what* you desire; it tells you *how* to desire" (*The Pervert's Guide to Cinema*) – which in turn implies that our desires are to some extent alien to ourselves, shaped and mediated in crucial ways by the public media discourses to which we are exposed even in the privacy of our homes.[33]

It is at this point that we must note that E.T.'s role as a representation of Elliott's unconscious shifts from being at first associated with the Id (e.g. Oedipal desire) to becoming an embodiment of the super-ego. If E.T., in the beginning, provides Elliott merely with a mirror image of his own psychic drives, then after his death and resurrection the alien becomes an awe-inspiring, messianic figure who urges Gertie to "[b]e good," and who thus voices – very much in the Name of the Lacanian Father – the moral imperative commonly associated with the super-ego (Homer 57–58; Thurschwell 48). In passing, we may observe that E.T. tells only the female child to be good, and that this is perhaps due to the misogynist bias that Phyllis Deutsch detects in Spielberg's film (12–13). More importantly, for the time being, we must note that E.T.'s death is the moment when the telepathic link between the alien and Elliott is finally broken, as if to emphasize that the boy has now moved beyond his earlier, narcissistic identification with the double or mirror-image, and instead accepted the symbolic call of a newfound father figure.[34] It is precisely such intimate notions as desire and the uncanny, as well as the question of how the father's material and symbolic position within the familial home relates to wider socio-historical contexts, which

33 For a more general account of this Lacanian claim that Žižek makes in *The Pervert's Guide to Cinema* (dir. Sophie Fiennes) see Žižek's *Looking Awry* (6). For two similar accounts of the self as inseparable from otherness see Julie Kristeva, *Strangers to Ourselves* (1988), and Paul Ricoeur, *Oneself as Another* (1990).

34 Note that Terry Eagleton describes the symbolic order as a structure in which we are "never entirely at home," in part because the imaginary always remains with us as a kind of excess (*Trouble with Strangers* 84).

will be explored in detail in the discussion of William Faulkner's *Absalom, Absalom!* in chapter four.

Alienation and Oppression at Home: Feminist and Marxist Critiques

Some of the most powerful critiques of the father's position within the family home have arguably come from feminist thinkers. The institution of marriage, for instance, has historically been deeply problematic for women – an insight that is memorably expressed by Bathsheba Everdene in Thomas Hardy's *Far from the Madding Crowd* (1874), when she explains to Liddy, her maid and confidante, why simply to run away from an unhappy marital union does not constitute a viable solution for her:

> A runaway wife is an encumbrance to everybody, a burden to herself, and a byword – all of which make up a heap of misery greater than any that comes by staying at home, though this may include the trifling items of insults, beating and starvation. Liddy, if you ever marry – God forbid that you ever should – you'll find yourself in a fearful situation; but mind this, don't you flinch. Stand your ground and be cut to pieces. (299)

In a deeply patriarchal society, where married women are seen as belonging to their husbands in the sense of being their rightful property, it seems illusory to Bathsheba that leaving her husband would result in anything as desirable as freedom. On the contrary, for a woman in Victorian Britain such an act would mean enduring consequences that are so severe that it appears preferable to Bathsheba to stay in a home where one is exposed to "insults, beating and starvation" – which is, as feminists have long pointed out, a sadly appropriate description of the kinds of home in which many women have been forced to live (Blunt and Dowling 125–126). In short, true to the belief so memorably expressed in the slogan that 'the personal is political,' feminist critics have explored the extent to which the private space of the home is in fact intricately related to, and indeed inseparable from, the gendered division of the public sphere characteristic of patriarchal society.[35]

One key historical moment in the construction of modern gender difference is the so-called Age of Enlightenment. Jean-Jaques Rousseau, for instance, argued that women were by nature made to be subjugated, dependent on the judgment of men, and unsuited to abstract and speculative thought (*Émile* 411, 418, and 448) – views vehemently opposed even at the time (e.g. by Mary Wollstonecraft in *A Vindication of the Rights of Women*). As Dorinda Outram points

35 For a highly accessible introduction to feminist criticism see Pam Morris, *Literature and Feminism.*

out, the ideas of philosophers like Rousseau attempted to limit women's sphere to the domestic world, and some historians suggest that industrialization contributed to such a 'sexual division of labor.' The association of women with the domestic sphere in fact preceded the period of industrialization, and as Outram notes the true Enlightenment innovation was its use of medical or biological 'evidence' to naturalize earlier ideas about gender difference (91). At the same time, Outram continues, women in fact assumed eminently important functions in the creation and maintenance of an Enlightenment public sphere, both as hosts of *salons* and as authors (94–96). Accordingly, critics like Amanda Vickery have cautioned against the assumption that men and women truly lived in entirely 'separate spheres' (413; see Sharon Marcus 6–7; Michael McKeon, *The Secret History of Domesticity* 168–170).

Nevertheless, there are of course countless literary texts that evoke this ideology of separate spheres, from little-known Victorian novels like Annie Lucas's *The City and the Castle* ("[F]rom the calm, tender eyes of a noble, loving wife, shone the faithful, comprehensive love, that makes the light of an earthly home"; 427) to African American interwar classics like Zora Neale Hurston's *Their Eyes Were Watching God* ("She's uh woman and her place is in de home"; 69). Similarly, Ania Loomba has shown that in nationalist struggles against colonial masters, women are "usually cast as mothers or wives, and are called upon to literally and figuratively reproduce the nation" (180). Male nationalists have, in other words, often deployed women's supposedly private position in the family home for eminently public purposes. The key feminist insight is, in short, that in the critical analysis of home, we need to pay close attention to the way in which home participates in, and perhaps even underpins, the gendering of social space (including the public-private divide).

In the case of *E. T.*, for instance, Phyllis Deutsch argues that Elliott's mother, Mary, is systematically devalued as a character as part of the film's promotion of a patriarchal agenda. Deutsch observes, among other things, that the male children in the film never blame the absent father for their parents' separation. Instead, they lovingly remember the father while directing feelings of frustration at their mother. Moreover, according to Deutsch the film emphasizes Mary's inadequacy as a single parent in a scene where she calls the police because Elliott has temporarily gone missing:

> [A] policeman grills Mary trying to find out if anything has happened in the family that might have caused her son to run away. Mary tearfully replies that her husband has gone and that "it hasn't been easy on the children." Clearly, she's the one at fault: she's at home and not doing a proper job raising the kids. [...] In the viewer's mind,

> daddy's departure is subliminally excusable: would you want to live with such an unstable woman? (12–13)

The film, Deutsch continues, in effect portrays Mary as a comic buffoon who "constantly misses the obvious," and the film's religious infrastructure only serves to support this misogynist bias because it moves "from father to king to God with sweeping grandeur," leaving "a lot of troubled women in its wake" (12). If Mary, by the end of the film, does seem more emotionally stable, then for Deutsch this is not a sign of her progress as a woman, but instead appears as related to a "nice male scientist" who stands next to Mary in the movie's final scene (13). All homes, in short, need a competent mother, but for Deutsch *E. T.* makes the sexist point that female competence ultimately depends on the presence of a male – and although Deutsch's account of the portrayal of Mary may be somewhat too scathing, her argument certainly supports William Alexander's more cautious claim that the film's "sexual politics are not the most advanced" (27).

Crucially, feminism's insistence that the privacy of the home is inseparable from societal structures of domination constitutes its most direct link to the Marxist tradition, according to which social alienation necessarily affects a person's entire being. In a sense, this Marxian insight is already encapsulated in the etymology of the word 'economy,' which nowadays refers predominantly to public activities in the capitalist market, but which originally derives from the management of the *oikos*: the Ancient Greek term for 'household' or 'family' (OED; see McKeon, *The Secret History of Domesticity* 7–8). Moreover, the importance for classic Marxism to pay close attention to the material shape of the home is evident in Friedrich Engels's *The Condition of the Working Class in England in 1844*:

> I assert that thousands of industrious and worthy people – far worthier and more to be respected than all the rich of London – [...] find themselves in a condition unworthy of human beings; and that every proletarian, everyone, without exception, is exposed to a similar fate without any fault of his own and in spite of every possible effort.

> But in spite of all this, they who have some kind of a shelter are fortunate, fortunate in comparison with the utterly homeless. In London fifty thousand human beings get up every morning, not knowing where they are to lay their heads at night. (43–44)[36]

The poor are either homeless or live in the most unworthy conditions, and Engels insists that in such filthy circumstances "only a physically degenerate race, robbed of all humanity, degraded, reduced morally and physically to bestiality, could feel comfortable and at home" (75). Engels argues, then, that the industrial proletariat suffers from such precarious conditions at home that their humanity itself threatens to become deformed.

Meanwhile, if Engels focuses on the material conditions in workers' homes, Marx turns his attention to the process of production that, he argues, reduces the workers' sense of belonging or being at home. According to Marx, the force underlying proletarians' sense of unbelonging is their continual experience of estranged or alienated labor:

> What, then, constitutes the alienation of labor?
>
> First, the fact that labor is *external* to the worker, i.e., it does not belong to his essential being; that in his work, therefore, he does not affirm himself but denies himself, does not feel content but unhappy, does not develop freely his physical and mental energy but mortifies his body and ruins his mind. The worker therefore only feels himself outside his work, and in his work feels outside of himself. He is at home when he is not working, and when he is working he is not at home. His labor is therefore not voluntary, but coerced; it is *forced* labor. It is therefore not the satisfaction

36 The German original runs: "[I]ch behaupte, dass Tausende von fleissigen und braven Familien, viel braver, viel ehrenwerther als sämmtliche Reichen von London, in dieser eines Menschen unwürdigen Lage sich befinden, und dass jeder Proletarier, jeder ohne Ausnahme, ohne seine Schuld und trotz allen seinen Anstrengungen, von gleichem Schicksal getroffen werden kann. – / Aber bei alledem sind diejenigen noch glücklich, die nur noch ein Obdach irgend einer Art haben – glücklich gegen die ganz Obdachlosen. In London stehen jeden Morgen funfzig [sic] Tausend Menschen auf, ohne zu wissen, wo sie für die nächste Nacht ihr Haupt hinlegen sollen" (45).

> of a need; it is merely a *means* to satisfy needs external to it. (*Economic and Philosophic Manuscripts* 74; original emphasis)[37]

Marx thus suggests that all humans have a right to feel at home when at work – indeed, that the freedom to choose one's work according to one's abilities and desires constitutes the very essence of humanity as such (whereas animals are not in general able to make such choices; *Economic and Philosophic Manuscripts* 74–75).[38] However, in Marx's view, for the vast majority, the capitalist system of production reduces work to a mere means of survival – i.e. to its exchange-value – which in turn leaves the experience of work devoid of any use-value: of the specifically human pleasure that one can gain through creative self-expression.

In the case of *E. T.*, the effects of a social system where exchange-value trumps use-value can be seen most clearly in the technocratic approach of most of the film's adults to non-human life. The scene at school in which Elliott and his classmates are set the task of anesthetizing and dissecting frogs, for instance, confronts us with a society that inoculates its children with a disregard for other life-forms in the name of scientific knowledge: perfect evidence for Louis Al-

---

37 The German original runs: "Worin besteht nun die Entäusserung der Arbeit? / Erstens, dass die Arbeit dem Arbeiter *äusserlich* ist, d. h. nicht zu seinem Wesen gehört, dass er sich daher in seiner Arbeit nicht bejaht, sondern verneint, nicht wohl, sondern unglücklich fühlt, keine freie phsysische und geistige Energie entwickelt, sondern seine Physis abkasteit und seinen Geist ruiniert. Der Arbeiter fühlt sich daher erst ausser der Arbeit bei sich und in der Arbeit ausser sich. Zu Hause ist er, wenn er nicht arbeitet und wenn er arbeitet, ist er nicht zu Haus. Seine Arbeit ist daher nicht freiwillig, sondern gezwungen, *Zwangsarbeit.* Sie ist daher nicht die Befriedigung eines Bedürfnisses, sondern sie ist nur ein Mittel, um Bedürfnisse ausser ihr zu befriedigen" (*Ökonomisch-philosophische Manuskripte* 514; original emphasis).

38 See Marx's remarks in the third volume of *Capital*: "[T]he realm of freedom does not commence until the point is passed where labor under the compulsion of necessity and of external utility is required. [...] Just as the savage must wrestle with nature, in order to satisfy his wants, in order to maintain his life and reproduce it, so civilized man has to do it, and he must do it in all forms of society and under all possible modes of production. [... There] always remains a realm of necessity. Beyond it begins that development of human power, which is its own end, the true realm of freedom, which, however, can flourish only upon that realm of necessity as its basis" (*Capital* 954–955). The German original runs: "Das Reich der Feiheit beginnt in der Tat erst da, wo das Arbeiten, das durch Not und äussere Zweckmässigkeit bestimmt ist, aufhört [...]. Wie der Wilde mit der Natur ringen muss, um seine Bedürfnisse zu befriedigen, um sein Leben zu erhalten und zu reproduzieren, so muss es der Zivilisierte, und er muss es in allen Gesellschaftsformen und unter allen möglichen Produktionsweisen. [... Es bleibt] immer ein Reich der Notwendigkeit. Jenseits desselben beginnt die menschliche Kraftentwicklung, die sich als Selbstzweck gilt, das wahre Reich der Freiheit, das aber nur auf jenem Reich der Notwendigkeit als seiner Basis aufblühen kann" (*Das Kapital* 355).

thusser's thesis that schools form part of what he calls ideological state apparatuses (132–133).[39] Given this kind of education, it is not surprising that the government agents and scientists do not pay any heed to E. T.'s needs and desires, but instead simply try to capture, immobilize, and exploit him in order to gain new knowledge. Accordingly, when the scientists finally get their hands on the alien, they do not hesitate to link him up to their machines and to isolate him from Elliott, his only friend – just as the industrial laborer's experience of mechanized work often isolates him or her from fellow workers. In short, inured to scientific violence through years of training and therefore no longer knowing what they do, the scientists hasten E. T.'s Christ-like death. (We may add, incidentally, that Jesus happened to be the son of a working man.) We will revisit the problem of alienated work, as well as the question of how it relates to gendered spaces and bodies, in the discussion in chapter five of Pat Barker's *Union Street.*

Nature, Technology, and Communication

To the extent that the social system depicted in *E. T.* seems to have fostered alienation from nature as well as alienation between men, we may also relate the film to some of the theories proposed by Jean-Jacques Rousseau. Arguing against Thomas Hobbes, and echoing Michel de Montaigne's concept of the noble savage (Garrard 125), Rousseau can be seen as the first secular theorist of alienation. Rousseau suggested that man in the state of nature had been virtuous and innocent but had since become corrupted through the pressures of society towards conformity and dissimulation. In the preface to *A Discourse on Inequality*, Rousseau calls the state of nature "a state which no longer exists, which perhaps never existed, and which will probably never exist" (68), thus admitting freely that the concept may merely be a theoretical fiction that does not necessarily refer to a particular historical reality.[40] Moreover, as Andrew Biro contends, Rousseau did not advocate a return to nature in the naive sense of abandoning society altogether; rather, Rousseau "tried to articulate solutions to the problem of alienation from nature" while at the same time conceiving of human

39 In her novel *Ceremony*, Leslie Marmon Silko formulates a similar critique of the school's role in accustoming children to a disrespect of animal life by contrasting it to Native American beliefs (incidentally also using frogs "bloated with formaldehyde" as an image to bring across the point; 194).

40 In the French original, the full sentence runs: "Car ce n'est pas une légére entreprise de démêler ce qu'il y a d'originaire & d'artificiel dans la Nature actuelle de l'homme, & de bien connoître un Etat qui n'existe plus, qui n'a peut-être point existé, qui probablement n'existera jamais, & dont il est pourtant nécessaire d'avoir des Notions justes pour bien juger de nôtre état présent" (lvii – lviii; the spelling of the 1755 edition is retained).

beings "in a social (or postnatural) state" (Biro 60).[41] For Rousseau, alienation is thus a historically conditioned phenomenon that can, for that very reason, be overcome (or at least mitigated) through changes to the social structure.

And indeed, *E. T.*, too, does not dream naively of total regression to some pristine state of nature, but instead develops a critique of society's alienation from nature precisely along Rousseauian lines. At the beginning of Spielberg's film, we encounter E. T. and his fellow aliens in the deep night of a Californian forest, peacefully engaged in collecting samples of plants. The aliens do not simply cut off these plants, but instead remove them together with their roots as well as some soil to ensure that they can continue to thrive. Subsequently, the film's *mise-en-scène* emphasizes the contrast between, on the one hand, the aliens' quietly harmonious presence in the forest, and, on the other, the disruptive government agents, who arrive in droning cars with glaring lights and exhaust pipes spewing forth their toxic fumes. The contrast between these cars – metallic, angular contraptions – and the aliens' soft-glowing, chubby spaceship could, indeed, scarcely be more pointed. At the same time, the scene makes clear that Spielberg's film is not hostile to technology as such. Rather, in showing that the ecologically sensitive aliens have mastered the technology of interplanetary space travel – an achievement that has so far eluded the technocratic humans – *E. T.* suggests that a more respectful kind of science (i.e. one not driven exclusively by the logic of exchange-value) would in the long run be both more productive and beneficent.

The idea, however, that the alien way of life could serve as a model for a better society no longer works if the aliens in *E. T.* are conceived as by nature fundamentally other than humans – and according to William Alexander the construction of such an essential difference is precisely the ideological point of Spielberg's film. We have already examined Alexander's suggestion that E. T., as a dark-skinned alien, must be interpreted in racialist terms. However, Alexander further contends that the film *E. T.* attempts to naturalize racial difference, and that the scene in which Elliott saves the frogs from being anesthetized and dissected is crucial to this ideological project: "Elliott, E. T. in mind, releases his frog and urges the other pupils to release theirs, chanting 'Back to

41 After all Rousseau maintains, in *The Social Contract*, that society is inevitable because "there is a point in the development of mankind at which the obstacles to men's self-preservation in the state of nature are too great to be overcome by the strength that any one individual can exert" (54; bk. 1, ch. 6). The French original runs: "Je suppose les hommes parvenus à ce point où les obstacles qui nuisent à leur conservation dans l'état de nature, l'emportent par leur résistance sur les forces que chaque individu peut employer pour se maintenir dans cet état primitif" (*Contrat social* 20).

the river and forest,' a refrain the other children pick up" (31). Both E.T. and the frogs, Alexander maintains, are thus portrayed as being "out of their native habitat"; they are, the implication is, depicted as naturally unfit for life in a white, suburban environment, and must therefore "go back to where they came from" (31–33). For Alexander, that is to say, *E.T.* superficially promotes tolerance and acceptance, but is ultimately an attempt at cementing exclusion. Accordingly, as the film progresses, E.T. becomes increasingly sick, which would only seem to confirm that there is indeed something in the earthly environment to which the alien is simply unable to adapt. At any rate, if Alexander's claim that *E.T.* naturalizes difference is correct, then this would undermine the idea that the aliens could become role models for the humans, as it hardly makes sense to emulate those who are clearly unfit to cope with the natural conditions that apply on earth.

However, Alexander's argument in fact fails to do justice to Spielberg's film because it does not take into account the central role of communication. Early on in the film, E.T. and Elliott are not really able to communicate with each other at all, and only gradually does the alien learn to use human language. Once he is able to make himself understood, however, E. T. is quick to point out to Elliott that he would like to re-establish contact with his fellow aliens: "E.T. phone home" (Mathison 100). Accordingly, we do not necessarily have to attribute the fact that E.T. becomes increasingly sick in the course of the film to his supposedly natural 'unfitness.' Instead, we may suggest that his illness is the consequence of a crushing sense of isolation: hostility from all sides in the host community, and an utter lack of communicative ties with the home community. Indeed, what supports this interpretation is the fact that E.T.'s resurrection towards the end of the film occurs at the precise moment when the other aliens, having picked up a signal of distress from a device that E.T. built especially to re-establish contact, are finally about to return to earth. E.T.'s illness thus does not serve to naturalize his absolute Otherness, but instead suggests that his suffering arises from a lack of communal support, either from aliens or from humans (with the exception of a handful of children, who are not in a position of power and on whom E.T. therefore cannot depend in the long run for protection).

Communication – or the lack of it – thus prove vital to the notion of home as it is encapsulated in *E.T.*, and several critics have likewise noted that communication in the form of language and cultural conventions is crucial to our sense of belonging.[42] For instance, in his study *Migration in World History*, Patrick Manning notes that those "who move from one community to another must learn not only a new language, but also an accompanying set of customs" (4). Likewise, Agnes Heller emphasizes the importance of cultural conventions for our sense of being at home:

> A home is always a human habitat, a network of human bonds and ties, a community of kind. At home, one talks without footnotes but one can talk without footnotes on the condition that one talks to someone who understands. And if one understands the other from a few words, allusions, and gestures, a common cognitive background is already presupposed. (10)

Heller emphasizes that communication is facilitated by a "common cognitive background," and Friedrich Nietzsche – who is otherwise notoriously skeptical about language and the value of communication (Grimm 24n26) – concedes that shared, lived experience greatly facilitates the exchange of ideas:

> It is not sufficient to use the same words to understand one another: we must also employ the same words for the same kind of internal experiences, we must in the end have experiences *in common*. On this account the people of one nation understand one another better than those belonging to different nations, even when they use the same language; or rather, when people have lived long together under similar circumstances (of climate, soil, danger, requirement, toil) there *originates* therefrom an entity that 'understands itself' – namely, a nation. (*Beyond Good and Evil* 213–214; § 268; original emphasis)[43]

42 See Evetts-Secker for a Jungian interpretation of the importance of formulaic expressions in creating "a language in which the soul is at home" (138).

43 The German original runs: "Es genügt noch nicht, um sich einander zu verstehen, dass man dieselben Worte gebraucht; man muss dieselben Worte auch für dieselbe Gattung innerer Erlebnisse gebrauchen, man muss zuletzt seine Erfahrung miteinander *gemein* haben. Deshalb verstehen sich die Menschen Eines Volkes besser unter einander als Zugehörige verschiedner Völker, selbst wenn sie sich der gleichen Sprache bedienen; oder vielmehr, wenn Menschen lange unter ähnlichen Bedingungen (des Klima's, des Bodens, der Gefahr, der Bedürfnisse, der Arbeit) zusammen gelebt haben, *so entsteht* daraus etwas, das 'sich versteht,' ein Volk" (*Jenseits von Gut und Böse* 253; § 268; original emphasis).

Nietzsche's remarks point to the eminently social nature of language, which acquires its meaning in reference to shared experiences, where words can be measured against their context in an intersubjective process of negotiation.[44]

To say that the seemingly immaterial homes of language and communication are social phenomena necessarily implies that the ability to communicate is determined by decidedly material conditions. As Aijaz Ahmad rightly insists, the idea of 'determination' is not to be understood as implying an utter lack of human agency; rather, it refers "to the givenness of the circumstance within which individuals *make* their choices, their lives, their histories" (6; original emphasis). For example, in Spielberg's film, E.T.'s ability to communicate with his fellow aliens is determined by the meager resources at his disposal: an electronic toy, an umbrella, and some other items he can find in Elliott's home. If E.T. nevertheless manages to build a device that allows him to send a signal of distress to his fellow aliens, then it is reasonable to assume that he would have been able to construct a much more powerful and reliable device if he had been welcomed by his host society and given access to a wider range of resources. John Durham Peters is thus right in insisting that communication is not merely a question of semantics, but "more fundamentally a political and ethical problem" (*Speaking into the Air* 30).

More generally, we can say that an individual's possibilities for 'home-making,' and specifically the odds for or against that individual's ability to maintain multiple and spatially dispersed homes, change significantly depending on the social and material resources at hand. For instance, while some theorists celebrate nomadic identities as an alternative to oppressive power structures (e.g. Deleuze, *Difference and Repetition* 45–47; Deleuze and Guattari, *A Thousand Plateaus*, 60; see also Tally, *Melville, Mapping and Globalization* 65–67), others emphasize that "the resources for self-invention are unequally distributed," and that accordingly the nomadic identities of a select few, though intended to subvert oppressive power structures, in fact depend on these oppressive structures (Peters, "Exile, Nomadism, and Diaspora" 34). Likewise, Blunt and Dowling have pointed out that the creation and maintenance of dia-

44 In an extended discussion, one would also have to bear in mind that not all languages have a word that is synonymous with home. Judith Flanders, for example, distinguishes between "home and house languages" (4). The home languages – English, the Germanic and Scandinavian languages, as well as the Finno-Ugric group – distinguish between the concepts of *home* and *house* (3). The Romance and Slavic languages, by contrast, "have just one word for both meanings" (4). See also Anna Wierzbicka, who in *Imprisoned in English* (2014) cautions against the uncritical assumption that concepts which exist in English – "the first ever global lingua franca" (64) – necessarily exist in all languages, even if they do not have a specific word for a given concept.

sporic homes is greatly facilitated by easy access to particular types of media and communication (206; see Manning 160). Moreover, given the importance for diasporic communities of everyday rituals of food preparation and consumption (Blunt and Dowling 216), it is clear that those who cannot afford the foodstuffs required are also excluded from communal rituals. We will revisit such considerations of the link between community, rituals, and forms of communication – as well as humankind's relation to the natural world (e.g. through the construction of a pastoral space) – in the discussion in chapter six of Jeffrey Eugenides's *The Virgin Suicides.*

Knowing Home: The Uses and Abuses of Defamiliarization

By way of concluding this introductory chapter, we need to explore briefly the importance of conventions for establishing a sense of home (as well as, more generally, the relation between home, familiarity, and knowledge). Commenting on the role of conventions, Theano S. Terkenli insists that it is precisely through repetition, routine, and ritual that we turn places into homes:

> [H]abits that repetitively unfold in specific contexts differentiate these locales or circumstances from the rest of the known world. [...] Over time an individual develops numerous behavioral, cognitive, and affective routines by investing resources and emotional commitment. The same process occurs at a group level in the creation of a collective home in the form of a common cultural background and a common homeland. (326)

The conventions and routines of home thus allow us to save both cognitive and affective energies, thus making it possible for us to employ these psychic energies for other purposes. This idea is not of recent origin, for as early as 1815, Percy Bysshe Shelley argued in his essay "On Life" that the "wonder of our being" is in a sense far too great, and that therefore we depend on a "mist of familiarity" that shields us "from an astonishment which would otherwise absorb and overawe" (633). In other words, the limited economy of psychic life renders familiarity eminently desirable.

At the same time, however, too much familiarity may blind us to the world around us, which is why the Russian Formalists and others before them insisted on a need for carefully administered doses of defamiliarization. The concept of defamiliarization or *ostranenie* ('making strange') was introduced by Victor Shklovsky in 1917 in an essay entitled "Art as Technique." In this essay, Shklovsky suggests that when "perception becomes habitual," it retreats "into the area of the unconsciously automatic" (19). To combat the resulting mental numbness, art must attempt to 'de-habitualize' perception:

> The purpose of art is to impart the sensation of things as they are perceived and not as they are known. The technique of art is to make objects 'unfamiliar,' to make forms difficult, to increase the difficulty and length of perception because the process of perception is an aesthetic end in itself and must be prolonged. (20)

According to Shklovsky, it is the form in which an object is presented in the work of art that forces us to perceive this object as if we were "seeing it for the first time" (21). In this way, defamiliarization may reveal the strangeness that lies hidden at the heart of the familiar – an idea that has prompted Nicholas Royle to observe that defamiliarization bears more than a passing resemblance both to Freud's notion of the uncanny and to the Heideggerian concept of existential angst (4). Likewise, Royle points out, the idea that defamiliarization may revolutionize our way of perceiving the world underpins Bertolt Brecht's concept of a *Verfremdungs-* or alienation effect (5).[45] This point, too, had already been developed by Percy Bysshe Shelley, in his 1821 essay "A Defence of Poetry":

> [Poetry] strips the veil of familiarity from the world, and lays bare the naked and sleeping beauty which is the spirit of its forms.
>
> [… I]t purges from our inward sight the film of familiarity which obscures from us the wonder of our being. It compels us to feel that which we perceive, and to imagine that which we know. It creates anew the universe after it has been annihilated in our minds by the recurrence of impressions blunted by reiteration. (698)

For Shelley, as for the Russian Formalists, it is poetry or art that re-infuses life and vitality into a universe annihilated by repetition, tearing the veil of familiarity from our eyes and thus allowing us to experience – and know – the world anew and, therefore, more profoundly.

In fact, the idea of familiarity as a threat to real understanding goes back even further, to Georg Wilhelm Friedrich Hegel, who claims, in the Preface to his *Phenomenology of Spirit*, that "the familiar, just because it is familiar, is not cognitively understood" (18; § 31).[46] Indeed, Hegel even posits a need for the style of truly philosophical writing to be so unfamiliar and difficult that such texts might have to be read repeatedly before they can be understood (39; § 63–65). Importantly, whereas Shelley and the Russian Formalists tend to see in defami-

---

45 See also Jacques Rancière: "[I]t is in the moments when the real world wavers and seems to reel into mere appearance, more than in the slow accumulation of day-to-day experiences, that it becomes possible to form a judgement about the world" (19).

46 The German original runs: "Das Bekannte überhaupt ist darum, weil es *bekannt* ist, nicht *erkannt*" (24).

liarization the essence of 'poetry' or 'literariness' – i.e. a primarily aesthetic technique – for Hegel it is a necessary step in the acquisition of true knowledge as such, and thus not strictly speaking 'merely' an artistic, but instead a philosophical enterprise. In a sense, it is this idea that Oscar Wilde picks up on in his dialogue "The Critic as Artist," where one of the interlocutors suggests:

> An age that has no criticism is either an age in which art is immobile, hieratic, and confined to the reproduction of formal types, or an age that possesses no art at all. [... T]here has never been a creative age that has not been critical also. For it is the critical faculty that invents fresh forms. The tendency of creation is to repeat itself. (254)

For Wilde's speaker as much as for Hegel, the new, unexpected, and unfamiliar is thus not the effect of the creative impulse, but instead the product of the "critical faculty."

In *E. T.* there is at least one scene that illustrates perfectly how it is possible implicitly to critique a particular state of affairs by confronting the audience with the familiar as seen through unfamiliar eyes. In the scene in question, Elliott tries to explain the contents of his room to E. T., but for the audience it is clear that the alien cannot but find Elliott's explanations confusing:

> Coke, see? We drink it. It's, uh, it's a drink. You know... food. [Showing E. T. two action figures.] These are toys. These are little men. This is Greedo, and then this is Hammerhead. [...] And look, they can even have wars. Look at this. [Taking two plastic fishes, a smaller one and a shark.] And look, fish. The fish eat the fish food. And the shark eats the fish. But nobody eats a shark. See, this is Pez. Candy. See, you eat it. You put the candy in here, and then when you lift up the head, the candy comes out, and you can eat it! You want some? [Pointing to his peanut-shaped piggybank.] Oh, this is a peanut. You eat it. But you can't eat this one, 'cause this is fake. This is money. See? We put the money in the peanut. You see? Bank. You see? [Showing E. T. a tiny toy car.] And then this is a car. This is what we get around in. [Offering the toy car to E. T.] You see? (Mathison 68–69)

What on earth, for instance, is E. T. to make of the idea that we "put the money in the peanut"? And how is he to understand Elliott's explanation that "this is a car. This is what we get around in" – given the fact that Elliott is showing him a *toy* car, which is far too small for any human to get around in? This notably comic scene in *E. T.* is, in short, also an exact application of one technique of defamiliarization that Shklovsy identifies in Tolstoy: making the familiar seem strange by prompting the audience to see things from an unfamiliar point of view, for example a horse's (21) – or, as in our case, an extra-terrestrial's. Suddenly we see the strangeness at the heart of a boy's room: it harbors fantasies of war – the fighting action figures – and generally reflects a world where the small fish are eaten by the sharks, and which, already, revolves around money and, of course, cars: that ultimate symbol of individual freedom through consumption. Terry Eagleton thus rightly insists that we "can engage with the wider world simply by recording what goes on at home" (*The English Novel* 322) – provided that we manage to see the familiar as if we were perceiving it for the first time.

At the same time, even if we accept that defamiliarization is a necessary technique for any critical enterprise – very much including the present one – we should not therefore see it as the binary opposite of a desire to belong. Rather, as Hegel suggests, the ultimate "aim of knowledge is to divest the objective world that stands opposed to us of its strangeness, and, as the phrase is, to find ourselves at home in it" – and this, for Hegel, involves a dialectical return to belonging as a complement to previous acts of self-alienation (*Logic* 289; § 194).[47] It is, presumably, the same idea that the German poet Novalis wanted to express in a frequently quoted aphorism: "Philosophy is actually homesickness – the *urge to be everywhere at home*" (*Philosophical Writings* 135; original emphasis).[48] To relinquish the quest for a sense of home altogether would thus defeat the very purpose of defamiliarization. Moreover, as Terry Eagleton observes, to indulge in the denigration of home, the familiar, and the everyday is tantamount to accepting a peculiarly modernist bias against the common life: "In the transition from realism to modernism, a fascination with the texture of everyday living gives way to a mandarin scepticism of it. Common experience is now the locus of illusion, not of truth" (*Trouble with Strangers* 277).[49] To assume, that is to say, that everything about the places we call home is false and coercive is just as problematic as blindly to accept everything that is familiar. When studying home, we may therefore want to bear in mind the words of Friedrich Dürrenmatt's Inspector Bärlach when he talks about the idea of loving one's country: "One should not be ashamed of one's love, [...] only it has to be stern and critical,

47 The German original runs: "Beim Erkennen ist es überhaupt darum zu tun, der uns gegenüberstehenden objektiven Welt ihre Fremdheit abzustreifen, uns, wie man zu sagen pflegt, in dieselbe zu finden" (*Die Wissenschaft der Logik* 351; § 195).

48 "Die Philosophie ist eigentlich Heimweh, ein Trieb überall zu Hause zu sein" (*Schriften* 179).

49 For an interesting recent overview of ideas concerning the concept of the everyday, see Bryony Randall, "A Day's Time: The One-Day Novel and the Temporality of the Everyday" (2016).

otherwise it turns into the love of a monkey" (183; my translation).[50] Home-making requires patience as well as, at times, critical effort. But ought we therefore to privilege the pain of unbelonging? It is this tension between alienation and belonging that lies at the heart of the six readings that follow, starting with *Moby-Dick* in chapter one.

50 The German original runs: "Man soll sich seiner Liebe nicht schämen, [...] nur muss sie streng und kritisch sein, sonst wird sie eine Affenliebe." In English translations, the inspector's last name is usually given as Barlach.

1 "Another Orphan": Trauma and Transcendental Homelessness in Herman Melville's *Moby-Dick: or, The Whale*

To understand home we need to understand homelessness, and in few other novels is home as fundamentally absent as in Herman Melville's *Moby-Dick: or, The Whale* (1851).[1] We find, for instance, that the crew of the Pequod and its monomaniac leader, Captain Ahab, spend most of the narrative far from home, with only one of the mariners returning from the voyage to tell the tale. We learn, too, that the loved ones who have remained at home can only communicate with the Pequod via letters entrusted to outward-bound whalers – letters that may take years to reach their addressees, and perhaps will never arrive at all (196; ch. 53). The sailors' physical absence from home is thus exacerbated by an almost complete lack of communicative ties to their home communities.

In what follows, we will focus in particular on Ishmael's and Ahab's sense of unbelonging, and on how it can be read in relation to such diverse ideas as Emersonian self-reliance, post-traumatic stress disorder, and Hegel's master-slave dialectic. We will begin the discussion by examining Ishmael's profound sense of alienation, which he attempts to combat through discursive constructions of universal belonging that seem persuasive but which, on closer inspection, turn out to be highly problematic. One way of interpreting Ishmael's alienation is to see it as arising from his lack of self-reliance – in contrast to Ahab, who in many ways embodies Emerson's ideal. At the same time, *Moby-Dick* undermines any simple binary opposition between Ishmael and Ahab, and the novel in effect constitutes a sustained critique of the concept of self-reliance as such. Moreover, we will find that both Ishmael and Ahab come from broken homes, and that both suffer from very particular kinds of unbelonging: social alienation in the case of Ishmael, and mental alienation (or 'madness') in the case of Ahab. Ultimately, though both experience moments of spiritual comfort that could in fact help them to combat alienation, neither Ishmael nor Ahab manages to overcome their profound sense of homelessness.

---

1 [51] I would like to thank Simone Heller-Andrist and Christa Schönfelder for their comments on early versions of this chapter, as well as Sarah Chevalier and Anja Neukom-Hermann for their feedback on the final version.

If belonging proves elusive for Melville's characters, for us as readers it is likewise difficult ever to feel at home in a novel that, from the very outset, confronts us with highly unusual kinds of textuality. The following, for instance, are the opening paragraphs of *Moby-Dick*:

> Etymology
>
> (*Supplied by a Late Consumptive Usher to a Grammar School*)
>
> [The pale Usher – threadbare in coat, heart, body, and brain; I see him now. He was ever dusting his old lexicons and grammars, with a queer handkerchief, mockingly embellished with all the gay flags of all the known nations of the world. He loved to dust his old grammars; it somehow mildly reminded him of his mortality.]
>
> *Etymology*
>
> "While you take in hand to school others, and to teach them by what name a whale-fish is to be called in our tongue, leaving out, through ignorance, the letter H, which almost alone maketh up the signification of the word, you deliver that which is not true."
>
> *Hackluyt.*
>
> "WHALE. * * * Sw. and Dan. *hval.* This animal is named from roundness or rolling; for in Dan. *hvalt* is arched or vaulted."
>
> *Webster's Dictionary.*

Even in purely formal terms, these paragraphs are likely to strike one as odd: square as well as round brackets, indented quotations, asterisks and a title – "Etymology" – that appears twice, once in a larger font and once in italics. Likewise, these paragraphs prove unsettling in terms of content, as they confront us with an eccentric figure who is no longer alive ("*Late* Consumptive Usher"; emphasis added), as well as with the twin possibility of mockery and untruth ("mockingly embellished," "you deliver that which is not true").[2] It does not help, moreover, that this first section on the etymology of the word *whale* is followed by a longer and equally puzzling section containing eighty quotations on whales from a seemingly random array of texts (e.g. the Book of Genesis, Montaigne's *Apology for Raimond Sebond*, and *Captain Cowley's Voyage round the Globe*). These "Extracts," as they are referred to in the text, were apparently "*Supplied by a Sub-Sub-Librarian*," whom the narrator calls a "painstaking burrower and grub-worm of a poor devil" (8; original emphasis). In short, the opening of *Moby-Dick* is one of the oddest in the literary canon, and perhaps the best indicator of just how unhomely it feels to most readers – including some leading

2 While the layout may vary from one edition to the next, it always remains striking and unusual.

literary critics – is the fact that they tend simply to ignore these sections, pretending instead that the novel opens with the first phrase of chapter one: "Call me Ishmael" (e.g. Eagleton, *How to Read Literature* 23; Edinger 22; Peretz 36).[3] More generally, we will find that *Moby-Dick* is "a work that breaks all boundaries of genre" (Robert K. Martin 11) – a novel that juxtaposes various styles and registers and that continually raises expectations which it then proceeds to thwart. In *Moby-Dick*, characters as well as readers thus find it exceedingly difficult to establish a sense of home; significantly, the novel's final word is "orphan" (427; "Epilogue").

Moby-Dick has often been read as a Great American Novel (Buell 138), and the desire to do so – i.e. to use it, as Nick Selby puts it, to "define what American literature might be" (8) – perhaps constitutes an indirect response to the fundamental sense of homelessness conveyed by the text: a desire to fill the void of unbelonging by turning Melville's novel itself into a symbolic key to the imagined community of the American nation.[4] And indeed, we will see that there is good reason to read Melville's tale as an allegory of the ship of the American state – a ship that has strayed dangerously far from its intended course. However, we will also find that the novel simultaneously discourages allegorical readings.[5] Like the Pequod's crew, readers are thus tossed to and fro on the stormy seas of *Moby-Dick*, unable to find that "final harbor, whence we unmoor no more" (373; ch. 114); like Ahab, we eventually begin to wonder "whether the world is anchored anywhere" (385; ch. 121). Both formally and thematically, *Moby-Dick* is thus a deeply agnostic novel: admitting to, even longing for, the possibility of transcendence, but failing truly to believe in the existence of a transcendental home. Indeed, Melville's novel even suggests that an unconditional belief in transcendence is likely to lead to personal as well as political disaster, and it is only in the most fleeting of moments that it seems possible to discern, on the horizon of *Moby-Dick*'s narrative universe, a utopian alternative

3 For a slightly different and more detailed reading of "Extracts" and "Etymology," see Robert T. Tally, Jr., *Melville, Mapping and Globalization* 54–61.

4 See Benedict Anderson, who defines the nation as "an imagined political community – and imagined as both inherently limited and sovereign" (6). For an illuminating discussion of the concept of the Great American Novel, see Lawrence Buell, "The Unkillable Dream of the Great American Novel: *Moby-Dick* as Test Case." One of Buell's key points in this essay is that "a great American novel project must be transnational and also transgeneric" (138).

5 See also Robert T. Tally, Jr., who notes the strong tendency by critics to read *Moby-Dick* "as an essentially American national narrative," but who himself emphasizes "the powerful postnational energies" of Melville's novel (*Melville, Mapping and Globalization* 51 and 54).

to orphaned existence: moments of common endeavor and bodily comfort in which the question of transcendence is suspended in favor of a home in the here and now.

Alienation and Home-Making Practices

The problem of homelessness and alienation proves central to Ishmael's narrative from the very beginning – and Ishmael provides us with notably contradictory explanations for his sense of 'unbelonging.' Looking back, as a narrator, to the time before he joined the Pequod's crew, Ishmael attempts to explain his fateful decision to go to sea. At first, Ishmael's light-hearted tone suggests that this decision was entirely incidental: "[H]aving little or no money in my purse, and nothing particular to interest me on shore, I thought I would sail about a little and see the watery part of the world" (18; ch. 1). However, we can reasonably doubt whether Ishmael's decision is indeed based merely on the whim of a moment, both because he in fact admits to a lack of financial resources ("little or no money") and because the phrase "nothing particular to interest me on shore" barely conceals a fundamental sense of isolation: Ishmael has no interest on shore – neither financial, nor intellectual, nor emotional. There is, in short, nothing and no one there who could make him want to stay. Ishmael's subsequent remarks confirm that we are dealing here with an underlying problem:

> Whenever I find myself growing grim about the mouth; whenever it is a damp, drizzly November in my soul; whenever I find myself involuntarily pausing before coffin warehouses, and bringing up the rear of every funeral I meet; and especially whenever my hypos get such an upper hand of me, that it requires a strong moral principle to prevent me from deliberately stepping into the street, and methodically knocking people's hats off – then, I account it high time to get to sea as soon as I can. (18; ch. 1)

Ishmael's use of the word "whenever" in this passage reveals that a profound sense of alienation is a recurring problem in his life, and that his going to sea is a rather desperate attempt to prevent himself from committing random acts of aggression against innocent bystanders ("methodically knocking people's hats off"). His genial tone should thus not seduce us into underestimating the extent of his crisis of unbelonging.

The idea that Ishmael's sense of alienation is more fundamental than it appears at first sight is confirmed by his very name, which constitutes an intertextual link to biblical exile. According to the bible, Ishmael is one of the sons of Abraham, and God prophesies before his birth that Ishmael's "hand will be against every man, and every man's hand against him" (Genesis 16: 12). The name Ishmael is therefore, as Wadlington Warwick observes, "a synonym for alienation between the name-bearer and all other men" (141). Moreover, the phrase Melville's first-person narrator uses to open his tale – "*Call* me Ishmael" (emphasis added) – sounds as if we were not given the narrator's real name, but instead a pseudonym chosen "for patently symbolic reasons" (Warwick 141; see also Eagleton, *How to Read Literature* 23).[6] Like the deceptively light-hearted passages discussed above, the narrator's name thus indicates that all is not well between him and his fellow men.

At the same time, it is possible to read the choice of the name Ishmael as one instance of what Samuel Kimball calls Ishmael's desire to "make a narrative home of homelessness" (541): to mitigate his own sense of alienation by refracting his experience through the stories of others. Sigmund Freud, for instance, suggests that comparisons and analogies have the capacity to reduce unfamiliarity: "[W]e compare the less familiar with the more familiar, [...] and use the comparison to explain the item that is more difficult and unfamiliar" (*The Joke and Its Relation to the Unconscious* 202; see Punter 90).[7] Accordingly, if the name is indeed a pseudonym adopted by Melville's narrator, then the implicit comparison between his own experiences and the familiar biblical story of Ishmael may be read as an attempt symbolically to reduce his sense of isolation. Perhaps more importantly, however, the intertextual reference serves to reduce unfamiliarity on the part of the reader – at least, that is, if we assume "that writer and audience possess a common knowledge" (Warwick 141), for the allusion only has this effect for those who are familiar with the biblical narrative. This, in turn, reminds us of the double-edged quality of intertextual home-making practices, as those readers who are unfamiliar with the biblical narrative may end up feeling excluded from the novel's implied readership (see introduction).

Examining further the biblical parallel established in *Moby-Dick*, we find that both the novel's narrator and the biblical Ishmael are treated badly by their step-mothers, which may imply that there is a link between alienation in later life and the lack of a stable childhood home. In the biblical account, Abraham's wife, Sarah, at first proves unable to bear children, and so Abraham "went in

---

6 Warwick further argues that the pseudonymous nature of the name is evidenced by the fact that no character ever calls the narrator Ishmael. While this claim is not quite correct – Captain Peleg does so when Ishmael enlists as a sailor on the *Pequod* (77; ch. 16) – the oversight does not invalidate Warwick's general point, since it is perfectly possible for narrators to misrepresent the 'actual' events, and to have characters use pseudonyms instead of the 'real' names.

7 "Es kommt hinzu, dass das Gleichnis einer Verwendung fähig ist, welche eine Erleichterung der intellektuellen Arbeit mit sich bringt, wenn man nämlich, wie zumeist üblich, das Unbekanntere mit dem Bekannten [...] vergleicht und durch diesen Vergleich das Fremdere und Schwierigere erläutert" (*Der Witz* 181).

unto Hagar," Sarah's maid, who eventually gave birth to Ishmael (Genesis 21: 16; KJV). Immediately there is strong tension between Sarah and her maid, and when many years later Sarah miraculously gives birth to Isaac, she urges Abraham to banish Ishmael and his mother: "Cast out this bondwoman and her son: for the son of this bondwoman shall not be heir with my son" (Genesis 21: 10; KJV). Initially Abraham is reluctant, but when God assures him that he will protect Ishmael, Abraham complies with Sarah's wish to have Ishmael removed from the community. The relationship between Sarah and her stepson can thus hardly be called particularly loving. Similarly, in *Moby-Dick*, the narrator recalls that his stepmother "was all the time whipping me, or sending me to bed supperless" (37; ch. 4). This, in turn, explains the narrator's choice of metaphor later in the novel, when he speaks of a "step-mother world, so long cruel – forbidding" (405; ch. 132). Never fully at home even as a child, Melville's Ishmael remains unable to belong in later years.[8]

The resulting desire to "make a narrative home of homelessness" (Kimball 541) explains, among other things, why Ishmael is so interested in the character of Perth, a blacksmith, whose alienation from society, too, is connected to a broken home. Ishmael introduces Perth, whose function on the level of plot is relatively marginal, with a detailed account of the story of his life.[9] Formerly an "artisan of famed excellence," with a "youthful, daughter-like, loving wife, and three blithe, ruddy children," Perth becomes fatefully addicted to alcohol and eventually goes bankrupt, with his wife and children dying in abject poverty (368–369; ch. 112):

> Death seems the only desirable sequel for a career like this; but Death is only a launching into the region of the strange Untried; it is but the first salutation to the possibilities of the immense Remote, the Wild, the Watery, the Unshored; therefore, to the death-longing eyes of such men, who still have left in them some interior compunctions against suicide, does the all-contributed and all-receptive ocean alluringly spread forth his whole plain of unimaginable, taking terrors, and wonderful, new-life adventures [...]. (369; ch. 112)

Forever estranged from the "equally abhorred and abhorring, landed world" (369; ch. 112), Perth seeks refuge in the oblivious infinity of the "all-receptive ocean" – partly because of "some interior compunctions against suicide." This latter point is important because Ishmael, too, has felt tempted to end his life,

8 McLoughlin, by contrast, argues that Ishmael's biblical name links all sailors to outcasts" (61).

9 Later in the novel, Perth forges a new harpoon for Ahab shortly before the climactic chase of Moby Dick (370–372; ch. 113).

but opts for going to sea instead, as a "substitute for pistol and ball": "With a philosophical flourish Cato throws himself upon his sword; I quietly take to the ship" (18; ch. 1). Both Perth and Ishmael, then, are trying to escape from the memories of broken homes, and going to sea is an attempt to prevent aggression not only against others, but also against themselves: a truly Freudian sublimation of a seemingly implacable death drive.

Of course, in Freudian psychoanalysis, the death drive is not merely the bane of unhappy individuals with difficult pasts, but a universal condition of human life.[10] Therefore, it is perhaps not surprising that Ishmael – after initially portraying his urge to go to sea as merely an incidental, individual problem – suddenly suggests that all humans necessarily suffer from a similar sense of alienation. Ishmael at first remains relatively cautious, asserting only that "*almost* all men in their degree, some time or other, cherish *very nearly* the same feelings towards the ocean" (18; ch. 1, emphasis added). However, he quickly abandons any such show of circumspection, suggesting instead that man's mysterious attraction to the ocean is an inevitable by-product of human selfhood as such:

> Why upon your first voyage as a passenger, did you yourself feel such a mystical vibration, when first told that you and your ship were now out of sight of land? Why did the old Persians hold the sea holy? Why did the Greeks give it a separate deity, and own brother of Jove? Surely all this is not without meaning. And still deeper the meaning of that story of Narcissus, who because he could not grasp the tormenting, mild image he saw in the fountain, plunged into it and was drowned. But *that same image, we ourselves see in all rivers and oceans.* It is the image of the ungraspable phantom of life; and this is the key to it all. (19–20; ch. 1; emphasis added)

Gone are such guarded phrases as "very nearly" or "almost." Instead, Ishmael now claims that all of us ("we ourselves") share Narcissus's fatal attraction to watery reflections.

Ishmael's theory thus has strong affinities with Jacques Lacan's account of the development of subjectivity. Lacan describes the mirror stage as an irreversible process of subject-formation through alienation:

10 The following passage may serve to exemplify Freud's position: "The fateful question for the human species seems to me to be whether and to what extent their cultural development will succeed in mastering the disturbance of their communal life by the human instinct of aggression and self-destruction" (*Civilization and Its Discontents* 111; see also Thurschwell 88–89). The German original runs: "Die Schicksalsfrage der Menschenart scheint mir zu sein, ob und in welchem Masse es ihrer Kulturentwicklung gelingen wird, der Störung des Zusammenlebens durch den menschlichen Aggressions- und Selbstvernichtungstrieb Herr zu werden" (*Das Unbehagen in der Kultur* 256).

> [T]he mirror stage is a drama whose internal pressure pushes precipitously from insufficiency to anticipation – and, for the subject caught up in its lure of spatial identification, turns out fantasies that proceed from a fragmented image of the body to what I will call an 'orthopedic' form of its totality – and to the finally donned armor of an alienating identity that will mark his entire mental development with its rigid structure. ("The Mirror Stage" 78)

Lacan is a notoriously difficult thinker, but Pam Morris has provided an excellent paraphrase of his argument regarding the mirror stage and its role in the formation of the subject:

> According to Lacan, at the mirror-phase of the infant's development, it achieves a joyful perception of itself as a unified being, physically separate and independent from its surrounding world – an image of itself such as it might indeed see in a mirror. This recognition of a specular image offers a wholly desirable self in contrast to the infant's actual state of total dependence, uncoordinated motor skills, and boundary uncertainty between itself and the world. It is, however, misrecognition, since self can never be identical to image. Thus the narcissistic desire for a unified self initiated in the mirror stage and pursued throughout life is always for a phantasy, for the imaginary ego-ideal. This first splitting of the subject into a perceiving self and a self as imaged is repeated in the next phase of development – entry into the Symbolic Order. A sense of individual subjectivity is constituted with the acquisition of the first person pronoun singular, but as with the specular image there exists an unclosable gap between the 'I' who speaks and the 'I' which is the subject of that discourse. These two phases of development, the mirror stage and entry into language, constitute the subject's sense of self as an autonomous individual, but, since this image is an imaginary ideal, the subject is decentred and driven always by narcissistic desire after the unified ego-ideal it can never attain. (*Dickens's Class Consciousness* 4–5)

As Morris observes, the Lacanian subject is decentered and driven by narcissistic desire, and Sean Homer rightly argues that Lacan defines the ego as "the effect of images" – a function of "misrecognition; of refusing to accept the truth of fragmentation and alienation" (Homer 25). All humans, in this view, are alienated, and in a sense the ego's work is to disguise this fact from the subject. The mystifying work of the ego in turn renders it necessary for exceptionally insightful individuals – such as Lacan or Ishmael – to draw our attention to the hidden fact of alienation as a universal human condition. In short, while Ishmael initially portrays his decision to go to sea as merely his own individual problem, he later tries to convince us that the condition is in fact rooted in the alienated subjecthood he shares with Narcissus and, indeed, with us all.[11]

Ishmael's Rhetorical Shifts

We ought to note, however, that Ishmael misrepresents the myth of Narcissus – a fact that should alert us to the possibility that his rhetoric, though powerful, may at the same time be misleading. In Ishmael's account, Narcissus dies by drowning, yet this is not the case in any of the extant versions of the myth. In traditional accounts, Narcissus either kills himself with a sword, or he dies of thirst because he no longer dares to disturb the water that reflects his beloved mirror-image (Bremmer 712; Grimal 302). Harrison Hayford is of course right in arguing that Ishmael's presentation of the myth is better suited to Melville's novel (660), since the story of Narcissus's death by drowning in the first chapter beautifully foreshadows the drowning of Ahab and his crew at the end of the *Moby-Dick.* However, in contrast to Hayford, we need to emphasize that Ishmael's version of the myth of Narcissus is "the key to it all" – as Ishmael himself puts it (20; ch. 1) – not because this story discloses a universal truth, but precisely because it constitutes a case of misrepresentation on Ishmael's part. After all, while Ishmael's Lacanian view of an inherently alienating selfhood may be convincing as such, it clearly fails to answer the question he originally posed to himself: What is it that compelled *him* (and not anyone else, or even all of us) to go to sea? A theory of universal alienation cannot explain Ishmael's particular choice, and accordingly we must remain skeptical of his rhetorical shift from contingent circumstances (lack of money and emotional "interest") via alienation as a recurring problem in his life ("whenever it is a damp, drizzly November in my soul") to alienation as a basic human condition. Indeed, rather than accepting Ishmael's interpretation of alienation as a universal truth, we should see it as yet another attempt to make a home of homelessness: a measure of Ishmael's desire to belong and simply be just like everyone else.

In order better to understand the problematic elision underlying Ishmael's rhetorical sleight of hand, we may adopt Richard Schmitt's distinction between, on the one hand, the precondition for alienation, and, on the other, alienation itself. According to Schmitt, alienation "is a threat in human lives because we live as persons we did not choose to be in a world not of our own making" (48). For Schmitt, the body illustrates well that though we may have a good deal of influence on our life, we can never fully control or understand it; we cannot

11 For extended discussions of the myth of Narcissus and its significance for literature and subjecthood in general see Jeffrey Berman, *Narcissim and the Novel* (1990) and Steven Bruhm, *Reflecting Narcissus: A Queer Aesthetic* (2001).

exist without a body, nor can we choose our body freely. Moreover, as our body constitutes both the basis of our existence and the root cause of our mortality, our relationship towards it is, in Schmitt's view, fundamentally ambivalent (46–47). Schmitt further contends that this ambivalence is related to Martin Heidegger's notion of *Geworfenheit* ('thrownness'):

> Because we are *geworfen* (thrown) into this world, we do not know it [...]. We find ourselves in the world, as we grow up, and need to discover its traits. We are not born understanding the world, nor do we know who we are ourselves but must discover that as life goes on. (48–49)

Just as the body is a home in which we can never feel fully at home, so do both the world and the self necessarily retain an unhomely (or uncanny) core.[12]

However, while all humans share this precondition for alienation, circumstances will shape the way in which they will have to confront it. Accordingly, Schmitt rightly insists that "the struggle against the precondition of alienation is much more difficult for some people than for others" – not least because some lives "are too burdened by external conditions" (51). Some people, that is to say, lack the material or mental resources to deal adequately with the fundamental ambivalence of the human condition, either because of individual experiences (e.g. a traumatic childhood), or because they live in societies that "systematically starve their members of the opportunities to learn how to live" (Schmitt 76).[13] In other words, while it is impossible to remedy the precondition of alienation – or what Dominick LaCapra has called "structural or existential trauma" (*History and Memory after Auschwitz* 47) – we may distinguish between those societies that enable their members to cope with the *Geworfenheit* of human existence, and those societies that withhold the necessary resources or even exacerbate alienation. Applying Schmitt's distinction to *Moby-Dick*, we can thus say that Ishmael subtly shifts from a more specific sense of alienation as the result of particular circumstances to the precondition for alienation (i.e. the idea that human selfhood itself makes alienation possible), thereby obscuring the biographical and social roots of his own condition.

And indeed, once we begin to view Ishmael's rhetoric more skeptically, we find that some of his other explanations, too, fail to solve the problems he pretends to address. For instance, after having – ostensibly – answered the question

12 Terry Eagleton is one of many critics who have expressed similar ideas: "Human beings move at the conjuncture of the concrete and the universal, body and symbolic medium; but this is not a place where anyone can feel blissfully at home" (*The Idea of Culture* 97).

13 Richard Schmitt here refers to a condition that Miranda Fricker has termed "hermeneutical injustice" (1).

why he decided to go to sea, Ishmael tries to explain why he chose to do so as a common sailor rather than as a passenger. The first reason he offers is, once again, pecuniary: "For to go as a passenger you must needs have a purse, and a purse is but a rag unless you have something in it" (20; ch. 1). Ishmael's decision is thus due primarily to his want of financial resources. However, he immediately adds that he would rather be a sailor than a passenger anyway because passengers generally "do not enjoy themselves much" (20; ch. 1). Moreover, Ishmael claims that he prefers being a "simple sailor" to being "a Commodore, or a Captain, or a Cook" because he strongly dislikes "all honorable and respectable toils" (20; ch. 1). Not only is this assertion at odds with his later arguments for the dignity of whaling (e.g. ch. 82, "The Honor and Glory of Whaling"); it is also difficult to reconcile Ishmael's first two explanations – lack of money, and a preference for lowly work – with the third reason he gives for deciding to become a sailor: "It is quite as much as I can do to take care of myself, without taking care of ships, barques, brigs, schooners, and what not" (20; ch. 1). In yet another rhetorical shift, Ishmael now claims that his becoming a sailor rather than a commander was not truly an act of choice, but instead derives from his awareness that he is barely able to take care of himself and therefore quite simply unable to assume any responsibility for others. There is thus, once again, a move from an apparently contingent cause – Ishmael's lack of money, combined with a proud disdain for the easy life of the passenger – to an underlying, more general problem in his life.

Furthermore, not content with this shift from free choice to inability, Ishmael then tries to remold his argument into a general philosophy of life. In order to explain why he is perfectly content to bear the indignities associated with the life of a common sailor, Ishmael resorts to a lofty notion of metaphysical justice:

> What of it, if some old hunks of a sea-captain orders me to get a broom and sweep down the decks? What does that indignity amount to, weighed, I mean, in the scales of the New Testament? [...] Who aint [sic] a slave? Tell me that. Well, then, however the old sea-captains may order me about – however they may thump and punch me about, I have the satisfaction of knowing that it is all right; that everybody else is one way or other served in much the same way – either in a physical or metaphysical point of view, that is; and so the universal thump is passed round, and all hands should rub each other's shoulder-blades, and be content. (21; ch. 1)

Ishmael here transforms what could be a cause for discontent – i.e. the fact that his decision to go to sea was dictated by poverty – into a philosophy of political quietism: one should simply be content with whatever life happens to offer because everybody is a slave in one way or another. Friedrich Nietzsche would, arguably, deride Ishmael's humility as one variant of what Nietzsche called "slave morality": a morality of the oppressed that values "the kind, helping hand," and that regards power as inherently evil (*Beyond Good and Evil* 203; § 260).[14] At any rate, even if we are less polemically inclined than Nietzsche, Ishmael's claim that he prefers working as a common sailor to being a commander "because of the wholesome exercise and pure air of the forecastle deck," as well as his suggestion that it is often "the commonality [who] lead their leaders," look suspiciously like wishful thinking (21; ch. 1). What Ishmael wants us to believe, in effect, is that he dislikes both the "honorable toils" of a commander (which he is unable to perform) and the comfort of the passenger (which he cannot afford), preferring instead a life of indignities because such indignities are, ultimately, shared equally by all – at least from a metaphysical point of view. In short, Ishmael prefers to do what he cannot help doing because it is morally correct anyway ("I have the satisfaction of knowing that it is all right"). This may be a comforting philosophy for our narrator (as well as for others who find themselves in dire straits), but it is hardly a convincing analysis of the situation. And indeed, even Ishmael himself admits that he is at a loss to explain why he decided to enlist on a "whaling voyage" rather than to join a merchant ship, as he had done on previous occasions. He concludes that this mystery must form "part of the grand program of Providence" (21–22; ch. 1). What began as a simple question of money – or, to be precise, the lack of it – has thus miraculously metamorphosed into the providential shape of a transcendental necessity.

The key point of the discussion so far is that Ishmael does everything in his rhetorical power to mitigate a fundamental sense of unbelonging. His humorous tone, for instance, constitutes an attempt to downplay the seriousness of the condition he describes. In addition, he goes out of his way to find other stories that are similar to his: the biblical Ishmael's, Perth's, and even the myth of Narcissus. However, Ishmael succumbs to the temptation to use these stories – particularly the myth of Narcissus – to diffuse the historical particularity of his situation; he no longer appears as an alienated outsider, but as someone who shares in a universal human condition. This strategy provides Ishmael with symbolical comfort, but it also comes at a political cost, as it leads him to embrace

14 In *Beyond Good and Evil*, Nietzsche describes slave morality as follows: "Supposing that the abused, the oppressed, the suffering, the unemancipated, the weary, and those uncertain of themselves, should moralise, what will be the common element in their moral estimates? [...] The slave has an unfavourable eye for the virtues of the powerful" (203; § 260). The German original runs: "Gesetzt, dass die Vergewaltigten, Gedrückten, Leidenden, Unfreien, ihrer selbst Ungewissen und Müden moralisieren: was wird das Gleichartige ihrer moralischen Wertschätzungen sein? [...] Der Blick des Sklaven ist abgünstig für die Tugenden des Mächtigen" (*Jenseits von Gut und Böse* 242; § 260).

a quietist worldview in which resistance to injustice finds little conceptual space. We discover, in short, that there is sometimes a very thin line between, on the one hand, the desire to belong, and, on the other, a problematic kind of moral conformism that impairs one's ability to question the status quo.

A Soul Not at Home: Ishmael, Ahab, and Emersonian Self-Reliance

Rather than accept Ishmael's own theories, we should therefore look for alternative explanations for his decision to go to sea, and one productive option is to regard it as resulting from a lack of what Ralph Waldo Emerson calls "Self-Reliance." Comparing Emerson's 1841 essay with Melville's novel, we find that there are many surprisingly literal links between the two texts.[15] For instance, in "Self-Reliance," Emerson explicitly mentions whaling (191), and he later writes of his preference for "the silent church before the service begins" (192) – a scene that Ishmael describes in great detail early on in *Moby-Dick* (ch. 7–8). Similarly, Ishmael's depiction of the Pacific Islander Queequeg's quick recovery from illness towards the end of the novel (366; ch. 110) echoes very closely Emerson's claim that the white man has lost the "aboriginal strength" that "the savage" still possesses (200). Given these strikingly direct parallels, it seems reasonable to bring the two texts into a more sustained dialogue.

For a start, we must note just how far Ishmael is from embodying Emerson's ideal of a self-reliant man. Ishmael's idea of a "joint-stock world" (64; ch. 13), for instance, closely parallels Emerson's notion that society "is a joint-stock company" ("Self-Reliance" 178) – yet Melville's narrator uses the expression in an emphatically positive sense (i.e. to explain why Queequeg risked his own life to save someone else's), whereas for Emerson the phrase designates a market-place mentality that leads to conformity and slavish dependence.[16] Given these diametrically opposed points of view, it is perhaps not surprising that Ishmael fails to heed one of Emerson's central admonitions: not to mistake "mechanical" (i.e. physical) isolation from society for "spiritual" isolation, which alone can lead to "elevation" (192). Emerson insists that "the great man is he who in the midst of the crowd keeps with perfect sweetness the independence of solitude" (181), and that a person "who travels to be amused, or to get somewhat he does not carry, travels away from himself" (198). For Emerson, the self-reliant man should thus

15 There is, in fact, historical evidence that Melville "was reading Emerson when he was composing *Moby-Dick*" (Gray 132). Indeed, Melville read sections of "Self-Reliance" either "not long before, and possibly during, his composition of *Moby-Dick*" (McLoughlin 79).

16 McLoughlin also notes that Ishmael's use of the concept is "a far cry from the concept of 'the joint-stock company' in 'Self-Reliance'" (80).

"be admonished to stay at home," and to put his genius "in communication with the *internal* ocean" (191–192; emphasis added).[17] Ishmael, by contrast, cannot stay "with perfect sweetness" amongst the crowd, but is tempted to knock people's hats off; he does not aim at spiritual elevation, but opts for mechanical isolation instead: for leaving home and traveling on the world's *external* seas.

Seeing that Ishmael fails to meet Emerson's standards of self-reliance, one might suppose that Ahab, the non-conforming and awe-inspiring commander of the Pequod, must figure as his polar opposite: a kind of Nietzschean *Übermensch* who, instead of subscribing to a humble "slave morality," manages to subordinate others to his will. According to Emerson, the self-reliant man does not obey the customs of society, but lives "wholly from within"; no law is sacred to him but that of his own nature: "[I]f I am the Devil's child, I will live then from the Devil" ("Self-Reliance" 179). It is a small step from this Emersonian belief that "the only right is what is after my constitution" (179) to Nietzsche's notion of the great individual who, rather than following external laws, creates his own values and laws (*Beyond Good and Evil* 208; § 262).[18] Nietzsche insists that mediocre people fear everything that lifts the individual up over the herd, and that therefore they decry such a person as evil (113; § 201).[19] By contrast, Nietzsche himself holds that truly "noble" men not only live beyond good and evil, but are also humanity's only hope for salvation:

---

17 See Emerson's warnings against an excess of "intellectual nomadism" in his essay on "History"; while the "home-keeping wit" faces the peril of "monotony and deterioration," the intellectual nomad "bankrupts the mind through the dissipation of power on a miscellany of objects" (161–162). Emerson's distinction between "intellectual nomadism" and the "home-keeping wit" will be discussed in more detail in the concluding chapter.

18 "[T]he greater, more manifold, more comprehensive life *is lived beyond* the old morality; the 'individual' stands out, and is obliged to have recourse to his own law-giving, his own arts and artifices for self-preservation, self-elevation, and self-deliverance" (*Beyond Good and Evil* 208; § 262; original emphasis). The German original runs: "[D]as grössere, vielfachere, umfänglichere Leben [lebt] über die alte Moral *hinweg* [...]; das 'Individuum' steht da, genöthigt zu einer eigenen Gesetzgebung, zu eigenen Künsten und Listen der Selbst-Erhaltung, Selbst-Erhöhung, Selbst-Erlösung" (*Jenseits von Gut und Böse* 248; § 262; original emphasis).

19 "[E]verything that elevates the individual above the herd, and is a source of fear to the neighbour, is henceforth called *evil*; the tolerant, unassuming, self-adapting, self-equalising disposition, the *mediocrity* of desires, attains to moral distinction and honour" (*Beyond Good and Evil* 113; § 201; original emphasis). The German original runs: "[A]lles, was den Einzelnen über die Herde hinaushebt und dem Nächsten Furcht macht, heisst von nun an *böse*; die billige, bescheidene, sich einordnende, gleichsetzende Gesinnung, das *Mittelmass* der Begierden kommt zu moralischen Namen und Ehren" (*Jenseits von Gut und Böse* 134; § 201; original emphasis).

> [W]here do *we* have to fix our hopes? In *new philosophers* – there is no alternative [...]. To teach man the future of humanity as his *will*, as depending on human will, and to make preparation for vast hazardous enterprises and collective attempts in rearing and educating, in order thereby to put an end to the frightful rule of folly and chance which has hitherto gone by the name of "history" [...] – for that purpose a new type of philosophers and commanders will some time or other be needed, at the very idea of which everything that has existed in the way of the occult, terrible, and benevolent beings might look pale and dwarfed. (117; § 203; original emphasis).[20]

Such a new philosopher or commander, for Nietzsche, has an "unalterable belief that to a being such as 'we,' other beings must naturally be in subjection, and have to sacrifice themselves" (212; § 265).[21] Nietzsche thus agrees with Emerson, who maintains that "the strong spirits will overpower those around them without effort" ("The Transcendentalist" 256). Indeed, George J. Stack has suggested that "the parallels between Nietzsche's depiction of the *Übermensch* and Emerson's scattered descriptions of sovereign individuals could be multiplied beyond necessity" (333), and accordingly Stack speaks of an elective affinity between the two philosophers.[22] Though Emerson is generally more optimistic than Nietzsche, retaining a belief in an "eternal trinity of Truth, Goodness, and Beauty" ("The Transcendentalist" 255; see Mikics 230), both philosophers share a sense that contemporary society weakens its members, and that there is a need for exceptional individuals (such as Ahab) who dare to fly in the face of custom.

If we now examine the episodes in which Ahab, the sovereign individual, overpowers the weaker humans around him, we once again find striking par-

20 "[W]ohin müssen *wir* mit unsren Hoffnungen greifen? Nach *neuen Philosophen*, es bleibt keine Wahl [...]. Dem Menschen die Zukunft des Menschen als seinen *Willen*, als abhängig von einem Menschenwillen zu lehren und grosse Wagnisse und Gesamt-Versuche von Zucht und Züchtigung vorzubereiten, um damit jener schauerlichen Herrschaft des Unsinns und Zufalls, die bisher 'Geschichte' hiess, ein Ende zu machen [...] – : dazu wird irgendwann einmal eine neue Art von Philosophen und Befehlshabern nöthig sein, an deren Bilde sich alles, was auf Erden an verborgenen, furchtbaren und wohlwollenden Geistern dagewesen ist, blass und verzwergt ausnehmen möchte" (*Jenseits von Gut und Böse* 138; § 203; original emphasis).

21 "[I]ch meine jenen unverrückbaren Glauben, dass einem Wesen, wie 'wir sind', andre Wesen von Natur unterthan sein müssen und sich ihm zu opfern haben" (*Jenseits von Gut und Böse*; 251–252; § 265).

22 See also Mikics, who notes as a shared concern of Emerson and Nietzsche "the wish to be perfected and to be guided by the allure of the exemplary (Emerson's central or representative man, Nietzsche's *Übermensch*)" (1); and Weber, who argues that the true man, for Emerson "just as later for Nietzsche, is necessarily beyond the common morality" (75).

allels between *Moby-Dick*’s plot and Emerson’s philosophical imagery. Ahab’s charismatic personality is first presented fully in a scene where he announces his quest for revenge against Moby Dick to the sailors under his command. The crew soon find themselves carried away by their captain’s rhetoric, gazing “curiously at each other, as if marveling how it was that they themselves became so excited” (138; ch. 36). Within a few moments, the sailors grow “frantic” (142; ch. 36), and Ishmael admits both to a dread in his soul – what Nietzsche would arguably interpret as the mediocre person’s fear of the exceptional – and to a “wild, sympathetical feeling” that made Ahab’s feud seem Ishmael’s own (152; ch. 41). Moreover, a later episode that illustrates Ahab’s power to dominate weaker spirits literalizes effectively a series of metaphors from Emerson’s essay “The Transcendentalist.” After Ahab, in a burst of rage, has destroyed his quadrant (378; ch. 118), we find the Pequod trapped in a thunderstorm and enveloped by glowing “corpusants” (i.e. St. Elmo’s fire). The sailors cower in superstitious fear and even utter “a half mutinous cry,” but Ahab snatches his harpoon – from the steel barb of which comes “a levelled flame of pale, forked fire” – and threatens to kill anyone who defies him (383; ch. 119). Let us now compare this to a passage from Emerson:

> [I]n society, besides farmers, *sailors*, and weavers, there must be a few *persons of purer fire* kept specially as gauges and meters of character; persons of a fine, detecting instinct, who betray the smallest accumulations of wit and feeling in the bystander. Perhaps too there might be room for the *exciters* and monitors; *collectors of the heavenly spark* with power to *convey the electricity to others*. Or, as the *storm-tossed vessel* at sea speaks the frigate or ‘line packet’ to learn its longitude, so it may not be without its advantage that we should now and then encounter rare and gifted men, to compare the points of our *spiritual compass*, and verify our bearings from superior chronometers. (“The Transcendentalist” 257; emphasis added)

Emerson mentions “exciters,” “sailors” and a “storm-tossed vessel”; we read of a “spiritual compass” and a “collector of heavenly sparks,” who can “convey the electricity to others.” In short, the episode in *Moby-Dick* incorporates Emerson’s imagery almost verbatim, which underlines Ahab’s position as a self-reliant, Emersonian individual (and simultaneously as a Nietzschean *Übermensch*). However, the catastrophic outcome of Ahab’s quest to kill Moby Dick ought to make us wary of reading Ahab’s self-reliance in an overly positive light – a point to which we will return.

Ahab, Trauma, and the Community of Suffering

While in many ways Ahab offers a stark contrast to Ishmael and his humble "slave morality," we must also acknowledge the many similarities between the two characters. For instance, like Ishmael, Ahab comes from a broken home; he is the son of a "crazy, widowed mother, who died when he was only a twelvemonth old" (78; ch. 16). In addition, both Ishmael and Ahab believe that the body (and material existence in general) is ultimately insubstantial when measured against the transcendent soul, for just as Ishmael sees in his body "but the lees" of his "better being" (45; ch. 7), Ahab insists that "immaterial are all materials" (396; ch. 128). Of course, John Wenke is right when he points out that Ahab – in contrast to Ishmael (and Emerson) – is an "inverted Platonist" who believes that the transcendent source of life is malignant (706). However, the key point in this context is that neither Ahab nor Ishmael question the idea of transcendence as such. Similarly, Ishmael's statement that humankind seems, for the most part, "a mob of unnecessary duplicates" (356; ch. 107) strongly resembles Ahab's view on the matter, which the latter makes explicit in a conversation with his first and second mates: "You two are the opposite poles of one thing: Starbuck is Stubb reversed, and Stubb is Starbuck; and ye two are all mankind; and Ahab stands alone among the millions of the peopled earth, nor gods nor men his neighbors!" (413; ch. 133). The many differences between Ishmael and Ahab should thus not blind us to the fact that they also share certain views and characteristics.[23]

As Wenke observes, this spiritual convergence between Ahab and Ishmael has "its culminating, and most teasing, manifestation" in one of world literature's great textual cruxes (710): a speech that has been attributed to both Ahab the character and Ishmael the narrator, and which is therefore worth quoting in its entirety:

> Oh, grassy glades! oh, ever vernal endless landscapes in the soul; in ye, [...] men yet may roll, like young horses in new morning clover; and for some few fleeting moments, feel the cool dew of the life immortal on them. Would to God these blessed calms would last. But the mingled, mingling threads of life are woven by warp and woof: calms crossed by storms, a storm for every calm. There is no steady unretracing progress in this life; [...] once gone through, we trace the round again; and are infants, boys, and men, and Ifs eternally. Where lies the final harbor, whence we unmoor no more? In what rapt ether sails the world, of which the weariest will never weary? Where is the foundling's father hidden? Our souls are like those orphans whose un-

23 For a reading that places much more emphasis on Ahab and Ishmael as polar opposites, see McLoughlin (67).

> wedded mothers die in bearing them: the secret of our paternity lies in their grave, and we must there to learn it. (373; ch. 114)

In the first edition of *Moby-Dick*, this speech on orphaned souls and man's fundamental homelessness was printed without quotation marks, and though they were added in later editions to make clear that the speech is Ahab's and not Ishmael's, their earlier absence points to a potential ambiguity that surely must, as Hershel Parker and Harrison Hayford put it with admirable understatement, have "implications for any critical argument that takes Ishmael and Ahab as embodying opposing values" (373n1). Both Ishmael and Ahab believe in transcendence, and both feel deeply alienated; both come from broken homes; and both become obsessed with Moby Dick: Ahab with capturing the whale itself, and Ishmael with mastering the telling of its tale.

If we ask why, precisely, Ahab is bent on killing Moby Dick, one possible answer is to relate his obsession to a post-traumatic crisis. Ahab was mutilated in an encounter with Moby Dick, losing his leg (108; ch. 28) and consequently suffering a profound violation of his bodily integrity: a defining characteristic of traumatic events (Fricke 14). Moreover, as is typical for the development of post-traumatic stress disorder (PTSD), some time elapses between the traumatic event and the appearance of the patient's post-traumatic symptoms:

> [When Ahab] received the stroke that tore him, he probably but felt the agonizing bodily laceration, but nothing more. Yet, when by this collision forced to turn towards home, and for long months of days and weeks, Ahab and anguish lay stretched together in one hammock, rounding in mid winter that dreary, howling Patagonian Cape; then it was, that his torn body and gashed soul bled into one another; and so interfusing, made him mad. (156; ch. 41)

This brief account opens with Ahab feeling an "agonizing bodily laceration" – in other words, the kind of sensory overload that, once again, is characteristic for traumatic events (Fricke 15–17). Later, like other victims of trauma (Schönfelder 64, 146), Ahab suffers from bouts of depression alternating with fits of feverish hyper-arousal, as well as from a pronounced desire to take revenge. Indeed, hyper-arousal and the desire for revenge coincide in the scene where Ahab discloses his desire to kill Moby Dick to the Pequod's crew. Only a few moments earlier, Ahab had seemed to be sunk in impenetrable gloom (131; ch. 34); however, Ahab now mesmerizes his rapt audience with a countenance that is "fiercely glad and approving" (137; ch. 35). Since post-traumatic crises negatively affect patients' interpersonal relationships (e.g. Herman 56), even the fact that Ahab generally remains "inaccessible" to the other members of the crew (*Moby-Dick* 131; ch. 34) may be the symptom of PTSD rather than simply a character trait. Moreover, in Dominick LaCapra's terms, Ahab's trauma is not structural or existential, but historical (i.e. it "is related to specific events"; *History and Memory after Auschwitz* 47).

Interestingly, in *Moby-Dick* Ahab feels drawn to others who have suffered from similarly traumatic experiences. For instance, when the Pequod meets a whaling ship from London, Ahab learns that its commander, Captain Boomer, has lost an arm because of Moby Dick. Ahab immediately wants to meet his fellow sufferer, and he greets Captain Boomer in an uncharacteristically sociable manner: "Aye, aye, hearty!" (336–337; ch. 100). Similarly, Ahab responds keenly to the fate of Pip, the black ship's boy who, on two occasions in the novel, becomes so frightened during the chase of a whale that he jumps overboard. While the first time the others immediately abandon the chase to pick Pip out of the water, the second time they simply leave him behind. Although the sailors rescue Pip once the chase is completed, from that traumatic moment "the little negro went about the deck an idiot" (321; ch. 93). Significantly, when Ahab becomes aware of Pip's altered condition, his reaction betrays intense emotions:

> Lo! ye believers in gods all goodness, and in man all ill, lo you! see the omniscient gods oblivious of suffering man; and, though idiotic, and knowing not what he does, yet full of the sweet things of love and gratitude. Come! I feel prouder leading thee by thy black hand, than though I grasped an Emperor's! (392; ch. 125)

Ahab, usually so "inaccessible," suddenly feels that community of suffering which, according to Iwona Irwin-Zarecka, often arises between people with shared experiences – especially if these experiences are of an "extraordinary if not traumatic quality" (47).

Of Masters and Slaves: Power, Isolation, and Recognition

What makes Ahab's affection for young Pip particularly notable is that the latter is depicted as the very lowest person on board the ship (Fanning 217). For instance, the narrator points out that, "if there happen to be an unduly slender, clumsy, or timorous wight in the ship, that wight is certain to be made a ship-keeper" (319; ch. 93). Moreover, when Pip jumps overboard for the first time, the second mate Stubb upbraids him for being a coward and explicitly warns him that he may not be picked up so quickly next time: "[A] whale would sell for thirty times what you would, Pip, in Alabama" (321). Stubb, in other words, brutally reminds Pip of his status as a potential slave – a powerful threat in antebellum America, where slavery remained a terribly real threat for someone like Pip.

Given Pip's position as the ship's 'symbolical slave,' it is productive to read the relationship between Ahab and Pip in the light of Hegel's account of the master-slave dialectic. In *Phenomenology of Spirit*, Hegel examines "how simple sensuous certainty mutates into a series of more advanced shapes of consciousness and, finally, into absolute knowing or speculative philosophy" (Houlgate 67). The analysis of the master-slave dialectic constitutes a crucial step in Hegel's argument, for it is intended to demonstrate that no self-conscious being can ever exist as an entirely self-sufficient entity. When two consciousnesses fight for recognition, one initially becomes the dominant "master" or "lord" (*Herr*), while the other assumes the subservient position of "slave" or "bondsman" (*Knecht*).[24] The master and the slave are, for Hegel, "two opposed shapes of consciousness; one is the independent consciousness whose essential nature is to be for itself, the other is the dependent consciousness whose essential nature is simply to live or to be for another" (115).[25] However, since for Hegel self-consciousness can only exist if it is recognized by another consciousness (112–114), the master also depends on the slave. This in turn renders the relationship between master and slave inherently unstable, for if the former depends on the latter, he cannot be seen as the unconditional master. Full self-consciousness is, then, only possible if recognition occurs between equals: when the master-slave dialectic is overcome or, to use Hegel's term, sublated (*aufgehoben*) in a higher unity (Findlay xvii; Houlgate 68).

If we read the relationship between Ahab and Pip in the light of this master-slave dialectic, it becomes significant that Ahab explicitly bemoans his inescapable dependence on others. Ahab, the supreme master of the Pequod, curses "that mortal inter-indebtedness" that makes it impossible for him to "be free as air" (360; ch. 108) – or, we might add, to be truly self-reliant. Fittingly, when Ahab inspects the images on a Spanish doubloon that he has nailed to the Pequod's main mast as a prize for whoever first sights Moby Dick, he reveals himself as the consummate narcissist:

> [L]ook here, – three peaks as proud as Lucifer. The firm tower, that is Ahab; the volcano, that is Ahab; the courageous, the undaunted, and victorious fowl, that, too,

---

24 Though the terms *slave* is a rather problematic translation of the term *Knecht*, I have decided to retain it not only because the phrase *master-slave dialectic* is commonly used in discussions of Hegel's *Phenomenology*, but also because Hegel does actually use the term *Sklav(e)* in other works (Buck-Morss 52n90).

25 "Beide Momente sind wesentlich [...] als zwei entgegengesetzte Gestalten des Bewusstseins; die eine das selbständige, welchem das Fürsichsein, die andere das unselbständige, dem das Leben oder das Sein für ein anderes, das Wesen ist" (*Phänomenologie des Geistes* 140–141).

> is Ahab; all are Ahab; and this round gold is but the image of the rounder globe, which, like a magician's glass, to each and every man in turn but mirrors back his own mysterious self. (332; ch. 99)

At this point in the novel, Ahab construes the entire world as merely a reflection of himself – which of course renders true recognition of another impossible. It is in the very next chapter, however, that Ahab meets Captain Boomer, and this meeting with a fellow sufferer is the first moment a chink appears in Ahab's armor of solipsism. Ahab's empathy for Pip is the next step in this process, and, crucially, one of the first things Ahab notices when he looks at Pip is the latter's inability to serve as his mirror: "I see not my reflection in the vacant pupils of thy eyes" (392; ch. 125). Whereas the pictures on the doubloon reflected only Ahab's image of himself, the eyes of the symbolical slave seem to mirror nothing at all. Thus recognizing Pip as a fellow homeless soul, Ahab immediately decides that his own cabin "shall be Pip's home henceforth" (392; ch. 125). In this way, the community of suffering between Ahab and Pip literally becomes the basis for a new and common home: a home made out of homelessness (as in Ishmael's rhetorical attempts to universalize his sense of unbelonging).[26]

At the same time, Ahab realizes that he can only continue his (self-)destructive quest to kill Moby Dick if he does not truly allow himself to accept others as equal human beings who, as such, are constitutive of his own, supposedly sovereign self. When Ahab finds that Pip's condition is "too curing" for his malady because "[l]ike cures like," he decides that they ought no longer to spend time together, and he hastily retreats when Pip tells him that he would prefer to "remain a part" of Ahab (399; ch. 129). Ahab is quite explicit about why he can no longer face Pip's presence: "If thou speakest thus to me much more, Ahab's purpose keels up in him" (399; ch. 129). He cannot, in other words, carry on with his single-minded quest if he acknowledges Pip the slave as constitutive of his own masterly self. Indeed, the very language Ahab uses expresses his inner conflict, for he distinguishes between the "me" that Pip addresses ("thou speakest thus to me"), and "Ahab," another self, to which he refers in the third person only ("Ahab's purpose keels up in him").

Though Pip ultimately obeys Ahab's command to leave him alone, the Pequod's captain never quite regains his earlier ability easily to deny other humans the recognition they demand. For instance, not much after his final exchange with Pip, Ahab looks into Starbuck's eyes and discovers the image of "the far

26 cf. Edwin F. Edinger on Ahab's reaction to Pip: "This is the first of several incidents indicating a growing self-awareness in Ahab, which begins to humanize him even if it is not sufficient to avert his tragic end" (109).

away home" there: the memory of his wife and child (406; ch. 132). Starbuck reacts by emphasizing that he, too, is a husband and father, before urging Ahab to abandon his quest for Moby Dick and, instead, to return to his loved ones. However, Ahab evades the presence of this too familiar Other – we learn that now his "glance was averted" – and instead muses upon the mysterious force that drives him onward:

> What is it, what nameless, inscrutable, unearthly thing is it; what cozzening, hidden lord and master, and cruel, remorseless emperor commands me; that against all natural lovings and longings, I so keep pushing, and crowding, and jamming myself on all the time [...]? Is Ahab, Ahab? Is it I, God, or who, that lifts this arm? But if the great sun move not of himself; but is as an errand-boy in heaven; nor one single star can revolve, but by some invisible power; how then can this one small heart beat; this one small brain think thoughts; unless God does that beating, does that thinking, does that living, and not I. (406–407; ch. 132)

Freud would, presumably, point out here that no ego is ever "master in its own house" because of the all-pervasive influence of the unconscious (*Introductory Lectures* 285).[27] Ahab, by contrast, insists that an external force – a malevolent, "hidden lord and master" – must be the cause of his self-alienation. And yet, the crucial point is that Ahab has doubts about his own mastery at all. Far from "defyingly" worshipping the hidden master, as he did not so long ago (382–383; ch. 119), Ahab now seems weary and on the verge of resignation. As readers, we may thus speculate that, had Ahab been given more time to converse with others and truly to reflect on his own situation, he might eventually have overcome his narcissistic isolation and decided to turn homewards instead.

What supports this interpretation is that, in *Moby-Dick*, isolation from others is not only portrayed as a symptom, but also a cause of mental alienation. For instance, in the case of Pip, it is quite clear that the boy's madness relates to his experience of absolute isolation after he had jumped overboard a second time, for "the awful lonesomeness" of the open ocean is intolerable to humans: "The intense concentration of self in the middle of such a heartless immensity, my God! who can tell it?" (321; ch. 93). In properly Hegelian fashion, Pip's self cannot survive without the presence of another; bereft of the presence of fellow human beings, the abandoned boy eventually becomes mad. I therefore agree with Sa-

27 The German original runs: "Die [...] empfindlichste Kränkung aber soll die menschliche Grössensucht durch die heutige psychologische Forschung erfahren, welche dem Ich nachweisen will, dass es nicht einmal Herr im eigenen Hause, sondern auf kärgliche Nachrichten angewiesen bleibt von dem, was unbewusst in seinem Seelenleben vorgeht" (*Vorlesungen zur Einführung* 295).

muel Kimball that, in *Moby-Dick*, "selfhood is defined relationally in terms of homelessness," in the sense that the self is haunted by the specter of abandonment and non-relation (546). Ahab, too, feels the intensity of this pressure, as he confesses to Starbuck after his last farewell to Pip:

> When I think of this life I have led; the desolation of solitude it has been; the masoned, walled-town of a Captain's exclusiveness, which admits but small entrance to any sympathy from the green country without – oh, weariness! heaviness! Guinea-coast slavery of solitary command! – when I think of all this; only half-suspected, not so keenly known to me before – and how for forty years I have fed upon dry salted fare – fit emblem of the dry nourishment of my soul! [...] – away, whole oceans away, from that young girl-wife I wedded past fifty, and sailed for Cape Horn the next day, leaving but one dent in my marriage pillow – wife? wife? – rather a widow with her husband alive! (405; ch. 132)

Ahab believes that he suffers from more than the common sailor's homesickness, though his absence from the loved ones at home is a burden, too. What makes his lot particularly difficult to endure is the "Captain's exclusiveness" – that "Guinea-coast slavery of solitary command" that has for so long isolated him from his crew, the only home available during the years he spent far from his native Nantucket. Once again mastery involves a kind of "slavery" – an insight that for many years Ahab had "only half-suspected."

The case of Ahab thus supports Terry Eagleton's claim that power is "naturally solipsistic": that it "tends to breed fantasy, reducing the self to a state of querulous narcissism" (*After Theory* 132). While the poor and disempowered cannot, according to Eagleton, afford to believe in a world that will simply bend to their every whim and desire, those in power regularly witness the apparent triumph of their own will over matter. Eagleton's position is thus not entirely unlike Nietzsche's, who posits a fundamental difference between "noble" and lower souls:

> In all kinds of injury and loss the lower and coarser soul is better off than the nobler soul: the dangers of the latter must be greater, the probability that it will come to grief and perish is in fact immense, considering the multiplicity of the conditions of its existence (Beyond Good and Evil 221; § 276)[28]

28 "Bei aller Art von Verletzung und Verlust ist die niedere und gröbere Seele besser daran als die vornehmere: die Gefahren der letzteren müssen grösser sein, ihre Wahrscheinlichkeit, dass sie verunglückt und zu Grunde geht, ist sogar, bei der Vielfachheit ihrer Lebensbedingungen, ungeheuer" (*Jenseits von Gut und Böse* 261–262; § 276).

Eagleton and Nietzsche thus share a sense that the elevated are also more vulnerable, for if their self is more sophisticated (or more inflated, depending on one's point of view), it is also more likely to collapse entirely when confronted with an insurmountable obstacle.[29] What is so poignant in Ahab's case, however, is that his progress towards a less inflated sense of self is brutally cut short in *Moby-Dick*. When Ahab examines the images on the Spanish doubloon, he is still lost in the solipsism of his power. However, he increasingly opens up to others due to his encounters with fellow sufferers: Captain Boomer and little Pip. Ahab is a tragic figure because, when the Pequod meets Moby Dick and thus its doom, he is so close to overcoming his thirst for vengeance, to abandoning his monomaniac quest, and to re-establishing a sense of belonging with the fellow human beings around him.

Moby-Dick is, then, not primarily an indictment of Ahab as a character, but a critique of the very idea that self-reliant *Übermenschen* ought to shape the fate of the world. Even Nietzsche himself in fact admits that this idea involves terrible risks: "[T]he necessity for such leaders, the dreadful danger that they might be lacking, or miscarry and degenerate: – these are *our* real anxieties and glooms, ye know it well, ye free spirits!" (*Beyond Good and Evil* 117; § 203; original emphasis).[30] For Emerson, failure also constitutes a possible outcome, yet he tends to portray it as an individual tragedy rather than as a threat to the fate of mankind as such ("The Transcendentalist" 252–253). In *Moby-Dick*, however, Ahab's tragedy is not individual, as virtually all his followers meet their doom – even Queequeg, who is arguably the most positive and heroic character in the novel (e.g. Cohen, *The Novel and the Sea* 185; Edinger 35; Flory 96–97). Only Ishmael survives to tell the tale, lost and abandoned: "another orphan" (427; "Epilogue"). If a self-reliant individual as damaged as Ahab for one reason or another assumes the position of supreme commander, this will likely lead to death and destruction. Accordingly, we can read *Moby-Dick* as a political allegory against the evils of power and the threat inherent in the idea of self-reliant mastery.

---

29 In his Jungian reading of Melville's novel, Edwin F. Edinger describes a notably similar dynamic: "[I]nflation is also an alienation insofar as being at a height separates one both from others and from the earthly realities of one's own being. A fall is necessary, but if it is too abrupt, or if the dissociation is too great, the descent can be a disaster" (52).

30 "[D]ie Notwendigkeit solcher Führer, die erschreckliche Gefahr, dass sie ausbleiben oder missrathen oder entarten könnten – das sind *unsere* eigentlichen Sorgen und Verdüsterungen, ihr wisst es, ihr freien Geister?" (*Jenseits von Gut und Böse* 138; § 203).

The Duty of Civil Disobedience

The remedy that the novel implicitly proposes against the evils of, on the one hand, Ahab’s unleashed ‘will to power,’ and, on the other, Ishmael’s (and others’) political quietism is what Henry David Thoreau calls civil disobedience. In his essay “Resistance to Civil Government” (published two years before *Moby-Dick*, and later renamed “Civil Disobedience”), Thoreau points out that law “never made men a whit more just; and, by means of their respect for it, even the well-disposed are daily made the agents of injustice” (387). In this view, the problem with the crew of the Pequod is that even those who condemn Ahab’s quest continue to obey their captain. This is particularly apparent in the case of Starbuck, who voices his outrage at Ahab’s desire for vengeance from the very outset of his commander’s quest (139; ch. 36), but who nevertheless continues to carry out Ahab’s orders. Importantly, the point here is not to argue that Starbuck should have killed Ahab when he had the chance to do so (ch. 123, “The Musket”) – and neither does Thoreau advocate violent resistance to governmental injustice. However, it is safe to assume that Thoreau would condemn Starbuck’s insistence on a “lawful way” to wrest Ahab’s power from him (387; ch. 123). Instead, Thoreau maintains that those “who, while they disapprove of the character and measures of a government, yield to it their allegiance and support, are undoubtedly its most conscientious supporters” (394). In other words, those who see that the law is unjust yet nevertheless choose to adhere to it are, according to Thoreau, the most morally objectionable of all. The legitimacy of command must, in Throeau’s view, derive from justice rather than from legal authority. Indeed, in the course of *Moby-Dick*, we learn of no fewer than two ships on which mutinies have taken place, which confirms that one of the novel’s central interests is the potential legitimacy of insubordination.[31]

Moby-Dick can thus be read as an allegory of the universal dangers of power and tyranny as well as of the potential remedies.[32] At the same time, many critics see Melville’s novel as a response to more specifically American ills: a supposedly democratic and egalitarian society that is in fact based on exploitation and exclusion. The fact that the novel is set on a whaling ship to some extent supports the idea that national concerns may be central to the novel, as the U.S. was preeminent amongst the nations engaged in whaling at the time (Osterhammel 557) – a preeminence that registers in *Moby-Dick* in moments of national pride,

31 Indeed, the similarity between the titles of the respective chapters – “The Town-Ho’s Story” and “The Jeroboam’s Story” (ch. 54 and 71) – makes it difficult not to see them as interrelated.

32 See C.L. R. James’s *Mariners, Renegades and Castaways* (1953) for a classic reading of Ahab as the embodiment of totalitarian impulses.

as when the narrator boasts "that the Yankees in one day, collectively, kill more whales than all the English, collectively, in ten years" (197; ch. 53). A whaling ship can thus be seen, with some justice, as a particularly American type of setting, and accordingly its allegorical significance might equally concern the U.S. in particular.

Critics who focus on this aspect of the novel generally highlight the discrepancy between, on the one hand, American ideals of equality, and, on the other, a highly exclusive political reality. Philip Armstrong nicely sums up this line of argument:

> As Melville was well aware, his nation's much vaunted ideal of democracy depended upon the exclusion of large sectors of the adult population. Many studies have shown how *Moby-Dick* satirically recognizes America's dependence upon the labor of Native Americans, African American slaves, and conscripted Pacific islanders. (1050)

The Pequod's three harpooneers – Queequeg, Tashtego, and Daggoo – are a Pacific islander, a Native American, and an African, respectively, and though their labor is essential, they are effectively barred from the higher levels of command. Moreover, if the Pequod is a symbol of the American state, then the fact that the ship is named after "a celebrated tribe of Massachusetts Indians, now extinct as the ancient Medes" (69; ch. 16) becomes harrowingly appropriate, for the United States themselves are founded on the basis of violent conquest.[33] We need to bear in mind this underlying concern with ethnic Others when reading Ishmael's assertion that "it was the whiteness of the whale that above all things appalled me" (159; ch. 42), and perhaps the significance of the white whale is indeed, as Margaret Cohen suggests, to challenge the "schematic use of whiteness in Western moralities" ("The Chronotopes of the Sea" 657). Moreover, if race is one of the critical faultlines in the novel, then Philip Armstrong points out that gender is another key problematic, since women are excluded from the allegorical ship of the state altogether, and Ahab's complaint about the distance from his wife "involves the Captain's recognition of the damage produced by the economic separation between the genders" (1050).

That the benefits of such a racially and sexually divided societal order are ultimately insubstantial except for those who are already in power is nicely illustrated in Melville's novel by the Spanish doubloon that Ahab has promised as a reward to whoever first sights Moby Dick. We have seen that the force of Ahab's rhetoric may serve to sway others to his purpose, yet when it comes to

---

33 The fact that the Pequots (or Pequods) were not actually extinct (see Parker and Hayford 69n4) is, I suggest, irrelevant here; what counts is that the allegorical ship of the state is named after a Native American tribe that was utterly dispossessed.

persuading his crew to join him on his quest for revenge against Moby Dick, the prospect of a financial reward is perhaps equally, if not more, effective (138; ch. 36). At any rate, when the Pequod finally encounters Moby Dick, Ahab claims that he himself "raised the White Whale first," and that "Fate reserved the doubloon" for him (408; ch. 133). Ahab, the captain (and part owner) of the allegorical ship of the state thus himself reaps the reward that he used earlier as a bait for those amongst his crew who remained reluctant to join him. In short, the financial reward promised for collaboration in the commander's morally dubious endeavor ultimately proves illusory.[34]

The Signs of Madness and Transcendence: A "Hideous and Intolerable Allegory"?

Moby-Dick thus invites at least two different kinds of allegorical readings: one that regards the novel as a general critique of power and the dangers of corruption, and another that focuses more particularly on the social ills of exclusion in the polity of the United States. At the same time, however, the text also discourages allegorical readings entirely. Admittedly, an allegorical reading of Ahab's story is strongly suggested in some of the novel's early chapters, in which Ishmael visits "a Whaleman's Chapel" in New Bedford. In these chapters, Ishmael suggests that "the world's a ship" and "the pulpit its brow" (47; ch. 8), with the preacher acting as "pilot-prophet" (53; ch. 9). Accordingly, if Ahab the pilot goes astray, then this involves grave allegorical dangers for the world. And yet, at other times the narrator explicitly urges readers to refrain from seeing Moby Dick as "a hideous and intolerable allegory" (172; ch. 45), emphasizing the realism of his tale instead (e.g. ch. 55, "Of the Monstrous Pictures of Whales"). Indeed, the narrator's attention to even the smallest details of whaling appears superfluous if we read his tale allegorically. It would therefore be better to say that *Moby-Dick* uneasily combines features both of a realist novel and of traditional allegory, without being fully at home in either genre.[35] The extent of the book's generic unbelonging is, in fact, reflected in the plethora of labels that critics have used to describe *Moby-Dick*, from "fable of the Real" (Eagleton,

34 Such a reading also ties in with Fredric Jameson's reminder that the sea may seem to promise adventure and escape from the mundane world of business, but is in fact itself a work-place and trading highway, and as such essential to capitalist development (*The Political Unconscious* 198).

35 For a similar argument see Jeremy Tambling, who suggests that in *Moby-Dick* allegorical significance "has faded in the age of realism; and the text cannot prove the validity of allegorical interpretation, save by asserting it" (*Allegory* 91).

Trouble with Strangers 216) to “monster anti-novel” (Hillis Miller, *On Literature* 73) and “modern epic” (Franco Moretti, *Modern Epic*).

Moby-Dick’s uneasy combination of allegorical imagery and novelistic realism is in many ways epitomized in Ahab, who constitutes a borderline figure between a ‘realistic,’ embodied individual with psychological depth, and a ‘flat,’ allegorical character. In his study of nineteenth-century realism, Fredric Jameson notes in passing that “allegory and the body [...] repel one another and fail to mix” (*Antinomies of Realism* 37), and it is indeed difficult to reconcile the allegorical readings proposed above with the idea that Ahab suffers from post-traumatic stress disorder. In other words, as soon as we focus on the realistic depiction of Ahab as a traumatized individual with a wounded body, we remain in the domain of literal meaning – which poses a problem for traditional forms of allegorical reading because, as Jeremy Tambling notes, allegory privileges the ‘spirit’ over the ‘letter’ of the word: “A spiritual reading says that the literal meaning is not as important as the allegorical message” (16). Accordingly, close attention to the ‘literal,’ realistic details of a character’s embodied mind distracts from the text’s allegorical message, which can only be revealed if the literal character disappears, or at least recedes from view. Perhaps this explains why, according to Angus Fletcher, an allegorical character’s way of acting typically is “severely limited in variety” (38), for by reducing the character’s ‘realistic’ complexity texts can foreground that character’s allegorical function.

Intriguingly, for Fletcher, this limited behavioral complexity of allegorical characters is open to two entirely different interpretations, one religious and the other secular. To tease out these two different interpretations, Fletcher imagines how an allegorical character would appear to us if we were to meet that character in real life:

> [W]e would say of him that he was obsessed with only one idea, or that he had an absolutely one-track mind, or that his life was patterned according to absolutely rigid habits from which he never allowed himself to vary. It would seem that he was driven by some hidden, private force; or, viewing him from another angle, it would appear that he did not control his own destiny, but appeared to be controlled by some foreign force, something outside the sphere of his own ego. (40–41)

In the context of a real-life situation, the allegorical character would “appear to be controlled by some foreign force,” and Fletcher notes that in religious views of the world such external forces are referred to as the demonic (39). By contrast, from a secular perspective, the character’s “one-track mind” and “rigid habits” appear as nothing other than psychological obsession. As Fletcher suggests, *Moby-Dick*’s portrayal of Ahab oscillates precisely between these two poles (61), and even Ahab himself wavers between a religious and a secular interpretation of his own condition: "I'm demoniac, I am madness maddened!" (143; ch. 37).

More generally, *Moby-Dick* as a novel oscillates between a realist understanding of madness as a psychological problem, and a religious interpretation of madness as demonic – i.e. a phenomenon with transcendental significance. For instance, when Ahab discloses his desire to take revenge on Moby Dick, the first mate Starbuck wavers between psychological and religious discourses, retorting that such a plan is "[m]adness" as well as "blasphemous" (139; ch. 36).[36] The notion that madness may in fact be linked to transcendence is stated most explicitly, however, in Ishmael's account of Pip's tragic fate:

> The sea had jeeringly kept his finite body up, but drowned the infinite of his soul. Not drowned entirely, though. Rather carried down alive to wondrous depths, where strange shapes of the unwarped primal world glided to and fro before his passive eyes [...]; and among the joyous, heartless, ever-juvenile eternities, Pip saw the multitudinous, God-omnipresent, coral insects, that out of the firmament of waters heaved the colossal orbs. He saw God's foot upon the treadle of the loom, and spoke it; and therefore his shipmates called him mad. So man's insanity is heaven's sense; and wandering from all mortal reason, man comes at last to that celestial thought, which, to reason, is absurd and frantic; and weal or woe, feels then uncompromised, indifferent as his God. (321–322; ch. 93)

Pip may be mad, but he was also confronted with visions of the divine, and accordingly for Ishmael the boy's "insanity is heaven's sense": the madness of the holy fool, which might hold the key to a kind of transcendental knowledge that other mortals seek in vain.

Ahab, too, refers at one point to Pip's "holiness" (391; ch. 125), which suggests that he shares with Starbuck and Ishmael a view of madness that Michel Foucault regards as typical of a much earlier historical period:

> In the Middle Ages and until the Renaissance, man's dispute with madness was a dramatic debate in which he confronted the secret powers of the world; the experience of madness was clouded by images of the Fall and the Will of God, of the Beast and the Metamorphosis, and of all the marvelous secrets of Knowledge. (*Madness and Civilization* xii)

36 It is interesting that some of the early critical reactions to *Moby-Dick* echo Starbuck's link between madness and blasphemy, with one reviewer reading the novel's "stylistic and formal incoherence" as "certainly blasphemous, and most probably insane" (Selby 18).

Foucault argues that, in the Middle Ages, the link between transcendence and madness constituted a theological given, and in *Moby-Dick* Ahab’s very name emphasizes this connection. “Ahab” is, as Ishmael points out early in the novel, the name of an idolatrous and ill-fated King of Israel denounced by the prophet Elijah, and we learn that it was given to Ahab by his “crazy, widowed mother” (78; ch. 16; see 1 Kings 18: 16–19). In other words, Ahab’s mother was mad when she chose his name – yet her choice also proves prophetic, for Ahab, too, is denounced by a man who calls himself Elijah. Indeed, Elijah had warned Ishmael and his friend Queequeg not to embark on the Pequod, and though Ishmael believes that Elijah “must be a little damaged in the head,” he is also riveted with the latter’s “insane earnestness” (87; ch. 19), confessing later that Elijah’s “diabolical incoherences” continue to haunt him (108; ch. 28). Moreover, by the end of Melville’s novel, we know that Elijah’s prophecies of doom have all come true, which in turn seems to confirm the earlier link between madness and “the marvelous secrets of Knowledge.” We are thus now in a position to understand what Georg Lukács means when, in his *Theory of the Novel*, he interprets madness as an objectivation of “transcendental homelessness” (61). Extraordinary mental states appear as demonic or prophetic in a world of faith, and it is only when the link to the transcendental home is severed that a purely secular concept of madness can emerge.

Let us be clear about the implications of these conflicting interpretations of madness for the larger theme of homelessness in *Moby-Dick*. What Emerson defines in positive terms as self-reliance – a kind of ‘splendid isolation’ from the mass of average beings – in Ahab appears as both mental and social alienation (i.e. his madness is linked to his being cut-off from other human beings).[37] The captain’s madness thus constitutes a state of unbelonging – provided that we subscribe to a secular interpretation of his condition. We have seen, however, that *Moby-Dick* also offers a competing interpretation of madness as the sign of transcendental connectedness (“insanity is heaven’s sense”), and perhaps this explains why Ahab is so afraid of spending more time with Pip. If recognition of the symbolical slave were indeed able to cure the master’s malady, then this

37 According to Johannes Völz, Emerson’s own thinking in fact “evolves from a theory of the individual as an aspiring self-reliant genius in which the Other is never absent, but generally pushed to the background from where it resurfaces as a *problem*, a theory of the individual who still strives to become the great man or genius, but who can become so only on the basis of what Emerson calls *representativeness*” (101). However, the aim of this chapter is not to provide a systematic account of the relation between Melville’s work and Emerson’s philosophy as it evolved over the years, but instead to use certain Emersonian ideas as one of several tools that may help us to explore the notion of home and belonging in *Moby-Dick*.

process might also force Ahab to face the possibility that his obsession is ‘mere’ madness, and that his quest for the white whale lacks any transcendental significance. Put differently: were Ahab to relinquish his belief in the “demoniac” nature of his quest, then this would force him to confront two kinds of trauma at one and the same time: the historical trauma of physical mutilation and mental illness (i.e. a recognition of his own madness, resulting from post-traumatic stress disorder), and the structural or existential trauma of transcendental homelessness. Faced with this double threat of unbelonging, Ahab holds fast to the obsessive quest that has given meaning to his life – and turns away from Pip forever.

We could say, then, that the ‘epic’ character Ahab shies away from the aesthetic of the novel, for according to Lukács the genre of the novel is a formal expression of transcendental homelessness (41). Lukács argues that the world of the epic (and, arguably, allegory) “is like a home, for the fire that burns in the soul is of the same essential nature as the stars” (29). The novel, by contrast, “is the epic of an age in which the extensive totality of life is no longer directly given, in which the immanence of meaning in life has become a problem” (56). As both Michael McKeon (*Theory of the Novel* 179) and John Neubauer (533–534) have noted, for Lukács this transcendental homelessness constitutes a fundamental loss, and Robert T. Tally Jr. rightly notes that the feeling Lukács evokes is akin to Martin Heidegger’s notion of existential angst (*Spatiality* 47). Lukács’s evaluation thus differs markedly from Mikhail Bakhtin’s, who finds in the genre of the novel “a certain linguistic homelessness of literary consciousness” that he sees as profoundly liberating because he believes it to be incompatible with oppressive, ‘monologic’ types of discourse (“Discourse in the Novel” 367; see McKeon, *Theory of the Novel* 318; Neubauer 541).

Despite such differences in evaluation between Lukács and Bakhtin, however, we should note that linguistic and transcendental homelessness in fact remain intimately related. The link between the two ideas is nicely expressed in Barry Unsworth’s historical novel *Morality Play*, set in fourteenth-century England, in which a former monk wonders whether it is morally acceptable for actors to perform a play based on a real-life crime rather than stories taken from scripture:

> God has not given us this story to use, He has not revealed to us the meaning of it. So it has no meaning, it is only a death. Players are like other men, they must use God’s meanings, they cannot make meanings of their own, that is heresy, it is the source of all our woes, it is the reason our first parents were cast out. [… I]f we make our own meanings, God will oblige us to answer our own questions, He will leave us in the void without the comfort of His Word. (74)

If meaning is not revealed (and thus transcendentally guaranteed), then according to Unsworth's narrator it necessarily becomes the problematic task of orphaned selves to create their own meaning in a comfortless void. In other words, if we lose the transcendental anchor of God's Word, meaning itself becomes arbitrary and linguistically homeless.

Of course, it is possible to disagree with Lukács's and Bakhtin's view of homelessness as an inherent characteristic of the novel as a genre, but the important point in our context is that *Moby-Dick*'s concern with both transcendental and linguistic homelessness is in fact apparent from the novel's very first page. In *Moby-Dick*'s opening section ("Etymology"; 7), the narrator tries to unravel the meaning of the word *whale* by venturing beyond the boundaries of English, his linguistic home:

חן	*Hebrew.*
khtoς,	*Greek.*
CETUS,	*Latin.*
WHÆL,	*Anglo-Saxon.*
HVAL,	*Danish.*
WAL,	*Dutch.*
HWAL,	*Swedish.*
HVALUR,	*Icelandic.*
WHALE,	*English.*
BALEINE,	*French.*
BALLENA,	*Spanish.*
PEKEE-NUEE-NUEE,	*Fegee.*
PEHEE-NUEE-NUEE,	*Erromangoan.*

In doing so, however, Melville's narrator merely highlights the arbitrary nature of linguistic signs (or, more precisely, the free-floating nature of the signifier, the meaning of which is not, in fact, transcendentally given). Moreover, in the novel's second section ("Extracts"), the narrator provides us with quotations on whales "from any book whatsoever, sacred or profane," and his use of the phrase "gospel cetology" beautifully encapsulates *Moby-Dick*'s characteristic oscillation between empiricist realism ("cetology") and allegorical or transcendental significance ("gospel"; 8). In short, while initially these two sections are bound to have an alienating effect on the reader, in retrospect we find that they are intimately related to the novel's key philosophical conflicts.

Losing Control: Madness, Obsession, and Homeless Narration

The novel's first two sections, moreover, highlight the extent to which the narrator's quest for the meaning of his story parallels Ahab's obsessive quest for meaning through his quest for revenge against Moby Dick.[38] The narrator's "systematized exhibition of the whale in his broad genera" (115; ch. 32); his promise to paint "something like the true form of the whale as he actually appears to the eye of the whaleman" (214–215; ch. 55); or his account of "the precise origin of ambergris" (317; ch. 92): these and other painstakingly detailed descriptions betray a well-nigh pathological obsession with the subject matter of whales. Put somewhat differently, we may say that readers who find themselves exasperated by *Moby-Dick*'s frequent essayistic digressions on every conceivable aspect of whaling have sensed something of vital importance: that the novel as a whole has an obsessive narrative structure that is, quite simply, apt to drive one mad.

Intriguingly, just as Ahab fails to sustain his narcissistic fantasy of mastery, Ishmael the narrator in many ways loses control over the story he tells – to the extent that his very identity as a narrator threatens to dissolve.[39] Ishmael's status as a realistically conceived narrator who simply relates his own experiences is in fact precarious at best, for there are many chapters in *Moby-Dick* that read like classically omniscient narration.[40] In the chapter entitled "The Doubloon," for instance, the narrator never refers to himself in the first person; instead, he uses impersonal phrases such as "it has been related" and "it has not been added," which could just as well be uttered by an extradiegetic, omniscient narrator (331; ch. 99). Moreover, it is unlikely that Ishmael, as a character, could actually have overheard what Ahab and Pip say to each other in the solitude of the Captain's cabin, and yet as a narrator he is able miraculously to provide us with all the details of this exchange (399–400; ch. 129). In addition, the narrator refers to himself in the first person in only one of the novel's final fifteen chapters; the

38 Presumably, this is why Eyal Peretz has suggested that Ahab's monomaniac desire to kill Moby Dick must be read as attempt on the captain's part to become "the origin of meaning" (60).

39 See also McLoughlin, who notes that "the narrator recedes into the background midway in the narrative" (62).

40 Robert T. Tally, Jr., too, has argued that Ishmael need not be read as a "monologic authority" (*Melville, Mapping and Globalization* (61).

other fourteen chapters conform to the paradigm of third-person omniscience.[41] More disturbingly still, at various points in the novel, the narrator’s voice disappears altogether, as in a chapter that presents us with Ishmael’s musings about the loss of identity that can occur to someone who meditates in solitude on the mast-head of a whaling ship (136; ch. 35). In the chapters that follow, the conventional form of narrative fiction slowly dissolves, transforming instead into something that resembles a play script rather than novelistic prose:

> HARPOONEERS AND SAILORS
> *(Foresail rises and discovers the watch standing, lounging, leaning, and lying in various attitudes, all singing in chorus.)*
> Farewell and adieu to you, Spanish ladies!
> Farewell and adieu to you, ladies of Spain!
> Our Captain’s commanded–
>
> 1ST NANTUCKET SAILOR
> Oh, boys, don’t be sentimental; it’s bad for the digestion! Take a tonic, follow me!
> (*Sings, and all follow.*)
> Our captain stood upon the deck,
> A spy glass in his hand,
> A viewing of those gallant whales
> That blew at every strand. (145–146; ch. 40)

In these dramatized passages, the narrator virtually disappears – and as if in panic-stricken response to this loss of narrative mastery, the next chapter opens with an emphatic re-assertion of textual presence: “I, Ishmael, was one of that crew” (152; ch. 41).

What is striking about Ishmael’s moments of narratorial dissolution is that they are always associated with either Ahab or Pip, the two other characters whose sense of self proves highly unstable in the course of *Moby-Dick.* A first example is the sequence of increasingly dramatized narrative discussed just now, which opens with Ahab announcing his quest for vengeance against Moby Dick (138–139; ch. 36) and ends with Pip voicing his fear of death and dissolution in a prayer to God (151; ch. 40). A second example occurs after the chapter in which Pip jumps overboard for a second time and in consequence remains abandoned for too long in the vast solitude of the ocean (“The Castaway”; ch. 93). This chapter precedes Ishmael’s account of how, when squeezing the spermaceti extracted from a slaughtered whale, he suddenly finds himself squeezing his co-la-

41 See Buell, who argues that the novel’s “first personness [...] disappears for the last part of the text save the epilogue” (146).

borer's hands – an experience that leads Ishmael to indulge in a strongly homoerotic fantasy of bodily union with his fellow sailors ("let us squeeze ourselves into each other") which he immediately proceeds to sublimate into a transcendental vision: "I saw long rows of angels in paradise, each with his hand in a jar of spermaceti" (323; ch. 94). Though Pip's traumatic isolation and Ishmael's erotic abandonment differ in many respects, they both involve a sense that the bounded nature of their selves is being dissolved. Finally, the scene in which Ahab mesmerizes his crew by catching the heavenly spark of St. Elmo's fire triggers another sequence of narratorial dissolution through an increasingly dramatized style of storytelling (ch. 118–122). We ought therefore to regard with skepticism Walter E. Bezanson's claim that Ishmael's voice "is there every moment from the genesis of the fiction in 'Call me Ishmael' to the final revelation of the 'Epilogue'" (647), as well as John Bryant's assertion that "it is always Ishmael who contains and controls" (80). Rather, Ishmael is a remarkably precarious narrator who continually struggles against his own dissolution; increasingly absent from the novel's plot as a character, he must even fear that his narratorial voice will be drowned in the maelstrom of his story.

Moby-Dick thus constitutes a prime example of what Rick Altman calls a multiple-focus narrative. In his *Theory of Narrative*, Altman suggests that there are three basic types of narrative fiction. In the first type, which Altman calls dual-focus narratives, the narrator shifts his attention back and forth between two groups (or two individuals) whose conflict is defined by stable binary oppositions (55). Such narratives, according to Altman, presuppose a set of universal values that are temporarily challenged by one or more characters, but ultimately reaffirmed by either the destruction or re-integration of those characters who have strayed (86–87). As one example of a dual-focus narrative, Altman cites Homer's *Iliad*, in which the Trojans violate supposedly universal values, and where the ultimate destruction of Troy reaffirms the Greek community (79–81). In single-focus narratives, by contrast, we typically concentrate on one main character who violates the symbolic laws of his or her community on a quest "into previously unexplored territory, behavior, or thought"; the emphasis, in other words, does not lie on reaffirming established values but instead on discovering new ones (Altman 189). One of Altman's examples for this second type of narrative is Nathaniel Hawthorne's *The Scarlet Letter*, which could easily have been told as a dual-focus narrative (with Hester Prynne embodying values opposed to the true Puritan faith of her community), but which instead concentrates entirely on Hester's quest for new and different values (Altman 99–118). While, in dual-focus narratives, the two opposing sets of values are ordered hierarchically and portrayed as objective, in single-focus narratives all values "remain subject to interpretation" (189). Nevertheless, even in single-focus stories there is a stable narrative center – i.e. the main character – and this distinguishes them from multiple-focus narratives, which "thrive on discontinuity" (243). In such stories, "we find ourselves transported by the narrator from one character to another" in an unpredictable, seemingly arbitrary manner (263). Multiple-focus narratives thus function, according to Altman, "like a mosaic," where the individual parts of the text "may mean something quite different" from the text as a whole (288).

Importantly, *Moby-Dick* initially looks very much like a single-focus narrative, and this creates expectations that the text subsequently proceeds to thwart. After plowing their way through *Moby-Dick*'s enigmatic introductory sections ("Etymology" and "Extracts"), readers are likely to react with considerable relief when the narrator invites them to call him Ishmael and join him on his narrative quest. We follow Ishmael to New Bedford, where he meets a new friend in Queequeg, who decides to accompany him on his journey. As is typical of single-focus narratives, the novel concentrates on its main character – until the moment when the Pequod sets sail (ch. 22). At this point, the narrative suddenly loses focus. Chapter 23, for instance, is devoted entirely to a character named Bulkington, whom we previously encountered only very briefly (ch. 3), and who will never again appear in the novel. Next comes the first of many essayistic excursions (ch. 24), and from this point on the story of Ishmael and his friend Queequeg recedes into the background, displaced by the tale of Ahab's quest. Even Ahab, however, sometimes disappears for long stretches of the text (e.g. ch. 74–80, or 92–98), making it impossible to construe him as a new and stable textual center. As readers, we thus experience a movement from fixity of narrative purpose to textual disorientation, and according to Altman this is typical of multiple-focus narratives in general: "Many texts invite a single-focus or dual-focus reading, only to undermine the reading in favor of a multiple-focus alternative" (255).[42]

Intriguingly, Altman describes the reader's condition in multiple-focus narratives as an experience of homelessness, and it is plausible to argue that *Moby-Dick*'s disjointed narrative structure effectively undermines any sense of spiritual belonging that we may gain from the narrator's assurances of deeper religious significance. Walter E. Bezanson, for instance, notes that readers expecting "classical form" will find *Moby-Dick* aesthetically unsatisfactory because

42 Compare these observations to Margaret Cohen's claim that "Melville breaks his contract with the reader of sea fiction" because his "remarkable poetics transgress poetic and generic expectation, across all the different scales of the novel" (*The Novel and the Sea* 186).

"explorations of structure suggest elaborate interrelations of the parts but do not lead to an overreaching formal pattern" (655).[43] This statement matches precisely Altman's characterization of how multiple-focus narratives affect their readers:

> Reading dual-focus and single-focus narrative, I always feel at home – whether it is the group-based home of the dual-focus texts or the single-focus identification with an individual. Coming to multiple-focus narrative with expectations developed in another world, I sense the new form as a loss, a lack, a diversion from the expected path. Trained to expect coherence [...], I can't feel at home in the multiple-focus world [...]. (285)

Altman compares this effect of disorientation to the paintings of Pieter Bruegel the Elder, which confront us with images of a multiple-focus world marked by the absence of a clear center: "We remain unable to image the drawing as a whole, to constitute visually any unity or hierarchy, to restore a center in terms of either interest or space" (200). In *Moby-Dick*, this absent center is, of course, symbolized by the white whale itself: a void that structures the entire narrative but that continues to elude both the novel's characters, its narrator, and its readers.

According to Altman, Bruegel's technique of de-centering is complemented in multiple-focus narratives by a clash of various styles, and Altman explicitly associates this strategy with the Russian Formalist's notion of defamiliarization (as well as with Bakhtin's concepts of dialogism and linguistic homelessness; Altman 217–221). In *Moby-Dick*, too, we encounter various contrasting styles – for instance in the novel's juxtaposition of satirical legal history (ch. 89–90) with picaresque episodes (ch. 91) and didactic treatises (ch. 92). In thus failing to follow any predictable trajectory, multiple-focus narratives challenge their readers to "stretch beyond the action-oriented and character-oriented questions of single-focus and dual-focus narrative" (Altman 263). Instead, Altman contends, "the multiple-focus form seeks out the *tertium quid* of conception" (269) – i.e. it encourages its disoriented, homeless readers to look for common thematic denominators, formal patterns, and recurring tropes.

43 The following complaint by a contemporary reviewer is a good example: "This is an ill-compounded mixture of romance and matter-of-fact. The idea of a connected and collected story has obviously visited and abandoned its writer again and again in the course of composition" ("[An Ill-Compounded Mixture]" 597).

Unraveling the "Weaver-God"

Let us examine how one such recurring trope – the image of the loom – can help us to bring into sharper focus some of *Moby-Dick*'s central concerns. We first encounter this recurring image in the title of the novel's very first chapter ("Loomings"), and already we are faced with significant ambiguities. The nautical meaning of the term *looming* is "land or ships beyond the horizon, dimly seen by reflection in peculiar weather conditions" (Parker and Hayford 18n1) – and indeed at this point in the narrative we do not yet 'see' the Pequod, but perceive it only dimly in Ishmael's reference to a "whaling voyage" on which he is about to embark (22; ch. 1). This specialized meaning of *looming* is thus relatively close to its more general – and often figurative – meaning as a "coming indistinctly into view" (OED): a vaguely foreshadowed, possibly ominous presence.[44] However, *looming* can also denote the "action or process of 'mounting' the warp on the loom" (OED), which is precisely what the narrator does in the novel's first chapter: he sets out to weave the web of his story.[45] The title "Loomings," in other words, simultaneously constitutes an authentic use of nautical jargon, an ominous expression of foreboding, and a playfully metafictional comment. From the outset, *Moby-Dick*'s concern with a realistic depiction of life at sea is thus counterpoised with a transcendental aura of prophecy as well as with an interest in the workings of textuality as such.

Moreover, when an actual loom appears later on in the novel, we are confronted once again with Ishmael's characteristic desire to imbue mundane facts with a deeper, transcendental significance. As he and Queequeg are "mildly employed weaving," Ishmael begins to lose himself in thoughts about the symbolical value of looms:

> [I]t seemed as if this were the Loom of Time, and I myself were a shuttle mechanically weaving and weaving away at the Fates. There lay the fixed threads of the warp subject to but one single, ever returning, unchanging vibration, and that vibration merely enough to admit of the crosswise interblending of other threads with its own. This warp seemed necessity; and here, thought I, with my own hand I ply my own shuttle and weave my own destiny into these unalterable threads. Meantime, Queequeg's impulsive, indifferent sword, sometimes hitting the woof slantingly, or crookedly, or strongly, or weakly, as the case might be; and by this difference in the concluding blow producing a corresponding contrast in the final aspect of the completed fabric; this savage's sword, thought I, which thus finally shapes and fashions both warp and woof; this easy, indifferent sword must be chance – aye, chance, free will, and necessity –

44 looming, *n¹* (OED Online, 2 August 2017; 2nd ed. 1989).
45 looming, *n²* (OED Online, 2 August 2017; 2nd ed. 1989).

> no wise incompatible – all interweavingly working together. The straight warp of necessity, not to be swerved from its ultimate course – its every alternating vibration, indeed, only tending to that; free will still free to ply her shuttle between given threads; and chance, though restrained in its play within the right lines of necessity, and sideways in its motions directed by free will, though thus prescribed to by both, chance by turns rules either, and has the last featuring blow at events. (179; ch. 47)

What is so extraordinary about Ishmael's reading of the loom as a model of how necessity, free will, and chance interact as the three shaping forces of our lives is that his initial interpretation is thoroughly agnostic, for "necessity" could designate natural and historical laws just as it might refer to any mysterious, providential design.

Characteristically, however, Ishmael later revises his original interpretation in order to salvage a transcendental meaning. In the passage quoted above, God is conspicuously absent from Ishmael's image of the "Loom of Time," but Ishmael later sets out on project of rhetorical readjustment by claiming that Pip, while abandoned during the chase of a whale, "saw God's foot upon the treadle of the loom" (322; ch. 94). Whereas God was at first merely an unnamed possibility, he now suddenly emerges as the omnipotent weaver. This image of the "weaver-god" returns a few chapters later, when Ishmael describes the lush landscape of a Pacific island:

> [T]he industrious earth beneath was as a weaver's loom, with a gorgeous carpet on it, whereof the ground-vine tendrils formed the warp and woof, and the living flowers the figures. [...] Through the lacings of the leaves, the great sun seemed a flying shuttle weaving the unwearied verdure. Oh, busy weaver! unseen weaver! – pause! – one word! – whither flows the fabric? what palace may it deck? wherefore all these ceaseless toilings? Speak, weaver! – stay thy hand! – but one single word with thee! Nay – the shuttle flies – the figures float from forth the loom; the freshet-rushing carpet for ever slides away. The weaver-god, he weaves; and by that weaving is he deafened, that he hears no mortal voice; and by that humming, we, too, who look on the loom are deafened; and only when we escape it shall we hear the thousand voices that speak through it. For even so it is in all material factories. The spoken words that are inaudible among the flying spindles; those same words are plainly heard without the walls, bursting from the opened casements. Thereby have villainies been detected. Ah, mortal! [...] be heedful; for so, in all this din of the great world's loom, thy subtlest thinkings may be overheard afar. (345; ch. 102)

The whole world has now become, for Ishmael, a text woven by God, the great master-weaver, who is supposedly deafened by the noise of his creative act. And yet, the idea that our "subtlest thinkings may be overheard afar" seems to imply that there is some transcendent connection – possibly with the ones who have escaped the loom (which may be Ishmael's poetic way of referring to the souls of the departed, as opposed to us mortals who "may be overheard afar").

Just like his earlier rhetorical maneuvers, Ishmael's remolded image of the "Loom of Time" thus expresses his deep yearning for a transcendental sense of belonging. At the same time, the idea that communication with God is entirely impossible, and that the transcendent weaver will neither cease his work nor ever react to human supplications must make us wonder how we could possibly know anything about this absent being. Moreover, it is telling that Ishmael introduces the problem of social alienation (i.e. the textile workers who are isolated from each other by the noise of the "material factories") only to shy away from it, as if afraid of the "villainies" that we might detect if we remained undistracted by transcendental re-imaginings.[46]

Visions of Home: Labor, Equality, and the Question of Gender

In *Moby-Dick*, the transcendental home remains out of reach, even as Ishmael refuses to relinquish his desire for it; time and again, this sole survivor of the Pequod's disaster uses all the rhetorical means at his disposal in an attempt to retrieve some grander meaning from the wreckage of his life at sea. Just like Ahab, in other words, Ishmael is unable to let go of Moby Dick; the specter of the whale continues to haunt him, and significantly he ends his tale, not on a note of hope and belonging, or with a scene of joyful homecoming, but instead as merely "another orphan."

It is remarkable how fundamentally absent home is in *Moby-Dick*. Both Ahab and Ishmael come from a 'broken' home (i.e. Ahab's mother was mad, while Ishmael's stepmother treated him badly – and we know virtually nothing about their fathers). Indeed, this lack of parental care may have something to do with the two characters' desperate attempts in later life to cling to the idea of a transcendent father (benevolent or malicious, as the case may be). In Ahab's case, things are made worse through the experience of trauma, and neither the power nor the solitude and isolation that come with the captain's office are likely to improve his condition, for while the former tends to foster a narcissistic sense of grandeur, the latter shuts Ahab off from human interaction (including therapeutic storytelling). In effect, Ahab as a character constitutes a study of the pathologies inherent in Emersonian self-reliance, and it is only when Ahab, the

---

46 My argument is similar to Christopher S. Durer's, who maintains that "the notion of the grand programme [of Providence] is present at the beginning, but is being corroded, undermined, and finally dismissed" (253). While Ishmael tries to emphasize the presence of God, the contradictions in his argument end up undermining his case.

ship's master, encounters Pip the 'slave,' who suffers from a similar condition, that the captain tentatively begins to re-establish a sense of belonging – a development that is tragically cut short when the Pequod finally meets Moby Dick. Ishmael, meanwhile, is in some ways merely a good-humored conformist, but if we pay close attention to his rhetorical shifts, we find that in fact his textual contortions constitute discursive attempts at home-making in the face of a deep sense of alienation. Crucially, though Ishmael's alienation may be rooted in some fundamental human condition (e.g. existential trauma or a human subjectivity that is necessarily based on lack), it is the lack both of financial resources and of any other kinds of interest that drive him away from a place that, given these circumstances, simply does not feel like home. Perhaps it is Ishmael's ardent desire finally to belong – to have a well-defined place in the world – that stops him from even contemplating civil disobedience as a means to prevent Ahab from abusing his power. Tragically, the Pequod's calamitous journey will leave Ishmael with such a mutilated sense of self that even his own narrative spins out of control, despite all his attempts to weave a discursive home out of the manifold strands of his story.

And yet, there are two brief moments in Melville's novel when Ishmael feels at home in the world, and both of these are strongly homoerotic. One of these two moments occurs, as we have seen, when Ishmael squeezes his co-workers' hands, filled with such an "abounding, affectionate, friendly, loving feeling" that he wishes to tell them: "let us squeeze ourselves universally into the very milk and sperm of kindness" (323). For one thing, we may note that Ishmael here alludes to a passage from Shakespeare's tragedy *Macbeth*, in which Lady Macbeth is afraid that her husband may be "too full o' th' milk of human kindness," and thus unable to seize the throne (1.5.16). From the reader's point of view, this reference to a canonical text conveys an intertextual sense of home at the very moment when Ishmael, too, feels that he belongs. At the same time, while the original metaphor thrives on associations of milk with motherhood and nourishment, Ishmael's use of the word "sperm" (ostensibly as a short form of spermaceti) adds to the image a decidedly masculine and sexual twist, leaving the familiar phrase strangely altered.[47] Byron R.S. Fone has suggested that "Melville constructs a fictional world in which the primary characters are outcasts from the land-locked world of (hetero-)sexual morality" (52), and perhaps Ishmael's alteration of the canonical text constitutes a stylistic correlative to the novel's revision of supposedly given moral codes.

47 At this point, one is almost obliged to point out that, in Melville's novel, a group of sturdy men join forces in order to extract sperm from a giant (Moby) Dick.

At any rate, the only similarly homely moment for Ishmael occurs much earlier in the novel, when he shares a bed with Queequeg at the Spouter-Inn in Nantucket. At the end of their first night together, Ishmael wakes up to find "Queequeg's arm thrown over me in the most loving and affectionate manner," so that an observer could have "almost thought I had been his wife." At this point, Ishmael's sensations are still "strange" rather than pleasant (36; ch. 4), but his vague sense of discomfort has clearly faded by the second night:

> How it is I know not; but there is no place like a bed for confidential disclosures between friends. Man and wife, they say, there open the very bottom of their souls to each other; and some old couples often lie and chat over old times till nearly morning. Thus, then, in our hearts' honeymoon, lay I and Queequeg – a cosy, loving pair. (57; ch. 10)

Ishmael and Queequeg are like a "cosy, loving pair," and every once in a while Queequeg affectionately throws his legs over Ishmael's because the two are now "entirely sociable and free and easy"; indeed, Ishmael loves to have Queequeg smoking by his side because the latter seems to be "full of such serene household joy" (57 and 58; ch. 11). In the comfort of a bed he shares with another man, Ishmael thus feels just as much at home as in the common labor of squeezing sperm with his equals on board the Pequod.[48]

These, then, are the glimpses of a utopian vision in a novel otherwise suffused with homelessness: equality and intimacy, shared work and bodily comfort – a home in this world rather than the next. In Ishmael's case, bodily comfort happens to mean physical contact with other men, and it may well be that he fails to feel at home in his native land because there is no real place there for same-sex relationships:

> Would that I could keep squeezing that sperm for ever! For now, [...] by many prolonged, repeated experiences, I have perceived that in all cases man must eventually lower, or at least shift, his conceit of attainable felicity; not placing it anywhere in the intellect or the fancy; but in the wife, the heart, the bed, the table, the saddle, the fire-side, the country [...]. (323; ch. 94)

Ishmael cannot imagine a real-life counterpart to his homoerotic "conceit" or "fancy," and instead believes that "man must eventually lower, or at least shift, his conceit of attainable felicity" by settling for a conventional home shared with "the wife." In a world where women are considered to be the natural

48 See also Robert K. Martin's more extended analysis of male friendship in *Moby-Dick* in his monograph on Melville, *Hero, Captain, and Stranger* (67–94).

home-makers, Ishmael is evidently unable to imagine an everyday home with another man at his side.[49]

It is therefore important to be clear about the limited nature of these visions of belonging. On the one hand, *Moby-Dick*'s utopian vision of equality and intimacy – of shared work and bodily comfort – transcends the divisions of gender because in theory both men and women can engage in common labor, and both men and women are able to heed the needs of other desiring human bodies. On the other hand, the utopian moments that are actually depicted in Melville's novel are shared only between men, and Ishmael as a narrator is unable to understand them as anything but fancies: pleasant, perhaps, but necessarily fleeting and insubstantial. In other words, unlike Emerson's self-reliant man, Ishmael and his ideas ultimately remain within the boundaries dictated by custom.

This latter point also explains why *Moby-Dick* ought properly to be understood not as a downright rejection of Emerson's ideas, but as a complex and searching critique. What Melville's novel does reject, through its portrayal of Ahab, is Emerson's belief that self-reliance as such is synonymous with spiritual isolation, and must always involve the will to dominate and sacrifice others. At the same time, *Moby-Dick* suggests that Ishmael is far too willing to accommodate to the status quo because he is afraid of standing apart, or appearing in any way as different from others. The point of the novel's critique, in short, is that isolation from others is neither splendid nor an end in itself, but only, at times, a tragic necessity when faced with widespread communal injustice – and it is this that Ishmael fails to grasp. *Moby-Dick* thus confronts us with two very different male figures, both of whom remain transcendentally homeless. Melville's women, meanwhile, stay behind on shore, as absent characters who merely serve to symbolize the conventional home. To overcome this ideological deadlock, we must now turn to George Eliot's *The Mill on the Floss*, where a female character takes center stage.

49 See Steven B. Herrmann for a Jungian reading of Melville's "portrait of same-sex marriage" (65).

2 “Whom She Belongs To”: Gender, Genre, and “Immovable Roots” in George Eliot’s *The Mill on the Floss*

While Melville’s *Moby-Dick* explores oceans of transcendental homelessness, George Eliot’s *The Mill on the Floss* (1860) dutifully attends to the home and the hearth.[1] The novel is set in the English provinces of the late 1820s to 1830s and focuses on the lives of the Tulliver family, owners of Dorlcote Mill on the banks of the Ripple, a small tributary to the river Floss.[2] The Tullivers have lived here “for generations” (217; bk. 3, ch. 9), and on one level *The Mill on the Floss* is about the family’s relation to the physical place that, for them, signifies home. At the same time, the novel focuses on the Tullivers’ relationships to their relatives, and to the larger community of St. Ogg’s. More specifically, the text examines the interdependence between home as a physical place and home as a complex network of social relations, as well as the factors that may enhance or diminish one’s sense of home. These factors include class and gender stereotypes, and the latter make it especially difficult for Maggie, the daughter of Mr. and Mrs. Tulliver, to maintain a sense of true belonging.

Importantly, the novel’s exploration of social prejudice is paralleled by a searching critique of literary conventions, styles, and genres – including the *Bildungsroman* (or novel of formation), the use of irony and nostalgia, and the vicissitudes of tragic theory in its Aristotelian form. In relating such stylistic and generic inquiries to the material problems of home and belonging, Eliot’s novel suggests that literary culture ought not be imagined as a rarefied aesthetic realm that can be understood in isolation from ideological and political struggles. The novel thus rejects any clear-cut separation between social and discursive modes of dispossession. Highlighting instead that discourse itself is a material product of social relations, *The Mill on the Floss* intimates that the quest for a just and inclusive society depends, at least in part, on a community’s repertoire of fictions of home. In doing so, it focuses less on the problem of transcendental

1 I would like to thank Simone Heller-Andrist and Christa Schönfelder for their comments on an early draft, as well as Sarah Chevalier and Anja Neukom-Hermann for feedback on the final version of this chapter.

2 According to Susan Meyer, “[v]arious temporal references in *The Mill on the Floss* make it clear that the novel is set in the rural England of the late 1820s to 1830s” (148).

homelessness, and more on the role of societal forces in determining the limits of our freedom to belong.

Home and the Bildungsroman

Critics have long discussed *The Mill on the Floss* as a novel of formation or *Bildungsroman* (e.g. Buckley 97 and Jost 106), and of all novelistic genres the *Bildungsroman* is perhaps most inextricably intertwined with the question of home. Home is, for instance, quite literally the genre's starting point:

> [T]he hero sets out from home in order to travel and see the world, and records his right and wrong turns. He falls in love, and has his first sexual experiences before finding, and eventually marrying, his ideal companion. He thus gains knowledge of the world, and his experiences modify his *Weltanschauung*. (Gemmeke 32)

Leaving his childhood home, the (male) protagonist will have to learn the ways of the world, and this experience will ultimately turn him into a mature and useful individual richly deserving of domestic bliss. By the end of his quest, the hero will, in other words, have learnt to reconcile his individual desires with the demands of society: "[E]xperiencing both defeats and triumphs, [he] comes to a better understanding of self and to a generally affirmative view of the world" (Hardin xiii). Indeed, as Franco Moretti points out, in the process of true *Bildung* the hero fuses external compulsion and internal impulses "into a new unity until the former is no longer distinguishable from the latter" (*Way of the World* 16). Desire and duty may jar at first, but any such discord will eventually be dissolved.

The only reason why such a dialectical fusion of societal imperatives and individual desire is conceivable is that the genre envisages *Bildung* itself as a kind of homecoming:

> [I]n *Bildung* one gives oneself over to something other than oneself, and by this process of giving over, becomes more fully oneself. Giving oneself over to something other is a going out to the other, so that *Bildung* involves the notion of leaving home [...] and going out into a new place that is strange and unfamiliar. As one comes to understand this other place, as it becomes familiar, *it comes to be a new home.* [...] It seemed strange simply because we did not recognise ourselves in it. (Coyne and Snodgrass 224; emphasis added)

Bildung allows the protagonist to recognize himself in what at first seemed an alien world, and the prototypical *Bildungsroman* narrativizes the "dialectical harmony" of such an experience of homecoming (Castle 8; see also Lukács 138; Slaughter 111). As harmony is the key term in the ideal version of *Bildung*, the hero's ultimate acceptance of society's demands must never be motivated by compulsion, fear, or disillusionment, but instead ought to result from his genuine identification with society's norms (Moretti, *Way of the World* 16).

Many critics recognize, however, that in practice the genre often falls short of this haromonic ideal, as witnessed by the many classic *Bildungsromane* that end neither in joyous affirmation nor with calm acceptance, but rather on a note of reluctant, at times painful, compromise. Indeed, for some critics, the genre's historical development follows a downward trajectory from early optimism to increasing gloom. Franco Moretti, for instance, posits that the truly optimistic phase of the genre, with its "beautiful balance" between the benefits and constraints of modern socialization, lasted only until the mid-nineteenth century, when "the atmosphere darkens" (*Way of the World* vi – vii). The case of *Great Expectations* (1860–1861) arguably constitutes a good example of this increasingly ambivalent atmosphere, as Dickens famously wrote two markedly different endings for his novel: a first one, where the protagonist's desire for his beloved remains forever unfulfilled (481–482); and a second version, where Pip can finally clasp Estella's hand, seeing "the shadow of no parting from her" (480; ch. 20). Dickens's first instinct was, in other words, to end on a pessimistic note, and it took a conscious effort of authorial revision to construct a somewhat more hopeful conclusion. And yet, even this second ending remains curiously ambiguous, as there are two entirely different ways of reading the phrase "the shadow of no parting": either as affirming that Estella and Pip will live happily ever after (i.e. 'no future parting is foreshadowed'), or as intimating that their common future will inevitably be cold and dreary (i.e. 'the fact that there will be no parting casts a shadow over their lives'). This is, to be sure, still far from despair – but it is not "dialectical harmony," either.[3]

There is good reason, then, for a more cautious assessment of the *Bildungsroman* as a genre, and accordingly Marianne Hirsch speaks of the protagonist's eventual accommodation to, rather than his affirmation of, the society in which he lives ("Novel of Formation" 298). Less optimistically still, Jeffrey L. Sammons's definition of the genre incorporates the possibility of the protagonist's utter failure ever to find a sense of being at home in the world:

> It does not much matter whether the process of *Bildung* succeeds or fails, whether the protagonist achieves an accommodation with life and society or not. [...] There must be a sense of evolutionary change within the self, a teleology of individuality, even if

---

3 In fact, Dickens himself seems to have recognized this ambivalence, for from the 1862 Library Edition onward, the final sentence appeared in a slightly different, less ambivalent form: "I saw no shadow of another parting from her" (Rosenberg 500–501).

> the novel, as many do, comes to doubt or deny the possibility of achieving a gratifying result. (41)

Sammons, in other words, is willing to consider as a *Bildungsroman* even a novel in which individual gratification ultimately remains irreconcilable with life in society – a novel, in short, that takes very much the same pessimistic stance as Sigmund Freud's *Civilization and Its Discontents.*[4] Accordingly, for Sammons, the key requirement for a *Bildungsroman* is not a happy outcome, but merely that *Bildung* – which he defines as "the early bourgeois, humanistic concept of the shaping of the individual self from its innate potentialities through acculturation and social experience to the threshold of maturity" – play a central part in the hero's quest (41). In this less sanguine view, the protagonist's leaving home still constitutes the genre's starting point, yet a regained sense of belonging may ultimately prove sadly elusive (Gemmeke 38).

Such an austere account of the genre fits well with Eliot's *The Mill on the Floss*, for the novel's heroine, Maggie, undoubtedly fails to harmoniously fuse her own desires with the demands and imperatives of her family and society at large. Even when Maggie is still a child, her relatives express misgivings and disapproval: Mr. Tulliver fears that his daughter is "[t]oo 'cute [i.e. acute, clever]" for a woman, and his wife bemoans both Maggie's unruly behavior and her brown skin, which "makes her look like a mulatter" (12; bk. 1, ch. 2). Aunt Pullet similarly frowns at her niece's dark complexion, suspecting that looking "like a gypsy" will stand in Maggie's way later in her life (58; bk. 1, ch. 7). Deborah Epstein Nord rightly notes that Maggie's relatives thus conflate her "anomalous femininity" with a sense of racial otherness (103), and to some extent this explains why, after a particularly severe scolding, little Maggie decides to run away and join a group of gypsies – an act that she sees as "the only way of escaping

---

4 Two brief excerpts may serve to exemplify Freud's position: "If civilization imposes such great sacrifices not only on man's sexuality but on his aggressivity, we can understand better why it is hard for him to be happy in that civilization" (*Civilization and Its Discontents* 73; "Wenn die Kultur nicht allein der Sexualität, sondern auch der Aggressionsneigung des Menschen so grosse Opfer auferlegt, so verstehen wir es besser, dass es dem Menschen schwer wird, sich in ihr beglückt zu finden"; *Das Unbehagen in der Kultur* 226). "Since civilization obeys an internal erotic impulsion which causes human beings to unite in a closely-knit group, it can only achieve this aim through an ever-increasing reinforcement of the sense of guilt" (*Civilization and Its Discontents* 96; "Da die Kultur einem inneren erotischen Antrieb gehorcht, der sie die Menschen zu einer innig verbundenen Masse vereinigen heisst, kann sie dies Ziel nur auf dem Wege einer immer wachsenden Verstärkung des Schuldgefühls erreichen"; *Das Unbehagen in der Kultur* 243).

opprobrium, and being entirely in harmony with circumstances" (88; bk. 1, ch. 11). The episode thus constitutes a variant of the Freudian family romance:

> [This alternate version] involves the fantasy not of social aggrandizement and aspiration, but of lowly or stigmatized birth. The desire to rival and defeat the parent can also express itself as the wish to escape from the bonds of obedience and conformity through the discovery of a secret non-English, non-white (to the extent that Englishness is defined as white) self. (Nord 12)

Feeling constricted and unhappy at home, in short, little Maggie makes a desperate attempt to venture out and find her place in the world.

Accordingly, Maggie's flight to the gypsies is more than merely a semi-comical episode about childish fantasies and youthful sorrows. Rather, given the symbolical status of Romani in 19th-century British culture, we must see Maggie's attempt to associate with gypsies as decidedly ominous. Deborah Epstein Nord has shown that, for many nineteenth-century writers (including George Eliot), gypsies symbolized the absence of a clearly defined homeland and therefore the lack of a "propitious future" (7). More generally, C. A. Bayly describes the nineteenth century as a period that saw a worldwide onslaught on nomadic forms of life – both in colonial territories and in long-established, independent states (Bayly 436–440; see also Maier 30). The British government in India, for example, idealized the settled (and tax-paying) peasant and, in 1871, introduced the Criminal Tribes Act in order to increase its control over itinerant and nomadic groups (Kerr 100; Osterhammel 225). Maggie's dark hair and her attempt to find a new home amongst the 'unsettled' gypsies thus associate her with a people that, for Eliot's contemporaries, tended to symbolize backwardness, dispossession, and ruin. The link between Maggie and gypsies can thus be seen as having the same function as her mother's repeatedly expressed fears that Maggie's wild nature will one day lead her to drown (e.g. 12 and 87; bk. 1, ch. 2 and ch. 10): foreshadowing that the novel must end in disaster, and that Maggie will fail to find a true home in the world.

A Woman's Place

To a large extent, the conflict that leads to Maggie's failure revolves around her relationship with her brother Tom. As a little girl, Maggie once says that she loves Tom "better than anybody in the world" (27; bk. 1, ch. 4), and she later tries to explain the well-nigh incestuous intensity of her attachment by the fact that her earliest memory is the image of Tom and herself standing hand in hand by the river Floss (249; bk. 1, ch. 1). At the same time, it is evident early on in the novel that Tom's clear-cut, rigid view of what is right and what is wrong conflicts sharply with Maggie's impulsiveness and intellectual curiosity. Nevertheless, as long as they are children they manage to avoid estrangement even when Tom's righteousness erupts into anger, for "Maggie and Tom were still very much like young animals, and so she could rub her cheek against his, and kiss his ear in a random, sobbing way, and there were tender fibres in the lad that had been used to answer to Maggie's fondling" (34; bk. 1, ch. 6). If childhood is at one point compared to Eden in Eliot's novel (155 and 159; bk. 2, ch. 7), then this is not because it is entirely free of conflict, but because it still holds the promise of forgiveness for Maggie.

However, it is precisely the abrupt and brutal nature in which childhood ends for Maggie and Tom that also destroys this bond of forgiveness. When their father loses a lawsuit over property rights (concerning irrigation works and the legitimate share of water power: 129; bk. 2, ch. 2), the proud man and his family suddenly find themselves bankrupt. Soon, many of the Tullivers' most cherished belongings are to be put up at auction, and it is this traumatic experience of dispossession that propels Maggie and Tom into the adult world of "remembered cares" (159; bk. 2, ch. 7). John Wakem, the lawyer who defeated Mr. Tulliver in court and whom the miller regards as evil incarnate, eventually buys the Tullivers' old mill. Wakem, relishing the opportunity to humiliate the old owner under the guise of a "benevolent action" (208; bk. 3, ch. 7), offers Mr. Tulliver the opportunity to stay on as manager of the mill – and thus as a dependent of the very man he loathes: "one o' them fine gentlemen as get money by doing business for poorer folks, and when he's made beggars of 'em he'll give 'em charity" (220; bk. 3, ch. 9). Formerly a version of the independent, land-owning English yeoman, Mr. Tulliver is now reduced to being a mere employee, and he never fully recovers from the blow.[5] In consequence, the responsibility to earn enough money to restore the lost home to the family falls almost entirely to Tom, who is at the time only sixteen years old. Mr. Tulliver, however, also urges Tom to write in the family bible that he will never forgive Wakem for what he has done to his father. It is a command that Tom executes "with gloomy submission" (220; bk. 3, ch. 9), and which expels him forever from the realm of forgiveness that he had shared with his sister before the sudden end of their childhood.

Maggie herself, meanwhile, is not only dismayed by her father's hatred of Wakem, but also suffers from the new "dreariness of a home where the morning

---

5 Similarly, in their reading of Eliot's novel as "a family tragedy," Jayne Elisabeth Archer, Richard Maggraf Turley and Howard Thomas argue that "[a]rable livings were being consumed by the transformation of agriculture into agri-business" (722) – a process they regard as "symptomatic of a widespread and irreversible disengagement from the land" (708).

brings no promise with it" (163; bk. 3, ch. 1). The family's material dispossession exacerbates Maggie's sense of spiritual unbelonging – a link that the novel symbolically highlights through the forced sale of her 'spiritual capital': her beloved books (197; bk. 3, ch. 6). At the same time, we saw in the discussion of Captain Ahab and Pip in chapter one that recognition of shared suffering may foster a feeling of mutual belonging. And indeed, Maggie finds a precarious sense of being at home in the presence of a fellow sufferer. Philip, lawyer Wakem's sensitive son – whom Maggie first met when he was Tom's schoolfellow in happier days – has a hump because of "an accident in infancy" (134; bk. 2, ch. 3). As a consequence Philip feels that he is an outcast with no one to "tell everything – no one who cares enough" (246; bk. 5, ch. 1). Earlier in the novel, Eliot's narrator suggests that "the gift of sorrow" is that it may serve to strengthen the "bond of human fellowship" (159; bk. 2, ch. 7), and when Maggie meets Philip again she finds herself responding to his pain. Admittedly, at first she is hesitant to accept Philip's offer of friendship, knowing that she would have to keep it a secret because both her father and Tom would forbid any association with the Wakem family. However, deciding that there is "such a thing as futile sacrifice for one to the injury of another" (247; bk. 5; ch. 1), Maggie ultimately agrees to meet Philip again. With each new meeting their friendship deepens, and in time Maggie even accepts Philip's professions of love, despite the fact that she remains uncertain as to the true nature of her feelings towards him (271–274; bk. 5, ch. 5).

Importantly, it is Tom who breaks up Maggie and Philip's relationship because of his inflexible notions of familial duty and, in particular, female respectability. When Tom finds out about Maggie and Philip's secret meetings, he angrily confronts his sister, threatening to tell Mr. Tulliver that Maggie is "a disobedient, deceitful daughter, who throws away her own respectability by clandestine meetings with the son of a man that has helped to ruin her father" (278; bk. 5, ch. 5). Tom then forces Maggie to lead him to Philip, and his reproaches to the latter, too, are explicitly patriarchal: "Do you pretend you had any right to make professions of love to her, even if you had been a fit husband for her, when neither her father nor your father would ever consent to a marriage between you?" (280). Maggie, disgusted at Tom's contemptuous treatment of both Philip and herself, vehemently reproaches her brother for his self-righteous attitude: "[Y]ou have always enjoyed punishing me – you have always been hard and cruel to me" (282). Tom, however, proves inexorable, and instead asks Maggie why she chooses to show her love through selfishness and deceit rather than by trying to improve their family's situation. Maggie's answer once again focuses on gender as the decisive factor: "Because you are a man, Tom, and have power, and can do something in the world" (282; bk. 5, ch. 6). Maggie thus explicitly frames her conflict with Tom in terms of the limitations she encounters as a woman, which relates their personal conflict to broader questions of societal prejudice.

In a similar vein, critics have long pointed out that a gender bias lies at the heart of overly optimistic assessments of the *Bildungsroman* as a literary genre. If we have so far used the masculine pronoun to refer to the prototypical hero of a *Bildungsroman*, then this is because the conventional story of a sturdy individual venturing out to explore the world constitutes – at least in a nineteenth-century context – a decidedly masculine ideal. For Susan J. Rosowski, such masculine quests find a feminine counterpart in what she calls the "novel of awakening":

> The novel of awakening […] also recounts the attempts of a sensitive protagonist to learn the nature of the world, discover its meaning and pattern, acquire a philosophy of life, but she must learn these lessons in terms of herself as a woman. […] The protagonist's growth results typically not with "an art of living," as for her male counterpart, but instead with a realization that for a woman such an art of living is difficult or impossible: it is an awakening to limitations. (313)

Where the *Bildungsroman* emphasizes the male protagonist's quest for independence, the novel of awakening focuses on the limits to freedom in the lives of women. Precisely because the limitations imposed on women are greater, Gregory Castle argues that novels of awakening "may be a better index of the subversive potential of the genre" than the texts featuring a male protagonist (21).[6]

According to Jane McDonnell, the subversive potential of novels of awakening arises, in particular, from the way in which they highlight the conflict between, on the one hand, the 'male' values of personal development and self-determination, and, on the other, "the ideals of renunciation and self-sacrifice so often demanded of nineteenth-century women" (379).[7] In the final two books of *The Mill on the Floss*, for instance, Maggie falls in love with Stephen Guest, heir to a local business and banking concern and fiancé of Maggie's cousin Lucy. At first, both Stephen and Maggie try to resist each other's mutual attraction, but they ultimately relinquish, with Stephen appearing to Maggie as a

6 For a related argument on the use of the *Bildungsroman* as a "genre of demarginalization," see Joseph R. Slaughter (135).

7 See also Fredric Jameson, who suggests that women, "not yet fully absorbed into capitalism and the vehicles of unpaid labor, are more likely narrative occasions for revolt and resistance than men" (*The Antinomies of Realism* 147).

"stronger presence that seemed to bear her along without any act of her own will" (376; bk. 6, ch. 13). Maggie elopes with Stephen and soon finds herself on a boat, floating down the river Floss. After a spell of fitful sleep, punctured by disturbing dreams, however, Maggie's struggle with her own conscience resumes, and she forces herself to leave Stephen and return home:

> I can't believe in a good for you, that I feel – that we both feel is a wrong towards others. We can't choose happiness either for ourselves or for another: we can't tell where that will lie. We can only choose whether we will indulge ourselves in the present moment, or whether we will renounce that, for the sake of obeying the divine voice within us – for the sake of being true to all the motives that sanctify our lives. (387; bk. 6, ch. 14)

It is important to note that Maggie's fateful decision is simultaneously conventional and brave, for while such an act of female renunciation would have been expected by Victorian readers, in Eliot's novel it also constitutes a reassertion of the protagonist's agency against her passive submission to her male partner's desire for a sort of escapism: to elope and, as Stephen puts it, "never go home again" (377; bk. 6, ch. 13).

And yet, Maggie is not rewarded for her painful act of renunciation by any semblance of poetic justice. Instead, she is ostracized by her home community in a way that, once again, highlights how gender difference impacts on one's chances to establish a sense of belonging. After Maggie's return to St. Ogg's, her behavior is widely judged as shameful – particularly by the 'respectable' women of the community, who could have forgiven her if Maggie had returned home married to Stephen, as a 'legitimate' member of (patriarchal) society, but who now ironically blame Maggie for her "unwomanly boldness and unbridled passion" (397; bk. 7, ch. 2). By contrast, public opinion regards Stephen's conduct as admittedly blameworthy, but also as understandable, even natural, in a young man. Eliot's contemporaries were, in other words, confronted with a novel whose heroine does precisely what, as a woman, she ought to do (i.e. resist the temptations of sexual desire), but who is not, in the end, rewarded for her act of renunciation. This outcome flies in the face of the Victorian expectations that Oscar Wilde brilliantly satirizes in *The Importance of Being Earnest*, in which Miss Prism sums up the moral of a three-decker novel she once wrote: "The good ended happily, and the bad unhappily. That is what fiction means" (273; 2.52–53). Marianne Hirsch has suggested that the *Bildungsroman* is an essentially didactic genre ("Novel of Formation" 298), and if it is true that the protagonist's *Bildung* in such texts is only a stand-in for the more important process of educating the audience, then in the case of *The Mill on the Floss* the awakening that matters most may be the reader's: a growing awareness of the gendered nature of social injustice, as well as of the limits of poetic justice as a reliable doctrine for moral guidance.

Tom's Education: Generational Conflict and Masculine Bildung

The picture is even more complex than this, however, for as Susan Fraiman suggests, *The Mill on the Floss* in fact juxtaposes a male and a female *Bildungsroman*: the story of Maggie's awakening, and the narrative of her brother's self-advancement (140–141).[8] Working his way up the social ladder, Tom becomes a respected partner in the local business and banking concern Guest & Co., and ultimately manages to restore to the family the lost mill and its position in society. At the same time, Fraiman rightly emphasizes that Tom remains unmarried and eventually drowns locked in an embrace with his younger sister, which constitutes a narrative refusal truly to validate his individual development (140). Indeed, far from becoming a well-rounded individual, Tom develops into a tragically one-dimensional man. Mr. Tulliver's dying wish was for Tom to "get the old mill back" (291; bk. 5, ch. 7), and accordingly Tom feels bound at all costs to return to the place that symbolizes home and respectability. To do so, however, Tom will have to suppress his "strong appetite for pleasure," for only by living a life of "abstinence and self-denial" can he ever hope to save the amount of money that is needed to pay the family debt and buy back the old mill (252; bk. 5, ch. 2). Tom's long-term cultivation of self-denial in turn explains why, towards the end of the novel, he assures his uncle Deane that he always wants to have plenty of work because there is nothing else he cares about much – a statement that even his "business-loving" relative considers "rather sad" (323; bk. 6, ch. 6). Moreover, when Tom finally 'succeeds' and moves back to Dorlcote Mill, we never see him derive any pleasure from owning the old home; though the mill eventually belongs to Tom, for some unfathomable reason he finds that he himself no longer feels that he truly belongs there.[9]

In part, this is because Tom follows his father's explicit commands to the letter while failing to grasp the spirit of his words (and, indeed, the father's actions, which frequently run counter to his own precepts). Mr. Tulliver's views may be as rigid as Tom's, but he is far less dogmatic when it comes to acting on his beliefs. This is evident, for instance, in how Mr. Tulliver treats his sister. After a quarrel with his wife's elder sister, the proud miller decides to settle all his debts

8 In a similar vein, Jerome Buckley considers *The Mill on the Floss* as a "contrapuntal Bildungsroman" (97).

9 Philip Fisher similarly argues that, by the end of the novel, what Tom holds "is the symbol of the past, not its substance" (533).

with Aunt Glegg and her husband. To do so, however, he must reclaim the money he has lent to his own sister Gritty, "who had married as poorly as could be" (52; bk. 1, ch. 7). Though initially he seems determined to reclaim what is his due, Mr. Tulliver ultimately cannot bring himself to take the money from his sister, for he suddenly realizes that Maggie, too, might one day depend on her brother for help (71; ch. I.8). On his deathbed, Mr. Tulliver accordingly urges Tom to take care of both Mrs. Tulliver and Maggie (291; bk. 5, ch. 7). For Tom, however, taking care of someone seems to comprise material security only, as becomes clear towards the end of the novel, when he assures his sister that he will always give her money if she is in need, while at the same time making it clear that, as a 'fallen' woman, she will no longer be welcome in his home (392–393; bk. 7, ch. 1). In thus neglecting Maggie's emotional needs, Tom violates the spirit of his father's dying wishes even as he attempts most scrupulously to obey them.

At the same time, it would be unfair to suggest that Mr. Tulliver's actions are always guided by lofty ideals, and indeed in at least one crucial respect he acts very selfishly towards his own son. When, early on in Eliot's novel, Mr. Tulliver explains why he wants to send Tom to a tutor, he admits that one of his motives is to keep the boy from becoming his rival:

> Why, if I made him a miller an' farmer, he'd be expectin' to take to the mill an' the land, an' a-hinting at me as it was time for me to lay by an' think o' my latter end. Nay, nay, I've seen enough o' that wi' sons. [...] I shall give Tom an eddication an' put him to a business, as he may make a nest for himself, an' not want to push me out o' mine. (15; bk. 1, ch. 3)

In this passage, Mr. Tulliver does not envision the family home as a "refuge from the competitive, insecure, amoral world of the market" (Howarth 169). Instead, he portrays it as a contested piece of property that the patriarch must protect even from his own son. Tom's education is thus not intended by his father to further the son's spiritual growth, but instead can be seen as Mr. Tulliver's conscious attempt to curb Tom's ambition to become a miller by thwarting or 're-directing' his talents.

There is, then, an important element of generational conflict to *The Mill on the Floss*, as suggested among other things by the narrator's differential use of names in the novel.[10] Generally speaking, Eliot's narrator refers to the older characters by their family names: 'Mr. and Mrs. Tulliver,' 'Aunt and Uncle Glegg,' or 'lawyer Wakem.' Indeed, even attentive readers may be forgiven for failing to remember, say, that Mr. Tulliver's first name is Jeremy, as it is mentioned only once and in passing (17; bk. 1, ch. 3). Moreover, while Mrs. Tulliver's first name – Elizabeth, or Bessy – occurs much more frequently (three and seventy-nine times, respectively), in all cases except one this happens in one of three particular contexts: (a) other characters use the name Bessy in passages of direct speech; (b) the name Bessy appears in indirect speech; and (c) the narrator calls Mrs. Tulliver Bessy in passages that are focalized through Mrs. Tulliver's husband or relatives (examples for each of these cases: 46–47; bk. 1, ch. 7). This stands in marked contrast with the narrator's virtually exclusive use of first names for Maggie, Tom, and Philip even when they are not seen through the eyes of other characters.[11] At first sight, the effect of this subtle, but nevertheless clear distinction seems relatively obvious, for by putting us, as it were, on a first-name basis with the younger characters while at the same time retaining a polite distance from their elders, the narrator arguably prompts us to identify more closely with the former rather than with the latter.

This, however, is only part of the picture, for, in addition to age or generation, another factor determining the narrator's use of first as opposed to family names is a character's social status and degree of economic independence. This is most readily apparent in the case of two characters who belong to an older generation than Maggie and Tom, but who both have long formed part of the Tulliver household as faithful servants to the family. Reflecting the fact that these servants are dependents, the narrator does not hesitate to refer to them by their first names, Kezia and Luke, even when they are not seen through the eyes of other characters (e.g. 211 and 213; bk. 3, ch. 8). The underlying logic at work here is that of the nineteenth-century household, which Fredric Jameson describes as "an ambiguous category":

> [The household] does not preserve the blood jealousies of the older clans but yet is not technically purely familial either, in the sense of some later extended family.

10 The ideas presented in this and the following paragraph derive from class discussions in the Bachelor-level seminar "*Bildungsroman* vs. Coming of Age: Victorian and Contemporary Versions of a Genre," which I taught at the University of Zurich in the spring semester 2013. The discussion itself was based on input by one of the seminar participants, Simay Altan, who first brought the narrator's differential use of proper names to my attention.

11 The same is true, incidentally, of Tom's childhood friend Bob Jakin (e.g. 255; bk. 5, ch. 2).

> Rather, these households very much include servants [...]. (*The Antinomies of Realism* 102)

In this particular social context, identity and honor are determined by an individual's position within a master's household. We can therefore say that, just as the common designation of slaves as 'boys' or 'girls' expresses their permanently subordinate position (Blackburn 11), so the narrator's use of first names for Kezia and Luke signals their 'lower' and dependent status, irrespective of these characters' age. However, while in one sense this aligns the two servants with the younger characters in Eliot's novel, the key difference is that, in theory, someone like Tom ought at one point to gain honor and independence by assuming his father's position as master of the household – and it is precisely this 'natural,' patriarchal succession that Mr. Tulliver proves himself desperate to prevent by sending Tom to school in order to learn a trade other than milling.

And yet, it is one of the many bitter ironies in *The Mill on the Floss* that Tom's schooling turns out to be doubly inadequate even from Mr. Tulliver's problematic point of view. For one thing, Mr. Tulliver originally wanted Tom to learn more about the practical world of business and less about things that lie "mostly out o' sight" (20; bk. 1, ch. 3). However, following the ill-founded advice of a friend, Mr. Tulliver sends Tom to Reverend Stelling, who provides the boy with the kind of classical education cherished by humanist proponents of *Bildung*, but largely irrelevant to a future Victorian tradesman. Tom's business-loving uncle Deane is later quick to point this out to the frustrated nephew:

> Your Latin and rigmarole may soon dry off you, but you'll be but a bare stick after that. Besides, it's whitened your hands and taken the rough work out of you. And what do you know? Why, you know nothing about book-keeping, to begin with, and not so much of reckoning as a common shopman. (190; bk. 3, ch. 5)

Contrary to his intention, Mr. Tulliver has thus failed to provide Tom with an education that would enable his son to "make a nest for himself." Moreover, Mr. Tulliver will eventually lose his beloved mill to lawyer Wakem and must then depend on Tom to restore it to the family. In a painfully ironic twist of fate, the son whom he regarded as a rival and threat to his property thus eventually becomes the miller's only hope to regain the lost home.

Importantly, however, despite these inauspicious circumstances, there are hints in Eliot's novel that Tom's education at Reverend Stelling's could have initiated a genuine process of *Bildung*. For instance, when Tom realizes that he is unable to master his academic subjects, the boy experiences for the first time that awakening to limitations that Susan J. Rosowski sees as typical of *female* protagonists. Tom had hitherto taken for granted that "all girls were silly" (35;

bk. 1, ch. 5), whereas he would, "when he was a man, be master of everything" (111; bk. 2, ch. 1). Now, Tom suddenly suspects that he may be "all wrong somehow" (113), and these doubts nullify "his boyish self-satisfaction," rendering him "more like a girl than he had ever been in his life" (118; bk. 2, ch. 1). However, if it is possible for a boy to become "more like a girl" simply because his education is ill-suited to his talents, then this also suggests that women's supposedly inferior nature is in fact the product of a societal structure that thwarts rather than fosters their development. Tom's experience of self-doubt could, we may therefore speculate, have led him to a deeper understanding not only of himself, but also of the constructed nature of gender difference.

Sadly, however, the seeds of this insight fall on thorny ground, for as Philip Fisher rightly contends, far from making Tom a better human being, his education ultimately "crushes and obscures his best traits" (540). When Maggie visits Tom at Reverend Stelling's and enthusiastically proclaims that she could master both Latin and Geometry, Tom finds his own prejudices confirmed rather than challenged by the male teacher:

> "Girls can't do Euclid; can they, sir?"
>
> "They can pick up a little of everything, I dare say," said Mr. Stelling. "They've a great deal of superficial cleverness; but they couldn't go far into anything. They're quick and shallow." (126; bk. 2, ch. 2)

While Tom delights in having his sense of superiority restored, Maggie is understandably dismayed at the thought that her readiness of mind should be the very sign of female inferiority – not least because it seems to confirm her father's fears that female intelligence can only lead to trouble (16; bk. 1, ch. 3). Indeed, Mr. Tulliver believes that Maggie's sharp wits compromise her value as a marriageable commodity, for he is certain that she will "fetch none the bigger price" for being clever (12; bk. 1, ch. 2). In this regard, Mr. Tulliver notably agrees with his arch-enemy, lawyer Wakem, who defines the social role of woman with brutally aphoristic precision: "We don't ask what a woman does – we ask whom she belongs to" (345; bk. 6, ch. 8) – an undoubtedly accurate statement, given that under the doctrine of coverture married women of the period had no legal identity independent of their husbands (e.g. Griffin 9). Teachers, fathers, and lawyers: where the status of women is concerned, the Victorian patriarchs in *The Mill on the Floss* are evidently in perfect agreement. In such an environment, it is little wonder that Tom's 'girlish' self-doubts fail in the long run to challenge his belief in male supremacy, for as Eliot's narrator suggests in a different context, "we are all apt to believe what the world believes about us" (65; bk. 65, ch. 8).

"Immovable Roots": Bildung and the Limits of Self-Determination

Both Tom and Maggie's stories thus focus on the problem of inadequate education. While Tom only reluctantly reconciles "himself to the idea that his school-time was to be prolonged and that he was not to be brought up to his father's business" (111; bk. 2, ch. 1), Maggie would be thrilled at the opportunity to stay at Reverend Stelling's. However, the boy Tom has to stay where he is, while Maggie, because she is a girl, is sent to "Miss Firniss's boarding school in the ancient town of Laceham on the Floss" (154; bk. 2, ch. 7). The place name "Laceham" provides us with some clues as to the kind of schooling Maggie can expect there: not geometry or Latin, but weaving decorative cloth ('lace' and 'hem'). Significantly, the narrator tells us virtually nothing about Maggie's time at Miss Firniss's boarding school – a gap in the story that highlights how irrelevant this type of schooling is for Maggie in terms of *Bildung* (i.e. the development of one's innate potential).[12] Jane McDonnell notes that unsatisfactory education is in fact a common theme in the *Bildungsroman*, and we could therefore conclude that *The Mill on the Floss* simply forms part of a larger movement for educational reform, leading to a system of schooling that would allow each individual, irrespective of gender, fully to develop his or her potential for true *Bildung*.

The story of Philip Wakem intimates, however, that changes in educational policy alone are not sufficient. We have seen that *The Mill on the Floss* incorporates two related but different *Bildungsromane*: the 'female' story of Maggie, and the 'male' story of her increasingly one-dimensional brother Tom. To these two plots, which explore the social inadequacies of institutionalized education, the story of Philip's development adds a third narrative, one that is crucial for the novel's critique of the *inherent* problems of the ideal of *Bildung*. Importantly, Maggie herself adheres to such a classical ideal of wide-ranging and 'well-rounded' intellectual formation, insisting that it is "a sort of clever stupidity only to have one sort of talent." Philip, however, believes himself "cursed with susceptibility in every direction," implying that the sheer breadth of his interests merely serves to dilute and disperse his intellectual faculties (266; bk. 5, ch. 3). Moreover, though Philip may be the intellectually most well-rounded individual in Eliot's novel, his physical "deformity" marks him as an outsider and makes it impossible for him to feel at home in the community of St. Ogg's (277; bk. 5, ch. 5). In other words, in the case of lawyer Wakem's son at least,

12 Given that Eliot's German was excellent, the name Firniss may be intended as a reference to the German word *Firnis*, which can be translated as 'varnish' or 'lacquer.' This in turn would strengthen the suggestion that the type of education reserved for girls focused mainly on surface accomplishments.

wide-ranging *Bildung* does not automatically lead either to personal fulfillment or to social success.

It is significant in this context that Philip does not suffer from a *congenital* 'deformity.' The fact that Philip's hump is due to an accident (134; bk. 2, ch. 3) rules out any suspicion, on the part of the readership, that Eliot might have intended Philip as an example of the fearful consequences of hereditary degeneration. Such racialist fears, though not yet widespread in 1860, were nevertheless growing amongst Eliot's contemporaries (Pick 178–179). If Philip had been born a 'deformed creature,' then it would be possible to interpret his failure to succeed in life as a kind of biological or eugenic inevitability. The purely contingent nature of Philip's 'deformity,' in contrast, highlights the inherent limits of the notion of self-determination that lies at the core of ideals of *Bildung*, for if one's ability to reach an ideal depends just as much on accident as on one's innate potential, then perhaps the ideal itself is in need of qualification. Put bluntly, we can say that through the story of Philip, Eliot's novel explores to what extent 'deformity' can render *Bildung* (in the sense of successful formation) difficult if not impossible. *The Mill on the Floss* thus complements the twin-narrative of Maggie and Tom's inadequate *Bildung* with what we may call Philip's 'novel of deformation.' In each of these three cases, the mental or spiritual ideal of *Bildung* is qualified by the problem of embodied existence: sexual difference with Maggie and Tom, and physical disability in the case of Philip. In short, Eliot's novel critiques, or at least questions, *Bildung*'s lofty idealism with a sober reminder of bodily limitations.

In addition, the notion of self-determination is circumscribed in *The Mill on the Floss* by the lasting impact of one's past and, more specifically, one's experiences as a child. We have already seen that the prejudices of relatives and teachers affect, and in many ways stunt, the development of both Maggie and Tom. Similarly, Philip's accident took place when he was still an infant, which means that he grew up with the experience of seeing people shrink from him "only because he was deformed" (247; bk. 5, ch. 1). Moreover, in a passage worth quoting at length, Eliot's narrator argues explicitly that one's childhood sets the boundaries of self-determination:

> [Tom experienced] the happiness of seeing the bright light in the parlor at home [...]; the happiness of passing from the cold air to the warmth and the kisses and the smiles of that familiar hearth, where the pattern of the rug and the grate and the fire-irons were "first ideas" that it was no more possible to criticise than the solidity and extension of matter. There is no sense of ease like the ease we felt in those scenes where we were born, where objects became dear to us before we had known the labor of choice, and where the outer world seemed only an extension of our own personality;

> we accepted and loved it as we accepted our own sense of existence and our own limbs. Very commonplace, even ugly, that furniture of our early home might look if it were put up to auction; an improved taste in upholstery scorns it; and is not the striving after something better and better in our surroundings the grand characteristic that distinguishes man from the brute, or, to satisfy a scrupulous accuracy of definition, that distinguishes the British man from the foreign brute? But heaven knows where that striving might lead us, if our affections had not a trick of twining round those old inferior things; if the loves and sanctities of our life had no deep immovable roots in memory. (127; bk. 2, ch. 1)

The narrator here suggests that, as children, we are not required to lead a self-determined existence – we do not yet know "the labor of choice" – and therefore we feel perfectly at ease in the "early home." To strive after "something better and better" may be in one sense what makes us human, but there is also an undercurrent of violence to this ideal of implacable progress, which for the narrator tends to hinge on a racist distinction between the supposedly progressive "British man" and the backward, primitive, "foreign brute." Countering such destructive fantasies of boundless (self-)invention and improvement, the narrator emphasizes that we can never entirely determine ourselves because our affections and convictions have "deep immovable roots" – roots not in blood or soil, but "in memory." [13]

Both Marx and Freud would, of course, agree that complete self-determination is in fact an illusion, and that the explanation for this lies in one's past. Marx stated his case most famously in "The Eighteenth Brumaire of Louis Bonaparte," published in 1852 (only a few years earlier than Eliot's novel):

> Men make their own history, but they do not make it just as they please in circumstances they choose for themselves; rather they make it in present circumstances, given and inherited. Tradition from all the dead generations weighs like a nightmare on the brain of the living. (32)[14]

While it is possible at any point in time for men – and women – to choose their course of action, Marx emphasizes that they can never select freely the context

---

13 Note that Eliot's argument is strikingly similar to Margaret Morse's claim that "[f]eelings and memories linked to home are highly charged, if not with meaning, then with sense memories that began before the mastery of language" (63) – i.e. in early childhood.

14 "Die Menschen machen ihre eigene Geschichte, aber sie machen sie nicht aus freien Stücken, nicht unter selbstgewählten, sondern unter unmittelbar vorgefundenen, gegebenen, überlieferten Umständen. Die Tradition aller toten Geschlechter lastet wie ein Alp auf dem Gehirne der Lebenden" (Marx, *Der achtzehnte Brumaire* 115).

of that particular choice. And, importantly, one of these contexts that lies entirely beyond our range of choice is the early childhood home: the place and the community where we grow up, and which can never be 'self-selected.' In a dialectical view of history, the 'starting point' called home necessarily remains part of everything that follows, albeit in what Hegel would call a 'sublated' form (in German, *aufgehoben*: the point of origin is at the same time canceled, kept in store, and lifted to a higher level; see J. Hillis Miller 28). Likewise, Sigmund Freud argues that the past establishes the limits of self-determination. Beyond these limits, Freud suggests, lies the realm of the unconscious, which is shaped crucially by our childhood experiences, and which makes it impossible for us ever to attain complete mastery over ourselves.

Like Freud and Marx, *The Mill on the Floss* is hostile to postmodern dreams of infinitely malleable, fluid identities – but not necessarily in a conservative or reactionary sense. Postmodern dreams of boundless self-fashioning appear problematic, for instance, in the light of recent findings regarding the long-term effects of malnutrition in the fetal stage and during childhood, which not only impair individuals' health, cognitive abilities, and labor productivity over the course of their lives, but which also heighten the chance that such individuals will lack the necessary resources to take sufficient care of their children: "It is therefore in no way fanciful to see the influence of the health and welfare of grandparents in the bodies of their grandchildren and the effect may be even longer lasting" (Floud et al. 37). Our own life is thus shaped by the lives of our ancestors – and not in the sense of ancestral spirits or fateful heredity, but in terms of the contingent yet long-lasting effects of detrimental living standards. Moreover, as Terry Eagleton maintains, change and flexibility are not inherently progressive or oppositional qualities:

> A faith in plurality, plasticity, dismantling, destabilizing, the power of endless self-invention – all this, while undoubtedly radical in some contexts, also smacks of a distinctly Western culture and an advanced capitalist world. [...] Capitalism may be upbraided for many defects, but a lack of dynamism is hardly one of them. (*Sweet Violence* xi)[15]

We may quite rightly insist that identity is neither simply given nor eternally fixed. At the same time, however, there would also be something callous about

15 See also Fredric Jameson, who argues that the "ambiguity of postmodernism as a philosophy" lies in the fact that "its progressive endorsement of anti-essentialist multiplicity and perspectivism also replicates the very rhetoric of the late-capitalist marketplace as such" (*Archaeologies of the Future*, 163) – a replication that Jameson finds "exceedingly suspicious" (ibid., 165).

telling someone like Mr. Tulliver that his "clinging affection for the old home as [...] part of himself" (217; bk. 3, ch. 9) is merely an instance of reactionary nostalgia.

Indeed, as Terry Eagleton points out elsewhere, the idea that unstable identities are always subversive and thus desirable is a claim "which it would be interesting to test out among the socially dumped and disregarded" (*After Theory* 16). Philip Fisher's remark that a "break in continuity is the death of what is meant by the self in *The Mill on the Floss*" has to be seen precisely in this context (522), for without a certain amount of material stability, it becomes extremely difficult to sustain a reasonably stable sense of self. Mr. Tulliver's attachment to the past may thus have much to do with an underlying sense of economic insecurity – at least according to Eliot's narrator, who contrasts the old miller's fear "that the country could never again be what it used to be" with the optimism of Mr. Deane, who is "attached to a firm of which the returns were on the increase," and who "naturally took a more lively view of the present" (64; bk. 1, ch. 7). If, in short, *The Mill on the Floss* insists perhaps too much on the importance of "immovable roots," we should not forget that it does so against a backdrop (or at least the fear) of material dispossession that, in turn, highlights the fragility of the place we call home.

Nostalgia, Mourning, and Ironic Distance: Novelistic Immaturity

Accordingly, we should read the novel's generally nostalgic mood not exclusively as a form of sentimental indulgence, but also as an implicit critique of social injustice and thus as a potential basis for resistance. The nostalgic mood of *The Mill on the Floss* is established in the very first chapter, through the narrator's dreamy remembrances of how Dorlcote Mill and its surroundings "looked one February morning many years ago" (8; bk. 1, ch. 1; see Boumelha 20):

> Just by the red-roofed town the tributary Ripple flows with a lively current into the Floss. How lovely the little river is, with its dark changing wavelets! It seems to me like a living companion while I wander along the bank, and listen to its low, placid voice, as to the voice of one who is deaf and loving. I remember those large dipping willows. I remember the stone bridge. (7; bk. 1, ch. 1)

This is not the detached, analytic tone one would expect from a "Study of Provincial Life" – the subtitle of Eliot's later novel *Middlemarch* – but the nostalgic voice of a narrator who longs for a time "when joys were vivid" (127; bk. 2, ch. 1). Instead of dismissing such nostalgic longings as sentimental, Kimberley K. Smith emphasizes their potential "as a mode of resistance" (523). Smith shows that the term nostalgia, which was coined in 1688 by the Swiss physician Johan

Hofer to denote a potentially fatal condition of homesickness, underwent a process of radical redefinition (509–510):

> [N]ostalgia evolved from a disease into an emotion [...]. The concept broadened and complicated: Once defined simply as a desire to return home, to a specific *place*, nostalgia was gradually being conceptualized as a longing to return to a former *time* – and usually a time that was only *imagined* to be better. (512; original emphasis)

Eventually, Smith continues, nostalgia was reduced to a sometimes painful, occasionally pleasant, but in either case unreliable, private emotion that is inevitably unrelated to any real political harm (519). For Smith, such a view of nostalgia mirrors a progressivist distrust towards any form of resistance to change, and is therefore "integral to the emotional regime of industrial capitalism" (522) – for if those who resist change are always and everywhere 'merely being nostalgic,' then their political objections can be conveniently disregarded.[16]

Accordingly, when reading the conclusion of *The Mill on the Floss*, we must not simply dismiss the novel's tone as nostalgic, but instead examine how such nostalgia contributes to the text's critique of *Bildung* and the genre of the *Bildungsroman*. The key for doing this lies in the problem of mourning, which according to Franco Moretti can have no more than episodic significance in the classical *Bildungsroman* because it "does not contribute to *Bildung*" ("The Comfort of Civilization" 132). Indicating a refusal to let go of the past, mourning constitutes an obstacle to the protagonist's smooth, evolutionary development – and, implicitly, to his or her 'progress.' Accordingly, while in the final chapter of *The Mill on the Floss* Eliot's narrator at first seems to argue that time has the power to heal all wounds, it soon becomes clear that this is not in fact the case:

> Nature repairs her ravages – repairs them with her sunshine, and with human labor. The desolation wrought by that flood had left little visible trace on the face of the earth, five years after. [...]
>
> Nature repairs her ravages, but not all. The uptorn trees are not rooted again; the parted hills are left scarred; if there is a new growth, the trees are not the same as the old, and the hills underneath their green vesture bear the marks of the past rending. To the eyes that have dwelt on the past, there is no thorough repair. (422; "Conclusion")

The Mill on the Floss does not, then, end on a confident note of progress, but with the image of two men – Philip and Stephen – who continue to visit Maggie's

---

16 Alison Blunt likewise argues that the widespread antipathy towards nostalgia may blind us to its "liberatory potential" (14). See also John Kirk, who emphasizes that there are "forms of nostalgic memory [...] which can be *enabling*" (606; original emphasis).

grave, feeling "that their keenest joy and keenest sorrow were for ever buried there" (422; "Conclusion"). As Susan Meyer points out, the novel's nostalgia "exerts a more memorable and stronger force than the energy of its forward movement" (131); the smooth river of progress finds itself checked by an indelible longing for the past. Only by forgetting the past can we hope to avoid mourning and nostalgia. However, since our identities must, for Eliot's narrator, have immovable roots in memory, to forget or deny the past would be tantamount to surrendering one's self – the very self so cherished by advocates of *Bildung*.

This is not to suggest that nostalgia ought to become a privileged discourse in our relation to the past. We should, however, be aware that to dismiss nostalgia out of hand means to surrender a potent resource for social critique. Nostalgia is, first and foremost, an experience of homelessness, and as such an indication of discontent with the present:

> [W]e should recognize that remembering positive aspects of the past does not necessarily indicate a desire to return there. Remembering the past should instead be seen as a way to express valid desires and concerns about the *present* – in particular, about its relationship (or lack of relationship) to the past. (Smith 523; original emphasis)

Nostalgia expresses desires and values that, in themselves, are neither necessarily sentimental nor illegitimate; after all, one reason for shying away from examining the past is, as Eliot's narrator puts it, that "mankind is not disposed to look narrowly into the conduct of great victors when their victory is on the right side" (207; bk. 3, ch. 7) – i.e. one's own. To dismiss any kind of longing for the past as 'mere nostalgia' may thus encourage, in both others and ourselves, an unwarranted sense of "ironic detachment" from both past injustice and present harm (Smith 515).[17]

In *The Mill on the Floss*, ironic detachment is in fact quite explicitly portrayed as a privilege that the dispossessed cannot afford. In a lengthy passage that is itself supremely ironic (Raymond Williams 172), Eliot's narrator satirizes the

17 Svetlana Boym distinguishes between two types of nostalgia: restorative nostalgia, which "attempts a transhistorical reconstruction of the lost home," and reflective nostalgia, which, at best, "can present an ethical and creative challenge" (xviii): "Reflective nostalgia does not pretend to rebuild the mythical place called home [...]. This type of nostalgic narrative is ironic, inconclusive and fragmentary. [...] The past is not made in the image of the present or seen as foreboding of some present disaster; rather, the past opens up a multitude of potentialities, nonteleological possibilities of historical development" (50). See also Kevis Goodman on Romantic nostalgia, which she regards as an attempt "to register the growing pains of historical existence" (196).

belief that using irony implies a lofty transcendence of one's limited, subjective point of view:

> In writing the history of unfashionable families, one is apt to fall into a tone of emphasis which is very far from being the tone of good society, where principles and beliefs are not only of an extremely moderate kind, but are always presupposed, no subjects being eligible but such as can be touched with a light and graceful irony. But then good society has its claret and its velvet carpets, its dinner-engagements six weeks deep, its opera and its faëry ball-rooms; rides off its ennui on thoroughbred horses; [...] gets its science done by Faraday, and its religion by the superior clergy who are to be met in the best houses – how should it have time or need for belief and emphasis? But good society, floated on gossamer wings of light irony, is of very expensive production; requiring nothing less than a wide and arduous national life condensed in unfragrant deafening factories, cramping itself in mines, sweating at furnaces, [...] or else, spread over sheepwalks, and scattered in lonely houses and huts on the clayey or chalky corn-lands [...]. This wide national life is based entirely on emphasis – the emphasis of want, which urges it into all the activities necessary for the maintenance of good society and light irony; it spends its heavy years often in a chill, uncarpeted fashion, amidst family discord unsoftened by long corridors. (238; bk. 4, ch. 3)

Irony, the narrator insists, is not an ideologically neutral device, but suffused with implicit value-judgments; an "unsoftened" hut is far less hospitable to "light irony" than a comfortable, wealthy home furnished with "velvet carpets." Indeed, given the depth of social injustice ("deafening factories," "the emphasis of want"), good society's well-tempered beliefs appear curiously exorbitant (or "extremely moderate," in the narrator's elegantly oxymoronic phrase). Accordingly, it would be a profound mistake to think that holding strong beliefs necessarily indicates blind fanaticism, whereas a properly ironic distance goes hand in hand with intellectual subtlety and independence.[18]

In addition, the narrator's argument also challenges the idea that irony is necessarily subversive, for it is difficult to imagine that the tone of "good society"

18 The historian E. P. Thompson makes a similar observation on the relationship between religious enthusiasm and social standing in his *The Making of the English Working Class*: "The rational Christianity of the Unitarians, with its preference for 'candour' and its distrust of 'enthusiasm', appealed to some of the tradesmen and shopkeepers of London, and to similar groups in large cities. But it seemed too cold, too distant, too polite, and too much associated with the comfortable values of a prospering class to appeal to the city or village poor. Its very language and tone served as a barrier" (31). For a particularly entertaining account of the relationship between class and irony, see Terry Eagleton's remarks on "a certain kind of English patrician" (*Across the Pond* 39).

constitutes a counter-hegemonic discourse. The narrator's point is thus not far from an observation Franco Moretti makes when noting irony's centrality in the history of the modern novel. How, Moretti wonders, could a stylistic device that has enjoyed almost unrivalled dominance in novelistic aesthetics simultaneously constitute a grave threat to the social order (*Way of the World* 97)? Rather than seeing the device as subversive, we should regard irony as a stylistic correlative to what Moretti posits as the great theme and political disposition of the *Bildungsroman*: compromise (*Way of the World* 10). This becomes more readily apparent if we examine Moretti's definition of compromise: "We can speak of compromise when conflicting principles have indeed reached an accord, but without having lost their diversity. They remain heterogeneous, and the agreement intrinsically precarious" (*Way of the World* 69). In agreement, but only precariously so – unified, yet remaining heterogeneous: it is a definition of compromise, but also a perfectly good description of how irony manages momentarily to unite fundamentally irreconcilable meanings: what Catherine Gallagher calls a characteristically modern "spirit of 'ironic' assent" (347).

Admittedly, *The Mill on the Floss*'s critique of irony is complicated by the fact that its narrator at the same time employs the device. There is irony, for instance, in the narrator's description of the "fashionably drest [sic] female in grief" as a "striking example of the complexity introduced into the emotions by a high state of civilization" (48; bk. 1, ch. 7). There is irony, too, in the narrator's attitude towards little Maggie, who, after running away from home to join the gypsies, mistakenly believes that she was really "gaining great influence over them," and that the gypsies would want her to become their queen (92; bk. 1, ch. 11). And there is irony, to give a third and final example, in the narrator's comments on the supposedly staggering backwardness of the past depicted in the novel:

> All this, you remember, happened in those dark ages when there were no schools of design; before schoolmasters were invariably men of scrupulous integrity, and before the clergy were all men of enlarged minds and varied culture. In those less favored days, it is no fable that there were other clergymen besides Mr. Stelling who had narrow intellects and large wants, and whose income, by a logical confusion to which Fortune, being a female as well as blindfold, is peculiarly liable, was proportioned not to their wants but to their intellect, with which income has clearly no inherent relation. (139–140; bk. 2, ch. 4)

The surface meaning of the passage is that the narrator's present is superior to the past, yet the idea that nowadays *all* schoolmasters are upright men, and *all* members of the clergy persons of enlarged minds and varied culture, is transparently excessive and, therefore, highly suspicious.[19] Moreover, if taken at face value, the link made in the passage between "female" and "logical confusion" would sit uneasily with the novel's general gender politics. In short, there is good reason to believe that the narrator's comments are not in fact intended to praise the present, but instead to ridicule those who subscribe to an overly optimistic progressivism.

And yet, it is important to recognize that ironic distance towards a particular ideology is not in fact the same as repudiating it. We have already examined some reasons why irony is not necessarily subversive, and Slavoy Žižek even suggests that "ideological identification exerts a true hold on us precisely when we maintain an awareness that we are not fully identical with it" (*The Plague of Fantasies* 27). Accordingly, we might read *The Mill on the Floss*'s use of irony as evidence of just how firmly the novel is committed to the liberal ideology of progress from which it ostensibly distances itself. After all, the narrator states quite clearly that suffering simply "belongs to every historical *advance* of mankind" (223; bk. 4, ch. 1; emphasis added). Suffering is, in other words, regrettable – but also an inevitable aspect of progress, which itself remains eminently desirable. Moreover, even according to the narrator's own theory of irony, the novel's use of the device would in fact mark *The Mill on the Floss* as yet another product of that 'good society' that depends on exploitation and widespread want. From either perspective, the novel seems curiously at odds with itself: satirizing the very 'good society' from which it has itself emerged, and embracing an idea of progress that, at the same time, it critiques through its pervasive mood of nostalgia.

Crucially, however, there is one respect in which Eliot's novel increasingly abandons the respectable stance of ironic distance, namely in relation to its protagonist, Maggie. We have already seen that, when still a child, Maggie at times serves as the butt of the narrator's irony. However, as the novel's heroine matures, the narrator identifies more and more uncompromisingly with her spiritual and emotional plight. Indeed, for F.R. Leavis it is precisely this lack of ironic distance towards Maggie's soulful yearnings that constitute the one great flaw of *The Mill on the Floss*:

> There is nothing against George Eliot's presenting this immaturity with tender sympathy; but we ask, and ought to ask, of a great novelist something more. 'Sympathy and understanding' is the common formula of praise, but understanding, in any strict sense, is just what she doesn't show. To understand immaturity would be to 'place' it, with however subtle an implication, by relating it to mature experience. (485)

---

19 On excessive praise as a classic strategy to create ironic effects, see Colebrook, *Irony* 10.

For Leavis, Eliot's novel of education remains scandalously immature because it does not moderate its protagonist's emotional intensity through properly ironic distance. In a similar vein, Virginia Woolf complains that the narrator's humor "controls" Maggie only as long as she is still a child, whereas this superior ironic poise is lost as the novel's protagonist matures – and it is this that separates it from *Middlemarch*, which Woolf has famously called "one of the few English novels written for grown-up people" ("George Eliot" 168–169). What upsets both Leavis and Woolf, in short, is that the narrator of *The Mill on the Floss* progressively – or, to their mind, regressively – abandons the mature tone of 'good society,' opting instead for a very unfashionable, emphatic identification with the adolescent heroine's struggle.

However, before analyzing in more detail some vital components of Maggie's struggle, we should perhaps rephrase the argument up to this point in terms of two different levels of critique: the mimetic or referential, and the literary or intertextual. On the one hand, we have seen that *The Mill on the Floss* constitutes a far-reaching critique of Victorian gender norms and their adverse effects on women and, at least to some extent, on men as well. As this kind of critique is linked to the state of affairs in the real world, we may – for lack of a better term – call it mimetic or referential. Eliot's novel highlights symbolically the extent to which Victorian gender norms are sustained by central pillars of the bourgeois order: fathers (Mr. Tulliver), preachers and educators (Reverend Stelling), as well as lawyers (Wakem). Importantly, the novel does not depict these patriarchs as a monolithic and unified front of oppression; rather, the text depicts them as engaged in deep conflict but nevertheless agreeing on one key issue: the inferiority of women as intellectually limited commodities that belong to the head of the family. The novel thus also portrays the family home as an institution that is deeply implicated in the reproduction of social injustice, even as it acknowledges the deep bonds of affection between father and daughter, or sister and brother. Moreover, like so many a *Bildungsroman*, it exposes important flaws in the educational system, and as such advocates social change.

Such referential critique is, however, complemented in the novel by what we might term literary or intertextual critique. This includes, for instance, the way in which *The Mill on the Floss* challenges some key tenets of the *Bildungsroman* as a genre by refusing to focus on Stephen Guest and instead juxtaposing three unsuccessful plots of formation: Maggie's, Tom's, and Philip's, none of whom will find a true home in this world. In combining these three plots, the text highlights the limits to self-determination, and thus qualifies an overly optimistic conception of human agency inherent to classical ideals of *Bildung*. Moreover, the novel questions the political innocence of irony as a stylistic device, and to some extent at least rejects what it portrays as a class-based stance. The strongest expression of this incomplete but significant repudiation is the narrator's increasing rejection of ironic distance from Maggie, which has led critics to accuse Eliot's novel as a whole of unseemly immaturity. Similar accusations could be leveled against the narrator's nostalgic tone, if one were to analyze nostalgia as merely a regressive yearning for an idealized childhood home. However, the novel cautions us against such a simplistic assessment of the nostalgic impulse, and instead pits it against a narrative of implacable progress in order to highlight the latter's emotional as well as social costs. If this last point threatens to collapse the distinction between referential and intertextual critique, then this is not a coincidence, but instead one of the novel's key arguments: that social critique ought not limit itself to what we might call the world's content, but must also pay attention to its style and its discursive arrangements of oppression. To put things somewhat differently: one's loss of home may derive from material deprivation or from one's lack of a proper place in the symbolic order – and, not infrequently, from a combination of the two.

Maggie's Dreams: Awakening and Romance

It is with these considerations in mind that we must now analyze Maggie's struggle, as an emotional conflict that arises from her desire to honor past duties and, at the same time, to strive towards future fulfillment; she wishes to develop as a 'free' individual without relinquishing the ancestral home that stands in the way of that very development. Maggie's passionate response – as a young woman who has lost the material security of home (and the social status associated with it) – to the writings of the late-medieval mystic Thomas à Kempis needs to be seen in this context. In à Kempis's ascetic philosophy, Maggie believes to have found a way of resolving the dilemma between individual desire and social limitations:

> [H]ere was a sublime height to be reached without the help of outward things; here was insight, and strength, and conquest, to be won by means entirely within her own soul [...]. It flashed through her like the suddenly apprehended solution of a problem, that all the miseries of her young life had come from fixing her heart on her own pleasure [...]; and for the first time she saw the possibility of shifting the position from which she looked at the gratification of her own desires – of taking her stand out of herself, and looking at her own life as an insignificant part of a divinely guided whole. (237; bk. 4, ch. 3)

Maggie finds herself doubly deprived: as a woman refused the benefits of education, and as a daughter suffering from the family's very material downfall.

This explains why the notion of "means entirely within her soul" must seem so appealing, as it involves neither intellectual nor material resources; it is a matter of the soul, not of the mind or the body. Maggie, in other words, hopes to solve these conflicts by discursively reframing her needs as merely "the gratification of her own desires," and as insignificant in the larger scheme of things. It is precisely the emphasis of want that leads Maggie to embrace an emphatic belief, in the hope that this will help her recover the "sense of home" that she has been unable to find in the "world outside the books" (194; bk. 3, ch. 5).

Significantly, it is Philip who ends Maggie's mystic dream of cheerful resignation by challenging its underlying assumptions about the nature of longing and desire. Ascetics like Thomas à Kempis assume that desire binds us to a fallen world to which we do not truly belong, and that therefore desire itself is the main obstacle to our quest for a lasting, transcendent home. Philip, however, questions Maggie's belief that denying her longings is the path to true belonging:

> It seems to me we can never give up longing and wishing while we are thoroughly alive. There are certain things we feel to be beautiful and good, and we *must* hunger after them. How can we ever be satisfied without them until our feelings are deadened? I delight in fine pictures; I long to be able to paint such. I strive and strive, and can't produce what I want. That is pain to me, and always *will* be pain, until my faculties lose their keenness [...]. (246; bk. 5, ch. 1; original emphasis)

Longing may mean suffering, Philip admits, but it is also essential to a fulfilling and truly human life. The German philosopher Ludwig Feuerbach, who claims that God is nothing but an outward projection of humankind's own essential nature, and whose *Das Wesen des Christenthums* (*The Essence of Christianity*) Eliot herself had translated into English in 1854, makes a case very similar to Philip's:

> I feel feeling [...] as belonging to my essential being, and, though the source of all sufferings and sorrows, as a glorious, divine power and perfection. What would man be without feeling? It is the musical power in man. (*The Essence of Christianity* 63; ch. 5)[20]

The only way to avoid suffering, Feuerbach argues, would be entirely to quench our feelings – that divine, "musical power in man" which defines what it means to be truly human.

---

20 "[Ich] empfinde die Empfindung [...] als zu meinem Wesen gehörig, und, obwohl als die Quelle aller Leiden, Schwächen und Schmerzen, doch als eine herrliche, göttliche Macht und Vollkommenheit. Was wäre der Mensch ohne Empfindung? Sie ist die musikalische Macht im Menschen" (*Das Wesen des Christenthums* 102–103).

What underlines this philosophical connection is that Feuerbach's musical metaphor repeatedly resurfaces in *The Mill on the Floss.* For instance, there are echoes of Feuerbach's metaphor in what Philip says to Maggie shortly after his attack on ascetic self-denial:

> I think there are stores laid up in our human nature that our understandings can make no complete inventory of. *Certain strains of music affect me so strangely*; I can never hear them without their changing my whole attitude of mind for a time, and if the effect would last, I might be capable of heroisms. (248; bk. 5, ch. 1; emphasis added)

Like Feuerbach, Philip here associates music both with our deepest feelings and our most heroic or divine powers.[21] Moreover, listening to Philip's pleas, Maggie herself feels as if "music would swell out, [...] persuading her that the wrong lay all in the thoughts and weaknesses of others, and that there was such a thing as futile sacrifice" (247; bk. 5, ch. 1). Similarly, toward the end of the novel, Philip assures Maggie in a moving letter that she has been, to his affections, "what light, what colour is to my eyes – what music is to the inward ear" (407; bk. 7, ch. 3). The musical imagery here becomes linked to the appreciation of light and colour, and hence with the "delight in fine pictures" that Philip had mentioned earlier on. In this way, the novel associates desire and longing with a thirst for the beautiful, the good, and the true – with, in short, the classical ideal of *Bildung* as a culture of the self that is entirely incompatible with an ascetic philosophy of self-denial (Boumelha 26–27).

Philip thus in one sense (re-)awakens Maggie's desires for knowledge and culture, and we may note in passing that his last name is, tellingly, Wakem ('wake 'em'). At the same time, however, *The Mill on the Floss* portrays desire itself as related to that dissolution of the conscious self that is characteristic of sleep and dreams. For instance, at one point we find little Maggie, who continually thirsts for the knowledge that can be gained from reading, "dreaming over her book" (15; bk. 1, ch. 3). Similarly, when she later runs off to join a group of gypsies, the experience at first seems to her as if "rehearsed in a dream" (91; bk. 1, ch. 11) – and we have seen that the episode as a whole can be read as a version of the Freudian family romance. Moreover, romantic love and sexual fulfillment, too, are associated with dreams, for the idea that she could ever have a lover seems to Maggie "like a dream – only one of the stories one imagines" (272; bk. 5, ch. 4). Significantly, towards the end of the novel, Maggie must literally wake up from "vivid dreaming" before she can bring herself to decide against an

---

21 See Levine for a more sustained discussion of the relationship between *The Mill on the Floss* and Ludwig Feuerbach's ideas.

elopement with Stephen Guest (381; bk. 6, ch. 14). Susan J. Rosowsksi's description of the 'female *Bildungsroman*' as typically revolving around a woman's awakening to limitations thus proves particularly accurate for *The Mill on the Floss*, in which Maggie's dreamlike desires clash, time and again, with the limitations imposed by reality.[22]

And yet, while this may suggest that the novel attempts to expose the insubstantiality of dreams by portraying them as the binary opposite of a realistic outlook on the world, the text in fact explores the complex interrelatedness of the "triple world of Reality, Books, and Waking Dreams" (225; bk. 4, ch. 2). We have seen, for instance, that books do inspire some of Maggie's dreams and desires. At the same time, however, Maggie is also very well aware of the unrealistic conventions of popular romances, where the "blond-haired young lady" invariably triumphs over the "dark woman" (270; bk. 5, ch. 4). Northrop Frye's claim that "romance is nearest of all literary forms to wish-fulfillment and dream" (186) is, therefore, not exactly true for Maggie, who is herself one of those dark women whose desires continually end up thwarted in popular romances. Accordingly, Maggie formulates her dreams in direct opposition to conventional romances, voicing the hope that she herself might one day be able to avenge all these "dark unhappy" heroines (270; bk. 5, ch. 4). Philip, who is passionately in love with Maggie, teasingly assures her that she could easily win a handsome young man away from a pretty, blond-haired woman such as her cousin, Lucy – and this is, of course, precisely what will happen in Eliot's novel. Maggie eventually wins Stephen Guest's love from pretty, blond-haired Lucy and, in this way, fulfills her daydream fantasy of revenge. In *The Mill on the Floss*, Maggie's dreams and desires thus not only take shape in relation to both everyday domestic reality and the imaginary worlds described in books; they also have an uncanny way of coming true, and of shaping the course of her own life.

The Tragedy of Wish-Fulfillment

This realization may in turn help us understand the novel's much-discussed, dream-like ending, in which Maggie and her brother Tom drown in a flood, and which is highly problematic when read in realist terms of narrative coherence and probability. Henry James, for instance, is one of many critics who have been uncomfortable with the novel's dramatic conclusion, and highly suspicious of its artistic merits: "As it stands, the *dénouement* shocks the reader most painfully. Nothing has prepared him for it; the story does not move towards it; it casts no

22 In a similar vein, Tom, is "awakened" from his "boyish dreams" when he learns that Mr. Tulliver has lost his lawsuit against lawyer Wakem (158; bk. 2, ch. 7).

shadow before it" (465). In a similar vein, F.R. Leavis suggests that the novel's ending belongs to "another kind of art" than the preceding sections; the flood in which Tom and Maggie perish constitutes a "*dreamed-of* perfect accident," but has "no symbolic or metaphorical value" (488; my emphasis). Less judgmentally, Jane McDonnell remarks that *The Mill on the Floss* moves from a realistic portrayal of Maggie towards a more supernatural mode of representation typical of such genres as the fairy tale or romance (400).

While Penny Boumelha agrees that the novel's ending abandons the realist mode, she is one of the few critics who also notes the crucial, metafictional effect of such a "flagrantly fantasied and contrived" conclusion:

> It acknowledges and makes unusually visible the formal-cum-ideological impasse that the novel has reached by virtue of its concentration on the development of a woman for whom no meaningful future [...] can be imagined. It breaks out of this impasse only by sweeping the novel out of its realist mode altogether. (29)

According to Boumelha, the ending of Eliot's novel serves to expose "the restricted possibilities of the world as it could be imagined by realism," and the shift to a world of fantasy and wish-fulfillment thus constitutes a critique of classic realism's unacknowledged limitations (32–33).[23] By flaunting the contrived nature of its conclusion – the flood arrives at the very moment of Maggie's utmost despair, when she wonders "how long it will be before death comes" (417; bk. 7, ch. 5) – *The Mill on the Floss* problematizes its status as fiction and highlights the link between generic conventions, narrative closure, and ideology.[24]

More specifially, Eliot's novel dismantles a central convention of the English *Bildungsroman*: its valorization of childhood, commonly expressed in endings that depict the protagonist's fairytale-like return to his or her original home. As Franco Moretti has pointed out, the hero's childhood is not only granted an emblematic prominence in the English *Bildungsroman*; in contrast to continental

---

23 See the subtitle of U.C. Knoepflmacher's 1968 study *George Eliot's Early Novels: The Limits of Realism*.

24 Terry Eagleton agrees that metafiction is an important aspect of Eliot's fiction: "It is with Eliot that realism in the English novel becomes theoretically self-conscious" (*The English Novel* 168). Kristie M. Allen also puts forward a reading of the ending as productively disruptive: "The novel's conclusion, thus, becomes a formal forging of new channels of ideas about the taken-for-grantedness of culture, the mind's processes of repetition, the cumulative moral effects of habit, and the kinds of self-reflective consciousness required to manifest our best selves" (847). Similarly, Jordan Baker posits that at the end of The Mill on the Floss "we find ourselves subject to a logic alien to the typical protocols of the realist novel" (229)

examples of the genre, the protagonist's most significant experiences also tend to be "those which *confirm* the choices made by childhood 'innocence'" (*Way of the World* 182; emphasis added):

> Can you picture a child reading *Wilhelm Meister, The Red and the Black, Lost Illusions*? Impossible. But *Waverley* and *Jane Eyre, David Copperfield* and *Great Expectations*: here we have the 'great tradition' of children's literature (and our era, less intimidated by sex, can easily add *Tom Jones*). [...] Could it in fact be that, deep down, these novels are fairy tales? (*Way of the World* 185)

In the fairytale world of the English *Bildungsroman*, Moretti points out, siblings often "magnetically attract the negative values of the narrative universe," as part of a broader tendency towards moral polarization into clear-cut rights and wrongs (*Way of the World* 186). If continental heroes are happy to leave (and even deliberately defy) their childhood homes, the youthful journeys of English protagonists are portrayed as enforced exile: "a long and bewildering detour" from the cherished stability of the original home (*Way of the World* 203).[25] The basic structure of the English *Bildungsroman* is, in short, regressive, and the often unlikely or even blatantly unrealistic plot twists needed to manufacture a happy ending – the rediscovery of long-lost relatives, or Rochester's voice supernaturally calling out to Jane Eyre over the distance of several miles – reveal the extent to which the endings of such novels are concerned, not with reality, but with poetic justice and wish-fulfillment. And of course, almost all of this is true for *The Mill on the Floss*, too: the sibling who attracts the negative values of the fictional universe (i.e. Tom); the protagonist's aversion to the idea of having to leave the childhood home; and the restoration of an 'innocent' childhood perspective through the reconciliation of Tom and Maggie, brought about by the flagrantly fantasized flood that concludes the novel. There is only one problem with this argument in connection with *The Mill on the Floss*: its ending

25 In Goethe's *Wilhelm Meisters Lehrjahre*, for instance, young Wilhelm is not at all unhappy to leave his childhood home: "Seines Vaters Haus, die Seinigen zu verlassen, schien ihm ein Leichtes" (37); the English translation runs: "It seemed to him the easiest thing in the world to leave his family and his father's house" (*Wilhelm Meister's Apprenticeship* 16). Similarly, the protagonist of a *Bildungsroman* by Stendahl is more than eager to venture forth into the world: "Pour Julien, faire fortune, c'était d'abord sortir de Verrières; il abhorrait sa patrie" (*Le rouge et le noir* 45; ch. 5); the English translation runs: "For Julien, making his fortune meant first and foremost getting out of Verrières; he loathed his native town" (*The Red and the Black* 26; ch. 5). Compare this to, say, Dickens's *David Copperfield*, the fifth chapter of which is entitled "*I am sent away from Home*" (73).

may be just as fantasized as all the others – but it is not truly a happy one. How can we make sense of this fantasy of doom?

Using Slavoj Žižek's Lacanian framework as an analytical tool, we can say that Eliot's novel 'traverses the ideological fantasy' that structures the English *Bildungsroman*, and in doing so confronts the generic tradition's traumatic kernel. Here is how Žižek defines fantasy:

> Fantasy conceals the fact that the Other, the symbolic order, is structured around some traumatic impossibility, around something which cannot be symbolized [...] – so what happens with desire after we 'traverse' fantasy? Lacan's answer, in the last pages of his *Seminar XI*, is drive, ultimately the death drive: 'beyond fantasy' there is no yearning or any kindred sublime phenomenon, 'beyond fantasy' we find only drive, its pulsation around the *sinthome*. (*Sublime Object of Ideology* 138–139; original emphasis)

For Lacan, fantasy serves to hide a traumatic kernel, and if we traverse it we will be confronted with the pulsation of the death drive around the so-called *sinthome*, which Žižek defines as "a knot, a point at which all the lines of the predominant ideological argumentation [...] meet" (*The Ticklish Subject* 206). This is a potentially liberating encounter, for Žižek suggests that if we untie the *sinthome*, then the efficiency of the corresponding ideological edifice is suspended (ibid.). Given that, for Žižek, ironic distance is one of the key ways in which we can "blind ourselves to the structuring power of ideological fantasy" (*Sublime Object of Ideology* 30), we may therefore speculate that abandoning irony may be one way to confront the traumatic kernel of ideological fantasies.

If we now apply this theoretical framework to Eliot's novel, then we can say that *The Mill on the Floss* manages to traverse the regressive fantasy of childhood that lies at the core of the English *Bildungsroman* precisely through its progressive abandoning of ironic distance, which is why the – expected and conventional – fairytale happy ending turns into a sublime depiction of a pulsating, semi-incestuous death drive:

> Tom, looking before him, saw death rushing on them. Huge fragments, clinging together in fatal fellowship, made one wide mass across the stream.
>
> "It is coming, Maggie!" Tom said, in a deep, hoarse voice, loosing the oars, and clasping her.
>
> The next instant the boat was no longer seen upon the water [... B]rother and sister had gone down in an embrace never to be parted [...]. (422; bk. 7, ch. 5)

Maggie is reunited with Tom, who in the course of the narrative has come to embody the Law of the Father, and both are obliterated in what one could call a literal 'stream of unconsciousness': a fantasized *Liebestod* in the flood unleashed by Maggie's death drive.[26] Once we foreground this submerged psychological drama, it seems almost too fitting that, in the course of the novel, Eliot's narrator incorporates references to two of psychoanalysis's favorite tragic narratives: Sophocles's *Oedipus* and Shakespeare's *Hamlet* (110 and 325; bk. 1, ch. 13 and bk. 6, ch. 6).

More than merely referring to these tragedies in passing, however, the narrator of *The Mill on the Floss* in fact launches a systematic analysis of the genre of tragedy and its relation to the story of Maggie and her family. Early on in the novel, Maggie already suspects that Tom's character and actions might make the "future in some way tragic" (15; bk. 1, ch. 3). Later, the narrator compares Maggie to the tragic hero of Sophocles's play *Ajax* (56; bk. 1, ch. 7) and even points explicitly to Aristotle's discussion of tragedy in his *Poetics* (85; bk. 1, ch. 10). At another point, the narrator challenges received ideas about the genre, relating this critique to more general problems of novelistic representation:

> Mr. Tulliver, you perceive, though nothing more than a superior miller and maltster, was as proud and obstinate as if he had been a very lofty personage, in whom such dispositions might be a source of that conspicuous, far-echoing tragedy, which sweeps the stage in regal robes, and makes the dullest chronicler sublime. The pride and obstinacy of millers and other insignificant people, whom you pass unnoticingly on the road every day, have their tragedy too; but it is of that unwept, hidden sort that goes on from generation to generation, and leaves no record – such tragedy, perhaps, as lies in the conflicts of young souls, hungry for joy, under a lot made suddenly hard to them, under the dreariness of a home where the morning brings no promise with it, and where the unexpectant discontent of worn and disappointed parents weighs on the children like a damp, thick air, in which all the functions of life are depressed; or such tragedy as lies in the slow or sudden death that follows on a bruised passion, though it may be a death that finds only a parish funeral. (163; bk. 3, ch. 1)

Against the classic Aristotelian dogma, the narrator maintains that tragedy is not confined to those whom one could call "lofty"; it may also afflict "insignificant people," who suffer from everyday conflicts and "the dreariness of a home where the morning brings no promise."[27] *The Mill on the Floss* is thus best un-

---

26 See, for instance, how Elisabeth Bronfen summarizes Freud's account of the psychological dynamics of fantasy: "[F]antasies try to jettison their origin but only find themselves drawn back to the repressed other scene from which they emerged" (209).

27 For a similar argument, see Meyer 129. Note that the narrator of Eliot's *Middlemarch* constructs a "home *epic*" for Dorothea Brooke, the heroine of that novel (*Middlemarch* 511; "Finale"; emphasis added – see Marotta 416).

derstood as an attempt not only to stage, but explicitly to conceptualize a novelistic version of domestic tragedy.[28]

In the course of this exploration of the genre of tragedy, the narrator takes particular issue with the idea of the tragic flaw (*hamartia*), understood as a defect of character. Various critics have recently rejected the traditional understanding of *hamartia* as an inherent flaw in the hero's character. Jennifer Wallace, for instance, argues that the Aristotelian notion of *hamartia* is "less about a character defect than about an error in judgment which led to a wrong decision or a wrong course of action" (118–119). It is this very idea – that *hamartia* refers to an error of judgment – which explains why John Drakakis and Naomi Conn Liebler maintain that *hamartia* is related to the notion of *dilemma*, defined as "the positioning of protagonist, represented community and audience alike between two choices of equal value both politically and morally" (9). If a character is faced with two choices of more or less equal value, then an "error in judgment" is of course far more likely to occur. Accordingly, Drakakis and Liebler insist that what may appear to be an innate character flaw in fact often has its roots, "not in the inner psychological life of the protagonist, but in the larger domain of culture" (8). Intriguingly, much the same stance is taken by the narrator in *The Mill on the Floss*:

> [Y]ou have known Maggie a long while, and need to be told, not her characteristics, but her history, which is a thing hardly to be predicted even from the completest knowledge of characteristics. For the tragedy of our lives is not created entirely from within. "Character," says Novalis, in one of his questionable aphorisms–"character is destiny." But not the whole of our destiny. Hamlet, Prince of Denmark, was speculative and irresolute, and we have a great tragedy in consequence. But if his father had lived to a good old age, and his uncle had died an early death, we can conceive Hamlet's having married Ophelia, and got through life with a reputation of sanity, notwithstanding many soliloquies, and some moody sarcasms toward the fair daughter of Polonius, to say nothing of the frankest incivility to his father-in-law.
>
> Maggie's destiny, then, is at present hidden, and we must wait for it to reveal itself like the course of an unmapped river; we only know that the river is full and rapid, and that for all rivers there is the same final home. (325; bk. 6, ch. 6)

28 Domestic tragedy had already appeared on the English stage in the early eighteenth century in plays such as George Lillo's *The London Merchant*, which was first performed in 1731 (Sanders 302 and Johann N. Schmidt 215; see Helgerson 13–76 for an account of its prehistory). Perhaps the most celebrated eighteenth-century example of tragedy in the English novel is Samuel Richardson's *Clarissa: or, The History of a Young Lady*, published in 1748 (Eagleton, *Sweet Violence* 201–202).

For Eliot's narrator, tragedy is not usually the direct consequence of a protagonist's inherent, tragic flaw, but the result of a fatal misfit between character and circumstances. If, that is to say, the classical *Bildungsroman* assumes that we can recognize ourselves in, and identify with, the wider world as our natural home (i.e. as a place in harmony with our selves), then tragedy focuses on dissonance and the possibility of breakdown. We can therefore read the ending of *The Mill on the Floss*, which constitutes such a blatant break with the novel's realist mode, not only as a critique of the doctrine that tragedy arises "entirely from within," but also as highlighting tragedy's impulse towards a violent disruption of what is conceived as the 'proper' order.

A tragic novel, then – yet at the same time a novel ending in wish-fulfillment? Can a narrative really be called a tragedy if the outcome fulfills the protagonist's deepest, death-driven, incestuous desires? Perhaps we must not only accept that it can, but even posit that such knowledge in fact deepens the tragic experience because it highlights the overwhelming pressures on the protagonist's self. In the course of Eliot's novel, we have come to see that Maggie may well be overly impulsive – but she is also intelligent, sensitive, and generous. Surely it deepens rather than dilutes the tragedy that such a person should find herself in a situation where her only remaining wishes are to be reunited with, and at the same time to take revenge against, her own brother, who has so often treated her with the harshest contempt. Maggie is "so young, so healthy" (415; bk. 7, ch. 5), yet by the end of the novel this only means to her that death is still a long time to come: she is doomed to live, and thus to experience further pain. So yes, Maggie's death in the flood at the end of the novel, locked in an erotically charged embrace with her brother, is a fantasy scenario that allows her to fulfill her conflicting desires. But it is deeply tragic that things should have come to such a pass: that this is indeed the only thing left for Maggie to desire. In *The Mill on the Floss*, Maggie's desire for "homecoming and reconciliation" can only be fulfilled by death and destruction (Fisher 522) because her society provides "no home, no help for the erring" (417; bk. 7, ch. 5). Nicholas Howe is therefore right when he suggests that thinking about home and homelessness has everything to do with how one defines "a just and decent society" (11). The tragic wish-fulfilment of Eliot's novel surely constitutes a plea for social change, even if it does not – is perhaps unable to – envision the precise nature of this change.

Capitalism and the Specter of Nomadic Existence

Indeed, despite a commitment to social reform, Eliot's novel seems afraid of any real historical change. More precisely, *The Mill on the Floss* is pervaded by a fear of the epochal changes that, in the course of the nineteenth century, were transforming the nature of family and home:

> By 1860, when George Eliot's novel first appeared, industrialization had transformed the nation [... T]he construction of railroads and other kinds of infrastructure had caused the razing of entire neighborhoods and a concentration of population in a small number of districts. The contrast between overcrowded, unhealthy urban centers and the open country, which represented the ideal of England, fostered sentimental longings for older, traditional ways of life. The competitive spirit fostered by the industrial system was viewed as infiltrating private lives, corrupting common feelings by aspirations to advance one's own status, even at the risk of abandoning domestic responsibilities. [...] In a work force that was moving from villages to cities, following employment opportunities as they developed, kinship ties had become tenuous, even to the point of giving way to more advantageous commercial connections. (Kilroy 119)

By the mid-Victorian period, which "marks the beginning of the greatest migration of peoples in history" (Hobsbawm, *Age of Capital* 193; see also Manning 149), the ties to the place where one had grown up – the childhood home so central to *The Mill on the Floss* – had lost much of their former meaning. There may therefore be something escapist about the fact that the novel is set in the early decades of the nineteenth century, when the notion of immovable roots perhaps seemed less problematic than it did in 1860, when Eliot's novel was published.[29] Moreover, Deirdre David points out that Maggie possesses qualities that align her with the "pre-industrial era" (603), and this lends symbolical significance to the fact that she and her brother Tom are killed by a piece of "machinery" carried towards them by the novel's apocalyptic flood (421; see also Fisher 521, Kreisel 99–100). Just when it seems that the old values of kinship and belonging have been reaffirmed, just when brother and sister are finally reunited, a machine – that most widely recognized symbol of the industrial age – kills off the two characters who, in their different and conflicting ways, refused to relinquish the ancestral home.

The novel's nostalgic longing for stable roots is thus only one of the ways in which *The Mill on the Floss* expresses deep misgivings about the extent to which the changes of the nineteenth century can be seen as progress rather than as destructive forces. Similar worries about a newly emerging, rootless society

---

29 Or, to be more precise, from the point of view of the 1860s, it was easier to imagine that the notion of immovable roots had seemed less problematic in earlier times. In other words, the point is not that early-nineteenth-century society was truly more stable; rather, the point is that Eliot and her contemporaries could plausibly imagine the past as simpler and less disrupted.

were to remain a concern in English fiction well into the early twentieth century, as we can see in E.M. Forster's *Howards End* (1910). In Forster's novel, the narrator fears that the course of modern societal development will eventually reduce humanity "again to a nomadic horde" (154; ch. 17):

> London was but a foretaste of this nomadic civilization which is altering human nature so profoundly, and throws upon personal relations a stress greater than they have ever borne before. Under cosmopolitanism, if it comes, we shall receive no help from the earth. Trees and meadows and mountains will only be a spectacle, and the binding force that they once exercised on character must be entrusted to Love alone. May Love be equal to the task! (256–257; ch. 31)

The age of urbanization and mass-migration, in this view, constitutes not progress, but a kind of regression to a more primitive, nomadic past. In such a 'nomadic age,' where the home is no longer rooted in a specific place, "Love" – or, as Maggie would put it, "the wayward choice of [...] passion" (381; bk. 6, ch. 14) – may remain the only binding force in people's lives.

This fear of an uprooted, nomadic civilization in fact also pervades little Maggie's escape to the gypsies, which soon turns into an experience of almost gothic terror:

> Her ideas about the gypsies had undergone a rapid modification in the last five minutes. From having considered them very respectful companions, amenable to instruction, she had begun to think that they meant perhaps to kill her as soon as it was dark, and cut up her body for gradual cooking; the suspicion crossed her that the fierce-eyed old man was in fact the Devil, who might drop that transparent disguise at any moment, and turn either into the grinning blacksmith, or else a fiery-eyed monster with dragon's wings. (95; bk. 1, ch. 11)

On the one hand, Deborah Epstein Nord is surely right in insisting that Maggie's excessive hopes and fears in this episode must be read as ironically exposing her childish "myopia and delusions" (16). On the other hand, it would be difficult to argue that Eliot's novel secretly propagates the gypsies' nomadic way of life as a desirable alternative to the Tullivers' respectable, settled existence. Rather, the narrative emphasizes the gypsies' comparative poverty ("We've got no tea nor butter"; 93; bk. 1, ch. 9), suggesting that one ought, perhaps, to pity, but certainly not emulate such a 'rootless' existence.

Similarly, *The Mill on the Floss* foregrounds the threats of rootlessness and nomadism in Maggie's relationship to Stephen Guest. For Maggie, abandoning her family and her home community to elope with Stephen would mean "for ever [to] sink and wander vaguely, driven by uncertain impulse" (382; bk. 6, ch. 14). Even Stephen's last name in fact emphasizes that Maggie cannot expect to find a stable home with him, for a 'guest' is, by definition, a person who is not staying in his or her own home, but only ever in someone else's. Moreover, Stephen is the prospective heir of Guest & Co., "a great mill-owning, ship-owning business [...], with a banking concern attached" (54; bk. 1, ch. 7), and thus a proponent of the very industrial-capitalist order that threatens to erode the ideal of home that Maggie (and, arguably, Eliot's novel) desperately tries to uphold.[30] Put more abstractly, the novel confronts Maggie with the choice between, on the one hand, a negative, personal kind of freedom from interference by the home community (i.e. asserting her right to be with Stephen, over and against the wishes of relatives, friends, etc.), and, on the other, the positive freedom of belonging to a community and participating in its daily life (i.e. remaining accepted and included).[31]

The Politics of Genre and Style Brought Home

Maggie's conflict cannot be solved within the realist parameters of the English *Bildungsroman*, and accordingly *The Mill on the Floss* ultimately abandons the world of realism for the realm of tragic wish-fulfillment and dreamlike dissolution. The prototypical *Bildungsroman* tells the story of someone who, after leaving home, manages to reconcile his or her own desires with the demands of society – someone who finds a place in the world, albeit at the cost of compromise. Whenever such a (more or less harmonious) homecoming becomes entirely impossible, we approach the tragic realm of 'unbelonging' that is characterized by a breakdown of both the social and the transcendental order. As Terry Eagleton points out, this tragic realm tends to be associated with "virile warriors and immolated virgins"; it confronts us with scapegoat figures who incarnate "the inner contradictions of the social order" and thus symbolize an entire society's failure in their own defeat (*Sweet Violence* ix and 280).

This idea that inner, hidden contradictions are exposed in tragedy also explains why Andrew Bennet and Nicholas Royle associate the tragic as such with psychoanalytic theory: both make the unconscious public (109). Freud himself

30 Importantly, to say that the new, industrial-capitalist order threatens the older social order is not to idealize the latter. See, for instance, Raymond Williams, who describes English history as "a story of growth and achievement, but for the majority of men it was the substitution of one form of domination for another: the mystified feudal order replaced by a mystified agrarian capitalist order, with just enough continuity, in titles and in symbols of authority, in successive compositions of a 'natural order', to confuse and control" (39).

31 On the notions of negative and positive liberty see, for instance, Isaiah Berlin's "Two Concepts of Liberty."

famously argued that the interpretation of dreams is “the royal road to a knowledge of the unconscious” (*Five Lectures* 33), and the fact that the tragic catastrophe in Eliot’s novel constitutes a departure from realism into a land of semi-incestuous, death-driven wish-fulfillment is thus merely a more than usually striking example of the secret affinity between tragedy, dreams, and the unconscious.[32]

Importantly, in *The Mill on the Floss* the critical exploration of tragedy and other literary concepts is linked explicitly to the novel’s thematic focus on home and dispossession. For instance, in a chapter entitled “What Had Happened at Home,” the narrator describes Mr. Tulliver’s loss of Dorlcote Mill, his beloved home, as a “tragedy” both for himself and for the family (as well as the servants) who depend on him (162–163 and 212; bk. 3, ch. 1 and 8). Similarly, as we have seen, the narrator believes that fashionable irony thrives only in the comfortable homes of the privileged who depend, for their comfort, on those who suffer from want and dispossession. Even the novel’s concern with popular romances, where the dark-haired heroine must always end unhappily, is in fact directly related to the events in Maggie’s own home, for both her parents and other relatives echo these prejudices in their misgivings about Maggie’s ‘gypsy-like’ dark hair. Literary conventions and stereotypes thus reinforce, and perhaps also create, social prejudices that, in turn, have real repercussions in domestic life. In short, we can say that *The Mill on the Floss* relates all its three major literary critical concerns – the critique of tragedy, of irony, and of popular romances – to problems of domesticity, home, and belonging, and thus to key themes of the *Bildungsroman.*

In doing so, Eliot’s novel presents a vision of home – that supposedly safe and private space – as permeated and shaped by fundamentally public forces. It also presents home as a gendered space owned by patriarchs who see the world mainly in terms of property relations. Reverend Stelling’s decision to teach, for instance, is not based on any desire on his part to contribute to the progress of civilization; he simply needs the money to finance his and his wife’s rather expensive lifestyle (113; bk. 2, ch. 1). Moreover, we have seen that Mr. Tulliver only decides to send Tom to a tutor because he wants to prevent the son from becoming his rival by one day claiming the mill as his own. Similarly, Mr. Tulliver fears that Maggie’s intelligence lowers her value as a marriageable commodity. Like Lawyer Wakem, Mr. Tulliver thus (at least occasionally) regards women as

32 “Die Traumdeutung ist in Wirklichkeit die Via Regia zur Kenntnis des Unbewußten, die sicherste Grundlage der Psychoanalyse und jenes Gebiet, auf welchem jeder Arbeiter seine Überzeugung zu gewinnen und seine Ausbildung anzustreben hat” (Freud, *Über Psychoanalyse* 32).

a piece of property, which suggests that belonging, for women, all to often means being owned by the male head of the household, rather than feeling at home in the family or the wider community.

Even Stephen Guest, who in many ways is the proponent of a younger, more 'advanced' generation of men, has no doubts that a woman's role in life is defined through and by her relation to men. For instance, in the scene where we first meet Stephen, he asks Maggie's cousin Lucy to "sing the whole duty of woman" from Handel's *The Creation* (297; bk. 6, ch. 1), and is thus immediately associated with a view of women in terms of their duty to men – a view sanctioned by official religious discourse. In a later scene, Stephen angrily "bursts forth" that a bazaar organized by the women of St. Ogg's takes "young ladies from the duties of the domestic hearth":

> I should like to know what is the proper function of women, if it is not to make reasons for husbands to stay at home, and still stronger reasons for bachelors to go out. If this goes on much longer, the bonds of society will be dissolved. (327; bk. 6, ch. 6)

The Father, the Teacher, the Lawyer, the Preacher, and even the young Capitalist thus all agree that belonging, for women, has little to do with a sense of ease, emotional attachment to people and places, or a modicum of control over their own lives. Consequently, it is not difficult to understand why Maggie urgently wishes for an occupation that would allow her to "get my own bread and be independent" (e.g. 402; bk. 7, ch. 2) – that would, in Virginia Woolf's terms, allow her to have a room of her own.

What makes matters even more difficult for Maggie is that, despite the injustices of a patriarchal society, there is much about her home to love and cherish: her father can be affectionate (as in the treatment of his sister, Mrs. Moss; 64–72; bk. 1, ch. 7) and often takes Maggie's side when others berate her; her mother may not really understand her, but always tries to protect her from harm; and Maggie is treated with genuine kindness not only by Philip, but also by Tom's boyhood friend Bob, who helps the Tullivers after they lose their mill (bk. 3, ch. 6), and who even takes Maggie into his home when most people in St. Ogg's treat her as an outcast because of her 'failed' elopement with Stephen Guest (bk. 7, ch. 1). In spite of patriarchal injustice, home thus means more to Maggie than merely pain and restriction; it also holds the promise of fulfillment, intimacy, and kindness – the positive freedom that comes from belonging to others, as opposed to a negative liberty that is defined through the absence of interference. It is true, of course, that the image of a carefree childhood, a time when Maggie and her brother "clasped their little hands in love, and roamed the daisied fields together" (422; bk. 7, ch. 5), is a nostalgic idealization. But it is also true that such moments of harmony do, at times, occur in *The Mill on the Floss* (as when Tom, at one point, tries to console little Maggie by kissing her and offering her a piece of cake – 34; bk. 1, ch. 5) – at least before Mr. Tulliver's embittered command of revenge thwarts the impulse toward forgiveness that characterized Tom in his younger years. At the end of Eliot's novel, Maggie must choose between this imperfect, but familiar home, and the vague promise of a 'nomadic' future with Stephen. It is very well possible that returning home is the wrong choice for Maggie (Eagleton, *The English Novel* 178), but this is in some ways beside the point, for the real tragedy is that she is forced by circumstances to make the choice at all.

One may, then, justifiably criticize *The Mill on the Floss* for its failure to see that one can, in fact, feel perfectly at home in a nomadic existence – whether it is a way of life inherited from one's forebears (as in the case of the gypsies), or whether it is freely chosen (as in the case of contemporary upper-class nomads who enjoy shuttling back and forth between the world's metropolitan centers). Yet Eliot's novel rightly emphasizes that nomadism is not a matter of positive, free choice for everyone. It is, as we have seen, not that for Maggie, who refuses the seductively modern choice of a 'rootless' existence and opts instead for a 'pre-modern' adherence to the familiar home. It is not necessarily so for the children of today's transnational elite, some of whom, according to recent studies, feel that they do not really belong anywhere (e.g. Blunt and Dowling 218–219). And nomadic existence is certainly not a free choice for those who suffer what J. Douglas Porteous and Sandra E. Smith refer to as domicide: "the deliberate destruction of home by human agency" (12). In nineteenth-century Britain, it was still possible to imagine that those who abandoned their homes did so freely, although for the poor this 'freedom' in fact often consisted in a desperate attempt to avoid economic hardship or even famine, as was the case in Ireland during the 1840s (Daunton 47; Harvie 506).[33] The first half of the twentieth century, however, would come to be dominated by the more directly enforced mass migrations precipitated by genocidal, total war (Manning 164). From the mid-nineteenth century onwards, in short, the threat of homelessness and exile became an increasingly real prospect for Europeans (as it had long been for the colonized and the enslaved). It is against this backdrop that we should read both the great Victorian domestic tragedy of *The Mill on the Floss*

33 See Dirk Hoerder, who notes that migrants "made and make decisions 'free' *under the constraints of economic conditions* that leave no room for life-projects or even survival. Their 'home' may be a society that is unfair and unsupportable, that does not permit sustainable lives" (474; original emphasis).

as well as the masterpieces of Modernist fiction – including Virginia Woolf’s *Mrs. Dalloway.*

3 "The Majesty of England": The Ethics of Home and the Imperial City in Virginia Woolf's *Mrs. Dalloway*

For European modernists after 1914, writing about home meant coming to terms with the impact of global war.[1] Consider, for instance, the novel that many believe to be the period's greatest achievement: James Joyce's *Ulysses* (1922), written abroad and named after a hero who, after a protracted and devastating war, can no longer seem to find his way home. At the same time, though the long nineteenth century had arguably come to a close with the armistice on November 11, 1918 (e.g. Osterhammel 88), to political commentators in the early 1920s the meaning of the historical moment was far less clear than it seems in hindsight. The United Kingdom, for instance, mourned the deaths of hundreds of thousands in the bloodiest conflict in human history, but the country had also emerged victorious from the war, and the British Empire in many respects appeared more unified and powerful a world system than ever (Jeffrey 13; see also North 54). Given this strange commixture of triumph and trauma, the profound sense of ambivalence that pervades English postwar novels like *Mrs. Dalloway* (1925) is hardly surprising.

In Woolf's novel, this sense of ambivalence revolves, specifically, around the nature of everyday life in London, the Empire's proud metropolitan center.[2] However, the novel's key question is not, as some critics suggest, whether or not it is *possible* to feel at home in the modern metropolis (Ellis 76; see also Hawthorn 78; Whitworth 153). Rather, *Mrs. Dalloway* explores whether, given the state of British society in the 1920s, to feel at home in the capital is morally *justifiable*. In the previous chapters, we mainly examined the factors that make it more difficult to feel at home for some characters than for others; accordingly, the focus was on the potential obstacles to an individual's sense of belonging. We have thus not yet asked whether there may be circumstances under which

---

1 I would like to thank Simone Heller-Andrist, Laura Marcus, and Christa Schönfelder for their comments on draft versions of this chapter, as well as Sarah Chevalier and Anja Neukom-Hermann for their feedback on the final version. For a detailed examination of the impact of World War I on modernist fiction, see Stevenson, *Literature and the Great War* (114–120, in particular).

2 See Bryony Randall (595–599) for more general comments on *Mrs. Dalloway* as a novel of the everyday.

one should not truly want to feel at home because the ethical price for belonging is simply too high. It is this question that we will address in the present chapter.

Part of the discussion will revolve around the way in which Woolf's novel constructs both geographical and discursive space. We will begin by examining how *Mrs. Dalloway* reflects and renegotiates English debates about the relative merits of the city and the country as sites of home. In particular, the novel dissects the familiar idyll of the English country house, laying bare some of its ideological limitations and pitting it against the pulsating and spectacular space of the modern city. At the same time, however, the space of the city also appears as very precisely delimited in Woolf's novel, at least for those associated with Clarissa Dalloway and her social circle. In part, the novel uses shifting narrative perspectives to open up this delimited social space, but even the scope of these narrative shifts has very precise boundaries, depending on the characters with whom they are associated. Ultimately, *Mrs. Dalloway* confronts us with characters whose discursive space of belonging is every much as confined and contested as their geographical room for maneuver in the city.

In order better to understand the conflicts between these characters, we will therefore have to shift the emphasis from the spatial dimensions of home to what we might call the temporality of belonging. In effect, the novel contrasts characters who – for various reasons – gravitate toward a timeless, mythical view of life with those who are more firmly rooted in historical time. The novel's postwar context is vital here, as the repression of history has much to do with a desire on the part of Clarissa, in particular, to evade questions of responsibility and social injustice. In consequence, Clarissa and others from her circle not only misread the novel's most tragic figures, Septimus and Lucrezia Warren Smith; they also fail to reflect on the extent to which their own sense of belonging depends on their social position within a political elite that is at least partly responsible for the disasters of the Great War. Importantly, *Mrs. Dalloway* does not fault these characters for their desire to belong. Rather, the novel emphasizes that their sense of belonging comes at a price, and it encourages us continually to judge whether this ethical price is worth paying. In its wanderings through the imperial city, *Mrs. Dalloway* thus constitutes nothing short of a narrative quest for an ethics of home.

The Country and the City

If debates about the modern metropolis as a problematic kind of home shed light on Woolf's novel, then this is in part because London has been a central reference point in such discussions since at least the period of the Enlightenment. Raymond Williams, for instance, points out that Enlightenment thinkers like Voltaire and Adam Smith disagreed fundamentally with regard to both the nature and the ethical value of the city as a site of home:

> Voltaire saw the pursuit of industry and urbane pleasure as the marks of the city and thence of civilisation itself. The golden age and the Garden of Eden, lacking industry and pleasure, were not virtuous but ignorant; the city, and especially London, was the symbol of progress and enlightenment, its social mobility the school of civilisation and liberty [...]. Adam Smith, rather differently, saw the city as securing the industry of the country: a centre of freedom and order but in its very dependence as a market and manufacturing centre liable to breed a volatile and insecure people. (144)

At a time when the modern industrial cities were only beginning to emerge, London was thus already envisaged as both an ideal home and a potentially dangerous space: the cradle of freedom and civilized order, but also a breeding ground for "volatile" urban masses.

In the late nineteenth century, similar arguments were waged in the field of sociology, though by now the metaphoric terms of the debate had shifted from the Enlightenment contrast between unruliness and order to an opposition – better suited to industrialized society – between organic and mechanical ways of life. In his *Gemeinschaft and Gesellschaft* (*Community and Society*, 1887), Ferdinand Tönnies suggested that the supposedly organic rural communities of the past were increasingly being replaced by a rationalized urban society dominated by merely mechanical relations of exchange (Delanty 32–33). Only sixteen years later, however, Émile Durkheim provocatively reversed Tönnies's thesis in *De la division du travail social* (*The Division of Labor in Society*, 1893) – an argument that Phil Hubbard has summarized succinctly:

> For Durkheim [...], traditional, rural life offered a form of *mechanical* solidarity with social bonds based on common beliefs, custom, ritual, routines, and symbols. Social cohesion was thus based upon the likeness and similarities among individuals in a society. Durkheim argued that the emergence of city-state [sic] signalled a shift from mechanical to *organic* solidarity, with social bonds becoming based on specialisation and interdependence. [...I]n contrast to feudal and rural social orders, urban society was one which allowed for the coexistence of social differences, with a complex division of labour (where many different people specialise in many different occupations) creating greater freedom and choice for individuals. (15–16; original emphasis)

Whereas in Tönnies's view rural society was organic because it was based on 'natural' kinship relations, Durkheim, by contrast, regarded such kinship relations as automatic or 'mechanical' because they lacked any element of freedom and individual choice (Delanty 38). In short, while Tönnies idealized life in the country, Durkheim – much like Voltaire a century before him – viewed rural existence as narrow-minded and stifling when compared with the exhilarating freedom of the city.

Such debates over the relative value of rural and urban homes arguably had a particularly strong resonance in Britain due to the very common cultural association of rural life with 'true Englishness.'[3] As David Gervais has shown, it was in the course of the nineteenth century, when the new, industrial cities emerged, that writers increasingly located true Englishness in the rural existence of a rapidly disappearing yeoman class (4). An example for this trend is the influential Garden City movement, which attempted to reintroduce some of the supposedly redemptive qualities of rural life into the city (Gifford 37; Hubbard 61). Even for city-dwellers, the English domestic ideal thus became associated with images of country mansions and rural cottages:

> London's residential neighborhoods exhibited a paradoxical symbiosis of the rural and the urban: paradoxical because, despite their identification as rural and even anti-urban, those suburban villas were also specifically and indelibly metropolitan, just as the song "Home, Sweet Home" (1823) invoked a prelapsarian village abode but was written for a melodrama set and performed in London. (Sharon Marcus 98–99)

A literary example of the privileged cultural position of the English countryside are the novels of Jane Austen, where narrative complications tend to occur in more urban areas, such as seaside towns or London itself, while the happy resolution takes the heroine to a (stately) home in the countryside (Moretti, *Atlas of the European Novel* 17–19).

Such ruralist ideals of Englishness continued to gain in importance during the Edwardian period, and by the 1920s constituted one of the most prominent features in national self-definitions (Howkins 63). The overwhelming majority of writers between 1910 and 1940 thus regarded as the most representative part of the nation a "favoured enclave of the English countryside, usually presented in pastoral terms as a tranquil idyll" (Baldick 305). In these pastoral visions of Englishness, the city tended to be construed as stimulating yet chaotic, filled with dirt, criminals, and other 'alien' elements; indeed, "the discourses of urban investigation that developed in the 1840s argued that especially in London, the city had overtaken and destroyed the home" (Sharon Marcus 101). The metrop-

---

3 This association is facilitated by the fact that in English the word *country* can refer both to a nation's rural area ('I prefer the country to the city') and to the nation as a whole ('England is my country'; see Raymond Williams 1).

olis, in short, was seen as undermining domestic ideals, while the country promised the timeless stability of a truly English home.[4]

Mrs. Dalloway, however, questions such ruralist prejudices from the outset by challenging the idea that rural life is stable and idyllic. Woolf's novel famously opens with Clarissa Dalloway stepping out of her London home in Bond Street to go and buy flowers for a party that she intends to give in the evening. The scene she encounters immediately reminds Clarissa of a more rural past at Bourton, the stately country home of her youth:

> What a lark! What a plunge! For so it had always seemed to her, when, with a little squeak of the hinges, which she could hear now, she had burst open the French windows and plunged at Bourton into the open air. How fresh, how calm, stiller than this of course, the air was in the early morning; like the flap of a wave; the kiss of a wave; chill and sharp and yet (for a girl of eighteen as she then was) solemn, feeling as she did, standing there at the open window, that something awful was about to happen [...]. (3)

On the one hand, Clarissa immediately associates the freshness of the morning air in the city with life in the country, though the air there had been "stiller than this of course." However, the rural stillness at Bourton is not an unequivocally positive feature for Clarissa; it seems like the "kiss of a wave" and yet somehow solemn, as if "something awful was about to happen." Moreover, later in the novel, we learn that Clarissa's rural past is indeed associated with a very personal tragedy, as her only sister was killed in the woods near Bourton by a falling tree (85). In contrast to common celebrations of rural England, there is thus, from the beginning, little sense in *Mrs. Dalloway* that homes in the country are necessarily more idyllic or carefree than city abodes.

Revisiting the Country House

Importantly, to say that *Mrs. Dalloway* constitutes a critique of countryside ideals is not to deny any idyllic dimension to Clarissa's more rural home at Bourton, as some pastoral scenes in Woolf's novel constitute a self-conscious reworking of the literary topos that Terry Gifford has called "country-house Arcadias" (66). This is particularly evident in those scenes that focus on Clarissa's intimate friendship with Sally Seton, whom Clarissa continues to remember with glowing affection: "Had not that, after all, been love?" (35). The loving

4 It is in part due to this anti-modern celebration of the countryside that the work of many English 'modernists' seems tame and insular when compared to avant-garde writing from the United States, Ireland, or the Continent (Esty 33–35).

relationship between the two women culminates, on the terrace at Bourton one star-lit night, in a glorious, passionate kiss:

> Then came the most exquisite moment of her whole life passing a stone urn with flowers in it. Sally stopped; picked a flower; kissed her on the lips. The whole world might have turned upside down! The others disappeared; there she was alone with Sally. (38)

Such celebrations of same-sex affection have long been characteristic of pastoral literature; homoerotic desire was, for instance, already a central concern in the *Idylls* of Theocritus (Holmes M. Morgan), and by the seventeenth century one of pastoral's primary interests was its "participation in fields of sexual deviation" (Bredbeck 200). It is thus possible to read the love scene between Sally and Clarissa not primarily as a moment of rural authenticity, but instead as a self-consciously literary evocation of pastoral conventions.

However, whereas pastoral texts generally allow the same-sex lovers more than merely a brief moment of bliss, in *Mrs. Dalloway* Sally and Clarissa are immediately interrupted by their friend Peter Walsh, who asks whether they have been star-gazing: "It was shocking; it was horrible! [... Clarissa] felt his hostility; his jealousy; his determination to break into their companionship" (39). The pastoral idyll of homoerotic desire is evoked only to be immediately shattered. It is thus fitting that shepherds – those staple ingredients of classical pastoral (Gifford 15) – are only hinted at in the vaguest of terms in *Mrs. Dalloway*, when we learn that Clarissa, in her youth at Bourton, owned a "great shaggy dog which ran after sheep" (65). Similarly, though the name of Clarissa's sister, Sylvia (Latin for 'forest' or 'woods'), carries strong pastoral associations (Abel 111), her death – being killed by a falling tree – gives this generic link a decidedly non-idyllic, black-humored twist.[5] The homely rural idyll of Clarissa's youth at Bourton is, in short, suffused with conflict, self-consciously artificial, and fragile at best.

If the general literary tradition of country-house Arcadias is reworked in *Mrs. Dalloway* to challenge common preconceptions about rural innocence and stability, the novel also more specifically refers to a novel by Jane Austen to broaden the scope of the domestic novel beyond the confines of the heterosexual courtship plot. As Raymond Williams notes, Jane Austen's novels are centrally concerned with estates, incomes, and social position as indispensable elements

---

5 It is, admittedly, possible to place Sylvia's death in the long-standing tradition of pastoral that highlights the presence of death even in Arcadia ('Et in Arcadia ego'; see Gifford 154; Heusser 183). However, naming someone who is killed by a tree 'Sylvia' nevertheless constitutes a peculiarly cruel variation on the motif.

of all the relationships that are formed (113). In order, Williams continues, to solve the ensuing conflict between economic interest and moral value, Jane Austen "guides her heroines, steadily, to the right marriages" (115); the transmission of wealth is secured through a match between those characters whom the narrative has revealed as being most worthy of it. At the beginning of the heroine's journey, her family home tends to be under threat; at the end, she is rewarded with an equally deserving husband and a new, far more exquisite home somewhere in rural England (Moretti, *Atlas of the European Novel* 18).

Elizabeth Abel astutely observes that this fictional universe is evoked in *Mrs. Dalloway* when Clarissa at first mishears her future husband's family name as "Wickham," thus linking him to arguably the most disreputable character in Austen's *Pride and Prejudice* (1813). According to Abel, this explicit intertextual reference draws attention to how Woolf's novel modifies the standard courtship plot of Austen's fiction:

> Woolf condenses the [...] moment that constitutes Austen's novel and locates it in a remembered scene thirty years prior to the present of her narrative [...]. Marriage in *Mrs. Dalloway* provides impetus rather than closure to the courtship plot, dissolved into a retrospective oscillation between two alluring possibilities as Clarissa continues to replay the choice she made thirty years before. (107)

The home of Clarissa's youth, Abel reminds us, was also the scene of her marriage choice, with Peter Walsh and Richard Dalloway as the two competing male suitors.[6] However, while Austen's novels conclude with the heroine reaching the goal of the 'right' marriage, the suggestion in *Mrs. Dalloway* that Richard is similar to Austen's deceitful George Wickham intimates that Clarissa may in fact have made the wrong choice. This suspicion is, if not explicitly confirmed, then at least kept alive by the fact that much of Woolf's novel focuses on Clarissa's lingering doubts, with the heroine sometimes thanking heaven that she refused to marry Peter, yet at other times wishing she had agreed to his proposal rather than to Richard's (50–51; see Bowlby 147). Whereas in Jane Austen's novels marriage at least superficially signifies happiness, maturity, and narrative closure, in *Mrs. Dalloway* the country-house world of romantic fulfillment becomes, instead, the past as prelude to the heroine's conflicts in later life, as well as a subtly playful intertextual reference point.

At the same time, we need to bear in mind that, by the 1920s, life in the actually existing English country houses had itself become a mode of playful perform-

6 While a long-term relationship between Clarissa and Sally never appears as an alternative to heterosexual marriage in *Mrs. Dalloway*, it is central in *The Hours* (1998), Michael Cunningham's appropriation of Woolf's novel.

ance for the nations' upper class. Since at least the late nineteenth century, the average stately home in the country had few (if any) remaining ties with rural life in the sense of agricultural work; such country houses were, rather, the setting for "ritual enactments" of country life, maintained "on the profits of industrial and imperial development" (Raymond Williams 282). In *Mrs. Dalloway*, we only have to listen to the rural daydreams of Clarissa's daughter, Elizabeth, to hear echoes of such upper-class performances as disconnected from the social reality of English farmers:

> She might be a farmer. [...] She might own a thousand acres and have people under her. She would go and see them in their cottages. [...] One might be a very good farmer – and that, strangely enough, [...] was almost entirely due to Somerset House. It looked so splendid, so serious, that great grey building. And she liked the feeling of people working. (149)

Hierarchy and privilege are central to this fantasy of rural England ("She might [...] have people under her"), and even Elizabeth acknowledges that Somerset House – situated in the heart of the city and, at the time, home to the government's principal tax and public record offices (Showalter 224n58) – is the main reason why someone like her might one day be able to style herself as a good 'farmer,' for it is the supposedly urban political and financial system that enables a small group of country-house owners to enjoy "the *feeling* of people working" (emphasis added). Importantly, to highlight the links between the country and the city is not to contradict Elizabeth Abel's observation that Clarissa herself sees Bourton as a pastoral world that is spatially and temporally disjunct from London, the sociopolitical world of her husband Richard (108). It does mean, however, that Woolf's novel as a whole portrays 'rural' country-house Arcadias as only superficially isolated from the city, whereas in fact they are part of the same overarching social system.[7] Accordingly, we must now leave the countryside and devote our attention to the urban spaces of *Mrs. Dalloway*.

Street Haunting: Flânerie, Gender, and Class

Just as *Mrs. Dalloway's* engagement with 'country-house England' constitutes a meticulous reworking of ruralist and pastoral traditions, its depiction of life in the city draws on an already existing image: the urban wanderer or *flâneur*. As Raymond Williams points out, the experience and perception of the modern city

7 Historically, the country and the city have been part of the same economic order since the agricultural and industrial revolutions of the eighteenth century, if not earlier (McKeon, *The Secret History of Domesticity* 689; Raymond Williams 98).

has been "associated, from the beginning, with a man walking, as if alone, in its streets" (233). Long before Williams, Walter Benjamin had devoted sustained theoretical attention to this key figure of modernity, and Sharon Marcus notes how in Benjamin's writings the city street sometimes appears curiously cozy – almost more homelike than city homes themselves (13–14). Indeed, what is ultimately at stake in Benjamin's as well as later discussions of *flânerie* is whether the urban wanderer's experience of the modern city can be described as a new way of belonging – a genuinely modern sense of home – or whether such urban experiences need to be understood in terms of increasing anomie and alienation.

The figure of the *flâneur* – around whom these problems coalesced – was, for most critics writing after Benjamin, predominantly male: the relatively privileged man of means who appears in the poems of Charles Baudelaire, or in such stories as Edgar Allan Poe's "The Man of the Crowd" (Parsons 4).[8] We also find such a privileged male *flâneur* in *Mrs. Dalloway*, in Clarissa's old friend Peter Walsh, whose life Woolf's heroine considers to have been a failure (8), but who nevertheless clearly belongs to imperial Britain's wealthy elite. In one of the many scenes from Woolf's novel in which Peter is wandering through the streets of London, he encounters an attractive young woman and decides secretly to follow her:

> [S]he's not married; she's young; quite young, thought Peter, the red carnation he had seen her wear as she came across Trafalgar Square burning again in his eyes and making her lips red. [...] There was a dignity about her. She was not worldly, like Clarissa; not rich, like Clarissa. Was she, he wondered as she moved, respectable? [... H]e was an adventurer, reckless, he thought, swift, daring [...] He was a buccaneer. (58)

Peter, the bourgeois man of means, turns the young woman who is "not rich, like Clarissa," into a spectacle for his own consumption: an erotic fantasy that he admits is "half made up" (59). And in this, too, he resembles the *flâneurs* in Baudelaire, where according to Deborah L. Parsons women are objectified by

8 Note, however, that recently critics have also traced accounts of female *flânerie* as far back as the mid-nineteenth century (e.g. Gleber 12).

the leisured male spectator while they themselves rarely appear in a position that would allow them to become the observers of others (25).[9]

At the same time, as Parsons rightly points out, there is an element of conscious parody about the way in which Peter observes the city, in "an attitude of rebellion yet ultimate conventionality" (73); Peter styles himself a "buccaneer," but he is in fact a much more common and decidedly less daring figure: a middle-aged man silently fantasizing about a much younger woman in an attempt to escape "(only of course for an hour or so) from being precisely what he was" (57). Indeed, we can see how far Peter is from being a true rebel in the scene that immediately precedes this fantasied 'adventure.' After a visit in Bond Street, Peter feels dissatisfied with Clarissa's conventionality (53), and he begins to reflect on his own position within the Dalloway's social circle:

> He was not old, or set, or dried in the least. As for caring what they said of him – the Dalloways, the Whitbreads, and their set, he cared not a straw – not a straw (though it was true he would have, some time or other, to see whether Richard couldn't help him to some job). (55)

Peter once again styles himself as a non-conformist, yet at the same time he hopes to profit from his association with the Dalloways. Even so, Peter would like to believe that his own private enthusiasms will, one day, stand revealed as prefiguring nothing less than the future of society as a whole:

> He had been sent down from Oxford – true. He had been a Socialist, in some sense a failure – true. Still the future of civilisation lies, he thought, in the hands of young men like that; of young men such as he was, thirty years ago; with their love of abstract principles; getting books sent out to them all the way from London to a peak in the Himalayas; reading science; reading philosophy. The future lies in the hands of young men like that, he thought. (55)

---

9 See for instance the following passage from Baudelaire's essay "The Painter in Modern Life," in which the gendered nature of the *flâneur* becomes increasingly apparent: "For the perfect *flâneur*, for the passionate spectator, it is an immense joy to set up a house in the heart of the multitude, amid the ebb and flow of movement, in the midst of the fugitive and infinite. To be away from home and yet to feel oneself everywhere at home; to see the world, to be at the centre of the world, and yet to remain hidden from the world – such are a few of the slightest pleasures of those independent, passionate, impartial natures which the tongue can but clumsily define. The spectator is a *prince* who everywhere rejoices in his incognito. The lover of life makes the whole world his family, just like the lover of the fair sex who builds up his family from all the beautiful women that he has ever found, and that are – or are not – to be found" (9). For a concise summary of Baudelaire's and Benjamin's ideas about the *flâneur* see Tally (*Spatiality* 95–99).

Tellingly, however, immediately after this imperial vision of a future created by intellectual 'renegades' like him, Peter witnesses a troop of boys parading "in uniform, carrying guns, [...] on their faces an expression like the letters of a legend written round the base of a statue praising duty, gratitude, fidelity, love of England" (55). This juxtaposition suggests, for one thing, that the real future may lie, not with bookish young men in love with abstract principles, but with uniformed boys carrying guns, "drugged into a stiff yet staring corpse by discipline" (56).[10] Moreover, it is important to note that this band of boys are on their way to the Cenotaph, a monument commemorating the dead of the Great War and, as such, one of the most "arresting emblems of the modern culture of nationalism" (Anderson 9). Typically Peter, though not entirely uncritical, ultimately remains convinced that, even if one laughed at such a display, "one had to respect it" (56). We are, significantly, not given a reason why, precisely, "one" ought to respect a militarization of everyday life; Peter merely asserts the fact as self-evidently the appropriate thing for an Englishman to do – which shows just how far Peter is from being a truly reckless "adventurer" or "buccaneer." As an urban wanderer in London, Peter corresponds to the literary figure of the *flâneur*, but as was the case with pastoral idylls and the romance of Austen's stately homes, *Mrs. Dalloway* evokes this figure in part to lay bare its conventional ideological bias.

This is not to suggest that wandering through the city is seen as an inherently reprehensible pursuit in Woolf's novel. On the contrary, *Mrs. Dalloway* to some extent celebrates the liberating potential that 'street haunting' can offer for women, in particular. Clarissa, for example, loves to wander through the streets of London, insisting that it is "better than walking in the country" (6). As Laura Marcus points out, through their entry into the public spaces of the city upper- and middle-class women in early twentieth-century literature frequently found "liberation from enclosure in the private, domestic sphere" of the home (61; see also Parsons 27).[11] Virginia Woolf's own essay on "Street Haunting" (1927) constitutes a particularly important document from this corpus of female literature about the city, for it explicitly suggests that one may feel a sense of liberation when leaving one's home – a home in which one sits "surrounded by objects

10 See also Pam Morris, *Jane Austen, Virginia Woolf and Worldly Realism* 66–67.

11 Note that Sharon Marcus has cautioned against an overly strict conception of separate spheres (without, however, denying the concept's heuristic value): "Feminist scholarship showed how a host of nineteenth-century discourses and practices defined the home as a private, cloistered space, advocated women's restriction to that space, and correspondingly excluded women from the easy commerce with the city's public spaces that was the privilege of many men. Crucial as that demonstration was, it anchored those divisions too securely and fixed their extent too widely" (6–7).

which perpetually express the oddity of our own temperaments and enforce the memories of our own experience" (177):

> [W]hen the door shuts on us, all that vanishes. The shell-like covering which our souls have excreted to house themselves, to make for themselves a shape distinct from others, is broken, and there is left of all these wrinkles and roughnesses a central oyster of perceptiveness, an enormous eye. (178)

Leaving the home is thus similar to breaking out of a constricting shell, and as we wander through the city, "everything seems miraculously sprinkled with beauty" (181); we can finally "leave the straight lines of personality" and explore more fully both our own potential and, imaginatively, the lives of others (187). Clarissa, in *Mrs. Dalloway*, clearly feels some of the euphoric delight described in Woolf's essay: after her "plunge" into the London streets, she encounters "what she loved: life; London; this moment of June" (4). For women like Clarissa, then, the streets of London may appear, not as the urban nightmare so frequently envisioned by mournful pastoralists, but as a counter-homely source of vitality and regeneration (Whitworth 153).

Nevertheless, if we compare *Mrs. Dalloway* and Woolf's essay on "Street Haunting" more closely, we find that there are limits to these texts' celebration of female *flânerie.* On the one hand, the two texts have much in common, for both open with a figure leaving the home and subsequently becoming enthralled by the sights and sounds of the city. On the other hand, according to Woolf's essay the ideal times for such wanderings are evenings in winter (177), while in *Mrs. Dalloway* Clarissa leaves her home around ten in the morning, on a day in mid-June (3–4). Consequently, if we take the essay's celebration of street haunting on winter evenings at face value, then this might imply a subtle critique of Clarissa Dalloway's wanderings, which take place at a different time of the day and year.[12] In addition, though it is true that Woolf's essay celebrates the liberating sense of dissolution that comes when one imaginatively merges with the darkening crowd, it also posits that there are both temporal and social limits to such delights:

> [T]o escape is the greatest of pleasures; street haunting in winter the greatest of adventures. Still as we approach our own doorstep again, it is comforting to feel the old possessions, the old prejudices, fold us round, and shelter and enclose the self, which has been blown about at so many street corners, which has battered like a moth at the

12 Perhaps it is significant, too, that in her essay Woolf singles out evenings rather than nights, for as Matthew Beaumont has shown, "[n]ightwalking is, in both the physical and the moral meanings of the term, deviant" (*Nightwalking* 5).

> flame of so many inaccessible lanterns, sheltered and enclosed. Here again is the usual door; here the chair turned as we left it and the china bowl and the brown ring on the carpet. (187)

Escaping to the city, this passage suggests, is a pleasure for those who know they can return, after a relatively brief period of time, to the "old possessions" and the comfort of their homes. The idea of flux and instability is thus, as we have already seen in the discussion of *The Mill on the Floss*, much more attractive for those with stable homes than for those who live, precariously, on the edge of a socio-economic abyss.[13] It is not purely coincidental, then, that in both *Mrs. Dalloway* and "Street Haunting" the forays into the city streets are, at least ostensibly, motivated by the protagonists' intention of buying non-essential commodities: a pencil in the essay (177), and flowers in the novel. In short, whether male or female, *flânerie* remains an unequivocally class-based aesthetics: a leisured way of consuming the sights and sounds of the city, and thus a kind of pleasure that is not equally available to all.

The importance of class to *Mrs. Dalloway*'s depictions of female *flânerie* is confirmed in a scene in which Elizabeth, Clarissa's daughter, boards an omnibus to travel through London's legal and commercial district, for here we discover just how small the world of the novel's *flâneurs* really is. We learn, early on in Woolf's novel, that for Clarissa the omnibus is a typically middle-class mode of transport (18), which in turn may explain why the narrator places so much emphasis on the unusual nature of Elizabeth's excursion: "Suddenly Elizabeth stepped forward and most competently boarded the omnibus, in front of everybody" (148). There is a palpable note of ridicule here, in the text's emphasis on Elizabeth's competence and daring, and it seems fitting that Elizabeth indulges in her classist daydreams about visiting farmers in their cottages precisely at this moment, for her trip on the omnibus is daring or "reckless" (148) only according to very narrow standards of upper-class respectability. Moreover, like Peter, Elizabeth does not indulge in her little act of rebellion for very long: "She

---

13 In Robin Lippincott's appropriation of Woolf's novel, *Mr. Dalloway* (1999), there is an interesting moment when Richard Dalloway encounters an old man selling violets in the street: "He had always warned Clarissa against giving to the poor – not because he didn't want to help them – he did – but because of his belief that giving did them no good, no good whatsoever. 'They must learn to help themselves,' he had told her. 'And *that* we can help them with – laws and whatnot.' But this was different. For he felt as though he could *be* this man – turned out; no home; alone. Such thoughts had occurred to him during the past year when life as he had known it had felt so very, so terribly threatened; fragile" (33). Though the sense of instability that worries Richard in this passage is not truly economic, it still leads him to look with new dread at the idea of material homelessness.

must go home. She must dress for dinner" (150; see Bowlby 146). On her way back to Bond Street, Elizabeth in fact herself defines the perspective from which her excursion seems adventurous: "[N]o Dalloways came down the Strand daily," and her mother surely "would not like her to be wandering off alone like this" (151–152). The Strand, incidentally, leads away from Westminster, the center of government, to the civil and commercial center of the city, and even in the early nineteenth century, Beau Brummell, a well-known arbiter of fashion, reportedly expressed great mortification at being discovered as far east as that (Roy Porter 99). The area is clearly beyond (as well as below) the socio-geographical circle within which the Dalloways and their likes are wont to move. To style Elizabeth's trip as a great, non-conformist act of resistance would thus mean to judge it from a very limited upper-class perspective – and, conversely, to expand the term resistance to a point where it no longer retains any real political meaning (Loomba 203).

We can say more generally, then, that *Mrs. Dalloway* maps the social limitations of its characters' homes onto the urban geography of London. David Dowling has meticulously traced the itineraries of five central characters in Woolf's novel – Clarissa, Richard, and Elizabeth, as well as Peter Walsh and Septimus Warren Smith – and his maps show that virtually all the action of the novel's present takes place in Westminster. Dowling's itineraries, in fact, cover more or less the same part of London as Franco Moretti's maps of the so-called silver-fork novels, a largely forgotten genre that thrived between 1810 and 1840 and which, according to Moretti, depicted not a city but a particular class: the fashionable part of English society that would never stray as far as London's East End (*Atlas of the European Novel* 79). Moreover, we find that none of the Dalloways even venture as far as Oxford Street, which according to one of Woolf's own essays "is not London's most distinguished thoroughfare," and was rather looked-down upon by the more fashionable people who shop in "secret crannies off Hanover Square, round about Bond Street" ("Oxford Street Tide" 199). And Bond Street is, of course, precisely where the Dalloways live: far from the working-class squalor of the East End tenements, and sheltered from the 'vulgar' middle-class display of Oxford Street, in one of the most affluent areas in the city of London. The physical location of the Dalloways' house, together with their everyday urban itineraries, thus allows us to define with great precision their 'home space' within the city of London – a space that may seem fluid and mobile, but which in fact is rigidly circumscribed by the boundaries of social class.

Modernist Spectacles and Pathologies of Narration

If *Mrs. Dalloway* nevertheless overcomes some of the social limitations of its urban geography, then this is because it incorporates a wide variety of distinct points of views and class perspectives. As Pam Morris points out, in Woolf's novel "figures from the lowest strata of social life appear fleetingly but recurrently at the margins of the narrative, representing an encroaching material otherness at the perimeter of the enclosed nation of the well-to-do" ("Woolf and Realism" 45). Indeed, in *Mrs. Dalloway*'s eleven sections, the narrator grants us temporary access to the thoughts, emotions, and perceptions of almost forty characters.[14] Some of these characters are closely associated with Clarissa: her husband Richard and her daughter Elizabeth, for instance, or old friends of the family like Peter Walsh. Other focalizers, however – such as the shell-shocked war veteran Septimus Warren Smith and his wife Lucrezia – have no direct connection with Clarissa, and some are clearly lower-class (e.g. the Irishwoman Moll Pratt, who sells flowers in the street). To understand the social scope of Woolf's novel we must therefore decide how best to interpret this wide range of perspectives: the relations between the various focalizers, as well as the way in which they are distributed throughout the text.

The first thing we need to note is that, much as is the case with *Moby-Dick* (see chapter one), Woolf's novel initially misleads the reader to expect a story organized around a dominant central character; it looks, in Rick Altman's terms, very much like a single-focus narrative (189). Even before we open the book,

14 While Woolf's novel is not divided into separate chapters, in the edition used here a total of eleven sections are indicated by spaces between paragraphs: section 1 (3–14), section 2 (14–31), section 3 (31–52), section 4 (52–62), section 5 (62–64), section 6 (64–70), section 7 (71–103), section 8 (103–165), section 9 (165–180), section 10 (181–204), and section 11 (204–213). The characters who are, at least briefly, focalized from within are: Clarissa Dalloway (3), Scrope Purvis (4), Miss Pym (13), Septimus Warren Smith (15), Lucrezia Warren Smith (16), Sir John Buckhurst (18), several men standing in the bow window of White's, a gentlemen's club (19), Moll Pratt (20), an anonymous policeman (20), Emily Coates (21), Mr. Bowley (21), Maisie Johnson (28), Carrie Dempster (29), Mr. Bentley (30), a seedy-looking man (30), Lucy, a servant in the Dalloway household (41), Peter Walsh (44), Lady Bradshaw (103), Sir William Bradshaw (104), Hugh Whitbread (104), Lady Bruton (114), Milly Brush (115), Richard Dalloway (115), Elizabeth Dalloway (134), Doris Kilman (135), Mr. Fletcher (146), Mrs. Gorham (146), Mrs. Filmer (165), Charles Morris and his family (175), Mrs. Walker (181), Ellie Henderson (184), Jim Hutton (193), Aunt Helena (196), Sally Seton (198), and Willie Titcomb (206). The page numbers indicate where focalization from within occurs for the first time for that particular character. While for the most part the characters listed above are clearly focalized from within, the cases of Sir John Buckhurst and the anonymous policeman are at least debatable. For more on the notion of 'focalization from within' see Shlomith Rimmon-Kenan (*Narrative Fiction* 75–76).

the novel's title, *Mrs. Dalloway*, cues us to see Clarissa as the central figure, and this expectation seems confirmed by the text's famous opening sentence: "Mrs. Dalloway said she would buy the flowers herself" (3). The novel opens with the eponymous character, whom we then follow on her mundane, but clearly defined narrative quest to buy flowers. The point of view in the opening paragraphs is organized firmly around Clarissa, and she remains the dominant focalizer throughout the novel's first section. It may therefore be due to the – relatively – traditional nature of the novel's opening section that Avrom Fleishman sees *Mrs. Dalloway* as "the fictional autobiography of a single character," with the other figures merely juxtaposed to and surrounding Clarissa (80; see also Baldick 202; Rachman 5).[15]

Indeed, there is a good case to be made that the opening section of *Mrs. Dalloway* constitutes a modification of, but not yet a radical departure from the standard techniques of Victorian narration. Admittedly, the narrative perspective in the text's first section is more markedly subjective than what we are used to from Victorian novels (Pam Morris, *Realism* 14):

> [H]aving lived in Westminster – how many years now? over twenty, – one feels even in the midst of the traffic, or waking at night, Clarissa was positive, a particular hush, or solemnity; an indescribable pause; a suspense (but that might be her heart, affected, they said, by influenza) before Big Ben strikes. There! Out it boomed. First a warning, musical; then the hour, irrevocable. The leaden circles dissolved in the air. Such fools we are, she thought, crossing Victoria Street. For Heaven only knows why one loves it so, how one sees it so, making it up, building it round one, tumbling it, creating it every moment afresh [...]. (4)

In this passage, the 'omniscient' narrator is still the one who speaks, but the narrator's voice threatens to disappear behind the densely poetic texture of Clarissa Dalloway's focalizing consciousness. Nevertheless, the first section of Woolf's novel retains a relatively stable narrative perspective, with flashbacks that grant us insight into Clarissa's past (e.g. 3 and 7–8); with other characters' perspectives occasionally complementing her point of view (Scrope Purvis and Miss Pym; 4 and 13); and with the heroine eventually reaching "Mulberry's the florists," the goal of her quest (13). Though later parts of the novel are more experimental, we should thus not forget that the first section of *Mrs. Dalloway*

15 It is not entirely clear why Fleishman calls the novel "the fictional *auto*biography" of its title character (emphasis added), as the novel is not in fact told in the first person.

constitutes a modification (or perhaps better: intensification) of, but not yet a break with, the conventions of realist fiction.[16]

Intriguingly, to the extent that the first section does modify these conventions, this is linked subliminally to an illness from which Clarissa has only recently recovered. In an essay entitled "On Being Ill" (1926), Woolf contends that illness can have a remarkable effect on a patient's attitude towards the world:

> Directly the bed is called for, or, sunk deep among the pillows in one chair, we raise our feet even an inch above the ground on another, we cease to be soldiers in the army of the upright; we become deserters. They march to battle. We float with the sticks on the stream; helter-skelter with the dead leaves on the lawn, irresponsible and disinterested and able, perhaps for the first time in years, to look round, to look up – to look, for example, at the sky. (104)

In mock-militaristic language ("soldiers in the army of the upright," "deserters," "march to battle"), Woolf describes how, in illness, we are no longer required to put on a brave face, and instead may allow ourselves simply to "float" on the stream of existence – which is not a bad description of the mood in *Mrs. Dalloway*'s first section. There, we learn that Clarissa's heart is likely to have been affected by a recent bout of influenza (4), and in the two moments in the first section when Clarissa is not the focalizing agent, the temporary bearers of narrative perspective note that Woolf's heroine looks old and somewhat frail (4 and 13–14). There is thus a sense that the stream-like narrative flow in the novel's first section, as well as the slight disruptions in point of view, are semi-pathological deviations from the narrative norm; they appear as the lingering symptoms of a feverish state of mind that, as Woolf insists in her essay, has the power to make us see familiar phenomena in a startlingly different light (105). Illness, in short, while in itself undesirable, also leads to defamiliarization, and may thus reveal aspects of the home that seemed intimately known as suddenly strange and little understood.[17]

At the same time, the modifications of narrative technique described so far are mild compared to the sudden fragmentation of perspective that characterizes the novel's second section, which is fittingly introduced in the text by the "vi-

16 See Anna Snaith's argument that Woolf "is not a stream of consciousness writer, since apart from rare, isolated phrases of direct interior monologue, she captures private thought through free indirect discourse" (68–69) – a technique that, as Snaith rightly points out, has been used in novels since the eighteenth century (67).

17 On the frequent link between modernist techniques of narration and crisis, madness, illness, and suicide see Franco Moretti, *Modern Epic* 169–176. (On page 171, Moretti explicitly cites Septimus as an example.)

olent explosion" of a car that backfires at the end of *Mrs. Dalloway*'s opening section, startling both Clarissa and Miss Pym the florist (14). Whereas in the first section Clarissa is clearly the dominant focalizer and organizing center, the second section confronts us with over ten focalizing agents, and Clarissa's point of view now constitutes only one among many. As in *Moby-Dicky*, after having essentially been led to expect a single-focus narrative, we are now thrust into that "state of homelessness" that Rick Altman sees as typical of multiple-focus narration (285), and the relative stability of the novel's opening section is increasingly lost in multiple points of view and a seemingly aimless, meandering storyline.

Indeed, in contrast to section one, which remains at least partially plot-driven (i.e. it tells the story of Clarissa Dalloway leaving her home in order to buy flowers for her party), the second section is organized by a logic of symbolic co-occurrence. The "violent explosion" that startles Clarissa also causes widespread commotion outside the flower shop, among the crowd in Oxford Street, because "a face of the very greatest importance" is briefly seen through one of the windows of the car that backfired: "Was it the Prince of Wales's, the Queen's, the Prime Minister's? Whose face was it? Nobody knew" (15). This entire scene adds little in terms of plot development; it is, at best, a convenient ploy to introduce Septimus Warren Smith, one of the novel's central characters, who just happens to be present (Lee R. Edwards 103). At the same time, however, the scene is charged with symbolic meaning – a meaning that a passage from Raymond Williams's *The Country and the City* can help us unravel:

> It is impossible to read the early descriptions of crowded metropolitan streets – the people as isolated atoms, flowing this way and that; a common stream of separated identities and directions – without seeing, past them, this mode of relationship embodied in the modern car: private, enclosed, an individual vehicle in a pressing and merely aggregated common flow [...]. (296)

The car around which, in *Mrs. Dalloway*, the "common stream of separated identities" is organized is also the symbolic embodiment of a typically urban kind of relationship: co-presence rather than community – a society organized around common spectacles rather than collaborative action.

Four decades after the publication of *Mrs. Dalloway*, Guy Debord suggested, in thesis six of *The Society of the Spectacle* (*La société du spectacle*, 1967), that the spectacles permeating our daily lives are not to be understood as mere ornaments added to the normal course of events; rather, in "all of its particular manifestations – news, propaganda, advertising, entertainment – the spectacle represents the dominant model of life" (8). For Debord, then, the spectacles of modernity are never innocent, but rather point to the power structures at work in society. More particularly, the fact that Debord mentions propaganda and advertising in his analysis is surely significant for an interpretation of *Mrs. Dalloway*; after all, while the car in the second section of Woolf's novel carries a half-recognized passenger who prompts the onlookers to think of "the majesty of England" (i.e. it serves as a means of imperial propaganda; 17), the airplane that suddenly attracts the crowd's attention towards the end of the same section turns out to be part of an elaborate advertising stunt (30–31). Both the car and the airplane in Woolf's novel thus provide the crowd with spectacles that are not mere ornament, but that instead represent the period's dominant political and economic interests: the monarchy as a symbol of government, and the promotion of consumerism in advanced capitalist societies. We can say, therefore, that the slightly feverish, but nevertheless stable narrative perspective that we find in the first section of *Mrs. Dalloway* is shattered, in the second, by the twin spectacles of advertising and propaganda, both of which appear in quintessentially modern symbolic shapes: a motor car and an airplane (22). Urban space thus not only appears as socially stratified in Woolf's novel, but also as commodified and pervaded by governmental strategies of power.

National Virtues and the Memory of War

If the "violent explosion" that marks the transition between sections one and two of *Mrs. Dalloway* is associated on one level with the urban spectacles of imperial and capitalist modernity, we must also consider a further layer of meaning that arises from the text's historical position as a postwar novel. More specifically, we can interpret the differences in narrative perspective between the novel's first two sections as a stylistic expression of the unequal impact of the Great War on two of the novel's main characters: Clarissa Dalloway and Septimus Warren Smith. In the first section of the novel, whenever Clarissa looks back on the war, she emphasizes the fact that the conflict is past:

> The War was over, except for some one like Mrs. Foxcroft at the Embassy last night eating her heart out because that nice boy was killed and now the old Manor House must go to a cousin; or Lady Bexborough who opened a bazaar, they said, with the telegram in her hand, John, her favourite, killed; but it was over; thank Heaven – over. (4–5)

Two aspects about this passage are important. First, there is something rather disturbing about the first half of the sentence, which sounds as if the real tragedy consisted, not in the actual fact of a young man's death, but in how his death affects the Foxcroft family estate; the Foxcrofts no longer have a direct heir, and in consequence their home will have to "go to a cousin." Second, though Clarissa acknowledges, dutifully, that the war is not really over for everyone, she is clearly not keen on giving the matter much thought: "it was over; thank Heaven – over." Revealingly, she later thinks of Lady Bexborough with her "perfectly upright and stoical bearing" as the "woman she admired most" (10). In fact, Clarissa wishes to be "like Lady Bexborough, slow and stately; rather large; interested in politics like a man; with a country house" (11). We may note in passing that once again, in this passage, country-house England serves as the idealized home of the English upper classes. More importantly, it seems that, for Clarissa, the most admirable thing one can do is to maintain, at all times, a stiff upper lip, and to try and carry on much as one did before the War – which is, as we have seen, precisely what happens in the novel's first section, in terms of both narrative structure and point of view: a modification of, but not yet a true break with Victorian realism.

However, whereas the first section shows us Clarissa managing to maintain her composure despite the impact of the War and her recent illness, the sudden bout of fragmentation in *Mrs. Dalloway*'s second section reveals the seriousness of Septimus Warren Smith's post-traumatic stress disorder (PTSD). Anne Whitehead has shown that a "fragmented narrative voice" is a typical feature of trauma fiction in general (84), and we know from Woolf's novel that Septimus suffers from the "deferred effects of shell shock" (201), the term used by contemporaries for PTSD.[18] The suspicion that the second section's fragmented perspective can be related to Septimus's condition is confirmed by the fact that he and his wife Lucrezia are, taken together, by far the section's most dominant focalizing agents. In the edition of the novel used for this chapter, the perspective is organized around either Septimus's or Lucrezia's point of view on seven of section two's seventeen pages (i.e. roughly 40 %). Clarissa, by comparison, who of all the other characters occupies most space in this section, is the focalizer on slightly less than two pages (i.e. not quite 12 %). Moreover, while the section's other characters – including Clarissa – act as focalizers only once, the narrative perspective returns to Septimus and Lucrezia after a substantial interruption (15–18 and 23–28). Both in terms of perspective structure and the fragmented narrative logic of trauma, in other words, there is good reason for us to regard the Warren Smiths as the key figures in the novel's second section.

And yet, this is not to say that the other focalizers in section two are unimportant. Rather, we can read their presence as indicative of a broader social

18 The term *post-traumatic stress disorder* was coined in 1980 (Manguno-Mire and Franklin 353).

vision associated with the Warren Smiths, as opposed to the narrowly enclosed, upper-class Dalloways. We have seen that the Dalloways' world is very precisely delimited, and it is fitting that, in the novel's opening section, the only focalizers apart from Clarissa are a neighbor "who lives next door" (4), and an employee in an expensive flower shop (14). This contrasts sharply with section two, which is associated primarily with Septimus and Lucrezia, and which includes focalizers as diverse as, on the one hand, Sir John Buckhurst and the wealthy group of men standing in the bow window of White's, a gentlemen's club (18 and 19), and, on the other, Moll Pratt, an Irishwoman who sells flowers in the street (20); Maisie Johnson, recently arrived from Edinburgh "to take up a post at her uncle's" (28); and Carrie Dempster, an elderly woman whose husband drinks too much (29). If *Mrs. Dalloway* can at all be said to represent the whole complexity of London society, then this is to a large part due to the novel's second section, for in no other section is the cast of focalizers equally diverse in terms of social class. In fact, the only other section with a comparably inclusive perspective is section eight – a section that is, once again, framed by the Warren Smiths: it opens in their home near the Strand, and it ends with Septimus committing suicide by throwing himself out of the window of their living room (103 and 164–165).

If there is an upper-class bias in *Mrs. Dalloway*, then it is for the most part linked to specific characters and should therefore not be regarded as a structural limitation of the novel or its author. At the same time, we cannot simply dismiss out of hand Jeremy Hawthorn's point that Woolf's novel renders the idiom of its upper-class characters much more successfully than the speech of their lower-class counterparts. For instance, Hawthorn quite rightly insists that a character like Mrs. Dempster, who speaks Cockney, would not normally use a phrase like "it seemed to her better to be [...] a little moderate in one's expectations" (29); the use of "one," in particular, strikes a false note in a passage that is otherwise at pains to mimic Mrs. Dempster's working-class idiom (e.g. "She had had a hard time of it"; see Hawthorn 103). Like all of Woolf's novels, then, *Mrs. Dalloway* is notably more at home in the genteel idiom of the English upper classes than in any 'lowlier' style of speech (Eagleton, *The English Novel* 308 and 320).

Even if one concedes, however, that there is a certain linguistic class-bias in *Mrs. Dalloway*, Hawthorn's concomitant suggestion that the novel as a whole tends to depict members of the lower classes as lacking in individuality, associating them with animality instead, is hardly convincing. Hawthorn's argument hinges on the idea that, in *Mrs. Dalloway*, any statement that appears within parentheses constitutes "some implied narrator-interruption of a character's stream of thoughts” (101). This explains why Hawhthorn interprets a phrase like “The mothers of Pimlico gave suck to their young,” which appears within parentheses in *Mrs. Dalloway* (7), as a narratorial interjection that denies the humanity of lower-class mothers by using the expression *to give suck*, which is usually reserved for animals. However, while Hawthorn is right in claiming that there is a disparaging quality to the statement, we may take issue with his more general claim that all statements in parentheses should be read as narratorial commentary in Woolf’s novel. In the following passage, for instance, in which Clarissa examines the expensive items displayed in a shop window, the statement made in parentheses most likely constitutes an afterthought on Clarissa’s part: “[T]he shopkeepers were fidgeting in their windows with their paste and diamonds, their lovely old sea-green brooches in eighteenth-century settings to tempt Americans (but one must economise, not buy things rashly for Elizabeth) [...]” (5). If, however, this as well as other statements in parentheses cannot automatically be ascribed to the narrator, then Hawthorn’s argument concerning the text’s general association of the lower classes with animality no longer holds true. The passage that refers to mothers ‘giving suck’ to their young, for instance, is not a narratorial interjection but instead associated with marginal presences impinging on Clarissa’s consciousness:

> [A]s for saying, as Peter did, that he [i.e. Hugh Whitbread] had no heart, no brain, nothing but the manners and breeding of an English gentleman, that was only her dear Peter at his worst; and he could be intolerable; [...] but adorable to walk with on a morning like this.
>
> (June had drawn out every leaf on the trees. The mothers of Pimlico gave suck to their young. Messages were passing from the Fleet to the Admiralty. Arlington Street and Piccadilly seemed to chafe the very air in the Park and lift its leaves hotly, brilliantly, on waves of that divine vitality which Clarissa loved. To dance, to ride, she had adored all that.) (7)

It is, at the very least, not absolutely clear whether the class bias of the expression “gave suck” is the narrator’s or Clarissa’s; the narrator’s voice and the focalizing consciousness are notoriously difficult to distinguish in *Mrs. Dalloway*, and interpretative caution is therefore in order (Garvey 60; Snaith 63–64). Quite tellingly, Hawthorn’s only other example for an association of the lower classes with animal-like behavior occurs in a part of the novel where the focalizer is Richard Dalloway (124–128; see Hawthorn 102). Accordingly, while it is difficult to deny the subtle linguistic class bias of *Mrs. Dalloway*’s genteel idiom, we should ascribe the novel’s more blatantly prejudiced statements, not to the narrator or to the text as a whole, but to Richard and Clarissa Dalloway, the text’s focalizers at the two points in question. This, in turn, confirms the observation made earlier that the novel's social vision is far less inclusive in the sections that focus on the Dalloways than in the parts of the novel that revolve around Septimus and his wife.

The fact that the segments centering on Septimus and Lucrezia are also the most socially inclusive is particularly noteworthy because this renders it deeply ironic that several characters in Woolf's novel construe Septimus's behavior as un-English.[19] Even Septimus's wife in fact worries that Septimus's condition is too conspicuous and therefore unseemly:

> [H]er husband, for they had been married four, five years now, jumped, started, and said, "All right!" angrily, as if she [i.e. Lucrezia] had interrupted him.
>
> People must notice; people must see. [...] Suppose they had heard him? She looked at the crowd. Help, help! she wanted to cry out to butchers' boys and women. [...] But failure one conceals. She must take him away into some park. (17)

Lucrezia – herself an outsider because she is an Italian expatriate – tries to hide Septimus's condition from others because she has understood an important characteristic of 'good' English society: "failure one conceals." Later, we learn that Dr. Holmes, the physician whom the Warren Smiths consult, believes that there is "nothing whatever seriously the matter" with Septimus (23); in fact, Dr. Holmes – whose name blends 'Dr. Watson' with 'Sherlock Holmes' and thus evokes an unsavory combination of medical care and criminal judgment (Bradshaw xxxii) – explicitly reminds Septimus of his "duty" as an English husband to pull himself together and "do something instead of lying in bed" (101). Much like Clarissa, Dr. Holmes thus regards stoical composure in the face of adversity as one of life's highest virtues – and a decidedly English one at that. As Alex Zwerdling observes, such "unruffled self-control has everything to do with the ability to retain power," and those who fail to maintain a stiff upper lip quickly become "outsiders in a society dedicated to covering up the stains" (72). Private misery must, at all cost, be concealed, and those who fail to do so are regarded as un-English even if they are in many ways more representative than those who succeed.

It is therefore particularly poignant that Septimus himself at first also subscribes to the view that one must conceal one's emotions, realizing too late that his real problem is precisely an inability to feel. Before the war, Septimus's employer, Mr. Brewer, thought very highly of Septimus's professional abilities, but

---

19 See also Tamar Katz: "*Mrs. Dalloway* analyzes nationalism acutely in the figure of Septimus Smith" (400).

was worried by the fact that the young man "looked weakly" (94). Serving as a soldier in the trenches in France, however, Septimus supposedly "developed manliness," and when his friend Evans was killed in combat, Septimus "congratulated himself upon feeling very little and very reasonably" (94–95). As Lee R. Edwards observes, the lesson that Septimus has learnt is that, in this society, becoming a 'real man' means that one must not feel (105).[20] For this reason, Septimus is at first not alarmed by the "emotional numbing" that is, in fact, a characteristic symptom of post-traumatic stress disorder (Manguno-Mire and Franklin 356). Soon after the armistice, however, Septimus begins to worry about a lasting absence of feeling:

> He looked at people outside; happy they seemed, collecting in the middle of the street, shouting, laughing, squabbling over nothing. But he could not taste, he could not feel. [...] He could reason; he could read, Dante for example, quite easily [...], he could add up his bill; his brain was perfect; it must be the fault of the world then – that he could not feel. (96)

Septimus explicitly suspects here that it is "the fault of the world" that he can no longer feel, and he is evidently not merely deluded in his belief because society does in fact hold the truth to be self-evident that the only proper way for an Englishman to behave is to endure, stoically, the horrors even of total war.

As Karen DeMeester contends, this silencing of emotions also impairs Septimus's ability to engage in therapeutic storytelling, which in turn renders it less likely that he will manage to recover from the effects of shell-shock (662). Bearing this in mind helps us to see that Septimus's disturbing hallucinatory fits are best read as a psychological safety valve for pent-up emotions:

> [H]e, Septimus, was alone, called forth in advance of the mass of men to hear the truth, to learn the meaning, which now at last, after all the toils of civilisation – Greeks, Romans, Shakespeare, Darwin, and now himself – was to be given whole to... "To whom?" he asked aloud. "To the Prime Minister," the voices which rustled above his head replied. The supreme secret must be told to the Cabinet; first that trees are alive; next there is no crime; next love, universal love, he muttered, gasping, trembling, painfully drawing out these profound truths which needed, so deep were they, so difficult, an immense effort to speak out, but the world was entirely changed by them for ever. (74)

20 I have made a similar argument concerning the debilitating effects of an ideal of stoical masculinity in my essay "Between the Wild West and Pastoral Peace" (224).

To a society that values emotional restraint above everything else, Septimus, in his severely traumatized state, responds with rapturous visions of "universal love." Dr. Holmes, however, remains unsympathetic and interprets even Septimus's suicide as an un-English, unmanly sign of weakness: "The coward!" (164). What *Mrs. Dalloway* shows is that a society's demand for emotional control or moderation can itself become excessive: that an unconditional requirement for self-restraint is in fact a form of moral extremism.[21]

History as the Return of the Repressed

Just as it is instructive to examine Septimus's 'failure' to comply with upper-class ideals of stoic composure, it is worth asking why Clarissa herself is unable to maintain her equanimity when confronted with Doris Kilman, the tutor and close friend of her daughter Elizabeth. The intensity of Clarissa's dislike for Miss Kilman is in fact quite startling:

> Miss Kilman would do anything for the Russians, starved herself for the Austrians, but in private inflicted positive torture, so insensitive was she, dressed in a green mackintosh coat. Year in year out she wore that coat; she perspired; she was never in the room five minutes without making you feel her superiority, your inferiority; how poor she was; how rich you were how she lived in a slum without a cushion or a bed or a rug or whatever it might be [...].
>
> It rasped [Clarissa ...], to have stirring about in her this brutal monster! [...] this hatred, which, especially since her illness, had power to make her feel scraped, hurt in her spine [...], and made all pleasure in beauty, in friendship, in being well, in being loved and making her home delightful rock, quiver, and bend as if indeed there were a monster grubbing at the roots, as if the whole panoply of content were nothing but self love! this hatred! (12–13)

The "hatred" Clarissa feels for Doris Kilman endangers, we learn, even her pleasure in "making her home delightful" – and it certainly departs from an ideal of emotional equipoise. The text makes clear, moreover, that Clarissa does not hate Miss Kilman because she objects to the idea of her daughter falling in love with someone of her own sex; rather, Elizabeth's blunder is that she has fallen for a "[h]eavy, ugly, commonplace" woman (137), quite unlike Clarissa herself, who had had the good sense of pining after the fascinating and more socially acceptable Sally Seton. Moreover, when we learn that Clarissa disdains Miss Kilman's piety because of her conviction that "religious ecstasy made people

21 Kazuo Ishiguro's *The Remains of the Day* (1989) presents us with an excellent literary case study of the consequences of 'hyper-English' emotional restraint in the character of the 'perfect' butler Stevens.

callous" (12), we should remember the discussion of George Eliot's *The Mill on the Floss* in chapter two, where the narrator points out that fervent beliefs tend to be deemed unfashionable by those who live in wealthy, comfortable homes (238; bk. 4, ch. 3) and who can therefore afford to retain a properly ironic distance.

The unseemly intensity of Doris Kilman's beliefs is, however, only one reason why Clarissa reacts with such disgust to her daughter's friend. Another, equally important reason is that Doris Kilman is of German descent and a teacher of history, for as such she reminds Clarissa of the very thing she would like to forget: the horrors of the Great War, for which the class to which Clarissa belongs was ultimately responsible. Miss Kilman, we learn early on in the novel, was treated badly during the war, "all her soul rusted with that grievance sticking in it, her dismissal from school during the War" (12). We have already seen that Clarissa is all too keen on emphasizing that the war is a thing of the past, which explains why the presence, or even the mere thought, of Doris Kilman is so unbearable for Clarissa. Moreover, if Maria DiBattista is right in arguing that Clarissa seeks "unhistorical happiness in plunging spontaneously into the present" (40), then Doris Kilman's "really historical mind" (*Mrs. Dalloway* 12) points us toward a fundamental conflict: the clash between, on the one hand, someone who did not suffer directly during the war and who displays an intense love for the present, and, on the other hand, a person who was treated unfairly and whose very presence serves as a reminder of historical injustice.[22]

This is of course not to say that we should see Doris Kilman as a flawless character, for she may indeed, as Alice van Buren Kelley insists (91–92), occasionally use religion merely as a shield, or be too possessive in her love for Elizabeth (see *Mrs. Dalloway* 144: "If she could grasp her, if she could clasp her, if she could make her hers absolutely and forever and then die; that was all she wanted"). The very name Kilman ('kill man'), moreover, hardly helps to paint Elizabeth's friend in a positive light. At the same time, however, we should be wary of situating Doris Kilman "at the negative pole" of the novel's value system (Kelley 92), as this would mean simply to accept Clarissa's problematic judgment. Instead, we need to recognize that the extent of Clarissa's disgust is entirely disproportionate to any real offence on Miss Kilman's part – a circumstance to which Clarissa readily admits: "[I]t was not her one hated but the idea of her, which undoubtedly had gathered into itself a great deal that was not Miss

22 Doris Kilman thus functions as a Jungian shadow that Clarissa notably fails to integrate into her sense of self.

Kilman" (12–13).[23] Characteristically, however, Clarissa does not accept any responsibility on her part; it is simply that "one" – not she herself – hates Miss Kilman, because of an "idea" that has, almost magically, "gathered into itself a great deal" that, in fact, has little to do with the real Miss Kilman. The text's very language – the impersonal pronoun, the passive voice – thus testifies to the extent to which Clarissa desires to repress her own agency and responsibility for injustice.

This evasion of responsibility is most clearly in evidence when Clarissa thinks of her husband's work in a government committee concerned with the Armenians, a people Clarissa cannot even distinguish from the Albanians:

> [Richard] was already halfway to the House of Commons, to his Armenians, his Albanians, having settled her on the sofa, looking at his roses. And people would say, "Clarissa Dalloway is spoilt." She cared much more for her roses than for the Armenians. Hunted out of existence, maimed, frozen, the victims of cruelty and injustice (she had heard Richard say so over and over again) – no, she could feel nothing for the Albanians, or was it the Armenians? but she loved her roses (didn't that help the Armenians?) – the only flowers she could bear to see cut. (131–132)

Clarissa's admission that she cares more about flowers and her parties than about the Armenians is problematic irrespective of historical context. However, if we bear in mind the extent of genocidal violence committed against the Armenians by the Ottoman military forces during World War I, then Clarissa's indifference surely is nothing short of appalling:

> We don't know the exact number of Armenians killed in the years following 1915 – or even the number living in Turkey. 1.2–1.4 million killed might be a reasonable guess for 1915–16. [... O]nly about 10 percent of the Armenians living in Turkey in 1914 remained in the country in 1922 – the most successful murderous cleansing achieved in the 20th century. (Mann 140)

Clarissa even muddles "Armenians and Turks" (134), and David Bradshaw rightly points out that doing so in the early 1920s "is only a little less bizarre than muddling Jews and Nazis would be in the latter half of the following decade" (xx).

Nevertheless, Lee R. Edwards attempts to defend Clarissa's 'apolitical' stance, readily conceding that Clarissa's roses may not help the Armenians much, but also wondering whether the usual schemes of politics – petitions, committees,

---

23 On how Doris Kilman is treated by Clarissa Dalloway, see, for example, Pam Morris: "Part of the misery she suffers is at the hands of Clarissa Dalloway. [... She] becomes a figment of her hatred rather than a real person" (65).

charitable donations – had done much good, either (110–111). And indeed it is true that British policies during and after the war remained largely ineffective, despite initial promises to hold those who committed the massacres responsible:

> Power politics intruded [...] and Britain found itself forced – by circumstances and by preference – to back away from its stated commitments to the Armenians. This found its clearest expression in the half-hearted attempts by the British authorities to bring arrested Young Turk leaders before a military or criminal tribunal after the war; most of those in British custody were ultimately released, with only a few trials of minor figures having taken place (resulting in few convictions). (Totten and Bartrop 20)

Given the British government's failure to keep its promises to the Armenian people, one could hardly blame Clarissa for being angered, perhaps even disillusioned. However, for her to opt for indifference – to care more about her roses and do nothing at all – is hardly the appropriate response, especially for someone so closely associated to the very governing class that has failed to keep its promises to the Armenians in the first place. This, however, is precisely what Clarissa prefers to do: to forget the war, and in particular to repress the fact that she is guilty by association. Accordingly, while we began the discussion of Woolf's novel with an emphasis on the *spatial* dimensions home (e.g. country-house Arcadias, or the social geography of imperial London), we must now turn to the problem of history, and thus the temporality of belonging.

Time on the Clock vs. Time in the Mind

At first sight, it seems plausible to relate a recurring hostility against clocks in *Mrs. Dalloway* to Clarissa's desire to repress historical responsibility. However, as Randall Stevenson has shown, such hostility against mechanical timepieces occurs frequently in modernist fiction in general, and was to some extent shared by contemporary philosophers like Henri Bergson, who believed that time exists as duration within the self: a seamless continuum of conscious states, rather than a sequence of mechanically divisible and measurable items (Stevenson, *Modernist Fiction* 105). There is, in the words of the narrator in Woolf's *Orlando*, a "discrepancy between time on the clock and time in the mind" (95), and precisely this discrepancy is highlighted in *Mrs. Dalloway* through one of its leitmotifs: the sound of a bell tolling the hour, penetrating even into the private space of the home and interrupting a character's introspective mood (e.g. 103, 139–140 and 204).[24]

---

24 The centrality of time is also evident in Woolf's working title for *Mrs. Dalloway*, "The Hours" (Jo-Ann Wallace 18; York 52).

According to Stevenson, there are historically specific reasons why Woolf and her contemporaries were so concerned with mechanical time and its impact on people's everyday lives. For one thing, Stevenson argues, the spread of the railways in the mid-nineteenth century had made it necessary to standardize time throughout Britain, and thus contributed to an increasingly strict regime of time-keeping. Moreover, the newly regulated working environment of the industrial factories ensured that standardized time became an everyday reality for millions of laborers (e.g. through the ritual of 'clocking in' and 'clocking out'; *Modernist Fiction* 113–114). The complexity of military action during the Great War, finally, depended on exact synchronization and thus contributed to the spread of wristwatches (116). For all these reasons, Stevenson suggests, mechanical timepieces not only became an increasingly prominent feature in people's lives; they also came to symbolize a growing mechanization of human existence, with individuals reduced to wheels and cogs in a soulless military-industrial machine.

And yet, while Stevenson's argument explains the general preoccupation with clocks in modernist fiction, it is important to note that in *Mrs. Dalloway*, characters' attitudes towards timepieces vary depending on their particular situation and social status. We can see this in a passage from Woolf's novel that Stevenson discusses in the course of his argument:

> Shredding and slicing, dividing and subdividing, the clocks of Harley Street nibbled at the June day, counselled submission, upheld authority, and pointed out in chorus the supreme advantages of a sense of proportion, until the mound of time was so far diminished that a commercial clock, suspended above a shop in Oxford Street, announced, genially and fraternally, as if it were a pleasure to Messrs. Rigby and Lowndes to give the information gratis, that it was half-past one. (*Mrs. Dalloway* 112; see Stevenson, *Modernist Fiction* 134)

Stevenson is surely right in claiming that the hostility directed in this passage at the clocks of Harley Street is related to a critique of the status quo ("counseled submission, upheld authority"). However, what Stevenson does not discuss is that the value judgments at this point in Woolf's novel are, in all likelihood, the narrator's and Lucrezia Warren Smith's, whereas other characters exhibit entirely different attitudes towards mechanical timepieces.[25] For instance, in the paragraph that immediately follows the passage quoted above, Hugh Whitbread – a pinnacle of respectability, and viewed by both Peter Walsh and Sally Seton as the embodiment of mindless conformism (7 and 79–80) – feels “gratitude” rather than hostility towards the clocks in Harley Street (112). Or, to give a second example, immediately after her husband’s suicide, even Lucrezia, hearing a clock striking the hour, thinks “how sensible the sound was; compared with all this thumping and whispering” (164). In moments of great emotional turmoil, an otherwise oppressive order may suddenly seem “sensible” and reassuring. Without denying the general validity of Stevenson’s observations, we nevertheless need to examine more closely when and why, precisely, Woolf’s characters react to timepieces in the way they do.[26]

If we pay attention to the details of Woolf’s text, we find that, for Clarissa, clocks are problematic not as symbols of an oppressive social order, but for two rather different reasons: on the one hand they remind her of human mortality, and on the other they threaten to thwart her efforts to repress the reality of historical change. The former idea is made explicit early on:

> [Clarissa] feared time itself, and read on Lady Bruton’s face, as if it had been a dial cut in impassive stone, the dwindling of life; how year by year her share was sliced; how little the margin that remained was capable any longer of stretching, of absorbing, as in the youthful years, the colours, salts, tones of existence, so that she filled the room she entered [...]. (32–33)

Lady Bruton’s face here becomes the dial of a clock that measures the (life-)time Clarissa has left. Of course, the idea that clocks are mementoes of human mortality is far from new and has long been central to the *carpe diem* theme (Stevenson 113). Yet for Clarissa, mechanical timepieces also symbolize more than

---

25 In the paragraph that precedes the excerpt quoted above, Lucrezia Warren Smith is the focalizing agent, and it is at least plausible that she continues to be the focalizing agent (as there is no explicit indication of a change in perspective). Moreover, the language used in the excerpt echoes a passage that occurs a few pages earlier in Woolf’s novel, where the point of view at first seems to be associated exclusively with the omniscient narrator. The phrase “Rezia Warren Smith devined it,” however, which occurs in that passage, suggests that the narratorial perspective (including the narrator’s value judgments) is, if not identical with, then at least similar to Lucrezia’s; the point of view is both the narrator’s and Lucrezia’s. Given the parallels between that earlier passage and the excerpt quoted above, I would argue for a similar combination of narratorial and character focalization in the second passage.

26 See Paul K. Saint-Amour, who notes that “[s]ometimes clock time tyrannizes in *Mrs. Dalloway*,” but who also suggests that “oftener the striking of a clock is the occasion for linking or shuttling among characters” (89).

the general principle of mortality, as we discover when the sound of a bell tolling the hour immediately makes her think of Doris Kilman:

> The sound of Big Ben flooded Clarissa's drawing-room, where she sat, ever so annoyed, at her writing-table; worried; annoyed. It was perfectly true that she had not asked Ellie Henderson to her party; but she had done it on purpose. [... W]hy should she invite all the dull women in London to her parties? Why should Mrs. Marsham interfere? And there was Elizabeth closeted all this time with Doris Kilman. Anything more nauseating she could not conceive. Prayer at this hour with that woman. And the sound of the bell flooded the room with its melancholy wave [...]. (128–129)

Here, the intrusion of time into the (supposedly inviolate) privacy of the home initially leads Clarissa to think of a dull acquaintance who would spoil her upcoming party – but her thoughts are then mysteriously propelled forward to her daughter's "nauseating" friendship with Miss Kilman, the history teacher with German roots. The two passages thus illustrate Clarissa's concerns with time: a 'universal' fear of mortality, and a very personal dislike of Doris Kilman. Both these impulses express a desire on Clarissa's part to stop time and halt the progress of history. Therefore, if at first sight Clarissa's dislike of clocks may seem similar to Lucrezia's, on closer inspection we find that the reasons for their hostility are fundamentally different. Whereas Clarissa fears the idea of history and mutability itself, Lucrezia dislikes clocks as symbols of a particular socio-historical order and thus desires change (except in moments of existential crisis – e.g. after her husband's suicide – when even Lucrezia appreciates the sense of order and predictability that clocks convey).

Everyday Myths

It is in the same context that we have to see the use of mythical elements in *Mrs. Dalloway*, for myth should not only be conceived as a departure from the "everyday time" that Mikhail Bakhtin sees as characteristic of the novel ("Forms of Time and the Chronotope in the Novel" 128; see Walder 9); it also constitutes an attempt to empty the past of its historical dimension. According to Franco Moretti, rewriting an event in mythical form means "freeing it from the profane world of causes and effects, and projecting into it the symbolic richness of the archetype" (*Modern Epic* 248). And perhaps the most effective way of abandoning the logic of cause and effect is to adapt myth's non-linear conception of time, which breaks down the distinction between past and present (Tobin 266). Because of this different conception of time, Roland Barthes suggests, mythical objects seem to "come from eternity"; they no longer appear in a linear, causal sequence – as produced or chosen – and in consequence "history evaporates," together with any notion of human responsibility, since no one can be responsible for a state of affairs that is eternal and unchangeable (151). In short, then, myth is a kind of discourse that purports to discover, underneath the mundane historical surface of everyday life, a deeper, unchanging, eternal reality.

In Woolf's novel, a concern with this shift from surface to depth is intimated continuously through the frequent use of water imagery.[27] Such imagery is omnipresent, for instance, in the opening paragraphs of *Mrs. Dalloway*, in which Clarissa plunges into a London morning in June 1923 just as she had "plunged at Bourton into the open air," which for her felt "like the flap of a wave" (3); we learn that she loves the city's "waves of divine vitality" (7), and the beauty of flowers is to Clarissa like "a wave which she let flow over her and surmount" the hatred she feels for Miss Kilman, that stern woman with her unduly historical mind (14). Similarly Septimus, looking out of the window of the Warren Smith's living room, notices how the "trees dragged their leaves like nets through the depths of the air; the sound of water was in the room" (153). In both cases, the narrator's language associates everyday occurrences with images of watery depths and blissful submergence, and perhaps the pervasive presence of aquatic metaphors in *Mrs. Dalloway* has contributed to critics' tendency to attribute a stream-like quality to Woolf's prose style (e.g. Love 71; Nalbantian 84; Naremore 91; Judith Ryan 191). At any rate, the recurrence of water imagery in the novel suggests a continual tension between mythical depths and the flow of everyday reality.[28]

The novel's most celebrated attempt to explore the mythical substratum of everyday life occurs in a scene in which an old beggar-woman sings a song in Regent's Park. The focalizer at this point in the text is Peter (Booker, *Techniques of Subversion* 174), whose train of thought is interrupted by the sound of the old woman's song, which "bubbled up" and "streamed away in rivulets over the pavement" – note, once again, the use of aquatic metaphors. Peter imagines the woman to have been singing "through all ages": "Still remembering how once in some primeval May she had walked with her lover, this rusty pump, this battered old woman with one hand exposed for coppers, the other clutching her

27 See Juan Eduardo Cilot, who insists that water alludes to the "connexion between the superficial and the profound" (175); see also Sánchez-Vizcaíno for the significance of water imagery in Woolf, William James, Henri Bergson, and Sigmund Freud. Many critics have, of course, noted Woolf's use of water imagery – e.g. Janine MacLeod (55) or Roger Poole (266).

28 It might, incidentally, be interesting to pursue the theoretical link between this definition of myth and Fredric Jameson's characterization of postmodernism as a schizophrenic "breakdown of temporality" that results in the experience of an isolated present of "heightened intensity" (*Postmodernism* 27).

side, would still be there in ten million years" (89–90). There are two reasons why the phrase "rusty pump" is important here. For one thing, it shows again that, when a lower-class character is implicitly dehumanized in Woolf's novel (i.e. the woman is not regarded as human, but merely as a rusty, mechanical thing), the perspective is invariably that of a member of the Dalloway circle. For another, a pump is an instrument designed to tap sources that lie buried deep beneath the ground, just like the life-giving, mythical meaning that supposedly lurks somewhere beneath the surface of everyday reality.

For Peter, a poor beggar-woman singing a song thus becomes an awe-inspiring mythical presence related to the archetypes of the eternal feminine and the earth-mother (e.g. Fleishman 84; Viola 244; Wyatt 443) – a timeless being who already existed "in some primeval May," and who "would still be there in ten million years":

> But the passage of ages had blurred the clarity of that ancient May day; [...] and she no longer saw, when she implored him (as she did now quite clearly) [...] black whiskers or sunburnt face but only a looming shape, a shadow shape, to which, with the bird-like freshness of the very aged she still twittered "give me your hand and let me press it gently" (Peter Walsh couldn't help giving the poor creature a coin as he stepped into his taxi) [...]; and her fist clutched at her side, and she smiled, pocketing her shilling, and all peering inquisitive eyes seemed blotted out, and the passing generations – the pavement was crowded with bustling middle-class people – vanished [...]. (90)

History – "the passing generations," the "bustling middle-class people" – disappears in this mythopoetic vision, and there remains only an ancient female lover with her eternal song. Crucially, the rhapsodic language of myth threatens to distract us from the 'superficial' sequence of events: Peter, when stepping into a taxi, is importuned by an old beggar-woman to whom he gives a shilling (though, it seems, rather unwillingly: he "couldn't help giving"). At the same time, if there is an evasion of reality in this scene, then it is either Peter's or the narrator's, but not, as Michael Whitworth rightly insists, the novel's as a whole (156), for the mythicizing sequence is immediately followed by Lucrezia Warren Smith's correctively prosaic perception of the same beggar-woman: "Oh poor old wretch!" (90). Whereas, in short, the mythopoetic vision of the privileged *flâneur* threatens to dazzle us with symbolic richness, the perspective of a beleaguered middle-class wife with a foreign background returns us to the sparse, historical prose of everyday life.

It is thus no coincidence that, in *Mrs. Dalloway*, the 'visionary' characters who sense a mythical unity underlying everyday existence – Clarissa, Peter, and

Septimus – are also, albeit in different ways, cut off from ordinary personal relationships. James Naremore, for instance, points to Peter's dream vision of himself as a "solitary traveler" as evidence of his sense of isolation (99; see *Mrs. Dalloway* 62–64).[29] Naremore also highlights Clarissa's tendency to retreat from people into her upper room and, most emphatically, to Septimus's post-traumatic estrangement from his wife and the world (110). Each of these three characters experiences moments of intense and isolated subjectivity during which they believe they have discovered a mysterious, transcendent cosmic unity. As Raymond Williams notes:

> This is the 'collective consciousness' of the myth, the archetype: the 'collective unconscious' of Jung. In and through the intense subjectivities a metaphysical or psychological 'community' is assumed, and characteristically, if only in abstract structures, it is universal; the middle terms of actual societies are excluded as ephemeral, superficial, or at best contingent and secondary. Thus a loss of social recognition is in a way made into a virtue: as a condition of understanding and insight. (246)

These characters' union with a "metaphysical or psychological 'community'" flows, as Margaret Blanchard astutely observes, from vision rather than from action; it consists in a solitary way of seeing the world, not in a collective attempt to interact with and change it – and thus, like *flânerie*, ultimately constitutes a luxury that depends on the socio-historical circumstances of the individual in question: "One can afford to conjure up a better world without trying to actualize it only if the world one lives in is tolerable as it is" (Blanchard 305). In the light of these observations, it becomes crucial to note that, of the novel's three 'visionary' characters, only Peter and Clarissa survive, whereas the more beleaguered and less privileged Septimus is unable to re-establish a sense of home in the world and therefore eventually takes his own life.

Misreading the Other

More generally, a key feature of Woolf's novel is that it continually emphasizes the parallels between, on the one hand, the Warren Smiths, and, on the other, the Dalloways and their circle – but only simultaneously to highlight the crucial differences between them. To neglect these differences would mean to misread the story of Septimus and Lucrezia much as it is misread by Peter Walsh early on in Woolf's novel. In a scene set in Regent's Park, Peter passes Septimus and Lucrezia, and while he acknowledges that he does not know enough about the two to interpret their behavior adequately, he nevertheless supposes that they

29 For an argument similar to Naremore's, see Carlson (57).

are merely "lovers squabbling" (77) – an assessment that gravely underestimates the depth of the Warren Smiths' personal crisis. The sense that Peter misreads events connected to the Warren Smiths is confirmed later, after Septimus has killed himself. Lucrezia's reaction to her husband's suicide is, understandably, a mixture between shock and resignation, and looking back on their married life she movingly concludes: "Of her memories, most were happy" (165). This mood of loving sadness at the end of the novel's eighth section is disrupted brutally by the opening sentences of section nine, in which Peter hears the sound of an ambulance – in all likelihood the very ambulance that is on its way to the Warren Smiths – and thinks: "One of the triumphs of civilization" (165). A moment of deep sadness for Lucrezia is thus, for Peter, comforting, even uplifting.

We must therefore keep the possibility of misinterpretation in mind when we proceed to Clarissa's interpretation of Septimus's suicide towards the end of Woolf's novel. When the psychiatrist Sir William Bradshaw mentions Septimus's suicide at her party, Clarissa's first reaction is one of anger and frustration: "What business had the Bradshaws to talk of death at her party?" (201). Irritated perhaps because the intrusion of death into her home reminds her of her general fear of mortality, Clarissa briefly retires to her room. There, Clarissa's mood soon changes, and initially she interprets Septimus's suicide as an indirect comment on her own ethical failures:

> They (all day she had been thinking of Bourton, of Peter, of Sally), they would grow old. A thing there was that mattered; a thing, wreathed about with chatter, defaced, obscured in her own life, let drop every day in corruption, lies, chatter. This he [i.e. Septimus] had preserved. Death was defiance. (202)

Clarissa admits, here, not only to a sort of emptiness in her life – her self appears "wreathed about with chatter" – but even to a fundamental sense of dishonesty ("corruption, lies"). By contrast, she believes, Septimus's suicide has allowed him to save his innermost self from the corruption that comes from living in society:

> Somehow it was her disaster – her disgrace. It was her punishment to see sink and disappear here a man, there a woman, in this profound darkness, and she forced to stand here in her evening dress. She had schemed; she had pilfered. She was never wholly admirable. She had wanted success. (203)

Given Clarissa's unflinching criticism of herself, it would be tempting to think that being confronted with Septimus's suicide constitutes a truly life-changing epiphany for her: a moment of recognition concerning the extent to which the suicide of a shell-shocked war veteran reflects on her own life (including her desire for "success," and the ethical price she has been willing to pay for it).

However, Clarissa ultimately shies away from her insight and characteristically reinterprets Septimus’s death in entirely apolitical terms.[30] The same, moreover, is true for at least one literary critic, who argues that Septimus’s case should not be regarded in its own right at all, but instead as merely enhancing that of Clarissa in order “to bring to the surface something buried deep in her own life” (Rachman 5). In this view, the story of the shell-shocked war veteran Septimus Warren Smith is not to be read in political terms, but merely as a means of individual self-discovery for Clarissa.[31] However, as John G. Hessler points out, the society that Clarissa has assembled at her party is “the same society that sent Septimus Warren Smith (and many others like him) to the trenches” (135), and we must bear this in mind when we read Clarissa’s final assessment of Septimus’s suicide:

> The young man had killed himself; but she did not pity him; with the clock striking the hour, one, two, three, she did not pity him, with all this going on. [...] She must go back to them. But what an extraordinary night! She felt somehow very like him – the young man who had killed himself. She felt glad that he had done it; thrown it away. The clock was striking. The leaden circles dissolved in the air. He made her feel the beauty; made her feel the fun. But she must go back. She must assemble. She must find Sally and Peter. (204)

While at first Clarissa had read Septimus’s suicide as highlighting her own failures, she ultimately sees his death as little more than an appeal for her to seize the day (he “made her feel the fun”); she does “not pity him,” and even feels “glad that he had done it.” In sharp contrast, Septimus himself had felt little joy when he killed himself, as Deborah Gut reminds us: “Instead, there is the terror of the hunted beast” (“Self-Evasion” 19). Septimus has not preserved his innermost self, as Clarissa would like to believe; rather, he has obliterated his entire self because he could not find a way to restore it from its fragmented, shell-shocked condition. Clarissa’s attempt to interpret a shell-shocked young man’s suicide as an uplifting spiritual triumph is chillingly inappropriate, as well as conveniently compatible with her political complacency.

---

30 This argument would be one piece of evidence in support of Dominic Head’s impressively broad thesis that “most of the accepted modernist ‘epiphanies’ are problematic” (21).

31 Margaret Blanchard suggests that Septimus’s suicide cannot be seen as a political gesture (302), and she is of course right in the sense that Septimus is unlikely to have intended it as such. This does not mean, however, that there is no political significance to his action, for – as is generally the case when it comes to interpretation – intentions do not determine entirely the meaning of the interpreted object.

The argument that Clarissa misreads Septimus's death is supported by another of *Mrs. Dalloway*'s leitmotifs: a quotation from Shakespeare's *Cymbeline* that highlights the differences, rather than the similarities, between Clarissa and Septimus. Early in the novel, Clarissa sees an open book in a shop window and there discovers the following lines: "Fear no more the heat o' the sun / Nor the furious winter's rages" (10). These are the opening lines of a funeral dirge from *Cymbeline*, sung by two male characters:

> ***Guiderius***. Fear no more the heat o'th'sun
> Nor the furious winter's rages;
> Thou thy worldly task hast done,
> Home art gone and ta'en thy wages.
> Golden lads and girls all must,
> As chimney-sweepers, come to dust.
> ***Arviragus***. Fear no more the frown o'th'great;
> Thou art past the tyrant's stroke;
> Care no more to clothe and eat;
> To thee the reed is as the oak.
> The sceptre, learning, physic, must
> All follow this and come to dust. (84; IV.ii.258–269)

One may note in passing that this dirge evokes the age-old Judeo-Christian topos of death as a return to God as man's original, true home, and that it also refers to the threat posed by "the tyrant's stroke" (a theme which, arguably, resonates more strongly with Septimus's rather than with Clarissa's story). More importantly, we need to bear in mind that the dirge in Shakespeare's play is sung for two sharply distinct characters: for Imogen, King Cymbeline's daughter who, much like Clarissa, remains virgin-like even after her marriage (*Mrs. Dalloway* 34: "she [i.e. Clarissa] could not dispel a virginity preserved through childbirth"; see King 103); and for Cloten, son of the king's second wife, a rather self-important and obtuse villain who was in fact killed by Guiderius, one of the two characters who sing the dirge. Hermione Lee thus overestimates the extent to which the Shakespearean intertext suggests a fundamental similarity between Septimus and Clarissa (31). What ought to be emphasized instead is that, for the audience of Shakespeare's play, the scene is ripe with irony, since the dirge aligns the fate of a lowly villain, killed by one of the singers, with that of a regal woman who – unbeknownst to the singers, but not the audience – is not even dead (i.e. Imogen has drunk a potion that induces a sleep which merely resembles death). The Shakespearean text thus presents us with two widely differing characters: a male figure who dies a violent death, and a female figure who may appear lifeless, but who in fact remains entirely unharmed and will be miraculously resurrected.

Given these differences, it is worth examining more closely at which points in *Mrs. Dalloway* Clarissa recalls the lines from *Cymbeline* that she finds in a book early on in the novel. If we do so, it becomes apparent that they serve mainly to provide her with a sense of consolation in moments of comparatively mild distress. For instance, the reference to *Cymbeline* is repeated for the first time when Clarissa learns that Lady Bruton has failed to invite her to a lunch party – an event that constitutes a "shock" in the eyes of Clarissa (32). Clarissa remembers the opening lines of the dirge again later, when she is mending a dress in the quiet of her room, "calm, content," and secluded from the world's troubles in her comfortable home: "Fear no more, says the heart, committing its burden to some sea, which sighs collectively for all sorrows, and renews, begins, collects, lets fall" (43). Here too, thinking of Shakespeare leads to reconciliation, and typically this sense of reconciliation is expressed in aquatic metaphors that create a mythical mood of rebirth and renewal. The third and last time Clarissa remembers the lines is, as we have seen, when she abandons her thoughts about Septimus's suicide and decides to go back to her party (204). In each of these scenes, then, the Shakespearean text has a consolatory function for Clarissa, though at the same time it is clear that she is not in fact suffering a great deal; her 'wounds' are, if not entirely illusory, then clearly not life-threatening.

This contrasts sharply with the case of Septimus, whose psychic wounds prove too deep for literary consolation to be effective. Before the war, Septimus used to admire Shakespeare and what he stood for; indeed, according to the narrator, Septimus "went to France to save an England which consisted almost entirely of Shakespeare's plays and Miss Isabel Pole," whose public lectures on Shakespeare Septimus had admired greatly (94). After the war, however, Septimus remains, for a long time, unable to derive any joy from Shakespeare:

> That boy's business of the intoxication of language [...] had shrivelled utterly. How Shakespeare loathed humanity – the putting on of clothes, the getting of children, the sordidity of the mouth and the belly! This was now revealed to Septimus; the message hidden in the beauty of words. The secret signal which one generation passes, under disguise, to the next is loathing, hatred, despair. Dante the same. Aeschylus (translated) the same. (97)

The very cultural artifacts that, for Septimus, used to express the highest human values now speak to him only of the deepest despair, and Julia Briggs rightly points out that, in part, Shakespeare has become tainted for Septimus because of the way he was used as a national icon in war-time propaganda (14; see also Gordon Williams 243).

Nevertheless, when Septimus later thinks of the lines from *Cymbeline* – “Fear no more the heat o’ th’ sun” – he seems to regain a sense of joy in the beauty of the bard’s words; he is lying on his sofa, resting and watching the play of light on the wall-paper in the sitting-room, and for a brief moment “not afraid” (153); despite everything, Septimus suddenly believes in recovery: “He would not go mad” (155). For once, Septimus proceeds from vision to action: He joins Lucrezia, who sits at the table and is working on a hat, and while they are employed in common labor Septimus even makes a few jokes, leading Lucrezia to exclaim that they “were perfectly happy now” (160; see Hawthorn 95). However, recovery lasts only for the briefest of moments, for when Dr. Holmes suddenly interrupts the scene, Septimus panics and throws himself out of the living-room window (163–164). While, in short, a few lines from Shakespeare may help Clarissa to reestablish a sense of home, beautiful words alone are not enough for Septimus to recover – which, incidentally, is a sobering reminder that the power of literature to make us feel at home in the world may not be as great as literary critics, in particular, would perhaps like to believe.

The Home of Civilization: Shakespeare, Britain, and the Empire

In addition to putting in relief the many contrasts between Clarissa and Septimus, the Shakespearean intertext of Woolf’s novel allows us to address one final issue that is crucial to *Mrs. Dalloway*’s exploration of home: imperial conquest and colonial domination.[32] *Cymbeline* is, among other things, a play about a war between a subject people – the Britons – and the Roman Empire, written at a time when the English were actively colonizing Scotland and Ireland, and beginning to venture further abroad (Innes 16; Floyd-Wilson 102). This, in turn, renders it significant that the other two Shakespearean texts referred to in *Mrs. Dalloway* are *Othello* (37–38 and 202) and *Antony and Cleopatra* (93 and 100): two other plays that are clearly related to questions of ethnic difference, imperial power, and colonization.[33]

---

32 For a general overview of the importance of anti-imperialism in Woolf’s novels, see Helen Carr’s article on “Virginia Woolf, Empire and Race,” as well as the chapters on Woolf in Rebecca Walcowitz’s *Cosmopolitan Style: Modernism beyond the Nation* (2006) and Paul Stasi’s *Modernism, Imperialism, and the Historical Sense* (2012).

33 Woolf’s novel also refers to Shakespeare’s sonnets, which Richard Dalloway dislikes because reading the sonnets “was like listening at keyholes” (82). In contrast to the plays, then, which relate to the novel’s concern with ethnicity and empire, the sonnets are related to the text’s examination of gender and ‘deviant’ sexuality.

In addition to noting the imperial implications of Shakespearean texts in *Mrs. Dalloway*, we need to consider Peter Walsh’s position as an agent of colonialism. Focusing on Peter’s role in the opening paragraphs of *Mrs. Dalloway*, for instance, we find that these passages not only revolve around an uneasy opposition between a ‘rural’ past and an urban present; rather, the novel’s opening also suggests that colonialism is omnipresent even at home. We have already seen that Clarissa is immediately reminded of her youth at Bourton when, at the beginning of the novel, she steps out on Bond Street to buy flowers for her party in the evening. Significantly, her reminiscences end with the image of her old friend Peter, a man “from a respectable Anglo-Indian family which for at least three generations had administered the affairs of a continent” (60), and whom Clarissa expects to “be back from India” one of these days (3). Clarissa’s thoughts thus return to present-day London from recollections of a country-house past via a colonialist ‘detour’: a man returning from India, that ‘jewel in the imperial crown’ which was so central to Britain’s geopolitical strategy of domination (e.g. Hobsbawm, *Age of Empire* 68–69).[34]

The opening of Woolf’s novel thus implicitly confirms Edward Said’s claim that, partly because of colonialism and its effects, the national home always already includes the foreign, colonial Other (*Culture and Imperialism* xxv). In an analysis of Jane Austen’s *Mansfield Park*, Said focuses specifically on the English country house as a site that may appear isolated from the wider world, but which in fact depends for its existence on “overseas sustenance” (89). Franco Moretti has questioned Said’s idea that the colonies were, in actual fact, economically indispensable for the English ruling classes (*Atlas of the European Novel* 24–27). However, as Ian Baucom points out, Said focuses not only on the notion of economic interdependence between empire and ‘motherland,’ but also “relates the ordered moral economy which the country house represents to the apt administration of colonial property” (166). Similarly, Susan Strehle insists that idealizations of Empire use a particular kind of home for their symbolic representation of national values (21), with the ideology of ‘true Englishness’ depending on the image of the very country-house Arcadias we have already dis-

34 This is not to deny the complexity of Peter’s character, whom, as Elizabeth Clea Lamont rightly insists, one should not reduce to a “colonialist power-monger” (174). It is merely to highlight his thematic function as the first palpably colonial(ist) presence in Woolf’s novel.

cussed, and whose ordered stability is envisioned not only as a remedy for the city's social ills, but also as a cure for the 'barbarism' of the colonies.[35]

Later, *Mrs. Dalloway* in fact makes explicit this link between a supposedly rational order at home – what the narrator calls "Proportion" – and Britain's ongoing imperial project. In section eight of Woolf's novel, the narrator introduces Sir William Bradshaw, a renowned London psychiatrist, as the most fervent believer in the idea of Proportion:

> Worshipping proportion, Sir William not only prospered himself but made England prosper, secluded her lunatics, forbade childbirth, penalised despair, made it impossible for the unfit to propagate their views until they, too, shared his sense of proportion – his, if they were men, Lady Bradshaw's if they were women (she embroidered, knitted, spent four nights out of seven at home with her son) [...].
>
> But Proportion has a sister, less smiling, more formidable, a Goddess even now engaged – in the heat and sands of India, the mud and swamp of Africa, the purlieus of London, wherever in short the climate or the devil tempts men to fall from the true belief which is her own – is even now engaged in dashing down shrines, smashing idols, and setting up in their place her own stern countenance. Conversion is her name and she feasts on the wills of the weakly, loving to impress, to impose, adoring her own features stamped on the face of the populace. (109)

Not only do Sir and Lady Bradshaw adhere strictly to a high-bourgeois model of separate spheres that, for women, revolves mainly around household duties ("she embroidered, knitted, spent four nights out of seven at home with her son"); the establishment of a supposedly disinterested and rational order turns out to be intimately related to a 'will to power' and domination – a fact that is, perhaps, hinted at even by Sir William Bradshaw's first name, which is not only quintessentially English (William the Conqueror, William Shakespeare), but which can also be parsed as 'will-I-am.' Less speculatively, we may note that, according to the narrator, assuming the 'white man's burden' (i.e. converting one's colonial subjects to English Proportion) generally leads to acts of violence: "dashing down shrines" and "smashing idols."

Some critics have commented on the fact that, precisely at this point in the novel, the narrator of *Mrs. Dalloway* seems to lose all sense of equanimity and

---

35 See Raymond Williams (281) and, in particular, Peter Borsay on the enlightenment culture of improvement: "[T]he improvers [believed in] a struggle between the forces of civilization and enlightenment, and those of barbarity and heathenism. It cannot be denied that some of this spirit was to infuse the class conflict that gained increasing strength in the early years of the nineteenth century and the spread of empire later in the century" (210).

moral proportion (e.g. Blanchard 299), seemingly contradicting Woolf's own belief, stated in her essay "Women and Fiction," that authors should never let bitterness or anger seep into their work (135).[36] Avrom Fleishman even suggests that the moral outrage expressed in this passage constitutes a stylistic 'lapse' that can be explained by Woolf's own experience of mental illness and her consequent dislike of psychiatrists (69; see also Jouve 251). Importantly, however, in her essay Woolf is careful to distinguish between, on the one hand, the "distortion" that partisanship may introduce into a literary text and, on the other, artistic weakness; for Woolf, distortion only "frequently" – and thus not necessarily – results in artistic weakness (135). Moreover, even if we were to assume that Woolf was indeed fundamentally opposed to authors expressing any strong convictions in works of fiction, we would still be faced with a paradox that haunts all forms of 'dogmatic relativism.' As Christopher Herbert puts it: "In a world where all nonrelativistic truth has been abolished, the relativity principle itself is proclaimed as a universal verity" (118). The assumption that everything is relative, and that art should therefore refrain from expressing strong partisanship, is itself an absolutist creed – and thus inherently contradictory. Accordingly, the narrator's 'lapse' from equanimity when faced with the 'ideal' of English Proportion is best understood as a novelistic counterpoint to an absolutist moral relativism that would render political critique entirely impossible.

It is therefore fitting that the very language the narrator uses to describe the twin sisters of Proportion and Conversion is suffused with a sense of 'unproportional,' excessive enjoyment ("*feasts* on the will of the weakly"; emphasis added). If domination can be associated with such boundless pleasure, then this belies any idea that Empire is truly based on order and proportion. Rather, the narrator envisages the imperial project as a profoundly narcissistic endeavor, concerned not with higher ideals but with admiring its "own features stamped on the face of the populace" (i.e. with remaking the world in its own image). Reversing the colonialist stereotype that 'natives' are child-like and in need of guidance (Loomba 181), in this passage the imperialists themselves appear as overly powerful and unpredictable children who throw tantrums whenever 'their' colonial subjects dare to frustrate the self-serving needs of the imperial masters.

We have already seen, in the case of Ahab in *Moby-Dick*, that power is apt to re-enforce such narcissistic delusions of grandeur (see chapter one), and we encounter the same phenomenon in *Mrs. Dalloway* in the figure of Lady Bruton

---

36 See also *A Room of One's Own*, where Woolf suggests that, in the case of *Jane Eyre*, "it is clear that anger was tempering with the integrity of Charlotte Brontë the novelist" (66).

and her colonialist "project for emigrating young people of both sexes born of respectable parents and setting them up with a fair prospect of doing well in Canada" (119). In the scene in question, Lady Bruton has just asked Hugh Whitbread, a government official, to help her write a letter to *The Times* in support of her project – and it is precisely at this point that *Mrs. Dalloway* highlights the extent to which the work of domestic servants turns Lady Bruton's home into a cocoon that shields her from the vicissitudes of everyday life:

> (The coffee was very slow in coming.)
>
> "The address?" murmured Hugh Whitbread; and there was at once a ripple in the grey tide of service which washed round Lady Bruton day in, day out, collecting, intercepting, enveloping her in a fine tissue which broke concussions, mitigated interruptions, and spread round the house in Brook Street a fine net where things lodged and were picked out accurately, instantly, by grey-haired Perkins, who had been with Lady Bruton these thirty years and now wrote down the address; handed it to Mr. Whitbread, who took out his pocket-book, raised his eyebrows, and slipping it in among documents of the highest importance, said that he would get Evelyn to ask him to lunch.
>
> (They were waiting to bring the coffee until Mr. Whitbread had finished.)
>
> Hugh was very slow, Lady Bruton thought. He was getting fat, she noticed. [...] She was getting impatient [...]. (118–119)

An army of domestics is employed in order to spare Lady Bruton any undesired interruptions, and the phrase "tide of service" – another instance of water imagery – dehumanizes the servants by turning them into a natural phenomenon, underlining the extent to which their efforts seem natural to Lady Bruton and her class. If Lady Bruton wants the food to be served, there will immediately be "a soundless and exquisite passing to and fro" (114); she has "only to nod" for her servants to be "instructed to quicken the coffee" (117). In such an environment, the object of desire – Lady Bruton's project of emigrating young people to Canada – "becomes inevitably prismatic, lustrous, half looking-glass, half precious stone"; it is a narcissistic mirror that reflects back only her own sense of self: "Emigration had become, in short, largely Lady Bruton" (119).

Once we recognize the profound significance of colonialism in Woolf's novel, the virtual absence of characters that could be described as colonial subjects must appear striking. Peter Walsh, though admittedly a kind of outsider due to his Anglo-Indian background (Lamont 174), is also the scion of a family of colonial administrators and thus hardly qualifies as a colonial subject, if by that term we mean someone who is *subjected* to colonial rule. Indeed, even though he sees himself as "disliking India, and empire, and army," he also experiences "moments of pride in England" and ultimately approves of "London; the season; civilisation," which he regards as a "splendid achievement" (60). What is striking here is that Peter thinks of London as "civilisation," in implicit contrast to the uncivilized disorder of 'the East.' Moreover, this particular moment of pride occurs only a few pages after the nationalistic display, discussed earlier, of a group of boys "in uniform, carrying guns," marching through the streets of London towards a "statue praising duty, gratitude, fidelity, love of England" (55). For all his sense of isolation and psychological complexity, then, Peter is a marginal figure only when seen from within the very narrow upper-class circle of the Dalloways, not from a broader social perspective.

Only two characters thus remain in *Mrs. Dalloway* whom we might plausibly describe as colonial subjects: the Irishwoman Moll Pratt, who sells flowers on the street (20), and a nameless "Colonial" who appears a little earlier in Woolf's novel (19). Of these two, only Moll briefly becomes a focalizing agent, as if in reward for the "loyalty" she feels towards the Prince of Wales, who – supposedly – passes by in a car ("she wished the dear boy well"). Moll, we learn, would even have liked to express her loyalty more clearly by tossing a bunch of roses into St. James's Street; however, she refrains from doing so because she finds a "discouraging constable's eye upon her" (20). Despite the fact that Moll is a loyal subject, in other words, her freedom is very precisely delimited in Woolf's text (as, incidentally, was that of the recently established Irish Free State; see Robbins 82–83).

It is instructive to compare the way in which the novel treats Moll with the fate of the nameless "Colonial," who reacts to the (assumed) presence of the Prince of Wales, not with expressions of loyalty, but by insulting the royal family – "which led to words, broken beer glasses, and a general shindy" (19). Colonial dissent is thus immediately silenced within the fictional world of *Mrs. Dalloway* (Bradshaw xxix; Snaith 73). Moreover, the "Colonial" never becomes the focalizer or bearer of narrative perspective. In fact, we do not even learn what, precisely, the "Colonial" said, and are therefore unable to judge whether he was purposely insulting the royal family in order to pick a fight, or whether he was merely trying to make a valid political point. In either case, it is clear that neither he nor Moll Pratt can express themselves freely in *Mrs. Dalloway* because they are at all times monitored closely by the – official as well as unofficial – guardians of the imperial nation, who are prepared violently to suppress any oppositional point of view.

Mrs. Dalloway and the Ethics of Home

The imperial nation is thus not a true homeland for its colonial subjects. Moreover, we have seen that the urban space of the imperial capital is not only very precisely delimited, but also not fundamentally different from those 'rural' country houses that are among the key symbolical markers of 'true' Englishness. Throughout, it has become clear that ideas about what it means to be truly English – such as the glorification of stoical composure – are not in the end separable from questions of gender (e.g. manliness vs. cowardice) or the vagaries of social class (e.g. Doris Kilman's unfashionably emphatic religious beliefs).[37] Accordingly, it is difficult for outsiders like Doris Kilman or Lucrezia Warren Smith to feel at home in the city of London. Likewise, in the wake of the Great War, "home" for Septimus ultimately comes to mean, not security or belonging, but the threat of being sent, against his will, to one of Sir William Bradshaw's or "[Dr.] Holmes's homes" (106–107). It is telling, moreover, how differently Clarissa reacts to Septimus and to Miss Kilman. Doris Kilman is a woman whom Clarissa actually meets, and whom she considers her "enemy":

> That was satisfying; that was real. Ah, how she hated her – hot, hypocritical, corrupt; with all that power; Elizabeth's seducer; the woman who had crept in to steal and defile (Richard would say, What nonsense!). She hated her: she loved her. It was enemies one wanted, not friends [...]. (191–192)

Clearly, Clarissa loves to hate Doris Kilman, and this contrasts sharply with her reaction to Septimus, who remains an anonymous and mostly imaginary presence in Clarissa's life. This, in turn, makes it easy for her to reinterpret Septimus's suicide as a metaphysical triumph that reconciles her with life – or, more precisely, with the current state of society, as well as her position in it.

We must, in other words, always bear in mind Septimus Warren Smith, Doris Kilman, and the general (mis-)treatment of the 'lower orders' – working-class people and colonial subjects – when we examine Clarissa's attempts at "making her home delightful" (13), and particularly when we discuss the hospitality she displays at her parties. Clarissa herself believes that giving parties is inherently positive and, quite simply, "her gift":

---

37 As Jo-Ann Wallace so aptly puts it, *Mrs. Dalloway* suggests "the complex relationship between various components of 'the social system': education, medicine, religion, class, politics, imperialism, and the military" (26). See also Jane Goldman, who suggests that Clarissa and Septimus inhabit a social world that is profoundly distorted by "patriarchal imperialism" (57).

> Here was So-and-so in South Kensington; some one up in Bayswater; and somebody else, say, in Mayfair. And she [i.e. Clarissa] felt quite continuously a sense of their existence; and she felt what a waste; and she felt what a pity; and she felt if only they could be brought together; so she did it. And it was an offering; to combine, to create; but to whom? (133–134)

There is genuine generosity here, in Clarissa's vision of spontaneous interconnection, and it resonates powerfully with Jacques Derrida's idea that hospitality is not just one virtue among many, but rather the key to "culture itself":

> Insofar as it has to do with the ethos, that is, the residence, one's home, the familiar place of dwelling, inasmuch as it is a manner of being there, the manner in which we relate to ourselves and to others, to others as our own or as foreigners, *ethics is hospitality* [...]. ("On Cosmopolitanism" 16–17; original emphasis)

Opening one's home to others and making them feel at ease is, for Derrida, the quintessentially ethical behavior, and Clarissa's hospitality surely is not without merit. Yet even if her "offering" is virtuous in principle, we must ask not only why Clarissa can afford such conspicuous displays of generosity, but also – as the text of *Mrs. Dalloway* itself suggests – to whom, precisely, her hospitality is offered ("but to whom?").

Michel Foucault's concept of heterotopic spaces can help us shed some light on the extent to which Clarissa's parties are anything but the disinterested works of art that she herself imagines them to be ("an offering for the sake of offering"; 134). In "Of Other Spaces," Foucault defines heterotopias as spaces that project an ideal vision of a particular society, but which in contrast to utopian spaces actually exist as real places within that society (e.g. theaters and museums; 24–26). Among the six principles of heterotopic spaces that Foucault outlines in his essay, the one that is crucial in our context is that they are, in general, "not freely accessible like a public place" (26).[38] This is, of course, also true for Clarissa's parties, which do not just bring together any sort of people, but only members of the London establishment, including the Prime Minister,

38 The six principles of heterotopias that Foucault indicates are: (a) there is no society that refrains from constructing heterotopic spaces (24); (b) the same heterotopic space can have different meanings in different historical periods (25); (c) heterotopias can juxtapose in a single real space "several sites that are in themselves incompatible" (ibid.); (d) most heterotopias are linked to particular "slices of time" (such as museums, which are associated with "indefinitely accumulating time"; 26); (e) heterotopias "presuppose a system of opening and closing that both isolates them and makes them penetrable" (ibid.); (f) with regard to all the spaces that remain, heterotopias either function as spaces of illusion or as spaces of compensation (27).

"this symbol of what they all stood for, English society" (189). Clarissa's hospitality may, in other words, be perfectly sincere and gesture toward a genuinely admirable ideal. However, her parties also conveniently help the Dalloways fulfill societal expectations and thus to uphold their privileged position.

This is, importantly, not to say that Woolf's novel constitutes a relentless indictment of its eponymous heroine. In fact, many critics would agree with Alex Zwerdling's suggestion that *Mrs. Dalloway* is "finally a sympathetic picture of someone who has surrendered to the force of conventional life and permitted her emotions to go underground" (78). And it is indeed understandable that Clarissa wants to plunge into the present in order to forget, not only her recent illness or human mortality in general, but also the horrors of the Great War. It is understandable, too, that she looks to literary works like *Cymbeline* for consolation, in order to maintain a sense of belonging. Moreover, even if we believe that the society portrayed in *Mrs. Dalloway* is profoundly unjust, it does not follow that Clarissa has a moral obligation to be unhappy, for the oppressed of the world gain nothing by the misery of others – even the unhappiness of the privileged.

What is problematic about Clarissa is thus not her desire to feel at home, nor even the fact that she actually manages to find a place in the world. The problem is, rather, that she is willing to do so in ways that not only fail to combat injustice (her refusal to engage with key political issues, such as the British government's role during and after the Armenian genocide), but that even help maintain the status quo (e.g. fulfilling her role as "perfect hostess"; see *Mrs. Dalloway* 8 and 67), and which occasionally add insult to injury (e.g. her treatment of Doris Kilman, who poses a threat to Clarissa's sense of home because she reminds her of things she would prefer to forget). Clarissa herself acknowledges a peculiar "hollowness" at the heart of her social triumphs – triumphs which, perhaps because she was "growing old, satisfied her no longer as they used" (191) – and even in the eyes of her old friend Sally, Clarissa appears as "at heart a snob" (208).

This leads us to what is perhaps the least acknowledged fact about *Mrs. Dalloway*, and one that is crucial to the novel's attempt to establish an ethics of home, namely that judgments of all kinds are passed continually in the novel by various characters and, occasionally, by the narrator.[39] If we look, for instance, at the first ten paragraphs of *Mrs. Dalloway*, we not only find Clarissa judging Peter Walsh and Hugh Whitbread, as well as reporting Peter and Richard's

---

39 Julia Carlson has rightly emphasized the importance of Peter as a critic of Clarissa's character (58), but she does not discuss the notion of judgment in more general terms.

judgments of "the admirable Hugh" (5); we also learn that Scrope Purvis, who – like the Dalloways – lives in Westminster, finds Clarissa a "charming woman" (4). Later in the novel, we have Dr. Holmes, whose name, as we have seen, suggests both medical care and criminal judgment, and who indeed does not hesitate to call Septimus a coward. Moreover, there is the narrator's judgment of Sir William Bradshaw and his love of Proportion, and even Doris Kilman's view of Clarissa is given some space: "She despised Mrs. Dalloway from the bottom of her heart" (141). Crucially, we also have Clarissa's reactions to the judgments of others:

> [S]omething that Peter had said, combined with some depression of her own, in her bedroom, taking off her hat; and what Richard had said had added to it [...]. That was it! Her parties! Both of them criticised her very unfairly, laughed at her very unjustly, for her parties. [...]
>
> Well, how was she going to defend herself? Now that she knew what it was, she felt perfectly happy. They thought, or Peter at any rate thought, that she enjoyed imposing herself; liked to have famous people about her; great names; was simply a snob in short. Well, Peter might think so. Richard merely thought it foolish of her to like excitement when she knew it was bad for her heart. It was childish, he thought. And both were quite wrong. What she liked was simply life. (132–133)

We learn here that both Peter and Richard are critical of Clarissa's enthusiasm for parties (though both, of course, nevertheless dutifully attend), and Clarissa's only defense is that she "simply" likes life. If Woolf's novel shows us anything, however, it is precisely that simply liking life is not enough – neither in the imperial city, nor in the seemingly pastoral environment at Bourton.

To love life "simply" thus ultimately proves inadequate in a novel that confronts us with multiple points of view in two related, but distinct senses: a 'technical' sense relating to vantage points from which the fictional world is perceived; and a 'political' sense pertaining to conflicting judgments and diverging opinions. Woolf's novel provides us with a broad, albeit far from all-inclusive or politically neutral range of focalizers, and thus immerses us in a sea of ethical judgments. And this continual and contradictory passing of judgment can hardly fail to have an effect on the reader. Put somewhat bluntly: Can anyone read, say, Clarissa's idea that Richard and Peter criticize her "very unfairly" without beginning to judge her, too? When doing so, we may disagree with Karen DeMeester's idea that Clarissa, like other members of her social class, merely domesticates the social evils that are "evident in England's perpetuation of its empire and its sacrifice of a generation to war" (665). But it is difficult to read *Mrs. Dalloway* without at least considering the ethical implications of Clarissa's home-making practices.

By choosing the title *Mrs. Dalloway,* Woolf – consciously or not – emphasized Clarissa's social position as successful wife to the government official Richard Dalloway (in contrast to, say, Samuel Richardson, who did not include the patronymic "Harlowe" in the title of his novel *Clarissa,* thus foregrounding the heroine's first name), and Clarissa Dalloway's social success in what is arguably an unjust system may well be considered an ethical failure (Hawthorn 43). At the very least, Woolf's novel examines how, precisely, its eponymous character tries to make a home in a world that is not of her own making and over which she – like all of us – has only limited control. At the same time, *Mrs. Dalloway* encourages us to consider the ethical price Clarissa is willing to pay for such belonging, and it makes these abstract costs concrete by counterpointing her successful quest for belonging with the story of Doris Kilman and, in particular, with the tragedy of Septimus, who quite literally embodies the traumatic kernel of Clarissa's ideological fantasy. Something awful may lurk at the center of even the most delightful home: a repressed but familiar, uncanny presence that haunts *Mrs. Dalloway* in the figure of Septimus. It is this kind of political uncanny that takes center stage in William Faulkner's *Absalom, Absalom!,* which precipitates us into a veritable nightmare of belonging.

4 "Everybody Seemed to Have to Have a Home": History, Innocence, and the Nightmare of Belonging in William Faulkner's *Absalom, Absalom!*

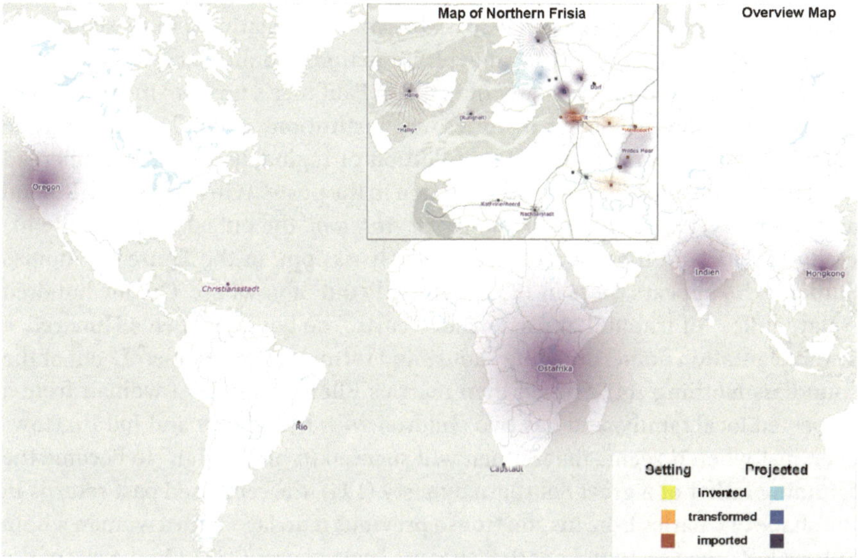

FIGURE 8: Storm's regionalism assumes a global dimension if one takes into account projected spaces.

Regionalism: the word evokes local color, boundedness, perhaps provinciality.[1] And yet, though there is a tendency in regionalist novels to depict their settings as pristine, authentic spaces outside of history (Kaplan 251–252), Philip Joseph rejects the notion that such novels are necessarily isolationist. Instead, Joseph argues that there have always been regional novels in which the local community remains "in dialogue with the outside world" (7). Likewise, Harilaos Stecopoulos argues that some novelists "counterintuitively found in regionalism

1 I would like to thank Christa Schönfelder and Simone Heller-Andrist for their comments on the first draft, as well as Sarah Chevalier for her feedback on the final version of this chapter. Parts of the chapter are based on my unpublished *Lizenziat* thesis, "Past the Game of Fiction."

the inspiration for transnational fiction" (24). The works of the German author Theodor Storm are a good example for this, for while virtually all of Storm's texts are set in the author's home region, Northern Frisia, this regional setting is opened up to the wider world through what Barbara Piatti has called projected spaces: locations that are remembered, dreamed of, or envisioned as future destinations (Piatti 362). As soon as one adds projected spaces to Storm's fictional universe, his regionalism in fact assumes truly global proportions (FIGURE 8).[2]

In the discussion that follows we will find that the regionalism of William Faulkner's *Absalom, Absalom!* (1936) is likewise transnational in its scope. *Absalom, Absalom!* is set in Yoknapatawpha, a fictional county located in the state of Mississippi and home to many of William Faulkner's novels.[3] In their ostensible focus on the particular histories and institutions of the Deep South, the Yoknapatawpha stories belong to a tradition of regionalism that had emerged as an important current in American fiction in the post-Civil-War period (Ruland and Bradbury 193). And yet, in *Absalom, Absalom!* the outside world quite literally intrudes on the town of Jefferson, Mississippi, in the figure of Thomas Sutpen, who appears there in 1833, seemingly out of nowhere. On one hundred square miles "of tranquil and astonished earth," he builds Sutpen's Hundred, a grand plantation home, dragging "house and formal gardens violently out of the soundless Nothing" (4). Sutpen then marries Ellen Coldfield, a woman from a respected local family, and has two children with her, Henry and Judith. However, just when it seems that Sutpen will succeed in his "design" to become the founding father of a great Southern dynasty (194), the repressed past returns in the shape of Charles Bon, his son from a previous marriage with a woman whom Sutpen left when he found out that she was "part negro" (283). On the eve of the American Civil War, Sutpen's design thus begins to falter, ultimately destroying his new family.

It is, however, only through the prism of several retellings that we come to know of Sutpen's relentless pursuit of a particular fiction of home, and the fact that his story is continually retold emphasizes the extent to which his catastrophic history continues, decades after the events in question, to haunt Quentin Compson and other members of Jefferson, his home community. We will see, moreover, that these regional hauntings are in fact intimately related not only to U.S. national history, but also to the country's geopolitical role in the nineteenth and early twentieth centuries. By allegorically encoding the his-

---

2 I would like to thank Barbara Piatti for allowing me to use the map in FIGURE 8.

3 Among the novels set in Yoknapatawpha county are *Sartoris* (1929), *The Sound and the Fury* (1929), *As I Lay Dying* (1930), *Light in August* (1932), *The Hamlet* (1940), *Go Down, Moses* (1942), *The Town* (1957), *The Mansion* (1959), and *The Reivers* (1962).

tory of slavery and racism, as well as the continuing U.S. involvement in the Republic of Haiti, the novel draws attention to the illusionary nature of fantasies of a new beginning, or dreams of splendid isolation. Instead, it evokes Karl Marx's famous dictum that "[t]radition from all the dead generations weighs like a nightmare on the brain of the living" ("The Eighteenth Brumaire of Louis Bonaparte" 32; see also chapter two), and gives literary form to this idea through equally Gothic tropes.[4] Moreover, *Absalom, Absalom!* uses a technique that we may call uncanny narration in order to make readers undergo a similarly nightmarish experience as one of the novel's protagonists, Quentin Compson.

In the preceding chapters, we have focused on the obstacles to belonging – social alienation, for instance, or injustices related to gender. In addition, we have examined the question of whether, at times, we ought to resist our urge to make ourselves at home because the ethical price to pay would simply be too high. In the discussion that follows, we will now have to examine what happens when someone would in fact prefer to leave the home behind, but finds to their horror that he or she simply cannot let go. In short, in assessing the potentially debilitating long-term impact of the family home and the wider community, *Absalom, Absalom!* constitutes an attempt to confront the nightmare of belonging, in order to unearth its potential as a basis for political action.

Postmemory: Excessive Past(s) and the Weight of History

The potentially overwhelming weight of history is made palpable in Faulkner's novel through the sheer multiplicity of interlocking and sometimes competing narratives that, collectively, reconstruct the story of Thomas Sutpen.[5] The novel opens in September 1909, with Quentin paying a visit to Miss Rosa Coldfield, an elderly lady who knew Sutpen personally (5). While the circumstances of Quentin's visit are related by an extra-diegetic, third-person narrator, the embedded story of Thomas Sutpen is told in the "grim haggard amazed voice" of Rosa Coldfield (3). In fact, of the first chapter's twenty pages, the final twelve consist almost exclusively of Miss Rosa's embedded tale, making her a second-level narrator who virtually takes over the telling of the story. Similarly, of the second chapter's twenty-three pages, only ten are told by the extra-diegetic third-person narrator, while the other thirteen consist of a monologue by Quentin's father. Not unlike Ishmael in *Moby-Dick*, then (see chapter one), the third-person narrator in *Absalom, Absalom!* repeatedly loses control over the

4 For a reading of Marx's ghostly imagery in "The Eighteenth Brumaire of Louis Bonaparte," see Jacques Derrida, *Specters of Marx* 133–155. For responses by Marxist critics, see Michael Sprinker, *Ghostly Demarcations.*

5 For a similar argument, see Heinrich Straumann, *Faulkner* 199–200.

narrative, speaking, for instance, only eight words in the twenty-four pages of chapter three. Later, in chapter five, the novel seems to dispose of the extra-diegetic perspective altogether, presenting us with another thirty-two pages of Miss Rosa's voice before, on the second-but-last page, the third-person narrator stages a surprise return. Instead of controlling and orchestrating the novel's many retellings, the 'omniscient' third-person narrator thus appears in a curiously precarious position and threatens to be drowned out by embedded narrative voices.[6]

Moreover, if the various retellings are well-nigh unmanageable in their totality, the embedded narrators appear similarly overwhelmed by their stories, which they recount in seemingly boundless sentences, as if compelled stylistically to recreate the enormity of the past. Consider, for instance, the following gargantuan sentence, spoken by Quentin's father:

> [Y]our grandfather never knew if it was Clytie who watched, kept in touch by some means, waited for the day, the moment, to come, the hour when the little boy would be an orphan, and so went herself to fetch him; or if it was Judith who did the waiting and the watching and sent Clytie for him that winter, that December of 1871;–Clytie who had never been further from Sutpen's Hundred than Jefferson in her life, yet who made that Journey alone to New Orleans and returned with the child, the boy of twelve now and looking ten, in one of the outgrown Fauntleroy suits but with a new oversize overall jumper coat which Clytie had bought for him (and made him wear, whether against the cold or whether not your grandfather could not say either) over it and what else he owned tied up in a bandana handkerchief – this child who could speak no English as the woman could speak no French who had found him, hunted him down in a French city and brought him away, this child with a face not old but without age, as if he had had no childhood, not in the sense that Miss Rosa says she had no childhood, but as if he had not been human born but instead created without agency of man or agony of woman and orphaned by no human being [...]. (159)

This lengthy quotation in fact constitutes only the first third of the sentence, and though the example may seem extreme, it is not at all uncharacteristic of the novel's overwhelming style. Too much, it seems, must be told:

> I will tell you what he [i.e. Sutpen] did and let you be the judge. (Or try to tell you, because there are some things for which three words are three too many, and three thousand words that many words too less, and this is one of them. It can be told; I could take that many sentences, repeat the bold blank naked and outrageous words

6 For a more detailed analysis of the competition (and even contradictions) between narrators see, for instance, Rimmon-Kenan, *Glance beyond Doubt* 43–64.

> just as he spoke them, and bequeath you only that same aghast and outraged unbelief I knew when I comprehended what he meant; or take three thousand sentences and leave you only that Why? Why? and Why? that I have asked and listened to for almost fifty years.) But I will let you be the judge and let you tell me if I was not right. (134–135)

Words, that is to say, cannot do justice to Sutpen's story ("three words are three too many, and three thousand words that many words too less"), and the enormity of the narrative task affects the very language in which Rosa – who is the narrator at this point – tells her tale: definite statements that she immediately qualifies ("I will tell you [...]. Or try to tell you"); adjectives crammed on top of each other ("bold bland naked and outrageous"); repetitions ("and let you be the judge," "will let you be the judge"), speculations ("could take"), and unresolved questions ("that Why? Why? and Why? that I have asked and listened to for almost fifty years"). If John Brannigan is right in suggesting that an "excess of memory and history is [...] the prototypical temporal condition of the twentieth century" (117), then perhaps *Absalom, Absalom!* is the century's paradigmatic novel, enacting this excessive temporality in the very texture of its convoluted style.

Nevertheless, much like Rosa Coldfield, Quentin is aware that even the most excessive of narrations cannot encompass the full reality of the past, but must instead select, rearrange, and condense its components. In order to tell Sutpen's story, the characters must thus distort the reality to which their tales purport to refer, thus adding to their material a dream-like quality:

> It (the talking, the telling) seemed (to him, to Quentin) to partake of that logic- and reason-flouting quality of a dream which the sleeper knows must have occurred, stillborn and complete, in a second, yet the very quality upon which it must depend to move the dreamer (verisimilitude) to credulity – horror or pleasure or amazement – depends as completely upon a formal recognition of and acceptance of elapsed and yet elapsing time as music or a printed tale. (15)

The "logic- and reason-flouting quality" of dreams finds its counterpart in the storyteller's need to manipulate time – to compress, for instance, the thirty-three years between Sutpen's arrival in Jefferson and his death in 1869 into a novel that one can read in only a few days. Such passages that discuss the precarious relationship between the reality of the past and its recreation as a text represent an explicit metafictional discourse in Faulkner's novel, and this explicit discourse in turn complements the novel's implicitly metafictional style (i.e. the extraordinarily long and complex sentences that flaunt the text's artificiality and constructedness). *Absalom, Absalom!* thus constitutes what Linda Hutcheon has termed a historiographic metafiction: a novel that "problematizes the very possibility of historical knowledge" (106).[7]

It is, in part, this problematic nature of attempts to reconstruct the past that Shreve, Quentin's roommate at Harvard College, finds stimulating and even exciting. "Let me play a while now," Shreve asks Quentin when the latter tries to interrupt his friend in the course of a free-flowing narrative improvisation on the story of Thomas Sutpen, and Norman W. Jones has rightly pointed out that there is a markedly homoerotic charge to the roommates' "back-and-forth storytelling" (334). We learn, for instance, that Shreve is "naked to the waist" (*Absalom* 176), and that the two roommates sometimes glare at one another "not at all as two young men might look at each other but almost as a youth and a very young girl might out of virginity itself" (240). Thus seduced by each others' imaginative prowess, Shreve and Quentin move further and further away from a version of the past based on verifiable fact, creating, "out of the rag-tag and bob-ends of old tales and talking, people who perhaps had never existed at all" (243): a dream-like historical fantasy driven by their mutual narrative desire.

However, while Shreve, a Canadian, is for the most part able to enjoy this game of narrative seduction, the Southerner Quentin finds himself unable to gain unadulterated pleasure from their flights of fancy because he is weighed down by the effects of collective historical trauma.[8] At one point in Faulkner's novel, Shreve and Quentin explicitly address this crucial difference in their relation to the past:

> [Shreve: I]t's something my people haven't got. [...] What is it? something you live and breathe like air? a kind of vacuum filled with wraithlike and indomitable anger and pride and glory at and in happenings that occurred and ceased fifty years ago? a kind of entailed birthright father and son and father and son of never forgiving General Sherman, so that forever more as long as your children's children produce children

---

7 It would be interesting to pursue in more detail how Faulkner's novel engages with the tradition of the historical novel as a genre, particularly with the model provided by Walter Scott. For instance, as Ian Duncan points out in an essay on *Waverley*, Scott "follows Shakespeare to make civil war the classical setting of historical fiction: it is the fiery, bloody rift in the fabric of common life through which history and national character become visible" (173). What Duncan says here about the role of the civil war and national character in Scott can, of course, equally well be applied to *Absalom, Absalom!* – an intertextual link that is made explicit in Faulkner's novel when we learn that Sutpen rides off to war on a "black stallion named out of Scott" (63).

8 For the distinction between existential and historical trauma see Dominick LaCapra, *History and Memory after Auschwitz* 46–48 (also discussed in the introduction of the present study).

> you wont be anything but a descendant of a long line of colonels killed in Pickett's charge at Manassas?"
> "Gettysburg," Quentin said. "You cant understand it. You would have to be born there."
> "Would I then?" (289)[9]

A particular way of relating to history is, Quentin and Shreve suggest here, passed on like a "birthright" from father to son, and can only be understood – if at all ("Would I then?") – by those for whom the South has always been home.[10]

Though Quentin has no personal recollections of the Civil War, he is thus unable to escape the impact of what Marianne Hirsch has called postmemory: memories handed down from one generation to the next, and therefore characterized by a deeply personal sense of emotional investment despite the temporal distance that separates the younger generation from the events concerned (*Family Frames* 22).[11] In *Absalom, Absalom!*, the story of Thomas Sutpen is part of this postmemory that Quentin 'inherits':

> [T]his first part of it, Quentin already knew. It was a part of his twenty years' heritage of breathing the same air and hearing his father talk about the man; a part of the town's – Jefferson's – eighty years' heritage of the same air which the man himself had breathed [...]. Quentin had grown up with that; the mere names were interchangeable and almost myriad. His childhood was full of them; his very body was an empty hall echoing with sonorous defeated names; he was not a being, an entity, he was a commonwealth. (7)

In the collective memory of Jefferson, Mississippi, Thomas Sutpen is such an overwhelming presence that Quentin is familiar with his story from childhood; Quentin's memories are "myriad," and his very self is not truly individual but instead "a commonwealth." Indeed, so heavily does postmemory weigh on Quentin that his sense of self threatens to collapse:

> [H]e would seem to listen to two separate Quentins now – the Quentin Compson preparing for Harvard in the South, the deep South dead since 1865 and peopled with

9 Note that expressions such as *don't* or *can't* are spelled without apostrophes throughout *Absalom, Absalom!*

10 The fact that Shreve imagines that this birthright is passed on from fathers to sons (rather than from mothers to daughters) would, incidentally, provide a good starting point for a feminist reading of Faulkner's novel.

11 I would like to thank Christa Schönfelder for bringing Hirsch's concept of postmemory to my attention.

> garrulous outraged baffled ghosts, listening, having to listen, to one of the ghosts who had refused to lie still even longer than most had [i.e. Miss Rosa], telling him about old ghost-times; and the Quentin Compson who was still too young to deserve yet to be a ghost but nevertheless having to be one for all that, since he was born in the deep South the same as she was [...]. (4)

Faced with the history of Sutpen and the Civil War, Quentin experiences himself as both disjointed ("two separate Quentins") and insubstantial ("a ghost"), and consequently cannot bring himself to share Shreve's sense of narrative exhilaration.

Thomas Sutpen and the Destruction of Home

If Quentin is unable truly to enjoy the game of historical reconstruction, the same is true of Rosa Coldfield, who in contrast to Quentin personally witnessed the destructive effects of Sutpen's design on Jefferson and, more particularly, on her own family. For one thing, Sutpen played a key role in the breakdown of the relationship between Rosa's father and his home community by proposing to him a dubious financial scheme – "one of those things that when they work you were smart and when they dont you change your name and move to Texas" (208). Though morally outraged by Sutpen's proposal, Mr. Coldfield realizes that he "couldn't quit thinking about it," and in order to "get it out of his mind" he decides to accept, fully expecting and even hoping that the scheme will fail (209). Consequently, Mr. Coldfield is appalled when Sutpen's unethical gamble eventually pays off:

> Mr Coldfield never did believe it would work, so when he saw that it was going to work, had worked, the least thing he could do was to refuse to take his share of the profits; [...] when he saw that it had worked it was his conscience he hated, not Sutpen; – his conscience and the land, the country which had created his conscience and then offered the opportunity to have made all that money to the conscience which it had created, which could do nothing but decline; hated that country so much that he was even glad when he saw it drifting closer and closer to a doomed and fatal war; [...] he would have joined the Yankee army [...], only he was not a soldier and knew that he would either be killed or die of hardship and so not be present on that day when the South would realise that it was now paying the price for having erected its economic edifice not on the rock of stern morality but on the shifting sands of opportunism and moral brigandage. (209)

In this episode, Rosa casts Sutpen in the role of the great tempter who seduces a morally upright man and leaves him fundamentally alienated from a home community that Rosa's father now views as irredeemably corrupt. Indeed,

Mr. Coldfield henceforth hates the South “so much that he was even glad when he saw it drifting closer to a doomed and fatal war.” After the outbreak of war, Mr. Coldfield closes his store to Confederate troops and also refuses to sell any goods to supporters of the Southern cause (64). Eventually, he locks up the store for good, and when it is looted by troops who were “doubtless abetted, if only vocally, by his own fellow citizens,” Mr. Coldfield withdraws to the attic of his home, shutting himself in and nailing the door behind him (65).

The reason why Rosa cannot forget this story is that it led directly to the irreversible destruction of everything she had previously thought of as home. From the point when her father shuts himself up in the attic, Miss Rosa secretly provides him with food, hauling up baskets of provision to him “at night by means of a well pulley and rope attached to the attic window” (65). Rosa does this even though she herself supports the Confederate cause – among other things by writing “odes to Southern soldiers” since the first day of her father’s self-incarceration. When, after three years of living in the attic, Mr. Coldfield finally refuses to eat and starves himself to death, the family’s financial assets are entirely depleted, and Rosa finds herself “not only an orphan, but a pauper too” (65–66). In a very real way, then, both the material and emotional security of Rosa’s family home was shattered by Thomas Sutpen, who proposed the dubious scheme that led to Mr. Coldfield’s alienation from the home community, as well as, indirectly, to his suicide.

In addition, we learn that Rosa’s is not the only home that Sutpen destroys in the relentless pursuit of his design to found a Southern planter dynasty. Before he came to Jefferson, Sutpen had worked as an “overseer or foreman or something to a French sugar planter” in Haiti (199). After saving the planter’s family during an uprising, Sutpen becomes engaged to marry his employer’s daughter, who soon gives birth to Sutpen’s first son, Charles (204, 212). However, when Sutpen finds out that his wife is not, as he had been led to believe, part Spanish, but “part negro” instead (283), he provides for her “and put[s] her aside” because, as a ‘mixed-race’ woman, she cannot be “adjunctive or incremental to the design” that Sutpen has in mind (194). Sutpen thus ruthlessly breaks apart the family home he has just established because it fails to correspond to the particular fiction of home that he obsessively pursues: a grand plantation manor owned by a ‘pure,’ white family clan.

However, while Sutpen believes that he can simply leave the past behind, the abandoned first plantation home ultimately brings about the destruction of his second home in Jefferson. As a young man, Charles, Sutpen’s first-born son, enrolls as a student at the same college as Henry, the son from Sutpen’s second marriage with Ellen Coldfield. Unaware that they are half-brothers, Charles and

Henry become close friends, and at one point Henry decides to take Charles home with him to Supten's Hundred. There, Charles meets Judith, Henry's sister, and he soon begins to court the young woman who is in fact his half-sister. When Sutpen finds his suspicion confirmed that Charles Bon is his first-bon son, he tries to convince Henry to put a stop to Charles and Judith's incestuous courtship. Henry, however, refuses to act against Charles, loving his friend so much that he prefers to repudiate "father and blood and home" instead (79). Seeing that even the threat of incest does not move Henry decisively to intervene, Sutpen, after a long period of waiting, ultimately reveals the secret of Charles's 'tainted' racial origin to Henry. Despite Henry's intense affection for Charles – Norman W. Jones even speaks of a "romance" between the two friends (348) – Henry cannot bear the thought of racial 'impurity,' as Charles himself observes toward the end of the novel: "So it's the miscegenation, not the incest, which you cant bear" (285). In a climactic scene, Henry shoots Charles at the gates of Sutpen's Hundred, his family home, and then disappears, leaving Sutpen bereft of a male heir and therefore, once again, foiled in his design to establish a great plantation dynasty.

And yet, if it is in some ways true that Sutpen's second home was destroyed by the return of a son from the first home, we must at the same time bear in mind that Sutpen's Hundred had never truly been a homely home. For instance, just as Sutpen's first marriage had "certainly not [been] about love" (200), we know that Sutpen never had any romantic interest in his second wife, Ellen Coldfield, but instead merely married her to gain respectability through "the shield of a virtuous woman" (9). When Ellen, on hear deathbed, asks Rosa to "save" her two children, or "Judith at least," from their father (10), it becomes quite clear that Sutpen's Hundred is a home only in the most impoverished sense of the term: a place of residence and physical shelter, but not, as Cleanth Brooks has pointed out, an emotional or psychological abode. The reason for this lack of interpersonal affection is that Sutpen's design, though ostensibly valuing the family, in fact views it as merely "incidental" (Brooks, *Towards Yoknapatawpha* 292). Perhaps 'instrumental' would be an even better term, for we can say that, for Supten, the family constitutes only a means to fulfilling his design, rather than an end in itself (Bollinger 214). Sutpen thus violates one of Kant's ethical imperatives, according to which rational beings must never be used as a means only:

> [T]he human being and in general every rational being *exists* as an end in itself, *not merely as a means* to be used by this or that will at its discretion; instead he must in

> all his actions, whether directed to himself or also to other rational beings, always be regarded *at the same time as an end* [...]. ("Groundwork" 79, original emphasis).[12]

In Marxist terms, Sutpen disregards the use-value of the members of his two families – their unique qualities and individual needs – reducing them to their exchange-value instead (i.e. to how much the wife and children can contribute toward his grand design).

The home at Sutpen's Hundred is thus built on the same logic as the system of plantation slavery, in which the unique qualities and needs of the slaves are seen as entirely irrelevant, and where the only question of importance is their exchange-value: how much can be got out of them. It is in part because slaves are reduced in this way to mere means of production, without rights of kinship, that Orlando Patterson has described them as the "quintessentially homeless" persons (162), and though Henry and Judith's situation at Sutpen's Hundred is incomparably better in terms of legal recognition and material comfort, the 'home' that Sutpen has built for them is founded on the same dehumanizing logic. It is understandable, then, that the only reason why Henry calls Sutpen's Hundred his home is that "everybody seemed to have to have a home" (263). Home, which for the fortunate is a place both of shelter and of kindness, for Sutpen's son constitutes nothing but an inescapable, oppressive obligation.

Knowledge and the Homes of Our Youth

If Sutpen's design thus has an enormously destructive effect on three different homes – the Coldfields' as well as his two plantation homes – the roots of his design reach back to his own precarious childhood home. Growing up in the mountains of Virginia, Sutpen only knew people "who lived in log cabins boiling with children like the one he was born in," in a society where "the land belonged to anybody" (179). While this description may initially tempt readers to imagine the Virginia home as a poor, but otherwise idyllic mountain community, Cleanth Brooks rightly observes that Sutpen in fact describes a "dog-eat-dog society" (*The Yoknapatawpha Country* 426). According to *Absalom, Absalom!*, everybody in this society "had just what he was strong enough or energetic enough to take and keep," and "the only colored people were Indians and you only looked down at them over your rifle sights" (179). In other words, the settler society that

12 The German original runs: "[D]er Mensch und überhaupt jedes vernünftige Wesen, *existiert* als Zweck an sich selbst, *nicht bloss als Mittel* zum beliebigen Gebrauche für diesen oder jenen Willen, sondern muss in allen seinen, sowohl auf sich selbst, als auch auf andere vernünftige Wesen gerichteten Handlungen, jederzeit *zugleich als Zweck* betrachtet werden" (Kant, *Grundlegung* 43; § 48).

Sutpen describes is characterized by endemic violence and only the most precarious sense of equality among whites, with the main principle of cohesion being the settlers' virulent fear of Native Americans. At the same time, even as a boy Sutpen sometimes overhears tales of a different society further south: a society governed by the rule of law and glowing with the splendor of plantation wealth. And yet, the boy never really pays much attention to such stories "because there was nothing in sight to compare and gauge the tales by and so give the words life and meaning" (180). What is emphasized here are the cognitive dimensions of the childhood home: they way in which familiar experiences function as yardsticks against which we measure the unfamiliar, and how some things may remain inconceivable because they are too different from anything we have encountered at home.[13]

It is, accordingly, the family's move away from the Virginia mountain home that brings about a first important change in young Sutpen's intellectual development. Interestingly, Sutpen's father decides to move south with his family shortly after the mother dies, and even though Sutpen does not "remember the reason if he ever knew it" (181), the sequence of events suggests a link between the domestic tragedy and the family's abandoning the old home. Moreover, the trauma of the loss of his mother may in part explain Sutpen's fixation on becoming a patriarch.[14] At any rate, when the Sutpens finally settle down again, they find themselves in a society that works very differently from the Virginia mountain community:

> [Supten] learned the difference not only between white men and black ones, but he was learning that there was a difference between white men and white men not to be measured by lifting anvils or gouging eyes or how much whiskey you could drink then get up and walk out of the room. That is, he had begun to discern that without being aware of it yet. He still thought that that was just a matter of where you were spawned and how; lucky or not lucky [...]. (183)

Society in the Deep South is based on entirely different laws and conventions, and sharply divided not only in terms of race (which, after all, had been the case in Virginia, too), but also in terms of class ("a difference between white men and

13 In this emphasis on the formative effect of the childhood home, *Absalom, Absalom!* is not unlike George Eliot's *The Mill on the Floss*. There, however, as we have seen in chapter 2, the enabling qualities of the home are foregrounded, whereas Faulkner's novel pays at least as much attention to the potentially debilitating effects of homes that are fundamentally flawed.

14 From a psychoanalytic and feminist perspective, the fact that the death of Sutpen's mother is mentioned only once and very briefly would support the idea that a repression of the motherly body is the driving force behind Faulkner's story.

white men"). It is a place where "regiments of niggers with white men watching them planted and raised things," and where a select group of white men living in big houses "owned all the land and the niggers and apparently the white men who superintended the work" (184). In this new society, young Sutpen also observes that many slaves wear "better clothes than he or his father and sisters had ever owned and ever expected to," and that some of these slaves also live in better-kept quarters than poor white laborers like the Sutpens. At the same time, the dwellings of poor whites still seem to the boy mysteriously "nimbused with freedom's bright aura, which the slave quarters were not for all their sound roofs and white wash" (184–185). Even though the family's geographical change of home confronts Sutpen with a new and different type of community, the boy is thus not yet prepared to abandon his belief that all white men are, if not economically, then at least legally and politically equal.

In Faulkner's novel, the family's physical removal from home is therefore a necessary first step, but not a sufficient condition for radically new knowledge and deeper insight on Sutpen's part. Instead, a 'cognitive restructuring' can only occur once additional factors come into play, and for Thomas Sutpen the decisive factor is an insult that undermines his previous trust in white equality and his own self-worth. When Sutpen is "thirteen or fourteen," his father sends him to his employer's plantation home to deliver a message, and the young boy looks forward to finally seeing the inside of the white master's mansion (185). However, a black servant not only stops Sutpen from entering the house, but even tells him "never to come to that front door again but to go around the back" (188). In consequence of this insult, everything Sutpen thought he knew and understood is suddenly cast in a different light:

> [H]e seemed to kind of dissolve and a part of him turn and rush back through the two years they had lived there like when you pass through a room fast and look at all the objects in it and you turn and go back through the room again from the other side and you find out you had never seen them before [...]. (186)

An experience of defamiliarization thus follows the black servant's insult, undermining not only Sutpen's self-image, but also his previously unquestioned belief that a rich man could never think himself superior to a poor white boy like Sutpen (185). Baffled rather than outraged, Sutpen turns away from the plantation manor and runs, "not toward home," but off into cave in the woods, "where he could be quiet and think" (188).

By having Sutpen run off into the woods and not toward home, the novel makes explicit that Sutpen's reconceptualization of society and his own place in it does not – perhaps cannot – happen in the most familiar surrounding of the home. Moreover, we soon learn just how profoundly the boy's perception of the family home changes through his dramatic experience of humiliation:

> [H]e began to think of *Home. Home* and […] he thought at first he was trying to laugh and […] he kept on telling himself it was laughing even after he knew better; home, as he came out of the woods and approached it, still hidden yet, and looked at it – the rough partly rotten log walls, the sagging roof […], the leanto room which they used for kitchen […], and his sister pumping rhythmic up and down above a washtub in the yard, her back toward him, shapeless in a calico dress and a pair of the old man's shoes unlaced and flapping about her bare ankles and broad in the beam as a cow, the very labor she was doing brutish and stupidly out of all proportion to its reward: the very primary essence of labor, toil, reduced to its crude absolute which only a beast could and would endure […]. (190–191)

The family home, previously "nimbused with freedom's bright aura," is now not even something to laugh at, but instead a place to be ashamed of for its poverty and squalor.[15] Whereas once Sutpen believed that all white men were created equal, he now recognizes that the dehumanizing poverty of white families (i.e. labor that is "stupidly out of all proportion to its reward," and "which only a beast could and would endure") is constitutive to the hierarchically divided social system he had thought he knew intimately and understood.

However, though Sutpen now recognizes the extent to which the 'private' life at home is shaped by 'public' social circumstances, the conclusions he draws from this insight fall short of their radical potential. In part, this is because Sutpen's upbringing has not provided him with the mental resources necessary to conceive of an appropriate response to his new insights. As Greg Forter observes, Sutpen for a time debates with himself the various ways in which he

---

15 A similar moment in which a character suddenly recognizes the abject poverty of his own, previously so familiar home occurs in Indra Sinha's novel *Animal's People* (2007). The novel's main character and narrator lives in a slum called Nutcracker in the fictional city of Khaufpur (modeled on Bhopal, the capital of the Indian state of Madhya Pradesh). When the protagonist hears someone observe that "this whole district looks like it was flung up by an earthquake," his home appears suddenly in an entirely new light: "On hearing Elli speak this one word, *earthquake*, something weird and painful happens in my head. Up to that moment this was Paradise Alley, the heart of the Nutcracker, a place I'd known all my life. When Elli says *earthquake* suddenly I'm seeing it as she does. Paradise Alley is a wreckage of baked earth mounds and piles of planks on which hang gunny sacks, plastic sheets, dried palm leaves. Like drunks with arms round each other's necks, the houses of the Nutcracker lurch along this lane which, now that I look, isn't really even a road, just a long gap left by chance between the dwellings. Everywhere's covered in shit and plastic. Truly I see how poor and disgusting are our lives" (106).

might respond to the black servant's insult, which emphasizes that "more than one response is conceivable" (Forter 276). Recognizing, for instance, that "they (the niggers) were not it, not what you wanted to hit" (*Absalom* 186), Sutpen could have developed a revolutionary yearning to level both class and racial hierarchies. However, the odds are stacked against such a response on Sutpen's part, as nothing in the boy's experience has prepared him to think beyond the color line: "[H]e was seeking among what little he had to call experience for something to measure it by, and he couldn't find anything" (188). Rather than conceiving of a kind of solidarity that transcends the boundaries of race, the first idea that comes to Sutpen's mind is simply to shoot the owner of the plantation (189) – an idea that arguably reflects the endemic violence of his Virginia mountain upbringing. At the same time, Sutpen senses that this "*wouldn't do no good*" (190; original emphasis), and still debating with himself, the insulted youth tries to find a more appropriate solution by drawing analogies between the current problem and his past experience:

> 'If you were fixing to combat them that had the fine rifles, the first thing you would do would be to get yourself the nearest thing to a fine rifle you could borrow or steal or make, wouldn't it?' and he said Yes. 'But this aint a question of rifles. So to combat them you have got to have what they have that made them do what he did. You got to have land and niggers and a fine house to combat them with. You see?' and he said Yes again. (192)

Building on the Virginia home's logic of gun-toting violence, Sutpen decides that he can only fight rich white men successfully if he rises to their social level, with "land and niggers and a fine house to combat them with." As is, perhaps, to be expected of a boy filled with the "self reliance of mountains and solitude" (195), Sutpen thus imaginatively models his "combat" against the white upper class on the individualist image of a gunfight, rather than envisaging a collective struggle of poor laborers – white and black – against the exploitative plantation owners.

It is, moreover, not only Sutpen's domestic background that severely limits his chances for dealing appropriately with his crisis of self-worth, for we also learn that he was sent to school only for "about three months one winter" (194). Sutpen's formal education thus proves woefully inadequate, too. One of the few things Sutpen remembers from his brief time at school is that the teacher once read to the class from a book about the West Indies, a place "to which poor men went in ships and became rich, *it didn't matter how*, so long as that man was clever and courageous" (195; emphasis added). The teacher's account of how colonial fortunes are made thus matches closely the way in which, according to

Franco Moretti, the colonies tend to be represented in nineteenth-century British novels: it is "the mythic geography – *pecunia ex machina* – of a wealth that is not really produced [...] but magically 'found' overseas" (*Atlas of the European Novel* 27). Combining the resources of his limited home experience with the teacher's misleading accounts of the West Indies, young Sutpen patches together his grand design of becoming a wealthy plantation owner.[16] He is aware that the accomplishment of the design will require "first of all and above all things money in considerable quantities and in the quite immediate future," and taking his teacher's ideologically distorted account of rags-to-riches careers in the West Indies at face value, Sutpen decides to leave the U.S. for Haiti (196). At this point in the novel, we know already that Sutpen will destroy several homes later in his life, but by emphasizing the highly inauspicious circumstances of his upbringing – inured to violence, and exposed to misleading information during his brief and unenlightening time at school – Faulkner's novel makes it possible for us to understand (though not condone) Sutpen's subsequent course of action.

Fantasies of Innocence: The American Adam

It is, in fact, precisely because Sutpen suffers from such an inauspicious upbringing that a seemingly outrageous claim made several times by Quentin's grandfather – namely that Sutpen's tragic flaw was "innocence" – gains at least some plausibility. Despite the fact that Sutpen ends up destroying one home after another, Quentin's grandfather insists that Sutpen at heart remained an innocent. Indeed, Grandfather Compson claims that Sutpen's innocence was already apparent in the latter's reaction to the black servant's insult:

> His trouble was innocence. All of a sudden he discovered, not what he wanted to do but what he just had to do, had to do it whether he wanted to or not, because if he did not do it he knew that he could never live with himself [...], never live with what all the dead men and women that had died to make him had left inside of him for him to pass on [...]. And that at the very moment when he discovered what it was, he found out that this was the last thing in the world he was equipped to do because he not only had not known that he would have to do this, he did not even know that it existed to be wanted, to need to be done, until he was almost fourteen years old. Because he was born in West Virginia, in the mountains [...]. (178)

16 In fact, Faulkner's novel also emphasizes that the father "probably" sent his son to school, "not to better himself," but out of "mere vindictive envy toward one or two men, planters, whom he had to see every now and then" (194). The two novels thus share the themes of patriarchal trouble, problematic father-son relationships, and inadequate schooling thus continues.

Explicitly related to his Virginia mountain background, Sutpen's innocence is also associated here with a lack of knowledge ("had not known that he would have to do this, he did not even know that it existed to be wanted, to need to be done"). Moreover, while it would seem that Sutpen must inevitably lose his innocence in the very moment of recognition, Quentin's grandfather maintains that this is not so. On the contrary, Supten kept his innocence "because after it [i.e. his innocence] finally told him what to do that night he forgot about it and didn't know he still had it" (194). Later, Quentin's grandfather defines Sutpen's supposed innocence in an almost biblical sense as a lack of knowledge of good and evil, for the man had "that innocence which believed that the ingredients of morality were like the ingredients of pie or cake and once you had measured them and balanced them and mixed them and put them into the oven it was all finished and nothing but pie or cake could come out" (212). It is possible, in short, to portray Sutpen as a victim of deleterious social circumstances: a young boy from a motherless home who was both intellectually and morally ill-equipped to deal with either the psychological or the societal pressures of an impoverished existence in the Deep South.[17]

If we therefore accept, for the time being, that the term 'innocence' may with some justice be applied to Thomas Sutpen, then it becomes easy to see that in many ways he corresponds to the type of figure that R. W. Lewis calls the American Adam. Michael Gellert argues that U. S. self-definitions have long involved the idea of a break with the past, and that this belief harks back to the Puritan notion "that America was the place for a new beginning in the history of mankind" (153). Gellert also notes that Thomas Jefferson – whose name the fictional town in *Absalom, Absalom!* carries – was among those who regarded the United States as a place where "the evils of the old European order [...] would no longer interfere with the people's ability to access their natural, God-given moral sense" (Gellert 149). For R. W. Lewis, it is from this particular view of history that the figure of the American Adam arises:

> America, it was said insistently from the 1820's onward, was not the end-product of a long historical process [...]; it was something entirely new. [...]
>
> The new habits to be engendered on the new American scene were suggested by the image of a radically new personality, the hero of the new adventure: an individual emancipated from history, happily bereft of ancestry, untouched and undefiled by the usual inheritances of family and race; an individual standing alone, self-reliant and

17 Of course, as Martin Gretchen notes, Sutpen initially wants to combat the Southern upper class but ultimately ends up joining and even defending it in the Civil War: "His personal fight becomes absorbed into the Southern conflict" (409).

> self-propelling, ready to confront whatever awaited him with the aid of his own unique and inherent resources. (5)

In this description, we can recognize a number of parallels to the figure of Thomas Sutpen: the emphasis on self-reliance, for instance, or the idea that it is possible to emancipate oneself from one's history and make a completely new beginning (as Sutpen tries to do twice, first in Haiti and then in Jefferson). Moreover, in terms of chronology, it is suggestive that Sutpen's life-changing experience of being insulted by a black servant, which lies at the origin of his design, occurs around 1820, and thus precisely when, according to Lewis, it became increasingly common in the American republic to emphasize a sense of historical rupture ("something entirely new").[18] There are, then, several reasons why it is possible for Quentin's grandfather to style Sutpen as a tragic version of the American Adam: a self-reliant and self-propelling figure of "heroic innocence" (Lewis 1) who embodies the New World's supposed potential for new beginnings, and who fails in his quest precisely because of his innocence.

At the same time, however, *Absalom, Absalom!* provides us with at least three different reasons why we should be wary of Grandfather Compson's portrayal of Sutpen as an Adamic innocent. The first of these reasons is that Sutpen's 'new beginning' in fact constitutes anything but a true break with his past. As we have seen, for instance, Sutpen's belief in self-reliant action and individual autonomy is itself part of his upbringing and cultural inheritance. Accordingly, Laurel Bollinger is right in suggesting that the figure of Sutpen exposes the myth of the autonomous individual who can simply leave his or her history behind (231). In addition, Faulkner's text is quite clear about the fact that Sutpen's reaction to the black servant's insult in part arises from his sense of duty to the past, for the boy believes that he could never again "live with what all the dead men and women that had died to make him had left inside of him for him to pass on" if he decided not to act (178). Paradoxically, then, Sutpen's attempt to break with the past is motivated by his sense of being bound and responsible to it. Finally, though Supten seems like a figure "of no discernible past" when he first appears in Jefferson (7), we know that the past later does come back to haunt him in the figure of Charles, the abandoned son from his first marriage. If, then, Faulkner's novel evokes the figure of the American Adam through the account of Sutpen given by Quentin's grandfather, it does so to critique the

18 We know from Faulkner's novel that Sutpen is thirteen or fourteen when the insult occurs (185), and as Sutpen was born in 1807 (*Absalom* 380), we can date the event to around 1820.

ideological dream that the figure embodies: the fantasy of a new beginning unburdened from the weight of history.

A second challenge to the narrative of innocence propagated by Quentin's grandfather is Miss Rosa's rendering of Sutpen as a demoniac Gothic villain. According to Quentin, his grandfather was Sutpen's "only friend" (220), and it is hardly surprising that a friend would want to depict Sutpen as innocent. By contrast, Rosa Coldfield has many reasons to detest Thomas Sutpen, since in her view he destroyed the home both of her father and of her sister Ellen, Sutpen's second wife. After Ellen's death, moreover, Sutpen adds insult to injury by telling Rosa that he might marry her if she were willing first to bear his child, in order to allow him to see whether it will be a boy or a girl: "if it was a boy and lived, they would be married" (228). Though Rosa at one point in the novel claims to have forgiven Sutpen, and even that she "had nothing to forgive" (138), much of what she says about the man in fact sounds rather like an indictment:

> [H]e was not articulated in this world. He was a walking shadow. He was the light blinded bat-like image of his own torment cast by a fierce demoniac lantern up from beneath the earth's crust and hence in retrograde, reverse; from abysmal and chaotic dark to eternal and abysmal dark completing his descending [...], clinging, trying to cling with vain unsubstantial hands to what he hoped would hold him, save him, arrest him – Ellen [...], myself, then last of all that fatherless daughter of Wash Jones's only child who, so I heard once, died in a Memphis brothel – to find severance (even if not rest and peace) at last in the stroke of a rusty scythe. (139)

In this heavily Gothic denouncement, Rosa associates Sutpen with netherworldly forces ("demoniac," "from beneath the earth's crust") and also invokes two other women on whose lives he wrought havoc: her sister Ellen and the fifteen-year-old Milly Jones, who, after Ellen's death and Rosa's refusal of Sutpen's 'proposal,' bears Sutpen's child but is then cast aside by him when he finds that she has given birth not to a male heir, but to a girl (an action that leads Milly's father to kill Sutpen with a scythe; 234). Drawing a sharp contrast between Rosa's and Grandfather Compson's account, *Absalom, Absalom!* thus lends support to Harald Welzer's thesis that memories are shaped by the desire for meaning of the person who remembers, and that socio-cultural story templates are used to establish the desired meaning (160, 186).[19] While, on the one hand, there is Quentin's grandfather, who uses the template of the American

19 See also Ulrike Hanna Meinhof (7): "As much as we might think that our self-constructions are our own, we always draw upon socially available resources with which we construct our experience of ourselves and the reality surrounding us."

Adam in his attempt retrospectively to absolve his friend, Rosa aims to exact narrative revenge by framing Sutpen as a Gothic villain.

A House Divided: From Biblical Intertext to National Allegory

If Rosa's Gothic counter-discourse and Sutpen's inability to make a new beginning challenge the image of Sutpen as an American Adam, a third challenge arises from the biblical title of Faulkner's novel, which aligns Sutpen, not with Adam, but instead with King David, and thus with a morally much more ambivalent figure. Even as a boy, Sutpen appears a bit like the young shepherd David in his belief that he might single-handedly defeat a seemingly invincible enemy: Goliath in the case of David, and the racist system of exploitation in the U.S. South in Sutpen's case. More importantly, however, the story of Sutpen's children in several ways parallels the story of the children of King David. According to the biblical tale, Absalom is one of King David's sons, and he kills his half-brother Amnon because the latter raped Tamar, Absalom's younger sister, just as Henry Sutpen will eventually kill his half brother Charles. Moreover, like Henry, Absalom ends up opposing his father (in Absalom's case leading a rebellion against the king). What connects the two stories, more broadly speaking, is a focus on domestic turmoil and its familial as well as dynastic consequences.

In addition, the precise context from which the novel's title is taken sheds some light on one of its key themes: on how history tends to come back to haunt us. In the biblical narrative, Absalom's rebellion against his father proves unsuccessful, and when King David learns that the son was killed after the battle, he utters a heart-rending cry of mourning that provides the source for Faulkner's title: "O my son Absalom, O Absalom, my son, my son!" (2 Samuel 19:4; KJV). As Peter von Matt rightly points out, the intensity of the king's grief is likely to appear puzzling to most readers, since Absalom wanted to kill David and was, from this perspective, justly punished for rising up against his father (28). For von Matt, the key to this interpretive puzzle lies in David's past, for the king, having fallen in love with Bathsheba, a married woman, conspired with one of his generals to ensure that Bathsheba's husband, Uriah, would be killed in battle (2 Samuel 11; see von Matt 28–29). The prophet Nathan subsequently foretold what the punishment for David's actions would be: "Thus saith the Lord, Behold, I will raise up evil against thee out of thine own house" (2 Samuel 12:11, KJV). Crucially, von Matt notes (28), it is in the very next episode that Absalom's name is first mentioned (2 Samuel 13:1). This suggests that it is Absalom who will be the instrument of divine retribution: the "evil" arising out of the king's own house. The sins of the father are, in this view, visited upon the son – which is, as we have seen, precisely what happens in Faulkner's novel, where both Henry and Charles become victims of their father's ruthless design.

As noted in the introductory chapter, it is tempting to see such allusions to biblical and other well known texts as home-making devices: a web of familiar intertextual references that makes a novel's readers feel more at home. However, in the case of *Absalom, Absalom!* there are a number of problems with this view. For one thing, it is only for readers who know the bible well that the title of Faulkner's novel could serve as guidance in the first place. For anyone who is unfamiliar with the details of the biblical narrative – i.e. the majority of the world population today, and arguably most Christians, too – the novel's title is enigmatic rather than helpful, especially since the reference is not explained or elaborated in the text. In other words, as we have seen in the case of Steven Spielberg's *E. T.*, religious intertexts can potentially serve as home-making devices, but their effect depends both on how, precisely, the references are deployed, and on readers' available intertextual repertoire.

Moreover, despite the parallels mentioned above, the plot of *Absalom, Absalom!* also differs in crucial respects from the biblical story. Unlike Thomas Sutpen, for instance, King David never asks Absalom to act against his half-brother (i.e. Absalom takes revenge for the rape entirely on his own initiative, whereas Sutpen himself urges his son Henry to take action). Similarly, unlike Absalom's half-brother Amnon, Charles does not rape his half-sister Judith, who would in fact be perfectly happy to marry Charles. Finally, while Absalom tries to depose his father and prematurely assume his position as David's successor, Henry rebels against his father by repudiating his home and thus refusing to become his dynastic heir at all. In short, while the biblical narrative may seem to provide Faulkner's readers with some reassuring interpretive guidance and thus make them feel more at home in the text, the manifold contrasts between the two stories end up complicating matters further.

Less conspicuous than these biblical intertext, but equally important in terms of the novels themes is its connection to Abraham Lincoln's 'House Divided' speech. In this speech, which Lincoln gave after he had won the Republican nomination for Senator from Illinois in 1858, the future President argued that a "house divided against itself" could not stand, and that the U.S. government would not "endure, permanently half *slave* and half *free*." (qtd. in McPherson 179; original emphasis). Lincoln's image of a "house divided against itself" draws on two distinct intertextual sources: a parable told by Jesus, who was accused of having driven out a demon with the help of Beelzebub, and who defended himself by insisting that this was impossible because the powers of evil were not a "house divided" (Mark 3:25), and a nineteenth-century American discourse that imagined the nation as reflected, and even embodied, in the domestic sphere: "Antebellum American writers celebrated the home as the symbol of 'America,' the site of nurture and republican fraternity, the embodiment of equality, affection, and toleration" (Egan 13). Given that the home was thus imagined as a symbol of the American nation, Ken Egan Jr. argues that stories about fallen houses (such as Edgar Allen Poe's "The Fall of the House of Usher") necessarily constituted a challenge to Antebellum (over-)confidence in enduring national stability (170–173). Focusing more specifically on *Absalom, Absalom!*, Eric Sundquist observes that both Lincoln and Supten try to save their 'house' from disintegrating, and in both cases it is the Civil War that forces a resolution of the crisis: "It is not by any means an analogy in which they or their designs are exactly duplicated but, rather, one in which they are mirror images in the sense that a mirror image reverses the figure to which it corresponds" (105) Just as is the case with the novel's biblical intertext, the links to Lincoln and his famous House Divided Speech are thus far from simple one-to-one correspondences; rather, they serve to increase the text's resonance and complexity because they create a dialectical tension between familiarity and alienation.

If we take the biblical intertext as a cue for allegorical decoding – allegory is, after all a scriptural mode of interpretation – and combine this with the text's reference to Lincoln's speech (which focused on the future of the American nation), then there is ample ground for us to attempt a reading of *Absalom, Absalom!* in terms of national allegory. In his introduction to the concept of allegory, Jeremy Tambling argues that the genre is still often misrepresented in modern literary studies as a rigid and abstract way of en- or decoding a text. At the same time, critics following the lead of Walter Benjamin and Paul de Man have challenged this view (Tambling, *Allegory* 1–2), and Fredric Jameson, too, insists that an allegorical reading does not necessarily constitute a narrowing or closing off of interpretive possibilities, but can instead lead to an "opening up of the text to multiple meanings, to successive rewritings" (*The Political Unconscious* 14). We have seen that both the biblical intertext and the thematic reference to Lincoln's speech add to the complexity of *Absalom, Absalom!*, and by systematically reading the novel as a national allegory, we will be able to perform precisely the kind of opening up that Jameson regards as the positive potential of allegorical interpretation.

Jameson himself has in fact commented on the concept of national allegory, making the controversial suggestion that it is "third-world texts," in particular, that "*necessarily* project a political dimension in the form of national allegory" ("Third-World Literature" 69; emphasis added). Aijaz Ahmad has rightly critized Jameson's rigid link between national allegory and "third-world texts" for its unwarranted, binary opposition between a unified West and a supposedly monolithic third-world Other (95). Among other things, Ahmad points out that Jameson overstates the presence of national allegory in 'third-world' literature while at the same time underestimating "the presence of analogous impulses in US cultural ensembles" (110). In the light of Ahmad's critique, we may speculate that there is a tendency toward national allegory in fiction from peripheral regions in general, irrespective of whether that periphery be located in the United States (e.g. the South), or in India, or elsewhere in the world. We may also ask whether a reader's distance from a particular location makes it easier for him or her to allegorize the literal level of a narrative because regional details seem to serve no real function except to add 'local color.' This would imply, conversely, that the greater the extent to which readers feel at home in a particular culture, the less likely (or willing) they are to 'devalue' the thick descriptions of everyday local life by recasting them as merely allegorical ciphers for broader, national concerns. Finally, the ways of reading allegorically may themselves differ vastly among different interpretive communities, to use a concept proposed by Stanley Fish. Fish argues that it is from the interpretive community to which they belong that readers learn how to construct the meaning of a text, and that such communities therefore "determine the shape of what is read rather than, as is usually assumed, the other way around" (14). If this is so, then it may be communally shaped interpretive desires, rather than any particular textual features, that would explain the decision to recast a novel – *Absalom, Absalom!*, for instance – in terms of a national allegory. Put differently: there are different ways of making oneself at home in a text, and these techniques of interpretive home-making may have much to do with our own communal and cultural belonging(s).

Plantation Domesticity: Slavery at Home

Though the concept of national allegory is far from problematic, a reading of *Absalom, Absalom!* in these terms quickly proves productive because the story of the origins of Sutpen's Hundred – Thomas Sutpen's plantation home – displays several links to the colonial conquest of the New World and the history of the United States, in particular. Early in the novel, for instance, we learn that Sutpen takes the land for his plantation "from a tribe of ignorant Indians" (10). Later, at a time when he had only one "gold Spanish coin" left, Sutpen engages a French architect to design the plantation manor subsequently built by black slaves (26; see also 31). These elements from the novel allegorically encode important aspects of the history of the New World, which the Spanish 'discovered' and then plundered because, among other things, of its rich supply of gold, and which involved the dispossession of Native Americans as well as the enslavement of black people. Moreover, the presence of the French architect can be read as an allegorical reference to the so-called Louisiana Purchase of 1803, in which the United States bought a huge territory – including the future state of Mississippi – from the French (Gordon S. Wood 368–370).[20] Sutpen's Hundred, the home of the family, is thus allegorically connected in *Absalom, Absalom!* to a broader continental and national history. In addition, we have already seen that Sutpen is a critical reworking of R.W. Lewis's figure of the American Adam, whose national and allegorical dimensions we need hardly emphasize further.

What we do need to re-examine, however, is the notion of innocence that forms such a crucial component of the idea of the American Adam, for we can rewrite allegorically the notion of innocence if we relate it to the cultural role of slavery in the United States. If *Absalom, Absalom!* critiques the figure of the American Adam by putting Sutpen's innocence in question in various ways – through Sutpen's inability truly to begin anew, by Rosa's Gothic version of Sutpen's story, and through that story's complicated intertextual relation to the story of King David and his son Absalom – then the fact that Sutpen is a slaveholder adds a crucial political twist to this critique. Carolyn Porter, for instance, has observed that the image of a slave-holding yet heroic innocent – this "wedding of the upwardly mobile American hero's dream of success to the Southern planter-aristocrat's paternalism" – is a particularly disturbing feature of Faulkner's novel (173). Indeed, what this combination in the allegorical figure of Thomas Sutpen highlights is that the United States' favored myth of national innocence is similarly troubled by the historical fact of slavery. The first sizeable shipment of Africans arrived in English-speaking North America as early as in 1619, and by the final decades of the seventeenth century slavery was starting to be systematically developed (e.g. Painter 22; Betty Wood 73–78). The 'peculiar institution' was thus well established when the American revolutionaries began to fight for independence, and numerous critics have commented on the paradox that the very men who feared 'enslavement' by the British, and who therefore declared their independence on the principle that all men were created equal, were themselves slaveholders (e.g. Middlekauff 119–126; Swaminathan 93).[21] Moreover, if we accept the view that the American Revolution was compromised

20 Elizabeth Maddock Dillon and Michael J Drexler note that, to this day, popular accounts of American history highlight its supposedly non-violent nature, ignoring "the bloody backdrop of the Haitian Revolution out of which" it emerged (8).

21 Thomas Jefferson – a Virginian like Sutpen and 'patron saint' of Quentin's fictional hometown – in many ways epitomized this paradox, for not only was he the author of the declaration of independence and a slave owner, but he also vocally advocated the view that the British were pursuing a "deliberate and systematical plan of reducing us to slavery" (8).

by the unresolved problem of slavery, and that these conflicts made a later national crisis like the Civil War virtually inevitable (Blackburn 141, 229 and 397–409; Osterhammel 768), then we can say that for the young nation, just as for Sutpen, a willful fantasy of innocence concerning the past returned violently to haunt the present. As Eric Sundquist puts it concisely, "Sutpen's crisis of innocence, as well as the flaw that engenders it [i.e. his first son's 'black blood'] is the nation's" (102). From the very beginning of U.S. history, the existence of slavery compromised the nation's revolutionary ideals expressed in the opening sentences of the Declaration of Independence – a challenge that the 'innocent' figure of Sutpen embodies.[22]

This challenge becomes all the more forceful if we consider that it was precisely around the time of Sutpen's childhood (i.e. in the early years of the nineteenth century) that there was a crucial shift of emphasis from domination toward 'innocence' in slaveholder ideology. This shift of emphasis was expressed through what Jeffrey Robert Young has called "plantation domesticity." Young argues that, to most eighteenth-century planters, the idea that there should be bonds of affection between slaves and their owners would have been entirely foreign; rather, the masters "despised and feared their bondservants" (124). By 1815, however, there was a growing assumption among planters that African Americans were human beings, albeit perpetually child-like ones (Young 131). As Richard Godden points out, the "peculiar institution peculiarly demanded that its managers view their slaves as a threat but also, and simultaneously, as children of limited will, as Sambos to be loved through subordination" (254). By thus figuring the enslaved as part of the extended family belonging to the plantation home, slave owners could both diffuse their own fears of a black insurrection and imagine themselves as stern but ultimately benevolent fathers (Gudemstad 82). The notion of plantation domesticity thus allowed slaveholders imaginatively to transfigure the daily violence of racist oppression into loving gestures of parental care.[23]

The link between Sutpen's 'innocence' and the "plantation domesticity" of slaveholder ideology initially seems at odds with the fact, observed by Richard Godden, that Sutpen differs from the more established Southern planters precisely in that he does not style himself as a benign fatherly figure in his dealings

22 See Gerald Horne's *The Counter-Revolution of 1776* (2014) for a particularly critical account of the link between the American Revolution and the institution of slavery.

23 In a deeply ironic reference to this paternalistic discourse of plantation domesticity, a Kentucky slave plantation in Toni Morrison's 1987 novel *Beloved* is called Sweet Home – a name about which one of the former slaves says early in the novel: "It wasn't sweet and it sure wasn't home" (14).

with the slaves (254–255). Instead, “naked and panting and bloody to the waist,” he engages in fierce wrestling matches with ‘his’ negroes, “perhaps as a matter of sheer deadly forethought toward the retention of supremacy, domination” (*Absalom* 21). There is little sense, in other words, that Sutpen is merely benevolently watching over his black children; rather, he fights them so fiercely that his son Henry – whom Sutpen at one point brings with him to watch the father wrestling the slaves – ends up “screaming and vomiting” (21). Given Sutpen’s disregard for even a show of plantation domesticity, it is tempting to conclude, with Cleanth Brooks, that Sutpen is ultimately not a representative or typical Southern planter (*Towards Yoknapatawpha* 292–294).

However, the idea that Sutpen is not representative jars with Brooks’s simultaneous claim that Sutpen “outdoes in his vehement orthodoxy” the established planters (*Towards Yoknapatawpha* 293). How, we must ask, can Sutpen be untypical yet somehow more orthodox than slaveholders from the older, long-established families? One way of reconciling Brooks’s seemingly contradictory claims is to read Sutpen as a literal return of the repressed for the other planters, who would prefer to mask and forget the necessarily violent nature of slavery. For the old-stock planters, the foundational violence of the system of plantation slavery lies buried deep in the past; their forefathers may have had to break the will of men and women who had been born free, but they themselves preferred to see themselves as benevolent fathers to their inherited, child-like, ‘domesticated’ slaves. Raymond Williams has commented on this very common illusion that long-established property is somehow more innocent than recently accumulated wealth:

> Very few titles to property could bear humane investigation, in the long process of conquest, theft, political intrigue [...], extortion and the power of money. It is a deep and persistent illusion to suppose that time confers on these familiar processes of acquisition an innocence which can be contrasted with the ruthlessness of subsequent stages of the same essential drives. (50)

To be confronted with “the ruthlessness of subsequent stages of the same essential drives”: this is what happens to the planters when Sutpen arrives in Jefferson to drag his plantation “violently” from the earth (*Absalom* 4). Sutpen truly is both unlike all the established planters and at the same time more representative than they are of the reality of a slave economy, for his ruthlessness renders visible the foundational violence that the ideology of plantation domesticity attempts to conceal.

If so far our allegorical ‘opening up’ of *Absalom, Absalom!* has been limited, for the most part, to the evil of slavery in the U.S. South, then Sutpen’s Virginia origin is the key element that allows us to recast his story in more broadly national, American terms. Edmund Sears Morgan has shown that the single most important good with which the revolutionary U. S. government bought the support of other nations in its struggle for independence was tobacco, produced on the Southern slave plantations, and particularly in Virginia:

> Virginia was the largest of the new United States, in territory, in population, in influence – and in slaveholding. Virginians owned more than 40 percent of all slaves in the new nation. It was Virginia slaves who grew most of the tobacco that helped buy American independence. [...] Virginians drafted not only the Declaration of Independence but also the United States Constitution of 1787 and the first ten amendments to it. And Americans elected Virginians to the presidency of the United States under that constitution for thirty-two out of the first thirty-six years of its existence. They were all slaveholders. (5–6)

We can therefore say, with Morgan, that to a large extent "Americans bought their independence by slave labor" (5), and that Virginia constitutes the key link between the slave economy and national politics. Sutpen's Virginia origin is thus crucial for the allegorical significance of *Absalom, Absalom!*, pointing as it does to the unsavory paradox that enslavement lies at the very heart of the United States' freedom as a nation.

The Specter of Race and Slavery Abroad

The reason why a re-examination of this genuinely American paradox was particularly urgent at the time when Faulkner wrote *Absalom, Absalom!* is that 'race relations' in the U.S. were in a deep state of crisis in the first decades of the twentieth century.[24] While the so-called Reconstruction of the post-Civil-War years initially prioritized black freedom and emancipation, the desire for national reconciliation between white Northerners and Southerners eventually "trumped race" (Blight 2). A new phase in race relations thus began in 1877, when federal troops were withdrawn from the Southern states and the North implicitly acquiesced in the South's demand that the region's dominant whites were to deal with the 'problem of race' on their own terms (Blackburn 429–432). As C. Vann Woodward notes, while it was not immediately apparent what precisely the "new status of the Negro" would be, it became clear by the early years

24 As Barbara J. Fields rightly notes, the term *race relations* is highly problematic: "Race relations as an analysis of society takes for granted that race is a valid empirical datum and thereby shifts attention from the actions that constitute racism-enslavement, disfranchisement, segregation, lynching, massacres, and pogroms-to the traits that constitute race" (151).

of the twentieth century that African Americans "would be effectively disfranchised throughout the South" through the system generally known as Jim Crow (6).[25] The fact that the various retellings of Sutpen's story take place between September 1909 and January 1910 in *Absalom, Absalom!* is thus significant, as it situates the novel's present at a time when race relations in the post-Civil-War South had arguably reached their nadir (e.g. Osterhammel 1210). In addition, we learn that Henry, Sutpen's son, secretly moves back to Sutpen's Hundred in 1905 (*Absalom* 140), and it is perhaps no coincident that this allegorical, racist specter from the Civil-War past returns home in the same year that W.E.B. Du Bois founded the Niagara Movement (Grossman 101), which called for racial equality and is generally considered a forerunner of the National Association for the Advancement of Colored People (NAACP). The latter was founded in the early months of 1909, and the title of the NAACP's monthly magazine, *The Crisis*, established in November 1910, bears eloquent witness to the social climate of the time (Ovington 16–17; Rampersad 472). The years 1909 and 1910 are thus not merely the temporal setting for the novel's various retellings (as well as for Quentin's eventual confrontation with Henry Sutpen; see *Absalom* 298), but also the period when the deepening crisis in race relations in the U.S. led to decisive developments in black self-emancipation. Henry, the long-lost son who killed his half-brother because of the latter's racial 'impurity,' returns – and dies – in Faulkner's novel precisely when the black emancipation movement began more directly to confront the social and legal consequences of Jim Crow.

Moreover, the fact that the most extended retelling of Thomas Sutpen's story – Quentin and Shreve's collaborative narrative – takes place not in the South, but at Harvard in Cambridge, Massachusetts, highlights the extent to which the North was involved in this crisis in race relations. According to Thadious M. Davis, segregationist practices had hardened not only in the South of Jim Crow, but throughout the nation, and they continued to do so after World War I, with the tacit approval of Woodrow Wilson's presidential administration (411). The Northern setting of the novel's retellings allegorically acknowledges the North's involvement in the country's racial crisis, and the fact that Shreve is Canadian extends the reach of *Absalom, Absalom!* even beyond the nation's boundaries.

If Shreve allegorically internationalizes the novel, then Sutpen's period of residence in Haiti from the early 1820s to about 1833 serves more concretely to highlight both historical and present dimensions of U.S. imperial policies. Haiti is described in *Absalom, Absalom!* as "halfway between the dark inscrutable

---

25 See Norman (4) on the complex history of the term *Jim Crow*.

continent from which the black blood [...] was ravished by violence, and the cold known land" from which Sutpen came (202). We never find out how exactly young Sutpen reaches Haiti, but we do learn that he ultimately worked as an "overseer or foreman or something to a French sugar planter," and that as such he helped quell a violent uprising (199). Commenting on this episode, Richard Godden insists that Sutpen's account of a slave revolt on Haiti in 1827 is anachronistic because "there were neither slavers nor French plantations" in the post-revolutionary 'black republic' (251).[26] By contrast, Leigh Anne Duck contends that, though formal slavery no longer existed in Haiti, the working conditions on the plantations were in fact virtually indistinguishable from those on the slave plantations of the U. S. South (34–35). John T. Matthews concurs with Duck's account:

> The Haitian Constitution of 1804 had abolished slavery, outlawed white landownership, and confiscated the property of French colonists [...]. Almost immediately mulatto offspring of former white landowners began to reclaim their land, violating the spirit of the measures and angering Emperor Dessalines. When Dessalines attempted to reinforce policies favoring Negroes, the mulatto class rebelled and Dessalines was assassinated. Meanwhile, agricultural failures stemming from the breakup of large plantations and the creation of small black-owned farms, especially in Haiti's southern region, led to reforms designed by President Jean Pierre Boyer to return peasants to laborer status on large farms. These measures constituted the notorious Rural Code [...]. (253)

Under the Rural Code, the rights of black laborers were so severely restricted that the historian Eric Williams describes the effects of the bill as "the restoration of slavery, minus the whip" (334). And indeed, if we look at the text of *Absalom, Absalom!*, we find that the black Haitian laborers – *de iure* freedmen – are depicted in such equivocal terms that their *de facto* status as quasi-slaves becomes apparent. Accordingly, as Matthews points out, even Sutpen himself "may not register that the black plantation workers he oversees are not technically slaves; he cares only that they may be treated that way" (253). Moreover, even if the novel's depiction of conditions in Haiti were incorrect (Blackburn 218), it would nevertheless have resonated strongly in the segregated United States of the early twentieth century, where African Americans were *de iure* equal but *de facto* increasingly discriminated against: "In sum, Thomas Supten travels to a locale shaped by economic and legal structures that prefigured post-Civil War

---

26 The military struggle in Haiti for independence from France ended in 1804 (Popkin 140), and the constitution established in 1805 proclaimed: "slavery is abolished forever" (qtd. in Popkin 2).

sharecropping in the U.S. South – the form of labor still experienced in Faulkner's era, by up to 80 percent of farmworkers in some regions" (Duck 35). The 'exotic' space of nineteenth-century Haiti thus suddenly appears as very close to home.

Moreover, Faulkner wrote *Absalom, Absalom!* at a time when the recent military occupation of Haiti by the U.S. was still frequently, and controversially, discussed in the national media.[27] The occupation of Haiti in 1915, which ended in 1934, had been justified by the island republic's economic instability, the causes of which reached back to the 1820s (i.e. precisely the time when Sutpen resided there):

> As part of the negotiations to achieve international recognition, in 1825 Haiti agreed to pay reparations to France to the tune of 150 million francs in gold. France had demanded these costs to compensate it for the costs of the war and also to pay the former plantation and slave-owners for losses. This move by France was supported by the United States [...]. (Street 4; see also Bryan 43)

The 1825 arrangement, which constitutes the root cause of Haiti's long-term financial instability, was thus supported by the slave-holding United States, whose government also withheld diplomatic recognition of the new black republic until 1862 (i.e. after the outbreak of the Civil War; see Herring 239; Gordon S. Wood 537). So crippling was Haiti's historical burden of reparation that it remained one of the island's major policy concerns even in the early decades of the twentieth century, despite the fact that Haitian governments had shown exemplary diligence in meeting debt payments (Hans R. Schmidt 32, 113, and 168; see also Popkin 152). In the meantime, and especially since work on the Panama Canal had begun in 1904, the U.S. showed itself more aggressively determined to maintain political stability in the Caribbean "as a means of preventing foreign encroachment that might threaten the developing American military, political, and economic hegemony in the area" (Hans R. Schmidt 43). If the Haitian republic's economic instability ultimately provided a rationale for U.S. intervention, this instability can in turn be traced back to the reparation

27 According to Ineke Bockting, it was in early 1934 that Faulkner began to combine four short stories which he had written between the late 1920s and the early 1930s into "a manuscript that he initially entitled *Dark House*"; by August 1934, Faulkner had decided on the title *Absalom, Absalom!* (1). When Faulkner began work on the novel, the U.S. troops were thus only just about to withdraw from Haiti.

payments the imposition of which the U.S. government had supported.[28] Put differently: At the time when Faulkner's novel was published, Haiti – much like the United States in general, and the South in particular – was still quite materially haunted by the unresolved conflicts between its revolutionary heritage and the historical burdens of racism and slavery. The allegory of *Absalom, Absalom!* is thus not, strictly speaking, national; rather, Faulkner's regionalist novel simultaneously constitutes a truly transnational allegory of the United States and its long-term entanglement in hemispheric policies of racialized injustice.

Gothic Revisited: Material Haunting and Uncanny Narration

This notion of material haunting makes it necessary for us to return to the genre of the Gothic and its larger role in Faulkner's novel, for it is precisely such historical remnants (or revenants) from the past that lie at the heart of this generic tradition. In admirably succinct fashion, Terry Eagleton has outlined how Gothic fiction, "this most subjectivist and supernatural of literary forms," is also a grossly materialist genre:

> [A]t its centre lie disputed wills and struggles over inheritance, secret legacies and financial double-dealing. [...] Gothic is a form in which the dead take command of the living – in which the clammy hand of the past stretches out and manipulates the present, reducing it to a hollow repetition of itself. The present is awash with spectres and revenants, with transmitted curses and rumours of primordial crimes; but it requires no great labour of decipherment to see in all this how the deadweight of property and inheritance moulds an upper-class world, and the novels are not shy of laying bare these connections themselves. (*Heathcliff and the Great Hunger* 194)

We have already seen how the "deadweight of property and inheritance" affects Thomas Sutpen and his design, as well as, more generally, the Southern States and U.S. American involvement in Haiti. In addition, one of the figures who most haunts Sutpen and his acknowledged son Henry is Charles Bon, the child who returns to reclaim his dynastic inheritance. Further, "secret legacies and financial double-dealing" pervade *Absalom, Absalom!*: in the dubious scheme Sutpen proposes to Rosa's father (who, in consequence, ends his life as a 'madman' in the attic), or in the figure of a lawyer hired by Charles's mother, Sutpen's first wife (a man whom Charles knows to be scheming for money; see *Absalom*

28 See also Jeremy D. Popkin, who cites internal factors – "above all, the failure to integrate the poorer classes of the population into society at a time when other countries were moving toward greater democracy" – but also emphasizes the "role of foreign economic interests and the intervention of foreign governments, particularly the United States" as explanations for Haiti's continuing problems (158; cf. Coupeau 53).

250). It is, once again, the Canadian outsider Shreve who comments on the importance of such material haunting – on the "defeated grandfathers and freed slaves (or have I got it backward and was it your folks that are free and the niggers that lost?) and bullets in the dining room table and such," which constantly remind white Southerners "to never forget" (289). In addition, Shreve's sly parenthetical question whether it might not be "the niggers that lost" reminds us that the white trauma of defeat in the Civil War, though real, is clearly not the full story. Tellingly, however, not a single black character assumes the role of embedded narrator in *Absalom, Absalom!*, which in some sense reproduces the practice of segregation on the level of the novel's narration (much as in *Mrs. Dalloway* colonial characters tend not to be focalized from within; see chapter 3).

Gothic fiction's concern with "guilty secrets from communal and family pasts" (Botting 115) is thus a key preoccupation in Faulkner's novel. As Fred Botting suggests, in the course of the nineteenth century Gothic styles became "domesticated" (123), leading to a kind of "homely Gothic": no longer set in gloomy castles or sublime Romantic landscapes, these texts focus on "horrors that are much closer to home" (113). One example of such 'homely horrors' would be the secret of Sutpen's abandoned first family. In addition, Rosa at one point evokes the trope of the haunted Gothic home when she tells Quentin about a mysterious presence in Sutpen's Hundred: "There's something in that house. [...] Something living in it. Hidden in it. It has been out there for four years, living hidden in that house" (140). Only later do we learn that this "something" is Henry Sutpen, who has returned in his old age to the house of his father, and who will eventually perish there when it burns to the ground.

Sutpen's Hundred, which had always been an 'unhomely' home, thus also becomes decidedly uncanny. As we saw in the introductory chapter, Freud argues that the uncanny arises from a return, in alienated form, of something repressed but long familiar ("The Uncanny" 148). In *Absalom, Absalom!*, the figures of Charles Bon and Henry are among the instances of this return of the repressed, as is the way in which Sutpen functions as a reminder of the inherent violence of slavery for the older and more established planters. More broadly, themes such as homoeroticism (Charles and Henry, as well as Quentin and Shreve) or incest and miscegenation (Charles and Judith) constitute a return of what has been repressed culturally in "Western history's long tradition of sexism, heterosexism, and racism" (Norman W. Jones 343). In staging these returns, Faulkner's novel plays on the "terrors and horrors of transgression" that Jeremy Tambling associates with the Gothic as a genre (7).

Crucially, beyond such uncanny returns on the level of content or theme, *Absalom, Absalom!* is also told in a style that can best be described as uncanny narration.[29] What this means is that the text uses particular stylistic techniques to create, within readers' minds, a rough equivalent to a repressed but long familiar knowledge, thus heightening the novel's emotional impact. The way in which this is done is, in part, through a combination of two techniques that we may call 'perceptual overload' and 'fragmentary exposition.' Consider, for instance, the following sentence, which appears toward the very beginning of the novel and which focuses on Quentin's familiarity with the story of Thomas Sutpen:

> It was a part of his twenty years' heritage of breathing the same air and hearing his father talk about the man; a part of the town's – Jefferson's – eighty years' heritage of the same air which the man himself had breathed between this September afternoon in 1909 and that Sunday morning in June in 1833 when he first rode into town out of no discernible past and acquired his land no one knew how and built his house, his mansion, apparently out of nothing and married Ellen Coldfield and begot his two children – the son who widowed the daughter who had not yet been a bride – and so accomplished his allotted course to its violent (Miss Coldfield at least would have said, just) end. (7)

In hindsight, we recognize that the passage already hints at the fact that Henry will kill the suitor of his sister, Judith, for the text mentions "the son [i.e. Henry] who widowed [i.e. killed the husband-to-be of] the daughter [i.e. Judith]." Moreover, a few pages later, Henry is described as a "murderer and almost a fratricide" (10), so that one could even guess that the prospective husband is Henry's half-brother. However, because these bits of expository information are dispersed throughout the text and often cryptically expressed (e.g. without the use of proper names, and formulated in an extremely circumlocutory manner), most readers are unlikely to be able consciously to process or remember the information.

This problem is exacerbated, moreover, by the incredibly long sentences characteristic of Faulkner's novel, which are so complex that, as readers, we struggle to understand the main point of the narrative and therefore miss a great

29 While Samuel Kimball uses the term *uncanny narration* in an article on *Moby-Dick* (see chapter one), he defines it in a much more general sense, noting that "'narration' and 'canny' share the same Indo-European root, *gno-*, meaning to know. Thus narration is in some sense a trope of the canny, a knowing how to tell, a telling knowledge; and to narrate includes the other side of the uncanny, the homeness of homelessness" (544–545).

deal of incidental information. At the same time, this 'superfluous' or excess information is arguably not simply lost altogether, but perceived and processed subliminally; it by-passes the conscious mind and is stored unconsciously, waiting to be (re)activated later on. The technique of uncanny narration thus first presents us with story fragments that are related to each other but dispersed throughout the text, subliminally familiarizing us with all the important information even as we fail to connect the dots consciously. The text then confronts us with the full story at some later stage, leading to the uncanny realization on our part that this 'unknown' story is in fact already familiar.

Perhaps the best example of this technique of uncanny narration is the way in which we learn that Charles's mother was "part negro" (283).[30] Before this crucial truth is revealed, fragments of information appear in no fewer than ten different passages dispersed throughout the novel.[31] To understand more clearly how the technique of uncanny narration works, we need to examine some of these lengthy passages in detail, as it is their cumulative effect that makes uncanny narration possible:

> (a) [Sutpen] told Grandfather how he had put his first wife aside, like eleventh and twelfth century kings did: 'I found that she was not and could never be, through no fault of her own, adjunctive or incremental to the design which I had in mind, so I provided for her and put her aside.' (194)

> (b) [Grandfather Compson described how Sutpen] granted that by certain lights there was injustice in what he did but that he had obviated that as much as lay in his power by being above-board in the matter; that he could have simply deserted her, could have taken his hat and walked out, but he did not: and that he had what Grandfather would have to admit was a good and valid claim, if not to the whole place which he alone had saved, as well as the lives of all the white people on it, at least that portion of it which had been specifically described and deeded to him in the marriage settlement which he had entered in good faith, with no reservations as to his obscure origin and material equipment, while there had been not only reservation but actual misrepresentation on their part and misrepresentation of such a crass nature as to have not only voided and frustrated without his knowing it the central motivation of his entire design, but would have made an ironic conclusion of all that he had suffered

30 Another example of the technique is the scene in which Sutpen is killed by Wash Jones, one of his tenants. Parts of this scene are told on page 139, 145, and 151 (among others), but the fact that Wash Jones killed Sutpen because the latter had disowned his child with Wash's daughter, Milly, is only stated explicitly on page 234.

31 The ten passages occur on the following pages of my edition of *Absalom, Absalom!*: 194, 199, 200, 205, 211–212, 218, 219, 220, 238, and 261.

> and endured in the past and all that he could ever accomplish in the future toward that design – which claim he had voluntarily relinquished, taking only twenty niggers out of all he might have claimed and which many another man in his place would have insisted upon keeping and (in which contention) would have been supported by both legal and moral sanction if not the delicate one of conscience [...]. (199)

In passage (a), we are told for the first time that there was something about Charles's mother that made her unsuitable for Sutpen's design, though what exactly the problem was remains unstated. In passage (b), we learn more about the situation: that there was "misrepresentation" on the part of the relatives, and that it is a kind of misrepresentation that would have been condemned by the dominant legal and moral order (i.e. Sutpen's reaction to this mysterious misrepresentation had "both legal and moral sanction if not the delicate one of conscience"). The key truth has not yet been revealed ('fragmentary exposition'), and this remains the case for some time to come:

> (c) [Sutpen] also told Grandfather, dropped this into the telling as you might flick the joker out of a pack of fresh cards without being able to remember later whether you had removed the joker or not, that the old man's wife had been a Spaniard [...]. (203)

> (d) [Sutpen: "The marriage was] an arrangement which I had entered in good faith, concealing nothing, while the other party or parties to it concealed from me the one very factor which would destroy the entire plan and design which I had been working toward, concealed it so well that it was not until after the child was born that I discovered that this factor existed [...]." (220)

> (e) [They] sat in that drawing room of baroque and fusty magnificence which Shreve had invented and which was probably true enough, while the Haiti-born daughter of the French sugar planter and the woman who Sutpen's first father-in-law had told him was a Spaniard (the slight dowdy woman with untidy gray-streaked raven hair coarse as a horse's tail, with parchment-colored skin and implacable pouched black eyes which alone showed no age because they showed no forgetting, whom Shreve and Quentin had likewise invented and which was likewise probably true enough) told them nothing because she did not need to because she had already told it [...]. (268)

Passage (c) both adds the information that the French planter's wife "had been a Spaniard" and serves as an implicit comment on Faulkner's own narrative technique, in which important information is "dropped into the telling as you might flick the joker out of a pack of fresh cards without being able to remember later." Next, in passage (d), there is a suggestion that the 'flaw' in Charles's mother was of the kind that can be detected after the birth of a child (though the causal relation is not in fact stated explicitly: "after the child was born [...] I discovered that this factor existed").[32] Finally, in passage (e), we get a description of Sutpen's first mother-in-law, who had "raven hair" and "parchment-colored skin," and who Sutpen had been told was of Spanish descent.

Against the backdrop of slavery, the U.S. South, and the history of Haiti, and taking all of this information together, it would, in theory, be possible to realize that the 'flaw' in Charles's mother must be racial in nature: a 'taint in her blood' that makes the marriage unsuitable in the eyes of the dominant white culture, with the claim that her mother is "a Spaniard" constituting the crucial act of misrepresentation on the part of her family. And yet, the fact that the five passages cited above are dispersed over seventy-four pages ('fragmentary exposition'), combined with the perceptual overload of Faulkner's style – particularly evident in passages (b) and (e) – renders it difficult for any reader even to process the information, let alone to put the various pieces together. Once the 'unknown' truth about Charles's mother is revealed in a straight-forward manner, however, the material that was subliminally perceived is (re)activated, generating on the part of the reader an uncanny sense of familiarity and belated recognition: it is strange but already long familiar.

Importantly, the technique of uncanny narration is not merely a way of sending shivers down readers' spines. Rather, it constitutes a stylistic correlative to the novel's concern with what we might call the nightmare of belonging. Much as is the case in a nightmare scenario, the novel's interminable sentences propel us inexorably forward, as if we were running from some obscure threat. At the same time, when reading *Absalom, Absalom!* there is a strong sense of not getting anywhere, in part because of the novel's frequent repetition of half-told stories. We have seen, for instance, that Rosa tells Quentin about a mysterious "something" hidden in Supten's Hundred quite early on in the novel (140), and four pages later the text states more precisely that "somebody" – i.e. a human being – is hidden there. And yet, much later in the novel, we still do not know "whatever it was that was up stairs, [...] hidden up there for almost four years" (280). At the same time, given that all the characters from the story that so haunts Quentin are either dead (e.g. Ellen, Judith, Charles Bon) or clearly not hiding at Sutpen's Hundred (e.g. Rosa), we in a sense already know that it can only be Henry who is hiding in his father's house, even if we are not consciously aware of this knowledge. When Quentin finally stands face-to-face with

32 In other words, a temporal relation (first A, then B) is processed as a causal relation, a cognitive mechanism which Rimmon-Kenan calls *post hoc, ergo propter hoc*, providing the following example: "Milton wrote *Paradise Lost*, then his wife died, and then he wrote *Paradise Regained*" (*Narrative Fiction* 17).

Henry, the nightmare of belonging thus reaches its uncanny climax not only for Quentin, but for the reader, too:

> *And you are---?*
> *Henry Sutpen.*
> *And you have been here---?*
> *Four years.*
> *And you came home---?*
> *To die. Yes.*
> *To die?*
> *Yes. To die.*
> *And you have been here---?*
> *Four years.*
> *And you are---?*
> *Henry Sutpen.* (298; original emphasis)

Though this is the first time in the novel that the truth about Henry's return home is revealed, for the reader the revelation constitutes a "hollow repetition" of the kind that Eagleton regards as characteristic of Gothic fiction in general (*Heathcliff and the Great Hunger* 194).[33] Even in terms of style, the dialogue is crammed with repetitions, and Quentin realizes that "waking or sleeping it was the same and would be the same forever as long as he lived" (298). Waking or sleeping, Quentin thus finds that he cannot escape the power of postmemory, which forever binds him to his haunted, conflicted home community. The aesthetic purpose of uncanny narration in *Absalom, Absalom!* is that it simulates or enacts this condition for the reader, who is similarly weighed down by the sheer mass of the novel's language, with its ceaseless stream of burdensome sentences and endlessly accumulating repetitions.

33 Note that the quotation from *Absalom, Absalom!* contains a narrative palindrome – "*To die. Yes. / To die? / Yes. To die.*" – embedded in a larger, 'semi-palindromic' passage. Christina Ljungberg suggests that such palindromes "focus attention on the very act of signification" (i.e. that they have an implicitly metafictional effect), and that "they bring into play the figure of reversal and thereby challenge the unidirectional linearity of human discourse, spoken or written" (248). Both observations fit Faulkner's novel perfectly. Moreover, Faulkner's revisions show that he reworked the manuscript version in a way that heightens the 'palindromic effect' of the published passage (Langford 358; I would like to thank Christina Ljungberg for bringing Faulkner's revisions to my attention).

The Weight of History and Loving One's Home

A region weighed down by a story from its past – a past that is as transnational as the region's present, ranging from France and Spain to Africa, Canada, and Haiti. It is a contested story that some attempt to frame in terms of innocence, while others tell it in the damning mode of the Gothic. It is a story of seemingly biblical proportions – about incest, fratricide, and war – with family homes being destroyed and a patriarch's dynastic designs thwarted. Through all of this, the region's black inhabitants continue to be denied their fundamental right to represent themselves: as narrators in the novel, but also as voters in Faulkner's present. It is difficult to think of any other novel in which the tradition of all dead generations weighs so palpably on the brains of the living – like an endless nightmare that we, as readers, are made to share through the technique of uncanny narration.

It is Quentin, in particular, who can barely cope with this nightmare of belonging to a region that is so deeply flawed. And yet, when at the end of *Absalom, Absalom!* Shreve asks Quentin why he hates the South, the latter denies that this is the case: "'I dont hate it,' Quentin said, quickly, at once, immediately; 'I dont hate it,' he said. *I dont hate it* he thought, panting in the cold air, the iron New England dark: *I dont. I dont! I dont hate it! I dont hate it!*" (303; original emphasis). Norman W. Jones interprets Quentin's surprising reaction as an unconscious denial of his homoerotic desire for Shreve (340), while most other critics read it rather straight-forwardly as Quentin's desperate attempt to repress his hatred for the South (e.g. Betina Entzminger 117; Fargnoli, Golay and Hamblin 25; Jameson, "Third-World Literature" 86).[34]

However, while such interpretations are certainly plausible, there is also a more intriguing possibility: that Quentin really does not hate the South. Quentin's reaction would then constitute, not a case of repression and denial, but rather a moment of horrified recognition of the fact that, despite everything he knows, he nevertheless cannot bring himself to hate the region that remains his only home. What leaves Quentin gasping in "the cold air" of New England, in other words, is his inability to hate a place he knows to be fundamentally corrupt – that in many ways would deserve his hatred. In a final twist to the novel's

---

34 Roger Lundin tries to strengthen the case that Quentin is torn apart by his hatred by pointing out that Quentin commits suicide five months later on (179) – at least according to *The Sound and the Fury*, a novel which also features a character named Quentin Compson. However, Lundin's argument is not unproblematic, for as Fargnoli, Golay and Hamblin (35) point out, Shreve has a different name in *Absalom, Absalom!* (genealogy: Shrevlin McCannon) than in *The Sound and the Fury* (Shreve MacKenzie), which suggests that despite the striking similarities between the characters in the two novels they are not necessarily identical.

emotional drama, it is not Quentin’s unconscious hatred, but his ineradicable love for home that lies at the heart of his nightmare of belonging (that is to say, he would prefer simply to hate it, if only he could).

What is left unstated in *Absalom, Absalom!*, but arguably implied by this final twist, is that in order to deal successfully with the weight of history, it is not enough for us merely to keep on retelling it. Admittedly, such a ‘working through’ of one’s story may constitute a necessary first step; after all, Quentin arrives at his recognition that he loves the South despite everything only through the therapeutic act of collaborative narrative reconstruction; in this sense, Shreve’s game of narrative seduction does have a positive effect after all. At the same time, however, the realization that ‘supernatural’ or Gothic hauntings are, in fact, material also means that historical (re-)interpretation must be followed by material changes if the ghosts of the past are ever to be laid to rest. If the home is found undeserving of a love that nevertheless proves ineradicable, then the only remaining course of action is to try and work towards changing that home.

Absalom, Absalom! makes clear that this is far from easy, and that it certainly cannot be achieved by indulging in fantasies of Adamic new beginnings. Rather, while some American ideologists (and supposedly many modernists) believed in the possibility of simply ‘making it new,’ Faulkner’s novel focuses on the obstinacy of socio-political reality and on the circumstances under which Americans in the 1930s had to try and make their own history: admirable ideals of freedom and equality, but also a heavy burden of racist oppression and imperialistic interference in other regions of the hemisphere.[35] This long history of injustice cannot, the text suggests, be redressed by the heroic actions of super-human individuals (as witnessed by the utter failure of Thomas Sutpen’s design single-handedly to defeat the plantation system that had destroyed his self-worth as well as his trust in the ideal of equality). We live, as Marx emphasizes, under circumstances not of our own making (see chapter two and above), and so heavy is the burden of our common history that only through a collective effort can we hope to escape the seemingly endless nightmare of belonging. Such unity, of course, never comes easily, especially in a society that is historically as deeply divided as Faulkner’s South – but it is all the more important for precisely that reason. However, to examine in more details the fissures within a particular

35 As Kurt Heinzelman points out, Ezra Pound is often erroneously credited with having coined the phrase ‘make it new’ in 1914. Though Pound did use the phrase “in canto 53, written probably in the early 1930s,” it was Ford Madox Hueffer (a.k.a. Ford Madox Ford) “who came closest in 1914 to saying the equivalent of ‘make it new,’ at least in the sense that phrase has come to possess” (131).

community, as well as the factors that might help to overcome them, we must now leave the rural South of Faulkner's novel and turn, instead, to the Northern English industrial town portrayed in Pat Barker's *Union Street.*

5 "People Still Living in the Derelict Houses": Realism, Class, and the Fragile Body in Pat Barker's *Union Street*

According to Michal Peled Ginsberg and Lorri G. Nandrea, the realist novel focuses on "the prosaic world of the everyday, of the common man, of the home and its cares" (246) – which is not a bad description of Pat Barker's *Union Street*, except that the latter tells the story, not of the common *man*, but of seven working-class *women* and their daily struggles during the economic crisis of the early 1970s.[1] The relation between realism, class, and gender will thus be central to the discussion that follows, and the body as a common ground for human vulnerability and finitude will help us connect these issues with the problem of home as physical shelter. This is particularly important because the body has been given relatively short shrift in the four preceding chapters; it features briefly in chapter one, in the discussion of Ishmael's few moments of bodily comfort – for example, when he shares a bed with Queequeg – but on the whole our embodied nature as human beings has not been an explicit theme. This will be redressed in the analysis of *Union Street*, a realist text that pays close attention to the materiality of working-class homes.

And yet, as a literary form, realism has frequently been associated, not with men and women from the lower orders, but with the rise of the middle class and, therefore, a decidedly bourgeois outlook (e.g. Jameson, *The Political Unconscious* 138; Watt 48). More specifically, Nancy Armstrong has shown that, whereas initially bourgeois novelistic discourse was directed against the aristocracy, from around the 1830s it turned instead to the industrial working class as the "target of moral reform" (20). If we accept this assessment, then it no longer comes as a surprise that, by the mid-nineteenth century, the British novel should have been "deeply biased against reflecting a working-class perspective on society" (Haywood 3). It would also be consistent with Terry Eagleton's claim that realism is "the form *par excellence* of settlement and stability" (*Heathcliff and the Great Hunger* 147), as well as with Franco Moretti's assertion that the nineteenth-century novel rested on the twin pillars of bourgeois existence and con-

1 [203] I would like to thank Simone Heller-Andrist and Rahel Rivera Godoy-Benesch for their comments on the first draft, as well as Sarah Chevalier for her feedback on this chapter.

servative beliefs (*The Bourgeois* 94). Catherine Belsey sums up this view of realism as a form that cannot prove truly unsettling for us today because, "however harrowing the events of the story, [...] the world evoked in the fiction, its patterns of cause and effect, of social relationships and moral values, largely confirm the patterns of the world we seem to know" (47). Stable, familiar, and reassuring: it is a view of realism as the discourse of the status quo.

There are, however, critics who disagree with this assessment, both on historical and on more theoretical grounds. Perhaps the most important historical objections come from scholars who have explored the cultural function of realist fiction in colonial settings. Derek Hand, for example, suggests that realism in pre-independence Irish fiction was not conformist, but in fact signified a revolutionary attempt to challenge centuries of colonialist misrepresentation (130). More generally, Neil Ten Kortenaar maintains that realism has often served "anti-colonial and subversive purposes" because it "located the truth of society in the untouchable, the coolie, the slave, the criminal, and the colonized" (1303). Turning to more theoretical objections to the idea that realism is necessarily conservative, we may cite the dramatist Lorraine Hansberry, who insists that an "artist creating a realistic work shows not only what *is* but what is *possible* – which is part of reality, too" (qtd. in Carter 32; original emphasis). Hansberry, in other words, maintains that realism is not limited to things as they are – as does Henri Lefebvre: "the negative and the possible are just as 'real' as the positive real" (319).[2] Indeed, for Pam Morris, these two characteristics of realist narratives – their ability to bridge global socio-cultural divides, and their power to discern alternatives to the present as part of reality itself – together constitute the "inherent utopianism" of the form (*Realism* 162). This leaves us with two starkly opposed views of realist fiction: either as a conservative discourse, or as emancipatory and even utopian.

Perhaps the best strategy is for us to assume that realism can serve both conservative and progressive political ends, and that a realist text like *Union Street* is inevitably marked by the genre's contradictory history: its historical association with bourgeois values, as well as its formal impulse ceaselessly to widen the social range of artistic representation (Cobley 79; Pam Morris, *Realism* 3). We will begin the discussion of *Union Street* by examining closely how the text establishes a parallel between dilapidated buildings and derelict, homeless human bodies as the material signs of economic crisis. These physical signs of dereliction also find an analogy in *Union Street*'s fragmented textual structure,

2 The French original runs: "Le négatif et le possible sont aussi 'réels' que le réel positif" (31).

though at the same time the text uses several discursive means to unify its narrative segments, thereby creating a dialectical tension between unity and fragmentation that, in turn, correlates with the contradictory pulls of female solidarity and intra-communal strife depicted in the story. We will see that one of the strongest unifying features of *Union Street* is a complex array of symbols that not only allow us to address the question of female identity, but also to reflect on realism as a literary mode (e.g. with mirrors appearing as problematic bearers of truth, or eyes linked to alienating as well as more beneficent kinds of vision). Indeed, it is through its use of intricate symbolical clusters, as well as by paying close attention to the fragile human body and its basic need for physical shelter, that *Union Street* appropriates and critiques the form of literary realism – in particular its long-standing equation of home with bourgeois domesticity. In so doing, *Union Street* works toward a truly progressive realism which never loses sight of the material condition of the working class, while at the same time exploring the symbolical forms of belonging that are specific to laboring human bodies.

Things Fall Apart: Dereliction and Fragmentation

Set in an unnamed Northern English industrial town in the early 1970s, *Union Street* evokes the well-established literary topos of the tightly-knit working-class community – only immediately to subvert it. As John Brannigan notes, for instance, the title *Union Street*, "seems to promise the intimate neighbourliness, shift-work routines, and cheerful endurance common to the popular, often nostalgic, imagination of working-class life" (14). However, the cozy warmth radiating from such familiar images is immediately dispelled by *Union Street*'s opening sentences: "There was a square of cardboard in the window where the glass had been smashed. During the night one corner had worked loose and scraped against the frame whenever the wind blew" (1). A makeshift cardboard cover barely keeps the elements at bay here, and Brannigan rightly notes that the smashed window of the opening scene is only "one of a number of images of exposure, of the lack of the protective shell that 'home' should represent" (19). This also explains the frequent use in Barker's text of the word *derelict* to describe the community's built environment: the "whole place was derelict," with "derelict streets," and rows of "derelict houses" (27, 64, 216; see Brannigan 18). From the very beginning, *Union Street* thus focuses our attention on the dilapidated condition of physical structures that ought to provide shelter and a sense of security, and in doing so the text highlights the concrete effects on people's homes of such seemingly abstract processes as economic downturns and recessions.

The destructive effects of an economy in crisis are not, however, limited to buildings and infrastructure in Barker's text. Rather, the narrative continually emphasizes the deleterious effects of deprivation on the human body. Indeed, *Union Street* uses the same word, "derelict," for both the neglect of the built environment and bodily harm, as if to underline that ultimately they result from the very same causes:

> [By the river,] a whole community had been cleared away: the houses waited for the bulldozers and the demolition men to move in, but they never came.
>
> [... S]till the houses stood. Officially empty, but not in reality. [...]
>
> [...H]owever carefully you trod sooner or later glass crunched under your feet or a sagging floorboard creaked and threatened to give way, and instantly [...] hidden life revealed itself, if only by a quickening of the silence. Tramps. Drunks. [...] These were not the drunks you meet wending a careful path home to the safety of hearth and bed. These were the hopeless, the abandoned, the derelict. (60)

An entire community has been "cleared away," we learn here, but the "derelict" remain, without a home that would provide "the safety of hearth and bed," and "abandoned" like the crumbling houses in which they seek shelter. Naturally, these "derelict" bodies will seek shelter anywhere, even in a public library (supposedly the home of cultured minds):

> They were dirty. They picked their noses and rolled the results between thumb and forefinger, making a pellet hard enough to be flicked away on to the floor. They made noises. They made smells. They were afraid. For the assistants in the library, lads and lasses in their late teens, had power over them and they knew it. They had the power of banning people from the library, of withholding warmth. So sandwiches were consumed furtively, a bit at a time. And those who were compelled to talk to themselves, thrashing out some unending internal feud, tried to do so quietly, though they did not always succeed. (223)

Books are sheltered, in other words, while human beings live under the continual threat of expulsion: this is one illustration of Walter Benjamin's well-known dictum that there is "no document of culture which is not at the same time a document of barbarism" ("Eduard Fuchs" 124). The poorest members of the society depicted in *Union Street* are shown to be out of place in both senses of the term: they have no place of their own, and they are perceived as incongruous and improper wherever they go.

In fact, if the "derelict" appear as dirty in the description cited above, then this is not exclusively a realistic rendering of their outward appearance (though it is that, as well). Rather, they also appear as dirty because dirt, in Mary

Douglas's famous definition, is simply "matter out of place" (*Purity and Danger* 44). More specifically, Douglas maintains that the systematic classification and ordering of matter always involves a "rejection of the inappropriate elements" – and this is, precisely, why the "derelict" are described as dirty in Barker's text. The "derelict" are characterized both by their abject, unruly corporeality – they pick noses, make noises, emanate smells – and by the frequent occurrence among them of mental disorder (which, incidentally, is indeed more prevalent amongst the poor because of the greater physical and social stresses to which they are exposed; see Ritter and Lampkin 37); they are both material bodies and the symbolical, 'dirty' excess that accumulates at the margin of the social system.[3]

The very language used to describe these 'dirty misfits' in fact emphasizes that people in a society who do not matter in some ways threaten to become mere matter. If we look, for instance, at the verbs in the passage describing the "derelict" in the public library, we find them shifting from the active voice ("picked noses") to a darkly humorous mock-active ("made smells") and, ultimately, to the passive voice ("sandwiches were consumed," "were compelled to talk to themselves"). Admittedly, the pattern is not perfectly consistent, as the final two verbs in the passage return to the active voice ("tried," "succeed"). At the same time, we need to bear in mind that the first of these two final verbs refers to the attempts on the part of the "derelict" to effect their own effacement by drawing as little attention to themselves as possible ("tried to do so quietly"), while the second appears in conjunction with a negation ("did not always succeed"). Much as is the case with the mock-active phrase "made smells," in other words, the agency that ultimately remains for the "derelict" is in fact a kind of non-agency, forced upon them by their lack of power and material resources. In *Union Street*, that is, people as well as houses end up "abandoned," "derelict," and – literally as well as figuratively – falling apart (Brannigan 17).

To some extent, this disintegration of minds and matter in Barker's text finds a parallel in *Union Street*'s structural fragmentation. Critics frequently refer to the book as a novel (e.g. Haywood 145; Hitchcock 55), and this label also appears

3 See Lucy Gallagher's essay "'He Had Always Believed That There Were Two Sorts of Women': The Female Body, Dirt, and Domesticity in Pat Barker's *Union Street*" for a highly illuminating discussion of how ideas about gender affect the cultural construction of bodily fluids as dirty.

on the front and back covers of various editions.[4] Moreover, the fact that the text's subdivisions are numbered from one to seven (and even labeled "chapters" in some editions) serves to emphasize whole-text coherence and thus to strengthen the association with the genre of the novel.[5] In fact, however, *Union Street* is divided into seven stories that can easily be read independently of each other (unlike the chapters – particularly the later ones – of a typical novel; see Fordham 142; Kirk 612). Forest Ingram has proposed the label *short-story cycle* for texts of this kind, which he sees as poised somewhere between, at one extreme, the typical novel with its tightly interwoven plotlines, and, at the other extreme, collections or anthologies of entirely unrelated stories (14). For Ingram, it is thus the individuality of the stories in terms of plot that separates the short-story cycle from the novel, while short-story cycles differ from a 'mere' collection of tales in the way in which they highlight "bonds of unity which make the many into a single whole" (19; see also Dunn and Morris 1).[6]

In other words, while the individual sections of short-story cycles usually lack any overarching coherence in terms of novelistic plot, such texts (e.g. James Joyce's *Dubliners* or Sherwood Anderson's *Winesburg, Ohio*) tend to be unified by other means, including the use of a common setting and a symbolically significant ordering of the individual units (Dunn and Morris 13–15). And indeed,

---

4 *Union Street* is, for example, referred to as a novel on the back cover of the edition used for the present study. In addition, the generic label appears prominently on the front cover of: Pat Barker. *Union Street & Blow Your House Down.* New York: Picador, 1999. The German equivalent of the label *novel*, *Roman*, appears on: Pat Barker. *Union Street.* Berlin: Orlanda Frauenverlag, 2001.

5 The sections are explicitly labeled as chapters in: Pat Barker. *Union Street & Blow Your House Down.* New York: Picador, 1999. In the edition used here, they are numbered in Roman numerals, from I – VII.

6 Maggie Dunn and Ann Morris have noted the astonishingly wide range of generic labels that have been proposed for the kinds of texts that Ingram describes: "*story cycle, short story cycle, multi-faceted novel, story novel, paranovel, loose-leaf novel, short story composite, rovelle* [sic], *composite, short story compound, integrated short story collection, anthology novel, modernist grotesque, hybrid novel, story chronicle, short story sequence, genre of return, short story volume*, and *narrative of community*" (4; original emphasis). While readily conceding that "terminology is hardly the most important factor in genre identification and theory," they themselves express a preference for the term *composite novel*, for three partly related reasons: (a) the term *composite novel* highlights the "kinship to the novel, the modern era's predominant literary genre"; (b) it emphasizes the "integrity of the whole"; and (c) it lacks the emphasis on "a circular path, a return to the beginning" that is implied in *short-story cycle*. I will, however, retain the term proposed by Ingram, only adding a hyphen to distinguish '*short-story* cycles' from 'short *story cycles*' (i.e. story cycles that are short).

the seven stories in *Union Street* are each set in the same Northern-English industrial town, as well as named after progressively older female characters:

I. KELLY BROWN (an eleven year old girl);
II. JOANNE WILSON (not yet twenty, unmarried but pregnant);
III. LISA GODDARD (married to an unemployed man, and pregnant with her third child);
IV. MURIEL SCAIFE (mother of two teenage children);
V. IRIS KING (about fifty years old, and mother of three daughters);
VI. BLONDE DINAH (a prostitute roughly sixty years of age);
VII. ALICE BELL (seventy-six years old, and very frail).

Thus, if in Shakespeare's *As You Like It* the character Jacques speaks of "the seven ages of man" (2.7.140–166), then the sequence of stories in Barker's text can be said to comprise "the seven ages of woman" (Rawlinson 20), from the onset of puberty through pregnancy and motherhood to old-age and death (see also Jolly 241). John Fordham may thus be oversimplifying matters when he regards the lack of any overarching plot coherence in *Union Street* as indicative of the "breakdown of working-class social coherence" (142; see also Kirk 612), since he neglects the countervailing elements of unity in Pat Barker's short-story cycle.

In fact, one of the key debates regarding short-story cycles centers precisely on what the genre's characteristically contradictory pull toward both unity and fragmentation implies for its representation of community. For Ingram, each short-story cycle's various strands "draw the co-protagonists [...] into a single community," to the extent that this community becomes the "central character" in such texts (22). Similarly, for J. Gerald Kennedy the experience of the interdependence of individual units that characterizes short-story cycles "poses a provocative analogy" to the basic structure of community (194). Rocío G. Davis, finally, notes that the passage "from individual stories to the whole [...] also marks the shift from the individual to the community" (24). At the same time, however, both Davis and Kennedy caution against an overly confident emphasis on unity and wholeness; rather, Davis sees the genre as characterized by a "struggle between cohesion and fragmentation" (17), and for Kennedy the glimpses of connection afford only "a partial and problematic view, ordinarily achieved by the suppression of [...] fissures and incongruities" (J. Gerald Kennedy 196–197). We are, in other words, confronted with three possible assessments of how the short-story cycle represents community: for Ingram, it is a form that gravitates toward communal unity; for Davis, a genre enacting a struggle between unity and fragmentation; and for Kennedy, a type of text in which the semblance of communal unity will, on closer inspection, always turn out to be founded on the suppression of gaps and fissures.

In the discussion of *Moby-Dick* in chapter one, we already encountered Rick Altman's idea of multiple-focus narratives, and it is illuminating to regard a short-story cycle like *Union Street* as one particular instance of this type of tale. Altman distinguishes multiple-focus narratives both from dual-focus narratives (which alternate "between two groups whose conflict provides the plot"; 55) and single-focus narratives (which follow a single individual on his or her narrative quest; 189). Moreover, Altman notes that a multiple-focus narrative often looks like a single-focus narrative at first, but then turns out to consist of a series of independent single-focus narratives that it juxtaposes to each other both to critique the single-focus system as such (254–256) and to "posit a level of unity beyond that of single individuals" (248). Further, while according to Altman dual-focus narratives revolve around conflicts over space and single-focus narrative around development in time, the multiple-focus form encourages readers to seek out the abstract, conceptual links between the narrative units (what Altman calls the "*tertium quid* of conception"; 269). Multiple-focus narratives – and, by implication, short-story cycles – thus do not allow the reader to remain comfortably immersed in the time and space of the multiple-focus world, but encourage a more meta-textual frame of mind instead (e.g. the "search for a hidden pattern"; 277). If we add to this Altman's conviction that "[m]ultiple-focus narration is the form of the little people" because it emphasizes collective, rather than individual, significance (281), then his analytical framework seems more than apt for a text like *Union Street*, in which dilapidated buildings and textual fragmentation complement the narrative's focus on the homeless, the "derelict," and the condition of the working-class.

Female Solidarity, Strife, and Surveillance

Union Street focuses in particular on the daily struggles of working-class women, so perhaps we ought to begin our quest for the *tertium quid* of multiple-focus conception by examining the text's depiction of female solidarity – which turns out to be sadly lacking even between women from the same family. For instance, just as *Union Street* opens with an emphasis on the crumbling physical structure of the Brown family home, the first interaction between female relatives that the text depicts is conflictual rather than harmonious. When the eleven-year-old Kelly is disturbed by the cardboard cover scraping over the sill of her smashed bedroom window, she turns over, still half asleep, and inadvertently throws an arm across the face of her sister Linda, with whom she shares a bed. The latter complains, understandably: "I wish you'd watch what you're doing. You nearly had my eye out there" (1). The two sisters then keep bickering for a while, and soon their mother joins the fray, contributing to the atmosphere of conflict: "For God's sake, you two, shut up! There's some of us still trying to sleep" (3). Indeed, familial tension remains high throughout the first pages of *Union Street*, with Kelly showing no attempt at disguising from the mother her hostile attitude to Arthur, Mrs. Brown's latest lover (5). More generally, conflicts between mothers and daughters abound in *Union Street*: there is a heated exchange between Lisa Goddard and her mother about whether or not she should leave her husband because he beats her (112); there is Muriel Scaife, who suffers from "a conflict of loyalties between her mother and her husband" (141); and there is a frightful fight between Iris King and her daughter Brenda, during which Iris physically assaults Brenda, calling her "a little whore" (184). In addition, we are told that, for the most part, Muriel Scaife has had a rather strained relationship with her sister-in-law (154–155). Likewise, Alice Bell is well aware that it would spell the end of her son's marriage if "he might one day have to offer her a home" because her daughter-in-law is dead set against it (236). The family, in short, is far from a bastion of female solidarity in the world depicted in *Union Street*.

The wider community of working-class women, moreover, is not a reliable source of solidarity either. According to Sarah Brophy, one symptom of distance rather than solidarity between women is the "gossip that forms the undercurrent of the community" in Barker's text (32). The shopkeeper Doris, for example, is eager "to share her outrage" about Mrs. Brown's supposedly scandalous love life with Iris King, who listens "avidly" to this latest bit of gossip (9–10). Distance is not limited to gossip, moreover, for we learn, too, that someone like Maureen Sullivan, who has "a houseful of kids but no husband," is respected for managing to eke out a living – "respected but *avoided*" (94; emphasis added). We also find Elaine Watson picking on her mentally retarded co-worker Lillian, with two of Elaine's friends, Barbara and Karen, excitedly watching the show, and Joanne Wilson the only one willing to intervene (91–93). There are, to be sure, some positive counter-examples as well, such as Iris King often taking care of other people's children (196), or the women from the community immediately offering their help when Alice Bell's health begins to deteriorate (236). Nevertheless, there is little in *Union Street* that would allow us to draw a straightforwardly idyllic picture of solidarity between its female characters.

This becomes particularly clear if for a moment we shift our attention from the notion of gender to race and ethnicity, as in the second section of *Union Street* racism clearly hampers female solidarity. In this section, we learn that Joanne Wilson – like many other women from the community – works at the local cake factory.[7] We are also told that "[n]obody liked it" when Big Bertha, a woman from the West Indies, starts working at the factory because she is "the first coloured worker there"; Elaine Watson in particular complains about Big Bertha's "nigger stink" (81), abusing and bullying her until one day Bertha has had enough and hits Elaine "full in the mouth" (83). Though the other women never approved of Elaine's aggressive behavior – which gossip attributes to the fact that Elaine's eldest sister had three children "to a nigger" (82) – they also refrain from taking Big Bertha's part, either before or after her violent confrontation with Elaine. Indeed, the women are "horrified" by Big Bertha's actions because "[m]en fought, sometimes man and wife fought, but violence between women was unthinkable," so that "[m]ore even than the colour of her skin," the ferocity of Big Bertha's attack confirms her as "an outsider amongst them" (82). Big Bertha, who for the longest time silently endured Elaine's cruelty, is thus left to fight on her own, only to be accused of unwomanly (and indeed, uncivilized) behavior when she eventually defends herself.

The name Big Bertha is significant in this context because it adds a layer of historical depth to this episode of contemporary racism by creating a strong intertextual link to Charlotte Brontë's *Jane Eyre* (Troy 9). According to Pam Morris, one long-standing problem for the relation between feminism and racism has been white feminists' assumption that they can speak for all women, irrespective of race (*Literature and Feminism* 165). However, this assumption is particularly problematic in Britain, where the development of feminism was influenced profoundly by the country's involvement in imperial endeavors (Burton 2; Midgley 1; Parry 38–39). In literary studies, arguably the best-known instance of this kind of entanglement is the character of Bertha in *Jane Eyre*, the madwoman in the attic of Rochester's mansion who, according to Sandra M. Gilbert and Susan Gubar's classic analysis, serves "as Jane's dark double," acting out the white protagonist's secret desire and, through her melodramatic death, paving the way for the novel's happy ending (360). We can thus say, with Simone Heller-Andrist, that "the formation of Western female individualism in *Jane Eyre* proceeds at the expense of Bertha" (212) – a circumstance famously critiqued in Jean Rhys's appropriation of *Jane Eyre* in her 1966 novel *Wide Sargasso Sea*. The fact that *Union Street* features a West-Indian character named Bertha thus links the seemingly local conflict between white women and a "coloured" co-worker to the long-term historical conflict between feminism and racism. Together with

7 This, incidentally, may be an ironic reference to the famous phrase "Then let them eat cake," erroneously attributed to Marie Antoinette, Queen of France, as a response to the idea that the poor lacked bread. (The phrase in fact comes from Rousseau and was uttered by an unidentified "*grande princesse*"; see Ó Gráda 196.)

the conflicts between members of the same family and between women in general, the focus on racism as a critical issue thus serves to challenge any starry-eyed visions of female working-class solidarity as simply a given. Instead, we are confronted once again with both unity and fragmentation: moments of neighborly help and solidarity that alternate with episodes of tension and even outright hostility.

As Sarah Brophy rightly notes, in *Union Street* the character of Iris King in many ways epitomizes this tension between solidarity and female conflict. Iris, Brophy argues, in some ways plays "the stereotypical role of indomitable working-class mother," as Barker's text in fact makes quite explicit:

> [Iris] mothered half the street. Kelly Brown and the Scaife children, Lisa Goddard's little lads – they all knew and loved their Iris. [...] And she sat with women in labour. Even laid out the dead, though there wasn't as much call for that now. [...]
>
> All this was meat and drink to her. She loved life [...] and took it for granted that life included old age, suffering and death. (*Union Street* 196)

Iris is mother to "half the street" (a role complemented by the fact that she works "full-time as a home help"; 185), so that one may be tempted to see her as the very model of solidarity and domestic care. In addition, Iris plays an important structural role in *Union Street*, as she is mentioned in each of *Union Street*'s seven stories and therefore appears as the "embodiment of connectedness in the narrative" (Brophy 33). And yet, we have also seen that Iris "avidly" participates in communal gossip (10), and that at one point she physically assaults her sixteen-year-old daughter Brenda for being pregnant ("I'll murder the little bitch"; 184). We learn, too, that Iris is highly judgmental of women who, like Mrs. Brown, fail to live up to her supposedly more respectable housekeeping standards (39). It is thus safe to agree with Brophy, who deems it impossible to regard Iris as an exclusively admirable character (33).[8]

Brophy also rightly observes that in *Union Street* the most troublesome aspects of Iris's character are related to her experience of growing up in a deeply troubled, 'broken' home. Abandoned by her mother when only six weeks old, Iris grew up with her father "in a series of boarding houses," some of which "weren't much better than brothels and some of them were brothels"; her father paid a "long succession of women to look after her" – with many of the women failing

8 I would thus be somewhat more reluctant than Roberto del Valle Alcalá to ascribe to Iris a "sustained rejection of the subaltern position accorded to working-class women," or to posit that she "embodies an attitude of refusal which in large measure corroborates the paramount importance accorded by revolutionary feminists like Federici to reproduction as the strategic axis of the class struggle" (203).

to do a good job (187). Living in Wharfe Street, the poorest part of town, Iris was so ill fed that she depended on vendors at the marketplace for free food (187–188), and later, when she was in her teens, Iris’s father used to beat her often (189). Though Iris has since worked her way up to a respected position in Union Street, she knows that Wharfe Street is “still in her” (186), and that her repeated bouts of depression – “a blackness she linked in her mind with those early years” – are unlikely ever to cease (195). It is, moreover, due to the total lack of safety during childhood that Iris falls “in love with the idea of marriage,” which she associates with the one thing she had never really had: “A home” (189). It is precisely the respectability of her home – this “home that she had toiled and sweated to create” (195) – that Iris now wants to protect at all cost. Accordingly, when Iris urges her daughter Brenda to have an abortion, this is only in part because she wants to avoid her being “stuck” with a baby for several years (201). Another important motive is that Brenda’s ‘stupidity’ poses a threat to Iris’s reputation in the community: a reputation that matters “more to her than anything else” because it is “the measure of her distance from Wharfe Street” (196; see also Brophy 33–34; Lucy Gallagher 42).

It is important to be clear about the extent to which Iris’s understanding of respectability corresponds to ideals of domesticity that are bourgeois in origin. Nancy Armstrong has shown that, in the eighteenth-century conduct books which were so vital to the rise of domestic fiction, one key characteristic of the ideal bourgeois female was that she was able to regulate her desires in order to allow her husband to accumulate capital: “Self-regulation alone gave a woman authority over the field of domestic objects and personnel where her supervision constituted a form of value in its own right” (81). As one conduct book quoted by Armstrong puts it, a woman who does not possess these virtues will be “incapable of perceiving her chief happiness to center at home,” and will instead “sally forth in quest of adventures”; such a woman prefers to put herself on display and be seen, rather than be vigilant and supervise her household – and it is this, Armstrong avers, that constitutes such a woman’s crime (77). Regulation of desire and an economy of vigilance and supervision: it is a fitting description for Iris King, who censures Mrs. Brown for going out pubbing and neglecting her household duties; who is livid at her own daughter’s “fucking and going on” (184), as well as “bloody sure” that sexual pleasure is not natural (198); and who, with her vigilant gaze, surveys and censures the entire community of female ‘malefactors.’

Of course, to say that Iris has internalized a particular ideology of middle-class domesticity is not to suggest that her views are entirely wrongheaded. For instance, though thoughts of respectability are an important motive for Iris, another reason why she wants her daughter Brenda to have an abortion is simply that the sixteen-year-old girl does not even "earn enough to keep herself" (200). This may appear like a brutally materialistic assessment on Iris's part, but it is difficult to dismiss her concerns as merely a kind of delusion, for the link between single motherhood and poverty had been a depressingly constant feature of twentieth-century British life (e.g. Kanji 131).[9] Moreover, if we bear in mind that "single mothers became a political debating point" in Britain in the late 1970s (McNeill, Blundell and Griffiths 48) – i.e. only a few years before *Union Street* was published – then it is reasonable to assume that readers would have recognized Iris's fears about her daughter's economic well-being as justified, especially given that the willingness to provide welfare support to single women was decreasing under the Conservative government of Margaret Thatcher (Kanji 132). In *Union Street*, Iris is thus correct in assuming that Brenda is likely to descend into poverty if she decides to keep her baby and raise it as a single mother: "The primary motivation for Iris's self-improvement has always been her desire for her daughters to have a better life than she did, and it is this that Brenda's pregnancy also undermines" (Lucy Gallagher 44).

However, rather than displaying any anger at the systemic conditions that render this scenario probable in the first place, Iris blames her daughter for what she sees as an exclusively individual failure – and this is the ideological point: for Iris, it is *only* her daughter's unregulated desire, and not at all the conspicuous lack of societal support, that constitutes an act of both economic and moral stupidity. Her daughter's 'domestic' failure thus remains privatized in two senses: hidden, as far as possible, from the gaze of others, and explained only as a private and never as also a public issue: bourgeois ideology at its best (or worst, depending on one's political outlook). Iris, in short, thinks exclusively within the framework of things as they are, and her particular, conservative brand of respectable domestic realism fails to envision any possibility of social change.

Significantly, Iris's very name intimates that she has internalized a class-based ideal of respectability and domestic womanhood. We have seen the extent to which Iris is in thrall to a bourgeois ideology of domestic respectability that is curiously at odds with her working-class status. If, therefore, we bear in mind

---

9 According to one survey, the overall poverty rate in the UK increased from 6 % in 1979 to 11 % in 1995, with the poverty rate among single mothers rising even more markedly, from 11 % to 28 % (Huber and Stephens 299). Matters were in many ways even worse in the USA, where the overall poverty rate rose from 17 % in 1979 to 19 % in 1994, with the poverty rate among single mothers increasing from an already staggering 42 % to 49 % (Huber and Stephens 299). Similarly, in a survey of Switzerland in 2010, of all forms of households, it is single parents – and particularly single mothers – who are at the highest risk of being poor (Guggisberg, Müller and Christin 18–20).

that in Britain the middle class and the aristocracy have historically been far more closely allied than elsewhere (e.g. Kocka 20), and that in the course of the nineteenth century even the aristocracy began to represent itself on the basis of the "model of middle-class domesticity" (Nancy Armstrong 74), then it seems eminently appropriate for Iris's last name to be "King": the patriarchal pinnacle of the ruling order. Moreover, if Iris's family name points to the issue of class, her function as guardian of respectability is aptly expressed in her first name, "Iris," which among other things refers to the part of the eye that controls the amount of light reaching the retina and thus hints at the panoptic power of Iris's ever watchful, relentlessly judgmental, disciplinary gaze.

Admittedly, the link between the name Iris and the Foucauldian concept of the panoptic gaze may seem far-fetched at first sight, but it ceases to do so once we realize the pervasive emphasis on eyes in *Union Street.*[10] The word *eye* appears at least once on no fewer than 96 of the 265 pages of the Virago Classics edition of *Union Street* – a remarkable 36 % – and in many of these cases, vision and sight are quite directly associated with power, panoptic or otherwise. There is, for instance, Lisa Goddard who, after losing her patience and hitting her three-year-old son in the supermarket, "raised her eyes and found a young girl staring at her," looking on silently, passing judgment (109). There is also Richard Scaife, twelve years old and afraid to be seen too often together with his mother because people might otherwise think of him as a "[b]it of a pouf" (141). And the examples could be multiplied at will: Big Bertha blowing out smoke that gets "into Elaine's eyes" (91); parents keeping "an eye" on their children (142); or Iris King's sister Laura, recently institutionalized and treated for schizophrenia, having "staring eyes" that unsettle almost everyone, including the elderly at the old people's home where she is now employed (178). In each of these cases, the gaze involves a sense of violation or power struggle, thus providing us with a solid figurative basis for interpreting Iris's first name as linked to her ambivalent role as panoptic matriarch of *Union Street.*

Identity and the Eye of the Beholder

Precisely because eyes, sight, and the gaze are continually linked to the notion of power in *Union Street*, they are also related to the construction and maintenance of identity. We find one negative image of this correlation in the scene in which Iris King and Brenda, her daughter, are confronted with the sight of Brenda's aborted baby:

---

10 Michel Foucault develops his ideas about panopticism in *Discipline and Punish* (1975). The key effect of panoptic power is to induce in the subject "a state of conscious and permanent visibility," which will in turn serve to discipline the subject's behavior (201).

> At the last moment she [i.e. Brenda] looked down and – "Eyes!" Iris said, putting a hand over her daughter's face, as the bag of membranes bulged out and burst.
>
> "I didn't see it, Mam," Brenda said. "I mean I just caught a glimpse … " She stopped. "I didn't see it."
>
> "Didn't you, love?"
>
> "No. No, I didn't see it." (215)

Trying to repress the fact of the baby's potential humanity and selfhood, Brenda convinces herself that she never actually saw "it" – which implies that looking at the baby would constitute an act of human recognition. This same link between sight and recognition is apparent when Kelly Brown is approached in a local park by a man who, she soon realizes, "had been watching her a long time" (14). Though Kelly is disconcerted by the intensity of the man's stare, it also exerts an inexorable power:

> He looked at her so intently. Other people – her mother, Linda, the teachers at school – merely glanced at her and then with indifference or haste, passed on. But this man stared at her as if every pore on her skin mattered. His eyes created her. And so she had to go with him. She could not help herself. (16)

As readers, we may shrink from the image of Kelly's only just pubescent body exposed to the gaze of a much older man, "whose eyes created her." At the same time, the passage makes clear that the gaze and vision are not inescapably threatening, alienating and objectifying; looking at others can also be a sign of recognition, and the narrator suggests that it is precisely the lack of such recognition from those closest to her that renders Kelly vulnerable to other, more dangerous kinds of visual exposure (Brannigan 20).

Put in more philosophical terms, *Union Street* creates a tension between vision as alienation and what Kelly Oliver has called the look of love. From Hegel through Sartre and Lacan, Oliver contends, there is a long philosophical tradition that regards the gaze as an inherently violent intrusion:

> [S]ight only serves to remind us of the abyss separating us from others. In these theories, vision creates a sense of lack, castration, or alienation, the sense of being cut off from the world, or being alone. [… W]hat we see when we recognize ourselves in or against the other is the distance between us that alienates us, not only from others but also from ourselves […]. (63)

Against such an exclusive focus on the alienating gaze, Oliver posits a look of love devoid of mastery and domination – a conception she derives from readings of Emmanuel Levinas and Maurice Merleau-Ponty, as well as from feminist philosophers like Julia Kristeva, bell hooks, and, in particular, Luce Irigaray:

> Irigaray's suggestions about the possibility of loving looks turn Sartre's or Lacan's anti-social gaze into a look as the circulation of affective psychic energy. The gaze does not have to be a harsh or accusing stare. [...]. Loving looks nourish and sustain the psyche, the soul, as well as the body. [... T]he caress, and the look as caress, do not fix an object for a subject, but open a realm in which the two remain two but cannot be separated. (71)

While at times Oliver's prose may be overly mellifluous, she remains convincing on the key point that there is not merely one kind of look; if there is a harsh stare that threatens us with symbolic castration, then by contrast the look of love – the "look as caress" – promises recognition and fulfillment. It is in this light that we must read a terrible scene in *Union Street* that depicts the death of Muriel Scaife's beloved husband John, whose eyes, the narrator emphasizes, "rolled about, frenzied and *unseeing*" (163, emphasis added): unable ever again to offer the look of love to his terrified wife and son (163).

Importantly, in *Union Street*, the objectifying gaze of mastery and domination is figured as non-seeing and thus death-like as well. For instance, when Iris King learns of her daughter's pregnancy, she is for a moment "literally blind with rage" (181) – and shortly afterwards she physically assaults her daughter (184). Perhaps the most forceful expression, however, of the link between the alienating gaze and bodily harm is *Union Street*'s association of non-seeing with rape. The stranger who watches Kelly in the park does not actually hurt her at that point in the story; he even protects her from a flock of geese who suddenly attack the girl when she is feeding the birds at the lake (17). However, when Kelly leaves to meet her friend Sharon at the nearby fun fair, a sense of menace remains, and several times Kelly feels that she is being watched by the man, "dressed all in black as he had been in the park" (19–20).[11] Increasingly panicked and queasy, Kelly leaves the fairground and soon finds herself doubled up, vomiting in the gutter – where suddenly she realizes that the man from the park is standing next to her: "Again she had the feeling that he had been there a long time" (22). Though the man promises to show her the way to a bus stop from where she can get back home, he in fact leads Kelly into an abandoned, derelict part of town. Here, Kelly feels exposed "like an insect crawling over an eyeball" (28), and when she ultimately finds herself trapped in a blind (!) alley, she turns around to look into the eyes of the man who approaches her, finding that "there was nothing there that she could reach"; she "closed her eyes, because his glazed

11 As John Brannigan has noted (77), the appearance of a man in black at the fun fair is one of many correspondences between *Union Street* and Pat Barker's fourth novel, *The Man Who Wasn't There*.

eyes and hanging face were too terrible to look at," but the man forces her to look at and touch his penis: a "single mucoid eye [that] leered at her from under the partially retracted foreskin" (29). This, indeed, is the 'male' gaze as the most extreme form of non-recognition: violating, objectifying, and blind to the female subject that has come within the grasp of its impersonal desire.[12] The man rapes Kelly, and climaxing in "a final, agonised convulsion," he looks at her afterward "as if he hated her more than anything else"; indeed, Kelly sees the thought "form in his eyes" that he could simply kill the object 'tainted' by his own lust (29–30). The man, however, refrains from further violating the girl, and with neither lust nor hate left to sustain the alienating gaze, he can no longer bear to look at her, his eyes skittering about "like ants" when Kelly tries to make eye contact (32). The castrating, annihilating, objectifying gaze, and the inability to offer the look of love: it is difficult to imagine a more harrowing juxtaposition of these two conflicting ways of seeing.

Union Street makes it clear that one consequence of the alienating gaze, as opposed to the look of love, is a fundamental kind of homelessness – both in Kelly's case and in the story of Alice Bell. Kelly, after being raped, believes that she "*was* what had just happened to her. It was between the man and her" – and "he was ... nothing!" (32). Later, Mrs. Brown will find Kelly determined to avoid the mother's concerned look (43). Conversely, other people will find themselves avoiding Kelly's "eyes of a curious naked amber: an animal's eyes" (46). Kelly, that is to say, is no longer able either to bestow or to receive the look of love; she is alienated from everyone else, and accordingly the "street was her home now" (48). The story of Alice Bell appears radically different at first sight. For the seventy-six-year-old woman, who unlike Iris used to be better off in the past (234–235), there are two main fears left in life: a pauper's funeral and the Workhouse (233). These fears explain why Alice, who has recently suffered an incapacitating stroke (245), is terrified by her son's suggestion that she move to the nearby "Home" (i.e. a home for the elderly):

> "But I don't want to go there."
> "Oh, you'll soon settle in." [...]
> "The Workhouse."
> "It's not the Workhouse now. In your day it was. It's all changed now." (257–258)

12 In a classic essay on mainstream cinema, Laura Mulvey claims that the Freudian notion of scopophilia – the pleasure associated with "taking other people as objects, subjecting them to a controlling and curious gaze" (587) – is a constitutive feature of the male gaze that structures the position of spectators in such films.

Ironically, the Home – which used to be that dreaded place, the Workhouse – is in fact an unhomely space that signifies the fundamental loss of control and belonging for Alice: "Her home. They were taking it away from her" (260). Alison Blunt and Robyn Dowling underline that homes, as sites of memory, continuity, and self-determination can become increasingly important for the elderly as their ability to move becomes restricted (114). And indeed, we learn in *Union Street* that, for Alice, everything in her home "was steeped in memory" (260) in this house that over the years has become "almost an extension of her own body" (234). John Brannigan thus rightly insists that, for Alice, there is a strong equation between a certain idea of home and her sense of identity, which explains why "Alice clings to what her home symbolizes [...] long after it has ceased to afford her the comforts of a home" (32). Or, as Alice herself sees it: "The dirt and disorder, the signs of malnutrition and neglect which to them were reasons for putting her away were, to her, independence" (260). It is this last symbolic refuge of Alice's self-determination that is being taken away on the recommendation of a social worker who, like Alice's son and daughter-in-law, fails to see how important her home is for the old woman: "She now understood the full indignity of rape. That man [i.e. the social worker], the expression in his eyes when he looked at her. The not-seeing" (260). If in Kelly's case rape undermines her sense of belonging, then in a kind of inverted mirror-image, for Alice it is the loss of the home that feels to her like rape. Moreover, in both cases, there is a refusal by others to recognize the needs and desires of someone who is unable to defend herself: a kind of "not-seeing" that reduces other human beings to mere objects.

A seemingly random episode in *Union Street* suggests that this kind of not-seeing is related to a worldview in which human beings are seen as mere means, and not as subjects who deserve to be regarded as ends in themselves (cf. the discussion of slavery in the chapter on *Absalom, Absalom!*). We have seen that Iris King's sister, Laura, has "staring eyes" and was recently treated for schizophrenia (178). When asked by Mrs. Sullivan, Iris explains the reason for Laura's temporary institutionalization:

> She was cleaning for this old man and one day she just took it into her head to set him on fire. One minute he was sat in his armchair, next he was up in flames. Or rather the chair was. He wasn't badly burned but [...] at that age the shock could have killed him. I said when I went to see her, I said, What d' y' want to do that for, Laura? She just turned around and said, Why not? He was no use. (179)

If others become mere means in a larger process – human resources, as it were – then there is no reason for them to continue existing as soon as they cease to be of use. It is an extreme view, and explicitly associated with mental illness in Barker's text. However, as Laura's inflexible stare is similar in kind to the unseeing looks in both Kelly's and Alice's stories, the political point is, arguably, that there is a larger, social problem underlying Laura's individual illness: a social system that consistently regards humans as means to ends, to be discarded if they cease to be 'useful.'

A Common Vision

The parallels between Kelly's and Alice's stories are emphasized further in a meeting between the two characters that is told twice in *Union Street*, the first time from Kelly's perspective. Crucially, for Kelly this meeting revolves around the possibility of regaining a sense of home and belonging. At the end of *Union Street*'s first section, on a cold late-winter day, Kelly is walking through the park – the very place where she first met her rapist – and is startled by the sight of the setting sun "obscured by columns of drifting brown and yellow smoke. A brutal, bloody disc, scored by factory chimneys, it seemed to swell up until it filled half the western sky" (64). Experiencing an odd "sensation of moving outside time," Kelly walks further into the park:

> Then a murmuring began and mixed in with it sharp, electric clicks, like the sound of women talking and brushing their hair at once. The noise became louder. She climbed to a ridge of higher ground and there at the centre was the tree, its branches fanned out, black and delicate, against the red furnace of sky. By now the murmur had become a fierce, ecstatic trilling, and when she looked more closely she saw that the tree was covered in birds that clustered along its branches as thick and bright as leaves, so that from a distance you might almost have thought that the tree was singing. (65)

It is a disturbingly beautiful vision, to which we shall return shortly. For the time being, however, the key thing to note is that Kelly does not find any consolation in it because she cannot "break out of that room inside her head" in which she is caught together with her rapist (65). As dusk settles, the lights go on in the houses bordering the park – "Homecomings," the narrator notes – and this is the very moment when Kelly notices what at first seems to her "nothing but a heap of rags" on a park bench in the cold February air (65–66). Soon, however, the girl discovers that there is an old woman wrapped tightly in these rags, peering back at Kelly "evidently unable to see her properly," her "eyes milky with cataract" (66). Kelly asks the old woman whether there is anybody expecting her "back home" (67), to which the women replies that she has come here to end her life, freezing to death on this bench in the park – an idea from which Kelly tries to dissuade her:

> “At least in a Home you’d get your meals.” She paused. Then burst out, “And they’d see you were warm. They’d see you had a fire.”
>
> “Is not the life more than meat and the body more than raiment?”
>
> She wasn’t quoting. She had lived long enough to make the words her own. (67)

The old woman’s biblical reply (cf. Matthew 6:25; KJV: “Is not the life more than meat, and the body than raiment?”) resonates with *Union Street*’s general themes, for while the text continually highlights that home must *begin* with material security, it also acknowledges that this in itself is not sufficient. Accordingly, though Kelly knows that she could disregard the old woman’s wishes and get ‘help,’ she accepts the woman’s claim to a modicum of agency and respect as a subject. “I won’t tell anybody,” Kelly says to the old woman, and if the look of love, according to Oliver, “does not pry or gaze, but caress” (69), then it is significant that the girl now reaches out and touches the old woman’s hand (*Union Street* 68). Kelly stays with the old woman until her eyes are closed, “in sleep, or unconsciousness, or death,” and then steps away from the bench, out of the park, and back into the streets of her community: “She was going home” (68–69) – and for John Brannigan, this conclusion to Kelly’s story suggests that the girl “resigns herself” to what her imperfect home has to offer (24).

However, while resignation does play a role in the section’s conclusion, it is arguably not the imperfect home to which Kelly resigns herself, but to the notion of human frailty and mortality as such – which makes a crucial difference in political terms. The idea that Kelly’s encounter with the old woman prompts the girl for the first time to confront her own mortality is explicit in *Union Street*: “[F]or the first time, she found it possible to believe in her own death. There was terror in this, but no sadness” (67). We have seen that Kelly’s traumatic experience of rape leads directly to a kind of homelessness on her part. Now, however, it is the realization that human life as such – not only her own – is vulnerable and exposed to suffering that makes it possible for her to regain some sense of value, to imagine herself as part of, rather than outside, the community, as well as to recover a concern for the others who live around her (Brophy 37).

Crucially, resigning oneself to the idea that human life is fragile and provisional does not mean the same as condoning the kind of violation and dereliction that we find everywhere in *Union Street*. Rather, it implies that such injustice can only be remedied if first we are willing to face the full terror of human frailty, and the full extent of present suffering, without resorting either to fatalism or despair (“There was terror in this, but no sadness”). Or, in the words of Antonio Gramsci: “It is necessary to create sober, patient people who do not despair in the face of the worst horrors and who do not become exuberant with every silliness. Pessimism of the intelligence, optimism of the will" (172). Not resignation to the broken state of these working-class homes, then, but a remorselessly clear view of things as they are: human frailty and mortality, the depth of economic privation, as well as the variety of conflicts that exist between working-class women, whose "discordant" voices Kelly hears on her way home (68; see Brophy 37). Realism, in other words, which in turn must serve as the starting point for any progressive politics worthy of the name.

Such a reading helps explain why the implications of the meeting between Kelly and the old woman are so different from the latter's point of view. The old woman, who remains unnamed in the first section of *Union Street*, is, of course, Alice, who in the text's seventh and final section experiences a moment of vision similar to Kelly's. The description of Alice's vision repeats parts of Kelly's almost verbatim, and it is therefore worth quoting at length:

> [A] murmuring began, as of the wind through summer trees or waves unfurling on the shore [... When Alice] looked at the skyline she saw that one tree stood out from the rest, its branches fanned out, black and delicate, against the red furnace of sky.
>
> [...] At first, it seemed to be bare like all the others, though with a jaggedness of outline that suggested not winter but death. By now the murmur had become a shout, a fierce, ecstatic trilling; and when she looked more closely, she saw that the tree was full of birds, clustering along its branches, as thick and bright as leaves. And all singing. But then, as she came closer still, as her white hair and skin took on the colours of blood and fire, she saw more clearly, and in a moment of vision cried. It isn't the birds, it's the tree. The tree is singing.
>
> The light was unbearably bright, bubbling in every vein, shaking her heart. She could not bear it. She shrank, she fell back. [...]
>
> But there was a child there, now, a girl, who, standing with the sun behind her, seemed almost to be a gift of the light. [...] Then it was time for them both to go.
>
> So that in the end there were only the birds, soaring, swooping, gliding, moving in a never-ending spiral about the withered and unwithering tree. (264–265)

Shrinking away from her overpowering experience, Alice finds Kelly "almost to be a gift of the light" – as if the girl herself were a symbol of solidarity and the continuation of life. Phrases from Kelly's vision (e.g. "By now the murmur had become a fierce, ecstatic trilling") are echoed very closely in this passage ("By now the murmur had become a shout, a fierce, ecstatic trilling"), which can be seen to suggest that the meaning of the vision is the same for both Alice and Kelly.

Critics have generally assumed that this is the case, though there is disagreement as to the political implications of the two characters' shared moment of vision. For Peter Hitchcock, for instance, the meeting between Kelly and Alice is "a strong statement on the sisterhood of class" (56). In a similar vein, Roberto del Valle Alcalá interprets their encounter as a moment that highlights the "irreversibility of resistance" (204), rather than as "a concession of defeat or confirmation of women's victimhood" (205). John Brannigan, by contrast, is hesitant, arguing that *Union Street*'s conclusion serves, not "to transcend the bleak depiction of dereliction presented throughout the novel, but to signal the possibility of an *imaginative* transformation of the structures which produce these material conditions," thus compelling us "to *conceive* of the functions and forms of 'home' and community anew" (33; emphasis added). Sarah Brophy likewise holds that the final union between Kelly and Alice "is more emblematic than it is political" (36), and Margaretta Jolly even wonders whether such visionary moments in Barker's work, which appeal to the body and spirit rather than the mind, might also imply that "material change and rational agency" are no longer feasible (236). The debate, in short, is reminiscent of the more general debate on realism as a form, questioning as it does whether the final moment of vision in *Union Street* carries with it a genuinely utopian impulse, or whether it merely serves imaginatively to dissolve the text's tensions in a politically void symbolical gesture.

What is lost out of sight in this debate is that, from the point of view of Alice, there really is not much hope left at the end of Barker's text, beyond imaginative consolation. We learn, for instance, that after Alice's stroke "it was obvious that the situation could not continue" – obvious "even to Mrs. Bell herself, though she would not admit it" (252). Later, when Alice tries to see herself "through a stranger's eyes," she finds it "no wonder they wanted her put away," and thinks of herself as "[r]ubbish. Ready for the tip" (259). This, accordingly, is Alice's crucial insight: "She searched among the wreckage for some fragment of hope, but there was none. Her life would not renew" (260). From Alice's own, single-focus perspective, in short, there truly is no hope left, only imaginative consolation. However, seen from the multiple-focus perspective of *Union Street* as a whole, the emphasis of Alice's insight shifts: "*Her* life would not renew" (emphasis added) – but others' lives might, including Kelly's, who thanks to her vision of the tree filled with birds is "alive with hope" when she finds Alice sitting on the bench in the park (67).

Put more abstractly, we may say that solving the interpretive puzzle posed by the meeting between Kelly and Alice involves a shift in focus from its meaning within the two separate stories to its significance for the reader as he or she reconsiders the text as a whole. Paul Ricoeur is one critic who has commented on the effect of symbolism on the reader, and a key point he makes is that symbols involve what one could call communicative excess: a symbol "says more than it says" and therefore "*invites us to think*, calls for an interpretation" (*The Conflict of Interpretations* 27–28; emphasis added). Franco Moretti in fact has made an intriguingly congruous suggestion, arguing that whereas 'pure' narrative is syntagmatic – in the sense that it concentrates on the relentless forward-flow of events (i.e. 'What comes next?') – symbolic scenes could be called paradigmatic because they entail an "urge to classify," and hence a more analytical attitude (i.e. 'Where does this fit, in the larger scheme of things?'; *Way of the World* 158). If this is the case, then the symbolism of *Union Street*'s 'twice-told' final scene constitutes a kind of wake-up call, akin to Slavoj Žižek's provocative advice in his book *On Violence*. There, Žižek suggests that too often a "fake sense of urgency" pervades contemporary discourses on violence and humanitarian crises – an urgency that is fundamentally anti-theoretical in that it discourages us from inquiring into the underlying causes of such crises: "There is no time to reflect: we have to *act now*" (5–6; original emphasis). However, Žižek continues, it may sometimes be more productive not to let oneself be drawn into the flow of current events, and instead to pause and reflect. In a similar vein, *Union Street*'s symbolical conclusion serves to redirect readers' attention, away from the forward-movement of the plot, and toward that *tertium quid* of conception which, according to Rick Altman, constitutes the crucial interpretive quest of multiple-focus readings in general.

Female Identity: Birds of a Feather

Ricoeur's ideas imply that symbolism may lead to a kind of alienation effect, making it impossible for readers to feel too comfortably at home in the fictional world of the text. Instead, symbols force us to examine the text from a certain critical distance – as exemplified by the discussion in this chapter of the symbolical role of eyes, sight, and visions in *Union Street*. If we now shift our attention to another figurative leitmotif in Barker's text – birds – we must therefore bear in mind Yuri Lotman's point that, in the case of symbols, to stop and think means at least two different things: on the one hand, to consider the symbol's "cultural memory" as it runs "vertically through the whole course of human history," and, on the other, to examine the network of symbolism as it is established and developed in one particular text (86). Put differently: though we must follow the general trajectory of symbols as they have historically migrated from one text to the next, we also need to find out how, precisely, these symbols are deployed in the particular text under study.

Starting with the symbolism of birds in cultural history in general, one key point for us to note is simply the wide array of meanings associated with avian imagery. Most dictionaries of symbols agree that in various cultures birds are linked to the soul, poetic inspiration and flights of fancy, as well as to prophecy: the winged messengers between Heaven and Earth (Cirlot 25; de Vries 47; Ferber 26; Lurker 773; Ronnberg 238). If we add to this Juan Eduardo Cirlot's description of the Tree of Life, with birds perched on the tree's branches representing the souls of the faithful (27), then we are immediately reminded of *Union Street*'s final vision of hope and renewal. Another component of this first cluster of symbolical meanings is that birds are frequently associated with freedom, or at least the desire for it (e.g. Ronnberg 240), pointing to a sense of possibility, transformation, and transcendence that forms part of the cultural memory stored in avian imagery. Moreover, a second cluster of avian associations revolves around femininity (e.g. de Vries 47), with the egg as a symbol of creation and regeneration (de Vries 158), and words like *chicks* even used colloquially to refer to girls or young women (OED).[13] Evidently, this gendered history, too, would render birds an appropriate symbol for *Union Street* and its focus on the lives of seven women. Meanwhile, a third and final cluster of associations relates birds to the notion of community and home, both because many birds build nests and because migratory birds leave but also always return home (Ferber 26, quoting Lévi-Strauss; cf. Ronnberg 238). In short, we have three clusters of symbolical associations – transcendence (or at least the longing for it), an association with femininity, and the link to the concept of home – that all seem admirably suited to *Union Street.*

However, at the same time we need to bear in mind that there is a complex and contradictory history of symbolism associated with individual birds (e.g. the albatross, the dove, or the eagle).[14] In this regard, the most basic observation to be made is that, in *Union Street*, the more 'aristocratic' birds – the eagle, nightingale, and owl, for example – tend to be missing (with the exception of swans, which appear twice; 16, 98), while the more common and 'homely' birds (geese, sparrows, and seagulls) take center stage. And once we think about it, this is not really surprising, as it ensures that the text's avian symbolism does not clash too forcibly with its realist aesthetic. It would, in other words, put a rather significant strain on the reader's willing suspension of disbelief to include soaring eagles and singing nightingales in the Northern-English industrial setting of a text like *Union Street.*

---

13 chick, *n*[1], 3b (OED Online, 3 August 2017; 2nd 1989).

14 A fuller list would include the albatross, cock, crow, cuckoo, dove, eagle, falcon, goose, hawk, lark, nightingale, owl, peacock, pelican, raven, sparrow, stork, swallow, and swan (see Ferber 27–28; Lurker 774; cf. Ronnberg 244–261).

This last point also leads us away from the more general cultural history of avian imagery to its particular use in *Union Street*, where birds appear in each of the seven sections (either as symbolical objects in the fictional world, or on the level of discourse, as metaphors and similes), and where there is a clear tendency for figurative fowl to be linked to female characters – though the connection is not entirely unequivocal. This becomes readily apparent from a (selective) survey of the many examples from *Union Street*'s seven sections:

1. When feeding "the ducks and geese and swans" at the lake in the park, Kelly Brown is attacked by the geese (17). At one point after having been raped, Kelly is tempted to kill an injured bird (63–64). Kelly is also moved, however, to find Alice Bell's throat "as vulnerable as a bird's," and later a group of women talking in front of a factory gate seem to her to make "a sound like the starlings had made" (68).
2. Near the lake in the park, Joanne Wilson tells her boyfriend Ken that she is expecting his child, and shortly after some geese and swans "begin sailing towards them in search of food" (98). Later in the story, Joanne confesses to a friend that sex with her boyfriend was brief and disappointing: "A sparrow couldn't 've farted quicker" (104).[15]
3. Lisa Goddard remembers that her husband once talked about the "bloody seagulls" that seemed drawn to the factory where he used to work ("a pest"); sometimes, a dead seagull would drop from the sky like a stone – killed, presumably, by the toxic fumes emanating from the factory's chimneys (121). Later in the story, Lisa gives birth to a baby daughter, to whom at first she does not feel any emotional connection. Eventually, however, Lisa manages to accept the baby daughter as her own; she then walks to the hospital window, carrying the girl in her arms, and sees "patches of trapped sky. Shadows of clouds and birds drifted across them" (139).
4. When Richard Scaife tells his father that he is reading a book about birds, he shows him the picture of a heron. The father, John, replies half-jokingly that this kind of knowledge is useless because "round here" there are no herons: "Only sparrows and starlings. And seagulls" (157). The father then points to a photograph in the newspaper of a woman posing naked and adds: "Only birds I ever fancy are in here" (ibid.).
5. Iris King, who is angry with her sixteen-year-old daughter for being pregnant, accidentally breaks an egg when working in the kitchen (201) – which

15 If we take into consideration that the Greeks associated sparrows with fertility, which is why in the Middle Ages sparrows could also be linked to unchastity and fornication (see Lurker 774), then the image Joanne uses becomes even more humorously apt.

seems doubly significant, given that the word *ovary* appears several times in this section of *Union Street* (205, 209). In addition, Iris uses the word "cock" (i.e. a male fowl) as a term of endearment for her daughter (217) – a usage derived from the word's metaphorical meaning as one "who fights with pluck and spirit" (OED).[16]

6. George Harrison uses the phrase "hawking it" (OED: "to carry about from place to place and offer for sale") to refer to Blonde Dinah's continuing to prostitute herself even at her advanced age (225).[17] George later has sex with Dinah, also spends the night with her but in the morning leaves before Dinah wakes up, feeling invigorated and encountering some birds on his way home: "Seagulls screamed and dived in the air above the river. And one detached itself from the rest to fly under the steel bridge; wings, briefly shadowed, gleamed in the restored light" (231).
7. Birds feature both in Alice Bell's mysterious vision (264) and in the very last sentence of *Union Street*, "soaring, swooping, gliding" around a "withered and unwithering tree" (265).

There are at least three things worth noting here. First, while it is possible to unify the various instances of avian imagery under the single umbrella term *birds*, we could also choose to emphasize difference: seagulls as opposed to sparrows, herons, or geese, for example. Second, though some images convey a sense of liberation (Lisa seeing birds drifting across the sky after finally finding an emotional connection to her baby daughter; a seagull whose wings gleam in "restored light"; or the birds we find "soaring, swooping, gliding" in the text's final sentence), others create an atmosphere of threat and oppression (Kelly being attacked by geese, but also herself tempted to kill a bird; seagulls falling dead from the sky; and Iris breaking an egg). Third, it is true that most of the images are related to female characters, yet some at least include a male perspective (Richard's father referring to women posing naked as birds; George Harrison thinking of Dinah as "hawking it"), and at least one instance is quite clearly directed at a male character (Joanne likening sex with her boyfriend to a sparrow farting). In fact, if we accept that Iris King is in thrall to a patriarchal, middle-class ideology, then it is peculiarly apt that she is the character who uses a term of endearment for her daughter – "cock" – that derives from the aggressive fighting spirit of a *male* bird and is also a slang term for *penis*. At any rate, given the strong, but not entirely straight-forward link between femininity

16 cock, *n*[1], II.8 (OED Online, 3 August 2017; 2nd ed. 1989).
17 hawk, *v*[2] (OED Online, 3 August 2017; 2nd ed. 1989).

and birds in *Union Street*, Ricoeur’s notion that symbols invite us to stop and think appears more pertinent than ever.

Perhaps what these somewhat equivocal clusters of identification imply is that female identity is best conceptualized along the lines of what Ludwig Wittgenstein calls “family resemblances.” According to Wittgenstein, when we look at a given category – for instance, the various kinds of objects we refer to as games – then we will find it impossible to determine a set of features shared by all the items belonging to this category. Instead, what we find are various degrees of relatedness – “a complicated network of similarities overlapping and criss-crossing” – and for Wittgenstein this kind of relationship is analogous to the network of resemblances that links members of the same family to each other (i.e. some have similar noses, others have similar ears, etc.; 36ᵉ, § 66).[18] Interpreting the figurative pattern of birds in *Union Street* in the light of these ideas, we can thus surmise that it is impossible to find one single set of characteristics that truly unites all women. Rather, there is a fuzzy set of features that signify femaleness, and each individual woman will share some (but not, as a rule, all) of these features. This not only makes it possible for two particular women to have virtually no characteristics in common and yet still remain associated with the category of woman as such; the fuzziness of the set also allows for its boundary to remain porous and permeable, so that one or several of the characteristic features of womanhood could, at the same time, be part of the fuzzy set that defines masculinity or manhood.[19] In other words, if in *Union Street* the female characters are subliminally presented as ‘birds of a feather,’ then the complexity of the text’s avian imagery also suggests that this does not at all imply an essentialist reduction of womanhood to a single core that stands in stable, binary opposition to manhood or masculinity.

Before proceeding to a third cluster of symbols in *Union Street* – mirrors, this time – let us take stock of the argument so far. We have seen that, in Barker’s text, the precarious state of the built environment finds a parallel in the “derelict” state of human bodies, as well as in the fragmentation of the text into semi-independent stories. Moreover, *Union Street* places strong emphasis on the conflicts between women, whether from the same family (e.g. Iris King physically

18 “Wir sehen ein kompliziertes Netz von Ähnlichkeiten, die ineinander übergreifen und kreuzen” (36; § 66).

19 The notion of fuzzy sets has recently come to great prominence in the study of literary genres (e.g. Marie-Laure Ryan 28. See also Michael Basseler on genre in general and the short story in particular (58), as well as Terry Eagleton on the genre of tragedy, which he sees as constituted “by a *combinatoire* of overlapping features rather than by a set of invariant forms or contents” (*Sweet Violence* 3).

assaulting her daughter because the latter has violated the rules of sexual respectability) or between women in general (with racism as one particularly violent conflict). At the same time, like other short-story cycles, *Union Street* balances these elements of fragmentation with various kinds of unity: a common setting (i.e. a Northern English working-class community); the ordering of individual stories to depict the lives of progressively older women; and what we could call figurative leitmotifs. Of these leitmotifs, eyes serve as symbols that highlight the opposition between an alienating, objectifying gaze and the look of love as a sign of intersubjective recognition. Both ways of seeing, therefore, are related to the constitution and maintenance of individual identity. By contrast, birds serve as a complex figure of collective female identity and, more generally, of communal belonging – which is one reason why they feature so prominently in the moment of vision that connects the stories of Kelly Brown and Alice Bell, who as victims of the non-seeing, objectifying gaze had both become isolated and, indeed, homeless.

Mirror, Mirror on the Wall: Reflection, Representation, and Realism

Turning to a third symbolical cluster in *Union Street* – mirrors – we briefly need to revisit the problem of individual identity because, in Barker's text, mirrors are shown to affect one's sense of self through their ability to reflect the human body. Joanne Wilson, for instance, who has recently found out that she is pregnant, at one point examines the reflection of her naked body in a mirror:

> She stood, pressing her hands fearfully against the still flat belly. No sign there at least. But her shoulder, her arms, her breasts! Blue veins showed up all over them, as intricately linked as the branches of a tree; all leading down to the nipples which themselves were bigger and browner than they had been a month ago. Some yellowish stuff had dried to form a crust over the skin. [...]
>
> Her body, from childhood so familiar, had become frightening. It occurred to her that it looked like another human face, with nipples instead of eyes, a powerful, barely-human face. By comparison, her real face seemed childish and unformed.
>
> She was afraid. 'What the hell am I going to do?' she asked that other, inhuman face, which was aware of no problem. (72)[20]

20 Note that the image of veins as similar to "the branches of a tree" is also used when Alice Bell examines her body in the mirror: "Silver branches spread out across her belly, springing from the sparsely-rooted hair. A tree in winter" (261). The metaphor is yet another link between the community of women and the symbolical tree of life that appears in Kelly's and Alice's moments of vision.

As was the case with the "derelict" in the local library, the description here focuses on the body as unruly matter: veins simply "showed up," together with some unidentifiable "yellowish stuff." Moreover, though Joanne's belly is "still flat," she knows that her body will soon betray the signs of her pregnancy to others, as if the body had a will entirely of its own. The supposedly supreme ego thus suddenly finds itself disturbingly powerless, lacking the sense of control that would enable it to feel at home in the body, which indeed appears like an alien, second self in the passage: "a powerful, barely-human face." In confronting Joanne with the sight of her body, the mirror thus forces a reassessment of her own identity; though her "real face seemed childish and unformed" when compared to that "other, inhuman face," she must somehow integrate the new knowledge forced upon her by the body into her conscious identity. The body thus constitutes the locus of the unconscious, which itself "is aware of no problem," but which through its symptoms and effects exerts a fearful pressure on our disturbingly fragile egos, whom the mirror confronts with reflections that may clash with our mental images of ourselves.[21]

We can in fact find the same mechanism at work in a different scene in *Union Street* as well, and ultimately the text highlights that it is impossible for individuals to escape the truth-telling function of the mirror. Kelly Brown, who in the aftermath of being raped has taken to roaming the streets at night, at one point in *Union Street* secretly enters the Victorian house of a well-to-do family who, Kelly speculates, have left the house for a short trip (51). Kelly explores the unfamiliar rooms and is particularly fascinated by the parents' bedroom. Though she knows that a "man slept there too," to Kelly the room's "flesh-coloured satin" and its "pink, flabby cushions" make it "a temple of femininity" (53). Suddenly, however, the girl is arrested in her exploration of this 'foreign' middle-class home when she sees her reflection in the bedroom mirror:

> She looked as wild and unkempt as an ape, as savage as a wolf. Only her hair, glinting with bronze and gold threads, was beautiful. [...] But she looked bad. She peered more closely in the glass and saw that the pores of her nose were bigger than they had been, and plugged with black. When Linda [i.e. Kelly's older sister] used the blackhead remover little worms of white stuff came wiggling out of the unblocked pores. Sud-

21 In psychoanalytic discourse, the key terms used to refer to our own self-image would be the *ideal-ego* and the *ego-ideal*, in connection to the *super-ego* (e.g. Felluga 142; Lacan, "Remarks on Daniel Lagache's Presentation" 562; Žižek, *How to Read Lacan* 79–80). In Jungian psychology, the key terms would be *shadow* and *persona* (e.g. Hopcke 13–16; Stein 106–109).

> denly, Kelly hated the mirror. On the man’s side of the bed was a heavy ashtray. She picked it up and threw it [...] against the glass. (54)

Once again, the mirror here appears as the harbinger of an unwelcome truth: ostensibly of Kelly’s looking “bad,” but perhaps more importantly of the fact that she is a young girl on the verge of sexual maturity – for this is, arguably, the significance of the comparison to her older sister Linda, whose symbolic role as a biologically mature female is made clear on the very first pages of *Union Street*, when Kelly finds her sister’s bloodied sanitary pads in a bottom drawer: “She looked at the hair in Linda’s armpits, at the breasts that shook and wobbled when she ran, and no, she didn’t want to get like that. And she certainly didn’t want to drip foul-smelling, brown blood out of her fanny every month” (3). Even before the rape, in other words, Kelly felt decidedly uneasy about the prospect of her body changing into that of a ‘grown woman.’ Now, after the rape, Kelly’s reaction to the reflection of her developing body is telling, for not only does she try and break the glass; she eventually fetches a pair of scissors and begins to cut off her hair – the only thing about her that still looks beautiful – in a desperate attempt to suppress her violated female body by making herself look boyish. Oscar Wilde, in the preface to *The Picture of Dorian Gray*, wrote that “[t]he *nineteenth century dislike* of Realism is the rage of Caliban, seeing his own face in a glass” (3), and there is a sense in this passage, too, that Kelly’s ‘animal’ rage (she is “unkempt as an ape, as savage as a wolf”) is tragically misguided – against herself, and against the mirror as the medium of a certain kind of truth, rather than against the man who raped her.[22] It is, perhaps, for this reason, that, by smashing the mirror, Kelly only ends up “trapping [...] her shattered face” in it (54): the image of a fragmented self that the mirror truthfully reflects.[23]

Crucially, it is not only reflections of the pubescent and the pregnant body that pose a threat, or at least challenge, to a stable sense of female identity, for in *Union Street* mirrors also reveal unpleasant truths about psychological and physical health as they affect the ageing body. Muriel Scaife, for instance, who has just lost her beloved husband, refrains from looking into her bedroom mirror because “it could show her only what she most feared to see: a woman, white-faced, sodden, and alone” (176). Similarly, when Iris King stands “in front

22 Note that John Brannigan (21) also associates Kelly’s rage with Caliban’s.

23 This is not to say that Lucy Gallagher is wrong in suggesting that Kelly’s violence, her “dirtying of herself and her environment is actually a step toward her recovery” (49). It is merely to emphasize that the truths contained in mirrors are not always welcome, at least not initially, and may trigger strong ‘defense mechanisms.’

of the mirror to tie the scarf around her head you could see that she wasn't well" (180). In both these cases, middle-aged women's reflections in the mirror have the power to reveal that something is amiss. Most brutally, however, the mirror reveals the truth about her mortal and, indeed, dying body to Alice Bell:

> Her hands came up. She hid herself from the mirror. For years she had avoided looking into it: the head it showed bore no relation to the person she thought she was. Inside herself, she was still sixteen. She had all the passion, all the silliness. Still there behind the gray hair and wrinkled skin. Now the dislocation between what the mirror showed and what she knew herself to be, was absolute. She would have liked to break the glass. (225)

While Alice tries to hold on to an ideal, timeless image of herself as she used to be ("the person she thought she was"), the mirror mercilessly confronts her with the truth of her impending death.

We can restate these crises of identity provoked by mirrors in more philosophical terms as conflicts between idealism and realism. Idealism, according to Pam Morris, "gives primacy to the consciousness, or mind or spirit that apprehends" rather than to the material world, and in aesthetic theory it has long been associated with art as an "intimation of timeless ideals" (*Realism* 50–52). In the scene where Alice hides herself from the mirror, it is precisely such a timeless ideal that is challenged by the mirror's truthful reflection of things as they are, not in the mind that apprehends, but in the world of objects, to which the human body belongs. And realism, for Pam Morris, derives precisely from an "acceptance that the objects of the world that we know by means of our sensory experience have an independent existence" (*Realism* 49–50). Accordingly, one aim of realism as an empiricist epistemology is to destroy idealist illusions about the world, and it is significant that, in *Union Street*, this process may lead to denial or, once again, feelings of rage, with Alice's desire to break the mirror reflecting Kelly's earlier desire to destroy the source of unwanted truth.

It would, however, be misleading to frame realism's "refusal of anodyne fantasy" (Eagleton, *The Event of Literature* 72) in exclusively destructive terms, as merely the destruction of idealist falsehoods. This becomes clear if we focus on the dual meaning of the word *representation* (Haywood 3). Just as political representation has historically been limited to certain groups (as a rule, property-owning men), aesthetic representation for centuries tended to exclude supposedly unseemly and low subject matter. The stuff of realism, by contrast, "is not selected for its dignity and nobility" – that is, it attempts to include *all* kinds of things, people, and experiences – and thus implies a truly democratic politics (Pam Morris, *Realism* 3).

In *Union Street*, the willingness to represent 'unseemly matters' is demonstrated forcefully in the chilling description of the abortion that Iris King's daughter has decided to undergo. As the doctors at the hospital refuse to perform the abortion, Iris and her daughter depend on the help of Irene, who lives in a run-down house on Wharfe Street. The procedure ends up taking much longer than Iris expected, and it ends with a description of the aborted fetus: "The baby clenched his fist feebly, lying on the floor of the lavatory with the *News of the World* spread over him" (215). Significantly, the newspaper here does not 'cover' the appalling event in the sense of reporting on it, but instead 'covers it up' and hides it from view. This, arguably, is a symbolic way of suggesting that certain kinds of events are not represented in the newspaper media. Accordingly, if one key function of the media in a democratic society is to represent the events that matter, and thus to provide the necessary input for public debate and political decision-making, then the image of the *News of the World* covering up the aborted child may imply that the contemporary press is not fulfilling its function properly. This, in turn, may explain why newspapers frequently remain "unopened" in *Union Street* (132), serving instead as blankets, padding, or fuel (4, 60, 232), as if the content of print media were entirely disconnected from the reality of life in a working-class community – the very kind of life that *Union Street*, as a realist text, attempts to represent.

At the same time, Barker's text does not simply oppose its own, supposedly more truthful realism to the failures of contemporary mass media, for *Union Street* at least hints at the potentially productive role of the media in general, and television in particular. To be sure, there are critical comments here, too: George Harrison, for instance, at one point says that people were "better off" when they did not have TV and had to make their own amusement instead (227). And yet, there is also a scene in which Kelly, having switched on the TV because her mother and sister are out, finds herself fascinated by a news report about sectarian conflict in Northern Ireland:

> [T]here was this young man, this soldier, and he was lying in a sort of cot, a bed with sides to it, and he was shouting out, great bellows of rage, as he looked out through the bars at the ward where nobody came. What caught her attention was: they'd shaved all his hair off. You could see the scars where they'd dug the bullets out. His head was like a turnip, a violent turnip, where they shot the bullets into his brain.
>
> The cameras switched to gangs of youth throwing stones. But his eyes went on watching her. (47–48)

Kelly, traumatized by the experience of rape, is suddenly confronted with an image to which she can relate: a violated body filled with rage, which provides a mirror-image to Kelly's own situation as well as a model for future behavior, for as we know she, too, will later cut off her hair until her head is "shorn" (54). An identification with the situation of others is thus one of the positive potentials that mediated images harbor. Admittedly, there are other positive functions that remain unexplored by Kelly (though as readers we are free to speculate, for example, that the troubles in Northern Ireland and the situation of working-class communities in Northern England may not be as unrelated as they appear at first sight). At any rate, the key point is that *Union Street* acknowledges the media's potential to bring politics home in both senses of the term: to cross the divide between public and private, and to help the audience understand the world in which they live. In principle, then, such 'daily mirrors' can have an emancipatory function, even if contemporary practice may at times be found wanting.

And of course, mirrors have long served as symbols for the truth-telling function of art as well – "to hold as 'twere the mirror up to nature" (*Hamlet* 297; 3.2.21–22) – and in particular of realist representation. "As a true reflector of external reality," Robert C. Holub observes, "the mirror is quite obviously the central image of realist aesthetics" (206–207). At the same time, however, Holub reminds us that realism only ever offers the "illusion" of faithfully reflecting the world (102), and one simple reason for this, Pam Morris notes, is that "words function completely differently from mirrors": they force the writer to order and select (*Realism* 5). The error in positing a one-to-one correspondence between fiction and reality is thus, according to Terry Eagleton, to regard "fiction as a mirror rather than as a work" (*The Event of Literature* 218); the literary work ought "to be seen not as a reflection of a history external to it, but as a strategic labour" (170).[24] In the light of such observations, the emphasis on the truth-telling function of mirrors in *Union Street* suddenly threatens to seem embarrassingly naïve.

This impression of naivety may become even stronger if we remember the role of mirrors in Lacanian accounts of identity formation. Elisabeth Bronfen has succinctly summarized Lacan's ideas about the role of mirrors in this process (see also the chapter on *Moby-Dick*):

> We recognize ourselves only through reflections, notably the images we fashion for ourselves, or the way we see ourselves reflected in the eyes of others. Yet as Jacques Lacan notes in his seminal essay on the mirror phase in psychic development, [...] the

24 See Pam Morris on George Lukács's useful distinction between "realism and the reassuring consensual convention of actualism" (*Jane Austen, Virginia Woolf and Worldly Realism* 8–9).

> act of recognizing oneself in a mirrored image is always inscribed by a misrecognition, for the image we see has undergone a double fracturing. It is not only an inversion of the figure it mirrors, but it returns to the subject only by a detour through an intermediary, namely as a representation. It thus harbors a disjunction between body and image [...]. (207; see Lacan, “The Mirror Stage” 78)

Two points are worth highlighting here: on the one hand, the importance of the body as the visible sign of the self, and, on the other hand, the element of disjunction between the body and the image formed on the basis of the reflection of one’s body in the mirror. Indeed, Sean Homer likewise emphasizes the importance of the body in the Lacanian mirror stage, for it is the reflected image of the body as “a total form” which, according to Homer, sustains the infant’s developing sense of mastery over the body (25). The key element of misrecognition lies, in other words, in the fantasy of a self that is not only unified, but also master in its own house: in full control of its own body. If this is so, however, then the use of mirrors in *Union Street* is not, after all, entirely naïve, for we have seen that one function of mirrors in Barker’s text is precisely to reflect back an image of the body as unruly matter that the ego repeatedly finds impossible to master.

Unspeakable: Reflections on the Limit of Discourse

While mirrors symbolize the possibility of recognizing the truth, *Union Street* nevertheless acknowledges that there are certain limits to its project of representing the real through the use of a fourth cluster of recurring symbols: gaping, spluttering, and speechless mouths. “Death,” Terry Eagleton insists, “is the limit of discourse, not a product of it” (*The Idea of Culture* 87), and we need to bear this in mind when examining how Barker’s text depicts the death of Muriel Scaife’s beloved husband, John:

> She [i.e. Muriel] ran back into the living-room and there was John, blood gargling from his mouth. Above the black hole his eyes rolled about, frenzied and unseeing. The flow of blood seemed to have stopped. [...]
>
> [...] He was choking on the blood. She began pulling out huge clots of it from his mouth. [...] Her fingers found a thick rope of blood, twined round it, and pulled. The clot slid out of his mouth, with the sound of a sink coming unblocked, and after it flowed a frothy, bright-red stream of blood, looking almost gay against the blackness of the other blood. (163)

If, as argued previously, the horror of John’s unseeing eyes is related to the loss of intersubjective recognition – the look of love gone forever – then this is complemented here by the frightening image of a human being silenced by his own blood: the body, our most intimate home, as at the same time the cause of suffering and, ultimately, death. It is surely no coincidence that Alice Bell, after her stroke, likewise experiences a profound sense of horror at "the sounds that glugged out of her mouth" – sounds which only slowly regain "some resemblance to speech" (245); indeed, even after Alice has recovered to some extent, when she is excited "her speech went altogether" (246). Scenes such as these, with their emphasis on mouths straining but failing to speak, are best understood as an engagement with the paradox of the unspeakable: to try and express what is in fact impossible to say. In theoretical terms, we would thus be confronted with the Lacanian Real as that which signifies the limits of signification (Homer 83).

This attempt to express the unspeakable surfaces repeatedly in *Union Street*, and if death constitutes one limit of discourse in Barker's text, then another is the fact of sexual difference. As Laura Mulvey has pointed out, sexual difference serves a key function in a patriarchal symbolic order: "The paradox of phallocentrism in all its manifestations is that it depends on the image of the castrated woman to give order and meaning to its world [... I]t is her lack that produces the phallus as symbolic presence" (585). From a patriarchal point of view, in other words, women can only serve as that constitutive absence that enables the symbolic order to function. Mulvey's comments help us unravel the meaning of a scene in *Union Street* in which George Harrison, after having had sex with Blonde Dinah, decides to inspect the sleeping prostitute's naked body:

> She was lying with her legs apart. [...] He had never actually seen it before. It was funny in a way. You spend your whole boyhood thinking about it, wondering what it's like; but when you finally get it you don't really *see* it.
>
> Almost against his will, he knelt down until it was on a level with his face. The lips gaped, still dribbling a little milky fluid. And there it was. A gash? A wound? Red fruit bitten to the core? It was impossible to say what it was like. (230–231; original emphasis)

The fact that George Harrison refers to Blonde Dinah's genitals only as "it" already indicates that he lacks a precise expression to refer to the object that has aroused his curiosity. In addition, the term "lips" to refer to Dinah's labia, as well as the use of the verb "gaped," further intimate a sense of the unspeakable, as if Dinah's vulva were a gaping mouth, dribbling fluid, but remaining stubbornly silent. As the passage continues, this sense of something that is impossible to say slowly combines with an undercurrent of violence ("gash," "wound," "bitten to the core") – and of course this makes sense within a patriarchal logic that posits women as the sign of lack and castration. Moreover, we need to bear in mind that the perspective here is a man's: George Harrison, the only male character who serves as a main focalizer in the seven sections of *Union Street*, and whose inquisitive, objectifying gaze is directed at a prostitute: the very embodiment of woman as merely a commodity (Brannigan 22).[25]

However, if womanhood as such is unspeakable within a patriarchal framework, then motherhood and the maternal may constitute a related, even more fundamental limit to discourse. According to Julia Kristeva, "the abject confronts us, on the one hand, with those fragile states where man strays on the territories of *animal*," but also, on the other hand, with our earliest attempts to release the psychological hold of the maternal (*Powers of Horror* 12–13; original emphasis). Paradoxically, then, the womb as our earliest home simultaneously figures as deeply unhomely in our psychic imaginary: the site of primal repression. It is thus hardly a coincidence that, in addition to death and sexual difference, the moment of birth also figures as well-nigh unspeakable in *Union Street*. In the case of Lisa Goddard, for instance, the protracted pains of labor ultimately render her inarticulate: "as the day wore on speech became too much of an effort" (128). In a similar vein, in the course of her abortion procedure Iris's daughter Brenda grips "the head of the bed, mouth wide open, lips stretched to splitting, like the other lips between her legs" (215). Lacan's Real and Kristeva's abject thus feature as limits to discourse and representation in *Union Street*. Sarah Brophy describes Pat Barker's texts as "[n]either realist novels nor psychoanalytic case studies, but partaking of and revising both genres" (25). However, if one agrees with Terry Eagleton that the achievement of Freudian psychoanalysis lies in providing us with "a materialist theory of the making of the human subject" (*Literary Theory* 141), then it is perhaps better to say that *Union Street* uses the insights of one materialist lineage of thought – psychoanalysis – to complement and reinvigorate that older materialism implied in the empiricist epistemology of realist aesthetics.[26]

The Body and Labor

The embodied nature of human existence is a necessarily central materialist concern, and we have seen that the body as unruly matter features prominently

---

25 Roberto del Valle Alcalá also argues that, in Barker's novel, the two extremes of rape and prostitution frame the "circumscription of life itself within the axis of capitalist accumulation. While rape embodies the most direct and extreme form of primitive accumulation, prostitution […] represents the proletarianization of women's reproductive labor power" – even as sexuality remains a site "also of resistance" (199)

26 The fact that realism has not always succeeded in staying true to this materialist project should not lead us to posit that it is an inherently idealist genre.

throughout *Union Street.* Indeed, Margaretta Jolly argues that, in Barker's work more generally, the body functions as "the visible face of psychological and social unreason" (235). In *Union Street* the best starting point for a detailed discussion of this claim is the relation between the female body and labor. More specifically, we can begin to understand how social pressures affect individual subjects by focusing on how *Union Street* exploits the dual meaning of labor as signifying both 'work' and 'giving birth.' This, for example, is how Barker's narrator describes the increasing intensity of Lisa Goddard's labor pains:

> There was something mechanical about their strength, their remorseless regularity. She felt them as extreme heat, as though she were being forced to stand too close to a furnace, to watch the door open, slowly [...].
>
> This rhythm went on hour after hour for most of the day until her whole being was subdued to it. (128)

The act of giving birth is couched here in language associated with industrial labor ("mechanical," "regularity," "furnace"), and John Brannigan rightly notes that such images indicate the extent to which factory work extends "into the mental and emotional life of the community" (26). The public, material conditions of working-class life appear, in other words, as powerful forces in the shaping of these characters' supposedly private interiority.

In this way, *Union Street* incorporates the Marxian notion that alienated labor affects human beings in their totality, including in their relations with one another. We can see this, for example, in a scene in which Joanne Wilson tells her unsuspecting boyfriend that she is pregnant. Ken, though far from pleased at the news, assures Joanne that they are "in it together" (99). However, when subsequently they have sex in an underpass, Joanne realizes that something is amiss:

> Ken was panting, and thrusting into her as though he hated her, grinding and screwing and banging hard enough to hurt. She was afraid for the baby and immediately knew what he was trying to do: he was trying to screw it out of her. She went cold, pressing herself back against the wall, but he fastened onto her with a terrible, monotonous power.
>
> There was something exciting in being used like this, in giving way to this impersonal, machine-like passion. (101)

Just like Lisa Goddard's labor pains, sex here is drawn into the sphere of industrial labor ("grinding and screwing and banging," "monotonous power," "machine-like passion"), setting up a parallel between capitalist production and biological as well as social reproduction. The same, moreover, is true for an earlier scene, in which Joanne, while working on the conveyer belt in the local cake factory, is trying to decide whether or not to keep her baby:

> She began the sequence of actions that she would perform hundreds of times that day. It took little effort once you were used to it and [...] it could be done almost automatically.
>
> Almost. But not quite. Now that she was alone – for in this roaring cavern of sound each woman *was* alone – she wanted to think about Ken, she wanted [...] to work out exactly how she was going to tell him about the baby. She couldn't do it. Each half-formed thought was aborted by the arrival of another cake. (85; original emphasis)

In terms of content, the passage makes clear that Joanne's working conditions affect her entire being, both interrupting her process of thought and isolating her from other women (with such isolation from others being a key effect of alienated labor for Marx). At the same time, the phrase "to work out" emphasizes that thinking itself is best conceived as intellectual labor, with Joanne's material surroundings thwarting her potential for mental creativity, and her thoughts continually "aborted" like unborn children (Rawlinson 27).

The relationship between creation, (re)production, and alienation is, however, as Susan Brophy has noted, illustrated most forcefully in the case of Lisa Goddard and her struggle emotionally to relate to her new-born daughter. Early on in Lisa's story, we learn that she barely manages to make ends meet because her occasionally violent husband is out of work and tends to spend far too much money on drink. It is difficult enough, under such circumstances, to take care of two little boys, and the mere idea of soon giving birth to a third child is virtually impossible for Lisa to bear: "She did not want this baby" (112); indeed, "[w]hen she first learned she was pregnant she had asked for an abortion," but the "doctor had told her there were no grounds" (132). Lisa, in other words, is neither provided with sufficient resources to take good care of the baby, nor legally granted control over her pregnant body. In this sense, it is entirely fitting that Lisa at first fails to recognize the baby as her own (133); to use Sarah Brophy's words, "Lisa is alienated from the baby, the product of her body and labor" (31). There is, in short, nothing natural or automatic about feelings of motherhood in *Union Street*, as Lisa finds to her dismay.

The political point here is that motherhood as such also ought be appreciated as cultural and, indeed, physical work. Kath Woodward, following feminist theorists like Adrienne Rich and Luce Irigaray, insists that motherhood "involves more than carrying a foetus and giving birth, although the stresses, strains and joys of delivery should not be underestimated"; more particularly, while "at some point there has to be a woman's body," motherhood is an eminently cultural concept (128) – as evidenced, for example, by the fact that societies expend an enormous amount of regulatory fervor to distinguish between 'good' and 'bad' mothers (131). This latter fact also documents that the supposedly natural phenomenon of motherhood is in many respects the result of (self-)discipline and work. Lisa Goddard, at any rate, is aware of the extraordinary effort that motherhood involves: "It took her all her time to cope with Kevin and Darren, whom she loved. How would she manage to care for this baby for whom she felt nothing?" (136). Under conditions of alienated labor, even such seemingly foundational and unshakeable social relations as the one between mother and daughter may thus slowly wither and die.

Crucially, it is the idea of common labor – in the sense of shared suffering and struggle – that ultimately allows Lisa to overcome her alienation from the baby daughter. Lisa experiences the first "stab of recognition" when one of the Sisters working at the hospital gives the baby a bath:

> Seeing it, red and howling, struggling in the nurse's hands, Lisa thought, Yes. And when it rose from the bath with dark and streaming hair the pain was so extreme that she had to turn aside; she could not bear to look.
>
> The feeling vanished. But it had given her hope. The time she spent simply staring at the baby increased. And then, one day, as she was changing its nappy, she found a smear of blood on the cloth. [...] Her heart contracted with fear. (137)

Seeing the baby struggling against adversity, Lisa for a brief moment recognizes something of herself in the daughter's pain. Margaretta Jolly is thus right in insisting that the body is also "a figure of hope" in Pat Barker's work (235), as it is in part the recognition of common suffering that serves as the basis of identification with others. Moreover, Lisa's "fear" for the baby's health arises as a by-product of the labor of caretaking that she devotes to her daughter's physical needs, as only the act of changing the baby's diapers makes it possible for her to discover the potentially worrying "smear of blood." To her relief, Lisa learns from a nurse that it is common for female infants to 'menstruate' at some point after being born: "All the female hormones in your blood get across to her, you see. Then when they stop, she starts to bleed" (137). And it is at this moment, after having both recognized herself in the baby's suffering and worked for the infant's physical well-being, that Lisa finally manages to accept the child as hers: "*My daughter*" (139; original emphasis).

But, one might object, is this not a misguided attempt once again to reduce femininity to women's reproductive and maternal functions? This kind of biological reductionism has, after all, been a strong tendency at least since the Age of Enlightenment (Outram 89–90), and women's supposedly natural role as the bearers of new life has frequently been used by men to deny them various rights (e.g. the right to vote and full citizenship; see, for example, Frevert 424–425). Ian Haywood is one critic who has raised such objections to the depiction of women in *Union Street* (146), but Margaretta Jolly insists that these criticisms fail to do justice to the complexity of Barker's text:

> [The] "feminine experience" of the body is problematized through its performance of unconscious social desires of class and sexuality. [...] A critique of "biological reductionism" [...] ignores the fact that within the societies in crisis that Barker explores, *biological* questions of physical survival – "stoicism," recovery, or simply birth itself – are fundamentals that must not be underestimated. For the poor, ill, or war-torn, the birth of new life and physical resistance are not necessarily "reductive" so much as astonishing. (242; original emphasis)

Rather than shying away from the body altogether, that is to say, *Union Street* uses those problems of human existence that arise from our embodied nature – birth, the need for sustenance and shelter, sexual difference, labor, and death – as a starting point for the recognition of commonality.

Moreover, *Union Street* does not posit such recognition as inherently comforting, but instead acknowledges that it may at times be downright frightening. This becomes clear in a harrowing scene that takes place right after Kelly's rape. When the rapist, after violating Kelly, wants her to leave as quickly as possible the girl refuses, not wanting "to go home yet" (30). Instead, Kelly demands that her rapist treat her to a drink at a nearby restaurant, threatening to shout for help if he refuses to come with her. Soon, we thus find the two of them – victim and perpetrator – sitting at the same table in a fish-and-chip bar whose walls are "lined with mirror-tiles," so that wherever Kelly looks, hers and the man's eyes meet:

> [A]s she continued to stare, she saw a slight movement, a crumbling almost, at the corner of the lids. Something was happening to his face. It was beginning to split, to crack, to disintegrate from within, like an egg when the time for hatching has come. She wanted to run. She didn't want to stay there and see what would hatch out of this egg. But horror kept her pinned to her chair. And the face went on cracking. And now moisture of some kind was oozing out of the corners of his eyes, running into cracks that had not been there a minute before, dripping, finally, into the open, the agonised mouth. She watched, afraid. And looked away. But that was no use.
>
> From every side his reflection leapt back at her, as the mirror-tiles filled with the fragments of his shattered face. (33)

Here, once again, we find the close attention to bodily matter so characteristic of Barker's prose: slight movements on a face, moisture oozing out of the corners of the man's eyes, and cracks forming where previously there had been none. In addition, the scene evokes each of the four symbolical clusters we have discussed: the image of something terrible hatching out of an egg (evoking the symbolism of birds); the emphasis on eyes, staring, and the desire to see (or not to see); the presence of mirrors and reflections; and, finally, the man's gaping mouth as yet another figure of the unspeakable. The terrible knowledge implied in all this is that even the rapist cannot ultimately be excluded from the common humanity that, for better or worse, we all share. And, understandably, Kelly tries to avoid and repress this knowledge, so that when later in the story her mother begins to cry the girl tries hard not to acknowledge Mrs. Brown's pain: "Her mother's face, crumbling, reminded her of The Man. She could not allow herself to feel pity" (59). The recognition of commonality can, in short, be a terrifying thing indeed, as Kelly learns in *Union Street*:

> His face remained. And would be there always, trailing behind it, not the cardboard terrors of the fairground, [...] but the real terror of the adult world, in which grown men open their mouths and howl like babies, where nothing that you feel, whether love or hate, is pure enough to withstand the contamination of pity. (57)

"The truth is rarely pure and never simple," says a character in Oscar Wilde's *The Importance of Being Earnest* (258), and it is precisely this realization which marks Kelly's entry into "the real terror of the adult world" (*Union Street* 57). Accordingly, if the common nature of the human body figures as a sign of hope in Barker's text, then once again it is not because our shared embodied nature effortlessly leads to solidarity, but because the body serves as a starting point from which community can be built, actively, as a difficult and wearisome kind of labor (Waterman 7).

Common Women, Common Men: The Body of Domestic Fiction

To explore further the idea that the body may serve as a common ground for the construction and maintenance of community, we need to return to the problem of female solidarity in *Union Street*, which is acknowledged as a complex task through the text's repeated reference to distorting mirrors. Significantly, mirrors at times distort reality to such an extent in *Union Street* that it becomes difficult even to interpret the reflected image. For instance, while giving birth, Lisa sees her face reflected in a steel surface so heavily curved that the mirror-image becomes "too distorted [...] to register anything so messily human as fear" (126). At the same time, however, Barker's text does not simply conflate distortion with misrepresentation. When Kelly and her friend Sharon Scaife attend a fun fair, for example, they meet Joanne Wilson – the protagonist of the second section of *Union Street* – at the "entrance to the Hall of Mirrors," a fairground attraction where the reflection of one's body is distorted in various ways: "Sharon Scaife, who was plump and suffered for it, had found a mirror that showed her long and stringy as a bean" (19). This moment is significant for at least two reasons. First, though the mirror clearly distorts, we must also note that Sharon in fact prefers the 'false' image to her real, "plump" self: "I quite like it" (ibid.). The text, in other words, acknowledges that distorted images can have a kind of utopian dimension, with the reflection hinting at an alternative to the present that is, or may be, preferable for the subject. Second, the scene is important because the Hall of Mirrors functions as a *mise en abyme* of the relation between the individual stories in *Union Street*, with each of the seven sections serving as a distorted reflection of – and indeed, on – the other six (hence the presence of Joanne Wilson, the protagonist of the second section, at the entrance of the hall of mirrors). Mirrors, in short, are the bearers of three complicated and interrelated truths in Barker's text: about the importance of the body (as well as ideal or idealized images of it) in the formation of identity; about the productive side of distortion (i.e. its potentially utopian dimension); and about the relation between the individual and the collective.

This latter point, incidentally, is the reason why figurative mirrors pervade the text of *Union Street*, serving as symbolical explorations of the commonality of women. For instance, at one point we find Kelly's mother looking at her daughter, startled to find that "we're alike": "There, in the lines of nose and chin, was her own face, glimpsed in a *distorting mirror*" (58; emphasis added). Similarly, for Joanne Wilson suddenly "every older woman became an image of the future, a reason for hope or fear" (94). More abstractly, Lisa Goddard's story mirrors Kelly's and Joanne's when Lisa reminisces about running through the park as a girl or working at the cake factory (113) – scenes with which we as readers are already familiar from the first two stories, but which now return in distorted shape in the third section of *Union Street*. The point is, then, that though each of these female figures is different from the other, they are nevertheless alike in some ways, as even George Harrison recognizes when he looks at the sleeping prostitute Blonde Dinah and realizes with a start that Dinah resembles his wife:

> She looked like Gladys lying there, her mouth open, a wisp of hair shaken with every breath. It disturbed him. She ought not to look like Gladys. He had always believed that there were two sorts of women: the decent ones and the rest. He felt that they should look different, for how could you tell them apart, how could you remember

they were different, if every sag, every wrinkle of their used bodies proclaimed that they were one flesh? (230)

George would like to think of all prostitutes as common, in the sense of being low and distinct from 'decent women,' but seeing his wife's body mirrored in Blonde Dinah's instead forces upon him a realization that they have much *in* common. Put differently, if there is a double meaning to the term *representation* – one political and another aesthetic – there is also a similar double meaning to realism's focus on 'the common': an attention to what is considered low and unseemly, but also, at the same time, an emphasis on what is shared, on our common nature as embodied beings.[27]

This commonality in various ways explicitly extends beyond girls and women in *Union Street*, to include boys and men as well. We have already seen that even the man who raped Kelly cannot be entirely abjected from the human community. Moreover, there are several moments of mirroring between male and female stories in Barker's text. For example, if Kelly Brown is disconcerted by the changes of her pubescent body (3), the same is true for Richard Scaife, whose "nose and ears seemed to have grown out of proportion to his face," and who does not know "what to do with his hands and feet" (140). Similarly, if Muriel Scaife and Alice Bell do not like to see their reflection in a mirror because it reveals unwelcome truths (176, 255), George Harrison for his part no longer goes to the public library because he, as a retired husband unwelcome at home and without enough money to spend all his time at the pub (221–222), hates to encounter the "derelict" who truly have no home left: "George was horrified to realise that the fear on everybody else's face was *reflected* in his own. He left at once and never went back" (223; emphasis added). In other words, George avoids reflecting on the "derelict" as mirrors to himself in order to avoid the unpleasant truth that, at some level, he and these smelly, homeless humans are, in fact, profoundly alike.

Perhaps the best way to start bringing together the various strands of the argument in this chapter is to address the criticism that some commentators have leveled against *Union Street* regarding its depiction of men. Ian Haywood, for instance, complains that for the most part men are depicted as violent and threatening, with sympathetic males either "inert" (Muriel Scaife's dying husband), ready to "undergo a feminist conversion" (George Harrison recognizing that his wife and Dinah are alike), or sexually unthreatening (146). The example

27 For an illuminating discussion of these two distinct meanings of the word *common* (i.e. what is shared vs. what is low) as they are contrasted in *Great Expectations*, see Pam Morris, *Dickens's Class Consciousness* (108–109).

Haywood gives for a sympathetic but 'sexually unthreatening' man is Joss, a close friend of Iris, who is ready to help Joanne Wilson when she needs him. However, Joss is also growth-restricted, leading Joanne to observe that he would be "a husband in a million, if only his arms and legs were the normal length" (*Union Street* 74). For Haywood, *Union Street*'s portrayal of men is thus overly limited and, ultimately, unfair. In fact, however, the depiction of the men in each of these cases is equivalent to the portrayal of women because of the *Union Street*'s strong focus on the effects of, and limits imposed by, the human body: illness and death for John Scaife (presumably due to toxic fumes he inhaled at work), ageing and retirement for George Harrison, and restricted growth for Joss.

Pat Wheeler is thus right in claiming that in Barker's novels "you cannot understand one gender in isolation from the other" (128).[28] Barker herself, moreover, has eloquently defended herself against the charge of demonizing men:

> I don't think I'm making a judgment about the two sexes, in the abstract, as it were. I think I'm writing about a scene in which the heavy industry which employed mainly men, and on which so many men from the working class relied for their sense of identity, is what's going. And the essence of the social changes in the book is the collapse of the men's identity. The women seem to be far more resilient in the face of this particular type of social change because they have their two roles in the home and outside it. The men seem to me to be very vulnerable to it. I think this is why [...] the men sometimes seem weaker than the women. (qtd. in Moseley 40)

According to Barker, the double-burden traditionally imposed on working-class women – wage labor as well as work in the home – suddenly becomes a resource in a situation of chronic unemployment and deindustrialization, as unlike the men's, the women's sense of worth is not dependent on one single scene of action. At the same time, the fact that the "derelict" who live on the margins of society are depicted in *Union Street* as anonymous beings of indeterminate gender suggests that, when pushed to extremes of deprivation, the shared fragility of the human body even transcends the division of gender. It is therefore the intersection of gender and class, rather than gender alone, which determines *Union Street*'s portrayal of men and women.

28 See also Roberto del Valle Alcalá, who notes that "*Union Street* is replete with male figures who have somehow deviated or been displaced from traditionally productive roles (as waged laborers and family breadwinners)," which results "in a general landscape of crisis which is not only punctuated by relative material poverty, but also by a radical disturbance of the sexual division of labor" (201).

If the body serves as the crucial site where this interaction between gender and class is negotiated and exposed, then this has to do with the repression of the body in more traditional forms of domestic realism. Consider, for instance, what Nancy Armstrong writes about the role of the body both in eighteenth- and nineteenth-century female conduct books as well as in domestic fiction of the period:

> A woman was deficient in female qualities if she, like the aristocratic woman, [...] aimed at putting the body on display [...]. For a woman to display herself in such a manner was the same as saying that she was supposed to be valued for her body and its adornments, not for the virtues she might possess as a woman and wife. By the same token, the conduct books found the laboring woman unfit for domestic duties because she, too, located value in the material body. [...] By implying that the essence of woman lay inside or underneath her surface, the invention of depths in the self entailed making the material body of the woman appear superficial. (75–76)

Middle-class, female domesticity is thus defined through a double negative: neither the spectacularly attractive, ornate body of the aristocratic lady, nor the material body of laboring women; instead, middle-class femininity involves an attempt "to subordinate the body to a set of mental processes that guaranteed domesticity" (Nancy Armstrong 76). Gender, class, *and a particular vision of home*, in short: these form the bedrock of English, bourgeois realism (together with certain assumptions about race and ethnicity, as acknowledged in *Union Street* through the story of the West Indian Big Bertha).

Synchrony, Diachrony, and the History of Class

Union Street focuses on seven working-class women, and it pays particular attention to the home and the body: to how it labors, to how vulnerable it is. However, in addition to this thematic concern, we also need to bear in mind the formal features discussed in this chapter, as they are the key to understanding *Union Street*'s attempt at finding an adequate way to represent class. Crucially, all of these formal features can be seen as revolving around the relation between synchrony and diachrony. For instance, in the individual stories of *Union Street*, we have what Rick Altman calls single-focus narratives, i.e. storylines which mainly proceed from one event to the next: individual diachrony. But individual diachrony is not good at representing community, as Hans-Georg Gadamer acknowledges when he talks about subjectivity and its relation to history as a collective experience:

> [H]istory does not belong to us; we belong to it. Long before we understand ourselves through the process of self-examination, we understand ourselves in a self-evident

> way in the family, society, and state in which we live. The focus of subjectivity is a distorting mirror. (278)[29]

The focus of subjectivity is a "distorting mirror" – and it is only by trying to take this distortion into account that we can understand the full extent to which we as individuals are shaped by, to which "we belong to history." *Union Street* acknowledges this very problem in its use of distorting mirrors as a symbol. Moreover, we have seen that the text's symbolism (birds, eyes, moments of vision, gaping mouths, and mirrors) constitutes a paradigmatic, analytical interruption of the narrative's syntagmatic flow – which is in fact another way of saying that narrative emphasizes diachrony, whereas symbolism tends towards synchrony.

While an emphasis of synchrony over diachrony is relatively unusual in European fiction, it is not uncommon in narrative traditions that emphasize the collective rather than the individual. The classic Chinese novel, for instance, tends to have as its protagonist not an individual, but a group or collective, and Franco Moretti sees this as the reason why such novels continually attempt to minimize narrativity ("The Novel" 168): "[W]hat really matters is not what lies 'ahead' of a given event, as in 'forward-looking' European prose, but what lies 'to the side' of it: all the vibrations that ripple across this immense narrative system – and all the *counter*-vibrations that try to keep it stable" ("The Novel" 169–170). Synchrony as opposed to diachrony, in other words: a focus on the collective, and an exploration of the social system. And this, we have seen, is what the multiple focus of the short-story-cycle format allows *Union Street* to achieve, with the text indeed showing how one event – Kelly being raped, for instance (29) – ripples across the narrative system only to reappear, obliquely, in the story of Muriel Scaife (149). Or, to give another example, in section two we find Joanne Wilson remembering how she saw Lisa Goddard at the supermarket, "weighed down with kids and shopping, pushing her belly in front of her like another self" (94); later – another narrative ripple – we learn that Lisa remembers seeing a "young girl" (Joanne?) watching her in the supermarket (109). *Union Street* is replete with such narrative ripples, which signify a move away from the individual life trajectory, towards the community and the social system.

29 "In Wahrheit gehört die Geschichte nicht uns, sondern wir gehören ihr. Lange bevor wir uns in der Rückbesinnung selber verstehen, verstehen wir uns auf selbstverständliche Weise in Familie, Gesellschaft und Staat, in denen wir leben. Der Fokus der Subjektivität ist ein Zerrspiegel" (*Wahrheit und Methode* 261).

And yet, there is a catch, because arguably what one loses by focusing on the social system are the very notions of causality and agency. Frederic Jameson writes about the relation between synchrony, diachrony, and causality:

> [I]t is as though the ever greater accumulation of facts about a given period (very much including our own) determines a gravitational shift from diachronic thinking (so-called linear history) to synchronic or systemic modeling. It is a shift that can be measured [...] by the increasing frequency of attacks on causality [...]. (*Archaeologies of the Future* 87)

The key point, for Jameson, is that this shift from diachronic thinking to synchronic or systemic modeling tends to affect our ability to conceive of alternative developmental paths:

> Diachronic causality, the single string of causes, the billard-ball theory of change, tends to isolate a causal line which might have been different, a single-shot effectivity (even an ultimately determining instance) which can very easily be replaced by an alternate hypothesis. But if, instead of this diachronic strand, we begin to posit causality as an immense synchronic interrelationship, as a web of overdetermination, a Spinozan substance made up of innumerable simultaneously coexisting cells or veins, then it is harder to object some causal alternative: all causes are already there [...]. (*Archaeologies of the Future* 88)

Increasing synchronic complexity thus comes at the cost of agency: "[W]inner loses, as Sartre liked to put it: the more airtight the synchronic system laid in place all around us, the more surely history itself evaporates in the process, and along with it any possibility of political agency or collective anti-systemic praxis" (Jameson, *Archaeologies of the Future* 89). This is in fact already implied in Franco Moretti's description of the synchronic narrative system of the Chinese novel, where we find vibrations and counter-vibrations that *keep the system stable* – and perhaps this systemic paralysis explains why John Brannigan believes that it is Kelly Brown's "*fate* to live out the lives of all the women depicted in *Union Street*" (27; emphasis added).

Given the conditions depicted in *Union Street*, stability – i.e. continuing deprivation, the permanence of crisis – is of course the last thing that is needed, and one may now begin to wonder whether the text's attempt to avoid the domestic fiction's ideological pitfalls have merely entangled it in a different kind of realism that, despite everything, proves to be a form of the status quo. To this pessimistic conclusion, we might object that *Union Street*'s realism is highly self-reflexive, in the sense of interrogating and exposing its own discursive limits. Think, for example, of the text's use of mirrors as figurative leitmotifs:

realism is a bit like a mirror – but how do mirrors work? How, in other words, do mirrors relate to individual identity, to life and the body, to truth? Or think of the gaping, speechless mouths in *Union Street*: What are the things that remain impossible to say? Does the unspeakable constitute not only a limit to discourse, but also its condition of possibility (in the sense of anchoring meaning in a hypothesized Real that must always remain just outside the reach of language)? Take, finally, the third symbolical cluster, eyes and vision: Who looks at whom, and with what purpose in mind? Is it the distanced, objectifying, alienating gaze, or a look of love that serves to connect and bind people together? Mirrors, mouths, eyes – reflection, telling, showing: in other words, the well-known literary critical problem of narrative perspective.

And narrative perspective is a vital issue in this context because the realist novel has so often been accused of adopting a middle-class point of view on working-class lives. John Brannigan has aptly summarized Raymond Williams’s comments on the problem: “[O]ne danger with realist representation of the working class is that it risks exercising a class division in its very form, between the ‘us’ of the narrator and reader, and the ‘them’ of its subject” (29). Brannigan has also shown in detail, however, that *Union Street* strives to avoid such narrative distance by two related means: first, by seamlessly shifting back and forth between a more objective narrative position and the subjectivities of the individual characters, thus avoiding the potentially solipsistic perspective of one single character (29–30); and second, by avoiding a narrative point of view that is superior to the characters’ collective perspective, with the narrator instead using an idiom that “is never far from the ways in which the characters might describe their own experiences,” and with the limits to the narrator’s knowledge corresponding, roughly, to the limits of collective communal knowledge (hence Blonde Dinah, the prostitute who lives on Wharfe Street, cannot become the main focalizer of section six, whereas George Harrison – who lives on Union Street – can; 30).[30] The narrator in *Union Street* is thus not “an omniscient being hovering over the story” (Brannigan 28), and against accusations that *Union Street*’s realism provides us with a cripplingly limited view, the text’s eminently self-reflexive qualities may serve as a first line of defense. The trouble, however, with this defense is that self-reflexivity is also a kind of irony that merely allows one to have one’s cake and eat it (Jameson, *Archaeologies of the Future* 177): one admits, in a meta-comment, that realism is limited and problematic – but one nevertheless continues to adhere to its conventions.

30 As Roberto del Valle Alcalá rightly notes (206), Barker would place the topic of prostitution at the center of her next novel, *Blow Your House Down* (1984).

A much stronger line of defense is that *Union Street* does not stop at constructing a more complex but potentially paralyzing synchronic system out of its individual, diachronic narratives. Instead, it takes this narrative system and tries, as it were, to fold it back into a diachronic trajectory, thus preparing the ground for a historical analysis of social class. To fully appreciate this idea, we do well to bear in mind E.P. Thompson's point that class is a thoroughly historical phenomenon; class is not a structure or category, but something that happens (9):

> If we stop history at a given point, then there are no classes but simply a multitude of individuals with a multitude of experiences. But if we watch these men [and women] over an adequate period of social change, we observe patterns in their relationships, their ideas, and their institutions. Class is defined by men [and women] as they live their own history, and, in the end, this is its only definition. (11)

Accordingly, *Union Street* does not follow the history of one individual, but at the end of each section stops time, tracks back to another individual, starts again, moves forward slightly, backtracks again: a synchronic multitude of individual experiences, encapsulated in separate stories – but arranged in a meaningful sequence, from the youngest to the oldest woman, which reintroduces diachrony into the narrative because humans, as historical actors, have memories.[31]

It is for this reason that the older women in *Union Street* are so important, as each new section adds, not only a new systemic ripple (associated with synchrony), but also an additional layer of memories (i.e. diachrony), reaching back further and further into the past, with Alice – a committed socialist (241) – serving as a veritable repository of memory: "There wasn't much she'd learned in the Depression that still made sense in the seventies. And yet. She was poorer now than she'd been then. And worse housed. Then, she'd had a lovely little Council house" (242). Economic crisis, in other words, is nothing new for Alice, but she remembers that in the past there was adequate public housing – as there is not in her present. We have seen that newspapers for the most part remain unread in *Union Street*, but this is not the case with Alice, who follows the "continued reports that the miners were about to go on strike" (239). Remembering,

31 Jonathan Sperber, writing about the European revolutions of 1848, argues that general theories of revolution tend to neglect "the role of memories and experience in human events": "What made 1848 different from 1789 was above all that in 1848 people remembered what had happened in 1789 and acted on those memories, thus creating a different outcome" (271). Memories, in other words, can lead to different historical outcomes.

following the news, engaging in political arguments with Mrs. Harrison (also elderly, but from a country background and a Tory; 241): Alice, the oldest woman in the text, most explicitly adds not only a layer of memory, but also an awareness of history and politics to *Union Street*'s narrative system.

Let us, one final time, re-examine the key points. In effect, the argument presented in the preceding paragraphs is inspired by Mark Rawlinson's comments on the relation between synchrony and diachrony in *Union Street*:

> [*Union Street* cues us] to start making sense of the diachronic or historical patterns in the lives which are opened to view by the narrative's synchronic snap-shots of female experience. It also points us, ironically, to all that divides the individuals who live check by jowl in the street [...]. (21)

However, while Rawlinson argues that the women's lives are "synchronic snap-shots," the seven sections in fact constitute individual diachronies that *Union Street* juxtaposes with one another in order to create a higher-level, collective synchrony. To avoid the potentially paralyzing stasis that tends to characterize such synchronic systems, *Union Street* then re-introduces diachrony – but a diachrony of a different order, which is only present in a virtual or symbolic space: as the memory of individual characters (particularly Alice Bell), and in the 'chronological' movement from the youngest to the oldest female character that we as readers can see and interpret. A collective diachrony, in short: the collective history of class, derived from a domestic realism that takes seriously the implications of the fragile human body and its need for shelter as a precondition for home and a sense of belonging.[32] It is with these findings in mind that we may now turn to the exploration of memory, myth, and collective identity in Jeffrey Eugenides's *The Virgin Suicides*.

32 Incidentally, anyone interested in cinematic adaptation as brazenly ideological rewriting might want to start with Martin Ritt's *Stanley & Iris* (1989). Ritt's film is – ostensibly – based on *Union Street* and tells the story of Iris (played by Jane Fonda!), who works in a factory and, there, meets Stanley, who cannot read (i.e. who is based on Muriel Scaife's husband, John). The film in effect turns Barker's account of the struggles of a Northern-English industrial community during the economic crisis of the 1970s into a story of individual upward mobility in the United States under Ronald Reagan, with Iris teaching Stanley how to read, and the two of them eventually getting married and moving to a nicer neighborhood.

6 "Saddened by a History We Knew Nothing About": Collective Memory and Rituals of Mourning in Jeffrey Eugenides's *The Virgin Suicides*

"It was the best of times, it was the worst of times": though it may seem far-fetched to begin this chapter with a comparison between Jeffrey Eugenides's *The Virgin Suicides* (1993) and Charles Dickens's *A Tale of Two Cities* (1859), the latter's opening line would in fact be a fitting epigraph for the former.[1] In its original context, Dickens's opening may be read as an expression of the narrator's ambivalence towards the world historical events depicted in the text: the French Revolution as a fundamental moment of historical rupture that, in the words of Immanuel Kant, "*is not to be forgotten*" (*The Conflict of the Faculties* 159; original emphasis).[2] Likewise, the notion of a fundamental break in historical continuity, as well as its impact on collective memory, are among the key themes of *The Virgin Suicides*. In Eugenides's novel, a group of now middle-aged boys find themselves unable to forget a sequence of events that took place in the early 1970s, in the suburban community of their youth. In those distant days, the boys' sense of unquestioned belonging is suddenly disrupted when Cecilia, the youngest of the five Lisbon sisters, tries to commit suicide by slitting her wrists in the bathtub. Cecilia survives the attempt, and following a psychiatrist's recommendation Mr. and Mrs. Lisbon for a time relax their strict domestic regime, even allowing their daughters to give a party. The sisters invite some boys from the community, but just as the party gets going, Cecilia excuses herself, goes upstairs and throws herself out of her bedroom window; her body impaled on the staked fence in front of the Lisbon's family home, the girl dies immediately. And yet, this terrible event is only the first blow to the boys' collective sense of belonging. Exactly one year after Cecilia's first suicide attempt, three of her sisters – Lux, Bonnie, and Therese – take their lives, with Mary, the last daughter, following only one month later. Even as adults, the neighborhood boys continue to be haunted by the Lisbon girls, their memories simultaneously

---

1 I would like to thank Diane Piccitto for her comments on the first draft, as well as Anja Neukom-Hermann for her feedback on the final version of this chapter (parts of which are based on my unpublished *Lizenziat* thesis, "Past the Game of Fiction").

2 In the German original, the corresponding phrase is: "ein solches Phänomen in der Menschengeschichte *vergisst sich nicht mehr*" (Kant, *Der Streit der Fakultäten* 67).

evoking the joys of adolescent love and the pain of personal trauma: the best and the worst of times. Though the boys' deeply personal recollection of historical rupture evidently differs from the world historical scope of Dickens's novel, the narrators in both texts display a deeply ambivalent relation to the past.

In the case of either text, however, we should not focus exclusively on the narrator's ambivalence, but instead also keep in mind the problem of polarization. The opening of *A Tale of Two Cities*, for instance, revolves around the clash between two starkly opposed evaluations of the past:

> It was the best of times, it was the worst of times, it was the age of wisdom, it was the age of foolishness, [...] it was the spring of hope, it was the winter of despair, [...] – in short, the period was so far like the present period, that some of its noisiest authorities insisted on its being received, for good or for evil, in the superlative degree of comparison only. (5; bk. 1, ch. 1)

According to Dickens's narrator, it is only the "noisiest authorities" who insist on such a polarized view of the past, and perhaps our sense of the narrator's ambivalence arises precisely from his attempt to adopt a – supposedly – more nuanced historical outlook: a synthesis, as it were, of two 'simplistic' interpretations. In the discussion that follows, we will see that the boys in *The Virgin Suicides*, too, try to dismiss competing and sharply delimited interpretations of the past in favor of their own, more cautious and provisional assessment.

In addition, polarization is a key concern in *The Virgin Suicides* because the early 1970s – i.e. the period in which the novel is set – occupy a critical position in American cultural memory. More specifically, 1974 is not only the year of the final four suicides in Eugenides's novel; it also marks the end of a period of upheaval in American history that can be said symbolically to begin with the assassination of John F. Kennedy on November 22, 1963, and which witnessed conflicts over the Civil Rights Movement, the emergence into mainstream discourse of second wave feminism, a new politics of gay pride, the sexual revolution and countercultural experiments, race riots, peaceful as well as violent protests against the Vietnam War, the Watergate scandal, and an oil crisis which brought to an end the postwar economic boom that Eric Hobsbawm, in *The Age of Extremes* (1994), has called the twentieth century's "Golden Age." It is a "Decade of Upheaval" (Blum et al. 851) that the historian James T. Patterson explicitly describes as a time of "rapidly rising polarization" (676), and the period has since become a focal point in discussions about the so-called culture wars in the United States – a term that James Davison Hunter introduced into the debate in 1991, only two years before *The Virgin Suicides* was published.[3]

Figure 9: Patrick Chappatte's cartoon "Kennedy, 50 Years Ago" seizes upon the widespread and problematic idea that the assassination of JFK in November 1963 marked the end of American innocence. © Chappatte in The International New York Times (21. November 2013)

Eugenides's novel is thus not only set in a quintessentially American cultural space (i.e. suburbia), but also at a time of crisis that continues to be perceived as a defining moment in national history, albeit in sharply polarized ways: "It was the best of times, it was the worst of times." This polarization, moreover, is frequently associated with the emergence of so-called identity politics. John Anner, for instance, speaks of a gradual shift within social justice movements in the wake of the 1960s from "broad, universalist goals" to "more specific struggles, often based on identity" (7; cf. Barbara Ryan 2–3). As we shall see, this historical context is relevant to *The Virgin Suicides* because the novel explores in detail the problem of collective identity – especially its construction and

3 This is, of course, not to suggest that the culture wars arose, as it were, out of nothing. See, for instance, Adam Laats's *Fundamentalism and Education in the Scopes Era*, which traces the origins of the debate back to the 1920s.

maintenance on the basis of a particular interpretation of the past, as well as its potentially exclusionary nature. In contrast to the previous chapters, the discussion of Eugenides's novel thus allows us to confront the inner workings of a group or collective: its myths of origins; its strategies of othering and marginalization; and its ritualized home-making practices. Indeed, in foregrounding the problem of communal belonging, we will be able to show that *The Virgin Suicides* not only comments on the role of identity politics in the history of the United States, but also critiques the widespread fantasy that the home – suburban as well as national – is, or ever was, entirely innocent (Figure 9).

The Voice of Collective Memory

As virtually all critics commenting on *The Virgin Suicides* recognize, it is crucial to address its highly unusual narrative voice, which speaks to us in the first-person plural. Francisco Collado-Rodríguez, for instance, observes that this plural voice is "of an uncertain condition," and that it represents "the collective perspective of an indeterminate number of mature men" (30; cf. Ciocoi-Pop 84; Dines 961; Heusser 179; Christian Long 359; Vanyova 49). Eugenides himself, meanwhile, has spoken of an "impossible narrator," whose voice it is difficult to locate precisely (Kehlmann and Eugenides 88).[4] Claudia Ioana Doroholschi, finally, defines the novel's plural narrator as a "shifting entity" with unclear boundaries:

> Any attempt to establish how many boys belong to this community, or what exactly their names are, is bound to fail. Sometimes one or more of the boys are detached from the group and become individualized, or referred to as "one of us," but the exact identity of those who tells [sic] the story remains indeterminate. (185)

Doroholschi rightly insists that one cannot tell for certain who belongs to this constantly shifting 'we,' and even the grammatical 'mistake' in her description – the phrase "those who tells" – is in fact peculiarly appropriate, as it encapsulates the conflicting pulls of group identity and individualized selves that render the novel's narrative voice so strangely haunting.[5]

---

4 On the differences in narrative voice between Eugenides's novel and Sophia Coppola's film adaptation of *The Virgin Suicides* see Hovland 260; McKnight 125–127; Richardson 52–53.

5 For more general accounts of the potential effects of first-person plural narration see Uri Margolin's "Telling Our Story," Amit Marcus's "*We* Are *You*," Alan Palmer's *Fictional Minds* (218–229), Monika Fludernik's "The Many in Action and Thought," and Natalya Bektha, "We-Narratives."

As Brian Richardson notes (52), there is one passage in *The Virgin Suicides* that indirectly reflects on this unusual narrative voice and its relation to collective identity. After Cecilia's suicide, the girl's diary eventually ends up in the boys' possession (41), and they proceed to study the book with well-nigh religious devotion:

> We know portions of the diary by heart now. [...] We passed the diary around, fingering pages and looking anxiously for our names. Gradually, however, we learned that although Cecilia had stared at everybody all the time, she hadn't thought about any of us. Nor did she think about herself. The diary is an unusual document of adolescence in that it rarely depicts the emergence of an unformed ego. [...] Instead, Cecilia writes of her sisters and herself as a single entity. It's often difficult to identify which sister she's talking about, and many strange sentences conjure in the reader's mind an image of a mythical creature with ten legs and five heads [...]. (42)

Unlike most coming-of-age narratives, the narrator maintains, Cecilia's diary does not depict the "emergence of an unformed ego" (i.e. an adolescent's path toward a 'fully-formed,' mature identity), but instead confronts the reader with an undifferentiated collectivity ("a single entity"). This, in turn, renders it difficult for the reader to identify individual members of the group – an effect that, according to Doroholschi, in fact applies to the novel's own collective narrative voice.

For Debra Shostak, these similarities are far from accidental. Rather, Shostak argues that we are dealing here with a classic case of narcissistic projection by a group of male voyeurs. The boys' use of the pronoun *we*, Shostak contends, "implies the effacement of the speakers' individuality and prepares for their conception of the Lisbon sisters as also de-individualized" (819). The narrators' portrayal of the Lisbon girls is thus, in Shostak's view, very much a projection of their own image onto the objects of their desire – and indeed, the phenomenon of narcissistic projection is itself indirectly acknowledged in the passage discussed above, for according to the narrator, Cecilia continually "stared at everybody all the time," without, however, truly thinking about them. This, arguably, is a good description of the boys' own voyeuristic idealization of the Lisbon sisters, who are the center of the boys' obsessive attention even as their reality as independent human beings continues to elude their male observers.

Accordingly, both Bree Hoskin (216) and Ceri Hovland (266) have observed that the Lisbon girls enter the boys' "collective memory" in distorted form, and it is precisely by exploring the idea of collective memory that we can understand more fully in which sense Eugenides's narrator is "impossible." Deriving his ideas about collective memory from the French sociologist Maurice Halbwachs, Jan Assmann observes that the most basic, "primal form" of a rupture between the past and the present is the "irremediable discontinuity" of death, for it is when someone dies that those left behind have to decide whether or not that individual is worth the effort of being remembered (19). More generally, Assmann contends that all groups face the question of what they must not allow themselves to forget; conversely, each of the components incorporated into a group's collective memory may provide us with clues regarding that community's most cherished values (16). Collective memories, in short, should not be envisioned as the random remains of times gone by; rather, according to Assmann, a group's stock of collective memories accumulates in a process of negotiation about which aspects of the past are to be considered significant, and this shared effort in turn fosters a sense of belonging among the members of the community (24).[6]

One implication of Assmann's observations is that we should not conceive of collective memory and identity as something solid or given. If Iwona Irwin-Zarecka maintains that collective memory is "best located not in the minds of individuals, but in the resources they share" (4), then this is in part to emphasize that collective memory is not simply the sum of several individuals' personal memories. Rather, only those components form part of a group's collective memory that are, as it were, made publicly accessible (for example in the form of written records and historical artifacts, but also in the form of shared oral accounts of personal memories). At the same time, however, personal memories form part of a group's potential resources of remembrance even when they have not (yet) been shared, for in principle these personal memories could be communicated if and when the need arises – at least, that is, as long as the individuals in question are still alive. Accordingly, though Irwin-Zarecka is right in emphasizing the shared, 'externalized' nature of collective memory in real-life groups, collective memory in the abstract also includes the information stored in the minds of individuals as one of its potential or virtual resources. Even in the case of real-life groups, moreover, Jan Assmann is careful to note that collective identity is necessarily "underpinned by factors that are purely symbolic," with the social body as such being "simply a metaphor – an imaginary construct" (113). Collective identity, in other words, "does not exist as a visible, tangible

6 In the German original, Assmann's elegant formula for this process runs: "Durch Zirkulation gemeinsamen Sinns entsteht 'Gemeinsinn'" (*Das kulturelle Gedächtnis* 140).

reality" (ibid.), and any attempt to personify it will necessarily be reminiscent of the ghostly: a disembodied, impossible voice.[7]

It is now no longer difficult to see that the first-person plural narrator of *The Virgin Suicides* is precisely such an impossible, symbolic personification of a group's collective identity. Therefore, we should not think of the narrator as merely a collection of individual voices (i.e. as a chorus of boys speaking together). Rather, the narrator's plural voice is the personification of an abstract, collective entity, and while each of the boys constitutes an individual part of the community of memory personified in this narrator, the collectivity itself remains qualitatively distinct from the sum of its parts.[8] A key passage from *The Virgin Suicides* illustrates this point, reflecting as it does on the "unnatural" way in which the narrator's collective memories accumulate:

> Our own knowledge of Cecilia kept growing after her death [...], with [... a] kind of unnatural persistence. Though she had spoken only rarely and had had no real friends, everybody possessed his own vivid memory of Cecilia. Some of us had held her for five minutes as a baby while Mrs. Lisbon ran back into the house to get her purse. Some of us had played in the sandbox with her, fighting over a shovel, or had exposed ourselves to her behind the mulberry tree that grew like deformed flesh through the chain linked fence. [...] A few of us had fallen in love with her, but had kept it to ourselves, knowing that she was the weird sister. (40)

The narrator here explains how various individuals and subgroups ("some of us") contribute to the group's collective memory, and initially one might imagine that the boys must have gotten together at some point to share their memories with one another. This, however, turns out not to be the case, for the narrator states explicitly that some group members refrained from revealing their memories to the others. More specifically, the narrator notes that "[a] few of us" had fallen in love with Cecilia yet had kept it, not to 'themselves' – as would be the more 'logical' way of putting it – but to "ourselves." Far from being a simple grammatical mistake, this phrase signals that the plural narrator, as a ghostly, entirely symbolic entity, has access even to those memories that the individual group members have refrained from sharing with their peers. The novel's narrator is impossible, in other words, because he is the disembodied, plural voice

7 "Die Evidenz kollektiver Identität unterliegt einer ausschliesslich symbolischen Ausformung. Den 'Sozialkörper' gibt es nicht im Sinne sichtbarer, greifbarer Wirklichkeit. Er ist eine Metapher, eine imaginäre Grösse, ein soziales Konstrukt" (*Das kulturelle Gedächtnis* 132).

8 This is why I refrain from using the term "choral narrator," suggested by Rachel McLennan (22).

of an abstract collectivity of middle-aged males engaged in a project of communal remembrance. And it is this plural narrator's discursive strategies of historical reconstruction that we must now proceed to examine more closely.

Fall from Grace: Myths of Origin and Founding Trauma

While there is little doubt that the Lisbon sisters' suicides would be perceived as disruptive in any community, Martin Heusser has shown that Eugenides's plural narrator draws on a specifically American version of pastoral aesthetics to portray the time before the suicides as a prelapsarian, suburban idyll. According to Heusser, pastoral rhetoric has been a defining feature of American self-descriptions from its earliest days, with the country being imagined as a "Garden of the World": a blessed new land in whose fertile soil a youthful nation can take root and prosper ("Et in Arcadia Ego" 176). In turn, it is this kind of imagery that, according to Heusser, informs American ideals of the suburb as a garden-like landscape "equally poised between the city and the wilderness" (ibid.). Moreover, just as the idea of a New World conjures up images of a space unburdened by history, so do pastoral landscapes appear as both secluded and outside the flow of historical time:

> The cardinal convention of the pastoral [...] is the opposition, explicit or implicit, between the idyllic pastoral environment and the reality of the world at large – the contrast between an ideal, secluded here and now, perfectly peaceful and timeless, and the outside world, haunted by continual change and death. ("Et in Arcadia Ego" 177)

Neither history nor death, Heusser notes, are supposed to disturb the peace of a self-enclosed, pastoral space – and if we examine how Eugenides's narrator describes life in the suburban community before Cecilia's suicide, then we find that his depiction of the boys' communal home as an earthly paradise matches these pastoral conventions precisely:

> There had never been a funeral in our town before, at least not during our lifetimes. The majority of dying had happened during the Second World War when we didn't exist and our fathers were impossibly skinny young men in black-and-white photographs on jungle airstrips [...]. Now our dads were middle-aged, [...] but they were still a long way from death. Their own parents, who spoke foreign languages and lived in converted attics like buzzards, had the finest medical care available and were threatening to live on until the next century. Nobody's grandfather had died, nobody's grandmother, nobody's parents, only a few dogs: Tom Burke's beagle, Muffin, who choked on Bazooka Joe bubble gum, and then that summer, a creature who in dog years was still a puppy – Cecilia Lisbon. (35)

In the narrator's account, death as such had of course always existed, but only in a different time and place. In the narrator's description, history and death form part of an external, historical wilderness of "jungle airstrips" and world wars – until, that is, Cecilia, the youngest of the Lisbon sisters, takes the decision to end her life.

The irruption of Cecilia's death into this pastoral suburban world thus constitutes, for the narrator, a fall from grace into a world of exile and death that is also imagined as the end of childhood innocence. As Heusser notes ("Et in Arcadia Ego" 181), the narrator portrays the immediate aftermath of Cecilia's suicide as a moment of intrusion by the world beyond the home community:

> From the roof of Chase Buell's house where we congregated [...] we could see, over the heaps of trees throwing themselves into the air, the abrupt demarcation where the trees ended and the city began. The sun was falling in the haze of distant factories, and in the adjoining slums the scatter of glass picked up the raw glow of the smoggy sunset. Sounds we usually couldn't hear reached us now that we were up high [...] – sounds of the impoverished city we never visited, all mixed and muted, without sense [...]. (35)

The irruption of violence and death is not only associated here with the realm of the sacred ("where we congregated"); it also propels the boys' gaze outward, beyond the boundaries of their home community, and suddenly history – in the form of industrial production, urban poverty, and pollution – manages to intrude, even as the meaning of its disturbing signs continues to elude the boys ("mixed and muted, without sense"). The boys keep watching for a while, and though later, one by one, they turn towards "home" (35), they will never recover their earlier sense of unquestioned and 'childish' communal belonging.

We need to be clear from the outset about the extent to which this image of a fall from pastoral suburban grace is in fact an entirely artificial construct (Heusser, "Et in Arcadia Ego" 179). Slavoj Žižek's notion of "the Fall" as one characteristic feature of ideological fantasies is useful in this context, for according to Žižek the Fall constitutes a decisive event in phantasmagoric narratives, but as such it has always already happened (*The Plague of Fantasies* 18). In addition, Žižek suggests that the Fall is a moment of symbolic castration that involves the "loss of something which the subject never possessed in the first place" (19). Both of these characteristics of the Fall suit the situation in *The Virgin Suicides* perfectly, for not only does the novel begin when the Fall has already happened (i.e. after the five suicides, which are already revealed as past in the novel's very first sentence); the group of now middle-aged men are also still turning their gaze back longingly toward girls whom they never actually "possessed" in the first place. As we saw earlier, the Lisbon sisters are idealized figures of youthful adoration – "a purely potential, nonexistent X," in Žižek's terms (19) – and only in those rare moments when the boys actually spend time with the Lisbons does the "revelation" come over them that the girls "weren't all that different" from their own sisters (123).[9] Moreover, even the narrator himself admits that the prelapsarian idyll of suburbia had in fact been a conscious construct or fantasy world established for the children by their parents. Accordingly, when they note that their parents remain surprisingly stoic in the face of Cecilia's death, the boys sense "how ancient they were, how accustomed to trauma, depressions, and wars. We realized that the world they rendered for us was not the world they really believed in" (55). The suburban community may have appeared Edenic to the group of boys, but this had never simply been the natural or true state of affairs.[10] Instead, as a fantasied fall from grace, the suicides become a kind of mythical moment of origin for Eugenides's plural narrator: an expulsion from the illusory plenitude of childhood innocence into a fallen subjecthood founded on absence or lack.[11]

We may summarize the argument so far by noting that Eugenides's novel constitutes a fiction of home in at least two different senses. On the one hand, *The Virgin Suicides* personifies collective belonging in the form of an impossible narrative voice that is unlikely to occur in a non-fictional text. On the other hand, the narrator draws on partly fictional models – a pastoral aesthetics, in particular – in his (re-)construction of a childhood home whose innocence was lost in one exceptional moment of rupture. The ideological fantasy of the boys' shared innocence and its tragic loss sustains the narrator as a plural subject. This loss thus constitutes the mythical moment of origin for the narrator as the personified voice of the boys' community of memory. Which begs the question: What, precisely, is the relation between myth and collective memory?

---

9 The fact that the girs are constructed as idealized adolescent fantasies has been widely commented upon in the critical literature; see, for instance, Hayes-Brady (212) and McLennan (30).

10 See also Martin Dines: "[I]t is not only the novel's narrators who appear to dwell in a 'timeless zone'; their parents also seek suspension from history" (963). Interestingly, the narrators' comments are echoed almost verbatim in Lynn Spigel's discussion of real-life suburbia in postwar America: "Postwar Americans – especially those being inducted into the ranks of middle-class ownership – must, to some degree, have been aware of the artifice involved in suburban ideals of family life. For people who had lived through the Depression and the hardships of the Second World War, the new consumer dreams must have seemed somewhat pretentious" (220).

11 See McLennan, who suggests that "the narrator(s) construct [the suicides] as their own point of origin" (27).

The Sacred Law of Authority

In the context of discussions about collective memory and identity the notion of myth is not to be understood as a story that is, in any straight-forward sense, untrue. Rather, as Jan Assmann rightly observes, myth is defined by its social function:

> Myth is foundational history that is narrated in order to illuminate the present from the standpoint of its origins. [...] Through memory, history becomes myth. This does not make it unreal – on the contrary, this is what makes it real, in the sense that it becomes a lasting, normative, and formative power. (38)[12]

Myth, for Assmann, is a performative discourse that creates, rather than merely reflects, a social reality. Moreover, in addition to its foundational role, myth may also serve as what Assmann calls a "contrapresent" – a function that sometimes conflicts with myth's foundational role because myth as contrapresent emphasizes "what has gone wrong, what has disappeared," and the present thus "finds itself dislocated or at the very least falling short of the great and glorious past" (62).[13] It is difficult to think of a better description of how, in *The Virgin Suicides*, the boys' loss of a mythical innocence provides the basis of their collective identity even as it instills their present with a lasting sense of lack and impairment: "scarred [...] forever, making us happier with dreams than with wives" (169). The sisters' suicides, as a foundational moment of loss, is the reason why the boys, as grown-ups, still gather in their "refurbished tree house," where they keep the "sacred objects" that document the myth of the Lisbon girls (246). The boys' attitude toward their collective myth of origin thus also bears out Dominick LaCapra's observation that an extremely destructive or disorienting event may become both a founding trauma and an occasion of "displaced sacralization" (*Writing History, Writing Trauma* 23) – a point to which we shall return shortly.

12 The German original runs: "Mythos ist eine fundierende Geschichte, eine Geschichte, die erzählt wird, um eine Gegenwart vom Ursprung her zu erhellen. [...] Durch Erinnerung wird Geschichte zum Mythos. Dadurch wird sie nicht unwirklich, sondern im Gegenteil erst Wirklichkeit im Sinne einer fortdauernden normativen und formativen Kraft" (52).

13 In the German original, Assmann characterizes this 'contrapresent' as follows: "Sie geht von Defizienz-Erfahrungen der Gegenwart aus und beschwört in der Erinnerung eine Vergangenheit, die meist die Züge eines Heroischen Zeitalters annimmt. Von diesen Erzählungen her fällt ein ganz anderes Licht auf die Gegenwart: Es hebt das Fehlende, Verschwundene, Verlorene, an den Rand gedrängte hervor und macht den Bruch bewusst zwischen 'einst' und 'jetzt.' Hier wird die Gegenwart weniger fundiert als vielmehr im Gegenteil aus den Angeln gehoben oder zumindest gegenüber einer grösseren und schöneren Vergangenheit relativiert" (79).

First, however, we ought to state clearly that the narrator, as the voice of the boys' collective identity, cannot ultimately wish to resolve the trauma of the girls' suicides because this would unravel the myth that underpins the group's existence. Importantly, this is not to suggest that the boys' desire for relief from the inordinate pressures of trauma is feigned or unreal; on the contrary, there is no doubt that "[s]ometimes, drained by this investigation," the boys long "for some shred of evidence, some Rosetta stone that would explain the girls at last" (170). At the same time, however, even in this passage the narrator uses the word *sometimes* to qualify the boys' desire for a final explanation. The reason for this is that the narrator himself cannot possibly desire the boys to overcome the suicides' negative effects because this shared experience of trauma is the only reason why the group as a community of suffering – and hence why the narrator – exists in the first place. The narrator, as a personification of collective memory, is thus caught in a double bind, for while on one level the whole purpose of the group he represents is to find collective ways of coping with trauma, he must at the same time prevent the boys from ever leaving their traumatic memories behind – for if this were to happen, then the community, and thus the narrator himself, would cease to exist. Accordingly, Rachel McLennan is right in insisting that, in the final analysis, the narrator is not truly interested in explaining or resolving the enigma of the past; instead, he wishes to legitimize his own mythical version of it: a version that sustains his identity as the personified voice of a group of middle-class, white, heterosexual American males (34).

Among the narrator's strategies of legitimation, his recourse to two discourses of power and authority is particularly striking: the language of religion and the idiom of the law. According to the narrator, for instance, the Lisbon girls at times appear "like a congregation of angels" (25), while Cecilia's "illuminated" diary looks "like a Book of Hours or a medieval Bible" (32). By using these and similar phrases, the narrator imbues the story of the Lisbon sisters with an aura of the sacred and thus as beyond question or close examination: "Please don't touch. We're going to put the picture back in its envelope now" (119). At the same time, the narrator deploys the discourse of law and legal inquiry to prevent accusations of downright mystification: "We've tried to arrange the photographs chronologically, though the passage of so many years has made it difficult. [...] Exhibit #1 shows the Lisbon house shortly before Cecilia's suicide attempt" (5). Referring to "documents" and "Exhibits" (e.g. 101) as well as to interviews conducted with various witnesses (e.g. 78), the narrator evokes an atmosphere of thorough investigation, trial, and judgment, with the boys meeting almost daily to "go over the evidence once again, reciting portions of Cecilia's journal" (238).

Tellingly, in this last quotation, the rituals of law (to "go over the evidence") and the realm of the sacred ("reciting" scripture) do not truly remain separate; rather, the narrator uses the combined authority of these two registers to bolster his own discursive authority. In this, *The Virgin Suicides* as a novel can in part be read as reflecting on the historical fact that the law, in 'archaic' societies, was indeed inseparable from the religious realm of the sacred, and that even today the law as a highly ritualized institution resembles the practices of religion (e.g. Stollberg-Rilinger 149–160; cf. Girard 24).

If the narrator of *The Virgin Suicides* uses certain types of discourses to lend authority to his account, he also continually works to dismiss as insufficient all attempts by others to explain why the Lisbon sisters might have killed themselves.[14] Journalists like Ms. Perl, for example, are portrayed as distorting and simplifying the Lisbons' suicides:

> Ms. Perl [...] single-handedly initiated the feeding frenzy of speculation that continues to this day. In her subsequent articles – one every two or three days for two weeks – she shifted her tone from the sympathetic register of a fellow mourner to the steely precision of what she never succeeded in being: an investigative reporter. Scouring the neighborhood in her blue Pontiac, she cobbled together reminiscences into an airtight conclusion, far less truthful than our own, which is full of holes. (222)

Just as he dismisses other "reporters" (224), the narrator here questions Ms. Perl's journalistic abilities ("what she never succeeded in being: an investigative reporter") before faulting her for her "airtight conclusions." More generally, the narrator claims that the boys are "forced to wander endlessly down the paths of hypothesis and memory" because no one has told the Lisbon girls' story to their "satisfaction" (224) – a word that has much to do with expectations and desires, but leaves open the question of factual truth. In a similar vein, the narrator objects to other attempts at explanation:

> Mr. Conley [...] said, "Capitalism has resulted in material well-being but spiritual bankruptcy." He went on to deliver a living room lecture about human needs and the ravages of competition, and even though he was the only Communist we knew, his ideas differed from everyone else's only in degree. Something sick at the heart of the country had infected the girls. Our parents thought it had to do with our music, our godlessness, or the loosening of morals regarding sex we hadn't even had. Mr. Hedlie mentioned that *fin-de-siècle* Vienna witnessed a similar outbreak of suicides on the part of the young, and put the whole thing down to the misfortune of living in a dying

14 As Bilyana Vanyova Kostova rightly notes, "the narrative clings unto uncertainty" (53).

> empire. It had to do with the way the mail wasn't delivered on time, and how potholes never got fixed, or the thievery at City Hall, or the race riots, or the 801 fires set around the city on Devil's night. (231)

However, even though the narrator ridicules the explanations put forward by the adults from the community ("the loosening of morals regarding sex we hadn't even had"), he later admits that the boys are at times tempted to accept such "general explanations, which qualified the Lisbon girls' pain as merely historic, springing from the same source as other teenage suicides" (238). Tellingly, the narrator refers to these explanations as "*merely* historic" (emphasis added) – and thus as inappropriate to the sacred truth of the Lisbon girls, which necessarily transcends the secular boundaries of history and reason, and which must remain forever unknowable:

> In the end we had pieces of the puzzle, but no matter how we put them together, gaps remained, oddly shaped emptinesses mapped by what surrounded them, like countries we couldn't name. [...] So much has been written about the girls in the newspapers, so much has been said over back-yard fences, or related over the years in psychiatrists' offices, that we are certain only of the insufficiency of explanations. (246–247)

Not entirely unlike some proponents of postmodern theory, the narrator is "certain" that there is no such thing as an absolute or even adequate truth, and that his version of the events is superior precisely because it recognizes its own "insufficiency."[15]

Of course, it would be unfair to regard the narrator's account as simply manipulative and misleading, for it clearly addresses the boys' emotional and psychological need to find "a story we could live with" (241). Moreover, as David Kennedy notes, "elegists are always faced with unsatisfactory resurrections, unfinished and unfinishable conversations" (21). Nevertheless, we must recog-

15 As Terry Eagleton notes, the rejection by some postmodern thinkers of the very idea of absolute truth rests on a fundamental misunderstanding of what this idea implies: "Absolute truth does not mean non-historical truth: it does not mean the kind of truths which drop from the sky, or which are vouchsafed to us by some bogus prophet from Utah. On the contrary, they are truths which are discovered by argument, evidence, experiment, investigation. A lot of what is taken as (absolutely) true at any given time will no doubt turn out to be false. Most apparently watertight scientific hypotheses have turned out to be full of holes. Not everything which is considered to be true is actually true. But it remains the case that it cannot just be raining from my viewpoint" (*After Theory* 108–109). Citing Bernard Williams, Eagleton adds that in effect "relativism is really a way of explaining away conflict," for if there is no such thing as truth, "then political radicals can stop talking as if it is unequivocally true that women are oppressed or that the planet is gradually being poisoned by corporate greed" (*After Theory* 109).

nize that in order to legitimize this version of the story, the narrator strategically discounts other versions of the past without really examining their respective merits. The narrator's construction and maintenance of the group's foundational myth is thus far from politically neutral or innocent, but instead depends on the systematic exclusion and disparaging of others: journalists, adults from within the community, and – as we shall see – those perceived as ethnically different.[16]

Old World Corruption and Ethnic Others

One example for the narrator's disparaging of ethnic difference is they way in which he subliminally attributes the irruption of death into the boys' youthful suburban idyll, not to conflicts arising from within the community, but instead to corrupting influences from the Old World. For instance, the narrator places great emphasis on the fact that, after Cecilia's first suicide attempt, "the most popular theory" held that Dominic Pallazolo, "the immigrant kid," was to blame (19). According to this theory, Dominic was hopelessly in love with a girl called Diana Porter, who one day left on vacation for Switzerland – an event that propelled Dominic into such depths of despair that he "climbed onto the roof of his relatives' house and jumped off" (without, however, hurting himself because his fall was broken by the "yard's calculated shrubbery"; 20). Dominic, the narrator observes, "looked frail, diseased, and temperamental, as we expected a European to look," and though he later distances himself from the theory that Cecilia killed herself because of Dominic (32–33), the fact remains that the first extended reference to ethnic otherness is also associated with the threat of disease and corruption, as if the boy's own, 'real' Americanness depended on Dominic as a negative foil – which of course it does, given that their own grandparents are immigrants who speak foreign languages (35; cf. Dines 970; McLennan 28). Moreover, as Martin Dines observes (971), after Cecilia's death Eugenides's narrator introduces more and more Old World figures into the scene of the American suburb: the Hessens, an "old German couple" (56); the Stamarowskis, whose house exudes an air of "Old World decay," in part because of the bats that circle over it and which, the boys believe, have "come with the Stamarowskis from Poland" (88–89); and, finally, "Old Mrs. Karafilis," who as a young woman during World War I had to flee from the Turks (172), and who is unsurprised by the Lisbon girls' deeds because – her grandson Demo claims – the "Greeks are a moody people" to whom suicide "makes sense" (174). In fact,

16 See Iwona Irwin-Zarecka, who notes that in order to construct a sense of community, "one almost inevitably needs the presence of the Other" (60).

even the Lisbons themselves are affected by this ethnic othering because their family name links them to Portugal, the "first European country to acquire an overseas empire" (Dias 68). In addition, the narrator continually emphasizes their Catholicism (Eugenides 8, 20, and 37), as if this Old World religion, too, played a part in the mysterious plague of death that has infected this all-American suburb located, according to the narrator, in a county bearing the "Anglo-Saxon" name Wayne (166).

And yet, things are not quite as straight-forward as that, for the narrator's own account continually reveals the precariousness of that Old World – read: non-Anglo-Saxon – otherness that he so desperately wants to maintain. Martin Dines, for instance, has observed that the Catholic Lisbons are also associated figuratively with the early history of Puritan settlement (972); their home contains "stark colonial furniture" as well as a "painting of Pilgrims plucking a Turkey" (*The Virgin Suicides* 25), and when dressed up for a ball the Lisbon sisters look "like pioneer women," with hairdos that have "the stoic, presumptuous qualities of European fashions enduring the wilderness," and wearing dresses that "look frontierish" (118). The narrator thus portrays the Lisbons both as archetypically American and as vaguely foreign (i.e. Catholics associated with continental Europe), and perhaps this disturbingly insistent cultural hybridity explains why the narrator feels unsettled in their sublime presence (cf. Dines 972).

At any rate, the truly threatening Others for the narrator are not those 'European' others from within the community, but the 'non-white' people who live, for instance, in that distant city beyond the demarcation line of trees. Tamara K. Hareven argues convincingly that, historically, the pastoral desire for a harmonious life in the garden-like suburbs is closely related to white, middle-class fears of racial and social Others, with the city representing immigration, ethnic conflict, and poverty (244). We have already seen that, in *The Virgin Suicides*, the city appears as "impoverished" (35), and the narrator also tells us that both the Lisbon girls and the boys recall the Detroit race riots of 1967, "when tanks had appeared at the end of our block and National Guardsmen had parachuted into our back yards" (124). This, together with the gunshots that the boys occasionally hear "coming from the ghetto" (36), creates an underlying sense of outside menace that binds the all-white suburban community together (Dines 967). The narrator himself is aware of the exclusionary nature of the suburb in which the boys grew up:

> Brave blacks had been slipping in for years, though they were usually women, who blended in with our maids. The city downtown had deteriorated to such a degree that most blacks had no other place to go. [...] Even though we'd always chosen to play

> Indians and not cowboys, considered Travis Williams the best kickoff returner ever and Willie Horton the best hitter, nothing shocked us more than the sight of a black person shopping on Kercheval. We couldn't help but wonder if certain 'improvements' in The Village hadn't been made to scare black people off. The ghost in the window of the costume shop, for instance, had an awfully pointed, hooded head, and the restaurant, without explanation, took fried chicken off its menu. (99)

Even though the boys are accustomed to the sight of black maids, and perfectly willing to admire dark-skinned Others on TV, the narrator confesses to a sense of shock when confronted with non-hierarchical intermingling. Moreover, while the narrator incorporates his reference to the Ku Klux Klan with great comic subtlety ("awfully pointed, hooded head"), the underlying threat is no less serious. After all, the narrator also makes clear that the Board of Commerce had long been worried about the "influx of blacks"; indeed, it is only temporarily – "[w]hile the suicides lasted, and for some time after" – that the "outflux of whites" becomes a matter of greater concern for the leaders of the community (99).[17]

Moreover, if the presence of blacks just beyond – and sometimes within – the boundaries of the boys' home community proves disturbing to the narrator, he also finds himself haunted by the repressed memory of America's pre-Columbian past. There is, for instance, a brief but telling reference to cowboys and Indians in the passage quoted above, and when the narrator mentions the "Anglo-Saxon" name of the county in which the boys grew up, he explicitly distinguishes them from "a parade of Indian county names, Washtenaw, Shiawassee" (166). Moreover, though Martin Dines rightly observes that "the biggest cliché in the book of American hauntings [is] the house built over an Indian burial ground" (962), he also fails to mention that *The Virgin Suicides*, too, recycles this well-worn device, for right after Cecilia's suicide, one boy insists that he found "an Indian arrowhead" buried in the Lisbon's lawn (55). Of course, there is more than just a hint of parody about this reference (as, indeed, there is about the bats hovering over the Stamarowski's house, or about the ghost with the pointed hood that evokes the Ku Klux Klan). And yet, if there is any truth to Freud's assertion that one function of jokes is to mask aggression, as well as genially to bribe listeners into taking the side of the person who tells the

17 See Bilyana Vanyova Kostova: "Although the cultural story of the suburb might appear ficticious, it is in fact a condemnation of the conformity, homoegenity and artificiality of the time, and a reflection of their disruption through the effects of the influx of black people, environmental decay, and people's disillusionment with the government in the 1970s" (51).

joke (*The Joke and Its Relation to the Unconscious* 98), then we should at least be wary of dismissing out of hand the idea that the narrator's remarks are ultimately more serious than they seem to be.[18]

What supports this idea is that the Lisbon girls themselves are repeatedly associated with Native American culture. Cecilia's diary, for instance, at one point mentions a commercial with a "weeping Indian paddling his canoe along a polluted stream" (44). In one photograph, moreover, the Lisbon sisters appear "sitting Indian-style" on the lawn in front of their home. Most ominously, however, we encounter the girls' images in a series of photographs in which they pose in "totem-pole shots, taken at a tourist attraction" (228–229). Mysteriously attracting the signs of a past that refuses to stay repressed, the Lisbon sisters at first appear as Catholic Europeans, then mutate into "pioneer women," and ultimately even seem to 'go native.' The narrator thus imbues the girls' gender difference with a haunting sense of racial and ethnic otherness: a porous, unstable identity that unsettles the boys' attempts at defining the boundaries of communal belonging.

Indeed, the boys seem to fear and adore the girls in equal measure, and there is a good case to be made that it is precisely for this reason that the narrator constructs the Lisbon sisters in terms of the sacred. According to René Girard, "[a]ll sacred creatures partake of monstrosity" (265), and there is indeed something monstrous about the boys' image of the girls as "a mythical creature with ten legs and five heads" (*The Virgin Suicides* 42). For the boys, the sisters transcend all the 'normal' boundaries of identity – of gender and race and even humanity – and some of them even imagine Lux as "a force of nature, impervious to chill, an ice goddess generated by the season itself" (150). The girls are thus both semi-divine objects of desire and castrating, racialized female demons who bring death and corruption into the boys' 'innocent' suburban world.

Gender Trouble: The Othering of Trip Fontaine

Once we recognize the narrator's strategic link between ethnic othering and gender difference, it no longer appears as an innocent detail that there is one

18 In *The Joke and Its Relation to the Unconscious*, Freud writes: "The joke will allow us to turn to good account those ridiculous features in our enemy that the presence of opposing obstacles would not let us utter aloud or consciously [...]. It will, further, bribe the listener with his own gain of pleasure into taking our side without probing very far" (98). The German original runs: "Der Witz wird uns gestatten, Lächerliches am Feind zu verwerten, das wir entgegenstehender Hindernisse wegen nicht laut oder nicht bewusst vorbringen durften [...]. Er wird ferner den Hörer durch seinen Lustgewinn bestechen, ohne strengste Prüfung unsere Partei zu nehmen" (*Der Witz und seine Beziehung zum Unbewussten* 85).

other character whom we encounter "sitting cross-legged like an Indian" (76). This other character is called Trip Fontaine: a focal point of gender trouble, and crucial in terms of plot because, in the narrator's account, he appears as the one individual who is most directly responsible for the suicides of Lux, Mary, Therese, and Bonnie (with the exception, perhaps, of the Lisbon parents). We learn about Trip that he falls in love with Lux Lisbon and that, despite Mr. and Mrs. Lisbon's strict rules about dating, he ultimately manages to convince the parents that he and three other boys ought to be allowed to accompany the four sisters to the homecoming ball. While Mary, Therese, and Bonnie return back to their family home by the agreed time, Lux and Trip stay behind to have sex on the football field, where Trip simply abandons the girl, not caring "how she got home" (138). Lux returns home much too late, and Mrs. Lisbon reacts by shutting "the house in maximum-security isolation" (141). A simple, by no means implausible explanation of the girls' suicides lies precisely in this experience of domestic entrapment, and Trip appears as largely responsible for their imprisonment in the narrator's reconstruction of the events. It is therefore significant that, from the very first moment that Trip appears in the text, the narrator describes him as disturbing preconceived notions about masculinity, desire, and gender difference:

> Only eighteen months before the suicides, Trip Fontaine had emerged from baby fat to the delight of girls and women alike. Because we had known him as a pudgy boy whose teeth slanted out of his open, trolling mouth like those of a deep-sea fish, we had been slow to recognize his transformation. In addition, our fathers and older brothers, our decrepit uncles, had assured us that looks didn't matter if you were a boy. We weren't on the lookout for handsomeness appearing in our midst, and believed it counted for little until the girls we knew, along with their mothers, fell in love with Trip Fontaine. Their desire was silent yet magnificent, like a thousand daisies attuning their faces toward the path of the sun. (69)

Socialized in a world where it is a woman's duty to be desirable rather than actively to desire, and where – according to the (heterosexual) men at least – "looks didn't matter if you were a boy," the narrator now witnesses the effect of masculine beauty on girls and women whose desire he perceives as "silent yet magnificent." In this way, the narrator not only frames Trip as the villain of the piece, but also identifies him as the source of anxiety regarding the meaning of masculinity.

What further complicates the challenge posed to the boys' beliefs by this male object of desire is the fact that Trip is also related to homosexuality. Shortly after Trip is introduced in the text, we learn that his father lives with another man, and the narrator is quick to conclude that this explains why the son's frequent (hetero)sexual exploits are tolerated by Mr. Fontaine: "[T]he iffiness of his own conduct prevented him from questioning the susurrations coming from under his son's door" (73–74). The narrator here explicitly associates Trip's disturbing desirability with the 'deviant' lifestyle of the father, as if growing up in an 'unconventional' household might explain Trip's 'perverted' masculinity. Importantly, the plural narrator never cares to elaborate how he – or indeed any of the boys – could possibly know the reason why Mr. Fontaine allows his son a considerable degree of sexual liberty; the narrator simply claims that it must be "the iffiness" of Mr. Fontaine's conduct that explains it all, without any evidence to prove his point.

Interestingly, on several occasions the narrator also tries to fend off an underlying sense that the boys might themselves be susceptible to any homoerotic interest in Trip. For instance, though the narrator describes Trip's good looks in lavish detail – noting the "tight seat of his jeans," as well as a tan that must have made "his nipples [look] like two pink cherries embedded in brown sugar" – he also insists that Trip's "musky scent, the coconut-oil smoothness of his face, the golden grains of intractable sand still glittering in his eyebrows" did not affect the boys "as it did the girls" (71). Read in isolation, the narrator's reassertion in this passage of the boys' heterosexual position may appear innocent enough. However, as soon as we examine it in the light of a later episode in which the boys fantasize about the taste of Lux Lisbon's strawberry lipstick the interpretive situation becomes more complex:

> Woody Clabault's sister had the same brand, and once, after we got into his parents' liquor cabinet, we made him put on the lipstick and kiss each one of us so that we, too, would know what it tasted like. Beyond the flavor of the drinks we improvised that night [...] we could taste the strawberry wax on Woody Clabault's lips, transforming them, before the artificial fireplace, into Lux's own. [... B]ut the next day we refused to remember that any of this had happened, and even now it's the first time we've spoken of it. At any rate, [...] it was Lux's lips we tasted, not Clabault's. (151)

The boys who, according to the narrator, remained relatively unaffected by the sight of Trip's cherry-like nipples are now even prepared to kiss another male – and though the narrator emphasizes that they were drunk, and that of course "it was Lux's lips" they tasted, he is also hesitant to talk about the experience, as if the boys' identity as heterosexual males depended on a complete rejection of any kind of queer desire. Moreover, what casts a particularly ironic light on the narrator's attempt to distinguish the boys' supposedly normal desires from 'deviant' same-sex attraction is the fact that the narrator seems to find nothing queer about their continuing fascination with five girls who have been dead for decades.

The best way to analyze the mechanism at play here is to use Eve Kosofsky Sedgwick's concept of homosexual panic. According to Sedgwick, the notion of homosexual panic attempts to describe the way in which "many twentieth-century western men experience their vulnerability to the social pressure of homophobic blackmail" (*Between Men* 89), and Jason Edwards has elegantly summarized the gist of Sedgwick's argument:

> Because solidarity between men within patriarchy generates and requires certain intense male bonds that are not readily distinguishable from the most reprobated homosexual bonds, Sedgwick believes that an endemic, almost ineradicable state of male homosexual panic was the normal condition of male heterosexual entitlement from the late nineteenth century onwards. (38)

In other words, in an environment of male privilege, tightly-woven groups of men – such as the grown-up boys in *The Virgin Suicides* – are likely to feel a continual need to portray their own homosocial community as free from, and fundamentally different to, any stigmatized forms of queer desire. Accordingly, it is possible for us to read the way in which the narrator of Eugenides's novel tries to keep Trip's disturbingly attractive sexuality at bay as in part a symptom of homosexual panic.[19]

As if to distance himself further from Trip's unsettlingly 'unmasculine' eroticism, the narrator once again resorts to his characteristic strategy of associating any kind of otherness with ethnic difference. We have already seen that Trip, like the Lisbon sisters, at one point appears "sitting cross-legged like an Indian," but there are many similar examples of a subtle process of ethnic othering. For instance, the narrator maintains that Trip's supposedly excessive masculine eroticism developed "during a trip to Acapulco," where Trip had sex with a recently divorced, much older woman (70). Mexico, as Martin Heusser has shown, often serves as a heterotopic space in American culture; the country is "associated with romantic myth, on the one hand, [...] and with backwardness and banditry, on the other" – which explains why Mexico can represent an entire spectrum of transgressions, "from the feared to the repressed to the secretly

19 Sedgwick later noted that the term *homosexual panic* also has an entirely different use as "a defense strategy that is commonly used to prevent conviction or to lighten the sentencing of gay-bashers" (the implication the defendant is less guilty if he suffers from a pathological aversion to homosexuals) – a use of which Sedgwick was unaware when she first introduced the term (*Epistemology of the Closet* 19).

desired" ("Mexicanness" 70; cf. Allatson 1485).[20] Mexico thus functions as a space of deviance in the U.S. cultural imaginary, and Trip seems somehow to have contracted the disease of sexual transgression on his brief stay in Acapulco. Moreover, the narrator places conspicuous emphasis on the "lustrous" tans of Trip and his father, which leaves their skins with a "mahogany hue":

> At dusk, Mr. Fontaine's and Trip's skins appeared almost bluish, and, putting on their towel turbans, they looked like twin Krishnas. [...] Marinated in baby oil, Mr. Fontaine and Trip boarded their air mattresses equipped with back rests and drink holders, and drifted beneath our tepid northern sky as though it were the Costa del Sol. We watched them, in stages, turning the color of shoe polish. (74)

In the narrator's account, Trip and his father are wont to engage in behavior that is decidedly un-American: fitting perhaps for "the Costa del Sol," but certainly not appropriate within the boundaries of a white suburb. As if in consequence of their 'foreign' behavior, Trip and Mr. Fontaine soon turn into literal non-whites, looking almost like "Krishnas" and "turning the color of shoe polish." Even though Trip and his father clearly form part of the boys' home community, the narrator's discourse transforms them into racialized others.

However, even such blatant ethnic and racial othering is not sufficient for Eugenides's narrator, for he also links Trip's difference to the 'lower' or working class. For one thing, if Trip's and his father's skins turn "the color of shoe polish," then this phrase carries with it classist as well as racist overtones, for "bootblacking" is one of the jobs where the historical link between race and class has been particularly strong (Vogel 52n20). Moreover, the narrator points out explicitly that the tans of Trip and his father were darker even than those of the "Italian contractors, working in the sun day after day" (74). When compared to the boys as a group of white, middle-class, male heterosexuals, Trip thus ends up appearing as wholly Other; he is the son of a gay father, desirable 'like a woman,' and poised precariously somewhere between a worker and a person of different racial and ethnic background.

And yet, despite the various strategies of othering that the narrator deploys against Trip, he nevertheless relies on him as a source of information, whereas he cannot bring himself to trust anyone who truly comes from outside the suburban community – a fact that is most readily apparent in the boys' reluc-

20 The parts of Jack Kerouac's *On the Road* that are set in Mexico may serve as one particularly famous example for the country's function as a heterotopic, more 'liberal' space where 'deviance' is far more acceptable (e.g. 250). Similarly, in Annie Proulx's "Brokeback Mountain," Mexico appears as the place where same-sex 'transgression' is possible (275).

tance to consult any actual members of the working class. As Rachel McLennan notes (28), the boys notably shy away from trying to gain any information from a character named Butch, who for a time is granted – limited – access to the Lisbons' family home:

> Butch, who cut the Lisbon grass, was [...] allowed inside for a glass of water, no longer having to drink from the outside faucet. Sweaty, shirtless, and tattooed, he walked right into the kitchen where the Lisbon girls lived and breathed, but we never asked him what he saw because we were scared of his muscles and his poverty. (22)

Whereas in other instances the narrator dismisses potential informants because, in his view, they "made terrible sources of information" (68), he admits that the boys cannot even bring themselves to ask Butch any questions because they are "scared" of his alien habitus ("shirtless, and tattooed") as well as of his poverty and the muscular body that testifies to Butch's routine engagement in physical labor. McLennan thus rightly speculates that the dismissal of the other potential informants on the basis of their 'improper' manner of speech may in fact reflect a middle-class bias against the supposedly coarse language of members of the working class (28).[21]

Before proceeding any further, it may be useful to draw together the two main strands of the argument so far: on the one hand, the narrator's strategies of othering, and, on the other hand, the ideas of myth and sacralization. We have seen that the narrator of *The Virgin Suicides* both idealizes and de-individualizes the Lisbon sisters, turning them into a kind of sacred monstrosity that is both part of the boys' home community yet also curiously other (as indicated by the girls' association with Europe, early American history, and Native American culture). In order to lend authority to his mythical account, the narrator not only combines the two discourses of the sacred and the law, but also disparages any alternative versions of the story. More specifically, the narrator argues that no one could ever fully explain the mystery of the Lisbon sister's actions because they are not "merely historic." This is telling because historical guilt is precisely what the narrator needs to erase from the boys' suburban home community in order to portray it as innocent: the history of Native American dispossession, for instance, or the policies of racial segregation pursued by many U.S. suburbs (cf. Millard 82).

However, in order to keep the suburb free from such intrusive forces, the narrator continually has to police the boundaries of the boys' home com-

21 The name "Butch" emphasizes the character's 'excessive' masculinity – a masculinity that is at the same time associated with queerness because the term *butch* can also denote a lesbian of (supposedly) masculine appearance.

munity, trying to stop it being 'infiltrated' or 'corrupted' by others. Conversely, anyone seen to upset the suburb's pastoral peace becomes the target of the narrator's othering – a strategy that is most readily apparent in the case of Trip Fontaine, who is associated with all kinds of others, and whom the narrator subtly frames as the villain of his story. Tellingly, however, the narrator not only admits that he had to "cobble together" the story of Trip and Lux's love affair; he also observes that it "began on a day when Trip Fontaine attended the wrong history class" (75), as if obliquely to admit that Trip has simply stumbled into a lesson about the past that happens not to be the right one for him. Trip, in short, ends up playing the role of a discursive scapegoat for the narrator.[22]

The Function of Sacrificial Violence

In order to understand more fully Trip's role as a discursive scapegoat, as well as its relation to the narrator's sacralization of the Lisbon girls, we need to examine in some detail René Girard's thesis that sacrifice is a means of deflecting intra-communal violence. In *Violence and the Sacred* (1972), Girard argues that all communities are threatened by the possibility of internal rivalry and conflict, and that sacrificial rites are one means of re-directing this type of violence in order to preserve the unity of the group in question (4–8). John Pahl has usefully summarized Girard's complex argument as a sequence of six basic steps:

1. **Mimetic Desire / Acquisitive Mimesis:** A subject (individual or group) imitates a rival's desire for an object
2. **Crisis of Differentiation / Rivalry:** Conflict for the object is threatened, or occurs
3. **The Scapegoat / Legitimation of Violence:** A scapegoat is identified whose elimination can resolve rivalry without fear of reprisal or escalating vengeance
4. **Sacrifice / Enactment of Violence:** The scapegoat is expelled or killed; the object's possession is clarified
5. **Restoration of Order:** Unanimity (temporarily) prevails
6. **Repetition, Masking, and Prevention through Religion:** Myth, ritual, prohibition, and (eventually) apotheosis of the victim ("the Sacred")

---

22 The idea of discursive sacrifice is inspired by a comment by Alex Woloch, who observes in a study of minor characters in fiction that narrative competition is often played out not only on the level of plot, but also on the level of discourse, with characters being "wounded, exiled, expelled, ejected, imprisoned, or killed" in the sense of being marginalized or excluded from the text and its telling (25).

> create a cycle of desire, enactment, and restoration that sanctions "legitimate" violence, but rules out unchecked rivalry (29)

According to Girard's model, an internal conflict arises from rivaling desires that are centered on the same object (steps 1 and 2). This conflict can be resolved if the group manages to agree on a surrogate victim or scapegoat (step 3) who is "expelled or killed" in an act that restores the unity of the group (steps 4 and 5; see Girard 84–86). Myth, ritual, and prohibition subsequently serve as means of stabilizing the outcome in order to prevent future outbursts of "unchecked rivalry" (step 6). In assuming a "mythico-ritual character," sacrificial violence is not only directed outward, but also "conceals the site of the original violence" (Girard 261).[23] In the process, the original violence is masked or disguised, and the group must to some extent misunderstand the nature of the sacrificial act for it to be effective (7). Ultimately, Girard contends, by "channeling its energies into ritual forms and activities sanctioned by ritual, the cultural order prevents multiple desires from converging on the same object" (158), and thus ensures its continuing existence.

The best way to apply Girard's model to *The Virgin Suicides* is to begin with the notion of internal rivalry and focus on those internal conflicts that could potentially tear the group of boys apart. The first of two sources of rivalry has to do with the role of the Lisbon girls as the objects of desire for the group of boys. As mentioned earlier, in Eugenides's novel we never learn precisely how many boys form part of the group. We do know, however, that their number exceeds that of the Lisbon sisters because, when Trip goes to the homecoming ball with Lux, it is only "some of us" who are chosen to accompany Mary, Therese, and Bonnie (115). The boys, in other words, are rivals in their desire for the Lisbon girls – and it is precisely this kind of internal rivalry that, according to Girard, can undermine the unity of a group and, thereby, threaten its very existence. Perversely, then, from the narrator's point of view the fact that the Lisbon sisters kill themselves constitutes a solution to the problem of internal rivalry, and it is thus no coincidence that he presents the scene of Cecilia's first suicide attempt in terms of a sacrificial rite:

> Mrs. Lisbon burst onto the porch, trailing Cecilia's flannel nightgown, and let out a long wail that stopped time. Under the molting trees and above the blazing, overexposed grass those four figures paused in tableau: the two slaves [i.e. the paramedics] offering the victim to the altar (lifting the stretcher into the truck), the priestess bran-

23 See also Girard's comments on myth: "Myths are the retrospective transfiguration of sacrificial crises, the reinterpretation of these crises in the light of the cultural order that has arisen from them" (67).

> dishing the torch (waving the flannel nightgown), and the drugged virgin rising up on her elbows, with an otherworldly smile on her pale lips. (6)

As part of his mythical reconstruction of the past (Shostak 818), the narrator describes this scene as a sacrificial act that is, of course, traumatizing for the boys as individuals. At the same time, from the point of view of the group the Lisbon girls' suicides constitute an act of terminal violence that, as Girard suggests, "can only be labeled sacrificial retrospectively, because it brought all hostilities to an end" (132). Put in the bluntest terms: had the girls lived, then the boys' friendship might not have survived.

If this interpretation seems disturbing and even callous, then this is in fact part of the point, for as Moshe Halbertal has noted in his study *On Sacrifice* (2012), feelings of guilt almost inevitably arise from the practice of sacrificial violence. According to Halbertal, sacrifice in the biblical sense "is a substitute for the violence that the offerer might himself deserve" (i.e. an act of atonement in the face of God; 32). Halbertal also contends that this view of sacrifice is incompatible with Girard's model, as the offerer is not motivated by a desire for violence, but instead by fear and anxiety. However, perhaps it is possible to reconcile Girard's and Halbertal's positions, for if communal conflict were to escalate, then everyone who is part of that community might become the victim of violence – which in turn would explain widespread feelings of fear and anxiety. A second disagreement between Halbertal and Girard relates to the question of the victim's innocence, for while Halbertal regards innocence as necessary because this renders the victim "capable of becoming a vehicle for ultimate projection" (33), Girard holds that the victim's innocence or guilt are simply irrelevant because it is the victim's status as "relatively indifferent" to – i.e. as not truly important for – the community that make him or her appear "sacrificeable" (4). Despite these differences, however, both Halbertal (34) and Girard (1) observe that the act of sacrifice itself always threatens to look like a crime because the sacrifice does not constitute a just punishment of the victim (for Halbertal because the victim is innocent, and for Girard because sacrifice has nothing to do with punishment in the first place). Without glossing over their fundamental disagreement, we can thus say that both Halbertal and Girard view acts of sacrifice as 'borderline crimes' that are, for that very reason, likely to lead to a sense of guilt on the part of those who commit – and benefit from – the sacrificial act.

This last point is crucial for a reading of *The Virgin Suicides* because guilt and mutual reproach are another factor that could lead to conflict within the group of boys. We have seen that, from the perspective of the group as a whole (i.e. from the narrator's point of view), the Lisbon suicides constitute a 'sacrifice' that solves the problem of internal rivalry. However, precisely because the boys *as a group* benefit from the suicides, their collective identity is haunted by a sense of guilt. In addition, there is the much more concrete sense of guilt that each of the boys is likely to feel because, as John R. Jordan and John L. McIntosh put it, in the aftermath of suicide "[g]uilt can be felt regarding what one did, did not do, imagined one might have done, and so forth" (31). Jordan and McIntosh also observe that one way of reacting to such feelings of guilt is to blame others and thereby cast the focus "away from oneself" (30). In the case of the group of boys in *The Virgin Suicides*, this could quickly lead to a vicious circle of mutual reproach and so undermine the boys' sense of communal belonging. There is thus a need for yet another surrogate victim, and this is – as we have seen – Trip Fontaine: the discursive scapegoat on whom the boys can shift the full weight of communal blame.

In the case of *The Virgin Suicides* at least, Halbertal's idea of the victim's necessary innocence thus works less well than Girard's model; after all, Trip's extremely insensitive treatment of Lux may well have contributed to the suicides, but this is not the true reason why the group of boys choses him as their primary scapegoat. Rather, what makes Trip 'sacrificeable' is that he is close to but not truly part of the community; because of his good looks and success with women (including Lux Lisbon), Trip has long been the object of envy and resentment for the boys, and his discursive destruction thus combines the sweet taste of revenge with the relief that comes when one is, finally, absolved from guilt. Tellingly, the final reference to Trip reports his dismissal in a letter clearly written by Lux Lisbon, one of the 'sacred' and adored girls:

> *Dear whoever,*
> *Tell Trip I'm over him.*
> *He's a creep.*
> *Guess Who* (192; original emphasis)

Trip's eradication on the level of discourse is thus sanctioned on the level of the story by an act of 'divine' rejection which simultaneously eliminates Trip as a rival for the group of boys.

And yet, Girard's model suggests that the sacrificial solution can only become permanent if its true function is masked or disguised, for instance through myth, ritual, or what Pohl calls the "apotheosis of the victim" (29). We have already seen that the Lisbon sisters' suicides constitute the primary act of 'sacrificial' violence in the sense that they solve the problem of intra-communal rivalry for the boys, and we have also examined the extent to which the narrator portrays them as semi-divine, mythical creatures. The discursive destruction of Trip, by contrast, constitutes a secondary act of sacrifice intended primarily to ward off mutual reproach and guilt, and accordingly Trip's "apotheosis" remains subtle and incomplete. Nevertheless, the narrator not only calls him a seducer "greater than Casanova" (72), but also notes that he and his father look like "Krishnas" (74). Trip is, in short, a sex-god, to whom all women from the suburban community supposedly turn "like a thousand daisies attuning their faces toward the path of the sun" (69), and whose stature in the narrator's account may not truly reach, but at least approaches the realm of the mythical.

Ritual, Rejection, and the Culture of Mourning

To say that the Lisbon sisters' suicides on one level constitute the solution to a communal problem is, importantly, not to deny its painful and traumatic nature for the boys. Indeed, if one function of their commemorative rituals is continually to retell their mythical story in order to disguise the troubling nature of sacrificial violence, then on another level these rituals are simply an attempt to cope with trauma. Moshe Halbertal's comments on religious rituals prove illuminating in this context, for according to Halbertal rituals serve to de-individualize the participants, who would otherwise have to face the overwhelming divine presence entirely on their own (15–16). Moreover, as a time-tested protocol for proper behavior, rituals provide supplicants with a sense of stability and security even in the presence of the sacred, and accordingly Halbertal describes them as procedures that allow believers to overcome the "anxiety of rejection" (18). Rituals, that is to say, symbolically express that one is not merely a forlorn individual, but instead part of a community whose members all suffer from the same fear: divine rejection and punishment.

Halbertal's comments are pertinent to *The Virgin Suicides* because, for the boys, the Lisbon sisters' suicides constitute an ultimate act of rejection by their semi-divine objects of desire. In the novel's final sentence, the narrator movingly expresses the boys' lasting sense of violation and bereavement:

> It didn't matter in the end how old they had been, or that they were girls, but only that we had loved them, and that they hadn't heard us calling, still do not hear us, up here in the tree house, with our thinning hair and soft bellies, calling them out of those rooms where they went to be alone for all time, alone in suicide, which is deeper than death, and where we will never find the pieces to put them back together. (249)

The boys' love for the Lisbon sisters may have been idealizing and voyeuristic, but nevertheless they did try to stay in touch with the Lisbons even after their parents had imprisoned them in their own home. For example, the boys eventually call the girls, barely saying a word but instead playing songs into the phone that "most thoroughly communicated our feelings" (195). When the sisters respond by playing songs like "Alone Again, Naturally" or "Candle in the Wind," the boys respond with "You've Got a Friend" or "Wild Horses" (196), trying to offer some kind of consolation. When the girls secretly invite the boys over to their home, pretending that they want to elope with them, the boys feel genuinely elated, not knowing that the girls will commit suicide while the boys are waiting for them, dreaming of their future together (212–213). It is therefore understandable that the boys take the suicides as a gesture that is directed against them personally, and they instinctively resort to the time-tested power of ritual to try and deal with the annihilating power of this ultimate gesture of rejection.[24]

If the precise shape of the boys' ritualistic acts of commemoration nevertheless appears pathological – one of their "most prized possessions" is the "titillating" report of one of Lux's gynecological exams (155) – then this may be quite simply because they have never been taught how to mourn. At school, for instance, during his speech at Convocation, the headmaster refers to Cecilia's suicide only obliquely, acknowledging that "it has been a long, hard summer for some of us here today," but also suggesting that "today begins a new year of hopes and goals" (104). Moreover, while the headmaster's wife in time manages to convince most teachers that the school ought to schedule a "Day of Grieving," her main argument for the project is that grief may be "natural," but "[o]vercoming it is a matter of choice" (ibid.). In the end, the "Day of Grieving" proves a total failure, at least according to the narrator's account:

> Most people remember the Day of Grieving as an obscure holiday. The first three hours of school were canceled and we remained in our home rooms. Teachers passed out mimeographs related to the day's theme, which was never officially announced, as Mrs. Woodhouse felt it inappropriate to single out the girls' tragedy. The result was that the tragedy was diffused and universalized. As Kevin Tiggs put it, "It seemed like we were supposed to feel sorry for everything that ever happened, ever." (104)

Not only is the day's theme "never officially announced"; it is also an event that fails to include either the Lisbon sisters (who "kept asking to be excused to go to the bathroom"; 105) or their father (a teacher at the school who only learned about the Day of Grieving when it was already "well under way"; 106). As a result, "all the healing was done by those of us without wounds" (105), and it therefore comes as no surprise that the success of the event remained a matter

24 See Bilyana Vanyova Kostova, who rightly notes that it is virtually impossible to decide unequivocally whether the boys should be seen as "bystanders, perpetrators or victims" (49).

of dispute (107). Moreover, in the aftermath of the other sisters' suicides, the only act of mourning that the narrator records is the dedication of a memorial bench to the Lisbon sisters: a "project that had been put in motion eight months earlier" after Cecilia's suicide and "was rededicated just in time to include the other girls" (231–232). Though the genuineness of such gestures need not be doubted, there nevertheless remains a sense that no one really tries to help the boys truly to deal with their traumatic experience of loss.

Interestingly, there are hints in Eugenides's novel that the suburban community's inability to mourn may have something to do with its broader cultural context. For one thing, the Greek grandmother of one of the boys confesses that she "couldn't understand how the Lisbon's kept so quiet, why they didn't wail to heaven or go mad"; more generally, she is unable to fathom why in America "everyone pretended to be happy all the time" (175). *The Virgin Suicides* thus at the very least raises the question of whether an inability to mourn may be a more widespread problem in the United States. The other passage from the novel that is relevant in this context relates to the ill-fated Day of Grieving, and more particularly to the comment by the headmaster's wife that "[g]rief is natural," whereas "[o]vercoming it is a matter of choice" (104). Intriguingly, the boys learn about this comment from a former teacher who now has "a job in advertising," and who actually used the same formula as a slogan for a dietary product: "Eating is natural. Gaining weight is your choice" (ibid.). The language is typical of advertising, which insinuates endless possibility ("Just do it!") and often involves an imperative to enjoy ("Enjoy Coke!"; see Žižek, *Enjoy Your Symptom* xvii). Terry Eagleton holds that such "pathological optimism" ultimately reflects "a fear of confronting loss" (*Across the Pond* 139), and if this is indeed the characteristic mood of capitalism in America, then *The Virgin Suicides* is at least partly a critique of this state of affairs.

Identity Politics: An Impossible Perspective

The Virgin Suicides is many things. It is a moving account of a group of boys trying to deal with the aftereffects of a traumatic experience of loss. It is also an analysis of collective identity: how it almost invariable relies on 'sacred' myths of origin; the extent to which it involves sacrificial practices of othering; and the importance of rituals that not merely represent, but in fact serve to create and maintain the unity of the group in question (Stollberg-Rilinger 13–14). Moreover, the novel constitutes an indictment of those societies that fail to provide its members with the adequate social resources for dealing with loss. The boys in *The Virgin Suicides* may be guilty of voyeurism, narcissistic projection, and exclusionary discourses of belonging; but while it would be easy to dismiss them as merely an unsavory collection of self-centered white, middle-class, heterosexual males, it is difficult to deny the traumatic nature of their experience.

It is crucial to insist that the boys' sense of being wronged and wounded is not merely illusionary because the novel's critique of identity politics would otherwise be far less convincing. Bilyana Vanyova provides a concise summary of the harmful effects explored in Eugenides's novel:

> Progressively, the narrator's narrative subtly connects the private suicides of the five sisters to their capacity to shake off the repressed public conformity of the suburb and, what is more, to expose its malfunctioning. Their refusal to live brings to the fore the social effects of heavily repressed collective wounds such as race riots, lay-offs, the impossibility of integration experienced by immigrants, or the ecological crisis. It also highlights the smothered adolescent erotic desire that injures not just the girls' sexual awakening [...] but also the narrator's [...]. (56)

For Vanyova, there is thus no doubt that the girls as well as the boys ought to be seen as real victims, their developing identities thwarted by their environment. On a more general level, Terry Eagleton contends that, though the categories of identity politics may be "ontologically empty," they nevertheless arise from real experiences of oppression:

> Women are not so much fighting for the freedom to be women – as though we all understood what exactly that meant – as for the freedom to be fully human; but that inevitably abstract humanity can be articulated in the here and now only through their womanhood, since this is the place where their humanity is wounded and refused. Sexual politics, like class or nationalist struggle, will thus necessarily be caught up in the very metaphysical categories it hopes finally to abolish; and any such movement will demand a difficult, perhaps ultimately impossible double optic, at once fighting on a terrain already mapped out by its antagonists and seeking even now to prefigure within that mundane strategy styles of being and identity for which we have as yet no proper names. ("Nationalism" 24)

For Eagleton, the politics of identity arises from a sense of being wounded on the basis of that ontologically empty identity, and just as it would be wrong to deny the reality of these wounds, it would be counterproductive to turn the wound itself into a kind of fetish. Instead, we need an "impossible double optic": staying firm in our commitment to these oppressed and wounded identities, but simultaneously bearing in mind that "our social, sexual, or racial identities" should not in fact be "all that important" ("Nationalism" 26).

In *The Virgin Suicides*, this impossible double optic is in some way expressed through the conflict between the collective narrator and the boys as individuals. The narrator, who is a personification of the group's collective identity, works to perpetuate the group's founding trauma, which is the only reason why the group still exists. By contrast, the boys as individuals are desperately trying to overcome their burdensome emotional and psychic wounds, and the support they seek from the other members of the group is mainly a means to this ultimate end (i.e. the particular group to which they belong is not all that important as an end in itself). The novel thus depicts a conflict between, on the one hand, identity politics as an end in itself, and, on the other, identity politics as mainly a means for creating the social conditions under which the identity for which one has been made to suffer and fight is no longer particularly important. We can also rephrase this idea in the form of a simple question: How can we avoid becoming trapped in an identity in which we have been forced to invest so much effort, but that we did not actually want thrust upon us in the first place?

The idea that *The Virgin Suicides* gives narrative form to the "impossible double optic" required in identity politics also allows us to formulate more precisely why the novel's setting, an American suburb in the early 1970s, is far from negligible or accidental. In the introduction to this chapter, we have seen that the period between, roughly, 1963 and 1974 is not only associated with an unprecedented polarization in American society – the so-called culture wars – but also with the emergence of identity politics as such. Second-wave feminism, black power, or gay liberation are among the most prominent examples of such 'identitarian' movements, and virtually all movements of this kind can be seen as challenges to the hegemonic power of white, middle-class, heterosexual males. From the point of view of those who happen to belong to this latter category, there is thus a real sense that the Decade of Upheaval between 1963 and 1974 constitutes a historical experience of loss – though of course what was lost were in fact the spoils of historical injustice and oppression. What *The Virgin Suicides* does, in effect, is to place us in the position of those who, as a group, are in a very real sense the victims of historical events beyond their control, but who at the same time fail to (or perhaps refuse) to grasp the extent to which the victimhood of others was not only far worse than their own, but in fact the very precondition for their earlier, privileged position.

More specifically, in *The Virgin Suicides*, the boys hold fast to an image of mythical innocence preceding the Lisbons' suicides, refusing to probe deeper into the exclusionary nature of the place they call home. Moreover, though the boys are right in suggesting that the Lisbon sisters' pain is not "*merely* historic" (231; emphasis added), this does not mean that socio-historical pressures play no part at all. For instance, the fact that no one tries to prevent Mr. and Mrs. Lisbon from effectively imprisoning their daughters in their suburban home arguably reflects a deep-seated cultural bias in favor of what Isaiah Berlin has called negative liberty (i.e. the freedom from interference; 121–122) – particularly when it comes to parents 'protecting' their daughters (i.e. to restricting the freedom of young women to participate in the life of the community, and thus their freedom to belong). Likewise, while the Lisbon girls may not have killed themselves *exclusively* because the United States in some ways looked like a "dying empire" in the early 1970s (*The Virgin Suicides* 231), the general atmosphere of pessimism may well have played a part. Accordingly, if the boys at one point confess that Old Mrs. Karafilis had been "shaped and saddened by a history we knew nothing about" (172), then perhaps this is an apt way for us to describe the boys' relation to the past of their own home community as well. At the same time, *The Virgin Suicides* as a whole in fact anatomizes collective belonging and the politics of identity, and as such the novel constitutes an attempt to understand its own historical moment: the emotional dynamics of the culture wars; the vagaries of identity politics; and a culture obsessed with fetishistic memory but lacking in historical understanding.

If Eugenides's novel nevertheless refuses simply to portray suburban communities as mindless spaces of conformity, or to condemn the boys' desire for home as such, then this should not be misconstrued as a sign of critical weakness. Rather, the degree of the novel's affection is a measure of its strength, for it is far easier to criticize those spaces of belonging with which we do not identify than to expose ourselves to the alienating flaws at the heart of the homes that we love and cherish. A critical but affectionate gaze: this has also been the aim of the present study, which we must now proceed to bring to a close.

Conclusion – The End of Intellectual Nomadism

The rhyme between *home* and *roam* may be one of the more hackneyed in the poetic repertoire, but it encapsulates beautifully the extent to which our inquiry into the concept of home has led us to travel wide and far.[1] Chapter one, for example, among other things focuses on Ishmael's attempts in *Moby-Dick* to combat alienation through discursive constructions of universal belonging, while chapter two examines the reasons why Maggie is ultimately unwilling to reconcile herself to the prospect of a 'nomadic' existence in *The Mill on the Floss.* A central theme in the discussion of *Mrs. Dalloway* in chapter three is Clarissa's willingness to evade questions of political responsibility in order to maintain her sense of belonging, whereas chapter four explores Quentin's nightmarish inability in *Absalom, Absalom!* to abandon his love for a home that in many ways would seem to deserve his hatred. Chapter five then turns to the parallels between crumbling houses and 'derelict' human bodies in *Union Street*, while the discussion of *The Virgin Suicides* in chapter six revolves around a group of boys and their ritualistic reenactment of communal identity. In Emersonian terms, one might say that we have engaged in "intellectual nomadism" in order to avoid the monotony and dullness that may easily befall a "home-keeping wit" ("History" 161–162).[2]

At the same time, it is worth taking seriously Emerson's warning that intellectual nomadism, if taken to extremes, "bankrupts the mind, through the dissipation of power on a miscellany of objects" ("History" 161) – for this warning allows us to explain some of the theoretical limitations of this study. Emerson's idea that intellectual nomadism may involve a "dissipation of power" alerts us

1 I would like to thank Nicole Frey Büchel for her comments on the first draft of this chapter, as well as Sarah Chevalier and Anja Neukom-Hermann for their feedback on the final version.

2 On Emerson's discussion of nomadism see John Durham Peters ("Exile, Nomadism, and Diaspora" 30–31). Emerson's conflation of a historical antagonism between "Nomadism and Agriculture" with two conflicting types of mental attitudes "in the individual" is not unproblematic, as it may serve to erase the specificity of nomadic existence ("History" 161). Moreover, Emerson's distinction between, on the one hand, the nomads of Africa (who are "constrained" to wander), and, on the other, Europeans and Americans (who follow the "nomadism of trade and curiosity"; ibid.) is clearly not immune to postcolonial critique. On nomadic thought, see also Deuleuze, *Difference and Repetition* 45–47. The link between Emerson's and Deleuze's ideas is discussed in Tally, *Melville, Mapping and Globalization* 65–68.

to the fact that human beings have limited energy and resources at their disposal, and that the amount of power we are able to dissipate depends to a large extent on our past and present experience of home and belonging. We are born helpless and depend on others to take care of us during the first years of our lives. If our basic childhood needs are met, then we have a greater chance of thriving as teenagers and as adults. Similarly, if our education is suited to our talents (unlike Tom's and Maggie's in *The Mill on the Floss*), and if there is a reasonable degree of security in our lives, then we are free to expend some energy on nomadic thought. Should these conditions not be met, however, then intellectual nomadism may either seem like a luxury that one cannot afford, or simply constitute a task that one does not know how to perform.[3] In chapter four, for instance, we noted that Thomas Sutpen's upbringing was extremely inauspicious: inured to violence, racism, and poverty, and deprived of adequate formal education, Sutpen ends up lacking vital mental resources that, in turn, help explain his obsessive quest for a fixed and destructive idea of home. Similarly, in chapter two, we discussed the narrator's idea in *The Mill on the Floss* that "light and graceful irony," as well as "extremely moderate" beliefs, are of "very expensive production," while those living in poverty and squalor tend to need strong and clear guiding principles to help them cope with "the emphasis of want" (238; bk. 4, ch. 3). If, in short, one's physical and mental development was thwarted in childhood and youth, or if one is engaged in a daily struggle for survival, then a desire for intellectual nomadism may simply be too much to ask. In addition, there is an important difference between choosing to engage in intellectual nomadism and being driven to do so because one's sense of home and belonging has been disrupted against one's will. It is this emphasis on home as a material basis for, and limit to, our cognitive engagement with the world which explains the relatively minor presence in this study of poststructural, postmodern and deconstructive theories, which too often have little to say about embodidness and human limitations – unlike postcolonial, psychoanalytic, feminist, and Marxist approaches.

Other limitations of our intellectual journey can less easily be justified. This study's marked theoretical predelictions within the disciplinary boundaries of literary and cultural studies are, for instance, compounded by a virtually complete absence of disciplines such as law (which are discussed, for instance, in Maria Donata Panforti, "The Home and the Law"), human biology (e.g. Elizabeth Cashdan, "Spatial Organization and Habitat Use"), or architecture and housing

3 Miranda Fricker provides a useful definition of what she terms hermeneutical injustice, which occurs "when a gap in collective interpretive resources puts someone at an unfair disadvantage when it comes to making sense of their social experiences" (1).

studies (e.g. Helen Long, *The Edwardian House*; Thomas Barrie, *House and House*). Similarly, the fact that all primary texts come from the core nations of the so-called Anglosphere (i.e. England and the United States), and that most of the theorists consulted are either northwestern Europeans – predominantly English, German, and French – or U.S. Americans must surely give us pause.[4] Much has undoubtedly fallen outside the purview of this study, and our supposedly nomadic forays into the fields of home and belonging in many ways stand revealed as decidedly provincial.

And yet, this is not to say that nothing has been gained from our inquiry into home and belonging. The remainder of the conclusion will attempt to highlight the most important findings. Rather than retrace our analysis of home and belonging step by step, we will rephrase the argument by addressing three underlying themes that have rarely surfaced as explicit concerns in the six chapters that make up this study: the concept of genre and its thematic as well as formal relation to home and belonging; the recurring problem of suicide as a symptom of unbelonging that allows us to reflect on the limited power of fiction; and the idea that fiction itself constitutes a home-making practice because it offers imaginary solutions to real-life contradictions (cf. introduction). We will examine each of these three concerns in a separate section and, in so doing, provide at least some sense of closure to this purposefully meandering exploration of home.

Genre and Home: From Content to Form

The last of the seven precepts outlined in the introduction suggests that any critical analysis of home must focus not only on the content or ingredients of home, but also on their formal arrangements. This need to take into account both form and content also applies to the discussion of genre and its relation to home and belonging. Indeed, form is arguably the more important category of the two because, on the level of content, the link between home and genre is relatively straight-forward and, therefore, not particularly interesting. In the case of the *Bildungsroman* or novel of formation, for instance, we are faced with a genre that has as its key concern the problem of a young person leaving the family home in order to find his or her place in the world (i.e. to establish a broader sense of social belonging as a well-adjusted and 'mature' individual). We have examined this generic tradition most thoroughly in the discussion of George Eliot's *The Mill on the Floss* (see chapter two), but the specific challenges associated with the transition to adulthood also play a role in other texts dis-

4 On the problematic history of the term *Anglosphere*, see Vucetic, *The Anglosphere* (2011).

cussed in this study. In *E. T.*, for instance, little Elliott must abandon his narcissistic self-absorption and learn to consider the feelings of others, while the eleven-year-old Kelly Brown in *Union Street* must come to terms not only with growing up in a precarious home, but also with the terrible experience of rape. To some extent, Kelly thus resembles the traumatized group of male adolescents in *The Virgin Suicides*, but while the latter remain trapped in a ritualistic reenactment of their founding trauma, Kelly finds a way of reestablishing a sense of belonging in a moving encounter with a frail and desperate old woman (i.e. her meeting with Alice Bell, to whom we shall return in the following section).

A second genre discussed in this study that has a close thematic relation to home is the Gothic, which at times even intersects with the narrative of *Bildung*. As noted in chapter four, in the course of the nineteenth century, Gothic narratives increasingly turned away from sublime landscapes and gloomy castles, and instead focused their attention on more domestic settings – a variant of the genre that Fred Botting has called the "homely Gothic" (113). *Absalom, Absalom!* is one example of this subgenre: a text that examines the ideology of plantation domesticity as well as the horrors of slavery, highlighting how the material remains of a supposedly superseded racial order continue to haunt Faulkner's protagonists, as well as the United States as a nation, well into the twentieth century (and, arguably, beyond). Moreover, we can detect echoes of the "homely Gothic" in the suburbs of *E. T.* and *The Virgin Suicides.* In the case of Spielberg's film, we have examined closely the way in which E. T. functions as Elliott's uncanny double, and we may now add the Gothic motif of a family home being taken over by powerful forces beyond the inhabitants' control (i.e. the agents of a notably paranoid government bent on maintaining 'homeland security'). Similarly, in *The Virgin Suicides*, the motifs of female incarceration and memories that refuse to stay buried have at least a remote kinship with the genre of the Gothic.[5] The 'derelict' people living in the crumbling houses of *Union Street*, finally, are in some ways modern-day variants of Gothic revenants or monsters: abject and unruly bodies that lurk in the marginal spaces of society, continually threatening to encroach beyond their narrow confines, and unable to live or die in peace.

Indeed, the list of genres that have some relation to home and belonging on the level of content could be extended almost indefinitely. Among the genres discussed in this study, for instance, there is tragedy as a genre of failure and unbelonging (chapter two); pastoral as a literary tradition that tries to envision an ideal, homely fusion between nature and culture (chapters three and six); and

5 See Martin Dines's "Suburban Gothic and the Ethnic Uncanny"; cf. Hoskin 214.

realism as the genre of the everyday, the familiar, the domestic (chapter five). To these, we might add others that are not discussed in this study: the Western as a genre of European settlement and native dispossession (e.g. Bronfen 96–97); film noir and its concern with traumatized war veterans returning home (e.g. Spicer 20); or comedy, which in its narrowest sense can be conceived of as celebrating communal reintegration (e.g. Stott 1).[6]

The truly interesting link between genre and home, however, concerns the level of form or style, and in particular the question of how genre theory conceives of texts as belonging to multiple genres. In recent decades, genre theorists from across the critical spectrum have insisted that individual texts do not simply belong to one particular genre, in the sense of being tied to the supposedly unchanging laws of a single category of texts; rather, a literary text belongs to a genre to the extent to which it participates in certain generic practices: engaging with genre conventions, revising and rejecting some of them, and as a rule combining practices associated with diverging generic traditions (e.g. Amigoni 58; Frow 3; Zagarell 502). In the case of *Moby-Dick*, for instance, we saw that the novel's strange opening sections ("Etymology" and "Extracts") are followed by several chapters that seem to set up Ishmael as the protagonist of a 'single-focus' narrative of *Bildung* – only to thwart these generic expectations later on, when the text's focus broadens and becomes much more diffuse. Nevertheless, Melville's text remains affiliated with the generic tradition of the *Bildungsroman*: not fully or exclusively at home in it, but retaining significant ties of belonging – just as individuals, too, can at least try to explore new ties without necessarily abandoning all their former associations. The discussion of other novels in the present study likewise focuses on intersecting and sometimes conflicting literary lineages (e.g. in the case of *Mrs. Dalloway*, which sets up a dialogue between the 'rural' genre of pastoral, the literary tradition of the marriage plot, and a series of texts focusing on urban *flâneurs*; or *Union Street*, which pits the conventions of novelistic, bourgeois realism against the aesthetic of the short-story cycle). Various generic affiliations may thus coexist in a primary text – sometimes peacefully, at other times uneasily – just as an individual's sense of belonging may involve a set of diverse, potentially conflicting loyalties (e.g. familial, professional, and national).

Moreover, if we agree with critics such as Aijaz Ahmad (251), Wai Chee Dimock (1383), and John Frow (2) in regarding genres as fields of knowledge, then there is an important cognitive dimension to the idea of multiple generic

6 Stott rightly notes, however, that comic reintegration may simultaneously be exclusionary if it relies on the "systematic humiliation of targeted groups" (105).

belonging. According to these critics, each genre constitutes a particular way of knowing the world and therefore invariably includes a set of epistemological blind spots. Each genre, that is to say, resembles Emerson's concept of the "home-keeping wit," which would prefer to find "all the elements of life in its own soil," but which would quickly become dull and monotonous without salutary "foreign intrusions" ("History" 162). Put in slightly different terms: a text's coupling of one genre with one or several others constitutes a discursive attempt to make use of various sets of knowledge in order to come to terms with particular narrative, political, and philosophical problems. *Moby-Dick*, for instance, evokes the generic tradition of allegory – with its historical link to the discourse of religion – as well as the secular empiricism of realist narration in its attempt to grapple with man's existential place in the world. It is an uneasy combination at best, and one that helps us to relate the particular concerns of Melville's text to broader cultural and historical rivalries.

This also implies that, in tracing the affinities and contradictions between a text's generic lineages, we can gain a better understanding of what Mikhail Bakhtin has called the "basic social tone" of a text's individual style ("Discourse in the Novel" 259). The discussion of *The Mill on the Floss*, for instance, has shown how the realist novel's appreciation of the common life serves as a corrective influence on tragedy's aristocratic prejudices, just as tragedy's focus on intractable moral dilemmas tempers the *Bildungsroman*'s 'realistic' aesthetic of homecoming, compromise, and social adjustment. Similarly, if *Absalam, Absalom!* is in part a Gothic tale, it also evokes traditional versions of the historical novel (with Thomas Sutpen's stallion explicitly "named out of [Walter] Scott"; 63), thus combining one genre's focus on the dark recesses of the human psyche with another's interest in the way broader political conflicts shape the individual. To the extent that a given text participates in more than one single generic tradition, it formally enacts the cognitive implications of multiple belonging: its productive opening up of new horizons, but also its potential to lead to conflict and contradictions that may prove daunting and, at times, psychologically crippling. It is this formal process of generic 'cross-examination,' rather than any particular theme or content, that constitutes the most productive way of linking the concept of genre to the ideas of home and belonging.

Not-Being-at-Home: Suicide and Unbelonging

The second underlying theme that we need to explore in this concluding chapter is the problem of suicide, which features explicitly in many of the primary texts discussed in this study: the traumatized war veteran Septimus Warren Smith, who throws himself out of a window in *Mrs. Dalloway*; Alice Bell in *Union*

Street, who prefers to end her life rather than move to an old people's home; or the five Lisbon sisters, whose suicides continue to haunt a group of neighborhood boys in *The Virgin Suicides*. There is, moreover, something markedly suicidal about Ahab's quest for the white whale in *Moby-Dick*, and we know that Ishmael regards going to sea as a "substitute for pistol and ball" (i.e. for committing suicide; *Moby-Dick* 18; ch. 1). In addition, we have seen that the conclusion of *The Mill on the Floss* in fact constitutes a fantasied fulfilment of an only half-admitted death wish on Maggie's part. *Absalom, Absalom!*, finally, is haunted intertextually by Quentin's suicide in Faulkner's earlier novel *The Sound and the Fury* (1929), and Quentin's sense of despair at the end of *Absalom, Absalom!* does little to lay this fearful specter to rest.[7]

The reason why it is important to acknowledge the pervasive presence of suicide in the primary texts chosen for this study is that acts of suicide can be understood as an extreme expression of unbelonging. In chapter six, we observed that the Lisbon sisters' suicides are in part a fundamental act of rejection: a disavowal of any claims on them by other human beings, including the group of neighborhood boys. Accordingly, when Eugenides's narrator speaks of "the outrageousness of a human being thinking only of herself" (248), then this is to register that suicide not only constitutes an act of self-violation, but also – in effect, if not necessarily in intention – a violent misdeed against all those whose sense of self is bound up with the person who decides to put an end to his or her life. Christian Baudelot and Roger Establet describe the "disproportionate" effect of a suicide on the lives of others:

> Mourning following a suicide is not like any other mourning. [...] It's distinguishing feature is an intense expression of suffering, but also of shock. It is a traumatic form of mourning that lasts longer than other forms and is more likely to generate more depression, anxiety, negative and painful feelings, and feelings of guilt and shame. The scars it leaves on the suicide's relatives remain indelible. The feeling of guilt it generates is often so painful that it drives some to punish themselves or even to commit suicide in an attempt to assuage their guilt. The suicide's closest relatives are the first to be affected, but the shock waves spread far beyond the inside circle. (2)

Accordingly, while some have argued that suicide can be seen as an assertion of freedom (e.g. Seneca; see Dollimore 32), there are also those who, like Jennifer Michael Hecht, emphasize that one reason why "suicide is wrong" is that "sui-

---

7 In addition, there is a character in *Absalom, Absalom!* that does not appear in the discussion of the novel in chapter four: Clytemnestra, the daughter of Thomas Sutpen and a slave woman, who at the end of the novel sets fire to Sutpen's plantation manor, perishing in the flames together with her half-brother Henry.

cide causes more suicide" (5). In other words, while suicide may constitute an act of liberation or self-assertion for the person who takes their own life, it can also rend apart existing communal and affective ties, thus escalating rather than protesting against existing violent dynamics.

In addition, while on the one hand the rejection implied in suicide may forcefully unsettle the sense of home and belonging of those who are left behind, on the other hand there is also strong evidence that suicide in fact arises from problems associated with the family home and the wider community. According to Mark A. Reinecke and Elizabeth R. Didie, for instance, suicidal behavior correlates strongly not only with "stressful life events" – e.g. "work or legal problems, [...] the loss of a loved one, and changes in residence" – but also with experiences in childhood or adolescence of "negative peer relationships, abuse and neglect, family instability, and a chaotic home environment" (214). Disrupted family homes thus feature prominently among the factors that influence suicidality (as, indeed, they do in the case of Ahab and Ishmael in *Moby-Dick* and, to a lesser but still important extent, Maggie's in *The Mill on the Floss*). At the same time, the existence of "at-risk populations" – including LGBTQ individuals, Native Americans, military personnel, the homeless, and incarcerated men and women (Worchel and Gearing 291) – suggests that larger socio-cultural factors also play a crucial role in individual experiences of unbelonging.[8]

Moreover, in addition to unhomely pasts or socio-cultural conditions hindering belonging, the problem of suicide also involves a frequently neglected dimension of home: the future as a subjective horizon of expectations. Reinecke and Didie, for instance, emphasize the importance of hopelessness in triggering suicidal behavior (209), and other researchers agree that a persistent lack of hope is among the main indicators for an increased risk of suicide (e.g. Vaillant and Blumenthal 4; Worchel and Gearing 92–94). If, in other words, a person stops believing that he or she could ever again feel at home in the world, then suicide becomes increasingly likely (as is the case with Alice Bell in *Union Street*, who – unlike Kelly Brown – is no longer able to envisage a more homely future for herself).

To the extent that literary narratives can mitigate stressful life experiences or underlying feelings of alienation, fictions of home can quite literally become a matter of life and death. Coming-out narratives, for instance, may alleviate a gay or lesbian teenager's current feelings of isolation and even help him or her to imagine a future of communal belonging. More generally, fictional genres

8 The fact that suicide rates worldwide have increased by 60 percent in the past forty-five years (Hecht 4) could thus be read as an indicator of increasing global unhomeliness.

familiarize individuals with a wide range of different story templates, which they can then use as cognitive resources when it comes to narrativizing their life experiences – an ability that is widely held to be a crucial factor in maintaining mental health (e.g. Engel et al., *Narrative in Health Care*). Conversely, the reiteration of negative stereotypes in fiction may have averse emotional effects, particularly on those who already suffer from a precarious sense of belonging (witness, for instance, Maggie's complaint in *The Mill on the Floss* that women who are "dark" like her always lose out against their "light-complexioned" rivals – a conventional pattern that Eliot's novel repeatedly associates with racist prejudices against 'darker' races; *The Mill on the Floss* 270; bk. 5, ch. 4; see also the discussion of Victorian views of gypsies in chapter two).

At the same time, we ought to be wary of overestimating the power of fiction to avert the tragedy of suicide (or any other real-life tragedies, for that matter). In *Mrs. Dalloway*, for instance, a quotation from Shakespeare's *Coriolanus* repeatedly provides Clarissa Dalloway with a sense of consolation – but the very same passage fails to prevent Septimus from committing suicide. In a similar vein, the group of boys in *The Virgin Suicides* try to console the Lisbon girls with rock songs played to them over the phone, but hopeful lyrics prove insufficient in preventing the sisters from taking their lives. Likewise, though the recognition of shared suffering constitutes a vital element of emotional support – e.g. for Ahab and Pip in *Moby-Dick*, or for Alice Bell and Kelly Brown in *Union Street* – the varied outcomes in each of these cases suggest that other factors play an equally decisive part. Indeed, the argument in chapter four regarding *Absalom, Absalom!* suggests that therapeutic storytelling has the power to alleviate the symptoms of unbelonging, as well as to alert us to the roots of this condition, but that long-term improvement may require more than continual narrativization – including a willingness to engage in, and fight for, material changes to communal homes. Fiction, in short, has the power to console, to raise our awareness of hitherto unsuspected dimensions of human experience, and even to instill us with utopian hopes for a better and more homely future. Nevertheless, in the final analysis it is collective human agency – and not narratives of belonging alone – that will change the world and, perhaps, make it a more hospitable place.

Home-Making: Imaginary Solutions to Real-Life Contradictions

Let us take stock. The first section of the conclusion focused on genres as fields of knowledge that intersect with one another in literary texts, in a manner that is akin to an individual's multiple and potentially conflicting ties of loyalty and belonging. We then turned to suicide as an extreme expression of unbelonging, and though fiction may at times serve to alleviate alienation, it is also crucial to retain a realistic sense of the limits of fiction's transformative, therapeutic power. This latter point, in turn, requires us to reexamine the claim made in the introductory chapter that fictions are best understood as home-making practices. What the discussion of suicide forces us to state more clearly is that fiction constitutes an *attempt* to enhance our sense of belonging. More precisely, the fictional compromise *tries* to provide us with imaginary solutions to real-life contradictions – which not only leaves open the possibility that the form of a particular fictional compromise may be entirely unconvincing, but also acknowledges that even the most accomplished imaginary compromise may fail to have any palpable effect in a given real-life situation. Fiction is a home-making practice, and like any such practice it may very well fail. At the same time, this does not reduce the heuristic value of fiction for cultural analysis, as it is the formulation of a particular problem, rather than the success of its imaginary solution, that tells us most about historical pressures and cultural needs.

In the case of *Moby-Dick*, for instance, one key contradiction that the novel attempts to resolve is the clash, in the mid-nineteenth-century United States, between a political culture embracing the value of individualism, and social pressures on a steadily increasing fraction of the population toward economic dependence and conformity. More precisely, cultural ideals of independence and the free individual's pursuit of happiness conflicted sharply with the reality of increasing social inequality, the spread of standardized industrial production, and the concomitant disciplining of a growing workforce engaged in semi-skilled wage labor: "a form of dependency that seemed to contradict the republican principles on which the country had been founded" (McPherson 23). In terms of its story, *Moby-Dick* rejects the sovereign individualism of Ahab (who dies at the end of the novel), and instead sides with the conformist wage-laborer Ishmael (who survives the disaster to tell the tale). In terms of discourse or style, however, few literary texts are as idiosyncratic and non-conformist as *Moby-Dick*, and we can therefore say that the novel's form salvages the very 'extremist' individualism that it rejects on the level of the story. In this way, *Moby-Dick* attempts to have its cake and eat it: a (more or less) elegant imaginary solution to an intractable real-life problem.

The distinction between story and discourse also allows us to understand how *The Mill on the Floss* tries to reconcile a Victorian ideology of progress with a political system built on the so-called respect for tradition. On the one hand, the mid-nineteenth century constituted a period of relief in Victorian England: "the huge debts left by the wars against the French had not proved crippling, the working classes had not revolted, the Chartist movement of the 1830s and

1840s had collapsed" (Colin Matthew 8). In addition, the hitherto fitful – and possibly negative – development of workers' living standards first stabilized and then began to improve in the course of the 1850s (e.g. Floud et al. 162–163; Hoppen 78–79); the concept of 'evolutionary' (as opposed to revolutionary) progress "came to permeate every aspect of Victorian life and thought" (H.C.G. Matthew 523). However, British political culture was at the same time deeply averse to change, dominated by an aristocracy that was not only the richest in Europe (Osterhammel 1068), but that had also been able to maintain a socio-political position that was nearly as strong as it had been a hundred years earlier (Niedhart 39–40). More generally, a 'respect for tradition' was as strong a force as the belief in scientific and moral progress, and it is this conflict that lies at the heart of *The Mill on the Floss.* On the level of the story, Eliot's novel aligns itself squarely with the forces of progress (e.g. Stephen Guest), and either kills off or condemns to a childless, 'barren' existence all the characters who cling to the past (Mr. and Mrs. Tulliver, Maggie, Tom, and Philip). On the level of discourse, however, the narrator's nostalgia belies the story's endorsement of progress, and while the story's 'reality principle' works steadfastly and remorselessly towards Maggie's extinction, the novel's discourse increasingly abandons any signs of 'mature' ironic distance toward the female protagonist. It is a strained compromise, to be sure – but a compromise of sorts, nevertheless.

If *The Mill on the Floss* revolves in part around the conflict between faith in progress and respect for the past, then a key conflict in *Mrs. Dalloway* is the clash between, on the one hand, the freedom from interference, and, on the other, the freedom to belong. Woolf's novel, we saw in chapter two, revels in the experience of urban anonymity even as it associates modernist fragmentation with illness, trauma, and the continual misreading of some of its characters by others. More precisely, on the level of the novel's story it is Clarissa and the other members of the Dalloway circle who appreciate most fully the freedom of moving through the imperial city, while Septimus and Lucrezia are the characters who feel most isolated and beleaguered amongst London's teeming multitudes. At the same time, the sections focusing on the Dalloway circle are stylistically more conservative (i.e. closest to the model of classic realism), while the sections revolving around Septimus and his wife embrace most fully the urban aesthetics of modernist fragmentation. Put differently, on the level of the story the Dalloways are associated with the pleasure of solitary urban wanderings (i.e. the freedom from interference), while the story of Septimus and Lucrezia revolves around the lack of human connection (i.e. the freedom to belong). Stylistically, however, it is the sections centering on the Dalloways that emphasize connection and coherence in point of view, whereas Septimus and Lucrezia's perspective appears in free-floating combination with various and contiguous others. This chiastic structure creates a sense of formal balance – and thus attempts to reconcile, in imaginary form, the class conflict between the small social set of the Dalloways and the multitude of perspectives associated with Septimus and his Italian wife.

In *Absalom, Absalom!*, the real-life problem that only too clearly confronts the United States of the 1930s is the seemingly intractable history of racial conflict. And yet, while Faulkner's novel pits against each other conflicting interpretations and elaborations of this traumatic past (e.g. Miss Rosa's and Grandfather Compson's), shuttling back and forth from one level of time to another, its breathless, interminable sentences provide the novel with an underlying and unified stylistic rhythm. Using the terms developed in chapter four, we could say that the stylistic technique of uncanny narration, used throughout the novel, serves to reconcile the story's conflicting interpretations of the past, as each of the characters appears equally burdened by the novel's onerous syntax. However, the novel's thematic insistence on the crushing weight of history is in some ways mitigated by the ease with which the narrative shifts from one temporal level to the next. If, in short, Faulkner's story presents us with characters locked in historical conflict, the novel's discourse flows like one great single stream across periods and individuals, counteracting the story's centripetal forces.

In *Union Street*, the conflict between fragmentation and unity is important, too, but here it revolves more specifically around the conceptual nexus between human agency and class. On the one hand, the novel continually insists on the extent to which its working-class characters are the victims of social circumstances, determined by environmental forces far beyond their individual control. On the other hand, *Union Street* tries to overcome its protagonists' entrapment in a single, overarching social structure by breaking its story up into seven discursively discrete segments that, taken together, provide us with a synchronic panorama of simultaneously independent and interconnected lives. At the same time, the novel tries to reintroduce a sense of diachronic movement because an emphasis on synchrony threatens to dissolve history and, along with it, any room for human agency (i.e. if there is no horizon of temporal progression, then it is difficult to see how one could possibly construct a better future). As discussed in chapter five, *Union Street* attempts to overcome this potential deadlock by arranging its seven stories in such a way that its more or less synchronic 'story-time' is combined with a discursive 'life-time' progression from Kelly Brown, the youngest character, through to the oldest, Alice Bell. Barker's novel thus imaginatively opens up a space for historical transformation – at a time when the real-life industrial working-class of Thatcherite Britain was all too evidently in disarray (Marwick 153: "The overriding economic fact was the shrinkage of Britain's industrial base"; cf Harris 112–115).

The Virgin Suicides, finally, attempts to reconcile two conflicting interpretations of American history in the second half of the twentieth century. According to the first of these interpretations, the postwar years up until, roughly, 1963 not only saw the United States at the height of its economic power; the period was also a time of social stability and a broad political consensus directed against the evils of Soviet communism. Over the next decade or so, this consensus fell apart, as 'special interest groups' supposedly precipitated the country's material and moral decline, resulting in the culture wars that continued to cripple U.S. political culture in the early 1990s. According to a second, competing narrative, the 1950s were a period of mind-numbing conformism and widespread oppression of women, ethnic minorities, and everyone who could be considered 'deviant' or 'queer.' It was only in the 1960s that the new social movements began finally to challenge these hegemonic structures, leading to landmark civil rights legislation and culminating in the exposure of government corruption from Vietnam to Watergate. The economic downturn of the 1970s then paved the way for a resurgence of the political right, which remained in power until January 1993 – and thus until the beginning of the year in which *The Virgin Suicides* was published. While in the first narrative, identity politics appears as one symptom of what went wrong with the country, in the second it constitutes the very foundation of the nation's social and political progress. At the same time, the early 1970s feature as a negative watershed in both these conflicting narratives, and it is precisely at this point in time that the Lisbon sisters take their lives. The key traumatic event of Eugenides's novel is thus linked to a moment in U.S. history that symbolizes a kind of negative consensus. Moreover, while the characters who remain traumatized by these events are male, white, middle-aged heterosexuals (i.e. the social group most strongly associated with the first historical narrative), their representation as a group is formally analogous to the wounded collective subjectivity that underpins the projects of identity politics commonly linked to the second interpretation of the nation's history. In this way, *The Virgin Suicides* proposes an imaginary solution to the U.S. culture wars, which in real life were (and still are) far from abating.

Admittedly, none of the fictional compromises outlined above will hold up to critical scrutiny, as it is always possible to detect imbalances, contradictions, and questionable assumptions that undermine or at least problematize the imaginary solution that a given text proposes. However, to unravel a fictional compromise tends to require a considerable amount of time and interpretive effort. If one simply reads a text without thinking about it a great deal, then even a rough, makeshift compromise may work perfectly. Indeed, a lack of stringency and closure may in fact turn out to be an advantage because this renders the compromise more pliable and thus less likely to cause palpable ideological friction.[9] In addition, we need to bear in mind that, like the symbolism of dreams, literary fictions involve various kinds of displacement and condensation; they are overdetermined and may therefore simultanously fulfill various functions for one and the same reader, as well as different functions for different readers.

Nevertheless, if a given work of fiction enjoys widespread success, then it is at least plausible to assume that some aspect of the work speaks to a common social need. The intellectual labor of literary analysis may then help us to unearth this shared socio-cultural need – and, more importantly, allow us to define the underlying conflict(s) from which the need for a fictional compromise arises. In this way, fiction and literary criticism, together, assume a diagnostic function: unable to solve any real-life conflicts, they can – potentially – alert us to hitherto unrecognized social problems. And since we must first recognize a problem before we can attempt to solve it, the joyfully pointless game of fiction may at the same time have a more directly practical use. By alerting us to unacknowledged real-life contradictions, fiction and literary criticism may – just possibly – contribute in some small way to our efforts at making this world a more just, more welcoming, more homely place for all.

Leave-Taking

Let us not be deceived: as mortal creatures, we will never be fully at home in this world; no matter how strong our ties of belonging, they will always remain haunted by the repressed but ineluctable knowledge that death will one day rend them apart. At the same time, we are united in our finitude, and this shared vulnerability must serve as the starting point for any truly progressive politics.[10] Moreover, as noted in the discussion of *Moby-Dick* in chapter one, we must distinguish between, on the one hand, our human finitude as the precondition for alienation, and, on the other, alienation proper, which to a large extent derives from social arrangements that inadequately distribute the burdens of human existence (Richard Schmitt 46–51). Unlike the existential trauma of human mortality and incompleteness, social arrangements may in fact be ameliorated, in the hope that they will one day approach more closely the ideal of

9 See Franco Moretti's point that "hegemony doesn't need purity – it needs plasticity, camouflage, collusion" ("The Novel" 177).

10 Writing from a Jungian perspective, Edward F. Edinger similarly emphasizes that "[a]ll human relationship is based on the fact of human weakness" (129).

a society that makes claims on each according to his or her abilities, and that attempts to provide for everyone according to their needs (Marx, "Critique of the Gotha Program" 321).[11] In such a society, we would still not be completely at home, but freer to belong to one another as equals who might even feel like saying, before the time comes for the parting of the ways:

> It's wonderful to be here,
> It's certainly a thrill.
> You're such a lovely audience,
> We'd like to take you home with us,
> We'd love to take you home.
> (The Beatles, "Sgt. Pepper's Lonely Hearts Club Band")

In the meantime, for some of us at least, Marx's ideal of a society that is more atuned to the needs and abilities of each of its members remains the most inspiring fiction of home.[12]

---

11 "Jeder nach seinen Fähigkeiten, jedem nach seinen Bedürfnissen!" ("Kritik des Gothaer Programms 282).

12 In addition to the friends I have mentioned already, I would like to thank Daniela Landert and Nicole Studer Joho for allowing me to test even the oddest ideas during coffee breaks, lunches, and other more or less ill-suited occasions.

Bibliography

Primary Sources

Anderson, Sherwood. *Winesburg, Ohio.* 1919. New York: Modern Library, 2002.

Austen, Jane. *Mansfield Park.* 1814. Ed. Kathryn Sutherland. Updated ed. Penguin Classics. London: Penguin, 2003.

—. *Pride and Prejudice.* 1813. Ed. Vivien Jones. Penguin Classics. London: Penguin, 2003.

Barker, Pat. *Blow Your House Down.* 1984. Virago Modern Classics 415. London: Virago, [2002].

—. *The Man Who Wasn't There.* 1989. New York: Picador, 1998.

—. *Union Street.* 1982. *Union Street.* Virago Modern Classics 414. London: Virago, [1990].

Barrie, J. M. *Peter Pan.* 1904/1911. Ed. Anne Hiebert Alton. Broadview Editions. Peterborough: Broadview, 2011.

Brontë, Charlotte. *Jane Eyre.* 1847. Ed. Margaret Smith. New ed. Oxford World's Classics. OUP, 2000.

Close Encounters of the Third Kind. Dir. Steven Spielberg. 1977. *Unheimliche Begegnung der dritten Art.* Disc 1. DVD (Code 2). Columbia Tristar Home Entertainment 2001.

Conrad, Joseph. *Heart of Darkness: Complete, Authoritative Text with Biographical and Historical Contexts, Critical History, and Essays from Five Contemporary Critical Perspectives.* 1899. Ed. Ross. C. Murfin. 2nd ed. Case Studies in Contemporary Criticism. Boston: Bedford/St. Martin's, 1996.

Cunningham, Michael. *The Hours.* 1998. New York: Picador, 2002.

Defoe, Daniel. *Robinson Crusoe.* 1719. Ed. John Richetti. Penguin Classics. London: Penguin, 2001.

Dickens, Charles. *A Tale of Two Cities.* 1859. Ed. Richard Maxwell. Updated ed. Penguin Classics. London: Penguin, 2003.

—. *David Copperfield.* 1850. Ed. Jeremy Tambling. Rev. ed. Penguin Classics. London: Penguin, 2004.

—. *Great Expectations.* Ed. Margaret Cardwell. 1860–1861. The Clarendon Dickens. Oxford: Clarendon Press, 1993.

Dürrenmatt, Friedrich. *Der Verdacht: Ein Kriminalroman.* 1951. *Gesammelte Werke 4: Romane.* Paperback ed. Zürich: Diogenes, 1996. 119–265.

E. T.: The Extra-Terrestrial. Dir. Steven Spielberg. 1982. *E. T.: Der Ausserirdische.* Collector's ed. Disc 3. DVD (Code 2). Universal, 2002.

Eliot, George. *Middlemarch: An Authoritative Text, Backgrounds, Criticism.* 1871–1872. Ed. Bert G. Hornback. Norton Critical Editions. New York: W. W. Norton, 2000.

—. *The Mill on the Floss: An Authoritative Text, Backgrounds and Contemporary Reactions, Criticism.* 1860. Ed. Carol T. Christ. Norton Critical Edition. New York: W. W. Norton, 1994.

Eugenides, Jeffrey. *The Virgin Suicides.* 1993. London: Bloomsbury, 2002.

Faulkner, William. *Absalom, Absalom!* 1936. Vintage International ed. New York: Vintage, 1990.

—. *The Sound and the Fury.* 1929. Vintage International ed. New York: Vintage, 1990.

—. "Wash." 1934. *Collected Stories.* New York: Vintage, 1995. 535–549.

Fielding, Henry. *The History of Tom Jones.* Ed. R. P. C. Mutter. Penguin Classics. London: Penguin, 1985.

Forster, E. M. *Howards End.* 1910. Ed. Oliver Stallybrass. Penguin Classics. London: Penguin, 2000.

Goethe, Johann Wolfgang von. *Wilhelm Meister's Apprenticeship.* 1795 / 1796. Ed. and trans. Eric A. Blackall, in cooperation with Victor Lange. Vol. 9 of *Goethe: The Collected Works.* Princeton Paperbacks. Princeton: Princeton UP, 1995.

—. *Wilhelm Meisters Lehrjahre.* 1795 / 96. München: Deutscher Taschenbuch Verlag, 2004.

Hardy, Thomas. *Far from the Madding Crowd.* 1874. Ed. Suzanne B. Falck-Yi. Oxford World's Classics. Oxford: OUP, 2002.

Hawthorne, Nathaniel. *The Scarlet Letter.* Penguin English Library. London: Penguin, 2012.

Heim, Scott. *Mysterious Skin.* 1995. New York: Harper Perennial, 1996.

Homer. *The Iliad.* Trans. Anthony Verity. Oxford World's Classics. Oxford: OUP, 2012.

Hurston, Zora Neale. *Their Eyes Were Watching God.* 1937. London: Virago, 1986.

Ishiguro, Kazuo. *The Remains of the Day.* 1989. London: Faber and Faber, 1996.

Joyce, James. *Dubliners.* 1914. Penguin Popular Classics. London: Penguin, 1996.

—. *Ulysses.* 1922. London: Penguin, 1992.

Kerouac, Jack. *On the Road.* 1957. Penguin Classics. London: Penguin, 2000.

Lawrence, D. H. *Lady Chatterley's Lover.* 1928. *Lady Chatterley's Lover; A Propos of Lady Chatterley's Lover.* By D. H. Lawrence. Ed. Michael Squires. Penguin Classics. London: Penguin, 2006. 3–302.

Lucas, Annie. *The City and the Castle: A Story of the Reformation in Switzerland.* London: T. Nelson and Sons, 1876.

Mathison, Melissa. "A Boy's Life: The Annotated, Illustrated Screenplay." *E. T.: The Extra-Terrestrial: From Concept to Classic.* New York: Newmarket Press, 2002. 43–148.

Melville, Herman. *Moby-Dick: An Authoritative Text, Before Moby-Dick: International Controversy, Reviews and Letters by Melville, Analogues and Sources, Reviews of Moby-Dick, Criticism.* 1851. Ed. Hershel Parker and Harrison Hayford. 2nd ed. Norton Critical Edition. New York: W. W. Norton, 2002.

Milton, John. *Paradise Lost.* 1667. Ed. Christopher Ricks. Penguin Classics. London: Penguin, 1989.

Morrison, Toni. *Beloved.* 1987. New York: Plume, 1998.

Poe, Edgar Allan. "The Fall of the House of Usher." 1839. *The Complete Illustrated Tales of Edgar Allan Poe.* London: Bounty Books, 2004. 51–66.

—. "The Man of the Crowd." 1840. *The Complete Illustrated Tales of Edgar Allan Poe.* London: Bounty Books, 2004. 211–217.

Proulx, Annie. "Brokeback Mountain." 1997. *Close Range: Wyoming Stories.* New York: Scribner, 1999. 253–283.

Rhys, Jean. *Wide Sargasso Sea.* 1966. London: Penguin, 1968.

Richardson, Samuel. *Clarissa: or, The History of a Young Lady.* 1748. 4 vols. Everyman's Library. London: Dent, 1965.

Rushdie, Salman. *Midnight's Children.* 1980. London: Penguin, 1991.

Scott, Walter. *Waverley: or, 'Tis Sixty Years Since.* 1814. Ed. Clare Lamont. Oxford World's Classics. Oxford: OUP, 1998.

Shakespeare, William. *As You Like It.* Ed. Juliet Dusinberre. The Arden Shakespeare, Third Series. London: Thomson Learning, 2006.

—. *Cymbeline.* Ed. John Dover Wilson. The Cambridge Dover Wilson Shakespeare. Cambridge: CUP, 2009.

—. *Hamlet.* Ed. Ann Thompson and Neil Taylor. The Arden Shakespeare: Third Series. London: Thomson Learning, 2006.

—. *Macbeth.* Ed. Nicholas Brooke. The Oxford Shakespeare. Oxford: OUP, 1990.

Silko, Leslie Marmon. *Ceremony.* 1977. New York: Penguin, 1986.

Sinha, Indra. *Animal's People.* 2007. New York: Simon & Schuster, 2009.

Stendahl. *Le rouge et le noir.* 1830. Ed. Michel Crouzet. Paris: Flammarion, 1964.

—. *The Red and the Black: A Chronicle of the Nineteenth Century.* 1830. Ed. Roger Pearson. Trans. Catherine Slater. Oxford World's Classics. Oxford: OUP, 1998.

Stoker, Bram. *Dracula.* 1897. Ed. Maurice Hindle. Penguin Classics. London: Penguin, 1993.

The Day the Earth Stood Still. Dir. Robert Wise. 1951. *Der Tag, an dem die Erde still stand.* Cinema Premium. DVD (Code 2). Twentieth Century Fox Home Entertainment, 2005.

The Virgin Suicides. Dir. Sophia Coppola. 1999. DVD (Code 2). Mediacs 2002.

Unsworth, Barry. *Morality Play.* 1995. Norton Paperback Fiction. New York: W. W. Norton, 1996.

Wilde, Oscar. *The Importance of Being Earnest: A Trivial Comedy for Serious People.* 1895. *Lady Windermere's Fan; Salomé; A Woman of No Importance; An Ideal Husband; The Importance of Being Earnest.* Ed. Peter Raby. Oxford World's Classics. Oxford: OUP, 1998. 247–307.

—. *The Picture of Dorian Gray.* 1890. Ed. John Bristow. Oxford World's Classics. Oxford: OUP, 2006.

Woolf, Virginia. *Mrs. Dalloway.* 1925. Ed. Stella McNichol. Penguin Classics. London: Penguin, 2000.

—. *Orlando: A Biography.* 1928. Ed. Rachel Bowlby. Oxford World's Classics. Oxford: OUP, 1998.

Secondary Sources

Abel, Elizabeth. "Narrative Structure(s) and Female Development: The Case of *Mrs. Dalloway.*" 1983. *Virginia Woolf's Mrs. Dalloway.* Ed. Harold Bloom. Modern Critical Interpretations. New York: Chelsea House, 1988. 103–125.

Achebe, Chinua. "An Image of Africa." *The Massachusetts Review* 18.4 (1977): 782–794.

Ahmad, Aijaz. *In Theory: Nations, Classes, Literatures.* 1992. Radical Thinkers 25. London: Verso, 2008.

Alcalá, Roberto del Valle. "Crisis, Reproduction, and Resistance in Pat Barker's *Union Street* and *Blow Your House Down.*" *LIT: Literature, Interpretation, Theory* 26 (2015): 194–214.

Alexander, William. "Send 'Em Back to Where They Came from: Another Look at *E.T.*" *North Dakota Quarterly* 51.3 (1983): 24–34.

Allatson, Paul. "Mexican American Stereotypes." *The Greenwood Encylopedia of Multiethnic American Literature.* Ed. Emmanuel S. Nelson. Vol. 3. Westport: Greenwood Press, 2005. 1484–1486.

Allen, Kristie M. "Habit in George Eliot's *The Mill on the Floss.*" *Studies in English Literature, 1500–1900* 50.4 (2010): 831–852.

Althusser, Louis. "Ideology and Ideological State Apparatuses (Notes towards an Investigation)." 1969. *Lenin and Philosophy and Other Essays.* Trans. Ben Brewster. New York: Monthly Review Press, 1971. 127–186.

Altman, Rick. *A Theory of Narrative.* New York: Columbia UP, 2008.

Alton, Anne Hiebert, ed. *Peter Pan.* 1904 / 1911. By J. M. Barrie. Broadview Editions. Peterborough: Broadview, 2011.

Amigoni, David. *The English Novel and Prose Narrative.* Elements of Literature. Edinburgh: Edinburgh UP, 2000.

"[An Ill-Compounded Mixture]." 1851. *Moby-Dick: An Authoritative Text, Before Moby-Dick: International Controversy, Reviews and Letters by Melville, Analogues and Sources, Reviews of Moby-Dick, Criticism.* Ed. Hershel Parker and Harrison Hayford. 2nd ed. Norton Critical Edition. New York: W. W. Norton, 2002. 597–598.

Anderson, Benedict. *Imagined Communities: Reflections on the Origin and Spread of Nationalism.* 1983. Rev. ed. London: Verso, 1991.

Anner, John. Introduction. *Beyond Identity Politics: Emerging Social Justice Movements in Communities of Color.* Ed. John Anner. Cambridge: South End Press, 1996. 5–14.

Antonsich, Marco. "Searching for Belonging: An Analytical Framework." *Geography Compass* 4.6 (2010): 644–659.

Arata, Stephen D. "The Occidental Tourist: *Dracula* and the Anxiety of Reverse Colonization." *Victorian Studies* 33.4 (1990): 621–645.

Archer, Jayne Elizabeth, Richard Marggraf Turley and Howard Thomas. "'Moving Accidents by Flood and Field': The Arable and Tidal Worlds of George Eliot's *The Mill and the Floss.*" *ELH* 82.2 (2015): 701–728.

Armstrong, Nancy. *Desire and Domestic Fiction: A Political History of the Novel.* Oxford: OUP, 1987.

Armstrong, Philip. "'Leviathan Is a Skein of Networks': Translations of Nature and Culture in *Moby-Dick.*" *ELH* 71 (2004): 1039–1063.

Arnold, Matthew. *Culture and Anarchy.* 1867–1868. Ed. Jane Garnett. Oxford World's Classics. Oxford: OUP, 2006.

Assmann, Jan. *Cultural Memory and Early Civilization: Writing, Remembrance, and Political Imagination.* 1992. Cambridge: CUP, 2011.

—. *Das kulturelle Gedächtnis: Schrift, Erinnerung und politische Identität in führen Hochkulturen.* C.H. Beck Kulturwissenschaft. München: C.H. Beck, 1992.

Bachelard, Gaston. *The Poetics of Space.* 1958. Trans. Maria Jolas. New York: Penguin, 2014.

Bade, Klaus J. *Europa in Bewegung: Migration vom späten 18. Jahrhundert bis zur Gegenwart.* 2000. Europa Bauen. München: C.H. Beck, 2002.

Bakhtin, Mikhail. "Discourse in the Novel." 1935. *The Dialogic Imagination: Four Essays.* 1975. Ed. Michael Holquist. Trans. Caryl Emerson and Michael Holquist. University of Texas Press Slavic Series 1. Austin: University of Texas Press, 1981. 259–422.

—. "Forms of Time and the Chronotope in the Novel: Notes towards a Historical Poetics." 1937. *The Dialogic Imagination: Four Essays.* 1975. Ed. Michael Holquist. Trans. Caryl Emerson and Michael Holquist. University of Texas Press Slavic Series 1. Austin: University of Texas Press, 1981. 84–258.

Baldick, Chris. *The Modern Movement: 1910–1940.* The Oxford English Literary History 10. Oxford: OUP, 2004.

Barrett, Eileen. "Unmasking Lesbian Passion: The Inverted World of *Mrs. Dalloway.*" *Virginia Woolf: Lesbian Readings.* Ed. Eileen Barrett and Patricia Cramer. The Cutting Edge: Lesbian Life and Culture. New York: New York UP, 1997. 146–164.

Barrie, Thomas. *House and Home: Cultural Contexts, Ontological Roles.* London: Routledge, 2017.

Barthes, Roland. *Mythologies.* 1957. Trans. Annette Lavers. Vintage Classics. London: Vintage, 1993. 109–159.

Basseler, Michael. "Theories and Typologies of the Short Story." *A History of the American Short Story: Genres – Developments – Model Interpretations.* Ed. Ansgar Nünning and Michael Basseler. WVT-Handbücher zum literaturwissenschaftlichen Studium 14. Trier: WVT Wissenschaftlicher Verlag Trier, 2001. 41–64.

Baucom, Ian. *Out of Place: Englishness, Empire, and the Locations of Identity.* Princeton: Princeton UP, 1999.

Baudelaire, Charles. "The Painter of Modern Life." 1863. *The Painter of Modern Life and Other Essay.* Ed. and trans. Jonathan Mayne. London: Phaidon, 1964. 1–40.

Baudelot, Christian and Roger Establet. *Suicide: The Hidden Side of Modernity.* 2006. Trans. David Macey. London: Polity, 2008.

Bayly, C. A. *The Birth of the Modern World, 1780–1914: Global Connections and Comparisons.* The Blackwell History of the World. Malden: Blackwell, 2004.

Beaumont, Matthew. *Nightwalking: A Nocturnal History of London.* London: Verso, 2015.

—. "Reclaiming Realism." Introduction *Adventures in Realism.* Ed. Matthew Beaumont. Malden: Blackwell, 2007. 1–12.

Bednik, Anna. "Bataille pour l'uranium au Niger." *Le monde diplomatique* June 2006: 16. [Translation available at www.pambazuka.org / en / category / socialmovements / 49 568, 18 August 2008.]

Bekhta, Natalya. "We-Narratives: The Distinctiveness of Collective Narration." *Narrative* 25.2 (2017): 164–181.

Belsey, Catherine. *Critical Practice.* 1980. 2nd ed. New Accents. London: Routledge, 2002.

Bender, Barbara. Introduction. *Contested Landscapes: Movement, Exile and Place.* Ed. Barbara Bender and Margot Winer. Oxford: Berg, 2001. 1–18.

Benjamin, Walter. *Charles Baudelaire: A Lyric Poet in the Era of High Capitalism.* London: Verso, 1997.

—. *Charles Baudelaire: Ein Lyriker im Zeitalter des Hochkapitalismus.* Suhrkamp Taschenbuch Wissenschaft. Frankfurt am Main: Suhrkamp, 1974.

—. "Eduard Fuchs, Collector and Historian." *The Work of Art in the Age of Its Technological Reproducibility and Other Writings on Media.* Ed. Michael W. Jennings, Brigid Doherty, and Thomas Y. Levin. Cambridge: Harvard UP, 2008. 116–157.

—. "Eduard Fuchs, der Sammler und der Historiker." *Zeitschrift für Sozialforschung* 6 (1937): 346–381.

Bennett, Andrew and Nicholas Royle. *Introduction to Literature, Criticism, and Theory.* 1995. 4th ed. Harlow: Pearson Longman, 2009.

Berlin, Isaiah. "Two Concepts of Liberty." 1958. *Four Essays on Liberty.* Oxford: OUP, 1969. 118–172.

Berman, Jeffrey. *Narcissism and the Novel.* New York: New York UP, 1990.

Berman, Marshall. *All That Is Solid Melts into Air: The Experience of Modernity.* New York: Verso, 1981.

Bezanson, Walter E. "*Moby-Dick*: Work of Art." 1953. *Moby-Dick: An Authoritative Text, Before Moby-Dick: International Controversy, Reviews and Letters by Melville, Analogues and Sources, Reviews of Moby-Dick, Criticism.* Ed. Hershel Parker and Harrison Hayford. 2nd ed. Norton Critical Edition. New York: W.W. Norton, 2002. 641–657.

Bhabha, Homi K. "Arrivals and Departures." Preface. *Home, Exile, Homeland: Film, Media, and the Politics of Place.* Ed. Hamid Naficy. New York: Routledge, 1999. vii – xii.

Biro, Andrew. *Denaturalizing Ecological Politics : Alienation from Nature from Rousseau to the Frankfurt School and Beyond.* Toronto: University of Toronto Press, 2005.

Blackburn, Robin. *The American Crucible: Slavery, Emancipation and Human Rights.* London: Verso, 2011.

Blanchard, Margaret. "Socialization in *Mrs. Dalloway.*" *Marxist Interpretations of Mailer, Woolf, Wright and Others.* Spec. issue of *College English* 34.2 (1972): 287–305.

Blickle, Peter. *Heimat: A Critical Theory of the German Idea of Homeland.* Studies in German Literature, Linguistics, and Culture. Rochester: Camden House, 2002.

Blight, David W. *Race and Reunion: The Civil War in American Memory.* Cambridge: Belknap Press of Harvard UP, 2001.

Blum, John M. et al. *The National Experience: A History of the United States.* 8th ed. Fort Worth: Harcourt Brace Jovanovich, 1993.

Blunt, Alison. *Domicile and Diaspora: Anglo-Indian Women and the Spatial Politics of Home.* RGS-IGB Book Series. Malden: Blackwell, 2005.

Blunt, Alison and Robyn Dowling. *Home.* Key Ideas in Geography. London: Routledge, 2006.

Bockting, Ineke. "*Absalom, Absalom!*" *A William Faulkner Encyclopedia.* Ed. Robert W. Hamblin and Charles A. Peek. Westport: Greenwood Press, 1999. 1–4.

Bollinger, Laurel. "'That Triumvirate Mother-Woman': Narrative Authority and Interdividuality in *Absalom, Absalom!*" *LIT: Literature, Interpretation, Theory* 9 (1998): 197–223.

Booker, M. Keith. *Alternate Americas: Science Fiction Film and American Culture.* Westport: Praeger Publishers, 2006.

—. *Techniques of Subversion in Modern Literature: Transgression, Abjection, and the Carnivalesque.* Gainesville: University of Florida Press, 1991.

Borsay, Peter. "The Culture of Improvement." *The Eighteenth Century: 1688–1815.* Ed. Paul Langford. Short History of the British Isles. Oxford: OUP, 2002. 183–210.

Botting, Fred. *Gothic.* New Critical Idiom. London: Routledge, 1996.

Boumelha, Penny. "George Eliot and the End of Realism." *Women Reading Women's Writing.* Ed. Sue Roe. Brighton: Harvester Press, 1987. 15–35.

Bowlby, Rachel. “Thinking forward through Mrs. Dalloway’s Daughter.” 1988. *Mrs. Dalloway and To the Lighthouse: Virginia Woolf.* Ed. Su Reid. New Casebooks. New York: St. Martin’s Press, 1993. 142–155.

Boym, Svetlana. *The Future of Nostalgia.* New York: Basic Books, 2001.

Bradshaw, David. Introduction. *Mrs. Dalloway.* By Virginia Woolf. Ed. David Bradshaw. Oxford World’s Classics. Oxford: OUP, 2000. xi – xlv.

Brannigan, John. *Pat Barker.* Contemporary British Novelists. Manchester: Manchester UP, 2005.

Brecht, Bertolt. “Dialektik und Verfremdung.” *Schriften zum Theater I.* Vol. 15 of *Gesammelte Werke.* Frankfurt am Main: Suhrkamp, 1967. 360–361.

Bredbeck, Gregory. Sodomy and Interpretation: Marlowe to Milton. Ithaca: Cornell UP, 1991.

Bremmer, Jan N. “Narkissos: Mythologie.” *Der neue Pauly: Enzyklopädie der Antike.* Ed. Hubert Cancik and Helmuth Schneider. Vol. 8. Stuttgart: Metzler, 2000. 712–713.

Briggs, Julia. *Reading Virginia Woolf.* Edinburgh: Edinburgh UP, 2006.

Bryson, Bill. *At Home: A Short History of Private Life.* New York: Doubleday, 2010.

Bronfen, Elisabeth. *Home in Hollywood: The Imaginary Geography of Cinema.* Film and Culture. New York: Columbia UP, 2004.

Brooks, Cleanth. *William Faulkner: The Yoknapatawpha Country.* New Haven: Yale UP, 1963.

—. *William Faulkner: Towards Yoknapatawpha and Beyond.* New Haven: Yale UP, 1978.

Brophy, Sarah. “Working-Class Women, Labor, and the Problem of Community in *Union Street* and *Liza’s England.*” *Critical Perspectives on Pat Barker.* Ed. Sharon Monteith et al. Columbia: University of South Carolina Press, 2005. 24–39.

Brower, Jordan. “*The Mill on the Floss,* Riparian Law, and the Difficulty of Judgment.” *ELH* 83.1 (2016): 211–232.

Bruhm, Steven. *Reflecting Narcissus: A Queer Aesthetic.* Minneapolis: University of Minnesota Press, 2001.

Bryan, Patrick E. *The Haitian Revolution and Its Effects.* Heinemann CXC History. Oxford: Heinemann, 1984.

Bryant, John. “*Moby-Dick* as Revolution.” *The Cambridge Companion to Herman Melville.* Ed. Robert S. Levine. Cambridge Companions to Literature. Cambridge: CUP, 1998. 65–90.

Bryson, Bill. *At Home: A Short History of Private Life.* New York: Doubleday, 2010.

Buck-Morss, Susan. *Hegel, Haiti, and Universal History.* Illuminations: Cultural Formations of the Americas. Pittsburgh: University of Pittsburgh Press, 2009.

Buckley, Jerome Hamilton. *Seasons of Youth: The Bildungsroman from Dickens to Golding.* Cambridge: Harvard UP, 1974.

Buell, Lawrence. "The Unkillable Dream of the Great American Novel: *Moby-Dick* as Test Case." *American Literary History* 20.1–2 (2008): 132–155.
Burton, Antoinette M. *Burdens of History: British Feminists, Indian Women, and Imperial Culture, 1865–1915.* Chapel Hill: The University of North Caroline Press, 1994.
Butler, Jeffrey, Robert I. Rotberg and John Adams. *The Black Homelands of South Africa: The Political and Economic Development of Bophuthatswana and KwaZulu.* 1977. Paperback ed. Perspectives on Southern Africa 21. Berkeley: University of California Press, 1978
Cardwell, Margaret. Introduction. *Great Expectations.* By Charles Dickens. Ed. Margaret Cardwell. The Clarendon Dickens. Oxford: Clarendon Press, 1993. xiii – lxvii.
Carlson, Julia. "The Solitary Traveller in *Mrs. Dalloway.*" *Virginia Woolf: A Collection of Critical Essays.* Ed. Thomas S. W. Lewis. New York: McGraw-Hill, 1975. 56–62.
Carr, Helen. "Virginia Woolf, Empire and Race." *The Cambridge Companion to Virigina Woolf.* Ed. Susan Sellers. 2nd ed. Cambridge Companions to Literature. Cambridge: CUP, 2010. 197–213.
Carter, Roland and John McRae. *The Routledge History of Literature in English: Britain and Ireland.* 1997. 2nd ed. London: Routledge, 2001.
Carter, Steven R. *Hansberry's Drama: Commitment amid Complexity.* Urbana: University of Illinois Press, 1991.
Cashden, Elizabeth. "Spatial Organization and Habitat Use." *Evolutionary Ecology and Human Behavior.* Ed. Eric Alden Smith and Bruce Winterhalder. Foundations of Human Behavior. New Brunswick: Transaction, 1992. 237–267.
Castle, Gregory. *Reading the Modernist Bildungsroman.* Gainesville: University of Florida Press, 2006.
Ciocoi-Pop, Ana-Blanca. "Suicide as Affirmation and Gender as a Conscious Choice: The Deconstruction of Identity in Jeffrey Eugenides' Major Novels." *American, British and Canadian Studies* 10 (2008): 80–90.
Cirlot, Juan Eduardo. *A Dictionary of Symbols.* Trans. Jack Sage. London: Routledge & Kegan Paul 1962.
Cobley, Paul. *Narrative.* New Critical Idiom. London: Routledge, 2001.
Cohen, Margaret. "The Chronotopes of the Sea." *Forms and Themes.* Vol. 2 of *The Novel.* Ed. Franco Moretti. Paperback ed. Princeton: Princeton UP, 2007. 647–666.
—. *The Novel and the Sea.* Translation / Transnation. Princeton: Princeton UP, 2010.
Collado-Rodríguez, Francisco. "Back to Myth and Ethical Compromise: García Márquez's Traces on Jeffrey Eugenides's *The Virgin Suicides.*" *Atlantis* 27.2 (2005): 27–40.
Conboy, Martin. *Journalism: A Critical History.* London: SAGE, 2004.
Coupeau, Steeve. *The History of Haiti.* The Greenwood History of the Modern Nations. Westport: Greenwood Press, 2008.

Coyne, Richard and Adrian Snodgrass. *Interpretation in Architecture: Design as a Way of Thinking*. Oxon: Routledge, 2006.

Daunton, Martin. "Society and Economic Life." *The Nineteenth Century: The British Isles: 1815–1901*. Ed. Colin Matthew. Short Oxford History of the British Isles. Oxford: OUP, 2000. 41–82.

Davis, Philip. *The Victorians: 1830–1880*. The Oxford English Literary History 8. Oxford: OUP, 2002.

Davis, Rocío G. "Asian American and Asian Canadian Short-Story Cycles." Introduction. *Transcultural Reinventions: Asian American and Asian Canadian Short-Story Cycles*. Ed. Rocío G. Davis. Toronto: TSAR, 2001. 1–26.

Davis, Thadious M. "Race and Region." *The Columbia History of the American Novel*. Ed. Emory Elliott. New York: Columbia UP, 1991. 407–436.

de Vries, Ad. *Dictionary of Symbols and Imagery*. Amsterdam: North-Holland, 1974.

Debord, Guy. *Society of the Spectacle*. 1967. Trans. Ken Knabb. London: Rebel Press, 1983.

Deirdre, David. "Maggie Tulliver's Desire." 1987. *The Mill on the Floss: An Authoritative Text, Backgrounds and Contemporary Reactions, Criticism*. Ed. Carol T. Christ. Norton Critical Edition. New York: W.W. Norton, 1994. 595–609.

Delanty, Gerard. *Community*. Key Ideas. London: Routledge, 2003.

Deleuze, Gilles. *Difference and Repetition*. 1968. London: Continuum, 2004.

Deleuze, Gilles and Félix Guattari. 1980. *A Thousand Plateaus: Capitalism and Schizophrenia*. London: Continuum, 2004.

DeMeester, Karen. "Trauma and Recovery in Virginia Woolf's *Mrs. Dalloway*." *Modern Fiction Studies* 44.3 (1998): 649–673.

Derrida, Jacques. "On Cosmopolitanism." 1997. *On Cosmopolitanism and Forgiveness*. Thinking in Action. London: Routledge, 2001. 1–24.

—. *Specters of Marx: The State of Debt, the Work of Mourning, and the New International*. 1993. Trans. Peggy Kamuf. Routledge Classics. New York: Routledge, 2006.

Deutsch, Phyllis. "*E. T.*: The Ultimate Patriarch." *Jump Cut* 28 (1983): 12–13. 9 April 2010 <http://www.ejumpcut.org/archive/onlinessays/JC28folder/ET.html>.

Dias, Jill. "Portugal: Empire Building in the Old World and the New." *The Age of Empires*. Ed. Robert Aldrich. London; Thames & Hudson, 2007. 68–91.

DiBattista, Maria. "*Mrs. Dalloway*: Virginia Woolf's Memento Mori." 1980. *Clarissa Dalloway*. Harold Bloom, ed. Major Literary Characters. New York: Chelsea House, 1990. 37–68.

Dillon, Elizabeth Maddock and Michael J. Drexler. "Haiti and the Early United States, Entwined." Introduction. *The Haitian Revolution and the Early United States*. Eds. Elizabeth Maddoch Dillon and Michael J. Drexler. Philadelphia: U of Pennsylvania P, 2016. 1–15.

Dimock, Wai-chee. "Genres as Fields of Knowledge." *PMLA* 122.5 (2007): 1377–1388.

Dines, Martin. "Suburban Gothic and the Ethnic Uncanny in Jeffrey Eugenides's *The Virgin Suicides*." *Journal of American Studies* 46 (2012): 959–975.

Dollimore, Jonathan. *Death, Desire and Loss in Western Culture.* New York: Routledge, 1998.

Doroholschi, Claudia Ioana. "Viewing Trip: Point of View and Meaning in the Novels of Jeffrey Eugenides." *Romanian Journal of English Studies* 6 (2009): 183–191.

Douglas, Mary. *Purity and Danger.* 1966. Routledge Classics. London: Routledge, 2002.

—. "The Idea of Home: A Kind of Space." *Home: A Place in the World.* Ed. Arien Mack. New York: New York UP, 1993. 261–281.

Dowling, David. *Mrs. Dalloway: Mapping Streams of Consciousness.* Twayne's Masterworks Studies 67. Boston: Twayne, 1991.

Drescher, Seymour. "Divergent Paths: The Anglo-American Abolitions of the Atlantic Slave Trade." *Migration, Trade, and Slavery in an Expanding World: Essays in Honor of Pieter Emmer.* Ed. Wim Klooster. European Expansion and Indigenous Response 2. Leiden: Koninklijke Brill, 259–288.

Du Bois, W. E. B. *The Suppression of the African Slave-Trade to the United States of America, 1638–1870.* 1896. *Writings: The Suppression of the African Slave Trade; The Souls of Black Folk; Dusk of Dawn; Essays and Articles.* By W. E. B. Du Bois. New York: The Library of America, 1986. 1–356.

Duck, Leigh Anne. "From Colony to Empire: Postmodern Faulkner." *Global Faulkner: Faulkner and Yoknapatawpha, 2006.* Ed. Annette Trefzer and Ann J. Abadie. Proceedings of the 33rd Annual Faulkner and Yoknapatawpha Conference, Oxford, UK, 23–27 July 2006. Jackson: UP of Mississippi, 2009. 24–42.

Duncan, Ian. "*Waverley* (Walter Scott, 1814)." *Forms and Themes.* Vol. 2 of *The Novel.* Ed. Franco Moretti. Princeton: Princeton UP, 2007. 173–180.

Dupre, Daniel S. "The South in the New Nation, 1790–1824." *A Companion to the American South.* 2002. Ed. John B. Boles. Paberback ed. Blackwell Companions to American History 3. Malden: Blackwell, 2004. 85–102.

Durer, Christopher S. "Mocking the 'Grand Programme': Irony and after in *Moby Dick*." *Rocky Mountain Review of Language and Literature* 36.4 (1982): 249–258.

Durkheim, Emile. *De la division du travail social.* 1893. 6th ed. Paris: Quadrige / PUF, 2004.

—. *The Division of Labor in Society.* 1893. New York: The Free Press, 1997.

Duyvendak, Jan Willem. *The Politics of Home: Belonging and Nostalgia in Europe and the United States.* Basingstoke: Palgrave Macmillan, 2011.

Eagleton, Terry. *Across the Pond: An Englishman's View of America.* New York: W. W. Norton, 2013.

—. *After Theory.* New York: Basic Books, 2003.

—. *Heathcliff and the Great Hunger: Studies in Irish Culture.* London: Verso, 1995.
—. *Literary Theory: An Introduction.* 1983. Anniversary ed. Minneapolis: University of Minnesota Press, 2008.
—. "Nationalism: Irony and Commitment." 1988. *Nationalism, Colonialism, and Literature.* By Terry Eagleton, Fredric Jameson and Edward Said. A Field Day Company Book. Minneapolis: University of Minnesota Press, 1990. 23–39.
—. *Sweet Violence: The Idea of the Tragic.* Malden: Blackwell, 2003.
—. *The English Novel: An Introduction.* Malden: Blackwell, 2005.
—. *The Idea of Culture.* Blackwell Manifestos. Malden: Blackwell, 2000.
—. *How to Read Literature.* Yale: Yale UP, 2013.
—. *Trouble with Strangers: A Study of Ethics.* Malden: Wiley-Blackwell, 2009.
Eco, Umberto. "Excess and History in Hugo's *Ninety-Three*." *Forms and Themes.* Vol. 2 of *The Novel.* Ed. Franco Moretti. Paperback ed. Princeton: Princeton UP, 2007. 274–294.
Edinger, Edward F. *Melville's Moby-Dick: An American Nekyia.* 1976. Studies in Jungian Psychology by Jungian Analysts 69. Toronto: Inner City Books, 1995.
Edwards, Jason. *Eve Kosofsky Sedgwick.* Routledge Critical Thinkers. London: Routledge, 2009.
Edwards, Lee R. "War and Roses: The Politics of *Mrs. Dalloway.*" 1977. *Clarissa Dalloway.* Ed. Harold Bloom. Major Literary Characters. New York: Chelsea House, 1990. 99–112.
Egan, Ken Jr. *The Riven Home: Narrative Rivalry in the American Renaissance.* Selinsgrove: Susquehanna UP, 1997.
Ellis, Steve. *Virginia Woolf and the Victorians.* Cambridge: CUP, 2007.
Ellison, David A., ed. *Home.* Spec. issue of *The South Atlantic Quarterly* 108.1 (2009).
Emerson, Ralph Waldo. "History." 1841. *Nature and Selected Essays.* Ed. Larzer Ziff. Penguin Classics. New York: Penguin, 2003. 149–173.
—. "Self-Reliance." 1841. *Nature and Selected Essays.* Ed. Larzer Ziff. Penguin Classics. New York: Penguin, 2003. 175–203.
—. "The Transcendentalist." 1842. *Nature and Selected Essays.* Ed. Larzer Ziff. Penguin Classics. New York: Penguin, 2003. 239–258.
Engel, John D. et al. *Narrative in Health Care: Healing Patients, Practitioners, Profession, and Community.* Oxon: Radcliffe, 2008.
Engels, Frederick. *Die Lage der arbeitenden Klasse in England: Nach eigner Anschuung und authentischen Quellen.* Leipzig: Otto Wigand, 1845.
—. *The Condition of the Working Class in England.* 1845. Ed. David McLellan. Oxford World's Classics. Oxford: OUP, 1999.
Entzminger, Betina. " 'Listen to Them Being Ghosts': Rosa's Words of Madness That Quentin Can't Hear." *College Literature* 25.2 (1998): 108–120.

Esty, Jed. *A Shrinking Island: Modernism and National Culture in England.* Princeton: Princeton UP, 2004.

Evetts-Secker, Josephine. *At Home in the Language of the Soul: Exploring Jungian Discourse and Psyche's Grammer of Transformation.* New Orleans: Spring Journal Books, 2012.

Falk, Francesca. *Eine gestische Geschichte der Grenze: Wie der Liberalismus an der Grenze an seine Grenzen kommt.* München: Wilhelm Fink, 2011.

Fanning, Susan Garbarini. "'Kings of the Upside-Down World': Challenging White Hegemony in *Moby-Dick.*" *"Ungraspable Phantom": Essays on* Moby-Dick. Ed. John Bryant, Mary K. Bercaw Edwards and Timothy Marr. Kent: Kent State UP, 2006. 209–223.

Fargnoli, A. Nicholas, Michael Golay and Robert W. Hamblin. *Critical Companion to William Faulkner: A Literary Reference to His Life and Work.* New York: Facts on File, 2008.

Felluga, Dino Franco. *Critical Theory: Key Concepts.* Routledge Key Guides. London: Routledge, 2015.

Ferber, Michael. *A Dictionary of Literary Symbols.* Cambridge: CUP, 1999.

Feuerbach, Ludwig. *Das Wesen des Christenthums.* 1841. 3rd. ed. Ludwig Feuerbach's sämtliche Werke 7. Leipzig: Otto Wiegand, 1849.

—. *The Essence of Christianity.* 1841. Trans. George Eliot. Great Books in Philosophy. Amherst: Prometheus, 1989.

Fields, Barbara J. "*Origins of the New South* and the Negro Question." 2001. *Racecraft: The Soul of Inequality in American Life.* By Karen E. Fields and Barbara J. Fields. Paperback ed. London: Verso, 2014. 149–169.

Findlay, J. N. Foreword. *Phenomenology of Spirit.* By Georg Wilhelm Friedrich Hegel. Trans. A. V. Miller. Oxford: Clarendon Press, 1977. v – xxx.

Fish, Stanley. *Is There a Text in This Class? The Authority of Interpretive Communities.* Cambridge: Harvard UP, 1980.

Fisher, Philip. "[Self and Community in *The Mill on the Floss*]." 1981. *The Mill on the Floss: An Authoritative Text, Backgrounds and Contemporary Reactions, Criticism.* Ed. Carol T. Christ. Norton Critical Edition. New York: W. W. Norton, 1994. 520–542.

Flanders, Judith. *The Making of Home.* London: Atlantic Books, 2014.

Fleishman, Avrom. *Virginia Woolf: A Critical Reading.* Baltimore: Johns Hopkins UP, 1975.

Fletcher, Angus. *Allegory: The Theory of a Symbolic Mode.* Ithaca: Cornell UP, 1964.

Flory, Wendy Stallard. "Melville, *Moby-Dick,* and the Depressive Mind: Queequeg, Starbuck, Stubb, and Flask as Symbolic Characters." *"Ungraspable Phantom": Essays on* Moby-Dick. Ed. John Bryant, Mary K. Bercaw Edwards and Timothy Marr. Kent: Kent State UP, 2006. 81–113.

Floud, Roderick et al. *The Changing Body: Health, Nutrition, and Human Development in the Western World since 1700.* New Approaches to Economic and Social History; NBER Series on Long-Term Factors in Economic Development. Cambridge: CUP, 2011.

Floyd-Wilson, Mary. "Delving the Root: *Cymbeline*, Scotland, and the English Race." *British Identities and English Renaissance Literature.* Ed. David J. Baker and Willy Maley. Cambridge: CUP, 2002. 101–115.

Fludernik, Monika. "The Many in Action and Thought: Towards a Poetics of the Collective in Narrative." *Narrative* 25.2 (2017): 139–163.

Fone, Byron R. S. *A Road to Stonewall: Male Homosexuality and Homophobia in English and American Literature, 1750–1969.* Twayne's Literature and Society Series 6. New York: Twayne, 1995.

Fordham, John. "Working-Class Fiction Across the Century." *The Cambridge Companion to the Twentieth-Century English Novel.* Ed. Robert L. Caserio. Cambridge Companions to Literature. Cambridge: CUP, 2009. 131–145.

Forter, Greg. "Freud, Faulkner, Caruth: Trauma and the Politics of Literary Form." *Narrative* 15.3 (2007): 259–285.

Foucault, Michel. *Discipline and Punish: The Birth of the Prison.* 1975. Trans. Alan Sheridan. 2nd ed. New York: Vintage, 1995.

—. *Madness and Civilization: A History of Insanity in the Age of Reason.* 1961. Trans. Richard Howard. New York: Vintage, 1988.

—. "Of Other Spaces." 1967 / 1984. Trans. Jay Miskowiec. *Diacritics* 16.1 (1986): 22–27.

Fox, Michael Allen. *Home: A Very Short Introduction.* Very Short Introductions. Oxford: OUP, 2016.

Fraiman, Susan. "*The Mill on the Floss*, the Critics, and the *Bildungsroman*." *PMLA* 108.1 (1993): 136–150.

Freud, Sigmund. *Civilization and Its Discontents.* 1930. Ed. and trans. James Strachey. New York: W. W. Norton, 1989.

—. *Das Unbehagen in der Kultur.* 1930. *Totem und Tabu; Das Unbehagen in der Kultur.* Köln: Anaconda, 2010. 179–256.

—. "Das Unheimliche." 1919. *Psychologische Schriften.* Studienausgabe. Frankfurt am Main: S. Fischer, 1970. 241–274.

—. *Der Witz und seine Beziehung zum Unbewussten.* Leipzig: Franz Deuticke, 1905.

—. *Five Lectures on Psycho-Analysis.* 1909. New York: W. W. Norton, 1989.

—. *Group Psychology and the Analysis of the Ego.* 1921. Trans. James Strachey. New York: Boni and Liveright, [1924].

—. *Introductory Lectures on Psycho-Analysis (Part III).* 1916–1917. Ed. James Strachey. The Standard Edition of the Complete Psychological Works of Sigmund Freud 16. London: Vintage, 2001.

—. *The Joke and Its Relation to the Unconscious.* 1905. Trans. Joyce Crick. Penguin Classics. London: Penguin, 2003.

—. "The Uncanny." 1919. *The Uncanny.* Penguin Classics. London: Penguin, 2003. 121–161.

—. *Über Psychoanalyse: Fünf Vorlesungen gehalten zur 20jährigen Gründungsfeier der University of Worcester Mass, September 1909.* Leipzig: Franz Deuticke, 1910.

—. *Vorlesungen zur Einführung in die Psychoanalyse.* 1916–1917. 3rd. ed. Leipzig: Internationaler Psychoanalytischer Verlag, 1926.

Frevert, Ute. "War." *A Companion to Nineteenth-Century Europe, 1789–1914.* 2006. Paperback ed. Blackwell Companions to History. Chichester: Wiley-Blackwell, 2009. 417–431.

Fricke, Hannes. *Das hört nicht auf: Trauma, Literatur und Empathie.* Göttingen: Wallstein, 2004.Gray, Richard. *A History of American Literature.* Blackwell: Malden, 2004.

Fricker, Miranda. *Epistemic Injustice: Power and the Ethics of Knowing.* 2007. Paperback ed. Oxford: OUP, 2009.

Frow, John. *Genre.* New Critical Idiom. London: Routledge, 2006.

Frye, Northrope. *Anatomy of Criticism: Four Essays.* 1957. Princeton: Princeton UP, 1971.

Gadamer, Hans-Georg. *Truth and Method.* 1960. London: Continuum, 2004.

—. *Wahrheit und Methode: Grundzüge einer philosophischen Hermeneutik.* 1960. 4th ed. Tübingen: Mohr, 1975.

Gallagher, Catherine. "The Rise of Fictionality." *History, Geography, and Culture.* Vol. 1 of *The Novel.* Ed. Franco Moretti. Paperback ed. Princeton: Princeton UP, 2007. 336–363.

Gallagher, Lucy. "'He Had Always Believed That There Were Two Sorts of Women: The Decent Ones and the Rest': The Female Body, Dirt, and Domesticity in Pat Barker's *Union Street.*" *Contemporary Women's Writing* 5.1 (2011): 36–51.

Garnett, Jane. "Religious and Intellectual Life." *The Nineteenth Century: The British Isles, 1815–1901.* Ed. Colin Matthew. The Short Oxford History of the British Isles. Oxford: OUP, 2000. 195–227.

Garrard, Greg. *Ecocriticism.* The New Critical Idiom. London: Routledge, 2004.

Garrity, Jane. *Step-Daughters of England: British Women Modernists and the National Imaginary.* Manchester: Manchester UP, 2003.

Garvey, Johanna X. K. "Difference and Continuity: The Voices of *Mrs. Dalloway.*" *College English* 53.1 (1991): 59–76.

Geary, Dick. "Socialism and the German Labour Movement before 1914." *Labour and Socialist Movements in Europe before 1914.* 1989. Ed. Dick Geary. Paperback ed. Oxford: Berg, 1992. 101–136.

Gellert, Michael. *The Fate of America: An Inquiry into National Character.* Dulles: Brassey's, 2001.

Gemmeke, Mascha. *Frances Burney and the Female Bildungsroman: An Interpretation of* The Wanderer: or, Female Difficulties. Münster Monographs on English Literature 28. Frankfurt am Main: Peter Lang, 2004.

George, Rosemary Marangoly. *The Politics of Home: Postcolonial Relocations and Twentieth-Century Fiction.* 1996. Berkeley: University of California Press, 1999.

Gervais, David. *Literary Englands: Versions of 'Englishness' in Modern Writing.* Cambridge: CUP, 1993.

Gilbert, Sandra M. and Susan Gubar. *The Madwoman in the Attic: The Woman Writer and the Nineteenth-Century Literary Imagination.* New Haven: Yale UP, 1979.

Gifford, Terry. *Pastoral.* New Critical Idiom. London: Routledge, 1999.

Ginsburg, Michal Peled and Lorri G. Nandrea. "The Prose of the World." *Forms and Themes.* Vol. 2 of *The Novel.* Ed. Franco Moretti. Paperback ed. Princeton: Princeton UP, 2007. 244–273.

Girard, René. *Violence and the Sacred.* 1972. Trans. Patrick Gregory. London: Continuum, 2005.

Gleber, Anke. *The Art of Taking a Walk: Flanerie, Literature, and Film in Weimar Culture.* Princeton: Princeton UP, 1999.

Gluzman, Michael. *The Politics of Canonincity: Lines of Resistance in Modernist Hebrew Poetry.* Contraversions. Stanford: Stanford UP, 2003.

Godden, Richard. "*Absalom, Absalom!*, Haiti, and Labor History: Reading Unreadable Revolutions." 1994. *William Faulkner's Absalom, Absalom! A Casebook.* Ed. Fred Hobson. Casbooks in Criticism. Oxford: OUP, 2003. 251–282.

Goldman, Jane. *The Cambridge Introduction to Virginia Woolf.* Cambridge Introductions to Literature. Cambridge: CUP, 2006.

Goodman, Kevis. "Romantic Poetry and the Science of Nostalgia." *The Cambridge Companion to British Romantic Poetry.* Eds. James Chandler and Maureen N. McLane. Cambridge Companions to Literature. Cambridge: CUP, 2008. 195–216.

Gramsci, Antonio. *Prison Notebooks.* Vol. 1. Ed. Joseph A. Buttigieg. European Perspectives. New York: Columbia UP, 1992.

Gray, Richard. *A History of American Literature.* Malden: Blackwell, 2004.

Griffing, Ben. *The Politics of Gender in Victorian Britain: Masculinity, Political Culture and the Struggle for Women's Rights.* Cambridge: CUP, 2012.

Grimal, Pierre. *The Dictionary of Classical Mythology.* 1951. Trans. A. R. Maxwell-Hyslop. Blackwell Reference. New York: Blackwell, 1985.

Grimm, Ruediger Hermann. *Nietzsche's Theory of Knowledge.* Monographien und Texte zur Nietzsche-Forschung 4. Berlin: de Gruyter, 1977.

Grossman, James R. "A Chance to Make Good: 1900–1929." *A History of African Americans since 1880.* Vol. 2 of *To Make Our World Anew.* Ed. Robin D. G. Kelley and Earl Lewis. Oxford: OUP, 2000. 67–130.

Gudmestad, Robert H. *A Troublesome Commerce: The Transformation of the Interstate Slave Trade.* Baton Rouge: Louisiana State UP, 2003.

Guggisberg, Martina, Bettina Müller and Thomas Christin. *Armut in der Schweiz: Konzepte, Resultate und Methoden.* Neuchâtel: Office féderal de la statistique, 2012. 26 July 2013 <www.bfs.admin.ch / bfs / portal / de / index / news / publikationen.Document.164 851.pdf>.

Guth, Deborah. "Clarissa Dalloway's Final Moment of Vision." *Twentieth-Century Literature* 36.1 (1990): 35–42.

—. "'What a Larke! What a Plunge!': Fiction as Self-Evasion in *Mrs. Dalloway.*" *The Modern Language Review* 84.1 (1989): 18–25.

Halpern, Rick and Enrico Dal Lago, eds. *Slavery and Emancipation.* Blackwell Readers in American Social and Cultural History. Malden: Blackwell, 2002.

Han, Béatrice. *Foucault's Critical Project: Between the Transcendental and the Historical.* 1998. Trans. Edward Pile. Stanford: Stanford UP, 2002.

Hand, Derek. *A History of the Irish Novel.* Cambridge: CUP, 2011.

Hardin, James. "Reflection and Action: Essays on the Bildungsroman." Introduction. *Reflection and Action: Essays on the Bildungsroman.* Ed. James Hardin. Columbia: University of South Carolina Press, 1991. ix – xxviii.

Hareven, Tamara K. "The Home and the Family in Historical Perspective." *Home: A Place in the World.* Ed. Arien Mack. New York: New York UP, 1993. 227–259.

Harvie, Christopher. "Revolution and the Rule of Law (1789–1851)." *The Oxford History of Britain.* Ed. Kenneth O. Morgan. Rev. ed. Oxford: OUP, 1999. 470–517.

Haslett, Moyra. *Marxist Literary and Cultural Theories.* Transitions. Basingstoke: Macmillan, 2000.

Hawthorn, Jeremy. *Virginia Woolf's* Mrs. Dalloway*: A Study in Alienation.* Text and Context. London: Sussex UP, 1975.

Hayes-Brady, Clare. "'Obviously, Doctor, You've Never Been a Thirteen-Year-Old Girl': Problematic Adolescence in *The Virgin Suicides.*" *'Forever Young?': The Changing Images of America.* Ed. Philip Coleman and Stephen Matterson. European Views of the United States 4. Heidelberg: Universitätsverlag Winter, 2012. 209–218.

Hayford, Harrison. "'Loomings': Yarns and Figures in the Fabric." *Moby-Dick: An Authoritative Text, Before Moby-Dick: International Controversy, Reviews and Letters by Melville, Analogues and Sources, Reviews of Moby-Dick, Criticism.* Ed. Hershel Parker and Harrison Hayford. 2nd ed. Norton Critical Edition. New York: W. W. Norton, 2002. 657–669.

Haywood, Ian. *Working-Class Fiction: From Chartism to Trainspotting.* Writers and Their Work. Plymouth: Northcote House, 1997.

Head, Dominic. *The Modernist Short Story: A Study in Theory and Practice.* Cambridge: CUP, 1992.

Hecht, Jennifer Michael. *Stay: A History of Suicide and the Philosophies Against It.* New Haven: Yale UP, 2013.

Hegel, Georg Wilhelm Friedrich. *Die Wissenschaft der Logik: Mit den mündlichen Zusätzen.* 1830. Vol. 1 of *Enzyklopädie der philosophischen Wissenschaften im Grundrisse.* Werke 8; Suhrkamp Taschenbuch Wissenschaft 608. Frankfurt am Main: Suhrkamp, 1986.

—. *Logic: With Prolegomena.* 1830. Trans. William Wallace. Oxford: Clarendon Press, 1874.

—. *Phänomenologie des Geistes.* 1807. Ed. Johann Schulze. 2nd ed. Georg Wilhelm Friedrich Hegel's Werke 2. Berlin: Duncker und Humblot, 1841.

—. *Phenomenology of Spirit.* 1807. Trans. A. V. Miller. Oxford: Clarendon Press, 1977.

Heidegger, Martin. *Being and Time.* 1927. Trans. Joan Stambaugh. SUNY Series in Contemporary Continental Philosophy. Albany: State University of New York Press, 1996.

—. "... dichterisch wohnet der Mensch ..." 1951. *Vorträge und Aufsätze.* 11th ed. Stuttgart: Klett-Cotta, 2009. 181–198.

—. "... Poetically, Man Dwells ..." 1951. *Poetry, Language, Thought.* Trans. Albert Hofstadter. New York: Perennial Classics, 2001. 211–227.

—. *Sein und Zeit.* 1927. 15th ed. Tübingen: Max Niemeyer, 2006.

Heinzelman, Kurt. " 'Make It New': The Rise of an Idea." *Make It New: The Rise of Modernism.* Ed. Kurt Heinzelman. Austin: University of Texas Press, 2004. 131–134.

Helgerson, Richard. *Adulterous Alliances: Home, State, and History in Early Modern European Drama and Painting.* 2000. Paperback ed. Chicago: The University of Chicago Press, 2003.

Heller, Agnes. "Where Are We at Home?" *Thesis Eleven* 41.1 (1995): 1–18.

Heller-Andrist, Simone. *The Friction of the Frame: Derrida's Parergon in Literature.* Swiss Studies in English 138. Tübingen: Narr Francke Attempto, 2012.

Herbert, Christopher. "*Mrs. Dalloway*, the Dictator, and the Relativity Paradox." *NOVEL* 35.1 (2001): 104–124.

Herman, Judith Lewis. *Trauma and Recovery.* 1992. New York: Basic Books, 1997.

Herring, George C. *From Colony to Superpower: U.S. Foreign Relations since 1776.* The Oxford History of the United States. Oxford: OUP, 2008.

Herrmann, Steven B. "Melville's Portrait of Same-Sex Marriage in *Moby-Dick*." *Jung Journal: Culture & Psyche* 4.3 (2010): 65–82.

Hessler, John G. "Moral Accountability in *Mrs. Dalloway*." 1978 *Clarissa Dalloway.* Ed. Harold Bloom. Major Literary Characters. New York: Chelsea House, 1990. 126–136.

Heusser, Martin. "Et in Arcadia Ego: The Pastoral Aesthetics of Suburbia in Jeffrey Eugenides' *The Virgin Suicides*." *American Aesthetics.* Ed. Deborah Madsen. SPELL: Swiss Papers in English Language and Literature 20. Tübingen: Gunter Narr, 2007. 175–189.

–. "'Why I Write about Mexico': Mexicanness in Katherine Anne Porter's 'Flowering Judas' and 'María Concepción'." *English on the Move: Mobilities in Literature and Language.* Ed. Annette Kern-Stähler and David Britain. SPELL: Swiss Papers in Linguistics 27. Tübingen: Narr Francke Attempto, 2012. 69–80.

Hill, John. *At Home in the World: Sounds and Symmetries of Belonging.* Zurich Lecture Series in Analytical Psychology. New Orleans: Spring Journal Books, 2010.

Hirsch, Marianne. "Between *Great Expectations* and *Lost Illusions*: The Novel of Formation as Genre." *Genre* 12.3 (1979): 293–311.

–. *Family Frames: Photography, Narrative and Postmemory.* Cambridge: Harvard UP, 1997.

Hitchcock, Peter. *Dialogics of the Oppressed.* Minneapolis: University of Minnesota Press, 1993.

Hobsbawm, Eric. Introduction [to the subsection "Exile: A Keynote Address"]. *Home: A Place in the World.* Ed. Arien Mack. New York: New York UP, 1993. 61–64.

–. *The Age of Capital: 1848–1875.* 1975. New York: Vintage, 1996.

–. *The Age of Extremes: A History of the World, 1914–1991.* 1994. New York: Vintage, 1996.

–. *The Age of Revolution: 1789–1848.* 1962. New York: Vintage, 1996.

Hoerder, Dirk. "Migrations and Belongings." *A World Connecting: 1870–1945.* Emily S. Rosenberg. A History of the World. Cambridge: Harvard UP, 2012. 433–589.

Holub, Robert C. *Reflections on Realism: Paradox, Norm, and Ideology in Nineteenth-Century German Prose.* Detroit: Wayne State UP, 1991.

Homer, Sean. *Jacques Lacan.* Routledge Critical Thinkers. London: Routledge, 2005.

Hönnighausen, Lothar. *Faulkner: Masks and Metaphors.* Jackson: UP of Mississippi, 1997.

Hopcke, Robert H. *Persona: Where Sacred Meets Profane.* Boston: Shambhala, 1995.

Horne, Gerald. *The Counter-Revolution of 1776: Slave Resistance and the Origins of the United States of America.* New York: New York UP, 2014.

Hoskin, Bree. "Playground Love: Landscape and Longing in Sofia Coppola's *The Virgin Suicides*." *Literature Film Quarterly* 35.3 (2007): 214–221.

Houlgate, Stephen. *An Introduction to Hegel: Freedom, Truth and History.* Malden: Blackwell, 2005.

Hovland, Ceri. "'We Felt That If We Kept Looking Hard Enough, We Might Begin to Understand How They Were Feeling and Who They Were': Point of View and Performance in *The Virgin Suicides*." *Journal of Adaptation in Film & Performance* 3.3 (2010): 259–270.

Howarth, Janet. "Gender, Domesticity, and Sexual Politics." *The Nineteenth Century: The British Isles: 1815–1901.* Ed. Colin Matthew. Short Oxford History of the British Isles. Oxford: OUP, 2000. 163–193.

Howe, Daniel Walker. *What Hath God Wrought: The Transformation of America, 1815–1848.* 2007. Paperback ed. Oxford History of the United States. Oxford: OUP, 2009.

Howe, Nicholas. Introduction. *Home and Homelessness in the Medieval and Renaissance World.* Ed. Nicholas Howe. Notre Dame: University of Notre Dame Press, 2004.

Howkins, Alun. "The Discovery of Rural England." *Englishness: Politics and Culture 1880–1920.* 1986. Ed. Robert Colls and Philip Dodd. Paperback ed. Beckenham: Croom Helm, 1987. 62–88.

Hubbard, Phil. *City.* Key Ideas in Geography. London: Routledge, 2006.

Huber, Evelyne and John D. Stephens. *Development and Crisis of the Welfare State: Parties and Policies in Global Markets.* Chicago: University of Chicago Press, 2001.

Hunter, James Davison. *Culture Wars: The Struggle to Define America.* New York: Basic Books, 1991.

Hutcheon, Linda. *A Poetics of Postmodernism: History, Theory, Fiction.* New York: Routledge, 1988.

Ingram, Forrest L. *Representative Short Story Cycles of the Twentieth Century: Studies in a Literary Genre.* De proprietatibus litterarum, series maior 19. The Hague: Mouton, 1971.

Innes, Paul. "*Cymbeline* and Empire." *Critical Survey* 19.2 (2007): 1–18.

Irwin-Zarecka, Iwona. *Frames of Remembrance: The Dynamics of Collective Memory.* New Brunswick: Transaction, 1994.

Iser, Wolfgang. *Das Fiktive und das Imaginäre: Perspektiven literarischer Anthropologie.* Frankfurt am Main: Suhrkamp, 1991.

—. *The Fictive and the Imaginary: Charting Literary Anthropology.* Baltimore: The Johns Hopkins UP, 1993.

Jaeggi, Rahel. *Entfremdung: Zur Aktualität eines sozialphilosophischen Problems.* Frankfurter Beiträge zur Soziologie und Sozialphilosophie 8. Frankfurt am Main: Campus, 2005.

James, C. L. R. *Mariners, Renegades and Castaways: The Story of Herman Melville and the World We Live In.* 1953. Reencounters with Colonialism: New Perspectives on the Americas. Hanover: Dartmouth College Press / UP of New England, 2001.

James, Henry. "The Novels of George Eliot." 1866. *The Mill on the Floss: An Authoritative Text, Backgrounds and Contemporary Reactions, Criticism.* Ed. Carol T. Christ. Norton Critical Edition. New York: W. W. Norton, 1994. 464–465.

Jameson, Fredric. "A Note on Literary Realism in Conclusion." *Adventures in Realism.* Ed. Matthew Beaumont. Malden: Blackwell, 2007. 261–271.

—. *Archaeologies of the Future: The Desire Called Utopia and Other Science Fictions.* 2005. London: Verso, 2007.

—. *Postmodernism: or, The Cultural Logic of Late Capitalism.* Post-Contemporary Interventions. Durham: Duke UP, 1991.

—. *The Antinomies of Realism.* London: Verso, 2013.

—. "The Experiments of Time: Providence and Realism." *Forms and Themes.* Vol. 2 of *The Novel.* Ed. Franco Moretti. Paperback ed. Princeton: Princeton UP, 2007. 95–127.

—. *The Political Unconscious: Narrative as a Socially Symbolic Act.* 1983. Routledge Classics. London: Routledge, 2002.

—. "Third-World Literature in the Era of Multinational Capitalism." *Social Text* 15 (1986): 65–88.

Jefferson, Thomas. "A Summary View of the Rights of British America (1774)." *The Essential Jefferson.* Ed. Jean M. Yarbrough. The American Heritage Series. Indianapolis: Hacket, 2006. 3–17.

Jeffrey, Keith. "British Isles / British Empire: Dual Mandate / Dual Identity." *The British Isles: 1901–1951.* Ed. Keith Robbins. Short Oxford History of the British Isles. Oxford: OUP, 2002. 13–41.

Jolly, Margaretta. "Toward a Masculine Maternal: Pat Barker's Bodily Functions." *Critical Perspectives on Pat Barker.* Ed. Sharon Monteith et al. Columbia: University of South Carolina Press, 2005. 235–253.

Jones, Norman W. "Coming Out through Histories Hidden Love Letters in *Absalom, Absalom!*" *American Literature* 76.2 (2004): 339–366.

Joseph, Philip. *American Literary Regionalism in a Global Age.* Baton Rouge: Louisiana State UP, 2007.

Jost, François. "La tradition du *Bildungsroman.*" *Comparative Literature* 21.2 (1969): 97–115.

Jouve, Nicole Ward. "Virginia Woolf and Psychoanalysis." *The Cambridge Companion to Virginia Woolf.* Cambridge Companions to Literature. Cambridge: CUP, 2000. 245–272.

Jung, C. G. "Archetypes of the Collective Unconscious." 1934. *The Archetypes and the Collective Unconscious.* Trans. R. F. C. Hull. 2nd ed. Collected Works of C. G. Jung 9.1. Princeton: Princeton UP, 1969. 3–41.

—. "Über die Archetypen des kollektiven Unbewussten." 1934. *Archetypen.* 16th ed. München: Deutscher Taschenbuch Verlag, 2010. 7–43.

Kant, Immanuel. *Der Streit der Fakultäten.* 1798. *Immanuel Kants Werke in acht Büchern.* Ed. Hugo Renner. Vol. 8. Berlin: Weichert, 1907. 1–90.

—. "Groundwork of The Metaphysics of Morals." 1785. *Practical Philosophy.* Ed. and trans. Mary J. Gregor. The Cambridge Edition of the Works of Immanuel Kant. Cambridge: CUP, 1996.

—. *Grundlegung zur Metaphysik der Sitten.* 1785. Ed. Jens Timmermann. Sammlung Philosophie 3. Göttingen: Vandenhoeck & Ruprecht, 2004.

–. *The Conflict of the Faculties.* 1798. Ed. and trans. Mary J. Gregor. Paperback ed. Norwalk: Abaris, 1992.

Kanji, Shireen. "What Stops Lone Mothers from Working? Insights from the UK's Millennium Cohort Study." *The Costs of Children: Parenting and Democracy in Contemporary Europe.* Ed. David G. Mayes and Mark Thomson. Cheltenham: Edward Elgar, 2012. 129–151.

Kaplan, Amy. "Nation, Region, and Empire." *The Columbia History of the American Novel.* Ed. Emory Elliott. New York: Columbia UP, 1991. 240–266.

Katz, Tamar. "Woolf's Urban Rhythm." *A Companion to Virginia Woolf.* Ed. Jessica Berman. Blackwell Companions to Literature and Culture. Malden: Wiley Blackwell, 2016. 397–410.

Kehlmann, Daniel and Jeffrey Eugenides. Interview. "Narrative Heat." *Checkpoints.* Spec. issue of *PEN America* 9 (2008): 88–96.

Kelley, Alice van Buren. *The Novels of Virginia Woolf: Fact and Vision.* Chicago: The University of Chicago Press, 1973.

Kennedy, David. *Elegy.* New Critical Idiom. London: Routledge, 2007.

Kennedy, David M. *Freedom from Fear: The American People in Depression and War, 1929–1945.* 1999. Paperback ed. The Oxford History of the United States 9. Oxford: OUP, 2001.

Kennedy, J. Gerald. "From Anderson's *Winesburg* to Carver's *Cathedral*: The Short Story Sequence and the Semblance of Community." *Modern American Short Story Sequences: Composite Fictions and Fictive Communities.* Ed. J. Gerald Kennedy. Cambridge: CUP, 1995. 194–215.

Kerr, Ian J. "On the Move: Circulating Labor in Pre-Colonial, Colonial, and Post-Colonial India." 2006. *Coolies, Capital, and Colonialism: Studies in Indian Labor History.* Ed. Rana P. Behal and Marcel van der Linden. International Review of Social History Supplements. Cambridge: CUP, 2006. 85–110.

Khair, Tabish. *Babu Fictions: Alienation in Contemporary Indian English Novels.* New Delhi: OUP, 2001.

Khazanov, Anatoly M. *Nomads and the Outside World.* 1983. Trans. Julia Crookenden. 2nd ed. Madison: The University of Wisconsin Press, 1994.

Kilroy, James F. *The Nineteenth-Century English Novel: Family Ideology and Narrative Form.* New York: Palgrave Macmillan, 2007.

Kimball, Samuel. "Uncanny Narration in *Moby-Dick.*" *American Literature* 59.4 (1987): 528–547.

King, Ros. *Cymbeline: Constructions of Englishness.* Studies in Performance and Early Modern Drama. Aldershot: Ashgate, 2005.

Kirk, John. "Recovered Perspectives: Gender, Class, and Memory in Pat Barker's Writing." *Contemporary Literature* 40.4 (1999): 603–623.

Klancher, Jon P. "From 'Crowd' to 'Audience': The Making of an English Mass Readership in the Nineteenth Century." *ELH* 50.1 (1983): 155–173.

Knoepflmacher, U.C. "Tragedy and the Flux: *The Mill on the Floss.*" 1968. *The Mill on the Floss: An Authoritative Text, Backgrounds and Contemporary Reactions, Criticism.* Ed. Carol T. Christ. Norton Critical Edition. New York: W.W. Norton, 1994. 502–520.

Kocka, Jürgen. "The Middle Classes in Europe." *The European Way: European Society during the Nineteenth and Twentieth Centuries.* Ed. Hartmut Kaelble. New York: Berghahn Books, 2004. 15–43.

Kortenaar, Neil Ten. "Realism / Magic Realism." *The Encyclopedia of Twentieth-Century Fiction.* Ed. Brian W. Shaffer. Malden: Wiley-Blackwell, 2011. 1303–1305.

Kostova, Bilyana Vanyova. "Collective Suffering, Uncertainty and Trauma in Jeffrey Eugenides's *The Virgin Suicides*: Of Bystanders, Perpetrators, and Victims." *Atlantis* 35.2 (2013): 47–63.

Kreisel, Deanna. "Superfluity and Suction: The Problem with Saving in *The Mill on the Floss.*" *NOVEL* 35.1 (2001): 69–103.

Krishnaswamy, Revathi. "Mythologies of Migrancy: Postcolonialism, Postmodernism, and the Politics of (Dis)location." *Linked Histories: Postcolonial Studies in a Globalized World.* Ed. Pamela McCallum and Wendy Faith. Calgary: University of Calgary Press, 2005. 91–108.

Kristeva, Julia. *Powers of Horror: An Essay on Abjection.* 1980. Trans. Leon S. Roudiez. European Perspectives. New York: Columbia UP, 1982.

—. *Strangers to Ourselves.* 1988. Trans. Leon S. Roudiez. European Perspectives. New York: Columbia UP, 1991.

Laats, Adam. *Fundamentalism and Education in the Scopes Era: God, Darwin, and the Roots of American Culture Wars.* New York: Palgrave Macmillan, 2010.

Lacan, Jacques. "Remarks on Daniel Lagache's Presentation: 'Psychoanalysis and Personality Structure'." 1960. *Écrits: The First Complete Edition in English.* Trans. Bruce Fink, in collaboration with Héloïse Fink and Russell Grigg. New York: W.W. Norton, 2006. 75–81.

—. "The Mirror Stage as Formative of the *I* Function as Revealed in Psychoanalytic Experience." 1949. *Écrits: The First Complete Edition in English.* Trans. Bruce Fink, in collaboration with Héloïse Fink and Russell Grigg. New York: W.W. Norton, 2006. 75–81.

LaCapra, Dominick. *History and Memory after Auschwitz.* New York: Cornell UP, 1998.

—. *Writing History, Writing Trauma.* Parallax. Baltimore: The Johns Hopkins UP, 2001.

Ladenson, Elisabeth. *Dirt for Art's Sake: Books on Trial from Madame Bovary to Lolita.* Ithaca: Cornell UP, 2007.

Laing, Stuart. "The Politics of Culture: Institutional Change in the 1970s." *The Arts in the 1970s: Cultural Closure?* Ed. Bart Moore-Gilbert. London: Routledge, 1994. 29–56.

Lamarque, Peter. *The Philosophy of Literature.* Foundations of the Philosophy of Arts. Malden: Blackwell, 2009.

Lamont, Elizabeth Clea. "Moving Tropes: New Modernist Travels with Virginia Woolf." *Alif: Journal of Comparative Poetics* 21 (2001): 161–181.

Langford, Gerald. *Faulkner's Revision of Absalom, Absalom! A Collation of the Manuscript and the Published Book.* Austin: U of Texas P, 1971.

Leavis, F. R. "The Early Phase." 1948. *The Mill on the Floss: An Authoritative Text, Backgrounds and Contemporary Reactions, Criticism.* Ed. Carol T. Christ. Norton Critical Edition. New York: W. W. Norton, 1994. 483–488.

Lefebvre, Henri. *Critique de la vie quotidienne 2: Fondements d'une sociologie de la quotidienneté.* Paris: L'Arche, 1961.

—. *Critique of Everyday Life: The One-Volume Edition.* 1947–1981. Trans. John Moore and Gregory Elliott. London: Verso, 2014.

Lee, Hermione. "*Mrs. Dalloway.*" 1977. *Virginia Woolf's Mrs. Dalloway.* Ed. Harold Bloom. Modern Critical Interpretations. New York: Chelsea House, 1988. 15–35.

Levine, George. "Intelligence as Deception: *The Mill on the Floss.*" 1965. *The Mill on the Floss: An Authoritative Text, Backgrounds and Contemporary Reactions, Criticism.* Ed. Carol T. Christ. Norton Critical Edition. New York: W. W. Norton, 1994. 489–502.

Ljungberg, Christina. "'Damn Mad': Palindromic Figurations in Literary Narratives." *Insistent Images.* Eds. Elżbieta Takowska, Christina Ljungberg and Olga Fischer. Iconicity in Language and Literature 5. Amsterdam: John Benjamins, 2007. 247–266.

Llyod-Smith, Allan. *American Gothic Fiction: An Introduction.* Continuum Studies in Literary Genre. New York: Continuum, 2004.

Locke, John. *Second Treatise of Government.* 1690. Ed. C. B. Macpherson. Indianapolis: Hackett, 1980.

Long, Christian. "Running Out of Gas: The Energy Crisis in 1970s Suburban Narratives." *Canadian Review of American Studies* 43.3 (2011): 342–369.

Long, Helen. *The Edwardian House: The Middle-Class Home in Britain, 1880–1914.* Manchester: Manchester UP, 1993.

Loomba, Ania. *Colonialism/Postcolonialism.* 2nd ed. New Critical Idiom. London: Routledge, 2005.

Lotman, Yuri M. *Universe of the Mind: A Semiotic Theory of Culture.* Trans. Ann Shukman. 1990. Paperback ed. Bloomington: Indiana UP, 2000.

Love, Jean O. *Worlds in Consciousness: Mythopoetic Thought in the Novels of Virginia Woolf.* Berkeley: University of California Press, 1970.

Lukács, Georg. *The Theory of the Novel: A Historico-Philosophical Essay on the Forms of Great Epic Literature.* 1916. Trans. Anna Bostock. Cambridge: MIT Press, 1971.

Lundin, Roger. *From Nature to Experience: The American Search for Authority.* American Intellectual Life. Lanham: Rowman & Littlefield, 2005.

Lurker, Manfred. "Vögel." *Wörterbuch der Symbolik.* Ed. Manfred Lurker. 4th ed. Kröners Taschenbuchausgabe 464. Stuttgart: Kröner, 1988. 773–774.

MacLeod, Janine. "Water and the Material Imagination: Reading the Sea of Memory against the Flows of Capital." *Thinking with Water.* Eds. Cecilia Chen, Janine MacLeod and Astrida Neimanis. Montreal: McGill-Queen's UP, 2013. 40–60.

Mackail, J.W. *The Life of William Morris.* 2 vols. London: Longmans, Green & Co., 1899.

Magistrale, Anthony. "Innocence Unrewarded: A Note on *E.T.* and the Myth of Adolescence." *Science-Fiction Studies* 11 (1984): 223–225.

Magnuno-Mire, Gina and C. Laurel Franklin. "Post-Traumatic Stress Disorder." *Handbook of Integrative Clinical Psychology, Psychiatry, and Behavioral Medicine: Perspectives, Practices, and Research.* Ed. Roland A. Carlstedt. New York: Springer, 2010. 353–377.

Maier, Charles S. "Leviathan 2.0: Inventing Modern Statehood." *A World Connecting: 1870–1945.* Ed. Emily S. Rosenberg. A History of the World. Cambridge: Harvard UP, 2012. 28–282.

Mann, Michael. *The Dark Side of Democracy: Explaining Ethnic Cleansing.* Cambridge: CUP, 2005.

Manning, Patrick. *Migration in World History.* Themes in World History. New York: Routledge, 2005.

Marcus, Amit. "*We* Are *You*: The Plural and the Dual in 'We' Fictional Narratives." *Journal of Literary Semantics* 37.1 (2008): 1–21.

Marcus, Laura. *Virginia Woolf.* 2nd ed. Writers and Their Work. Tavistock: Northcote House, 2004.

Marcus, Sharon. *Apartment Stories: City and Home in Nineteenth-Century France Paris and London.* Basingstoke: Palgrave Macmillan, 1999.

Margolin, Uri. "Telling Our Story: On 'We' Literary Narratives." *Language and Literature* 5.2 (1996): 115–133.

Marotta, Kenny. "*Middlemarch*: The "Home Epic." *Genre* 15.4 (1982): 403–420.

Marshall, P.J. "1783–1870: An Expanding Empire." *The Cambridge Illustrated History of the British Empire.* Ed. P.J. Marshall. Cambridge: CUP, 1996. 24–51.

Martin, Gretchen. "Vanquished by a Different Set of Rules: Labor vs. Leisure in William Faulkner's *Absalom, Absalom!*" *Mississippi Quarterly* 61.3 (2008): 397–416.

Martin, Robert K. *Hero, Captain, and Stranger: Male Friendship, Social Critique, and Literary Form in the Sea Novels of Herman Melville.* Chapel Hill: The University of North Carolina Press, 1986.

Marx, Karl. *Capital: A Critique of Political Economy.* Vol. 3. Ed. Frederick Engels. Chicago: Charles H. Kerr, 1909.

—. "Critique of the Gotha Program." 1875. *Selected Writings.* Ed. Lawrence H. Simmons. Indianapolis: Hacket, 1994. 315–332.

—. *Das Kapital: Kritik der politischen Ökonomie.* Vol. 3. Ed. Friedrich Engels. 6th ed. Hamburg: Otto Meissners Verlag, 1922.
—. "Der achtzehnte Brumaire des Louis Bonaparte." 1852. *Werke.* By Karl Marx and Friedrich Engels. Vol. 8. Berlin: Dietz, 1960. 111–207.
—. *Economic and Philosophical Manuscripts of 1844.* 1844. *Economic and Philosophical Manuscripts of 1844 and the Communist Manifesto.* Trans. Martin Milligan. Great Books in Philosophy. New York: Prometheus Books, 1988. 13–168.
—. "Kritik des Gothaer Programms." 1875. *Karl Marx Lesebuch.* Ed. Klaus Körner. München: Deutscher Taschenbuch Verlag, 2008. 276–295.
—. *Ökonomisch-philosophische Manuskripte aus dem Jahre 1844.* 1844. *Karl Marx: Schriften und Briefe, November 1837–1844.* 2. Aufl. Karl Marx · Friedrich Engels: Werke 40. Berlin: Dietz, 1990. 465–588.
—. "The Eighteenth Brumaire of Louis Bonaparte." 1852. *Later Political Writings.* Ed. Terrell Carver. Cambridge Texts in the History of Political Thought. Cambridge: CUP, 1996. 31–127.
Massey, Doreen. "A Place Called Home?" *The Question of 'Home.'* Ed. Angelika Bammer. Spec. issue of *New Formations* 17 (1992): 3–15.
Matthews, John T. "Recalling the West Indies: From Yoknapatawpha to Haiti and Back." *American Literary History* 16.2 (2004): 238–262.
McBride, Theresa. "Women's Work and Industrialization." *The Industrial Revolution and Work in Nineteenth-Century Europe.* Ed. Lenard R. Berlanstein. Rewriting Histories. London: Routledge, 1992. 63–80.
McDonagh, Josephine. "Space, Mobility, and the Novel: 'The Spirit of Place Is a Great Reality'." *Adventures in Realism.* Ed. Matthew Beaumont. Malden: Blackwell, 2007. 50–67.
McDonnell, Jane. " 'Perfect Goodness' or 'The Wider Life': *The Mill on the Floss* as Bildungsroman." *Genre* 15.4 (1982): 379–402.
McKeon, Michael. *The Secret History of Domesticity: Public, Private, and the Division of Knowledge.* 2005. Paperback ed. Director's Circle Book. Baltimore: The Johns Hopkins UP, 2007.
—. *Theory of the Novel: A Historical Approach.* Baltimore: The Johns Hopkins Press, 2000.
McKnight, Stephanie. "Happier with Dreams: Constructing the Lisbon Girls through Non-Diegetic Sound in *The Virgin Suicides.*" *True to the Spirit: Film Adaptation and the Question of Fidelity.* Ed. Colin McCabe, Rick Warner and Kathleen Murray. Oxford: OUP, 115–129.
McLachlan, Shelley and Peter Golding. "Tabloidization in the British Press: A Quantitative Investigation into Changes in British Newspapers, 1952–1997." *Tabloid Tales:*

Global Debates over Media Standards. Ed. Colin Sparks and John Tulloch. Critical Media Studies. Oxford: Rowman & Littlefield, 2000. 75–90.
McLennan, Rachel. "Chasing After the Wind: The Adolescent Aporias of Jeffrey Eugenides." *Writing America into the Twenty-First Century: Essays on the American Novel.* Ed. Elizabeth Boyle and Anne-Marie Evans. Newcastle upon Tyne: Cambridge Scholars, 22–38.
McLoughlin, Michael. *Dead Letters to the New World: Melville, Emerson, and American Transcendentalism.* Literary Criticism and Cultural Theory. New York: Routledge, 2003.
McNeill, Patrick, Jonathan Blundell and Janis Griffiths. *Sociology AS: The Complete Companion.* Cheltenham: Nelson Thornes, 2003.
McPherson, James. *Battle Cry of Freedom: The Civil War Era.* 1988. With a new afterword by the author. Oxford History of the United States. Oxford: OUP, 2003.
Meinhof, Ulrike Hanna. *The Language of Belonging.* Language and Globalization. Basingstoke: Palgrave Macmillan, 2005.
Meyer, Susan. *Imperialism at Home: Race in Victorian Women's Fiction.* Reading Women Writing. New York: Cornell UP, 1996.
Middlekauff, Robert. *The Glorious Cause: The American Revolution, 1763–1789.* 1982 / 2005. 2nd paperback ed. The Oxford History of the United States. Oxford: OUP, 2007.
Midgley, Clare. *Feminism and Empire: Women Activists in Imperial Britain, 1790–1865.* London: Routledge, 2007.
Mikalachki, Jodi. "The Masculine Romance of Roman Britain: *Cymbeline* and Early Modern English Nationalism." *Shakespeare Quarterly* 46.3 (1995): 301–322.
Mikics, David. *The Romance of Individualism in Emerson and Nietzsche.* Series in Continental Thought. Athens: Ohio UP, 2003.
Millard, Kenneth. *Coming of Age in Contemporary American Fiction.* Edinburgh: Edinburgh UP, 2007.
Miller, J. Hillis. *Others.* Princeton Paperbacks. Princeton: Princeton UP, 2001.
Moretti, Franco. *Atlas of the European Novel: 1800–1900.* 1997. Paperback ed. London: Verso, 1999.
—. *Modern Epic: The World System from Goethe to García Márquez.* 1994. Trans. Quintin Hoare. London: Verso, 1996.
—. "Planet Hollywood." 2001. *Distant Reading.* London: Verso, 2013. 91–105.
—. *Signs Taken for Wonders: Essays in the Sociology of Literary Form.* 1983. Trans. Susan Fischer, David Forgacs and David Miller. Rev. ed. London: Verso, 1988.
—. *The Bourgeois: Between History and Literature.* London: Verso, 2013.
—. "The Comfort of Civilization." *Representations* 12 (1985): 115–139.
—. "The Novel: History and Theory." 2008. *Distant Reading.* London: Verso, 2013. 159–178.

—. *The Way of the World: The* Bildungsroman *in European Culture.* 1987. Trans. Albert Sbragia. New ed. London: Verso, 2000.

Morgan, Edmund Sears. *American Slavery, American Freedom: The Ordeal of Colonial Virginia.* 1975. New York: W.W. Norton, 2003.

Morgan, Holmes M. "Pastoral." 16 Nov 2002. Glbtq: An Encyclopedia of Gay, Lesbian, Bisexual, Transgender, and Queer Culture. Ed. Claude J. Summers. 20 July 2010 <www.glbtq.com / literature / pastoral.html>.

Morley, David. *Home Territories: Media, Mobility and Identity.* Comedia. London: Routledge, 2000.

Morris, Pam. *Dickens's Class Consciousness: A Marginal View.* New York: St. Martin's, 1991.

—. *Jane Austen, Virginia Woolf and Worldly Realism.* Edinburgh: Edinburgh UP, 2017.

—. *Literature and Feminism: An Introduction.* Oxford: Blackwell, 1993.

—. *Realism.* New Critical Idiom. London: Routledge, 2003.

—. "Woolf and Realism." *Virginia Woolf in Context.* Ed. Bryony Randall and Jane Goldman. Cambridge: CUP, 2012. 40–51.

Morse, Margaret. "Home: Smell, Taste, Posture, Gleam." *Home, Exile, Homeland: Film, Media, and the Politics of Place.* Ed. Hamid Naficy. AFI Film Readers. New York: Routledge, 1999. 63–74.

Moseley, Merritt. "Pat Barker (8 May 1943 –)." *British and Irish Novelists since 1960.* Ed. Merritt Moseley. Detroit: Gale, 2003. 39–48.

Moslund, Sten Pultz. "The Presencing of Place in Literature: Toward an Embodied Topopoetic Mode of Reading." *Geocritical Explorations: Space, Place, and Mapping in Literary and Cultural Studies.* Ed. Robert T. Tally, Jr. New York: Palgrave Macmillan, 2011. 29–43.

Mugerauer, Robert. *Heidegger and Homecoming: The Leitmotif in the Later Writings.* New Studies in Phenomenology and Hermeneutics. Toronto: U of Toronto P, 2008.

Mühlheim, Martin. "Between the Wild West and Pastoral Peace: Nature, Gender, and Tragedy in Annie Proulx's 'Brokeback Mountain'." *Forces of Nature: Natural(-izing) Gender and Gender(-ing) Nature in Discourses of Western Culture.* Ed. Bernadette Hyner and Precious McKenzie Stearns. Newcastle upon Tyne: Cambridge Scholars Press, 2009. 210–241.

—. "Past the Game of Fiction: History, Reconstruction, and Ideology in Five Narratives from the English-Speaking World." Lizenziat Thesis. University of Zurich, 2004.

—. "Resisting Governmental Illegalization: Xenophobia and Otherness in Steven Spielberg's *E.T.: The Extra-Terrestrial.*" *Experiencing Otherness: Multidisciplinary Perspectives.* Eds. Hassan Bashir and Susmita Roy. At the Interface. Oxford: Inter-Disciplinary Press, 2014. 3–12.

Mulvey, Laura. "Visual Pleasure and Narrative Cinema." 1975. *Literary Theory: An Anthology.* Ed. Julie Rivkin and Michael Ryan. Malden: Blackwell, 1998. 585–595.

Nalbantian, Suzanne. *Memory in Literature: From Rousseau to Neuroscience.* Basingstoke: Palgrave Macmillan, 2003.

Naremore, James. *The World without a Self: Virginia Woolf and the Novel.* New Haven: Yale UP, 1973.

Nelson, Cary. "1936, Madrid: The Heart of the World." *The Edinburgh Companion to Twentieth-Century Literatures in English.* Ed. Brian McHale and Randall Stevenson. Edinburgh: Edinburgh UP, 2006. 82–97.

Neubauer, John. "Bakhtin versus Lukács: Inscriptions of Homelessness in Theories of the Novel." *Creativity and Exile: European/American Perspectives II.* Spec. issue of *Poetics Today* 17.4 (1996): 531–546.

Nietzsche, Friedrich. *Beyond Good and Evil.* 1886. Trans. Helen Zimmern. New York: The Modern Library, 1917.

—. *Jenseits von Gut und Böse: Vorspiel einer Philosophie der Zukunft.* Leipzig: C. G. Naumann, 1900.

Nord, Deborah Epstein. *Gypsies & the British Imagination, 1807–1930.* New York: Columbia UP, 2006.

Norman, Brian. *Neo-Segregation Narratives: Jim Crow in Post-Civil Rights American Literature.* Athens: University of Georgia Press, 2010.

North, Michael. "1922, Paris, New York, London: The Modernist as International Hero." *The Edinburgh Companion to Twentieth-Century Literatures in English.* Ed. Brian McHale and Randall Stevenson. Edinburgh: Edinburgh UP, 2006. 48–57.

Noyes, John K. "Nomadic Landscapes and the Colonial Frontier: The Problem of Nomadism in German South West Africa." *Colonial Frontiers: Indigenous-European Encounters in Settler Societies.* Ed. Lynette Russell. Studies in Imperialism. Manchester: Manchester UP, 2001. 198–215.

Novalis. *Philosophical Writings.* Trans. and ed. Margaret Mahony Stoljan. Albany: State University of New York Press, 1997.

—. *Schriften.* Vol. 2. Jena: Eugen Diederichs, 1907.

Ó Gráda, Cormac. *Famine: A Short History.* Princeton: Princeton UP, 2009.

O'Donoghue, Brendan. *A Poetics of Homecoming: Heidegger, Homelessness and the Homecoming Venture.* Newcastle upon Tyne: Cambridge Scholars Publishing, 2011.

Oliver, Kelly. "The Look of Love." *Hypatia: A Journal of Feminist Philosophy* 16.3 (2001): 56–78.

Osterhammel, Jürgen. *Die Verwandlung der Welt: Eine Geschichte des 19. Jahrhunderts.* 2009. 5th ed. Historische Bibliothek der Gerda Henkel Stiftung. München: C. H. Beck, 2010.

Outram, Dorinda. *The Enlightenment.* 1995. 3rd ed. New Approaches to European History. Cambridge: CUP, 2013.

Ovington, Mary White. "How the NAACP Began." *NAACP: Celebrating a Century: 100 Years in Pictures.* By Julian Bond et al. Layton: Gibbs Smith, 2009. 12–17.

Pahl, Jon. *Empire of Sacrifice: The Religious Origins of American Violence.* New York: New York UP, 2010.

Painter, Nell Irvin. *Creating Black Americans: African-American History and Its Meanings, 1919 to the Present.* Oxford: OUP, 2006.

Palmer, Alan. *Fictional Minds.* Frontiers of Narrative. Lincoln: University of Nebraska Press, 2004.

Panforti, Maria Donata. "The Home and the Law – A Comparative Law Contribution." *Constructions of Home: Interdisciplinary Studies in Architecture, Law, and Literature.* Ed. Klaus Stierstorfer. AMS Studies in Cultural History 9. New York: AMS Press, 2010. 3–12.

Parker, Hershel and Harrison Hayford, eds. *Moby-Dick: An Authoritative Text, Before Moby-Dick: International Controversy, Reviews and Letters by Melville, Analogues and Sources, Reviews of Moby-Dick, Criticism.* By Herman Melville. 2nd ed. Norton Critical Edition. New York: W.W. Norton, 2002.

Parry, Benita. "Problems in Current Theories of Colonial Discourse." *The Post-Colonial Studies Reader.* Ed. Bill Ashcroft, Gareth Griffiths and Helen Tiffin. London: Routledge, 1995. 36–44.

Parsons, Deborah L. *Streetwalking the Metropolis: Women, the City and Modernity.* Oxford: OUP, 2000.

Patterson, James T. *Grand Expectations: The United States, 1945–1974.* 1996. Paperback ed. The Oxford History of the United States. Oxford: OUP, 1997.

Patterson, Orlando. "Slavery, Alienation, and the Female Discovery of Personal Freedom." *Home: A Place in the World.* Ed. Arien Mack. New York: New York UP, 1993. 159–187.

Peretz, Eyal. *Literature, Disaster, and the Enigma of Power: A Reading of* Moby-Dick. Stanford: Stanford UP, 2003.

Peters, John Durham. "Exile, Nomadism, and Diaspora: The Stakes of Mobility in the Western Canon." *Home, Exile, Homeland: Film, Media, and the Politics of Place.* Ed. Hamid Naficy. New York: Routledge, 1999. 17–41.

—. *Speaking into the Air: A History of the Idea of Communication.* 1999. Chicago: Chicago UP, 2000.

Piatti, Barbara. *Die Geographie der Literatur: Schauplätze, Handlungsräume, Raumphantasien.* 2008. 2nd ed. Göttingen: Wallstein, 2009.

Pick, Daniel. *Faces of Degeneration: A European Disorder, c. 1848–c. 1918.* 1989. Paperback ed. Ideas in Context. Cambridge: CUP, 1993.

Plaks, Andrew H. "The Novel in Premodern China." *History, Geography, and Culture.* Vol. 1 of *The Novel.* Ed. Franco Moretti. Paperback ed. Princeton: Princeton UP, 2007. 181–213.

Poole, Roger. *The Unknown Virgina Woolf.* 1978. New ed. Cambridge: CUP, 1995.

Popkin, Jeremy D. *A Concise History of the Haitian Revolution.* Viewpoints / Puntos de Vista: Themes and Interpretations in Latin American History. Wichester: Wiley-Blackwell, 2012.

Porter, Carolyn. "*Absalom, Absalom!*: (Un)Making the Father." *The Cambridge Companion to William Faulkner.* Ed. Philip M. Weinstein. Cambridge Companions to Literature. Cambridge: CUP, 1995. 168–196.

Porter, Roy. *London: A Social History.* 1995. Paperback ed. Cambridge: Harvard UP, 1998.

Porteous, J. Douglas and Sandra E. Smith. *Domicide: The Global Destruction of Home.* Montréal: McGill-Queen's UP, 2001.

Punter, David. *Metaphor.* New Critical Idiom. London: Routledge, 2007.

Rachman, Shalom. "Clarissa's Attic: Virginia Woolf's *Mrs. Dalloway* Reconsidered." *Twentieth-Century Literature* 18.1 (1972): 3–18.

Racz, Imogen. *Art and the Home: Comfort, Alienation and the Everyday.* London: I. B. Tauris, 2015.

Rakove, Jack N, ed. *The Annotated U.S. Constitution and Declaration of Independence.* Cambridge: Harvard UP, 2009.

Ramos, Peter. "Beyond Silence and Realism: Trauma and the Function of Ghosts in *Absalom, Absalom!* and *Beloved.*" *The Faulkner Journal* 23.2 (2008): 47–66.

Rampersad, Arnold. "1901; 1903, W. E. B. Du Bois's *The Souls of Black Folk* Rebukes Booker T. Washington's *Up from Slavery*: The Problem of the Color Line." *A New Literary History of America.* Ed. Greil Marcus and Werner Sollors. Cambridge: The Belknap Press of Harvard UP, 2009. 469–473.

Rancière, Jacques. *Proletarian Nights: The Workers' Dream in Nineteenth-Century France.* 1981. Translated by John Drury. London: Verso, 2012.

Randall, Bryony. "A Day's Time: The One-Day Novel and the Temporality of the Everyday." *New Literary History* 47 (2016): 591–610.

Rawley, James A. and Stephen D. Behrendt. *The Transatlantic Slave Trade: A History.* 1981. Rev. ed. Lincoln: University of Nebraska Press, 2005.

Rawlinson, Mark. *Pat Barker.* New British Fiction. London: Palgrave Macmillan, 2010.

Reinecke, Mark A. and Elizabeth R. Didie. "Cognitive-Behavioral Therapy with Suicidal Patients." *Assessment, Treatment, and Prevention of Suicidal Behavior.* Ed. Robert I. Yufit and David Lester. Hoboken: John Wiley, 2005. 205–234.

Richardson, Brian. *Unnatural Voices: Extreme Narration in Modern and Contemporary Fiction.* Theory and Interpretation of Narrative. Columbus: Ohio State UP, 2006.

Ricoeur, Paul. *Oneself as Another.* 1990. Trans. Kathleen Blamey. Paperback ed. Chicago: The University of Chicago Press, 1994.

—. *The Conflict of Interpretations.* 1969. London: Continuum, 2004.

Rimmon-Kenan, Shlomith. *A Glance beyond Doubt: Narration, Representation, Subjectivity.* Theory and Interpretation of Narrative. Columbus: Ohio State UP, 1996.

—. *Narrative Fiction: Contemporary Poetics.* New Accents. London: Routledge, 1983.

Ritter, Lois A. and Shirley Manly Lampkin. *Community Mental Health.* Sudbury: Jones & Bartlett Learning, 2012.

Ritz, E. "Entfremdung." *Historisches Wörterbuch der Philosophie.* Ed. Joachim Ritter, Gottfried Gabriel and Karlfried Gründer. Vol. 2. Darmstadt: Wissenschaftliche Buchgesellschaft, 1972.

Robbins, Keith. "The British Way and Purpose." *The British Isles: 1901–1951.* Ed. Keith Robins. The Short Oxford History of the British Isles. Oxford: OUP, 2002. 74–100.

Roberts, Adam. *Science Fiction.* 2000. 2nd ed. New Critical Idiom. London: Routledge, 2006.

Ronnberg, Ami, ed. *The Book of Symbols: Reflections on Archetypal Images.* Köln: Taschen, 2010.

Rosenberg, Edgar. "Putting an End to *Great Expectations.*" *Great Expectations: Authoritative Text, Backgrounds, Contexts, Criticism.* By Charles Dickens. Ed. Edgar Rosenberg. Norton Critical Editions. New York: W.W. Norton, 1999. 491–527.

Rosowski, Susan J. "The Novel of Awakening." *Genre* 12.3 (1979): 313–332.

Rousseau, Jean-Jacques. *A Discourse on Inequality.* 1755. Ed. and trans. Maurice Cranston. Penguin Classics. London: Penguin, 1984.

—. *Contrat social: ou, Principes du droit politique.* Genève: Marc-Michel Bousquet, 1766.

—. *Discours sur l'origine et les fondemens de l'inégalité parmi les hommes.* Amsterdam: Marc Michel, 1755.

—. *Émile: ou, De l'éducation.* New ed. Paris: Garnier, 1866.

—. *The Social Contract: or, The Principles of Political Right.* 1766. *Discourse on Political Economy and The Social* Contract. Ed. Christopher Betts. Oxford World Classics. Oxford: OUP, 1999. 43–175.

Royle, Nicholas. *The Uncanny.* Manchester: Manchester UP, 2003.

Rubenstein, Roberta. *Home Matters: Longing and Belonging, Nostalgia and Mourning in Women's Fiction.* New York: Palgrave Macmillan 2001.

Ruland, Richard and Malcolm Bradbury. *From Puritanism to Postmodernism: A History of American Literature.* New York: Penguin, 1992.

Ruotolo, Lucio. "The Unguarded Moment: *Mrs. Dalloway.*" 1986. *Virginia Woolf's Mrs. Dalloway.* Ed. Harold Bloom. Modern Critical Interpretations. New York: Chelsea House, 1988. 127–144.

Rushdie, Salman. "Imaginary Homelands." 1982. *Imaginary Homelands: Essays and Criticism 1981–1991.* London: Granta, 1992. 9–21.

Russell, Patricia Read. "Parallel Romantic Fantasies: Barrie's *Peter Pan* and Spielberg's *E. T.: The Extraterrestrial." Children's Literature Association Quarterly* 8.4 (1983): 28–30.

Ryan, Barbara. "Identity Politics: The Past, the Present, and the Future." Introduction. *Identity Politics and the Women's Movement.* Ed. Barbara Ryan. New York: New York UP, 2001. 1–16.

Ryan, Judith. *The Vanishing Subject: Early Psychology and Literary Modernism.* Chicago: The University of Chicago Press, 1991.

Ryan, Marie-Laure. "Toward a Definition of Narrative." *The Cambridge Companion to Narrative.* Ed. David Herman. Cambridge Companions to Literature. Cambridge: CUP, 2007. 22–35.

Rybczynski, Witbold. *Home: A Short History of an Idea.* 1986. New York: Penguin, 1987.

Said, Edward. *Culture and Imperialism.* A Borzoi Book. New York: Alfred A. Knopf, 1993.

—. *Reflections on Exile and Other Essays.* Convergences: Inventories of the Present. Cambridge: Harvard UP, 2000.

Saint-Amour, Paul. K. "*Mrs. Dalloway*: Of Clocks and Clouds." *A Companion to Virginia Woolf.* Ed. Jessica Berman. Blackwell Companions to Literature and Culture. Malden: Wiley Blackwell, 2016. 79–94.

Sammons, Jeffrey L. "The Bildungsroman for Non-Specialists: An Attempt at Clarification." *Reflection and Action: Essays on the Bildungsroman.* Ed. James Hardin. Columbia: University of South Carolina Press, 1991. 26–45.

Sánchez-Vizcaíno, María Jesús López. "The Waters of the Mind: Rhetorical Patterns of Fluidity in Woolf, William James, Bergson and Freud." 1 January 2007. *PsyArt: An Online Journal for the Psychological Study of the Arts.* 6 May 2011 <http://www.psyartjournal.com/article/show/jess_lpez_snchez_vizcano-the_waters_of_the_mind_rhetorical_patter>.

Sanders, Andrew. *The Oxford Short History of English Literature.* 1994. 3rd ed. Oxford: OUP, 2004.

Sandten, Cecile and Kathy-Ann Tan. "Home: Concepts, Constructions, Contexts." Introduction. *Home: Concepts, Constructions, Contexts.* Trier: WVT Wissenschaftlicher Verlag Trier, 2016. 1–8.

Sarti, Raffaella. *Europe at Home: Family and Material Culture, 1500–1800.* 1999. Trans. Allan Cameron. New Haven: Yale UP, 2002.

Schermerhorn, Calvin. *Money over Mastery, Family over Freedom: Slavery in the Antebellum Upper South.* Studies in Early American Economy and Society, from the Library Company of Philadelphia. Baltimore: The Johns Hopkins UP, 2011.

Schmidt, Hans R. *The United States Occupation of Haiti, 1915–1934.* 1971. New Brunswick: Rutgers UP, 1995.

Schmidt, Johann N. "Von der Restauration zur Vorromantik." *Englische Literaturgeschichte.* Ed. Hans Ulrich Seeber. 3rd ed. Weimar: J.B. Metzler, 1999. 149–216.

Schmitt, Richard. *Alienation and Freedom.* Boulder: Westview Press, 2003.

Schönfelder, Christa. *Words and Wounds: Childhood and Family Trauma in Romantic and Postmodern Fiction.* Lettre. Bielefeld: Transcript, 2013.

Scarry, Elaine. *The Body in Pain: The Making and Unmaking of the World.* Oxford: OUP, 1985.

Sebeok, Thomas. "Enter Textuality: Echoes from the Extra-Terrestrial." *Poetics Today* 6.4 (1985): 657–663.

Sedgwick, Eve Kosofsky. *Between Men: English Literature and Male Homosocial Desire.* 1985. With a new preface by the author. Gender and Culture. New York: Columbia UP, [1993].

—. *Epistemology of the Closet.* 1990. Updated ed. Berkeley: University of California Press, 2008.

Selby, Nick. *Herman Melville: Moby-Dick.* Columbia Critical Guides. New York: Columbia UP, 1998.

Shelley, Percy Bysshe. "A Defense of Poetry." 1821. *The Major Works.* Ed. Zachary Leader and Michael O'Neill. Oxford World's Classics. Oxford: OUP, 2003. 674–701.

—. "On Life." 1815. *The Major Works.* Ed. Zachary Leader and Michael O'Neill. Oxford World's Classics. Oxford: OUP, 2003. 633–636.

Showalter, Elaine. "Notes." *Mrs. Dalloway.* By Virginia Woolf. Ed. Stella McNichol. Penguin Classics. London: Penguin, 2000. 215–225.

Shklovsky, Victor. "Art as Technique." 1917. *Modern Criticism and Theory: A Reader.* Ed. David Lodge. London: Longman, 1988. 16–30.

Shostak, Debra. "'A Story We Could Live With': Narrative Voice, the Reader, and Jeffrey Eugenides's *The Virgin Suicides.*" *Modern Fiction Studies* 55.4 (2009): 808–832.

Slaughter, Joseph R. *Human Rights, Inc.: The World Novel, Narrative Form, and International Law.* New York: Fordham UP, 2007.

Smith, Kimberley K. "Mere Nostalgia: Notes on a Progressive Paratheory." *Rhetoric & Public Affairs* 3.4 (2000): 505–527.

Snaith, Anna. *Virginia Woolf: Public and Private Negotiations.* Basingstoke: Palgrave Macmillian, 2000.

Spigel, Lynn. "From Theatre to Space Ship: Metaphors of Suburban Domesticity in Postwar America." *Visions of Suburbia.* Ed. Roger Silverstone. London: Routledge, 1997. 217–239.

Sobchack, Vivian. " 'Is Any Body Home?': Embodied Imagination and Visible Evictions." *Home, Exile, Homeland: Film, Media, and the Politics of Place.* Ed. Hamid Naficy. AFI Film Readers. New York: Routledge, 1999. 45–61.

Spicer, Andrew. *Film Noir.* Inside Film. Harlow: Pearson Education, 2002.

Sprinker, Michael, ed. *Ghostly Demarcations: A Symposium on Jacques Derrida's Specters of Marx.* 1999. Radical Thinkers. London: Verso, 2008.

Stack, George J. *Nietzsche and Emerson: An Elective Affinity.* Athens: Ohio UP, 1992.

Stam, Robert. *Literature through Film: Realism, Magic, and the Art of Adaptation.* Malden: Blackwell, 2005.

Stasi, Paul. *Modernism, Imperialism, and the Historical Sense.* Cambridge: CUP, 2012.

Stecopoulos, Harilaos. "Regionalism in the American Modernist Novel." *The Cambridge Companion to the American Modernist Novel.* Ed. Joshua Miller. Cambridge Companions to Literature. Cambridge: CUP, 2015. 21–34.

Stein, Murray. *Jung's Map of the Soul: An Introduction.* Chicago: Open Court, 1998.

Stevenson, Randall. "1916, Flanders, London, Dublin: 'Everything Has Gone Well'." *The Edinburgh Companion to Twentieth-Century Literatures in English.* Ed. Brian McHale and Randall Stevenson. Edinburgh: Edinburgh UP, 2006. 35–47.

—. *Modernist Fiction: An Introduction.* Lexington: The UP of Kentucky, 1992.

—. *Literature and the Great War: 1914–1918.* Oxford Textual Perspectives. Oxford: OUP, 2013.

Stierstorfer, Klaus, ed. *Constructions of Home: Interdisciplinary Studies in Architecture, Law, and Literature.* AMS Studies in Cultural History 9. New York: AMS Press, 2010.

Stirling, Kirsten. *Peter Pan's Shadows in the Literary Imagination.* New York: Routledge, 2012.

Stollberg-Rilinger, Barbara. *Rituale.* Campus Historische Einführungen. Frankfurt am Main: Campus, 2013.

Stone, Donald D. "House and Home in Thomas Hardy." *Nineteenth-Century Fiction* 39.3 (1984): 292–304.

Stott, Andrew. *Comedy.* New Critical Idiom. London: Routledge, 2005.

Straumann, Barbara. *Figurations of Exile in Hitchcock and Nabokov.* Edinburgh: Edinburgh UP, 2008.

Straumann, Heinrich. *Faulkner.* Frankfurt am Main: Athenäum, 1968.

Street, Anne M. *Haiti 2004.* CIIR Briefing. London: Catholic Institute for International Relations, 2004.

Strehle, Susan. *Transnational Women's Fiction: Unsettling Home and Homeland.* London: Palgrave Macmillan, 2008.

Sundquist, Eric. *Faulkner: The House Divided.* 1983. Paperback ed. Baltimore: The Johns Hopkins UP, 1985.

Swaminathan, Srividhya. *Debating the Slave Trade: Rhetoric of British National Identity, 1759–1815.* Ashgate Series in Nineteenth-Century Transatlantic Studies. Farnham: Ashgate, 2009.

Tally, Robert T., Jr. *Melville, Mapping and Globalization: Literary Cartography in the American Baroque Writer.* Continuum Literary Studies. London: Continuum, 2009.

—. *Spatiality.* New Critical Idiom. London: Routledge, 2013.

Tambling, Jeremy. *Allegory.* New Critical Idiom. London: Routledge, 2010.

—. "Repression in Mrs. Dalloway's London." 1989. *Mrs. Dalloway and To the Lighthouse: Virginia Woolf.* Ed. Su Reid. New Casebooks. New York: St. Martin's Press, 1993. 57–70.

Terkenli, Theano S. "Home as a Region." *The Geographical Review* 85.3 (1995): 324–334.

Thompson, E.P. *The Making of the English Working Class.* 1963. A Pelican Book. Harmondsworth: Penguin, 1968.

Thoreau, Henry David. "Civil Disobedience." 1849. *Walden and Civil Disobedience.* Penguin Classics. New York: Penguin, 1986. 383–413.

Thurschwell, Pamela. *Sigmund Freud.* Routledge Critical Thinkers. London: Routledge, 2000.

Tobin, Patricia. "The Time of Myth and History in *Absalom, Absalom!*" *American Literature* 45.2 (1973): 252–270.

Tomasulo, Frank P. "The Gospel According to Spielberg in *E.T.: The Extra-Terrestrial.*" *Quarterly Review of Film & Video* 18.3 (2001): 273–282.

Tönnies, Ferdinand. *Gemeinschaft und Gesellschaft: Grundbegriffe der reinen Soziologie.* 1887. 2nd ed. Darmstadt: Wissenschaftliche Buchgesellschaft, 1988.

Totten, Samuel and Paul R. Bartrop. *Dictionary of Genocide.* Westport: Greenwood Press, 2008.

Trachtenberg, Alan. Introduction [to "Home as Place and Center for Private and Family Life"]. *Home: A Place in the World.* Ed. Arien Mack. New York: New York UP, 1993. 211–212.

Troy, Maria Holmgren. "Matrix, Metamorphosis, and the Readymade in *Union Street, Liza's England* and *Another World.*" *Re-Reading Pat Barker.* Ed. Pat Wheeler. Newcastle upon Tyne: Cambridge Scholars, 2011. 1–12.

Turner, John. "Governers, Governance, and Governed: British Politics since 1945." *The British Isles since 1945.* Ed. Kathleen Burk. The Short Oxford History of the British Isles. Oxford: OUP, 2003. 19–61.

Vaillant, George E. and Susan J. Blumenthal. "Suicide Over the Life Cycle: Risk Factors and Life-Span Development." Introduction. Ed. Susan J. Blumenthal and David J. Kupfer. Washington: American Psychiatric Press, 1990. 1–14.

Vickery, Amanda. "Golden Age to Separate Spheres? Review of the Categories and Chronology of English Women's History." *The Historical Journal* 36.2 (1993): 383–414.

Viola, André. " 'Buds on the Tree of Life': A Recurrent Mythological Image in Virginia Woolf's *Mrs. Dalloway.*" *Journal of Modern Literature* 20.2 (1996): 239–247.

Vogel, Todd. "The New Face of Black Labor." *The Black Press: New Literary and Historical Essays.* Ed. Todd Vogel. New Brunswick: Rutgers UP, 2001. 37–54.

Völz, Johannes. "'The Most Indebted Man': Emerson, Recognition, and the Reconfiguration of Non-Conformity." *Conformism, Non-Conformism and Anti-Conformism in the Culture of the United States.* Ed. Antonis Balasopoulos, Gesa Mackenthun and Theodora Tsimpouki. European Views of the United States 1. Heidelberg: Universitätsverlag Winter. 101–117.

Vucetic, Srdjan. *The Anglosphere: A Geneaology of a Racialized Identity in International Relations.* Stanford: Stanford UP, 2011.

von Matt, Peter. *Verkommene Söhne, missratene Töchter: Familiendesaster in der Literatur.* 1995. 4th ed. München: Deutscher Taschenbuch Verlag, 2004.

Wadlington, Warwick. "Ishmael's Godly Gamesomeness: Selftaste and Rhetoric in *Moby-Dick.*" 1972. *The Critical Response to Herman Melville's Moby-Dick.* Ed. Kevin J. Hayes. Critical Responses in Arts and Letters 13. Westport: Greenwood Press, 1994. 131–152.

Walcowitz, Rebecca. *Cosmopolitan Style: Modernism beyond the Nation.* New York: Columbia UP, 2006.

Walder, Dennis. "The Genre Approach." *The Realist Novel.* Ed. Dennis Walder. Approaching Literature. London: Routledge, 1995. 3–32.

Wallace, Jennifer. *The Cambridge Introduction to Tragedy.* Cambridge Introductions. Cambridge: CUP, 2007.

Wallace, Jo-Ann. Introduction. *Mrs. Dalloway.* By Virginia Woolf. Ed. Jo-Ann Wallace. Broadview Editions. Toronto: Broadview Press, 2013. 9–34.

Waterman, David. *Pat Barker and the Mediation of Social Reality.* Amherst: Cambria Press, 2009.

Watt, Ian. *The Rise of the Novel.* 1957. 2nd ed. Berkeley: University of California Press, 2001.

Weber, Tobias. "On the Verge of To-Day: Emerson and the Emergence of the American Age." Diss. University of Zurich, 2011. 31 October 2013 <http://opac.nebis.ch/ediss/20111235.pdf>.

Welzer, Harald. *Das kommunikative Gedächtnis: Eine Theorie der Erinnerung.* 2002/2005. 3rd. ed. Beck'sche Reihe 1669. München: C.H. Beck, 2011.

Wende, Peter. *Das Britische Empire: Geschichte eines Weltreichs.* 2008. Beck'sche Historische Bibliothek. München: C.H. Beck, 2012.

Wenke, John. "Ahab and 'the Larger, Deeper Part'." 1995. *Moby-Dick: An Authoritative Text, Before Moby-Dick: International Controversy, Reviews and Letters by Melville, An-*

alogues and Sources, Reviews of Moby-Dick, Criticism. Ed. Hershel Parker and Harrison Hayford. 2nd ed. Norton Critical Edition. New York: W.W. Norton, 2002. 702–711.

Wheeler, Pat. "Transgressing Masculinities: *The Man Who Wasn't There.*" *Critical Perspectives on Pat Barker.* Ed. Sharon Monteith et al. Columbia: University of South Carolina Press, 2005. 128–143.

Whitworth, Michael. "Virginia Woolf and Modernism." *The Cambridge Companion to Virginia Woolf.* Ed. Susan Sellers. Cambridge Companions to Literature. Cambridge: CUP, 2000. 146–163.

Wierzbicka, Anna. *Imprisoned in English: The Hazards of English as a Default Language.* Oxford: OUP, 2014.

Wilde, Oscar. "The Critic as Artist – Part I." 1891. *The Major Works.* Ed. Isobel Murray. Oxford World's Classics. Oxford: OUP, 2000. 241–266.

Williams, Eric. *From Columbus to Castro: The History of the Caribbean.* 1970. New York: Vintage, 1984.

Williams, Gordon. *British Theatre in the Great War: A Revaluation.* 2003. Paperback ed. London: Continuum, 2005.

Williams, Raymond. *The Country and the City.* 1973. Paperback ed. Oxford: OUP, 1975.

Winnicott, D.W. *Home Is Where We Start From.* 1986. New York: W.W. Norton, 1990.

Wittgenstein, Ludwig. *Philosophical Investigations: The German Text with an English Translation.* Trans. G.E.M. Ascombe, P.M.S. Hacker and Joachim Schulte. 4th ed. Chichester: Wiley-Blackwell, 2009.

Wollstonecraft, Mary. *A Vindication of the Rights of Women.* Revolutions. London: Verso, 2010.

Woloch, Alex. *The One vs. the Many: Minor Characters and the Space of the Protagonist in the Novel.* Princeton: Princeton UP, 2003.

Wood, Betty. "The Origins of Slavery in the Americas, 1500–1700." *The Routledge History of Slavery.* Ed. Gad Heuman and Trevor Burnard. Routledge Histories. Abingdon: Routledge, 2011. 64–79.

Wood, Gordon S. *Empire of Liberty: A History of the Early Republic, 1789–1815.* 2009. Paperback ed. The Oxford History of the United States. Oxford: OUP, 2011.

Wood, Robin. *Hollywood from Vietnam to Reagan – and Beyond.* 1986. Rev. ed. New York: Columbia UP, 2003.

Woodward, C. Vann. *The Strange Career of Jim Crow.* 1955. Commemorative ed. With a new afterword by William S. McFreely. Oxford: OUP, 2002.

Woodward, Kath. *Understanding Identity.* London: Arnold, 2002.

Woolf, Virginia. *A Room of One's Own.* 1929. *A Room of One's Own; Three Guineas.* Ed. Michèle Barrett. Penguin Classics. London: Penguin, 2000. 3–114.

—. "George Eliot." *The Common Reader.* 1925. Ed. Andrew McNeillie. A Harvest Book. San Diego: Harcourt, 1984. 162–172.

—. "On Being Ill." 1926. *Selected Essays*. Ed. David Bradshaw. Oxford World's Classics. Oxford: OUP, 2008. 101–110.
—. "Oxford Street Tide." 1932. *Selected Essays*. Ed. David Bradshaw. Oxford World's Classics. Oxford: OUP, 2008. 199–203.
—. "Street Haunting: A London Adventure." 1927. *Selected Essays*. Ed. David Bradshaw. Oxford World's Classics. Oxford: OUP, 2008. 177–187.
—. "Women and Fiction." 1929. *Selected Essays*. Ed. David Bradshaw. Oxford World's Classics. Oxford: OUP, 2008. 132–139.
Worchel, Dana and Robin E. Gearing. *Suicide Assessment and Treatment: Empirical and Evidence-Based Practices*. New York: Springer, 2010.
Wyatt, Jean M. "*Mrs. Dalloway*: Literary Allusion as Structural Metaphor." *PMLA* 88.3 (1973): 440–451.
Yeoman, Ann. *New or Neverland: Peter Pan and the Myth of Eternal Youth – A Psychological Perspective on a Cultural Icon*. Studies in Jungian Psychology by Jungian Analysts 82. Toronto: Inner City Books, 1998.
York, R. A. *The Rules of Time: Time and Rhythm in the Twentieth-Century Novel*. London: Associated UPes, 1999.
Young, Jeffrey Robert. *Domesticating Slavery: The Master Class in Georgia and South Carolina, 1670–1837*. Chapel Hill: The University of North Caroline Press, 1999.
Zagarell, Sandra A. "Narrative of Community: The Identification of a Genre." *Signs: Journal of Women in Culture and Society* 13.3 (1988): 498–527.
Zimbaro, Valerie P. *Encyclopedia of Apocalyptic Literature*. ABC-Clio Literary Companions. Santa Barbara: ABC-Clio, 1996.
Žižek, Slavoj. *How to Read Lacan*. London: Granta, 2006.
—. *Looking Awry: An Introduction to Jacques Lacan through Popular Culture*. 1991. Paperback ed. Cambridge: MIT Press, 1992.
—. *On Violence: Six Sideways Reflections*. London: Profile Books, 2008.
—. *The Pervert's Guide to Cinema*. Dir. Sophie Fiennes. 2006.
—. *The Plague of Fantasies*. 1997. The Essential Žižek. London: Verso, 2008.
—. *The Sublime Object of Ideology*. 1989. The Essential Žižek. London: Verso, 2008.
—. *The Ticklish Subject: The Absent Centre of Political Ontology*. 1999. Paperback ed. London: Verso, 2000.
Zwerdling, Alex. "*Mrs. Dalloway* and the Social System." *PMLA* 91.1 (1977): 69–82.

Index

Images

COVER ILLUSTRATION: © by Laura Barrett, used by permission

FIGURE 1: The idea of home ranges across various scales (diagram adapted from Fox 19).

FIGURE 2: The iconography of the Sacred Heart of Jesus is reflected in E. T.'s glowing heart. (Image of the Sacred Heart of Jesus taken from https://infovaticana.com / wp-content / uploads / 2013 / 10 / mar.jpg, 4 August 2017, public domain; screenshot from *E. T.: The Extra-Terrestrial* – © Amblin/Universal Studios, used by permission.)

FIGURE 3: Michelangelo's depiction of the creation is echoed in official ads for *E. T.* (Image by Michelangelo taken from https://en.wikipedia.org / wiki / The_Creation_of_Adam#/media / File:Creaci%C3%B3n_de_Ad%C3%A1n_(Miguel_%C3%81ngel).jpg, 4 August 2017, public domain; ad for *E. T.: The Extra-Terrestrial* taken from https://media.senscritique.com / media / 000 016 040 539 / source_big / E_T_l_extra_terrestre.jpg, 4 August 2017, public domain.)

FIGURE 4: Elliott is placed symbolically between a small child and two more adult figures. (Screenshot from *E. T.: The Extra-Terrestrial* – © Amblin/Universal Studios, used by permission.)

FIGURE 5: E. T. happens to hide right next to a monkey doll. (Screenshot from *E. T.: The Extra-Terrestrial* – © Amblin/Universal Studios, used by permission.)

FIGURE 6: The globe next to E. T. shows two 'non-white' continents: Africa and Asia. (Screenshot from *E. T.: The Extra-Terrestrial* – © Amblin/Universal Studios, used by permission.)

FIGURE 7: Government officials invade the home they are supposed to protect. (Screenshot from *E. T.: The Extra-Terrestrial* – © Amblin/Universal Studios, used by permission.)

FIGURE 8: Storm's regionalism assumes a global dimension if one takes into account projected spaces. (Map by Barbara Piatti, used by permission.)

FIGURE 9: Patrick Chappatte's cartoon "Kennedy, 50 Years Ago" seizes upon the widespread and problematic idea that the assassination of JFK in November 1963 marked the end of American innocence. (in The International New York Times 21 November 2013. © Chappatte)

Schweizer Anglistische Arbeiten (SAA)

Begründet von Bernhard Fehr

Herausgegeben von Andreas Fischer (Zürich), Martin Heusser (Zürich) und Daniel Schreier (Zürich)

Bisher sind erschienen:

Frühere Bände finden Sie unter:
http://www.narr-shop.de/reihen/s/schweizer-anglistische-arbeiten-saa.html

111
Stefanie Meier
Animation and Mechanization in the Novels of Charles Dickens
1982, 165 Seiten
€[D] 22,–
ISBN 978-3-7720-1566-3

112
Jörg Waldvogel
Licht- und Glanzwörter im modernen Englisch
1983, 336 Seiten
€[D] 29,–
ISBN 978-3-7720-1567-0

113
Annabeth Naef-Hinderling
The Search for the Culprit:
Dickens's Conflicting Self- and Object-Representations
1983, 149 Seiten
€[D] 19,90
ISBN 978-3-7720-1584-7

114
Barbara Glutz von Blotzheim-Maier
Angst und Schreckangst
1990, 82 Seiten
€[D] 14,90
ISBN 978-3-7720-1603-5

115
Hugo Schwaller
„This Sceptered Sway"
Sovereignty in Shakespeare's Comedies
1988, II, 251 Seiten
€[D] 34,–
ISBN 978-3-7720-1656-1

116
Neff-Mayson
Redemption
1990
€[D] 24,–
ISBN 978-3-7720-1676-9

177
Lotti Arter-Lamprecht
Deutsch-englischer Sprachkontakt
1992, 152 Seiten
€[D] 27,–
ISBN 978-3-7720-1930-2

118
Karin Schmidli
Models and Modifications Early African-American Women Writers
From the Slave Narrative to the Novel
1995, XIV, 204 Seiten
€[D] 29,–
ISBN 978-3-7720-2430-6

119
Marianne Dada-Büchel
Katherine Mansfield's Dual Vision
Concepts of Duality and Unity in Her Fictional Work
1995, XII, 286 Seiten
€[D] 39,–
ISBN 978-3-7720-2431-3

120
Thomas Honegger
From Phoenix to Chauntecleer
Medieval English Animal Poetry
1996, X, 288 Seiten
€[D] 43,–
ISBN 978-3-7720-2432-0

121
Esther Loehndorf
The Master's Voices
Robert Browning, the Dramatic Monologue, and Modern Poetry
1997, VIII, 210 Seiten
€[D] 39,–
ISBN 978-3-7720-2433-7

122
Michael C. Prusse
"Tomorrow is Another Day"
The Fictions of James Gordon Farrell
1997, XII, 237 Seiten
€[D] 39,–
ISBN 978-3-7720-2434-4

123
Thomas Hermann
»Quite a Little About Painters«
Art and Artists in Hemingway's Life and Work
1997, XII, 240 Seiten
€[D] 39,–
ISBN 978-3-7720-2435-1

124
Verena Bühler Roth
Wilderness and the Natural Environment
Margaret Atwood's Recycling of a Canadian Theme
1998, VIII, 206 Seiten
€[D] 34,–
ISBN 978-3-7720-2436-8

125
Ruth Frehner
The Colonizers' Daughters
Gender in the Anglo-Irish Big House Novel
1999, XIV, 256 Seiten
€[D] 39,–
ISBN 978-3-7720-2437-5

126
David Stamm
A Pathway to Reality
Visual and Aural Concepts in Dorothy Richardson's "Pilgrimage"
1999, VIII, 267 Seiten
€[D] 39,–
ISBN 978-3-7720-2438-2

127
Katharina Gutmann
Celebrating the Senses
An Analysis of the Sensual in Toni Morrison's Fiction
2000, VIII, 232 Seiten
€[D] 39,–
ISBN 978-3-7720-2439-9

128
Yvonne Studer
Ideas, Obsessions, Intertexts
A Nonlinear Approach to Russell Hoban's Fiction
2000, XII, 539 Seiten
€[D] 48,–
ISBN 978-3-7720-2440-5

129
Sandra Engler
„A Career's Wonderful, but Love Is More Wonderful Still“
Femininity and Masculinity in the Fiction of Mills & Boon
2004, XIV, 204 Seiten
€[D] 44,–
ISBN 978-3-7720-8065-4

130
Roger Meyenberg
Capel Lofft and the English Sonnet Tradition 1770–1815
2005, XVIII, 334 Seiten
€[D] 49,–
ISBN 978-3-7720-8104-0

131
Sarah Chevalier
Ava to Zac
A Sociolinguistic Study of Given Names and Nicknames in Australia
2006, XVI, 219 seiten
€[D] 39,–
ISBN 978-3-7720-8139-2

132
Cordula Hawes-Bilger
War Zone Language
Language and the Conflict in Northern Ireland
2007, 399 Seiten
€[D] 74,–
ISBN 978-3-7720-8200-9

133
Nicole Frey Büchel
Perpetual Performance
Selfhood and Representation in Byron's Writing
2007, X, 224 Seiten
€[D] 52,–
ISBN 978-3-7720-8201-6

134
Sabina J. Müller
Through the Mythographer's Eye
Myth and Legend in the Work of Seamus Heaney and Eavan Boland
2007, XII, 291 Seiten
€[D] 58,–
ISBN 978-3-7720-8215-3

135
Lukas Bleichenbacher
Multilingualism in the Movies
Hollywood Characters and Their Language Choices
2008, XIV, 236 Seiten
€[D] 54,–
ISBN 978-3-7720-8270-2

136
Stefan Daniel Keller
The Development of Shakespeare's Rhetoric
A Study of Nine Plays
2009, 310 Seiten
€[D] 58,–
ISBN 978-3-7720-8324-2

137
Lukas Rosenberger
The Swiss English Hypothesis
2009, XVI, 254 Seiten
€[D] 58,–
ISBN 978-3-7720-8333-4

138
Simone Heller-Andrist
The Friction of the Frame
Derrida's *Parergon* in Literature
2012, 277 Seiten
€[D] 58,–
ISBN 978-3-7720-8426-3

139
Philipp Gwerder
Gothic Identities
War, Atrocities and Doubles in Philip Caputo's Fiction
2013, 294 Seiten
€[D] 60,–
ISBN 978-3-7720-8460-7

140
Gaby Frey
Private Goes Public: Self-Narrativisation in Brian Friel's Plays
€[D] 58,–
2015, IX, 261 Seiten
ISBN 978-3-7720-8534-5

141
Nicole Studer-Joho
Diffusion and Change in Early Middle English
Methodological and Theoretical Implications from the LAEME Corpus of Tagged Texts
2014, XVIII, 231 Seiten
€[D] 58,–
ISBN 978-3-7720-8539-0

142
Dieter Studer-Joho
A Catalogue of Manuscripts Known to Contain Old English Dry-Point Glosses
2017, 306 Seiten
€[D] 58,–
ISBN 978-3-7720-8617-5

143
Martin Mühlheim
Fictions of Home
Narratives of Alienation and Belonging, 1850-2000
2018, 384 Seiten
€[D] 78,–
ISBN 978-3-7720-8637-3